"LINDA HOWARD MAKES OUR SENSES
COME ALIVE."
—*CATHERINE COULTER*

"LINDA HOWARD IS AN
EXTRAORDINARY TALENT."
—*ROMANTIC TIMES*

Acclaim for her sensational novels . . .

SHADES OF TWILIGHT

"[A] sizzler. . . . Ms. Howard is an extraordinary talent. . . . [Her] unforgettable novels [are] richly flavored with scintillating sensuality and high-voltage suspense."

—*Romantic Times*

SON OF THE MORNING

"Linda Howard offers a romantic time-travel thriller with a fascinating premise . . . gripping passages and steamy sex."

—*Publishers Weekly*

"A complex tale that's rich with detail, powerful characters and stunning sensuality. . . . It's no wonder that Linda Howard is the best of the best."

—*CompuServe Romance Reviews*

LINDA HOWARD

Shades of Twilight

Son of the Morning

POCKET BOOKS
New York   London   Toronto   Sydney

POCKET BOOKS, a division of Simon & Schuster, Inc.
1230 Avenue of the Americas, New York, NY 10020

Shades of Twilight copyright © 1996 by Linda Howington
Son of the Morning copyright © 1997 by Linda Howington

ISBN-13: 978-1-4165-1714-6
ISBN-10:   1-4165-1714-6

This Pocket Books trade paperback edition January 2006

10 9 8 7 6 5 4 3 2 1

POCKET and colophon are registered trademarks of Simon & Schuster, Inc.

For information regarding special discounts for bulk purchases, please contact Simon & Schuster Special Sales at 1-800-456-6798 or business@simonandschuster.com

Shades of Twilight and *Son of the Morning* were previously published individually by Pocket Books

Manufactured in the United States of America

Shades of Twilight

To

Beverly Beaver, a wonderful woman and dearly loved friend, for all the years of camaraderie and support, as well as taking the time to escort me around Tuscumbia and Florence, tell me who is sleeping with whom, and show me where all the bodies are buried. (Just joking, folks . . . you hope.)

And to Joyce B. R. Farley, sister extraordinaire. Here's to dolls, both blond and redheaded; tricycles with no brakes; attack roosters; graveyards for socks; hair rollers and bonfires; makeup and Molotov cocktails. You're the only other person I know who understands the reason behind wearing a Groucho mask and a tiara in public—and the only other person I know who's done it.

(For the curious: if you wear a Groucho mask and a tiara, people will figure you're either important, or crazy. Either way, they'll leave you alone. Try it some day when you're feeling grouchy and don't want to be bothered.)

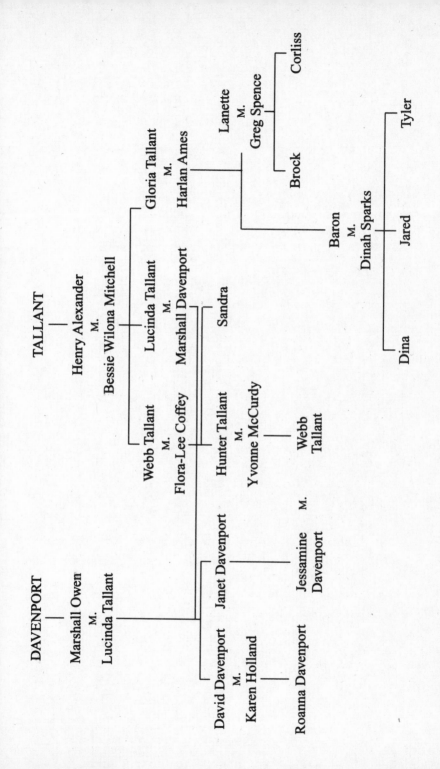

Prologue

She heard her own soft cries, but the pleasure exploding in her body made everything else seem unreal, distanced somehow from the hot magic of what he was doing to her. The noon sunlight wormed its way through the rustling leaves overhead, blinding her, dazzling her as she arched upward against him.

He wasn't gentle with her. He didn't treat her like a hothouse flower, the way the other boys did. Until she'd met him, she hadn't known how boring it was to always be treated like a princess. To the others, the Davenport name had made her a prize to be sought but never sullied; to him, she was just a woman.

With him, she *was* a woman. Though she was nineteen, her family treated her as if she were still a child. The protectiveness had never chafed her, until two weeks ago when she'd met him for the first time.

Naive and innocent she might be; stupid she wasn't. She knew when he'd introduced himself that his family was little better than white trash, and that *her* family would be horrified that she had even spoken to him. But the way his muscled torso had strained the fabric of his too-tight T-shirt had made her mouth go dry, and the swaggering masculini-

1

ty of his walk had started a strange tighening deep in her abdomen. His voice had lowered seductively when he spoke to her, and his blue eyes had been hot with promise. She'd known then that he wouldn't limit himself to hand-holding or necking. She knew what he'd wanted of her. But the wild response of her body was out of her experience, beyond her control, and when he asked her to meet him, she had agreed.

She couldn't get away at night without everyone knowing where she went, but it was easy to go out alone for a ride during the day and easy to arrange a meeting place. He had seduced her that very first time, stripping her naked beneath this very same oak tree—no, she couldn't pretend that it was a seduction. She had come here knowing what would happen, and she had been willing. Despite the pain of the first time, he had also shown her a wild pleasure she hadn't known existed. And every day, she came back for more.

He was crude sometimes, but even that excited her. He had been proud that he was the one to "bust her cherry," as he'd put it. Sometimes he said something, with a sneer in his voice, about a Neeley screwing a Davenport. Her family would be horrified if they knew. But still she dreamed, dreamed of how he would look in a nice suit and with his hair freshly cut and neatly combed as they stood together and informed the family that they were going to get married. She dreamed of him going to work at one of the family businesses and showing everyone how smart he was, that he could rise above the rest of his family. He would be a gentleman in public, but in private he would roll her on the bed and do these nasty, delicious things to her. She didn't want that part to change at all.

He finished, groaning with his climax, and almost immediately rolled off of her. She wished he would hold her for a moment before withdrawing, but he didn't like to cuddle when the weather was so hot. He stretched out on his back, the sunlight dappling his naked body, and almost immediately began dozing. She didn't mind. With two weeks' experience, she knew that he would awaken ready to make love again. In the meantime, she was content to simply watch him.

He was so exciting that he made her breath catch. She lifted herself onto her elbow beside him and reached out with one lightly exploring finger to trace the cleft in his chin. The corners of his mouth twitched, but he didn't awaken.

The family would have a collective conniption fit if they knew about him. The family! She sighed. Being a Davenport had ruled her life from the day she was born. It hadn't all been onerous. She loved the clothes and jewelry, the luxury of Davencourt, the prestigious schools, the sheer snobbery of it all. But the rules of behavior had chafed; sometimes she wanted to do something wild, just for the hell of it. She wanted to drive fast, she wanted to jump fences that were too high, she wanted . . . this. The rough, the dangerous, the forbidden. She loved the way he would tear her delicate, expensive silk underwear in his hurry to get to her. That perfectly symbolized all she wanted in this life, both the luxury and the danger.

That wasn't what the family wanted for her, however. It was assumed that she would marry the Heir, as she thought of him, and take her place in Colbert County society, with lunches at the yacht club, endless dinner parties for business and political associates, the dutiful production of two little heirs.

She didn't want to marry the Heir. She wanted this instead, this hot, reckless excitement, the thrill of knowing that she flirted with the forbidden.

She ran her hand down his body, sliding her fingers into the thatch of pubic hair that surrounded his sex. As she had expected, he stirred, wakening, and his sex did, too. He gave a low, rough laugh as he lunged upward, rolling her down to the blanket and settling on top of her.

"You're the greediest little bitch I've ever screwed," he said and shoved roughly into her.

She flinched, more from the deliberate crudity of his words than the force of his entry. She was still wet from the last time, so her body accepted him easily enough. But he seemed to like saying things that he knew would sting her, his eyes narrowed as he watched her reaction. She knew what it was, she thought, and forgave him. She knew he wasn't entirely comfortable being her lover, he was too aware of the social distance between them, and this was his way of trying to bring her nearer to his own level. But he didn't have to bring her down, she thought; she was going to bring him up.

She tightened her thighs around him, slowing his strokes so she could tell him before the growing heat in her loins made her forget what she wanted to say. "Let's get married next week. I don't care about a big wedding, we can elope if—"

He paused, his blue eyes flashing down at her. "Married?" he asked and laughed. "Where'd you get a stupid idea like that? I'm already married."

He resumed thrusting. She lay beneath him, numb with shock. A light breeze stirred the leaves overhead, and the sunlight pierced through, blinding her. *Married?* Granted, she didn't know much about him or his family, only that they weren't respectable, but a wife?

Fury and pain roared through her, and she struck out at him, her palm lashing across his cheek. He slapped her in return and caught her wrists, pinning them to the ground on each side of her head. "Goddamn, what's wrong with you?" he snapped, temper flaring hotly in his eyes.

She heaved beneath him, trying to throw him off, but he was far too heavy. Tears stung her eyes and ran down her temples into her hair. His presence inside her was suddenly unbearable, and each stroke seemed to rasp her like a rusty file. In her paroxysm of pain, she thought she would die if he continued. "You liar!" she shrieked, trying to jerk her hands free. "Cheat! Get *off* me! Go—go screw your *wife!*"

"She won't let me," he panted, hammering at her with cruel enjoyment of her struggles plain in his expression. "She just had a kid."

She screamed with rage and managed to jerk one hand

4

free, clawing him across the face before he could grab her. Cursing, he slapped her again, then drew back and swiftly flipped her onto her stomach. He was on her before she could scramble away, and she screamed again as she felt him plunge deep into her. She was helpless, flattened by his weight, unable to reach him to either hit or kick. He used her, hurting her with his roughness. Not five minutes before, the rough handling had excited her, but now she wanted to vomit, and she had to clench her teeth hard against the hot, rising nausea.

She pressed her face into the blanket, wishing she could smother herself, that she could do anything other than simply endure. But worse than the pain of betrayal, of realizing that she was nothing more than a convenience to him, was the bitter knowledge that it was her fault. She had brought this on herself, eagerly sought him out and not only let him treat her like a piece of trash, but enjoyed it! What a fool she was, spinning fairy tales of love and marriage to justify what was nothing more than a walk on the wild side.

He finished, grunting with his climax, and pulled out of her to fall heavily beside her. She lay where she was, trying desperately to pull the shattered pieces of herself back into some semblance of humanity. Wildly, she thought of revenge. With her torn clothes and the marks of his hand on her face, she could hurry home in very real hysterics, charge him with rape. She could make it stick, too; after all, she was a Davenport.

But it would be a lie. The fault, the weakness, was hers. She had welcomed him into her body. These last few minutes after she had changed her mind were little enough punishment for her monumental stupidity. It was a lesson she would never forget, the humiliation and sense of worthlessness a mental hair shirt she would wear for the rest of her life.

The burden of guilt pressed down on her. She had willingly traveled down this path, but now she had had enough. She would marry the Heir, the way everyone expected her to do, and spend the rest of her life being a dutiful Davenport.

Silently she sat up and began dressing. He watched her with drowsy malice in his blue, blue eyes. "What's the matter?" he sneered. "Did you think you were something special to me? Let me tell you something, baby: snatch is snatch, and your fancy name don't make yours anything special. What I got from you, I can get from any other bitch."

She put on her shoes and stood up. The pain of his words lashed at her, but she didn't let herself react to them. Instead she merely replied, "I won't be back."

"Sure you will," he said lazily, stretching and rubbing his chest. "Because what you got from me, you *can't* get anywhere else."

She didn't look back at him as she walked to where her horse was tied and painfully hauled herself into the saddle, the motion accomplished without her usual grace. The thought of returning to be used like a whore made the nausea rise hot and bitter in her throat again, and she wanted to kick him for his malicious, supreme confidence. She would forget the heated, soul-destroying pleasure he had given her and content herself with the life that had been planned for her. She could think of nothing worse than to come crawling to him and see the triumph in his eyes as he took her.

No, she thought as she rode away, *I won't come back. I'd rather die than be Harper Neeley's whore again.*

BOOK ONE

An End and a Beginning

CHAPTER
1

"What are we going to do with her?"

"God knows. *We* certainly can't take her."

The voices were hushed, but Roanna heard them anyway and knew they were talking about her. She curled her skinny little body into a tighter knot, hugging her knees to her chest as she stared stolidly out the window at the manicured lawn of Davencourt, her grandmother's home. Other people had yards, but Grandmother had a lawn. The lawn was a deep, rich green, and she had always loved the feel of her bare feet sinking into the thick grass, like walking on a live carpet. Now, however, she had no desire to go outside and play. She just wanted to sit here in the bay window, the one she had always thought of as her "dreaming window," and pretend that nothing had changed, that Mama and Daddy hadn't died and she'd never see them again.

"It's different with Jessamine," the first voice continued. "She's a young lady, not still a child like Roanna. We're simply too old to take on someone that young."

They wanted her cousin Jessie, but they didn't want *her*. Roanna stubbornly blinked to hold back the tears as she listened to her aunts and uncles discuss the problem of what to "do" with her and list the reasons why they'd each be glad to take Jessie into their homes, but Roanna would simply be too much trouble.

"I'll be good!" she wanted to cry but held the words inside just as she held the tears. What had she done that was so terrible they didn't want her? She tried to be a good girl, she said "ma'am" and "sir" when she talked to them. Was it because she had sneaked a ride on Thunderbolt? No one ever would have known if she hadn't fallen off and torn her new dress and gotten it dirty, and on Easter Sunday, at that. Mama had had to take her home to change clothes, and she'd had to wear an old dress to church. Well, it hadn't exactly been old, it had been one of her regular church dresses, but it hadn't been her gorgeous new Easter dress. One of the other girls at church had asked her why she hadn't worn an Easter dress, and Jessie had laughed and said because she'd fallen in a pile of horse doo-doo. Only Jessie hadn't said doo-doo, she'd used the bad word, and some boys had heard, and soon it was all over church that Roanna Davenport had said she'd fallen in a pile of horseshit.

Grandmother had gotten that disapproving look on her face, and Aunt Gloria's mouth had pursed up like she'd bitten into a green persimmon. Aunt Janet had looked down at her and just shook her head. But Daddy had laughed and hugged her shoulder and said that a little horseshit never hurt anybody. Besides, his Little Bit needed some fertilizer to grow.

Daddy. The lump in her chest swelled until she could barely breathe around it. Daddy and Mama were gone forever, and so was Aunt Janet. Roanna had always liked Aunt Janet, even though she'd always seemed so sad and hadn't liked to cuddle much. Still, she'd been a lot nicer than Aunt Gloria.

Aunt Janet was Jessie's mama. Roanna wondered if Jessie's chest hurt the way hers did, if she'd cried so much that the insides of her eyelids felt like sand. Maybe. It was hard to tell what Jessie thought. She didn't think a grubby kid like Roanna was worth paying any attention to; Roanna had heard her say so.

As Roanna stared unblinkingly out the window, she saw Jessie and their cousin Webb come into view, as if she had dreamed them into being. They walked slowly across the yard toward the huge old oak tree with the bench swing hanging from one of the massive lower limbs. Jessie looked beautiful, Roanna thought, with all the unabashed admiration of a seven-year-old. She was as slim and graceful as Cinderella at the ball, with her dark hair twisted into a knot at the back of her head and her neck rising swanlike above the dark blue of her dress. The gap between seven and thirteen was huge; to Roanna, Jessie was *grown,* a member of that mysterious, authoritative group who could give orders. That had happened only within the last year or so, because though Jessie had always before been classified as a "big girl" to Roanna's "little girl," Jessie had still played dolls and indulged in the occasional game of hide-and-seek. No longer, though. Jessie now disdained all games except Monopoly and spent a lot of time playing with her hair and begging Aunt Janet for cosmetics.

Webb had changed, too. He had always been Roanna's favorite cousin, always willing to get down on the floor and wrestle with her, or help her hold the bat so she could hit the softball. Webb loved horses the way she did, too, and could occasionally be begged into riding with her. He got impatient with that, though, because she was only allowed to ride her old slowpoke pony. Lately, Webb hadn't wanted to spend any time with her at all; he was too busy with other things, he'd say, but he sure seemed to have a lot of time to spend with Jessie. That was why she'd tried to ride Thunderbolt on Easter morning, so she could show Daddy that she was old enough for a real horse.

Roanna watched as Webb and Jessie sat down in the swing, their fingers laced together. Webb had gotten a lot bigger in the past year; Jessie looked little sitting beside him. He was playing football, and his shoulders were twice as wide as Jessie's. Grandmother, she'd heard one of the aunts say, doted on the boy. Webb and his mama, Aunt Yvonne, lived here at Davencourt with Grandmother, because Webb's daddy was dead, too.

Webb was a Tallant, from Grandmother's side of the family; she was his great-aunt. Roanna was only seven, but she knew the intricacies of kinship, having practically absorbed it through her skin during the hours she'd spent listening to the grown-ups talk about family. Grandmother had been a Tallant until she'd married Grandpa and turned into a Davenport. Webb's grandfather, who had also been named Webb, was Grandmother's favorite brother. She had loved him a whole lot, just as she had loved his son, who had been Webb's father. Now there was only Webb, and she loved him a whole lot, too.

Webb was only Roanna's second cousin, while Jessie was her first cousin, which was a lot closer. Roanna wished it were the other way around, because she would rather be close kin to Webb than to Jessie. Second cousins weren't much more than kissing cousins, was what Aunt Gloria had said once. The concept had so intrigued Roanna that at the last family reunion she had stared hard at all her relatives, trying to see who kissed who, so she would know who wasn't really kin. She had figured out that the people they saw only once a year, at the reunion, were the ones who did the most kissing. That made her feel better. She saw Webb all the time, and he didn't kiss her, so they were closer than kissing cousins.

"Don't be ridiculous," Grandmother said now, her voice cutting sharply through the muted arguments over who would be stuck with Roanna, and jerking Roanna's attention back to her eavesdropping. "Jessie and Roanna are both Davenports. They'll live here, of course."

Live at Davencourt! Equal parts of terror and relief displaced the misery in Roanna's chest. Relief that someone wanted her after all, and she wouldn't have to go to the Orphans' Home like Jessie had said she would. The terror came from the prospect of being under Grandmother's thumb all day, every day. Roanna loved her grandmother, but she was a little afraid of her, too, and she knew she'd never be able to be as perfect as Grandmother expected. She was always getting dirty, or tearing her clothes, or dropping something and breaking it. Food somehow always managed to fall off her fork and into her lap, and sometimes she forgot to pay attention when reaching for her milk, and knocked the glass over. Jessie said she was a clumsy clod.

Roanna sighed. She always *felt* clumsy, fumbling around under Grandmother's eagle eye. The only time she wasn't clumsy was when she was on a horse. Well, she had fallen off Thunderbolt, but she was used to her pony and Thunderbolt was so fat she hadn't been able to get a good grip with her legs. But usually she stuck to the saddle like a cocklebur, that's what Loyal always said, and he took care of all Grandmother's horses so he should know. Roanna loved riding almost as much as she had loved Mama and Daddy. The upper part of her felt like she was flying, but with her legs she could feel the horse's strength and muscles, as if *she* was that strong. That was one good part about living with Grandmother; she would be able to ride every day, and Loyal could teach her how to stay on the bigger horses.

But the best part was that Webb and his mama lived here, too, and she'd see him every day.

Suddenly she jumped down from the window seat and raced through the house, forgetting that she was wearing her slick-soled Sunday shoes instead of her sneakers until she skidded on the hardwood floor and almost slid into a table. Aunt Gloria's sharp admonition rang in the air behind her, but Roanna ignored it as she wrestled with the heavy front door, using all of her slight weight to tug it open enough that she could slip through. Then she was running across the lawn toward Webb and Jessie, her knees kicking up the skirt of her dress with every step.

Halfway there the knot of misery in her chest suddenly unwound, and she began sobbing. Webb watched her coming, and his expression changed. He let go of Jessie's hand and held his arms out to Roanna. She hurled herself into his lap, setting the swing to bumping. Jessie said sharply, "You're making a mess, Roanna. Go blow your nose."

But Webb said, "Here's my handkerchief," and wiped Roanna's face himself. Then he simply held her, her face buried against his shoulder, while she sobbed so violently that her entire little body heaved.

"Oh, God," Jessie said in disgust.

"Shut up," Webb replied, holding Roanna closer. "She's lost her parents."

"Well, I lost my mama, too," Jessie pointed out. "You don't see me squalling all over everybody."

"She's just seven," Webb said while he smoothed Roanna's tousled mop of hair. She was a pest most of the time, tagging along after her older cousins, but she was just a little kid, and he thought Jessie should be more sympathetic. The late afternoon sun slanted across the lawn and through the trees, catching in Roanna's hair and highlighting the glossy chestnut, making the strands glitter with gold and red. Earlier in the afternoon they had buried three members of their family, Roanna's parents and Jessie's mother. Aunt Lucinda had suffered the most, he thought, because she had lost both of her children at once: David, Roanna's daddy, and Janet, Jessie's mama. The huge weight of grief had bowed her down under the past three days, but it hadn't broken her. She was still the backbone of the family, lending her strength to others.

Roanna was quieting down, her sobs dwindling into occasional hiccups. Her round little head bounced against his collarbone as, without looking up, she scrubbed her face with his handkerchief. She felt frail in his strong young arms, her bones not much bigger than matchsticks, her back only about nine inches wide. Roanna was skinny, all pipestem arms and legs, and small for her age. He kept patting her while Jessie wore a long-suffering expression, and eventually one slanted, tear-wet eye peeped out from the security of his shoulder.

"Grandmother said that Jessie and I are going to live here, too," she said.

"Well, of course," Jessie replied, as if any other place would be unacceptable. "Where else would I live? But if I were them, I'd send you to the Orphans' Home."

Tears welled in that eye again and Roanna promptly reburied her face in Webb's shoulder. He glared at Jessie, and she flushed and looked away. Jessie was spoiled. Lately, at least half the time he thought she needed a good spanking. The other half of the time he was enthralled by those new curves to her body. She knew it, too. Once this summer, when they were swimming, she had let the strap of her bathing suit top fall down her arm, baring the upper part of one breast almost to the nipple. Webb's body had reacted with all the painful intensity of recent adolescence, but he hadn't been able to look away. He had just stood there, thanking God that the water was higher than his waist, but the part of him that had been above water had been dark red with mingled embarrassment, arousal, and frustration.

But she was beautiful. God, Jessie was beautiful. She looked like a princess, with her sleek dark hair and dark blue eyes. Her features were perfect, her skin flawless. And now she would be living here at Davencourt with Aunt Lucinda . . . and with him.

He returned his attention to Roanna, jostling her. "Don't listen to Jessie," he said. "She's just spouting off without knowing what she's talking about. You won't ever have to go anywhere. I don't think there *are* any orphanages anymore."

She peeked out again. Her eyes were brown, almost chestnut colored like her hair, just without the red. She was the only person on either the Davenport or Tallant sides of the family who had brown eyes; everyone else had either blue or green eyes or a mixture of the two. Jessie had teased her once, telling her that she wasn't really a Davenport because her eyes were the wrong color, that she'd been adopted. Roanna had been in tears until Webb had put a stop to that, too, telling her that she had her mother's eyes, and he knew she was a Davenport because he remembered going to see her in the hospital nursery when she'd just been born.

"Was Jessie just teasing?" she asked now.

"That's all it was," he replied soothingly. "Just teasing."

Roanna didn't turn her head to look at Jessie, but one small fist darted out and hammered Jessie on the shoulder, then was quickly retracted back into the safety of his embrace.

Webb had to swallow a laugh, but Jessie erupted into fury. "She hit me!" she shrieked, lifting her hand to slap Roanna.

Webb shot his hand out, catching Jessie's wrist. "No, you don't," he said. "You deserved it for telling her that."

She tried to jerk away but Webb held her, his grip tightening and his darkened eyes telling Jessie that he meant business. She went still, glaring at him, but he ruthlessly exerted his will and superior strength, and after a few seconds she sullenly subsided. He released her wrist, and she rubbed it as if he had really hurt her. He knew better, though, and didn't feel guilty as she intended. Jessie was good at manipulating people, but Webb had seen through her a long time ago. Knowing her for the little witch she was, though, only made it more satisfying that he had forced her to back down.

His face flushed as he felt himself getting hard, and he shifted Roanna slightly away from him. His heart was beating faster, with excitement and triumph. It was just a little thing, but suddenly he knew that he could handle Jessie. In those few seconds their entire relationship had changed, the casually close ties of kinship and childhood becoming the past, while the more intricate, volatile passions of male and female took their place. The process had been happening all summer long, but now it was completed. He looked at Jessie's sulky face, her lower lip pouting, and he wanted to kiss her until she forgot why she was pouting. Maybe she didn't quite understand yet, but he did.

Jessie was going to be his. She was spoiled and sulky, her emotions volcanic in intensity. It would take a lot of skill and energy to stay on top of her, but someday he would be there physically as well as mentally. He had two trump cards that Jessie didn't yet know about: the power of sex, and the lure of Davencourt. Aunt Lucinda had talked to him a lot the night of the car wreck. They had been sitting up alone, Aunt Lucinda rocking and quietly weeping as she dealt with the death of her children, and finally Webb had worked up the courage to approach and put his arms around her. She had broken down then, sobbing as if her heart would break—the only time she had so completely given in to her grief.

But when she had composed herself, they had sat alone far into the early hours of the morning, talking in hushed tones. Aunt Lucinda had a great reservoir of strength, and she had brought it to bear on the task of securing Davencourt's safety. Her beloved David, heir to Davencourt, was dead. Janet, her only daughter, was equally beloved but had not been suited in either nature or desire to handle the massive responsibilities involved. Janet had been quiet and withdrawn, her eyes dark with an inner pain that never quite went away. Webb suspected it was because of Jessie's father—whoever he was. Jessie was illegitimate, and Janet had never said who had fathered her. Mama said it had been a huge scandal, but the Davenports had closed ranks and the upper echelon of Tuscumbia society had been forced to accept both mother and child or face Davenport retaliation. Since the Davenports were the wealthiest family in the northwest quarter of Alabama, they had been able to carry it off.

But now, with both her children dead, Aunt Lucinda had to safeguard the family properties. It wasn't just Davencourt, the center jewel; it was stocks and bonds, real estate, factories, timber and mineral rights, banks, even restaurants. The sum total of Davenport holdings required an agile brain to understand it and a certain quality of ruthlessness to oversee it.

Webb was fourteen, but the morning after that long midnight talk with Aunt Lucinda, she had taken the family lawyer into the study, closed the door, and designated Webb as the heir apparent. He was a Tallant, not a Davenport, but he was her adored brother's grandson, and she herself had been a Tallant, so that wasn't a great hindrance in her eyes. Perhaps because Jessie had started life with such a huge strike against her, Aunt Lucinda had always shown a marked preference for Jessie over Roanna, but Aunt Lucinda's love was never blind. As much as she might wish otherwise, she knew Jessie was too volatile to take up the reins of such a huge enterprise; given a free hand, Jessie would have the family bankrupt within five years of attaining her majority.

Roanna, the only other direct descendant, wasn't even considered. She was only seven, for one thing, and completely unruly. It wasn't that the child was disobedient, exactly, but she had a definite talent for finding disaster. If there was a mud puddle within a quarter mile, Roanna would somehow manage to fall in it—but only if she was wearing her best dress. If she was wearing expensive new slippers, she would accidentally step into a horse pile. She constantly turned over, dropped, or spilled whatever was in her hands or merely nearby. The only talent she had, apparently, was an affinity for horses. That was a big plus in Aunt Lucinda's eyes, as she, too, loved the animals, but unfortunately didn't make Roanna any more acceptable in the role of main heiress.

Davencourt was going to be his, Davencourt and all the vast holdings. Webb looked up at the huge white house sitting like a crown in the middle of the lush green velvet of the lawn. Deep, wide verandas completely encircled the house on both stories, the railings laced with delicate ironwork. Six enormous white columns framed the front portico, where the veranda widened at the entrance. The house had an air of graciousness and comfort, imparted by the cool shade promised by the verandas, and the airy spaciousness, indicated by the vast expanse of windows. Double French doors graced each bedroom on the upper story, and a Palladian window arched majestically over the center entrance.

Davencourt was a hundred and twenty years old, built in the decade before the war. That was why there was a gently curving staircase on the left side, to provide a discreet entrance to the house for carousing young men, back when the bachelors of the family had slept in a separate wing. At Davencourt, that wing had been the left one. Various remodelings over the past century had done away with the separate sleeping quarters, but the outside entrance to the second floor remained. Lately, Webb had used the staircase a time or two himself.

And it was all going to be his.

He didn't feel guilty over being chosen to inherit. Even at fourteen, Webb was aware of the force of driving ambition within him. He *wanted* the pressure, the power of all that Davencourt entailed. It would be like riding the wildest stallion alive but mastering it with his own force of will.

It wasn't as if Jessie and Roanna had been disinherited, far from it. They would still both be wealthy women in their own right when they came of age. But the majority of the stocks, the majority of the power—and all the responsibility—would be his. Rather than being intimidated by the years of hard work that lay before him, Webb felt a fierce joy at the prospect. Not only would he own Davencourt, but Jessie came with the deal. Aunt Lucinda had hinted as much, but it wasn't until a few moments ago that he'd realized fully what she meant.

She wanted him to marry Jessie.

He almost laughed aloud in exultation. Oh, he knew his Jessie, and so did Aunt Lucinda. When it became known that he was going to inherit Davencourt, Jessie would instantly decide that she, and no one else, would marry him. He didn't mind; he knew how to handle her, and he had no illusions about her. Most of Jessie's unpleasantness was due to that massive chip on her shoulder, the burden of her illegitimacy. She deeply resented Roanna's legitimate status and was hateful to the kid because of it. That would change, though, when they married. He would see to it, because now he had Jessie's number.

Lucinda Davenport ignored the ongoing chatter behind her as she stood at the window and watched the three young people sitting in the swing. They belonged to her; her blood ran in all three of them. They were the future, the hope of Davencourt, all that was left.

When she had first been told of the car accident, for a few dark hours the burden of grief had been so massive that she had felt crushed beneath it, unable to function, to care. She still felt as if the best part of herself had been torn away, with huge gaping wounds left behind. Their names echoed in her mother's heart. *David. Janet.* Memories swam through her mind, so that she saw them as tiny infants at her breast, rambunctious toddlers, romping children, awkward adolescents, wonderful adults. She was sixty-three and had lost many people whom she had loved, but this latest blow was almost a killing one. A mother should never outlive her children.

But in the darkest hour, Webb had been there, offering her silent comfort. He was only fourteen, but already the man was taking shape in the boy's body. He reminded her a lot of her brother, the first Webb; there was the same core of hard, almost reckless strength, and an inner maturity that made him seem far older than his years. He hadn't flinched from her grief but had shared it with her, letting her know that despite this massive loss, she wasn't alone. It was in that dark hour that she had seen the glimmer of light and known what she would do. When she had first broached to him the idea of training to take over the Davenport enterprises, of eventually owning Davencourt itself, he hadn't been intimidated. Instead his green eyes had gleamed at the prospect, at the very challenge of it.

She had made a good choice. Some of the others would howl; Gloria and her bunch would be outraged that Webb had been chosen over any of the Ameses, when after all they were the same degree of kin to Lucinda. Jessie would have good cause to be angry, for she was a Davenport and direct kin, but as much as she loved the girl, Lucinda knew Davencourt wouldn't be in good hands with her. Webb was the best choice, and he would take care of Jessie.

She watched the small tableau in the swing play itself out in silence and knew that Webb had won that battle. The boy already had the instincts of a man, and a dominant man at that. Jessie was sulking, but he didn't give in to her. He continued comforting Roanna, who as usual had managed to cause some sort of trouble.

Roanna. Lucinda sighed. She didn't feel up to assuming the care of a seven-year-old, but the child was David's daughter, and she simply couldn't allow her to go anywhere else. She had tried, out of fairness, but she couldn't love Roanna as much as she loved Jessie, or Webb, who wasn't even her grandchild, but a great-nephew.

Despite her fierce support for her daughter when Janet was pregnant without benefit of a husband, Lucinda had expected to, at best, tolerate the baby when it came. She had been very much afraid that she would actively dislike it, because of the disgrace it represented. Instead she had taken one look at the tiny, flowerlike face of her granddaughter and fallen in love. Oh, Jessie was a high-spirited handful with her share of faults, but Lucinda's love had never wavered. Jessie *needed* love, so much love, soaking up every snippet of affection and praise that came her way. It hadn't been a starvation diet; from her birth, she had been cuddled and kissed and made over, but for some reason it had never been quite enough. Children sensed early when something about their lives was out of kilter, and Jessie was particularly bright; she had been about two when she had started asking why *she* didn't have a daddy.

And then there was Roanna. Lucinda sighed again. It had been as difficult to love Roanna as it was easy to love Jessie. The two cousins were total opposites. Roanna had never been still long enough for anyone to cuddle her. Pick her up for a hug, and she was squirming to get down. Nor was she pretty the way Jessie was. Roanna's odd mix of features didn't fit her small face. Her nose was too long, her mouth too wide, her eyes narrow and slanted. Her hair, with its un-Davenport-like tinge of red, was always untidy. No matter what she wore, give her five minutes and the garment would be dirty and likely torn. She favored her mother's people, of course, but she was definitely a weed in the Davenport garden. Lucinda had looked hard, but she couldn't see anything of David in the child, and now any resemblance would have been doubly precious had it existed.

But she would do her duty by Roanna, and try to mold her into some sort of civilized being, one who would be a credit to the Davenports.

Her hope, though, and the future, lay with Jessie and Webb.

CHAPTER
2

*L*ucinda wiped away the tears as she sat in Janet's bedroom and slowly folded and packed away her daughter's clothing. Both Yvonne and Sandra had offered to do this for her, but she had insisted on doing it alone. She didn't want anyone to witness her tears, her grief; and only she would know which items were precious, because of the memories, and which could be discarded. She had already performed this last task at David's house, tenderly folding away shirts that still faintly carried the scent of his cologne. She had wept, too, for her daughter-in-law; Karen had been well liked, a cheerful, loving young woman who had made David very happy. Their things had been stored in trunks at Davencourt for Roanna to have when she was older.

It had been a month since the accident. The legal formalities had promptly been taken care of, with Jessie and Roanna permanently installed at Davencourt and Lucinda as their legal guardian. Jessie, of course, had settled right in, commandeering the prettiest bedroom as her own and cajoling Lucinda into redecorating it to her specifications. Lucinda admitted that she hadn't needed much cajoling, because she understood Jessie's fierce need to regain control of her life, impose order on her surroundings again. The bedroom was only a symbol. She had spoiled Jessie shamelessly, letting her know that even though her mother had died, she still had a family who supported and loved her, that security hadn't vanished from her world.

Roanna, however, hadn't settled in at all. Lucinda sighed, holding one of Janet's blouses to her cheek as she pondered David's daughter. She simply didn't know how to get close to the child. Roanna had resisted all efforts to get her to choose a bedroom, and finally Lucinda had given up and chosen for her. A sense of fairness had insisted that Roanna's bedroom be at least as big as Jessie's, and it was, but the little girl had merely looked lost and overwhelmed in it. She had slept there the first night. The second night, she had slept in one of the other bedrooms, dragging her blanket with her and curling up on the bare mattress. The third night, it had been yet another empty bedroom, another bare mattress. She had slept in a chair in the den, on the rug in the library, even huddled on the floor of a bathroom. She was a restless, forlorn little spirit, drifting around in search of a place of her own. Lucinda estimated that the child had now slept in every room of the house except for the bedrooms occupied by others.

When Webb got up every morning, the first thing he did was go on a Roanna hunt, tracking her down in whichever nook or cranny she had chosen for the night, coaxing her out of her blanket cocoon. She was sullen and withdrawn, except with Webb, and had no interest in anything but the horses. Frustrated, not knowing what else to do, Lucinda had given her unlimited access to the horses, at least for the summer. Loyal would look out for the child, and Roanna had an uncommonly good touch with the animals anyway.

Lucinda folded the blouse, the last one, and put it away. Only the contents of the nightstand remained, and she hesitated before opening the drawers. When that was finished, it would all be finished; the townhouse would be emptied, closed, and sold. All traces of Janet would be gone.

Except for Jessie, Janet had left precious little of herself.

After she'd gotten pregnant, most of her laughter had died, and there had always been sadness in her eyes. Though she'd never said who fathered Jessie, Lucinda suspected it was the oldest Leath boy, Dwight. He and Janet had dated, but then he'd gotten in an argument with his father and enlisted and somehow ended up in Vietnam in the early days of the war. Within two weeks of setting foot in that miserable little country, he'd been killed. Over the years Lucinda had often looked at Jessie's face, searching for some resemblance to the Leaths but instead saw only pure Davenport beauty. If Dwight was Janet's lover, then he had been mourned until the day of her death, because she had never dated anyone else after Jessie's birth. It wasn't that she hadn't had the opportunity either; despite the awkwardness of Jessie's illegitimacy, Janet was still a Davenport, and there were plenty of men who would have wanted her. The lack of interest had all been on Janet's part.

Lucinda had hoped for more for her daughter. She herself had known deep love with Marshall Davenport and had wished the same for her children. David had found it with Karen; Janet had known only pain and disappointment. Lucinda didn't like to admit it, but she had always sensed a certain restraint in Janet's manner toward Jessie, as if she were ashamed. It was the way Lucinda had expected to feel but hadn't. She wished Janet could have gotten past the pain, but she never had.

Well, putting off an unpleasant chore wouldn't make it any less unpleasant, Lucinda thought, unconsciously straightening her spine. She could sit here all day musing over the intricacies of life, or she could get on with it. Lucinda Tallant Davenport wasn't one to sit around whining; right or wrong, she got things done.

She pulled open the top drawer of the nightstand, and tears filled her eyes again at the neatness of the contents. That was Janet, tidy to the bone. There was the book she'd been reading, a small flashlight, a box of tissues, a decorative tin of her favorite peppermint candy, and a leather-bound journal with the pen still stuck between the pages. Curious, Lucinda wiped away her tears and pulled out the journal. She hadn't known that Janet kept one.

She smoothed her hand over the journal, knowing full well what information might be on the pages. It could be only private comments on day-to-day life, but there was the possibility that here Janet had divulged the secret she'd carried to her grave. At this late date, did it really matter who Jessie's father was?

Not really, Lucinda thought. She would love Jessie no matter whose blood ran in her veins.

But still, after so many years of wondering and not knowing, the temptation was impossible to resist. She opened the journal to the first page and began reading.

Half an hour later, she blotted her eyes with a tissue and slowly closed the journal, then placed it on top of the pile of clothes in the last box. There hadn't been all that much to read: several anguished pages, written fourteen years ago, then very little after that. Janet had made a few notations, marking Jessie's first tooth, first step, first day in school, but for the most part the pages were blank. It was as if Janet had stopped living fourteen years ago, rather than just a month. Poor Janet, to have hoped for much and settled for so little.

Lucinda smoothed her hand over the journal's leather cover. Well, now she knew. And she had been right: it didn't make any difference at all.

She picked up the roll of masking tape and briskly sealed the box.

BOOK TWO

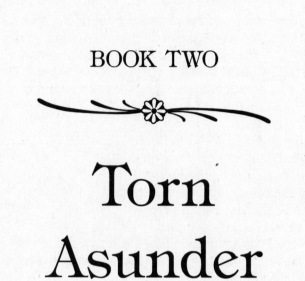

Torn Asunder

CHAPTER

3

*R*oanna bounced out of bed with the dawn, hurrying to brush her teeth and drag her hands through her hair, then scrambling into jeans and a T-shirt. She grabbed her boots and socks on the way out the door and ran barefoot down the stairs. Webb was driving up to Nashville, and she wanted to see him before he left. She didn't have any particular reason other than that she seized every opportunity to have a few private minutes with him, precious seconds when his attention, his smiles, were only for her.

Even at five o'clock in the morning, Grandmother would have had her breakfast in the morning room, but Roanna didn't even pause there on her way to the kitchen. Webb, while thoroughly comfortable with the wealth that was at his disposal, didn't give a snap of his finger for appearances. He would be scrounging around in the kitchen, preparing his own breakfast since Tansy didn't come to work until six, then eating it at the kitchen table.

She burst through the door, and as she had expected, Webb was there. He hadn't bothered with the table and was instead leaning against the cabinet while he munched on a jelly-spread slice of toast. A cup of coffee steamed gently beside his hand. As soon as he saw her, he turned and dropped another slice of bread into the toaster.

"I'm not hungry," she said, poking her head into the huge double-doored refrigerator to find the orange juice.

"You never are," he returned equably. "Eat anyway." Her lack of appetite was why, at seventeen, she was still skinny and barely developed. That and the fact that Roanna never simply *walked* anywhere. She was a perpetual motion machine: she skipped, she bounded, occasionally she even turned cartwheels. At least, over the years, she had finally settled down enough to sleep in the same bed every night, and he no longer had to search for her every morning.

Because it was Webb who'd made the toast, she ate it, though she rejected the jelly. He poured a cup of coffee for her, and she stood beside him, munching dry toast and alternately sipping orange juice and coffee, and felt contentment glowing warmly deep in her middle. This was all she asked out of life: to be alone with Webb. And to work with the horses, of course.

She gently inhaled, drawing in the delicious scents of his understated cologne and the clean, slight muskiness of his skin, all mingled with the aroma of the coffee. Her awareness of him was so intense it was almost painful, but she lived for these moments.

She eyed him over the rim of her cup, her whiskey brown eyes glinting with mischief. "The timing of this trip to Nashville is pretty suspicious," she teased. "I think you just want to get away from the house."

He grinned, and her heart flip-flopped. She seldom saw that cheerful grin any more; he was so busy that he didn't have time for anything but work, as Jessie consistently, relentlessly complained. His cool green eyes warmed when he smiled, and the lazy charm of his grin could stop traffic. The laziness was deceptive, though; Webb worked hours that would have exhausted most men.

"I didn't plan it," he protested, then admitted, "but I jumped at the chance. I guess you're going to stay in the stables all day."

She nodded. Grandmother's sister and her husband, Aunt Gloria and Uncle Harlan, were moving in today, and Roanna wanted to be as far from the house as possible. Aunt Gloria was her least favorite of aunts, and she didn't care much for Uncle Harlan either.

"He's a know-it-all," she grumbled. "And she's a pain in the—"

"Ro," he said warningly, drawing out the single syllable. Only he ever called her by the abbreviation of her name. It was one more tiny connection between them for her to savor, for she thought of herself as Ro. Roanna was the girl who was skinny and unattractive, clumsy and gauche. Ro was the part of herself who could ride like the wind, her thin body blending with the horse's and becoming part of its rhythm; the girl who, while in the stables, never put a foot wrong. If she had her way, she'd have *lived* in the stables.

"Neck," she finished, with a look of innocence that made him chuckle. "When Davencourt is yours, are you going to throw them out?"

"Of course not, you little heathen. They're family."

"Well, it isn't as if they don't have a place to live. Why don't they stay in their own house?"

"Since Uncle Harlan retired, they've been having trouble making ends meet. There's plenty of space here, so their moving in is the logical solution, even if you don't like it." He ruffled her untidy hair.

She sighed. It was true that there were ten bedrooms in Davencourt, and since Jessie and Webb had gotten married and now used only one room, and since Aunt Yvonne had decided to move out last year and get a place of her own, that meant seven of those bedrooms were empty. Still, she didn't like it. "Well, what about when you and Jessie have kids? You'll need the other rooms then."

"I don't think we'll need seven of them," he said drily, and a grim look entered his eyes. "We may not have any kids anyway."

Her heart jumped at that. She had been down in the dumps since he and Jessie had married two years ago, but she had really dreaded the idea of Jessie having his babies. Somehow that would have been the final blow to a heart that hadn't had much hope to begin with; she knew she'd never had a chance with Webb, but still a tiny glimmer lingered. As long as he and Jessie didn't have any children, it was as if he wasn't totally, finally hers. For Webb, she thought, children would be an unbreakable bond. As long as there were no babies, she could still hope, however futilely.

It was no secret in the house that their marriage wasn't all roses. Jessie never kept it a secret when she was unhappy, because she made a concerted effort to make certain everyone else was just as miserable as she was.

Knowing Jessie, and Roanna knew Jessie very well, she had probably planned to use sex, after they were married, to control Webb. Roanna would have been surprised if Jessie had let Webb make love to her before they were married. Well, maybe once, to keep his interest keen. Roanna never underestimated the depths of Jessie's calculation. The thing was, neither did Webb, and Jessie's little plan hadn't worked. No matter what tricks she tried, Webb seldom changed his mind, and when he did it was for reasons of his own. No, Jessie was *not* happy.

Roanna loved it. She couldn't begin to understand their relationship, but Jessie didn't appear to have a clue about the type of man Webb was. You could appeal to him with logic, but manipulation left him unswayed. It had given Roanna many secretly gleeful moments over the years to watch Jessie try her feminine wiles on Webb and then throwing fits when they didn't work. Jessie just couldn't understand it; after all, it worked on everyone else.

Webb checked his watch. "I have to go." He swiftly gulped the rest of his coffee, then bent to kiss her forehead. "Stay out of trouble today."

"I'll try," she promised, then added glumly, "I *always* try." And somehow seldom succeeded. Despite her best efforts, she was always doing something that displeased Grandmother.

Webb gave her a rueful grin on his way out the door, and

their eyes met for a moment in a way that made her feel as if they were co-conspirators. Then he was gone, closing the door behind him, and with a sigh she sat down in one of the chairs to pull on her socks and boots. The dawn had dimmed with his leaving.

In a way, she thought, they really were co-conspirators. She was relaxed and unguarded with Webb in a way she never was with the rest of the family, and she never saw disapproval in his eyes when he looked at her. Webb accepted her as she was and didn't try to make her into something she wasn't.

But there was one other place where she found approval, and her heart lightened as she ran to the stables.

When the moving van drove up at eight-thirty, Roanna barely noticed it. She and Loyal were working with a frisky yearling colt, patiently getting him accustomed to human handling. He was fearless, but he wanted to play rather than learn anything new, and the gentle lesson required a lot of patience.

"You're wearing me out," she panted and fondly stroked the animal's glossy neck. The colt responded by shoving her with his head, sending her staggering several paces backward. "There has to be an easier way," she said to Loyal, who was sitting on the fence, giving her directions, and grinning as the colt romped like an oversized dog.

"Like what?" he asked. He was always willing to listen to Roanna's ideas.

"Why don't we start handling them as soon as they're born? Then they'd be too little to shove me all over the corral," she grumbled. "And they'd grow up used to humans and the things we do to them."

"Well, now." Loyal stroked his jaw as he thought about it. He was a lean, hard fifty and had already spent almost thirty of those years working at Davencourt, the long hours outside turning his brown face into a network of fine wrinkles. He ate, lived, and breathed horses and couldn't imagine any job more suited to him than the one he had. Just because it was customary to wait until the foals were yearlings before beginning their training didn't mean it had to be that way. Roanna might have something there. Horses had to get used to people fooling around with their mouths and feet, and it might be easier on both horses and humans if the process started when they were foaled rather than after a year of running wild. It should cut down on a lot of skittishness as well as making it easier on the farriers and the vets.

"Tell you what," he said. "We won't have another foal until Lightness drops hers in March. We'll start with that one and see how it works."

Roanna's face lit up, her brown eyes turning almost golden with delight, and for a moment Loyal was struck by how pretty she was. He was startled, because Roanna was really a plain little thing, her features too big and masculine for her thin face, but for a fleeting moment he'd gotten a glimpse of how she would look when maturity had worked its full magic on her. She'd never be the beauty Miss Jessie was, he thought realistically, but when she got older, she'd surprise a few people. The idea made him happy, because Roanna was his favorite. Miss Jessie was a competent rider, but she didn't love his babies the way Roanna did and therefore wasn't as careful of her mount's welfare as she could have been. In Loyal's eyes, that was an unforgivable sin.

At eleven-thirty, Roanna reluctantly returned to the house for lunch. She would much rather have skipped the meal entirely, but Grandmother would send someone after her if she didn't show up, so she figured she might as well save everyone the trouble. But she had cut it too close, as usual, and didn't have time for more than a quick shower and change of clothes. She dragged a comb through her wet hair, then raced down the stairs, sliding to a halt just before she opened the door to the dining room and entered at a more decorous pace.

Everyone else was already seated. Aunt Gloria looked up at Roanna's entrance, and her mouth drew into the familiar disapproving line. Grandmother took in Roanna's wet hair and sighed but didn't comment. Uncle Harlan gave her one of his insincere used-car-salesman smiles, but at least he never scolded her, so Roanna forgave him for having all the depth of a pie pan. Jessie, however, went straight on the attack.

"At least you could have taken the time to dry your hair," she drawled. "Though I suppose we should all be grateful you showered and didn't come to the table smelling like a horse."

Roanna slid into her seat and fastened her gaze on her plate. She didn't bother responding to Jessie's malice. To do so would only provoke even more nastiness, and Aunt Gloria would seize the chance to put in her two cents' worth. Roanna was used to Jessie's zingers, but she wasn't happy at all that Aunt Gloria and Uncle Harlan had moved into Davencourt, and she felt she would doubly resent anything Aunt Gloria said.

Tansy served the first course, a cold cucumber soup. Roanna hated cucumber soup and merely dabbled her spoon around in it, trying to sink the tiny green pieces of herb that floated on top. She did nibble on one of Tansy's homemade poppy seed rolls and gladly relinquished her soup bowl when the next course, tuna-stuffed tomato, was served. She liked tuna-stuffed tomato. She devoted the first few minutes to painstakingly removing the bits of celery and onion from the tuna mixture, pushing the rejects into a small pile at the edge of her plate.

"Your manners are deplorable," Aunt Gloria announced as she delicately forked up a bite of tuna. "For heaven's sake, Roanna, you're seventeen, plenty old enough to stop playing with your food like a two-year-old."

Roanna's scant appetite died, the familiar tension and nausea tightening her stomach, and she cast a resentful glance at Aunt Gloria.

"Oh, she always does that," Jessie said airily. "She's like a hog rooting around for the best pieces of slop."

Just to show them she didn't care, Roanna forced herself to swallow two bites of the tuna, washing them down with most of her glass of tea to make certain they didn't lodge halfway.

She doubted it was tact on his part, but she was grateful anyway when Uncle Harlan began talking about the repairs needed on their car and weighing the advantages of buying a new one. If they could afford a new car, Roanna thought, they could certainly have afforded staying in their own house, then she wouldn't have to put up with Aunt Gloria every day. Jessie mentioned that she would like a new car, too; she was bored with that boxy four-door Mercedes Webb had insisted on buying for her, when she'd told him at least a thousand times she wanted a sports car, something with style.

Roanna didn't have a car. Jessie had gotten her first car when she was sixteen, but Roanna was a rotten driver, forever drifting off into daydreams, and Grandmother had stated that, in the interest of the safety of the citizens of Colbert County, it was best not to let Roanna out on the roads by herself. She hadn't resented it all that much, because she would much rather ride than drive, but now one of her demon imps raised its head.

"I'd like to have a sports car, too," she said, the first words she'd spoken since entering the dining room. Her eyes were round with innocence. "I've got my heart set on one of those Pontiac Grand Pricks."

Aunt Gloria's eyes rounded with horror, and her fork dropped into her plate with a clatter. Uncle Harlan choked on his tuna, then began laughing helplessly.

"Young lady!" Grandmother's hand slammed against the table, making Roanna jump guiltily. Some people might think her mispronunciation of Grand Prix had been the result of ignorance, but Grandmother knew better. "Your behavior is inexcusable," Grandmother said icily, her blue eyes snapping. "Leave this table. I'll speak to you later."

Roanna slipped from her chair, her cheeks red with embarrassment. "I'm sorry," she whispered and ran from the dining room but not fast enough to keep from hearing Jessie's amused, malicious question:

"Do you think she'll *ever* be civilized enough to eat with *people?*"

"I'd *rather* be with the horses," Roanna muttered as she slammed out the front door. She knew she should go back upstairs and change into boots again, but she desperately needed to get back to the stables, where she never felt inadequate.

Loyal was eating his own lunch in his office, while he read one of the thirty horse care publications that he received each month. He caught sight of her through the window as she slipped inside the stable and shook his head in resignation. Either she hadn't eaten anything, which wouldn't surprise him, or she was in trouble again, which wouldn't surprise him either. It was probably both. Poor Roanna was a square peg who stubbornly resisted all efforts to whittle down her corners so she would fit into the round hole, and never mind that most people happily whittled on their own corners. Burdened with almost constant disapproval, she merely hunkered down and resisted until the frustration grew too strong to be repressed, then struck out, usually in a way that only brought more disapproval. If she'd had even one-half of Miss Jessie's meanness, she could have really fought back and forced everyone to accept her on her own terms. But Roanna didn't have a mean bone in her body, which was probably why animals loved her so much. She was chock-full of mischief, though, and that only caused more trouble.

He watched as she drifted from stall to stall, trailing her fingers over the smooth wood. There was only one horse in the stable, Mrs. Davenport's favorite mount, a gray gelding who had injured his right foreleg. Loyal was keeping him quiet today, with cold packs on the leg to ease the swelling. He heard Roanna's crooning voice as she stroked the gelding's face, and he smiled as the horse's eyes almost closed with ecstasy. If her family gave her half the acceptance the horses did, he thought, she would stop fighting them at every turn and settle into the life into which she had been born.

Jessie drifted down to the stables after lunch and ordered one of the hands to saddle a horse for her. Roanna rolled her eyes at Jessie's lady-of-the-manor airs; she always caught and saddled her own horse, and it wouldn't hurt Jessie to do the same. To be honest, she never had any trouble catching a horse, but Jessie didn't have that knack. It only showed how smart horses were, Roanna thought.

Jessie caught her expression out of the corner of her eye and turned a cool, malicious look on her cousin. "Grandmother's furious with you. It was important to her that Aunt Gloria be made to feel welcome, and instead you went into your hick act." She paused ever so slightly and let her gaze drift over Roanna. "If it *is* an act." Having delivered that zinger, so subtly sharp that it slid between Roanna's ribs with barely a twinge, she smiled faintly and walked away, leaving only the miasma of her expensive perfume behind.

"Hateful witch," Roanna muttered, waving her hand to disperse the too-heavy scent while she stared resentfully at her cousin's slim, elegant back. It wasn't fair that Jessie should be so beautiful, know how to get along in public so perfectly, be Grandmother's favorite, and have Webb, too. It just wasn't *fair*.

Roanna wasn't the only one feeling resentful. Jessie seethed with it as she rode away from Davencourt. *Damn* Webb! She wished she'd never married him, even though it was what she'd set her sights on from girlhood, what everyone had taken for granted would happen. And Webb had taken it more for granted than anyone else, but then he'd always been so damn cocksure of himself that sometimes she nearly died with the urge to slap him. That she never had was due to two things: one, she hadn't wanted to do anything that would hurt her chances of ruling supreme at Davencourt when Grandmother finally died; and two, she had the uneasy suspicion that Webb wouldn't be a gentleman about it. No, it was more than a suspicion. He might pull the wool over everyone else's eyes, but she knew what a ruthless bastard he was.

She had been a fool to marry him. Surely she could have gotten Grandmother to change her will and leave Davencourt to her instead of to Webb. After all, *she* was a Davenport, not Webb. It should have been hers by right. Instead she'd had to marry that damn tyrant, and she'd made a big mistake in doing so. Chagrined, she had to admit that she'd overestimated her own charms and her ability to influence him. She thought she'd been so smart, refusing to sleep with him before marriage; she'd liked the idea of keeping him frustrated, liked the image of him panting after her like a dog after a bitch in heat. It had never been quite that way, but she'd cherished the image anyway. Instead, she'd been infuriated to learn that, rather than suffering because he couldn't have her, the bastard had simply been sleeping with other women—while he insisted she be faithful to him!

Well, she'd shown him. He was an even bigger fool than she was if he really believed she'd kept herself "pure" for him all those years while he was out screwing those bitches he met in college and at work. She knew better than to mess up her own playground, but whenever she could get away for a day or a weekend, she quickly found some lucky guy to take the edge off, so to speak. Attracting men was disgustingly easy—just give them a whiff and they came running. She'd done it the first time at the age of sixteen and had immediately discovered a delicious source of power over men. Oh, she'd had to do some pretending when she and Webb had finally married, whimpering and actually squeezing out a tear or two so he'd think his big bad pecker was actually hurting her poor little *virginal* pussy, but inside she'd been gloating that he'd been so easy to fool.

She'd also been gloating because now she was finally going to have the power in their relationship. After years of having to sweetly kowtow to him, she'd thought she had him where she wanted him. It was humiliating to remember how she'd thought he'd be more easily handled once they were married and she had him in bed with her every night. God knows, most men thought with their peckers. All of her discreet liaisons over the years had told her that she wore them out, that they couldn't keep up with her, but they'd all said it with big smiles. Jessie took pride in her ability to screw a man into limp exhaustion. She'd had it all planned: screw Webb's brains out every night, and he'd be putty in her hands during the day.

But it hadn't worked out that way at all. Her cheeks burned with humiliation as she guided her horse across a shallow creek, taking care that the water didn't splash on her shiny boots. For one thing, more often than not she was the one who was left exhausted. Webb could go at it for hours, his eyes remaining cool and watchful no matter how she panted and jerked her hips and worked him over, as if he knew she regarded it as a competition and was damned if he'd let her win. It hadn't taken her long to learn that he could outlast her, and she would be the one left lying exhausted on the twisted sheets, her loins throbbing painfully from such hard use. And no matter how hot the sex, no matter how she sucked or stroked or did anything else, once it was finished and Webb was out of bed, he went about his business as if nothing had happened, and she could just make the best of it. Well, damned if she would!

Her biggest weapon, sex, had proven to be ineffective against him, and she wanted to scream at the injustice of it. He treated her as if she were a disobedient child rather than an adult, and his wife. He was nicer to that brat, Roanna, than he was to her. She was sick and tired of being left at home every day while he roamed all over the nation, for God's sake. He said it was business, but she was certain that at least half of his "urgent" trips were conceived at the last moment just to prevent her from doing something fun. Just last month he'd had to fly to Chicago the morning before they were supposed to go on vacation in the Bahamas. And then there was the trip to New York last week. He'd been gone for three days. She'd begged to go with him, dying with excitement at the thought of the shops and theaters and restaurants, but he'd said he wouldn't have time for her and left without her. Just like that. The arrogant bastard; he was probably screwing some silly little secretary and didn't want his wife around to mess up his plans.

But she had her revenge. A smile broke across her face as she reined in the horse and spotted the man who was already lying stretched out on the blanket beneath the big tree, almost hidden in the secluded little cove. It was the most delicious revenge she could have imagined, made all the sweeter by her own uncontrolled response. It frightened her sometimes that she desired him so savagely. He was an animal, totally amoral, as ruthless in his way as Webb was, though without the cool, precise intellect.

She remembered the first time she'd met him. It hadn't been long after Mama's funeral, after she had moved into Davencourt and wheedled Grandmother into letting her redecorate the bedroom she'd chosen. She and Grandmother had been in town to choose fabrics, but Grandmother had run into one of her cronies in the fabric shop and Jessie had quickly gotten bored. She had already chosen the fabric she liked, so there was no reason to hang around listening to two old biddies gossip. She had told Grandmother she was going to the restaurant next door to get a Coke and made her escape.

She *had* gone there; she had learned early that she could get away with a lot more if she simply did what she really wanted to do after she'd done what she'd said she was going to do. That way she couldn't be accused of *lying,* for heaven's sake. And people knew how impulsive teenagers were. So, icy Coke in hand, Jessie had then whisked herself down to the newsstand where dirty magazines were sold.

It wasn't really a newsstand, but a grimy little store that sold hobby kits, a smattering of makeup and toiletries, some "hygienic" items such as rubbers, as well as newspapers, paperbacks, and a wide selection of magazines. The *Newsweek*s and *Good Housekeeping*s were prominently displayed up front with all the other acceptable magazines, but the forbidden ones were kept on a rack behind a counter in back, and kids weren't supposed to go back there. But old man McElroy had arthritis real bad, and he spent most of his time sitting on a stool behind the checkout counter. He couldn't really see who was in the back area unless he stood up, and he didn't stand up very often.

Jessie gave old man McElroy a sweet smile and wandered over to the cosmetic section, where she leisurely inspected a few lipsticks and selected a sheer pink lip gloss, her reason for being there should she get caught. When a customer claimed his attention, she whisked herself out of sight and slipped into the back area.

Naked women cavorted on various covers, but Jessie spared them only a brief disdainful glance. If she wanted to see a naked woman, all she had to do was strip off her clothes. What she liked were the nudist magazines, where she could see naked men. Most of the time their peckers were small and limp, which didn't interest her at all, but sometimes there would be a picture of a man with a nice, long, fat one sticking out. The nudists said there was nothing sexy about running around naked, but Jessie figured they lied. Otherwise, why would those men be getting hard like Grandmother's stallion did when he was about to mount a mare? She had sneaked into the stables to watch whenever she could, though everyone would have been horrified, just *horrified,* if they'd known.

Jessie smirked. They didn't know, and they wouldn't. She was too smart for them. She was two different people, and they didn't even suspect. There was the public Jessie, the princess of the Davenports, the most popular girl in school who charmed everyone with her high spirits and who refused to experiment with alcohol and cigarettes the way all the other kids did. Then there was the real Jessie, the one she kept hidden, the one who slipped the paperback porn books under her clothes and smiled sweetly at Mr. McElroy as she left his store. The real Jessie stole money from her grandmother's purse, not because there was something she couldn't have just for the asking, but because she liked the thrill of it.

The real Jessie loved tormenting that little brat, Roanna, loved pinching her when no one could see, loved making her cry. Roanna was a safe target, because no one really liked her anyway and they would always believe Jessie rather than her if she carried tales. Lately, Jessie had begun to really hate the brat, rather than just disliking her. Webb was always taking up for her, for some reason, and that made Jessie furious. How dare he take Roanna's side instead of hers?

A secret little smile curved her mouth. She'd show him who was boss. Lately she had discovered a new weapon, as her body had grown and changed. She had been fascinated by sex for years, but now physically she was beginning to match her mental maturity. All she had to do was arch her back and take a deep breath, thrusting out her breasts, and Webb would stare so fixedly at them that it was all she could do to keep from laughing. He'd kissed her, too, and when she rubbed her front against him, he had started breathing real deep, and his pecker had gotten hard. She had thought about letting him do it to her, but an innate cunning had stopped her. She and Webb lived in the same house; she would be taking too much of a chance that others would find out, and that might change the image they had of her.

She had just reached out for one of the nudist magazines when a man spoke behind her, his voice low and raspy. "What's a pretty little gal like you doin' back here?"

Alarmed, Jessie snatched her hand back and whirled to face him. She was always so careful not to let anyone see her in this section, but she hadn't heard him approach. She stared up at him, blinking wide, startled eyes at him as she prepared to go into her act of the innocent young girl who had wandered back here by accident. What she saw in the hot, impossibly blue eyes looking down at her made her hesitate. This man didn't look as if he would believe any explanation she could make.

"You're Janet Davenport's kid, ain't you?" he asked, still keeping his voice low.

Slowly, Jessie nodded. Now that she'd had a good look at him, a strange thrill ran through her. He was probably in his thirties, way too old, but he was really muscular and the expression in those hot blue eyes made her think he must know some really nasty things.

He grunted. "Thought so. Sorry about your mama." But even as he said the conventional words, Jessie had the feeling that he didn't really care one way or the other. He was looking her up and down in a way that made her feel peculiar, as if she belonged to him.

"Who are you?" she whispered, casting a weather eye toward the front of the store.

A feral grin bared his white teeth. "The name's Harper Neeley, little darlin'. Mean anything to you?"

She caught her breath, because she knew the name. She had snooped through Mama's things on a regular basis. "Yes," she said, so excited she could barely stand still. "You're my daddy."

He'd been surprised that she'd known who he was, she thought now, watching him as he lazed beneath the tree while he waited for her. But as excited as she'd been at meeting him, he really hadn't given a damn that she was his daughter. Harper Neeley had a bunch of kids, at least half of them bastards. One more, even if that one was a Davenport, didn't mean anything to him. He'd approached her just for the hell of it, not because he really cared.

Somehow, that had excited her. It was like meeting the secret Jessie, walking around in her father's body.

He fascinated her. She had made a point of meeting with him occasionally over the years. He was rough and totally selfish, and she often felt as if he were laughing at her. It infuriated her, but whenever she saw him, she still felt that same electric excitement. He was so nasty, so totally unacceptable to her social circle . . . and he was hers.

Jessie couldn't remember exactly when the excitement had turned sexual. Maybe it had always been like that, but she just hadn't been ready to recognize it. She had been so focused on bringing Webb to heel, so careful to indulge herself only when she was safely away from her home area, that it simply hadn't occurred to her.

But one day, about a year ago, when she had seen him, the usual excitement had suddenly sharpened, turned almost feral in its intensity. She had been furious with Webb— what was new about that?—and Harper had been right there, his thickly muscled body enticing her, his hot blue eyes drifting down her body in a way no father should ever look at his daughter.

She had hugged him, cuddled against him, sweetly called him "Daddy," and all the while she had been rubbing her breasts against him, rolling her hips against his pecker. That was all it had taken. He'd laughed down at her, then crudely grabbed her crotch and shoved her to the ground, where they had gone at each other like animals.

She couldn't stay away from him. She had tried, knowing how dangerous he was, knowing that she had no power to control him, but he drew her like a lodestone. There were no games she could play with him, because he knew her exactly for what she was. There was nothing he could give her and nothing that she wanted from him, except for the mindless, heated sex. No one had ever screwed her the way her daddy did. She didn't have to gauge her every reaction or try to manipulate his response; all she could do was simply lose herself in the hot nastiness of the sex. Whatever he wanted to do to her, she was willing. He was trash, and she loved it, because he was the best revenge she could ever have chosen. When Webb got into bed beside her at night, it served him right that he was sleeping with a woman who, only hours before, had been sticky with Harper Neeley's leavings.

CHAPTER

4

*R*oanna stared after Jessie as she rode away from Davencourt, up toward the hilly part of the Davenport lands. Jessie usually preferred a less demanding ride, over fields or level pastures. Why would she deviate from custom? Come to think of it, she had ridden that way a couple of times before, and Roanna had noticed it but not paid attention to it. For some reason, this time she was puzzled.

Maybe it was because she still felt resentful at Jessie's last zinger, though God knows it hadn't been any worse than the usual cut at her fragile self-esteem. Maybe it was because she, unlike everyone else, *expected* Jessie to be up to no good. Maybe it was that damn perfume. She hadn't been wearing it at lunch, Roanna thought. A scent that strong would have been noticed. So why had she doused herself with perfume before going for a ride by herself?

The answer dawned on her with blinding clarity. "She's got a boyfriend!" she whispered to herself, almost overcome with shock. Jessie was slipping around behind Webb's back and seeing someone! Roanna almost suffocated on her indignation on Webb's behalf. How could *any* woman, even Jessie, be fool enough to jeopardize her marriage to him?

Quickly she saddled Buckley, her current favorite, and set

out in the same direction she'd seen Jessie take. The big gelding had a long, slightly uneven gait that would have been jarring to a less experienced rider but covered distance at a fast clip. Roanna was used to his stride and settled herself into his rhythm, moving fluidly with the motion as she kept her eyes on the ground, following the fresh imprints of Jessie's horse.

Part of her didn't believe Jessie really had a boyfriend—it was just too good to be true, and besides, Jessie was too smart to drop her bread butter-side down—but she couldn't resist the tantalizing possibility that she might be right. Gleefully she began plotting some vague revenge against Jessie for the years of hurts and slights, though she didn't know exactly what she could do. Real revenge wasn't part of Roanna's makeup. She was far more likely to punch Jessie in the nose than she was to plot and carry through some long-term plan, and she would get a lot more enjoyment out of it. But she simply couldn't pass up the opportunity to catch Jessie doing something she shouldn't; it was usually she who was goofing up and Jessie who was pointing it out.

She didn't want to overtake Jessie too quickly, so she reined Buckley to a walk. The July sun broiled down so white and merciless that it should have washed out the colors of the trees, but it didn't. The top of her head burned from the heat. Usually she crammed a baseball cap on her head, but she was still dressed in the silk blend slacks and shirt she had worn to lunch, and the baseball cap, like her boots, was in her bedroom.

Dawdling was easy in that heat. She stopped and let Buckley drink from a small stream, then resumed her leisurely tracking. There was a slight breeze blowing into her face, which was why Buckley caught the scent of Jessie's mount and gave a soft whicker, alerting her. She immediately backtracked, not wanting the other horse to alert Jessie to her presence.

After tethering Buckley to a small pine, she quietly made

her way through the trees and up a small hill. Her thin-soled sandals slipped on the pine needles, and she impatiently kicked them off, then clambered barefooted the rest of the way to the top.

Jessie's mount was about forty yards below and to the left, calmly cropping a small patch of grass. A large, moss-covered rock jutted up just over the crest of the hill, and Roanna crept over to crouch behind its bulk. Carefully she peeked around it, trying to locate Jessie. She could hear voices, she thought, but the sounds were odd, not really words.

Then she saw them, almost directly below her, and sank weakly against the hot surface of the rock, shock clanging through her body. She had thought to catch Jessie meeting with one of her friends from the country club, maybe necking a little, but not *this*. Her own sexual experience was so severely limited that she couldn't have formed the images in her mind.

A bush partially concealed them, but still she could see the blanket, Jessie's pale, slim body, and the darker, more muscled form of the man on top of her. They were both stark naked, he was moving, and she was clinging to him, and they were both making sounds that made Roanna cringe. She couldn't tell who he was, could only see the top and back of his dark head. But then he moved off Jessie, rising up on his knees, and Roanna swallowed hard as she stared at him, her eyes huge. She had never seen a naked man before, and the shock was jarring. He pulled Jessie up on her hands and knees and slapped her rear, laughing harshly at the hot, guttural sound she made, then he was driving into her again the way Roanna had once glimpsed two horses doing it, and dainty, fastidious Jessie was clawing at the blanket and arching her back and rotating her butt against him.

Bile rose hotly in Roanna's throat, and she ducked down behind the rock, pressing her cheek against the rough stone. She closed her eyes tight, trying to control the urge to vomit.

She felt numb and sick with despair. My God, what would Webb do?

She had followed Jessie out of a perverse, mischievous desire to cause trouble for her hateful cousin, but she had expected something minor: teasing kisses, if another man was involved at all, maybe meeting some of her friends and slipping away to a bar or something. Years ago, after she and Jessie had first come to live at Davencourt, Webb had sternly neutralized Jessie's spitefulness by threatening to spank her if she didn't stop tormenting Roanna, a threat Roanna had found so delicious that she had spent days trying to provoke Jessie, just so she could watch her hateful cousin get her rear end warmed. Amused, Webb had finally taken her aside and warned her that the punishment could come her way, too, if she didn't behave herself. That same impish impulse had prompted her today, but what she had found was far more serious than she had anticipated.

Roanna's chest burned with impotent rage, and she swallowed convulsively. As much as she disliked and resented her cousin, she had never thought Jessie was stupid enough to actually be unfaithful to Webb.

Nausea rose again, and she quickly turned around to drape her arms across her drawn-up knees and rest her head on them. Her movements scraped against some small gravel, but she was too far away for them to hear the slight noises she was making, and at the moment she was too sick to care. They weren't paying much attention to anything around them anyway. They were too busy pumping and humping. God, how silly it looked . . . and how gross, all at the same time. Roanna was glad she wasn't any closer, glad that the bush had hid at least part of them.

She could just *kill* Jessie for doing this to Webb.

If Webb knew, he might kill Jessie himself, Roanna thought, and a chill ran through her. Though he normally controlled it, everyone who knew Webb well was aware of his temper and took care not to arouse it. Jessie was a fool, a stupid, malicious fool.

But she probably thought she was safe from discovery, since Webb wouldn't be back from Nashville until tonight. By then, Roanna thought sickly, Jessie would be all freshly bathed and perfumed, waiting for him and wearing both a pretty dress and a smile, and silently making fun of him because only a few hours earlier she'd been screwing in the woods with someone else.

Webb deserved better than that. But she couldn't tell him, Roanna thought. She could never tell anyone. If she did, the most likely outcome would be that Jessie would lie her way out of it, saying that Roanna was just jealous and trying to make trouble, and everyone would believe her because Roanna *was* jealous, and everyone knew it. Then both Webb and Grandmother would be angry with her rather than with Jessie. Grandmother stayed exasperated at her most of the time anyway for one reason or the other, but she couldn't bear for Webb to be mad at her.

The other possibility would be that Webb *did* believe her. He might really kill Jessie, and then he would be in trouble. She couldn't bear for anything to happen to him. He might find out some other way, but she couldn't do anything to prevent that. All she could do was not say anything herself and pray that if he did find out, he wouldn't do anything to get himself arrested.

Roanna slipped from her place of concealment behind the rock and quickly made her way back over the hill and through the stand of pine trees to where she had tethered Buckley. He blew a soft greeting and shoved his nose at her. Obediently she stroked the big head, scratching behind his ears, but her mind wasn't on what she was doing. She mounted him and quietly walked him away from the scene of Jessie's adultery, heading back to the stables. Misery weighed heavily on her thin shoulders.

She couldn't understand what she'd seen. How could any woman, even Jessie, not be satisfied with Webb? Roanna's childhood hero worship had only intensified in the ten years she had been living at Davencourt. At seventeen, she was painfully aware of other women's response to him, so she knew it wasn't just her opinion. Women stared at Webb with unconscious, or maybe not so unconscious, yearning in their eyes. Roanna tried not to look at him that way, but she knew she wasn't always successful, because Jessie sometimes said something sharp to her about mooning around Webb and making a pest of herself. She couldn't help it. Every time she saw him, it was as if her heart gave a great big leap before starting to beat so fast that sometimes she couldn't breathe, and she would get warm and tingly all over. Lack of oxygen, most likely. She didn't think love caused tingles.

Because she did love him, so much, in a way Jessie never would or could.

Webb. His dark hair and cool green eyes, the slow grin that made her dizzy with delight. The tall, muscled body that made her go both hot and cold, as if she had a fever; that particular reaction had been bothering her for a couple of years now, and it got worse whenever she watched him swimming and he was wearing only those tight brief trunks. His deep, lazy voice, and the way he scowled at everyone until he'd had his morning coffee. He was only twenty-four, but he ran Davencourt, and even Grandmother listened to him. When he was displeased, his green eyes would get so cold that they looked like glacier ice, and the laziness of his tone would abruptly vanish, leaving his words clipped and cutting.

She knew his moods, how he looked when he was tired, how he liked his laundry done. She knew his favorite foods, his favorite colors, which professional sports teams he liked, what made him laugh, what made him frown. She knew what he read, how he voted. For ten years she had absorbed every little detail about him, turning toward him like a shy little violet reaching for the light. Since her parents had died, Webb had been both her defender and her confidant. It was to him that she had poured out all her childish fears and fantasies, he who had comforted her after nightmares or when she felt so alone and frightened.

But for all her love, she had never had a chance with him

and she knew it. It had always been Jessie. That was what hurt most of all, that she could offer herself to him body and soul, and he would still have married Jessie. Jessie, who sometimes seemed to hate him. Jessie, who was unfaithful.

Tears burned Roanna's eyes, and she dashed them away. There was no point in crying about it, though she couldn't help resenting it.

From the time she and Jessie had come to live at Davencourt, Webb had watched Jessie with a cool, possessive look in his eyes. Jessie had dated other boys, and he had dated other girls, but it was as if he allowed her only so much rope, and when she reached the end of it, he would haul her back in. He had been in control of their relationship from the start. Webb was the one man Jessie had never been able to wrap around her finger or intimidate with her temper. A single word from him could make her back down, a feat even Grandmother couldn't match.

Roanna's only hope had been that Jessie would refuse to marry him, but that hope had been so slim as to be almost nonexistent. Once Grandmother had announced that Webb would inherit Davencourt itself plus her own share of the Davenport business concerns, which was fifty percent, it had been a foregone conclusion that Jessie would have married him even if he'd been the meanest, ugliest man on the earth, which he wasn't. Jessie had inherited Janet's twenty-five percent, and Roanna had her father's twenty-five percent. Jessie saw herself as the princess of Davencourt, with the promise of becoming its queen by marrying Webb. There was no way she would have accepted a lesser role by marrying someone else.

But Jessie had been fascinated by Webb, too. The fact that she couldn't control him as she did other boys had both irritated and entranced her, keeping her dancing around his flame and to his tune. Probably, with her overweening conceit, she had thought that once they were married she'd be able to control him with sex by bestowing or withholding her favors according to how he pleased her.

If so, she had been disappointed in that, too. Roanna

knew that their marriage wasn't happy and had been secretly pleased. Suddenly she was ashamed of herself for that, because Webb deserved to be happy even if Jessie didn't.

But how she had gloated every time Jessie hadn't gotten her way! She always knew, because although Webb might control his temper, Jessie never made any attempt to do so. When she was angry, she raged, she pouted, she sulked. In the two years they had been married, the fights had come more and more frequently, with Jessie's yelling heard all over the house, to Grandmother's distress.

Nothing Jessie did, however, could sway Webb from whatever decision happened to displease her. They were locked in almost constant battle, with Webb determined to oversee Davencourt and do his best by their investments, a job that was grinding and often kept him working eighteen hours a day. To Roanna, Webb was obviously adult and responsible, but he was still only twenty-four and had told her once that his age worked against him, that he had to work twice as hard as others to prove himself to older, more established businessmen. That was his primary concern, and she loved him for it.

A workaholic husband, however, wasn't what Jessie wanted in life. She wanted to vacation in Europe, but he had business meetings scheduled. She wanted to go to Aspen at the height of the ski season; he thought it was a waste of time and money because she didn't ski and wasn't interested in learning. All she wanted was to see and be seen. When she lost her driver's license due to four speeding tickets within six months, she would have blithely continued driving and counted on the Davenport influence to keep her out of trouble, but Webb had confiscated all of her car keys, sternly ordered everyone not to let her borrow theirs, and made her sit at home for a month before hiring a driver for her. What had enraged her even more was that she had tried to hire a driver herself, but Webb had anticipated her and stymied that. It hadn't been difficult; there weren't that many limousine services in the Shoals area, and none who would cross him. Only Grandmother hadn't received the rough end of Jessie's tongue during that hellish month when she'd been grounded like a rebellious teenager.

Maybe sleeping with other men was Jessie's revenge against Webb for not letting her have her way, Roanna thought. She was willful enough and spiteful enough to do it.

Bitterly, Roanna knew that she would have made Webb a much better wife than Jessie had, but no one had ever considered it, least of all Webb. Roanna was abnormally observant, a trait developed from a lifetime of being shoved to the side. She loved Webb, but she didn't underestimate his ambition. If Grandmother had made it plain that she would be very pleased if he married Roanna, the way she had with Jessie, then very probably they would now be engaged. Granted, Webb had never looked at her the way he'd looked at Jessie, but she'd always been too young. With Davencourt in the balance, he would have chosen her, she knew he would. She wouldn't have cared that he'd wanted Davencourt more than he wanted her. She would have married Webb on any terms at all, grateful just to get any part of his attention. Why couldn't it have been her? Why Jessie?

Because Jessie was beautiful, and had always been Grandmother's favorite. Roanna had tried hard at first, but she had never been as graceful or as socially adept, or had Jessie's good taste in clothing and decorating. She would certainly never be as pretty. Roanna's mirror wasn't rose tinted; she could plainly see her straight, heavy, untidy hair, more brown than red, and her bony, angular face with her weird, slanted brown eyes, the bump on the bridge of her long nose, and her too-big mouth. She was rail thin and clumsy, and her breasts were just barely there. Despairing, she knew that no one, especially no man, would ever willingly choose her over Jessie. At seventeen, Jessie had been the most popular girl in school, while Roanna, at the same age, had never had a real date. Grandmother had arranged for her to have "escorts" to various functions she'd been forced to attend, but the boys had obviously been shanghaied by their mothers for the duty, and Roanna had always been embarrassed and tongue-tied. None of the draftees had ever volunteered for another opportunity for her company.

But since Webb's marriage, Roanna had tried less and less to fit herself into the mold Grandmother had chosen for her, the appropriate social mold of a Davenport. What was the point? Webb was lost to her. She had begun withdrawing, spending as much time as she could with the horses. She was relaxed with them in a way she never was with people, because the horses didn't care how she looked or if she'd knocked over yet another glass at dinner. The horses responded to her light, gentle touch, to the special crooning note in her voice when she talked to them, to the love and care she lavished on them. She was never clumsy on a horse. Somehow her thin body would move into the rhythm of the powerful animal beneath her, and she would become one with it, part of the strength and grace. Loyal said he'd never seen anyone ride as good as she did, not even Mr. Webb, and he rode as if he'd been born in a saddle. Her riding ability was the only thing about her that Grandmother ever praised.

But she would give up her horses if she could only have Webb. Here was her chance to break up his marriage, and she couldn't take it, didn't dare take it. She couldn't hurt him that way, couldn't take the chance that he would lose his temper and do something irrevocable.

Buckley sensed her agitation, the way horses do, and began to prance nervously. Roanna jerked her attention back to what she was doing and tried to soothe him, patting his neck and talking to him, but she couldn't give him her full attention. Despite the heat, cold chills roughened her skin, and again she felt as if she might vomit.

Loyal was far more attuned to horses than he was to people, but he frowned when he saw her face and came over to take Buckley's reins as she swung down from the saddle. "What's wrong?" he asked bluntly.

"Nothing," she said, then rubbed a shaky hand over her face. "I think maybe I got too hot, that's all. I forgot my cap."

"You know better'n that," he scolded. "Go on up to the house and drink some cold lemonade, then rest up for a while. I'll take care of Buck."

"You told me to always take care of my own horse," she said, protesting, but he cut her off with a wave of his hand.

"And now I'm tellin' you to go on. Scat. If you don't have enough sense to take care of yourself, I don't know that you can take care of Buck."

"All right. Thanks." She managed a weak smile, because she knew she must really look sick for Loyal to bend his rule about the horses, and she wanted to reassure him. She was sick, all right, sick at heart, and so full of impotent rage that she thought she might explode. She *hated* this, hated what she'd seen, hated Jessie for doing it, hated Webb for letting her love him and putting her in this situation.

No, she thought as she hurried up to the house, stricken by the idea. She didn't hate Webb, could never hate him. It would be better for her if she didn't love him, but she could no more stop that than she could stop the sun from rising the next morning.

No one saw her when she slipped in the front door. The huge hall was empty, though she could hear Tansy singing in the kitchen, and a television played in the den. Probably Uncle Harlan was watching one of the game shows he liked so much. Roanna moved silently up the stairs, not wanting to talk to anyone right now.

Grandmother's suite was at the front of the house, the first door on the right. Jessie and Webb's suite was the front one on the left side. Over the years, Roanna had finally settled on one of the back bedrooms, away from everyone else, but to her dismay she saw that Aunt Gloria and Uncle Harlan had chosen the middle suite on the right side of the house, and the door was standing open, Grandmother's and Aunt Gloria's voices coming from within. Listening, Roanna could also make out the voice of the housekeeper,

Bessie, as she worked to unpack their clothes. She didn't want to see any of them, especially didn't want to give Aunt Gloria the opportunity to start in on her, so she reversed her steps and went out the double French doors onto the upper-story gallery that completely encircled the house. Using the gallery, she went around the house in the opposite direction until she came to the French doors that opened into her own bedroom and gained sanctuary.

She didn't know how she could ever look at Jessie again without screaming at her and slapping her stupid, hateful face. Tears dripped down her cheeks, and angrily she dashed them away. Crying never had done any good; it hadn't brought back Mama and Daddy, it hadn't made anyone like her any better, it hadn't kept Webb from marrying Jessie. For a long time now she had fought back her tears and pretended that things didn't hurt her even when she felt as if she would choke on her hidden pain and humiliation.

But it had been such a shock, seeing Jessie and that man actually doing it. She wasn't stupid, she'd been to an R-rated movie a couple of times, but that really never showed anything except the woman's boobs and everything was all prettied up, with dreamy music playing in the background. And once she'd glimpsed the horses doing it, but she hadn't really been able to see anything because she'd sneaked out to the stables for that very purpose and hadn't been able to find a good vantage point. The noises had scared her, though, and she'd never tried that again.

Reality was nothing like the movies. It hadn't been romantic at all. What she'd seen had been raw and brutal, and she wanted to blot it out of her memory.

She took another shower, then collapsed across the bed, exhausted from her emotional upheaval. Perhaps she dozed; she wasn't certain, but all of a sudden the room was darker as twilight gathered, and she realized she had missed supper. Another black mark against her, she thought, and sighed.

She felt calmer now, almost numb. To her surprise she was even hungry. She pulled on some clean clothes and trudged down the back stairs to the kitchen. Tansy had already cleaned up the dishes and gone home, but the industrial-size stainless-steel refrigerator would be full of leftovers.

She was nibbling at a cold chicken leg and a roll, with a glass of tea at her elbow, when the kitchen door opened and Webb strolled in. He looked tired, and he'd removed both coat and tie, the coat slung over his shoulder and hanging from one crooked finger. The top two buttons on his shirt were open. Roanna's heart gave its customary jump when she saw him. Even when he was tired and disheveled, he looked like heaven. The sickness roiled in her stomach again at the thought of what Jessie was doing to him.

"Are you still eating?" he teased with mock amazement, green eyes twinkling.

"Got to keep my strength up," she said, striving for her usual flippancy, but she couldn't quite achieve it. There was a somberness in her tone that she couldn't hide, and Webb gave her a sharp glance.

"What've you done now?" he asked, taking a glass down from the cabinet and opening the refrigerator door to pour himself some iced tea.

"Nothing unusual," she assured him, and even managed a wry, crooked smile. "I opened my big mouth at lunch, and both Grandmother and Aunt Gloria are mad at me."

"So what did you say this time?"

"We were talking about cars, and I said that I wanted one of the Pontiac Grand Pricks."

His broad shoulders heaved as he controlled a spasm of laughter, turning it into a cough. He dropped into the chair beside her. "My God, Ro."

"I know." She sighed. "It just popped out. Aunt Gloria made one of her snide remarks about the way I eat, and I wanted to get her goat." She paused. "It worked."

"What did Aunt Lucinda do?"

"She sent me from the table. I haven't seen her since." She picked at the roll, reducing it to a pile of crumbs, until

Webb's strong hand suddenly covered hers and stilled the movements.

"Had you eaten anything before you left the table?" he asked, and there was a stern tone in his voice now.

She made a face, knowing what was coming. "Sure. I had a roll and some tuna."

"A whole roll? How much tuna?"

"Well, probably not an entire roll."

"More than you've eaten of this one?"

She eyed the demolished bread on her plate, as if judiciously weighing each crumb, and was relieved to be able to say, "More than that."

It wasn't much more, but more was more. His expression told her he wasn't fooled, but he let that slide for now. "All right. How much tuna? How many bites?"

"I didn't *count* them!"

"More than two?"

She tried to remember. She knew she'd taken a couple of bites just to show Aunt Gloria that her verbal swipe had fallen short of the mark. She might try to evade the truth, but she wouldn't lie outright to Webb, and he knew it, so he would continue to pin her down with explicitness. With a little sigh she said, "About two, I guess."

"Did you eat anything afterward? Until now, that is?"

She shook her head.

"Ro." He turned his chair toward hers and put his arm around her thin shoulders, hugging her to him. His heat and strength enveloped her the way it always had. Roanna burrowed her untidy head against that broad shoulder, bliss overtaking her. When she'd been young, Webb's hugs had been a haven for a terrified, unwanted little girl. She was older now, and the quality of her delight had changed. There was a heady, faintly musky scent to his skin that made her heart beat faster, and made her want to cling to him.

"You have to eat, baby," he said cajolingly, but with a firm undertone. "I know you get upset and lose your appetite, but I can tell that you've lost even more weight. You're going to damage your health if you don't start eating more."

"I know what you're thinking," she charged, lifting her head from his shoulder to scowl at him. "But I don't make myself throw up or anything like that."

"My God, how could you? There's never anything in your stomach to be thrown up. If you don't eat, soon you won't have the strength to work with the horses. Is that what you want?"

"No!"

"Then eat."

She looked at the chicken leg, her expression miserable. "I try, but I don't like the taste of most food, and p-people are always criticizing how I eat and the food turns into this big wad that I can't swallow."

"You ate toast this morning with me and swallowed just fine."

"You don't yell at me or make fun of me," she muttered.

He stroked her hair, pushing the dark chestnut strands away from her face. Poor little Ro. She had always hungered for Aunt Lucinda's approval, but was too rebellious to modify her behavior to get it. Maybe she was right; it wasn't as if she was a juvenile delinquent or anything like that. She was just different, a quirky wildflower growing in the middle of a sedate, well-ordered southern rose garden, and no one knew quite what to make of her. She shouldn't have to beg for her family's love or approval; Aunt Lucinda should just love her for what she was. But for Aunt Lucinda, perfection was her other granddaughter, Jessie, and she had always made it plain that Roanna fell short in every category. Webb's mouth tightened. In his opinion, Jessie was far from perfect, and he was sick and tired of waiting for her to grow out of some of that selfishness.

Jessie's attitude, too, had a lot to do with Roanna's inability to eat. He had let this rock on for years while he devoted himself to the herculean task of learning how to run Davencourt and all the Davenport business concerns, packing four years of college into three and then going after his master's degree in business, but it was obvious now that the situation *wasn't* going to resolve itself. For Roanna's sake, he was going to have to put his foot down, with Aunt Lucinda as well as Jessie.

Roanna needed calm, peaceful surroundings where her nerves could settle down and her stomach relax. If Aunt Lucinda and Jessie—and now Aunt Gloria, too—wouldn't or couldn't let up on the criticism that they constantly leveled at Roanna, then he wouldn't let Roanna eat with them. Aunt Lucinda had always insisted that they be at the table together, that Roanna conform to social standards, but he was going to override her on this. If she would eat better with her meals served on a tray in the peacefulness of her bedroom, or even out in the stables if she preferred, then that was where she'd have them. If being separated from the family made her feel exiled, rather than the relief he thought it would be, then he'd eat out in the stable with her. This simply couldn't go on, because Roanna was starving herself to death.

Impulsively he scooped her onto his lap, the way he'd done when she was a youngster. She was about five-seven now, but not a lot heavier, and fear clutched at him as he encircled her alarmingly frail wrist with his long fingers. This little cousin had always appealed to his protective side, and what he had always loved best about her was her pluckiness, her willingness to fight back without regard for the consequences. She was full of wit and mischief, if only Aunt Lucinda would stop trying to obliterate those very traits.

She had always snuggled up to him like a kitten and did so now automatically, rubbing her cheek against his shirt. A faint twinge of physical awareness surprised him, making his dark eyebrows draw together in a puzzled frown.

He looked down at her. Roanna was woefully immature for her age, without the normal social skills and defenses teenagers developed in the course of interacting with each other. Faced with disapproval and rejection at home as well as at school, Roanna had responded by withdrawing, so she had never learned how to interact with the kids in her age group. Because of that, subconsciously he had always thought of her as still being a child in need of his protection, and maybe she did still need it. But even if she wasn't quite an adult, physically she was no longer a child either.

He could see the curve of her cheek, her long, dark lashes, the translucence of her temple where the fragile blue veins lay just beneath the surface. The texture of her skin was smooth, silky, and carried the sweet warm scent of womanhood. Her breasts were very small but very firm, and he could feel the nipple, as small and hard as a pencil eraser, of the breast that was nestled against him in her half-turned position. The twinge of awareness intensified into a sudden, definite throb in his loins, and he was abruptly conscious of how round her buttocks were and how they nestled so sweetly on his thighs.

He barely bit back a growl as he shifted her a little, just enough that the side of her hip wasn't rubbing against his hardening penis. Roanna was remarkably innocent for her age, having never dated; he doubted she had ever even been kissed. She had no idea what she was doing to him, and he didn't want to embarrass her. It was his fault for taking her on his lap as if she were still a kid. He'd just have to be more careful from now on, though this was probably a fluke. It had been over four months since he'd had sex with Jessie, because he'd gotten so damn sick and tired of her trying to manipulate him with her body. Their encounters weren't about making love; they were a contest of domination. Hell, he doubted Jessie even understood the concept of making love, of the mutual giving of pleasure. But he was young and healthy, and four months of denial had left him extremely edgy, so much so that even Roanna's skinny body could arouse him.

He jerked his mind back to the issue at hand. "Let's make a deal," he said. "I promise that no one else will say anything to you about how you eat, and if anyone does, you tell me and I'll take care of it. And you, sugar, will start eating regular meals. Just for me. Promise."

She looked up at him, and her whiskey brown eyes held that soft, adoring glow she reserved for him. "All right," she whispered. "For you." Before he had any inkling what she was going to do, she curved her arm around his neck and pressed her sweet, soft, innocent mouth against his.

From the moment he'd scooped her onto his lap, Roanna had been almost breathless with longing and intense excitement. Her love for him flooded her, making her want to moan with pleasure at his touch, at the way he was holding her so close. She rubbed her cheek against his shirt, and felt the heat and resilience of his flesh beneath the fabric. Her nipples throbbed, and blindly she pressed hard against his chest. The resulting sensation was so acute that it shot straight down between her legs, and she had to clench her thighs against the heat.

Then she felt it, that sudden hardness against her hip, and with a thrill she realized what it was. She had seen a naked man for the first time that afternoon, and the shock of the act she'd witnessed had left her weak and nauseated, but this was different. This was Webb. And this meant he wanted her.

The realization shattered her with delight. She stopped thinking. He moved her so that she couldn't feel him against her hip anymore, and he was talking. She watched him, her gaze fastened on his beautiful mouth, barely absorbing his words. He wanted her to eat, just for him.

"All right," she whispered. "For you." She would do anything for him. Then the longing grew so intense she couldn't hold it back any longer, and she did what she had wanted to do for so long that it seemed like her entire life had been spent craving this. She put her arm around his neck and kissed him.

His lips were firm and warm, and hinted of a tantalizing taste that made her quiver with need. She felt him jerk, as if startled, felt his hands move to her waist and tighten as if he would lift her away from him. "No," she sobbed, suddenly terrified that he would push her away. "Webb, please. Hold me." And she tightened her hold on him and kissed him even harder, shyly daring to lick his lips the way she'd seen it done in a movie.

He quivered, a long shudder running through his muscled body, and his hands clenched on her. "Ro—" he began, and her tongue slipped in between his opened lips.

He groaned, his entire body tensing. Then suddenly his mouth opened and moved, and control of the kiss was no longer hers. His arms closed around her, hard, and his tongue moved deep into her mouth. Roanna's neck bent back under the pressure, and her senses dimmed under the onslaught. She had thought about kissing, even practiced it on her pillow at night, but she hadn't realized a kiss could make her feel so hot and weak, or that his taste would be so delicious, or that the feel of him against her would unleash such terrible longing. She twisted on his lap, seeking to get closer, and fiercely he turned her so that her breasts were against his chest.

"You two-timing bastard!"

The shriek battered Roanna's ears. She leaped from Webb's lap, her face white as she pivoted to face her cousin. Jessie's features were twisted with rage as she stood just inside the door, glaring at them, her hands clenched into white-knuckled fists.

Webb got to his feet. Dull red stained his cheeks, but his gaze was steady as he too faced his wife. "Calm down," he said in an even tone. "I can explain."

"I just bet you can," she sneered. "This should be good. Damn you, no wonder you haven't been interested in touching me! All this time you've been fucking this stupid little whore!"

A red mist edged Roanna's vision. After what Jessie had been doing this afternoon, how dare she talk to Webb like this over a kiss! Without realizing she even moved, suddenly she found herself in front of Jessie, and she shoved her against the wall so hard that her head slammed against it.

"Roanna, stop it!" Webb said sharply, catching her and roughly setting her aside.

Jessie straightened and shoved her hair out of her eyes. Quick as a cat, she lunged past Webb and slapped Roanna across the face with all the strength in her arm. Webb grabbed her and swung her to one side, holding her with a firm grip on the collar of her blouse while he caught Roanna by the nape of her neck.

"That's enough, God damn it," he said with clenched teeth. Webb didn't normally swear in front of women, and the fact that he did now was a measure of his anger. "Jessie, there's no sense in letting the whole house in on this. We'll talk about it upstairs."

"We'll talk about it upstairs," she mimicked. "We'll talk about it right here, damn you! You want to keep it quiet? Tough shit! By tomorrow night, everyone in Tuscumbia is going to know you've got a taste for young ass, because I'm going to yell it on every corner!"

"Shut up," Roanna growled, ignoring her burning cheek and glaring her hate at Jessie. She tried to wriggle free of Webb's punishing hold on her neck, but he merely tightened his grip.

Jessie spat at her. "You've always been after him, you slut," she hissed. "You set it up for me to find you two together like this, didn't you? You knew I was coming down to the kitchen. You weren't content to fuck him behind my back, you wanted to lord it over me for once."

The scope of the lie stunned Roanna. She darted a glance at Webb and saw the sudden suspicious, condemning glare in his eyes. "Both of you shut up," he growled, his voice so low and icy that chills ran down her back. "Jessie. Upstairs. Now." He released Roanna and all but frog-marched Jessie to the door. He paused there to flick Roanna with a glacier gaze that cut like a whip. "I'll take care of you later."

The door swung shut behind them. Roanna sank weakly against the cabinets and covered her face with her hands.

Oh, God, she'd never meant for anything like this to happen. Now Webb hated her, and she didn't think she could bear it. Pain welled in her, tightening her throat, choking her. She had never been a match for Jessie in slyness and cunning, and Jessie had proved it once again, effortlessly spewing out the lie that would turn Webb against her. Now he thought she'd caused all this deliberately, and he would never, never love her.

Grandmother wouldn't forgive her for this ruckus. She rocked back and forth, overwhelmed with misery, wondering if she'd be sent away. Jessie had been telling Grandmother that Roanna should go away to some girl's college up north, but Roanna hadn't wanted to go and Webb had supported her, but now she doubted Webb would lift a finger if they wanted to send her to the Gobi Desert. She had caused him so much trouble he'd never forgive her, even if she could convince him that Jessie lied, which she doubted. In her experience, they always believed Jessie.

In the space of a few minutes, her entire world had crumbled around her. She had been so happy, those few, sweet moments in his arms, and then it had turned to hell. She would likely have to go away, and she'd lost Webb forever.

It wasn't fair. Jessie was the one who was the whore. But Roanna didn't dare tell, couldn't tell, no matter what happened. She couldn't defend herself against the vicious lies Jessie was even now telling about her.

"I hate you," she whispered thinly to her absent cousin. She cowered against the cabinets like a frightened little animal, her heart pounding against her ribs with a force that almost made her faint. "I wish you would die."

CHAPTER
5

*R*oanna lay huddled tensely in her bed. She was cold with misery despite the heat of the summer night, and sleep was as distant now as it had been when she had first escaped upstairs to her room.

The hours since Jessie had caught her kissing Webb had been a nightmare. The uproar had, of course, brought the rest of the household running. There was no need for questions, because Jessie had screamed curses at both Webb and Roanna the entire time he was dragging her upstairs, but both Grandmother and Aunt Gloria had hammered Roanna with endless queries and accusations anyway.

"How *dare* you do such a thing?" Grandmother had asked, glaring at Roanna with eyes as cold as Webb's had been, but Roanna remained mute. What could she say? She shouldn't have kissed him; she knew it. Loving him was no excuse, at least not one that would matter to the unanimous condemnation she faced.

She couldn't defend herself by pointing to Jessie's behavior. Webb might hate her now, but still she couldn't tell something that would so hurt him and might cause him to do something rash. She would rather take all the blame herself than risk anything bad happening to him. And in the final analysis, Jessie's actions didn't excuse her own. Webb was a married man; she shouldn't have kissed him. She writhed inside with shame at what her heedless, impulsive act had caused.

The battle raging upstairs had been clearly audible to everyone else. Jessie had always been unreasonable when thwarted and doubly so when her vanity was involved. Her screams had sliced over the deep rumble of Webb's voice. She'd called him every filthy name imaginable, using words that Roanna had never heard spoken aloud before. Grandmother was usually able to overlook anything Jessie did, but even she winced at the language being used. Roanna heard herself called a whore, a horse-faced little slut, and a stupid animal good only for barnyard screwing. Jessie had threatened to have Grandmother cut Webb out of her will—hearing this, Roanna had darted a terrified look at Grandmother, because she would die if she'd cost Webb his inheritance, but Grandmother had lifted her elegant brows in surprise at hearing this threat—and to have Webb arrested for statutory rape.

Of course, Grandmother and Aunt Gloria had instantly believed that Roanna had been sleeping with Webb, and this brought their hard glares and recriminations down on her again, though Uncle Harlan had merely lifted his thick gray brows and looked amused. Embarrassed, miserable, Roanna had shaken her head dumbly, not knowing any way to defend herself that they would believe.

Webb wasn't a man to take threats lying down. Until then, he'd been furious but kept his temper under control. Now there was a crash, and the sound of glass breaking, and he roared: "Get a goddamn divorce! I'll do whatever it takes to get rid of you!"

He'd come down the stairs then, his face hard and set, his eyes burning cold and green. His furious gaze touched on Roanna, and his eyes narrowed, making her shudder with dread, but he didn't stop. "Webb, wait," Grandmother said, reaching out a staying hand. He ignored her, slamming out of the house. A moment later they saw the headlights of his car slice across the lawn.

Roanna didn't know if he'd returned yet, because only loud vehicles could be heard from inside the house. Her eyes burned as she stared up at the ceiling, darkness weighing down on her like a blanket, suffocating her.

What hurt most of all was that Webb hadn't trusted in her; even knowing Jessie, he'd believed her lies. How *could* he think for one moment that she would deliberately do anything that would cause him any trouble? Webb was the center of her existence, her one champion; if he turned away from her, then she had no foundation, no security in this world.

But fury and disgust had been in his eyes when he'd looked at her, as if he couldn't stand the sight of her now. Roanna curled in a ball, whimpering with the pain that seemed so overwhelming she thought she could never recover from it. She loved him; she wouldn't have turned away from him, no matter what he did. But he had turned away from her, and she shrank in on herself as she realized what the difference was: he didn't love her. She hurt all over, as if she'd bruised herself in this headlong crash into the brick wall of reality. He'd liked her, been amused by her, maybe felt some sort of family tie with her, but he hadn't loved her the way she wanted him to love her. With sudden, shattering clarity, she saw that he'd felt sorry for her, and the humiliation of it scoured her raw inside. Pity was never what she'd wanted from Webb or from anyone else.

She'd lost him. Even if he gave her the chance to defend herself and if he then believed her, it would still never be the same again. He thought she had betrayed him, and his lack of trust was a betrayal of her. That knowledge would always be there in her heart, an icy, burning knot to mark her loss.

She had always clung fiercely to Davencourt and to Webb, resisting any effort to pry her loose. Now, for the first time, she thought about going away. There was nothing left here, she might as well go away to college the way everyone wanted her to and start fresh, where people didn't know her and have preconceived ideas about how she should look and act. Before, the very thought of leaving Davencourt had brought panic, but now she felt only relief. Yes, she wanted to get away from everyone and everything.

But first, she would fix things for Webb. One last gesture of love, and then she would put all this behind her and move on.

She glanced at the clock as she got out of bed. It was after two; the house was silent. Jessie was probably asleep, but Roanna frankly didn't give a damn. She could just wake up and listen, for once, to what Roanna had to say.

She didn't know what she would do if Webb were there, but she didn't really expect him to be. He'd been in such a temper when he'd left that he probably hadn't returned yet, and even if he had, he wouldn't crawl into bed with Jessie. He'd either be downstairs in the study or asleep in one of the other bedrooms.

She didn't need a light; she had wandered Davencourt so much at night that she knew all of its shadows. Silently she drifted down the hallway, her long white nightgown making her look like a ghost. She *felt* like a ghost, she thought, as if no one ever really saw her.

She paused in front of the door to Webb and Jessie's suite. A light was still on inside; a thin bright ribbon was visible at the base of the door. Deciding not to knock, Roanna turned the knob. "Jessie, are you awake?" she asked softly. "I want to talk to you."

The shrill scream tore through the soft fabric of the night, a long, raw sound that seemed to go on and on, straining, until it broke on a hoarse note. Lights flared in various bedrooms, even down in the stables where Loyal had his own apartment. There was a gabble of sleepy, confused voices crying out, asking questions, and the thud of running feet.

Uncle Harlan was first to reach the suite. He said,

"Godawmighty," and for once the too-smooth, too-hearty tone was absent from his voice.

Her hands stuffed into her mouth as if to keep another scream from escaping, Roanna slowly backed away from Jessie's body. Her brown eyes were wide and unblinking, the expression in them curiously blind.

Aunt Gloria rushed into the room despite Uncle Harlan's belated attempt to stop her, with Lucinda close behind. Both women stumbled to a halt, horror and disbelief stunning them to immobility as they took in the gory scene. Lucinda stared at the tableau presented by her two grand-daughters, and every vestige of color washed out of her face. She began to tremble.

Aunt Gloria put her arms around her sister, all the while staring wildly at Roanna. "My God, you've killed her," she blurted, each word rising with hysteria. "Harlan, call the sheriff!"

The driveway and courtyard were a snarl of vehicles parked at random angles, bar lights flashing eerie blue strobes through the night. Every window in Davencourt blazed with light, and the house was crowded with people, most of them wearing brown uniforms, some of them wearing white.

All of the family, except for Webb, sat in the spacious living room. Grandmother was weeping softly, her hands ceaselessly twisting a delicately embroidered handkerchief as she sat with slumped shoulders. Her face was ravaged with grief. Aunt Gloria sat beside her, patting her, murmuring soothing but meaningless words. Uncle Harlan stood just behind them, rocking back and forth on his toes, importantly answering questions and offering his own opinions on every theory or detail, soaking in the limelight currently shining on him because of his luck in being the first one on the scene—discounting Roanna, of course.

Roanna sat alone on the opposite side of the room from everyone else. A deputy stood nearby. She was dully aware that he was a guard, but she couldn't bring herself to care.

She was motionless, her eyes dark pools in a colorless face, her gaze both unseeing and yet encompassing as she stared unblinkingly across the room at her family.

Sheriff Samuel "Booley" Watts paused just inside the doorway and watched her, wondering uncomfortably what she was thinking, how she felt about this silent but implacable rejection. He assessed the thin frailty of her bare arms, noted how insubstantial she looked in that white nightgown, which wasn't much whiter than her face. The pulse at the base of her throat beat visibly, the rhythm too fast and weak. With the experience of thirty years in law enforcement behind him, he turned to one of his deputies and said quietly, "Get one of the paramedics in here to see about the girl. She looks shocky." He needed her lucid and responsive.

The sheriff had known Lucinda for most of his life. The Davenports had always been hefty contributors to his campaign funds when election time rolled around. Politics being what they were, he'd done a lot of favors for the family over the years, but at the base of their longtime relationship was genuine liking. Marshall Davenport had been a tough, shrewd son of a bitch but a decent one. Booley had nothing but respect for Lucinda, for her inner toughness, her refusal to relax her standards in the face of modern decline, her business acumen. In the long years after David's death, until Webb had become old enough to begin taking over some of the burden, she had run an empire, overseen a huge estate, and raised her two orphaned granddaughters. Granted, she'd had the benefit of immense wealth to smooth the way for her, but the emotional burden had been the same on her as it would have been on anyone else.

Lucinda had lost too many loved ones, he thought. Both the Davenport and Tallant families had suffered untimely deaths, people taken too young. Lucinda's beloved brother, the first Webb, had died in his forties after being kicked in the head by a bull. His son, Hunter, had died at the age of thirty-one when his small plane crashed in a violent thunderstorm in Tennessee. Marshall Davenport had been only sixty when he died from a burst appendix that he ignored, thinking it was just an intestinal upset, until the infection had become so massive his system couldn't fight it off. Then both David and Janet, as well as David's wife, had been killed in that car wreck ten years ago. That had nearly broken Lucinda, but she'd stiffened her spine and soldiered on.

Now this; he didn't know if she could bear up under this latest bereavement. She'd always adored Jessie, and the girl had been mighty popular in the elite society of Colbert County, though Booley himself had had his own reservations about her. Sometimes her expression had seemed cold, emotionless, like that of some of the killers he'd seen through the years. Not that he'd ever had any trouble with her, never been called on to cover up any minor scandals; whatever Jessie was really like, under the flirtatiousness and party manners, she'd kept her nose clean. Jessie and Webb had been the sparks in Lucinda's eyes, and the old girl had been nearly bursting a seam with pride when the two kids had gotten married a couple of years ago. Booley hated what he had to do; it was bad enough that she'd lost Jessie, without involving Webb, but it was his job. Politics or not, this couldn't be swept under the carpet.

A stocky paramedic, Turkey MacInnis, entered the room and crossed to where Roanna was sitting, hunkering down in front of her. Turkey, so called because of his ability to imitate a turkey call without benefit of any gizmos, was both competent and soothing, one of the better paramedics in the county. Booley listened to the casual matter-of-fact voice as he asked the girl a few questions, assessing her responsiveness as he flicked a tiny penlight in her eyes, then took her blood pressure and counted her pulse. Roanna answered the questions in a flat, almost inaudible tone, her voice sounding strained and raw. She regarded the paramedic at her feet with a total lack of interest.

A blanket was fetched and wrapped around her, and the paramedic urged her to lie down on the sofa. Then he brought her a cup of coffee, which Booley guessed to be heavily sweetened, and cajoled her into drinking it.

Booley sighed. Satisfied that Roanna was being taken care of, he couldn't put off his onerous duty any longer. He rubbed the back of his head as he walked over to the small group on the other side of the room. For at least the tenth time, Harlan Ames was recounting the event as he interpreted it, and Booley was getting heartily sick of that greasy, too-loud voice.

He sat down beside Lucinda. "Have you found Webb yet?" she asked in a strangled tone, as more tears slipped down her cheeks. For the first time, he thought, Lucinda looked her age of seventy-three. She had always given the impression of being lean and strong, like the finest stainless steel, but now she looked shrunken in her nightgown and robe.

"Not yet," he said uncomfortably. "We're looking for him." That was an understatement if he'd ever made one.

There was a slight disturbance at the door, and Booley looked around, frowning, but relaxed when Yvonne Tallant, Webb's mother, strode into the living room. Technically no one was supposed to be allowed in, but Yvonne was family, even though she had distanced herself several years back by moving out of Davencourt into her own little house across the river in Florence. Yvonne had always been a woman with an independent streak. Just now, though, Booley wished she hadn't shown up, and he wondered how she'd found out about the trouble here tonight. Ah, hell, no use worrying about it. That was the trouble with small towns. Someone in dispatch, maybe, had called home and said something to a family member, who'd called a friend, who'd called a cousin who knew Yvonne personally and had taken it upon herself to let her know. That was always how it worked.

Yvonne's green eyes swept the room. She was a tall, slim woman with streaks of gray in her dark hair, the type described more as handsome than pretty. Even at this hour, she was impeccably clad in tailored slacks and a crisp white blouse. Her gaze lit on Booley. "Is it true?" she asked, her voice cracking a little. "About Jessie?" Despite Booley's own reservations about Jessie, she had always seemed to get along with her mother-in-law. Besides, the Davenport and Tallant families were so close that Yvonne had known Jessie from the cradle.

Beside him, Lucinda gulped on a sob, her entire body trembling. Booley nodded an answer at Yvonne, who closed her eyes against welling tears.

"Roanna did it," Gloria hissed, glaring across the room at the small, blanket-wrapped figure lying on the sofa.

Yvonne's eyes flew open, and she gave Gloria an incredulous look. "Don't be ridiculous," she snapped, and purposefully strode over to Roanna, crouching down beside her and stroking the tumbled hair back from the colorless face, murmuring softly to her as she did. Booley's opinion of Yvonne jumped up several notches, though he doubted, from the look on her face, that Gloria shared it.

Lucinda bowed her head, as if unable to look across the room at her other granddaughter. "Are you going to arrest her?" she whispered.

Booley took one of her hands in his, feeling like a meaty, clumsy ox as his thick fingers folded around her cold, slender ones. "No, I'm not," he said.

Lucinda shuddered slightly, some of the tension leaving her body. "Thank God," she whispered, her eyes squeezing shut.

"I'd like to know why not!" Gloria shrilled from Lucinda's other side, rearing up like a wet hen. Booley had never liked Gloria nearly as much as he did Lucinda. She'd always been prettier, but Lucinda had been the one who'd caught Marshall Davenport's eye, Lucinda who had married the richest man in northwest Alabama, and envy had nearly eaten Gloria alive.

"Because I don't think she did it," he said flatly.

"We saw her standing right over the body! Why, her feet were in the blood!"

Irritably, Booley wondered why that was supposed to

have any significance. He reached for patience. "From what we can tell, Jessie had already been dead for several hours before Roanna found her." He didn't go into the technical details about the progression rate of rigor mortis, figuring Lucinda didn't need to hear it. It wasn't possible to pin down the exact time of a death unless it was witnessed, but it was still a sure thing that Jessie had died at least a couple of hours before midnight. He didn't know why Roanna had paid her cousin a visit at two in the morning—and he'd definitely find out—but Jessie had already been dead.

The little family group was frozen, staring at him as if they couldn't comprehend this latest twist. He took out his little notebook. One of the county detectives normally would have done the interviewing, but this was the Davenport family, and he was going to give the case his personal attention.

"Mr. Ames said that Webb and Jessie had a lulu of a fight tonight," he began, and saw the sharp look that Lucinda gave her brother-in-law.

Then she took a deep breath and squared her shoulders as she mopped at her face with the mangled handkerchief. "They argued, yes."

"What about?"

Lucinda hesitated, and Gloria stepped into the breach. "Jessie caught Webb and Roanna carrying on in the kitchen."

Booley's gray eyebrows rose. Not much surprised him anymore, but he felt mildly astonished at this. Dubiously, he glanced at the frail, huddled little form across the room. Roanna seemed, if not childish, still oddly childlike, and he wouldn't have figured Webb for being a man who was turned on by that. "Carrying on, how?"

"*Carrying on,* that's how," Gloria said, her voice rising. "My God, Booley, do you want me to draw you a picture?"

The idea of Webb having sex with Roanna in the kitchen struck him as even more unlikely. He was never surprised at the depth of stupidity supposedly smart people could exhibit, but this didn't ring true. Odd, that he could see Webb committing murder, but not fooling around with his little cousin.

Well, he'd get the true story about the kitchen episode from Roanna. He wanted something else from these three. "So they were arguing. Did the argument turn violent?"

"Sure did," Harlan replied, only too eager to take the spotlight again. "They were upstairs, but Jessie was screaming so loud we could hear every word. Then Webb yelled at her to get a divorce, that he'd do anything to get rid of her, and there was the sound of glass breaking. Then Webb came storming downstairs and left."

"Did any of you see Jessie after that, or maybe hear her in the bathroom?"

"Nope, not a sound," Harlan said, and Gloria shook her head. No one had tried to talk to Jessie, knowing from experience that it was better to let her cool down first or her fury would erupt on the erstwhile mediator. Lucinda's expression was one of growing disbelief and horror as she realized where Booley's questioning was headed.

"No," she said violently, shaking her head in denial. "Booley, no! You can't suspect Webb!"

"I have to," he replied, trying to keep his voice gentle. "They were arguing, violently. Now, we all know Webb has quite a temper when he's stirred up. No one saw or heard a peep out of Jessie after he left. It's a sad fact, but any time a woman's killed, it's usually her husband or a boyfriend who does it. This hurts me bad, Lucinda, but the truth is Webb is the most likely suspect."

She was still shaking her head, and tears were dribbling down her wrinkled cheeks again. "He couldn't. Not Webb." Her voice was pleading.

"I hope not, but I have to check it out. Now, what time was it when Webb left, as near as you can remember?"

Lucinda was silent. Harlan and Gloria looked at each other. "Eight?" Gloria finally offered, uncertainty in her voice.

"About that," Harlan said, nodding. "That movie I wanted to watch just had come on."

Eight o'clock. Booley considered that, chewing on his lower lip as he did so. Clyde O'Dell, the coroner, had been doing his job for just about as long as Booley had been doing his, and was damn good at guessing the time of death. He had both the experience and the knack for adding the degree of rigor with the temperature factor and coming up with pretty close to the right answer. Clyde had put the time of Jessie's death at "Oh, ten o'clock or thereabouts," with a rocking motion of his hand to indicate the actual time could slip either way. Eight o'clock was a mite early, and though it was still within the realm of possibility, that did throw a bit of doubt into the mix. He had to make damn sure of his case before he presented it to the county prosecutor, because old Simmons was too slick a politician to take on a case involving the Davenports and Tallants unless he was sure he could make it stick. "Did anyone hear a car or anything later on? Did Webb maybe come back?"

"I didn't hear anything," Harlan said.

"I didn't either," Gloria confirmed. "You'd have to be driving a transfer truck before we could hear it in here, unless maybe we were in bed and the balcony doors were open."

Lucinda rubbed her eyes. Booley had the feeling she wished her sister and brother-in-law would shut the hell up. "We can't normally hear anyone driving up," she said. "The house is very well insulated, and the shrubbery deadens the sound, too."

"So he could have returned and you wouldn't necessarily have known it."

Lucinda opened her mouth, then closed it without replying. The answer was obvious. The upstairs balcony that circled the huge, elegant old house was accessible from the outside stairs on Webb and Jessie's side of the house. Moreover, each bedroom had double French doors that opened onto the balcony; it would have been ridiculously easy for anyone to go up those stairs and enter the bedroom without anyone else in the house seeing them. From a security standpoint, Davencourt was a nightmare.

Well, maybe Loyal had heard something. His apartment in the stables probably wasn't as soundproof as this massive old house.

Yvonne left Roanna's side and came to stand right in front of Booley. "I heard what you've been saying," she said quietly, her tone even despite the way her green eyes were boring a hole in him. "You're barking up the wrong tree, Booley Watts. My son didn't kill Jessie. No matter how mad he was, he wouldn't have hurt her."

"Under normal circumstances, I'd agree with you," Booley replied. "But she was threatening to have Lucinda cut him out of her will, and we all know what Davencourt means to—"

"Bullshit," Yvonne said firmly, ignoring the way Gloria's mouth tightened like a prune. "Webb wouldn't believe that for a second. Jessie always exaggerated when she was mad."

Booley looked at Lucinda. She wiped her eyes and said faintly, "No, I would never have disinherited him."

"Even if they divorced?" he pressed.

Her lips trembled. "No. Davencourt needs him."

Well, that undercut a damn good motive, Booley thought. He wasn't exactly sorry. He would hate like hell to have to arrest Webb Tallant. He'd do it, if he could build a strong enough case, but he'd hate it.

At that moment a flurry of voices came from the front entrance, and they all recognized Webb's deep voice as he said something curt to one of the deputies. Every head in the room, except Roanna's, swiveled to watch as he strode into the room, flanked by two deputies. "I want to see her," he said sharply. "I want to see my wife."

Booley got to his feet. "I'm sorry about this, Webb," he said, his voice as tired as he felt. "But we need to ask you some questions."

CHAPTER
6

Jessie was dead.

They hadn't let him see her, and he desperately needed to, because until he saw it for a fact himself, Webb found it impossible to truly believe it. He felt disoriented, unable to sort out his thoughts or feelings because so many of them were contradictory. When Jessie had yelled at him that she wanted a divorce, he'd felt nothing but relief at the prospect of being rid of her, but . . . dead? Jessie? Spoiled, vibrant, passionate Jessie? He couldn't remember a day of his life when Jessie hadn't been there. They had grown up together, cousins and childhood playmates, then the fever of puberty and sexual passion had locked them together in an endless game of domination. Marrying her had been a mistake, but the shock of losing her was numbing. Grief and relief warred, tearing him apart inside.

Guilt was there, too, in spades. Guilt, first and foremost, because he could feel relief at all, never mind that for the past two years she had done her best to make his life hell, systematically destroying everything he'd ever felt for her in her relentless quest for the fawning adoration she'd thought she wanted.

And then there was the guilt over Roanna.

He shouldn't have kissed her. She was only seventeen, damn it, and an immature seventeen at that. He shouldn't have held her on his lap. When she had suddenly thrown her arms around his neck and kissed him, he should have gently pushed her away, but he hadn't. Instead he'd felt the soft, shy bloom of her mouth under his, and her very innocence had aroused him. Hell, he'd already been aroused by the feel of her round bottom on his lap. Instead of breaking the kiss, he had deepened it, taking control, thrusting his tongue into her mouth for an explicitly sexual kiss. He'd turned her in his arms, wanting to feel those slight, delicate breasts against him. If Jessie hadn't walked in at that point, he probably would have had his hand on those breasts and his mouth on the sweetly pebbled nipples. Roanna had been aroused, too. He'd thought she was too innocent to know what she was doing, but now he saw it differently. Inexperienced wasn't the same as innocent.

No matter what he'd done, he doubted Roanna would have lifted a hand or spoken a word to stop him. He could have taken her there on the kitchen table, or sitting astride his lap, and she would have let him.

There was nothing Roanna wouldn't do for him. He knew it. And that was the most horrible thought of all.

Had Roanna killed Jessie?

He'd been furious with both of them, and with himself for allowing the situation to happen. Jessie had been screaming her filthy insults, and abruptly he'd been so fed up with her that he knew it was the end of their marriage for him. As for Roanna—he never would have thought she was devious enough to set up the scene in the kitchen, but when he'd looked at her after Jessie's vicious accusation, he hadn't seen shock on Roanna's too-open, too-expressive face; he'd seen guilt. Maybe it was caused by the same dismay he'd been feeling, because they shouldn't have been kissing, but maybe . . . maybe it was more. For an instant he had seen something else, too: hate.

They all knew that Roanna and Jessie didn't get along, but he'd also known for quite some time that, for Roanna, the animosity had been very bitter. The reason for it had been obvious, too; only a blind fool could have missed seeing how much Roanna adored him. He hadn't done anything to encourage her, romantically speaking, but neither had he discouraged her. He was fond of the little brat, and that unquestioning hero worship of hers had definitely stroked his ego, especially after one of the endless battles with Jess. Hell, he supposed he loved Ro, but not in the way she wanted; he loved her with the amused exasperation of an older brother, he worried about her lack of appetite, and he felt sorry for her when she was humiliated by her own social awkwardness. It hadn't been easy for her, forever being cast as the ugly duckling to Jessie's beautiful swan.

Could she have believed that ridiculous threat Jessie had made, about having him cut out of Aunt Lucinda's will? He'd known it was nonsense, but had Roanna? What would she have done to protect him? Would she have gone to Jessie, tried to reason with her? He knew from experience that reasoning with Jessie was wasted effort. She would have turned on Roanna like a bear on fresh meat, dredging up even more hateful things to say, vicious threats to make. Would Roanna have gone to such extreme lengths to stop Jess? Before that episode in the kitchen, he would have said no way, but then he'd seen the expression on Roanna's face when Jessie burst in on them, and now he wasn't certain.

They said she'd been the one to find Jessie's body. His wife was dead, murdered. Someone had bashed her head in with one of the andirons from the fireplace in their suite. Had Roanna done it? Could she have done it deliberately? Everything he knew about her said no, at least to the second question. Roanna wasn't cold-blooded. But if Jessie had taunted her, made fun of her looks and her feelings for him, made more of those stupid threats, maybe then she could have lost her temper and hit Jessie.

He sat alone in Booley's office, bent over with his head cradled in his hands as he tried to bring some sort of order to the turmoil of his thoughts. Evidently he was the prime suspect. After the fight he and Jess had had, he supposed that was logical. It made him so angry he wanted to punch someone, but it was logical.

He hadn't been arrested, and he wasn't particularly worried, at least not about that. He hadn't killed Jess, so unless some evidence was fabricated against him, there was no way to prove that he had. He was needed at home to take care of things. From the brief glimpse he'd had of her, Aunt Lucinda had been devastated; she wouldn't be up to making the funeral arrangements. And Jess was his wife; he wanted to do this last service for her, mourn her, grieve for the girl she had been, the wife he had hoped for. It hadn't worked out for them, but still she hadn't deserved to die like that.

Tears burned his eyes, dripped through his fingers. Jess. Beautiful, unhappy Jess. He had wanted her to be a partner rather than a parasite that constantly demanded more and more, but it hadn't been in her nature to give. There hadn't been enough love in the world to satisfy her, and eventually he had stopped even trying.

She was gone. He couldn't bring her back, couldn't protect her.

But what about Roanna?

Had she killed his wife?

What should he do now? Tell Booley his suspicions? Throw Roanna to the wolves?

He couldn't do it. He didn't, couldn't, believe that Roanna would deliberately have killed Jessie. Hit her, yes. The blow might even have been struck in self-defense, because Jessie was—had been—perfectly capable of physically attacking Roanna. Ro was only seventeen, a juvenile; if she were arrested and tried and found guilty, her sentence would be light, for the crime. But even a light sentence would be a death sentence for her. Webb knew as sure as he was sitting there that Roanna wouldn't survive so much as a year's sentence to a juvenile detention hall. She was too frail, too vulnerable. She would stop eating altogether. And she would die.

He thought of the scene at the house. He'd been hustled out of the house before he'd been able to speak with anyone, though his mother had tried. But what he'd seen in that brief moment was branded on his mind: Yvonne, fiercely protective, ready to do battle for him, but then he'd expected nothing else from his stalwart mother; Aunt Lucinda, staring at him with numb grief; Aunt Gloria and Uncle Harlan, horrified, fascinated accusation in their eyes. No doubt about it, they thought he was guilty, damn them. And Roanna, in pale and frozen isolation on the other side of the room, not even lifting her head to look at him.

He'd spent the past ten years protecting her. It had become second nature to him. Even now, as angry as he was at her, he couldn't stop the instinct to shield her. If he thought she'd done it deliberately, that would be different, but he didn't. So here he was, protecting with his silence the girl who had probably killed his wife, and the bitterness of the choice filled his gut.

The office door opened behind him and he straightened, brusquely wiping the remaining dampness from his eyes. Booley walked around the desk and sank heavily into the creaky leather chair, his shrewd eyes on Webb's face, taking note of the evidence of tears. "I'm sorry about this, Webb. I know it's a shock."

"Yeah." His voice was rough.

"I got a job to do, though. You were heard telling Jessie you'd do anything to get rid of her."

The best way through this minefield, Webb figured, was to tell the truth—up to a point, when it would be best to say nothing at all. "Yeah, I said it. Right after I told her to get a divorce. I meant I'd agree to any settlement."

"Even giving up Davencourt?"

"Davencourt isn't mine to give, it's Aunt Lucinda's. That decision would be hers."

"Jessie threatened to have Lucinda cut you out of her will."

Webb gave an abrupt shake of his head. "Aunt Lucinda wouldn't do anything like that just because of a divorce."

Booley crossed his arms behind his head, linking his fingers to form a cradle for his skull. He studied the young man before him. Webb was big and strong, a natural athlete; he had the strength to crush Jessie's skull with one blow, but had he done so? He abruptly changed the subject. "Supposedly Jessie caught you and Roanna at some hanky-panky in the kitchen. Want to tell me about it?"

Webb's eyes flashed with a hint of the cold, ferocious fury he was holding bottled up inside. "I was never unfaithful to Jess," he said shortly.

"Never?" Booley let a little doubt slide into his tone. "Then just what did Jessie see that set her off?"

"A kiss." Let Booley have the unvarnished truth, as far as it went.

"You kissed Roanna? For God's sake, Webb, don't you think she's a mite young for you?"

"Damn it, of course she's too young!" Webb snapped. "It wasn't like that."

"Wasn't like what? What do you have going with her?"

"I don't have anything going with her." Unable to contain himself any longer, Webb lunged to his feet, causing Booley to tense and automatically lay his big hand on the butt of his pistol, but he relaxed when Webb began pacing the confines of the small office.

"Then why did you kiss her?"

"I didn't. She kissed me." Initially, that is. Booley didn't need to know the rest of it.

"Why'd she do that?"

Webb rubbed the back of his neck. "Roanna's like a kid sister to me. She was upset—"

"Why?"

"Aunt Gloria and Uncle Harlan moved in today. She doesn't get along with Aunt Gloria."

Booley made a grunting sound, as if he could understand that. "And you were . . . comforting her?"

"That, and trying to get her to eat. If she's upset or

nervous, she can't eat, and I was worried about what this would do to her."

"You think she's—what's the word—aner-something? Starving herself to death?"

"Anorexic. Maybe. I don't know. I told her that I'd talk to Aunt Lucinda and make the others stay off her back, if she would promise to eat. She threw her arms around my neck and kissed me, Jessie walked in, and all hell broke loose."

"Is that the first time Roanna's kissed you?"

"Except for pecks on the cheek, yes."

"So there's nothing at all romantic going on between the two of you?"

"No," Webb said, the word clipped.

"I heard she's got a crush on you. A sweet young girl like that, a lot of men would be tempted."

"She depends on me a lot, has since her folks died. It's no big secret."

"Was Jessie jealous of Roanna?"

"Not to my knowledge. She had no reason to be."

"Even though you get along real good with Roanna? From what I hear, you and Jessie hadn't been getting along at all. Maybe she was jealous about that."

"You hear a lot, Booley," Webb said tiredly. "Jessie wasn't jealous. She threw temper tantrums whenever she didn't get her way. She was mad at me for going to Nashville this morning, and when she saw Roanna kissing me, that was just an excuse to raise hell."

"The argument turned violent, didn't it?"

"I threw a glass and broke it."

"Did you hit Jessie?"

"No."

"Have you ever hit her?"

"No." He paused, and shook his head. "I spanked her ass once when she was sixteen, if that counts."

Booley restrained a grin. Now wasn't the time for amusement, but Jessie getting her rear end tanned was something he'd liked to have seen. A lot of kids nowadays, boys and girls both, would benefit greatly from the same treatment.

Webb would have been just seventeen at the time, but he'd always been older than his years.

"What happened then?"

"Jessie was getting more and more out of control. I left before things could get out of hand."

"What time did you leave?"

"Hell, I don't know. Eight, eight-thirty."

"Did you go back?"

"No."

"Where did you go?"

"I drove around a while, over to Florence."

"Did anybody you know see you, so they can verify it?"

"I don't know."

"What did you do? Just drive around?"

"For a while, like I said. Then I went to the Waffle Hut on Jackson Highway."

"What time did you get there?"

"Ten o'clock, maybe."

"What time did you leave?"

"After two. I didn't want to come home until I'd cooled down."

"So you were there about four hours? I reckon the waitress would remember that, don't you?"

Webb didn't reply. He thought it likely, because she had tried several times to strike up a conversation, but he hadn't been in the mood for chitchat. Booley would check it out, the waitress would verify his presence, and that would be the end of it. But who would Booley look at as a suspect then? Roanna?

"You can go on home," Booley said after a minute. "Don't guess I have to tell you to stick close. No going out of town on business trips or anything like that."

Webb's gaze was cold and hard. "I'd hardly be scheduling a business trip when I have to bury my wife."

"Well, as to that. Considering the nature of her death, there's gotta be an autopsy. Normally that only delays the funeral a day or two, but sometimes it can be longer. I'll have to let you know." Booley leaned forward, his jowly face earnest. "Webb, son, I'll tell you plain, I don't know about this. It's a sorry fact that when a woman gets killed, it's usually her husband or boyfriend who did it. Now, you've never struck me as the type, but then neither have a lot of other folks I've wound up arresting. I gotta suspect you, and I gotta check everything out. On the other hand, if you have any suspicions yourself, I'd appreciate hearing about them. Families always have their little twists and secrets. Why, your folks were sure Roanna had killed Jessie, and they were treating her like she was poison or something, until I told them that I didn't think she'd done it."

Booley was a country-plain, unsophisticated good old boy, but he'd been in law enforcement for a long time, and he knew how to read people. In his way, he used the same tactics Columbo had made famous on television, just kind of easing around and carrying on casual conversations and putting the pieces together. Webb resisted the invitation to confide in the sheriff, instead saying, "May I go now?"

Booley waved a meaty hand. "Sure. But like I said, stick close to home." He heaved his bulk out of the chair. "I might as well drive you home myself. It's already morning, so I'm not going to get any sleep anyway."

Roanna was hiding, not the way she had when she was little by crawling under furniture or burrowing deep in a closet, but nevertheless she had removed herself from the grim, hushed activity in the house. She had retreated to the bay window where once she had watched Webb and Jessie sit in the garden swing, while behind her the rest of the family had discussed what to do with her. She was still wrapped tight in the blanket the paramedic had put around her, holding the edges together with cold, bloodless fingers. She sat watching the slowly arriving dawn, ignoring the hum of voices behind her, shutting it all out.

She tried not to think about Jessie, but no amount of effort could erase that bloody scene from her mind. She didn't have to actively *think* about it, it was just there, like the window. Death had so altered Jessie that at first Roanna had simply stood there, gaping at the body without quite realizing that it was real, or even recognizing her cousin. Her head had been oddly misshapen, flattened around a huge open wound where her skull had literally been cracked open. She had been awkwardly sprawled with her neck bent as her head rested against the raised rock hearth.

Roanna had turned on the light when she'd entered the suite, blinking her eyes as she tried to adjust her vision, and walked around the sofa on her way to the bedroom to wake Jessie and talk to her. She had literally stumbled on Jessie's sprawled legs, and stared down in silent stupefaction for a long moment before she realized what she was seeing and began to scream.

It wasn't until later that she realized she'd been standing on blood-soaked carpet and that her bare feet were stained red. She didn't remember how they had gotten clean, if she had washed them or someone else had.

The window reflected the scene behind her, the swarm of people coming and going. The rest of the family had arrived, singly and in pairs, adding their questions and tears to the confusion.

There was Aunt Sandra, Webb's aunt on his father's side, which made her Grandmother's niece. Aunt Sandra was a tall, dark-haired woman with the Tallant good looks. She had never married, instead pursuing an advanced education in physics, and now worked for NASA in Huntsville.

Aunt Gloria's daughter and her husband, Lanette and Greg Spence, had arrived with their two teenagers, Brock and Corliss. Corliss was Roanna's age, but they had never gotten along. No sooner had they arrived than Corliss had slipped up to Roanna and whispered, "Were you really standing in her blood? What did she look like? I heard Mama tell Daddy that her head was cracked open like a watermelon."

Roanna had ignored the avid, insistent voice, keeping her face turned toward the window. "Tell me!" Corliss insisted.

A vicious pinch on the back of her arm made Roanna's eyes sting with tears, but she stared straight ahead, refusing to acknowledge her cousin in any way. Eventually Corliss had given up and left to badger someone else for the gory details she craved.

Aunt Gloria's son, Baron, lived in Charlotte; he and his wife and three kids were expected to arrive later in the day. Even without them, that meant ten family members were grouped in the living room or around a comforting pot of coffee in the kitchen, with the makeup of the groups changing as people shifted back and forth.

No one was allowed to go upstairs yet, though Jessie had long since been taken away, because the investigators were still taking pictures and gathering evidence. With the deputies and all the others there in various official capacities, the big house was teeming with people, but still Roanna managed to shut them all out. She felt very cold inside, a strange chill that had spread to every cell of her body and formed a protective shell, keeping her inside and everyone else outside.

The sheriff had taken Webb away, and she had nearly choked on her guilt. This was all her fault. If only she hadn't kissed him! She hadn't done it on purpose, but then none of the messes she caused were on purpose.

He hadn't killed Jessie. She knew it. She'd wanted to scream at them for even thinking something so ugly about him. Now that was all Aunt Gloria and Uncle Harlan were talking about, how shocking it was, as if he'd already been tried and convicted. Only a few hours before, they had been equally convinced that Roanna was the killer.

Webb couldn't do something like that. He could kill; somehow Roanna knew that Webb would do whatever was necessary to protect those he loved, but killing under those circumstances wasn't the same as murder. No matter how nasty Jessie had been, no matter what she'd said or even if she'd attacked him with a poker or something, he wouldn't have harmed her. Roanna had seen him tenderly helping a foal into the world, sitting up all night with a sick animal, taking turns with Loyal walking a colicky horse for hours on end. Webb took care of his own.

It wasn't her fault Jessie was dead, but because Roanna loved Webb and hadn't been able to control her stupid impulses, it had set in motion a chain of circumstances that caused Webb to be blamed for Jessie's death. She had no idea who had killed Jessie, her thoughts hadn't gone that far; she only knew that it wasn't Webb. With every cell in her body, she knew he couldn't have done it, just as she knew this was all her fault and he'd never forgive her.

When Sheriff Watts had taken Webb away for questioning, Roanna had been paralyzed with shame. She hadn't even been able to lift her head and look at him, sure that she would see nothing but hatred and contempt in his eyes if he happened to look at her, and she knew that she couldn't have borne it.

She had never felt so alone, as if there was an invisible bubble around her, preventing anyone from getting close. She could hear Grandmother behind her, softly weeping again, and hear Aunt Gloria's murmured attempts at consolation, but it didn't quite touch her. She didn't know where Uncle Harlan was; she didn't care. She would never forget the way they had accused her of killing Jessie, the way they had pulled back from her as if she had the plague. Even when Sheriff Watts had said he didn't think she'd done it, none of them had approached or apologized. Not even Grandmother, though Roanna had heard the soft "Thank God" she'd uttered when the sheriff had said he thought she was innocent.

All her life she'd tried so hard to earn these people's love, to be good enough, but she had never succeeded. Nothing about her had ever equaled the standards of the Davenports and Tallants. She wasn't pretty, she wasn't even presentable. She was clumsy, untidy, and had the unfortunate habit of saying the most appalling things at the most inappropriate time.

Deep inside her, something had given up. These people had never loved her, never would. Only Webb had cared, and now she had messed that up, too. She was alone in a fundamental way that left a huge, aching void inside. There was something devastating in knowing that if she simply walked out of this house and never came back, no one would care. The despair that she had faced earlier, when she realized that Webb didn't love her or trust her, had settled into mute acceptance.

All right, so they didn't love her; that didn't mean she had no love to give. She loved Webb with every fiber in her body, something that wasn't going to change no matter how he felt about her. There was also love for Grandmother, despite her obvious preference for Jessie, because after all it had been Grandmother who had firmly said, "Roanna will live here, of course," easing the terror of a seven-year-old who had abruptly lost everything. Even though she had more often found disapproval than approval from Grandmother, she still felt enormous respect and affection for the indomitable old woman. She hoped that someday she could be as strong as Grandmother, rather than the bumbling, unwanted fool she was now.

Both of the people Roanna loved had lost someone dear to them. All right, so she herself had despised Jessie; Grandmother and Webb hadn't. It wasn't her fault that Jessie was dead, but if Webb were blamed for it, that definitely would be her fault because of that kiss. Who really had killed Jessie? The only person who readily sprang to mind was the man she had seen with Jess the day before, but she had no idea who he was and wasn't certain she could either describe him now or even identify him if he walked in the door. Her shock had been so great that she hadn't paid a great deal of attention to his face. If she had decided before to keep quiet about what she'd seen, her reasons now were even more crucial. If Sheriff Watts found out that Jessie had been having an affair, he would see that as a motive for Webb to kill her. No, Roanna decided dazedly, she would only hurt Webb by disclosing what Jessie had been doing.

A murderer would go free. Roanna thought about that,

but her reasoning was simple: telling the sheriff about it wouldn't guarantee that the murderer was caught, because she couldn't give him any more information than that, and Webb would be harmed. For Roanna, there was no question of justice or truth, and she was too young and unsophisticated for subtleties of philosophy. The only thing that mattered was protecting Webb. Right or wrong, she would keep her mouth shut.

She watched as a county car silently rolled up the long driveway and stopped. Webb and Sheriff Watts got out and walked toward the house. Roanna watched Webb; her gaze stuck to him like a magnet to steel. He was still dressed in the clothes he'd worn yesterday, and he looked exhausted, his hard face shadowed with both fatigue and a day's growth of beard. At least he was home, she thought, her heart leaping, and he wasn't in handcuffs. That must mean the sheriff wasn't going to arrest him.

As the two men walked up the semicircle of brick-paved sidewalk, Webb glanced up to where she sat in the big bay window, outlined by the lights behind her. Though it still wasn't full daylight, Roanna saw the way his face hardened, then he looked away from her.

She listened to the confused, awkward flurry of family members behind her when Webb entered the house. Most of them didn't speak to him, but instead made an effort to make their own conversations seem casual. Under the circumstances, the effort was ridiculous, and they merely sounded stilted. Only Yvonne and Sandra rushed to him, and were gathered into his strong arms. In her reflective window, Roanna watched him bend his dark head down to them.

He released them and turned to Sheriff Watts. "I need to shower and shave," he said.

"Upstairs is off-limits for now," the sheriff replied.

"There's a bath with a shower next to the kitchen. Would you have a deputy bring me some clean clothes?"

"Sure." The arrangements were made, and Webb left to

clean up. The voices behind her resumed a more normal rhythm. Watching them, Roanna could tell that both Aunt Yvonne and Aunt Sandra were furious with the others.

Then suddenly her view of the room was blotted out as Sheriff Watts appeared directly behind her. "Roanna, do you feel up to answering some questions?" he asked in a tone so gentle it seemed out of place, coming from such a rough, burly man.

She clutched the blanket even tighter and silently turned around.

His huge hand closed over her elbow. "Let's go where it's quieter," he said, helping her to slide from the window seat. He wasn't quite as tall as Webb but was easily twice as wide. He was built like a wrestler, with a barrel chest and thick belly, and without any jiggle to his middle.

He led her into Webb's study, seating her on the sofa rather than in one of the big leather armchairs, and eased down beside her.

"I know it's hard for you to talk about it, but I need to know what happened tonight, and this morning."

She nodded.

"Webb and Jessie were arguing," Sheriff Watts said, watching her carefully. "Do you know—"

"It was my fault," Roanna interrupted, her voice flat and hollow and strangely raspy. Her brown eyes, usually so lively and full of golden lights, were dull and haunted. "I was in the kitchen trying to eat when Webb came home from Nashville. I—I'd missed supper. I was upset . . . Anyway, I k-kissed him, and that's when Jessie came in."

"You kissed him? He didn't kiss you?"

Miserably Roanna nodded. It didn't matter that, after a few seconds, Webb had held her tight and returned her kiss. She had initiated it.

"Has Webb ever kissed you?"

"Some. Mostly he ruffles my hair."

The sheriff's lips twitched. "I mean on the mouth."

"No."

"Do you have a crush on him, Roanna?"

She went still, even the breath halting in her chest. Then she squared her thin shoulders and gave him a look of such naked despair that he swallowed. "No," she said with pitiful dignity. "I love him." She paused. "He doesn't love me, though. Not like that."

"Is that why you kissed him?"

She began to rock back and forth, the movement slight but significant as she fought to control her pain. "I know I shouldn't have done it," she whispered. "I knew it then. I never would have done anything to cause Webb so much trouble. Jessie said I'd done it on purpose, that I knew she was coming down, but I didn't. I swear I didn't. He was being so sweet to me, and all of a sudden I couldn't resist it. I just grabbed him. He never had a chance."

"What did Jessie do?"

"She just started screaming at us. She called me all sorts of ugly names, and Webb, too. She accused us of—you know. Webb tried to tell her it wasn't like that, but Jessie never listened to anybody when she was pitching one of her fits."

The sheriff put his hand over hers, patting it. "Roanna, I have to ask you this, and I want you to tell me the truth. Are you sure there's nothing between you and Webb? Have you ever had sex with him? This is a serious situation, honey, and nothing but the truth will do."

She gave him a blank look, then hot color washed into her white face. "No!" she sputtered, and turned an even darker red. "I've never—with anyone! I mean—"

He patted her hand again, mercifully interrupting her mangled reply. "There's no need to be embarrassed," he said kindly. "You're doing the smart thing, placing such a high value on yourself."

Miserably Roanna thought that she didn't have a high value on herself at all; if at any time Webb had so much as crooked his finger at her, she would have come running and let him do whatever he wanted to her. Her virginity was due to his lack of interest, not her own morals.

"What happened then?" he prompted.

"They went upstairs, still arguing. Or rather, Jessie was. She was screaming at him, and Webb was trying to calm her down, but she wouldn't listen."

"Did she threaten to have him cut out of Lucinda's will?"

Roanna nodded. "But Grandmother just looked surprised. I was so relieved, because I couldn't have stood it if I caused Webb to lose Davencourt."

"Did you hear anything violent happening in their room?"

"Some glass breaking, then Webb yelled at her to go ahead and get a divorce, and he left."

"Did he tell her he'd do anything to get rid of her?"

"I think so," Roanna answered readily, knowing that the others had likely confirmed this. "I don't blame him. I'd have added my allowance to her alimony, if that would have helped."

The sheriff's lips twitched again. "You didn't like Jessie?"

She shook her head. "She was always hateful to me."

"Were you jealous of her?"

Roanna's lips trembled. "She had Webb. But even if she hadn't, I know that he wouldn't be interested in m-me. He never has been. He was nice to me because he felt sorry for me. After she caused such a ruckus last night—I mean after *I* caused it—I decided I might as well go away to college the way they'd been wanting me to do. Maybe then I could make some friends."

"Did you hear anything from their room last night after Webb left?"

Roanna shuddered, an image of Jessie as she'd last seen her flashing through her brain. She gulped. "I don't know. Everybody was mad at me, even Webb. I was upset and went to my room. It's at the back of the house."

"All right now, Roanna, I want you to think carefully. When you go up the stairs, their rooms are across the front hall to the left. If there's a light on in the room, you can see it under the door. I checked that myself. When you went to your room, did you look in that direction?"

She remembered that very well. She had cast a fearful

glance at Jessie's door, afraid she would come storming out of it like the Wicked Witch in *The Wizard of Oz,* and she had tried to be very quiet so Jessie wouldn't hear her. She nodded.

"Was there a light on?"

"Yes." She was certain of it, because otherwise she would have thought Jessie had gone on into the connecting bedroom and thus wouldn't hear her.

"Okay, now tell me about later, when you found her. What time was it?"

"After two. I hadn't been asleep. I kept thinking how I'd messed everything up and caused Webb so much trouble."

"You were awake the entire time?" the sheriff asked sharply. "Did you hear anything?"

She shook her head. "I told you, my bedroom's on the back, away from everyone else. It's real quiet back there. That's why I like it."

"Could you tell when the others came up to bed?"

"I heard Aunt Gloria in the hall about nine-thirty, but my door was closed and I couldn't tell what she was saying."

"Harlan said that he started watching a movie about eight. It shouldn't have been off at nine-thirty."

"Maybe he finished watching it in their room. I know they have a television in there, because Grandmother had a connection run for them before they moved in."

He pulled out his notebook and scribbled a few words, then said, "Okay, let's go back to when you went to Jessie's room this morning. Was the light on then?"

"No. I turned it on when I went in. I thought Jessie was in bed, and I was going in there to wake her up so I could talk to her. The light was bright, and I couldn't see good for a few minutes, and I—I stumbled over h-her."

She shuddered again and started shaking. The bright color of a moment before leached out of her face, leaving it chalky again.

"Why were you going to talk to her?"

"I was going to tell her that it wasn't Webb's fault, that he didn't do anything wrong. It was just me—being stupid, as usual," she said dully. "I never meant to cause him any trouble."

"Why not wait until morning?"

"Because I wanted to fix it before then."

"Then why didn't you talk to her before you went to bed?"

"I was a coward." She gave him an ashamed look. "You don't know how nasty Jessie could be."

"I don't think you're a coward at all, honey. It takes guts to say something's your fault. A lot of grown-ups never do learn how to do it."

She began rocking again, and the haunted look came back. "I didn't want anything bad to happen to Jessie, not bad like that. I'd have laughed if her hair fell out or something. But when I saw her head . . . and the blood . . . I didn't even recognize her at first. She was always so beautiful."

Her voice trailed off, and Booley sat in silence beside her, thinking hard. Roanna said she'd turned on the light. All doorknobs and light switches had already been dusted for fingerprints, so it should be her print on that particular switch, something easy enough to check. If the light had been on when she'd gone to her room, and off when she went to talk to Jessie, then that meant either Jessie had turned off the light herself after Webb had gone, or someone else had. Either way, Jessie had been alive when Webb had left the house.

That didn't mean he couldn't have returned later and gone up the outside stairs. If his alibi at the Waffle Hut checked out, though, that meant they likely didn't have enough circumstantial evidence to charge him. Hell, there was no motive anyway. He wasn't having an affair with Roanna, not that Booley had pinned much credence to that theory to begin with. It had been a shot in the dark, nothing more. The hard facts were, Webb and Jessie had argued over something Roanna said was her fault while totally absolving Webb. Jessie had threatened him with the loss of Davencourt, but no one had believed her, so that didn't count. In a temper, Webb had yelled at her to go ahead and get a divorce, and slammed out of the house. Jessie had been alive then, according to both Roanna's testimony and the coroner's estimate of time of death, based on the degree of rigor mortis and the temperature of Jessie's body. No one had seen or heard anything. Webb had been at the Waffle Hut close to the time of Jessie's death. Now, they weren't talking about any great distance here, nothing that couldn't be driven in about fifteen or twenty minutes, so it was still within the realm of possibility that he could have returned, bashed her in the head, and then calmly driven to the Waffle Hut to establish his alibi, but the odds of convincing any jury of that were pretty slim. Hell, the odds of convincing the county prosecutor to press charges on that basis were even slimmer.

Someone had killed Jessie Tallant. Not Roanna. The girl was so painfully open and vulnerable, he doubted she knew how to lie. Besides, he'd have bet money she didn't have the strength to pick up that andiron, which was one of the heaviest he'd ever seen, specially made for the oversize fireplaces here in Davencourt. Someone strong had killed Jessie, pointing to a man. The two other men at Davencourt, Harlan Ames and the stableman, Loyal Wise, had no motive.

So, the killer was either Webb—and unless Webb confessed, Booley knew there was no way of proving it—or a stranger. There was no sign of forced entry, but to his amazement he'd discovered that none of the people here locked their balcony doors, so force wouldn't have been necessary. Nor was there anything stolen, which would have given them robbery as a motive. The plain fact was, Jessie was dead for no good reason that he could tell, and it was damn hard to make a murder charge stick without giving a jury a motive it could believe.

This was one murder that wasn't going to be solved. He could feel it in his bones, and it made him sick. He didn't like for law-breaking slime to get away with so much as stealing a pack of chewing gum, much less murder. It didn't make any difference that Jessie had evidently been a bitch of the first water; she still hadn't deserved to have her head bashed in.

Well, he'd try. He'd check out all the angles, verify Webb's alibi, and present what he had to Simmons, but he knew the prosecutor was going to say they didn't have a case.

He sighed, got to his feet, and looked down at the forlorn little figure still on the sofa, and he was moved to offer her some comfort. "I don't think you give yourself enough credit, honey. You aren't stupid, and you aren't a coward. You're a sweet, smart girl, and I like you fine."

She didn't reply, and he wondered if she'd even heard him. She'd been through so much in the last twelve hours, it was a wonder she hadn't cracked under the strain. He patted her on the shoulder and quietly left the room, leaving her alone with her regrets, and her nightmare images.

CHAPTER

7

*T*he next few days were hell.

The entire Shoals area, which consisted of Tuscumbia, Muscle Shoals, Sheffield, and Florence, the four towns that butted together where Colbert and Lauderdale Counties met at the Tennessee River, were riveted by the spectacle of the bloody murder of a member of Colbert County's premier family and the ensuing investigation of her husband as the killer. Webb was as well known, if not quite as respected yet, as Marshall Davenport had been, and of course everyone who was anyone had known Jessie, the star of the local top society. Gossip ran rampant. Webb hadn't been arrested, and Sheriff Watts would say only that he had been questioned and released, but as far as everyone was concerned that was as good as saying he'd done it.

Why, look at how his only family treated him, the whispers ran. Lucinda cried every time she saw him, and she couldn't bring herself to talk to him yet. Gloria and Harlan Ames were convinced Webb had killed Jessie, and though publicly they didn't say anything, they had made a few comments to their closest friends, the "just between you and me" kind. The more moral souls were disapproving when the confidential gossip was spread, but that didn't stop it from growing like kudzu.

Gloria and Harlan's two children, Baron and Lanette, kept their respective families as far away from Webb as they could.

Only Webb's mother, Yvonne, and his aunt Sandra seemed convinced of his innocence, but of course they would be. He'd always been Sandra's favorite, while she practically ignored Gloria's grandchildren. A definite rift was growing in the family. And as for Roanna, who had discovered the body, she was said to be suffering from shock and had all but sequestered herself. She had always been like a puppy dog at Webb's heels, but not even she had anything to do with him. Word was that they hadn't spoken since Jessie's death.

The insidious vines of gossip spread the rumor that Jessie had been savagely beaten before she'd been killed; someone else said she'd been mutilated. They said that Webb had been caught *in flagrante delicto* with Roanna, the little cousin, but credulity stopped short of actually believing that. Maybe he'd been caught, but with *Roanna?* Why, she was skinny as a rail, unattractive, and had no idea how to make herself appealing to a man.

Anyway, obviously Webb had been caught with *someone,* and gossip ran hot with speculation on the unknown woman's identity.

The autopsy on Jessie's body was completed, but the results weren't released pending the results of the investigation. Funeral arrangements were made, and so many people attended the service that the church couldn't hold everyone. Even people who hadn't known her personally attended out of curiosity. Webb stood alone, an island around which everyone else moved but never quite touched. The minister extended his sympathies. No one else did.

At the cemetery, it was much the same thing. Lucinda was heartbroken, weeping uncontrollably as she stared at Jessie's flower-laden casket, supported on brass rails over the raw, open mouth of the grave. It was a hot summer day, without a cloud to mar the sky, and the white-molten sun soon had everyone dripping with sweat. Handkerchiefs and miscellaneous bits of paper were used to languidly fan perspiring faces.

Webb sat on one end of the first row of folding chairs that had been placed under the canopy for the immediate family. Yvonne sat beside him, firmly holding his hand, and Sandra sat beside her. The rest of the family had taken the other chairs, though no one seemed eager to be the one sitting directly behind Webb. Finally Roanna slipped into that chair, a frail wraith who had grown even thinner in the days since Jessie's murder. For once, she didn't stumble or drop anything. Her face was white and remote. Her dark chestnut hair, usually so untidy, was pulled sternly back from her face and tied with a black bow. She had always jittered around, as if she had too much energy to control, but now she was oddly still. Several people gave her curious glances, as if not quite certain of her identity. Her too-big features, so unsuited for the thinness of her face, somehow looked better suited to the remote severity that now swathed her. She still wasn't pretty, but there was something . . .

The prayers were said, and the mourners tactfully steered away from the gravesite so the casket could be lowered and the grave filled. No one actually left the cemetery, except for a few who had other things to do and couldn't wait around any longer for something to happen. The rest milled around, pressing Lucinda's hand, kissing her cheek. No one approached Webb. He stood alone, just as he had at the funeral home and then the church, his expression hard and closed.

Roanna stood it as long as she could. She had avoided him, knowing how he must hate her, but the way people were treating him made her bleed inside. She moved to his side and slipped her hand into his, her cold, frail fingers clinging to the hard, warm strength of his. He glanced down at her, his green eyes as welcoming as ice.

"I'm sorry," she whispered, her words audible only to

him. She was acutely aware of all the avid eyes trained on them, speculating on her gesture. "It's all my fault people are treating you like this." Tears swam in her eyes, blurring his outline as she looked up at him. "I just wanted you to know that I didn't . . . I didn't do it on purpose. I didn't know Jessie was coming downstairs. I hadn't talked to her since lunch that day."

Something flickered in his eyes, and he drew in a long, controlled breath. "It doesn't matter," he said, and gently but firmly removed his hand from her grip.

The rejection was like a blow to the face. Roanna swayed under the impact, her expression stark with despair. Webb muttered a curse under his breath and reluctantly lifted his hand to steady her, but Roanna stepped back. "I understand," she said, still in a whisper. "I won't bother you anymore." Then she slipped away, as insubstantial as a black-clad ghost.

Somehow she kept her control. It was easier now, as if the layer of ice that encased her kept everything from spilling out. Webb's rejection had almost cracked the ice, but after the initial blow, the layer had thickened in self-defense, becoming even stronger. The hot sun beat down on her, but Roanna wondered if she would ever be warm again.

She had scarcely slept since the night she'd found Jessie's body. Every time she closed her eyes, the bloody image seemed to be painted on the inside of her eyelids, where she couldn't escape it. Guilt and misery kept her from eating more than a few bites, and she had lost even more weight. The family was being kinder to her, perhaps because of their own guilt about the way they had treated her immediately after she'd found Jessie's body, when they had thought Roanna had killed her cousin, but it didn't matter. It was too little, too late. Roanna felt so distant from them, from everything, that sometimes it was as if she wasn't even there.

After the grave had been filled and the multitude of flowers positioned to cover the raw earth, all of the family and a good many others drove back to Davencourt. The upstairs had been off-limits for two days, then Sheriff Watts had simply sealed off the murder scene and let the remainder of the floor be used, though everyone had felt strange at first. Only Cousin Baron and his family were staying at the house, though, since all of the other relatives lived close by. Webb hadn't slept at Davencourt since Jessie's murder. He spent his days there, but at night he went to a motel. Aunt Gloria had said that she was relieved, because she wouldn't have felt safe with him in the house at night, and Roanna had wanted to slap her. Only a desire not to cause Grandmother more stress had restrained her.

Tansy had prepared huge amounts of food to feed the expected crowd and had been glad of the opportunity to keep herself busy. People wandered in and out of the dining room where the buffet had been arranged, filling plates and returning to gather in small groups where they discussed the situation in hushed voices.

Webb shut himself in the study. Roanna walked down to the stables and stood at the fence, finding comfort in watching the horses graze. Buckley saw her and trotted over, thrusting his head over the fence to be patted. Roanna hadn't been riding since Jessie's death; in fact, this was her first visit to the stables. She scratched behind Buckley's ears and crooned soothingly to him, but her mind wasn't on what she was saying, it was just automatic noise. He didn't seem to mind, though; his eyes half closed in delight, and he made a grunting noise.

"He's missed you," Loyal said, coming up behind her. He had changed out of the suit he'd worn to the funeral and was now clad in his more familiar khakis and boots.

"I've missed him, too."

Loyal propped his arms on the top railing and surveyed his kingdom, his gaze warming as he watched the sleek, healthy animals he loved. "You don't look too good," he said bluntly. "You need to take better care of yourself. The horses need you."

"It's been a bad time," she replied, her voice lifeless.

"Sure has," he agreed. "It still don't seem real. And it's a shame how folks are treating Mr. Webb. Why, he no more killed Miss Jessie than I did. Anybody who knows anything about him would know that." Loyal had been extensively questioned about the night of the murder. He'd heard Webb leave and agreed with everyone else that the time was between eight and eight-thirty, but hadn't heard any cars after that until the sheriff had been called and the county vehicles arrived on the scene. He'd been awakened from a sound sleep by Roanna's scream, a sound that could still make him wince when he remembered it.

"People only see what they want to see," Roanna said. "Uncle Harlan just likes the sound of his own voice, and Aunt Gloria's a fool."

"What do you reckon will happen now? With them living here, I mean."

"I don't know."

"How's Miss Lucinda holding up?"

Roanna shook her head. "Dr. Graves is keeping her on mild sedatives. She loved Jessie a lot. She still cries all the time." Lucinda had been frighteningly diminished by Jessie's death, as if this had been one blow too many for even her nature. She had pinned all her hopes for the future on Webb and Jessie, and now it looked as if her plans had been destroyed, with Jessie dead and Webb suspected of her murder. Roanna had kept waiting for Grandmother to go to Webb and put her arms around him, tell him that she believed in him. But for whatever reason, whether Grandmother was too paralyzed with grief or maybe because she *did* think Webb could have killed Jessie, it hadn't happened. Couldn't Grandmother see how much Webb needed her? Or was she in so much pain that she couldn't see his?

Roanna felt nothing but dread for the coming days.

"We got the results of the autopsy back," Booley said to Webb the day after the funeral. They were in Booley's office again. Webb felt as if he'd spent more time there since Jessie's death than he had anywhere else.

The initial shock had passed, but the grief and anger were

still bottled up inside him, all the more potent for having to be kept under restraint. He didn't dare let his control slip, or his rage would explode over everyone: his so-called friends, who had stayed as far away from him as if he'd been a leper; his business associates, some of whom had seemed secretly pleased at his trouble, the bastards; and most of all his loving family, who all apparently thought him a murderer. Only Roanna had approached him and said she was sorry. Because she'd accidentally killed Jessie herself, and was afraid to say so? He couldn't know for certain, no matter what he suspected. What he did know was that she too had avoided him, Roanna who had always done her best to stay right at his heels, and that she was definitely feeling guilty about something.

He couldn't help worrying about her. He could tell that she wasn't eating, and she was alarmingly pale. She had changed in other, more subtle ways, too, ways he couldn't analyze because he was still so angry he couldn't focus on those tiny differences.

"Did you know Jessie was pregnant?" Booley asked.

If he hadn't already been sitting, Webb's legs would have folded beneath him. He stared at Booley in silent shock.

"I guess not," Booley said. Damn, this case had as many hidden little twists as a maze. Webb was still the best bet for Jessie's killer, which wasn't saying much, but the evidence wasn't there. There wasn't much evidence, period; no witnesses and no known motive. He couldn't convict a gnat on the evidence he had. Webb's alibi had checked out, Roanna's testimony had established that Jessie had been alive when Webb had stormed out, so they had nothing but a corpse. A pregnant corpse, as it turned out.

"She was about seven weeks along, according to the report. Had she been puking or anything?"

Webb shook his head. His lips felt numb. Seven weeks. The baby wasn't his. Jessie had been cheating on him. He swallowed the lump in his throat, trying to consider what this meant. He'd had no indication she'd been unfaithful, and there hadn't been any gossip either; in a small town, there would have been gossip, and Booley's investigation would have turned up something. If he told Booley that the baby wasn't his, that would be considered a believable motive for killing her. But what if her lover had killed her? Without even a guess as to who the man might be, there was no way of finding out, even assuming Booley would listen to him.

He had kept quiet when he thought Roanna might have killed Jessie, and now he found himself forced into the same position again. For whatever reason, because he couldn't bring himself to destroy Ro or because disclosing that Jessie's baby wasn't his and bringing even more suspicion down on his own head, his wife's murderer was going to go unpunished. The impotent rage welled up again, eating him alive like acid; rage at Jessie, at Roanna, at everyone, and most of all at himself.

"If she knew," he finally said, his voice hoarse, "she hadn't told me."

"Well, some women know right off, and some don't. My wife didn't miss a period for four months with our first; we had no idea why she was throwing up all the time. Don't know why they call it morning sickness, because Bethalyn puked all hours of the day and night. We never knew what would set it off. But now, with the others, she knew pretty soon. Guess she learned how to spot it. Anyway, I'm sorry about this, Webb. About the baby and all. And, uh, we'll keep the case open, but frankly we don't have jack shit to go on."

Webb sat for a moment, staring at the whiteness of his knuckles as he gripped the arms of the chair. "Does this mean you're not investigating me anymore?"

"I guess it does."

"I can leave town?"

"Can't stop you."

Webb stood up. He was still pale. He stopped at the door and looked back at Booley. "I didn't kill her," he said.

Booley sighed. "It was a possibility. I had to check it out."

"I know."

"I wish I could find the killer for you, but it don't look good."

"I know," Webb said again and quietly closed the door behind him.

Sometime during the short drive to the motel, he made his decision.

He packed his clothes, checked out of the motel, and drove back to Davencourt. His gaze was bitter as he surveyed the grand old house, crowning a slight rise with its graceful and gracious wings spread wide, like welcoming arms. He had loved it here, a prince in his own kingdom, knowing that one day it would all be his. He had been willing to work himself into the ground for the sake of his kingdom. He had married the chosen princess. Hell, he had been more than willing to marry her. Jessie had been his since that long ago day when they had sat in the swing beneath the huge old oak and fought their first battle for dominance.

Had he married her out of pure ego, determined to show her that she couldn't play her little games with him? If he were honest, then yes, that had been part of the reason. But the other part had been love, a strange love compounded of a shared childhood, a shared role in life, and the sexual fascination that had existed between them since puberty. Not a great foundation for marriage, he knew now. The sex had burned itself out pretty damn fast, and their old bonds hadn't been strong enough to hold them together after the attraction was gone.

Jessie had been sleeping with another man. *Men,* for all he knew. Knowing Jessie as he did, he realized she had probably done it out of revenge, because he hadn't kowtowed to her every whim. She'd been capable of just about anything when thwarted, but somehow he'd never expected her to cheat on him. Her reputation in Tuscumbia and Colbert County had been too important to her, and this wasn't some fast-lane big city where lovers came and went and no one paid much attention to it. This was the South, and in some ways still the Old South, where appearances and genteel manners held sway, at least in the middle and upper echelons of society.

But she'd not only slept with someone else, she had neglected to use birth control. Again, out of revenge? Had she thought it would be a delicious joke on him to present him with a child not his own?

In one short, hellish week, his wife had been murdered, his entire life and reputation had been destroyed, and his family had turned on him. He had gone from prince to pariah.

He was fed up with it all. Booley's bombshell today had just topped it off. He had worked like hell for years to keep the family in the manner to which they'd become accustomed, meaning the lap of luxury, sacrificing his private life and any chance he might have had of making a real marriage with Jessie. But when he'd needed his family in a united front, supporting him, they hadn't been there. Lucinda hadn't accused him but neither had she backed him, and he was tired of dancing to her tune. As for Gloria and Harlan and their bunch, to hell with them. Only Mother and Aunt Sandra had believed in him.

Roanna. What about her? Had she set this entire nightmare in motion, striking out at Jessie without any regard to the damage she would do to him? Somehow, on a different level, Roanna's betrayal was more bitter than the others. He'd gotten so accustomed to her adoration, to the comfortable companionship he'd had with her. Her quirky personality and unruly tongue had amused him, made him laugh even when he was so dead tired he was about to fall on his face. *Grand Pricks,* indeed, the little imp.

At the funeral, she'd said that she hadn't deliberately set up that scene in the kitchen, but guilt and misery had been written all over that thin face. Maybe she had, maybe she hadn't. But she too had avoided him, when he'd have sold his soul for comfort. Booley didn't consider Roanna a suspect in Jessie's murder, but Webb couldn't forget the look of hate he'd seen in Roanna's eyes, or the fact that she'd had the chance. Everyone in the house had had the chance to do it, but Roanna was the only one who'd hated Jessie.

He just didn't know. He'd kept his mouth shut to protect her even though she hadn't supported him. He'd kept his mouth shut about Jessie's baby not being his, letting another possible murderer off scot-free, because he himself would have been the more likely suspect. He was goddamn tired of being caught in the middle.

To hell with them all.

He stopped the car in the driveway and stared at the house. Davencourt. It was the embodiment of his ambition, a symbol of his life, the heart of the Davenport family. It had a personality all its own, an old house that had sheltered generations of Davenports within its graceful wings. Whenever he was away on a business trip and thought of Davencourt, in his mind's eye he always saw it surrounded by flowers. In spring, the azalea bushes rioted with color. In summer, the roses and old maids took their bow. In fall there were the chrysanthemums, and in winter the pink and white camellia bushes. Davencourt was always in bloom. He'd loved it with a passion he'd never felt for Jessie. He couldn't put the blame for this totally on the others, because he too was guilty, in the final analysis marrying for the legacy rather than the woman.

To hell with Davencourt, too.

He parked at the walk and went in the front door. The conversation in the living room stilled abruptly, as it had been doing for the past week. He didn't even glance into the room as he strode into the study and seated himself behind the desk.

He worked for hours, completing paperwork, drawing up forms, returning active control of all the far-flung Davenport enterprises into Lucinda's hands. When it was finished, he got up and walked out of the house, and drove away without looking back.

BOOK THREE

The
Return

CHAPTER

8

Bring Webb back for me," Lucinda said to Roanna. "I want you to convince him to come home."

Roanna's face didn't show her shock, though it reverberated through her entire body. With controlled grace she replaced her tea glass on the dainty coaster without even the tiniest betraying rattle. Webb! Just the sound of his name still had the power to slice through her, bringing up the old painful longing and guilt, even though it had been ten years since she'd last seen him, since anyone had seen him.

"Do you know where he is?" she asked composedly.

Unlike Roanna's, Lucinda's hand did shake as she set down her glass. Her eighty-three years sat heavily on Lucinda, and the constant tremor in her hands was just another of the tiny ways her own body was failing her. Lucinda was dying, in fact. She knew it, they all knew it. Not immediately, not even soon, but it was summer now and it wasn't likely she'd see another one. Her iron will had stood up to a lot, but had slowly bowed under the inexorable crush of time.

"Of course. I hired a private investigator to find him. Yvonne and Sandra have known all along, but they wouldn't tell me," Lucinda said with a mixture of anger and exasperation. "He's kept in touch with them, and both of them have visited him occasionally."

Roanna veiled her eyes with her lashes, careful not to let any expression show through. So they had known all this time. Unlike Lucinda, she didn't blame them. Webb had made it perfectly plain he had no use for the rest of the family; he had to despise them, and herself most of all. She didn't blame him, considering. Still, it hurt. Her love for him was the one emotion she hadn't been able to block. His absence had been like a slow-bleeding wound, and in ten years it hadn't healed but still seeped pain and remorse.

But she had survived. Somehow, by locking away all other emotions, she had survived. Gone was the coltish, exuberant girl, brimming over with energy and mischief, that she'd been. In her place was a cool, remote young woman who never hurried, never lost her temper, and seldom even smiled, much less laughed aloud. Emotions were paid for with pain; she had learned a bitter lesson when her impulsiveness, her stupid emotionalism, had ruined Webb's life.

She had been worthless and unlovable the way she'd been, so she had destroyed herself and built a new person from the ashes, a woman who would never know the heights but would no longer sink to the depths either. Somehow she had set in motion the chain of events that had cost Jessie her life and banished Webb from theirs, so she had grimly set herself to the task of atonement. She couldn't replace Jessie in Lucinda's affection, but at least she could stop being such a burden and disappointment.

She had gone to college—at the University of Alabama, as it happened, rather than the exclusive all-girl's college that had previously been considered—and gotten a degree in business management so she could be of some help to Lucinda in running things, since Webb was no longer there to take care of everything. Roanna didn't like anything about her courses but forced herself to study hard and get good grades. So what if she found it boring? It was a small enough price to pay.

She had forced herself to learn how to dress, so Lucinda

wouldn't be embarrassed by her. She had taken a course to improve her poor driving skills, she had learned how to dance, how to apply makeup, to make polite conversation, to be socially acceptable. She had learned how to control the wild exuberance that had so often gotten her into trouble as a child, but that hadn't been difficult. After Webb had disappeared, her problem had been in working up any enthusiasm for life rather than the opposite.

She could think of nothing she dreaded more than having to face Webb again.

"What if he doesn't want to come back?" she murmured.

"Convince him," Lucinda snapped. Then she sighed, and her voice gentled. "He always had a soft spot for you. I need him back here. *We* need him. You and I together have managed to keep things going, but I don't have much time left and your heart and soul isn't in it the way Webb's was. When it came to business, Webb had the brain of a computer and the heart of a shark. He was honorable but ruthless. Those are rare qualities, Roanna, the kind that aren't easily replaced."

"That's why he may not forgive us." Roanna didn't react to Lucinda's dismissal of her competence in managing the family empire. It was nothing less than the truth; that was why the burden of decision-making rested, for the most part, on Lucinda's increasingly frail shoulders, while Roanna implemented them. She had trained herself, disciplined herself, to do what she could, but her best would never be good enough. She accepted that and protected herself by not letting it matter. Nothing had really mattered anyway for the past ten years.

Pain flickered across Lucinda's lined face. "I've missed him every day that he's been gone," she said softly. "I'll never forgive myself for what I let happen to him. I should have let folks know that I believed in him, trusted him, but instead I wallowed in my own grief and didn't see what my neglect was doing to him. I don't mind dying, but I can't go easy until I make things right with Webb. If anyone can bring him back, Roanna, you can."

Roanna didn't tell Lucinda that she had reached out to Webb at Jessie's funeral, and been coldly rebuffed. Privately she thought that she had less chance of convincing Webb to come home than anyone else did, but that was something else she'd taught herself: if she couldn't manage to block out her feelings, then her private pain and fears were just that, private. If she kept them inside, then no one but she knew they were there.

It didn't matter what she felt; if Lucinda wanted Webb home, she would do what she could, no matter the cost to herself. "Where is he?"

"In some godforsaken little town in Arizona. I'll give you the folder of information the investigator gathered for me. He's . . . done well for himself. He owns a ranch, nothing on the scale of Davencourt, but it isn't in Webb to fail."

"When do you want me to leave?"

"As soon as possible. We need him here. *I* need him. I want to make my peace with him before I die."

"I'll try," Roanna said.

Lucinda looked at her granddaughter for a long moment, then a tired smile quirked her mouth. "You're the only one who doesn't put on that fake cheerfulness and tell me I'll live to be a hundred," she said, a hint of acerbic approval in her voice. "Damn fools. Do they think I don't know that I'm dying? I have cancer, and I'm too old to waste my time and money on treatment when old age is going to get me pretty soon anyway. I live in this body, for God's sake. I can tell that it's slowly shutting down."

There was no response that wouldn't sound either falsely cheerful or callous, so Roanna made none. She was often silent, letting conversation flow around her, not thrusting out any verbal oars to deflect the tide her way. It was true that everyone else in the household tried their best to ignore the situation, as if it would go away if they didn't acknowledge it. It wasn't just Gloria and Harlan now; somehow, within a year of Jessie's death and Webb's departure, Gloria had managed to move more of her family into Davencourt. Their son, Baron, had decided to remain in Charlotte, but everyone else was there. Gloria's daughter, Lanette, had moved in her entire family: husband Greg and children Corliss and Brock. Not that they were children; Brock was thirty, and Corliss was Roanna's age. Lucinda had let the house fill, perhaps in an effort to banish the emptiness left by losing both Jessie and Webb. Assuming Roanna could convince Webb to return—a major assumption—she wondered what he would make of all this. True, they were all his cousins, but somehow she thought he might be rather impatient with them for taking advantage of Lucinda's grief.

"You know that I changed my will after Webb left," Lucinda continued after a moment, taking another sip of tea. She gazed out the window at the profusion of peach-colored roses, her favorite, and squared her shoulders as if bracing herself. "I made you the main heir; Davencourt and most of the money would go to you. I think it's only fair to tell you that if you can convince Webb to come back, I'll redo it in his favor."

Roanna nodded. That wouldn't make any difference to her efforts; nothing would. She would do her best to talk Webb into coming back but not let herself feel any personal loss when Lucinda changed her will. Roanna accepted that no matter how hard she tried, she simply didn't have the knack for business that Lucinda and Webb possessed. She wasn't a risk taker, and she couldn't muster any enthusiasm for the game of big business. Davencourt would be better off with him in charge and so would the myriad financial investments and interests.

"That was the deal I made with him when he was fourteen," Lucinda continued, her voice abrupt and her shoulders still held stiffly erect. "If he would work hard, study, and train himself to take care of Davencourt, it would all be his."

"I understand," Roanna murmured.

"Davencourt . . ." Lucinda stared out over the perfectly manicured lawn, the flower gardens, the pastures beyond where her beloved horses bent their sleek, muscular necks to graze. "Davencourt deserves to be in the best hands. It isn't just a house, it's a legacy. There aren't many like it left, and I have to choose who I think will be the best caretaker for it."

"I'll try to bring him back," Roanna promised, her face as still as a pond on a hot summer day, when no breeze existed to ripple the surface. It was the face she lived behind, a face of indifference, unreadable and serene. Nothing could pierce the safe cocoon she had woven for herself, except Webb, her only weakness. Despite herself, her thoughts drifted. To have him back . . . it would be heaven and hell combined. To be able to see him every day, listen to his voice, secretly hug his nearness to her in the long, dark nights when all her nightmares became real . . . that was the heaven. The hell was in knowing that he despised her now, that every look he gave her would be one of condemnation and disgust.

But, no, she had to be realistic. She wouldn't be here. When Lucinda—she never thought of her as Grandmother anymore—died, Davencourt would no longer be her home. It would be Webb's, and he wouldn't want her here. She wouldn't see him every day, perhaps not at all. She would have to move out, get a job, face the real world. Well, at least with her degree and experience, she should be able to get a decent job. Maybe not in the Shoals area; she might have to move, in which case it was certain she'd never see Webb. That, too, didn't matter. His place was here. Her thoughtless actions had cost him his inheritance, so it was only right that she do what she could to return it to him.

"Doesn't it matter to you?" Lucinda asked abruptly. "That you'll lose Davencourt if you do this for me?"

Nothing matters. That had been her mantra, her curse, for ten years. "It's yours to leave to whomever you want. Webb was your chosen heir. And you're right; he'll do a much better job than I ever could."

She could tell that her quiet, even voice disturbed Lucinda in some way, but injecting any passion in her words was beyond her.

"But you're a Davenport," Lucinda argued, as if she wanted Roanna to justify her own decision for her. "Some folks would say Davencourt should be yours by right, because Webb is a Tallant. He's my blood relative, but he isn't a Davenport, and he isn't nearly as closely related to me as you are."

"But he's the better choice."

Gloria came into the living room in time to hear Roanna's last comment. "Who's the better choice?" she demanded, sinking into the depths of her favorite chair. Gloria was seventy-three, ten years younger than Lucinda, but while Lucinda's hair was unabashedly white, Gloria still stubbornly resisted nature and kept her fluffy curls tinted a delicate blond.

"Webb," Lucinda answered tersely.

"Webb!" Shocked, Gloria stared at her sister. "For goodness sake, what could *he* possibly be the better choice for, except the electric chair?"

"To run Davencourt, and the business side of things."

"You have to be joking! Why, no one would deal with him—"

"Yes, they would," Lucinda said, steel in her voice. "If he's in charge, *everyone* will deal with him, or wish they hadn't been so stupid."

"I don't see why you even brought up his name anyway, since no one knows where he—"

"I found him," Lucinda interrupted. "And Roanna is going to talk him into coming back."

Gloria rounded on Roanna as if she had suddenly sprouted two heads. "Are you out of your mind?" she breathed. "You can't mean to bring a murderer among us! Why, I'd never be able to close my eyes at night!"

"Webb isn't a murderer," Roanna said, sipping her tea and not even glancing at Gloria. She had stopped thinking of Gloria as *Aunt,* too. Sometime during the awful night after Webb had walked out of their lives, the titles of kinship had faded from the way she thought of people, as if her emotional distance couldn't accommodate them anymore.

The people in her family now were simply Lucinda, Gloria, Harlan.

"Then why did he disappear like that? Only someone with a guilty conscience would run away."

"Stop that!" Lucinda snapped. "He didn't run, he got fed up and left. There's a difference. We let him down, so I can't blame him for turning his back on us. But Roanna's right; Webb didn't kill Jessie. I never thought he did."

"Well, Booley Watts certainly did!"

Lucinda dismissed Booley's thoughts with a wave of her hand. "It doesn't matter. *I* think Webb's innocent, there was no evidence against him, so as far as the law's concerned he's innocent, and I want him back."

"Lucinda, don't be an old fool!"

Lucinda's eyes glittered with a sudden ferocity that belied her age. "I think it's safe to say," she drawled, "that no one has ever considered me a fool, old or otherwise." *And lived to tell it,* was the unspoken message in her tone. Eighty-three or not, dying or not, Lucinda still knew the full range of her power as matriarch of the Davenport fortune, and she wasn't shy about letting other folks know it, too.

Gloria backed down and turned on Roanna, the easier target. "You can't mean to do it. Tell her it's crazy."

"I agree with her."

Fury sparked in Gloria's eyes at the murmured statement. "You *would!*" she snapped. "Don't think I've forgotten that you were crawling into bed with him when—"

"Stop it!" Lucinda said fiercely, half rising from her chair as if she would physically attack her sister. "Booley explained what really happened between them, and I won't let it be blown out of proportion. I won't let you badger Roanna either. She's only doing what I asked her to do."

"But why would you even *think* of bringing him back?" Gloria moaned, dropping her aggressiveness, and Lucinda sank back into her chair.

"Because we need him. It takes both Roanna and me to handle things now, and when I die, she'll be buried in work."

"Oh, pish tosh, Lucinda, you're going to outlive—"

"No," Lucinda said briskly, cutting through the statement she'd heard so many times before. "I am *not* going to outlive all of you. I don't want to even if I could. We need Webb. Roanna's going to get him and bring him home, and that's that."

The next night, Roanna sat in the shadows of a small, dingy cantina, her back to the wall as she silently watched a man lounging on one of the stools around the bar. She had been watching him for so long and so hard that her eyes ached from the strain of peering through the dim, smoky interior. For the most part anything she might have heard him say was drowned out by the ancient jukebox in the corner, the clatter of billiard balls striking together, the hum of curses and conversation, but every so often she could discern a certain tone, a drawl, that she knew beyond doubt was his as he made some casual comment to either the man beside him or to the bartender.

Webb. It had been ten years since she'd seen him, ten years since she had felt alive. She had known, accepted, that she still loved him, was still vulnerable to him, but somehow the dreary procession of ten years' worth of days had dulled her memory of how sharp her response to him had always been. All it had taken was that first glimpse of him to remind her. The flood of sensation was so intense that it bordered on pain, as if the cells of her body had been jolted back to life. Nothing had changed. She still reacted just the way she had before, her heart beating faster and excitement zinging through every nerve ending. Her skin felt tight and hot, the flesh beneath it pulsing, aching. The hunger to touch him, to be close enough that she could smell the unique, never-forgotten male muskiness of his scent, was so strong that she was almost paralyzed with need.

But for all her longing, she couldn't work up the courage to walk to his side and get his attention. Despite Lucinda's determined confidence that she could convince him to come home, Roanna didn't expect to see anything in that green gaze except dislike—and dismissal. The anticipation of pain kept her in her chair. She had lived with the pain of his loss every day for the past ten years, but that ache was familiar, and she *had* learned to live with it. She wasn't certain she had the endurance to bear up under any new pain, however. A new blow would crush her, perhaps beyond recovery.

She wasn't the only woman in the bar, but there were enough curious male glances her way to make her nervous. Webb's wasn't one of them; he was oblivious to her presence. It was only because she deliberately didn't attract attention that she had so far been left alone. She had dressed plainly, conservatively, in dark green slacks and a cream camp shirt, hardly the costume of a woman out on the town and looking for trouble. She didn't look anyone in the eye and didn't gaze around with interest. Over the years she had developed the knack of being as unobtrusive as possible, and it had stood her in good stead tonight. Sooner or later, though, some cowboy was going to work up enough nerve to ignore her "stay away" signals and approach her.

She was tired. It was ten o'clock at night, and her plane had left Huntsville at six o'clock that morning. From Huntsville she had flown to Birmingham, then from Birmingham to Dallas—with a stop at Jackson, Mississippi. In Dallas, she had endured a four-hour layover. She had arrived in Tucson at four twenty-seven, mountain time, rented a car, and driven south on Interstate 19 to Tumacacori, where Lucinda's private detective said Webb now lived. According to the information in the file, he owned a small but prosperous cattle ranch in the area.

She hadn't been able to find him. Directions notwithstanding, she had wandered around looking for the correct road, returning time and again to the interstate to get her bearings. She had almost been in tears when she had finally run across a local who not only knew Webb personally, but had directed Roanna to this seedy little bar just outside Nogales, where Webb was in the habit of stopping whenever he had to go to town, which he'd done this particular day.

The desert night had fallen with color and drama on the drive to Nogales, and when the kaleidoscope of hues had faded, it had left behind a black velvet sky full of the biggest, brightest stars she'd ever seen. The starkly beautiful desolation had calmed her, so that by the time she managed to find the bar, her usual remote expression was firmly in place.

Webb had been there when she'd walked in; he was the first person she'd seen. The shock had almost felled her. His head was turned away from her and he hadn't so much as glanced around, but she knew it was him, because every cell in her body screamed in recognition. She had gone quietly to one of the few empty tables, automatically choosing the one in the darkest corner, and here she still sat. The waitress, a tired-looking Hispanic woman in her late thirties, came by every so often. Roanna had ordered a beer the first time, nursed it until it was warm, then ordered another. She didn't like beer, didn't normally drink at all, but thought she should probably order or she'd be asked to leave the table to make room for customers who did.

She looked down at the scarred surface of the table, where numerous knife blades had carved a multitude of initials and designs as well as random scratches and gouges. Waiting wasn't going to make it any easier. She should just get up and walk over to him and get it over with.

But still she didn't move. Hungrily her gaze moved back to him, drinking in the changes ten years had made.

He'd been twenty-four when he'd left Tuscumbia, a young man, mature for his age and burdened with responsibilities that would have felled a lesser person, but still *young*. At twenty-four he hadn't yet learned the full range of his own strengths, his personality had still been a bit malleable. Jessie's death and the ensuing investigation, and the way he'd been ostracized by both family and friends, had hardened him. The ten years since had hardened him even more. It was evident in the grim line of his mouth and the cool, level way he surveyed the world around him, marking him as a man who was prepared to take on the world and bend it to his will. Whatever challenges he had faced, he had been the victor.

Roanna knew some of those challenges, because the file on him was thorough. When rustlers had been decimating his herd of cattle and the local law enforcement hadn't been able to stop it, Webb had single-handedly tracked the four rustlers and followed them into Mexico. The rustlers had spotted him and started shooting. Webb had shot back. They had kept each other pinned down for two days. At the end of those two days, one rustler had been dead, one severely injured, and another suffered a concussion after falling off a rock. Webb had been slightly wounded, a crease that burned along his thigh, and suffered from dehydration. But the rustlers had decided to cut their losses and get away the best they could, and Webb had grimly herded his stolen cattle back across the border. He hadn't been bothered by rustlers since.

There was an air of danger about him now that hadn't been there before, the look of a man who meant what he said and was willing to back it up with action. His character had been honed down to its steel core. Webb had no weaknesses now, certainly not any leftover ones for the silly, careless cousin who had caused him so much trouble.

He wasn't the man she had known before. He was harder, rougher, perhaps even brutal. She realized that ten years had wrought a lot of changes, in both of them, but one thing had remained constant, and that was her love for him.

Physically, he looked tougher and bigger than he had before. He'd always had the muscular build of a natural athlete, but years of grueling physical work had toughened him to whipcord leanness, coiled steel waiting to spring. His shoulders had broadened and his chest deepened. His forearms, exposed by his turned-back cuffs, were thick with muscle and roped with veins.

He was darkly tanned, with lines bracketing his mouth and radiating out from the corners of his eyes. His hair was longer, shaggier, the hair of a man who didn't get into town for a haircut on a regular basis. That was another difference:

it was no longer "styled," it was simply cut. His face was darkened by a shadow of beard, but it couldn't hide a newly healed cut that ran along the underside of his right jaw, from ear to chin. Roanna swallowed hard, wondering what had happened to him, if the injury had been dangerous.

The investigator's file said that Webb had not only bought the small ranch and quickly turned it into a profit-making enterprise, but that he had been systematically buying other parcels of land, not, as it turned out, to expand his ranch, but for mining. Arizona was rich in minerals, and Webb was investing in those minerals. Leaving Davencourt hadn't impoverished him; he'd had some money of his own, and he'd used it wisely. As Lucinda had pointed out, Webb had a rare talent for business and finance, and he'd been using it.

As prosperous as he was, though, you couldn't tell it from his clothes. His boots were worn and scuffed, his jeans faded, and his thin chambray shirt had been washed so many times it was almost white. He was wearing a hat, a dark brown, dusty one. Nogales had a reputation for toughness, but all in all, he fit right in with the rough crowd here in this dingy bar in the small desert border town that was as different from Tuscumbia as the Amazon was from the Arctic.

He had the power to destroy her. With a few cold, cutting words he could annihilate her. She felt sick at the risk she would be taking in approaching him, but she kept seeing the hope that had been in Lucinda's eyes when she'd kissed Roanna good-bye that morning. Lucinda, shrunken with age, diminished by grief and regrets, indomitable but no longer invincible. The end, perhaps, was closer than she wanted them to know. This might be her last chance to heal the rift with Webb.

Roanna knew exactly what she was risking, financially, if she could talk Webb into coming home. As Lucinda's will stood now, she was the major heir of Davencourt and the family financial empire, with some modest bequests going to Gloria and her offspring, some to Yvonne and Sandra, and pensions as well as lump sum amounts settled on the long-time domestic staff: Loyal, Tansy, and Bessie. But Webb had been groomed to be the heir, and if he returned, it would be his again.

She would lose Davencourt. She had blocked her emotions, hadn't let Lucinda see the pain and panic that had threatened to break through her protective barrier. She was human; she would regret losing the money. But Davencourt was worth more to her than any fortune. Davencourt was home, sanctuary, dearly beloved, and every inch familiar. It would tear her heart out to lose Davencourt, but she had no illusion that she would be welcome there if Webb inherited. He would want all of them out, including her.

But he could better care for it than she could. He had been raised with the understanding that, through his alliance with Jessie, Davencourt would be his. He had spent his youth and his young manhood training himself to be the best custodian possible for it, and it was Roanna's fault that he'd lost it.

What price atonement?

She knew the price, knew exactly what it would cost her.

But there was Lucinda, desperately wanting to see him before she died. And there was Webb himself, the exiled prince. Davencourt was his rightful place, his legacy. She owed him a debt she could never repay. She would give up Davencourt to get him to return. She would give up anything she had.

Somehow, her body moving without conscious will, she found herself on her feet and walking through the swirling smoke. She stopped behind him and to the right, her gaze fevered and hungry as she stared at the hard line of his cheekbone, his jaw. Hesitantly, both yearning for the contact but dreading it, she lifted her hand to touch his shoulder and draw his attention. Before she could, however, he sensed her presence and turned his head toward her.

Green eyes, narrowed and cool, looking her up and down. One dark eyebrow lifted in silent question. It was the look of a man on the prowl assessing a woman for availability, and desirability.

He didn't recognize her.

Her breath was rapid and shallow, but she felt as if she wasn't drawing in enough air. She dropped her hand, and ached because the brief contact she had so dreaded had been denied her. She wanted to touch him. She wanted to go into his arms the way she had when she was little, lay her head on his broad shoulder, and find refuge from the world. Instead she reached for her hard-won composure and said quietly, "Hello, Webb. May I talk to you?"

His eyes widened a little, and he swiveled on the bar stool so that he faced her. There was a brief flare of recognition, then incredulity, in his expression. Then it was gone, and his gaze hardened. He looked her over again, this time with slow deliberation.

He didn't say anything, just kept staring at her. Roanna's heart pounded against her ribs with sickening force. "Please," she said.

He shrugged, the movement straining his powerful shoulders against his shirt. He pulled a few bills from his pocket and tossed them on the bar, then stood, towering over her, forcing her to step back. Without a word he took her arm and steered her toward the entrance, his long fingers wrapped around her elbow like iron laces. Roanna braced herself against the tingle of delight caused by even that impersonal contact, and she wished she had worn a sleeveless blouse so she could feel his hand on her bare skin.

The door of the squat building slammed shut behind them. The lighting inside had been dim, but still she had to blink her eyes to accustom them to the darkness. Haphazardly parked vehicles crouched in the darkness, bumpers and windshields reflecting the blinking red neon of the BAR sign in the window. After the close, smoky atmosphere of the bar, the clear night air felt cold and thin. Roanna shivered with a sudden chill. He didn't release her but pulled her across the grit and sand of the parking lot to a pickup truck. Taking his keys out of his pocket, he unlocked the driver's side door, opened it, and thrust her forward. "Get in."

She obeyed, sliding across the seat until she was on the passenger side. Webb got in beside her, folding his long legs beneath the steering wheel and pulling the door shut.

Every time the sign blinked, she could see the iron set of his jaw. In the enclosed cab she could smell the fresh, hard odor of the tequila he'd been drinking. He sat silently, staring out the windshield. Hugging her arms against the chill, she too was silent.

"Well?" he snapped after a long moment when it became evident she wasn't exactly rushing into speech.

She thought of all the things she could say, all the excuses and apologies, all the reasons why Lucinda had sent her, but everything boiled down into two simple words, and she said, "Come home."

He gave a harsh crack of laughter and turned so that his shoulders were comfortably wedged against the door and the seat. "I *am* home, or near enough."

Roanna was silent again, as she often was. The stronger her feelings, the more silent she became, as if her inner shell tightened against any outbreak that would leave her vulnerable. His nearness, just hearing his voice again, made her feel as if she would shatter inside. She wasn't even able to return his gaze. Instead she looked down at her lap, fighting to control her shivering.

He muttered a curse, then shoved the key into the ignition and turned it. The motor caught immediately and settled into a powerful, well-tuned hum. He pushed the temperature control lever all the way over into the heat zone, then twisted his torso to reach behind the seat. He pulled out a denim jacket and tossed it into her lap. "Put that around you before you turn blue."

The jacket smelled of dust and sweat and horses and ineffably of Webb. Roanna wanted to bury her face in the fabric; instead she pulled it around her shoulders, grateful for the protection.

"How did you find me?" he finally asked. "Did Mother tell you?"

She shook her head.

"Aunt Sandra?"

She shook her head again.

"Damn it, I'm not in the mood for guessing games," he snapped. "Either talk or get out of the truck."

Roanna's hands tightened on the edges of the jacket. "Lucinda hired a private detective to find you. Then she sent me out here." She could feel his hostility radiating from him, a palpable force that seared her skin. She'd known she didn't have much chance of convincing him to return, but she hadn't realized how violently he disliked her now. Her stomach twisted sickeningly, and her chest felt hollow, as if her heart no longer lived there.

"So you didn't come on your own?" he asked sharply.

"No."

Unexpectedly he reached out and caught her jaw, his fingers biting into the softness of her skin as he wrenched her head around. A purr of soft menace entered his voice. "Look at me when you're talking to me."

Helplessly she did so, her eyes eating him, tracing every beloved outline and committing it to memory. This might be the last time she ever saw him, and when he sent her away, another piece of her would die.

"What does she want?" he asked, still holding her face in his grip. His big hand covered her jaw from ear to ear. "If she simply missed my smiling face, she wouldn't have waited ten years to find me. So what is it she wants from me?"

His bitterness was deeper than she'd expected, his anger still as hot as it had been the day he'd walked out of their lives. She should have known, though, and Lucinda should have, too. They'd always been aware of the force of his character; that was why, when he'd been only fourteen, Lucinda had picked him as her heir and the custodian of Davencourt. Their betrayal of him had been like pulling a tiger's tail, and now they had to face his fangs and claws.

"She wants you to come home and take over again."

"Sure she does. The good people of Colbert County

wouldn't dirty themselves by doing business with an accused murderer."

"Yes, they would. With Davencourt and everything else belonging to you, they'd have to, or lose a lot of their own income."

He gave a harsh bark of laughter. "My God, she must really want me back if she's willing to buy me! I know she's changed her will, presumably in your favor. What's gone wrong? Has she made a few bad decisions, and now she needs me to pull the family's financial ass out of the fire?"

Her fingers ached to reach out and smooth away the anger that lined his forehead, but she restrained herself, and the effort it cost her was reflected in her voice. "She wants you to come home because she loves you and regrets what happened. She needs you to come home because she's dying. She has cancer."

He glared at her in the darkness, then abruptly released her jaw and turned his head away. After a moment he said, "God *damn* it," and viciously slammed his fist against the steering wheel. "She's always been good at manipulating people. God knows, Jessie came by it honestly."

"Then you'll come?" Roanna asked hesitantly, unable to believe that was what he meant.

Instead of answering, he turned back to her and caught her face in his hand again. He leaned closer, so close she could see the glitter of his eyes and smell the alcohol on his breath. Dismayed, she abruptly realized he wasn't exactly sober. She should have known, she'd watched him drinking, but she just hadn't thought—

"What about you?" he demanded, his voice low and hard. "All I've heard is what Lucinda wants. What do *you* want? Do you want me to come home, little-Roanna-all-grown-up? How did she get you to do her dirty work for her, knowing that you'll lose a lot of money and property if you succeed?" He paused. "I assume that's what you meant, that if I go back she'll change her will again, leaving it all to me?"

"Yes," she whispered.

"Then you're a fool," he whispered derisively in return, and released her face. "Look, why don't you trot on back, like the good little lapdog you're turned into, and tell her you gave it your best shot but I'm not interested."

She absorbed the pain of that blow, too, and shoved it into her inner shell where the damage wouldn't show. The expression she turned to him was as smooth and blank as a doll's. "I want you to come home, too. Please."

She could feel his intensifying focus as it settled on her, like a laser beam finding its target. "Now, why would you want that?" he asked softly. "Unless you really are a fool. Are you a fool, Roanna?"

She opened her mouth to answer but he laid one callused finger across her lips. "Ten years ago you started it all by offering me a taste of that skinny little body. At the time, I thought you were too innocent to know what you were doing, but I've thought about it a lot since then, and now I think you knew exactly how I was reacting, didn't you?"

His finger was still covering her lips, lightly tracing the sensitive outline. This was what she had dreaded most, having to face his bitter accusations. She closed her eyes and nodded.

"Did you know Jessie was coming down?"

"No!" Her denial moved her lips against his finger, making her mouth tingle.

"So you kissed me because you wanted me?"

What did pride matter? she thought. She had loved him, in some form, her entire life. First she had loved him with a child's hero worship, then with an adolescent's violent crush, and finally with a woman's passion. The last change had, perhaps, taken place when she had watched Jessie cheating on him with another man and knew she couldn't tell, because to do so would hurt Webb. When she'd been younger, she would have been gleeful at the prospect of getting Jessie in trouble, and told immediately. That time she had put Webb's welfare above her own impulses, but then she had surrendered to another impulse when she kissed him, and he had ended up paying the price anyway.

His finger pressed harder. "Did you?" he insisted. "Did you want me?"

"Yes," she breathed, abandoning any scrap of pride or self-protection. "I always wanted you."

"What about now?" His voice was hard, inexorable, pushing her toward an end she couldn't see. "Do you want me now?"

What did he want her to say? Maybe he just wanted her complete humiliation. If he blamed her for everything that had happened, perhaps this was the price he wanted *her* to pay.

She nodded.

"How much do you want me?" Abruptly his hand slipped inside the jacket and closed over her breast. "Just enough to give me a feel, tease me? Or enough to give me what you offered ten years ago?"

Roanna's breath wheezed to a stop in her chest, frozen with shock. She stared helplessly at him, her dark eyes so huge that they dominated her pale face.

"Tell you what," he murmured, his big hand still burning her breast, lightly squeezing as if testing the firm resilience of her flesh. "I paid for this ten years ago, but I never got it. I'll go back and take care of business for Lucinda—if you'll give me what everyone thought I'd had then."

Numbly, she realized what he meant, realized that the years had made him even harder than she'd suspected. The old Webb never would have done such a thing—or perhaps he'd always had the capability for such ruthlessness but hadn't needed to use it. The iron was much closer to the surface now.

This, then, was his revenge against her for her juvenile romantic ambush, which had cost him so much. If he went back home he would have Davencourt as his payment, but he wanted Roanna's personal payment, too, and his price was her body.

She looked at him, at this man she had loved forever.

"All right," she whispered.

C H A P T E R

9

*T*he motel room was small and dingy, with a chill that went all the way to her bones. Roanna was certain there had to be better motels in Nogales, so why had he brought her here? Because it was closest or to show her how little she meant to him?

It would take a great deal of ego to think she meant anything to him at all, and ego was one thing Roanna didn't have. She felt small and shriveled inside, and a new guilt had been added to the burden she already carried: he thought he was punishing her, and in a way he was, but a secret part of her was suddenly, dizzily ecstatic that soon she would be lying in his arms.

The secret part was small, and deeply buried. She felt the shame he meant her to feel, and the humiliation. She didn't know if she'd have the courage to go through with it, and desperately she thought of Lucinda, ill and diminished with age, needing Webb's forgiveness before she could die in peace. Could she do this, lie down and let him coldly use her body, even for Lucinda?

But it wasn't just for Lucinda. Webb needed revenge just as much as Lucinda needed forgiveness. If this would help him even the scales, if he could then return to Davencourt, then Roanna was willing to do it. And deep inside, that secret little part of her was giddy with selfish delight. No matter what his reasoning, for a brief time he would be hers, the experience held to her heart and savored during the empty years ahead.

He tossed his hat onto the chair and sprawled on his back on the bed, bunching the pillow up behind his head for support. His narrowed green eyes raked down her body.

"Take off your clothes."

Stunned again, she stood there with her arms hanging at her sides. He wanted her to strip down naked, just like that, with him lying there watching?

"I guess you've changed your mind," he drawled, sitting up and reaching for his hat.

Roanna pulled herself together and reached for the buttons of her shirt. She had decided to do it, so what did it matter if he wanted to look at her first? Shortly he would be doing much more than looking. The enormity of what *she* was doing was what shook her, and her hands trembled as she struggled with the buttons. Odd how difficult this was, to bare herself for him, when she had dreamed of it for years. Was it because she had always dreamed he came to her in love, and in reality it was the opposite?

But it didn't matter, she told herself over and over, using the litany as protection against thinking too much. It didn't matter, it didn't matter.

The buttons were finally undone, and the shirt hung open. She had to keep moving or she'd lose her nerve entirely. With a quick, nervous movement she pulled the cloth off her shoulders and let it drop down her arms. She couldn't look at him, but she felt his gaze on her, narrowed and intense, waiting.

Her bra had a front clasp. Briefly, trembling with cold and embarrassment, she wished it was a sexy, lacy thing, but instead it was plain white, designed for concealment rather than enticement. She unhooked it and pushed the straps down, so that this garment too dropped to the floor at her feet. The cold air swirled around her breasts, making her nipples pucker into tight buds. She knew her breasts were small. Was he looking at them? She didn't dare glance at him to see, because she was terrified she would see disappointment in his gaze.

She didn't know how to undress to please a man. Mortified at her own awkwardness, she knew that there had to be a way to do it gracefully, to tease and interest a man with the slowly revealed promise of her flesh, but she didn't know what that way was. All she knew how to do was unbutton, unhook, unzip, like a schoolgirl changing clothes for gym class.

The best thing to do then was to get it over with before she lost her nerve. Hurriedly she kicked off her sandals, unzipped her slacks, and bent over to push them down. It was icy in the room now, her skin rough with chills.

Only her panties remained now, and her meager supply of nerve was almost gone. Not giving herself time to think, she hooked her thumbs in the waistband and pushed this last garment down to her feet and stepped out of them.

Still he didn't speak, didn't move. Her hands made a brief, aborted motion, as if she would cover herself, but then she let her arms fall to her side again and she simply stood there, staring blindly at the worn carpet beneath her bare feet, wondering if it was possible to die of embarrassment. She forced herself to eat these days but she was still thin, a meager offering on the altar of revenge. What if her naked body wasn't desirable enough for him to have an erection? What if he laughed?

He was completely silent. She couldn't even hear him breathing. Darkness edged her vision, and she fought to drag oxygen into her constricted lungs. She couldn't look at him, but she had the sudden panicked thought that he might have had more to drink than she'd imagined, and gone to sleep while she'd been undressing. What a comment that would be on her practically nonexistent charms!

Then the whisper came, low and rough, and she realized he hadn't fallen asleep, after all: "C'mere."

She closed her eyes, trembling as relief threatened to buckle her knees, and edged toward the whisper.

"Closer," he said, and she moved until her knees bumped the side of the bed.

He touched her then, his hand sliding up the outside of her left thigh, callused fingertips sliding over the softness of her skin and rasping nerve endings to life, leaving a trail of heat behind. Up, up, he moved his hand over the column of her thigh and around to the roundness of her bottom, his long fingers cupping the cool undercurve of both cheeks and burning them with his heat. She quivered, and tried to control the sudden, fierce need to rub her bottom against his hand. She didn't quite succeed; her hips moved in a barely perceptible shimmy.

He gave a low laugh, his fingers tightening on the flesh beneath him. He stroked her buttocks, shaping his palm to the underside of each one as if he could imprint the soft female shape on his hand, and running his thumb down the crease between them.

Roanna began to tremble violently under the combined lash of pleasure and shock, and no amount of willpower could stop the betraying tremors. No one had ever touched her there. She hadn't known that this slow caress could make an empty ache begin between her legs, or make her breasts feel hard and tight. She squeezed her eyes even more tightly together, wondering if he would touch her breast again and if she could bear it if he did.

But it wasn't her breasts that he touched.

"Spread your legs."

His voice now was so low and raspy that she wasn't certain she'd heard him, and yet part of her knew she had. A dull roaring began in her ears, even as she felt herself shifting her stance so that her thighs were open enough to admit his exploration, and felt his hand slipping between her legs.

He ran his fingers along the closed, tender folds, feeling their softness, gently squeezing. Roanna stopped breathing. Tension stretched in her body, pulling tight in an agony of waiting that threatened to shatter her. Then one long finger boldly slipped into the closed slit, opening her, probing with unerring skill, and pushed deep up into her body.

Roanna couldn't stop the cry that broke from her lips, though she quickly choked it off. Her knees trembled and threatened again to buckle. She felt as if she was held erect only by his hand between her legs, his finger inside her. Oh, God, the sensation was almost unbearable, his finger big and rough, rasping against her tender inner flesh. He withdrew it, then quickly pushed it into her again. Over and over he stabbed the finger inside her, and rubbed his thumb against the little nub at the top of her sex.

Helplessly she felt her hips begin to move against his hand, heard breathy little moans forming in her throat and slipping free. In the quietness of the room she could hear his breathing, heard how hard and fast it was coming. She wasn't cold now; great waves of heat were breaking over her, and the pleasure was so acute it was almost painful. Desperately she reached down and seized his wrist, trying to pull his hand away from her, because it was too much, she couldn't bear it. Something drastic was happening to her, something even more drastic was about to happen, and she cried out in sudden fear.

He ignored her efforts as if she were holding his hand rather than trying to push it away. She could feel him probing at her, trying to work a second finger into her alongside the other, felt her body's sudden panicked resistance. He tried again, and she flinched.

He went still, and his low curse exploded in the silence.

Then everything turned upside down as he grabbed her and pulled her down onto the bed, turning her, dragging her across his body to lie beside him. Roanna's eyes flew open to combat the sudden dizziness, then she wished she'd kept them closed.

He leaned over her so close she could see the black striations in his green eyes, so close she could feel the heat of his breath on her face, smell the tequila. She was sprawled on her back with her right leg draped over his hip. His hand still rested between her open thighs, one fingertip moving restlessly around and around the tender opening that had grown moist for him.

She felt another wave of mortification, that she was naked while he was still fully clothed, that he was touching her in her most private place and watching her face while he did so. She felt her cheeks and breasts heat, turn pink.

He moved his finger back into her again, probing deep, and all the while he held her gaze with his. Roanna couldn't hold back another moan, and she yearned for the dubious comfort of her closed eyes, but she couldn't look away. His dark brows drew together over the fierce green glitter of his eyes. He was angry, she realized in confusion, but it was a hot anger instead of the cold disgust she would have expected.

"You're a virgin," he said flatly.

It sounded like an accusation. Roanna stared up at him, wondering how he'd guessed, wondering why he sounded so angry. "Yes," she admitted, and blushed again.

He watched the flush pinken her breasts, and she saw the way the glitter in his eyes deepened. His gaze focused intently on her breasts, on her hardened nipples. He removed his hand from between her legs, his finger damp from her body. Slowly, still staring fixedly at her breasts, he stroked her nipple with that wet finger, spreading her own juices on the tightly puckered nub. A rough, hungry sound rumbled in his throat. He leaned over her and fastened his lips around the nipple he had just anointed, sucking hard on it, taking her taste into his mouth.

The pleasure almost shattered her. The fierce pressure, the rasp of his tongue and teeth, sent pure fire racing through her. Roanna arched in his arms, crying out, and her hands clenched in his hair to hold his head in place. He moved to her other breast and sucked just as hard on that nipple until it too was dark red and wet, and painfully erect.

Reluctantly he lifted his head, staring at his handiwork with feral concentration and hunger. His lips, like her nipples, were red and wet, and slightly parted as his breath moved hard and fast between them. The heat radiating from his big body dispelled any lingering chill she might have felt.

"You don't have to do this," he said, the words so harsh they sounded as if they'd been ripped from his throat. "It's your first time . . . I'll go back anyway."

Disappointment pierced her, sliding like a dagger straight into her heart. All color faded from her face, and she stared at him with a stricken expression in her eyes. Taking off her clothes had been difficult, but once he'd touched her, she had been gradually losing herself in a rising tide of sensual delight, despite the shock she felt at every new caress. The secret part of her had been delirious with ecstasy, savoring every touch of those hard hands, waiting with barely restrained eagerness for more.

Now he wanted to stop. She didn't entice him enough for him to continue.

Her throat closed. A strained whisper was all that could escape the sudden constriction. "Don't—don't you want me?"

The plea was faint, but he heard it. His eyes dilated until only a thin circle of green shimmered around the fierce pools of black. He caught her hand and dragged it down his body, pressed it hard over his straining penis despite her instinctive effort to pull away, an action that underscored her innocence.

Roanna froze in wonder. She felt the hard ridge under the denim. It was long and thick, the heat of it burning through the heavy fabric, and it pulsed with a life of its own. She turned her hand, grasping him through his jeans. "Please, Webb. I want you to do it," she gasped.

For a terrifying moment she thought he would still refuse, but then with a sudden, violent motion he jackknifed off the bed and began stripping off his clothes. She was only dimly aware that he watched her as she watched him. She couldn't keep the fascination from her face as she stared at his body, the broad shoulders and hairy, muscled chest, the ridged abdomen. Carefully he maneuvered the zipper down, then pushed his shorts and jeans off with one motion. She blinked, startled, at his pulsing erection as it thrust forward when freed from the restraint of his jeans. Another blush warmed her cheeks.

He paused, sucking in deep breaths.

Suddenly terrified of doing anything that would make him stop, Roanna held herself still and quiet, forcing herself to look away from his body. She thought she would die if he turned away from her now. But he wanted to do it; she knew he did. She was inexperienced, but that wasn't the same as ignorant. He was very hard, and he wouldn't be if he wasn't interested.

The glare of the light was right in her eyes. She wished he'd turned it off, but didn't ask. The mattress dipped under his weight, and she spread her hands to balance herself, because the cheap mattress didn't give much support.

He didn't give her any time to think, to perhaps change her mind, not even time to panic. He moved on top of her, his hard thighs pushing between hers and spreading them, and his shoulders blotted out the light. Roanna barely sucked in a deep breath before he set his hands on either side of her skull, holding her head as he leaned down and covered her mouth with his. His tongue probed, and she parted her lips to accept it. Simultaneously she felt his hot, rock-hard penis begin pushing at the soft entrance between her legs.

Her heart jumped violently, banging against her ribs. She made a faint sound of apprehension, but his mouth smothered it as he deepened the kiss, penetrating her with both tongue and penis.

It wasn't easy, despite her arousal, despite the dampness that readied her for him. Somehow she had thought he would simply slip into her, but it didn't work that way. He rocked his hips back and forth, forcing himself a little deeper into her with each motion. Her body resisted the increasing pressure; the pain surprised her, dismayed her. She tried to endure it without reaction, but it grew progressively worse with each inward thrust.

She groaned, her breath catching. If she had expected him to stop, she was mistaken. Webb merely tightened his arms and held her firmly beneath him, controlling her with weight and strength, all of his intent and attention focused on penetrating her. She dug her nails into his back, weeping now from the pain. He pushed harder and her tender flesh gave under the pressure, stretching around his thick length as he surged deep inside. Finally he was in her to the hilt, and she writhed helplessly beneath him as she tried to find some level of ease.

Now that his masculine goal was accomplished, he set about soothing her, not withdrawing, but using touch and voice to reassure and calm her. He continued to hold her head in his hands, and he crooned to her as he kissed the salty tears from her cheeks. "Shh, shh," he murmured. "Just lie still, sweetheart. I know it hurts, but it'll ease off in a minute."

The endearment soothed her as nothing else could have. He couldn't truly hate her, could he, if he called her "sweetheart"? Slowly she calmed, relaxing from her frantic struggle to accommodate him. Some of his own tenseness eased, and until then she hadn't realized how tightly drawn his muscles had been. Panting, she softened around him, beneath him.

Her breathing calmed, became deeper. Now that she wasn't in such distress some of her pleasure returned. With growing wonder she felt him deep inside her, pulsing with arousal. This was Webb who penetrated her so intimately, Webb who cradled her in his arms. Only an hour before she had watched him from across a dimly lit bar, dreading the moment when she had to approach him, and now she was naked under his powerful body. She looked up at him and met his brilliant green gaze, studying her as intently as if he could see through her to the bone.

He kissed her, quick, hard kisses that had her mouth trying to catch his, begging for more, preparing her for more. "Are you ready?" he asked.

She didn't know what he meant. She gave him a bewildered look, and a tight smile twitched his lips.

"For what?"

"To make love."

She looked even more confused. "Isn't that what we're doing?" she whispered.

"Not quite. Almost."

"But you're . . . inside me."

"There's more."

Confusion changed to alarm. *"More?"* She tried to draw back from him, pressing herself into the mattress.

He grinned, though it looked as if the effort cost him. "Not more of me. More to do."

"Oh." The word was drawn out, filled with wonder. She relaxed beneath him again, and her thighs flexed around his hips. The movement caused a reaction inside her; his sex jumped, and her enveloping sheath tightened around the thick intruder, caressing him. Webb's breath hissed between his teeth. Roanna's eyes grew heavy lidded, slumberous, and her cheeks pinkened. "Show me," she breathed.

He did, beginning to move, at first thrusting into her in a slow, delicious rhythm, then gradually quickening his pace. Hesitantly she responded, her body lifting to his as her excitement soared. He shifted his weight to one elbow and reached down between their bodies. She gasped as he stroked her tightly stretched entrance, her flesh so sensitive that the slightest touch jolted through her like lightning. Then he moved his attention to the nodule he'd touched before, rubbing his fingertip back and forth across it, and Roanna felt herself begin to dissolve.

It happened fast under his ruthless, sensual assault. He didn't ease her into climax, he hurled her into it. He gave her no mercy, even when she bucked under his hand in an effort to escape the intensity of it. The fierce, rapidly increasing sensation burned her, melted her. He rode her harder, thrusting deep, and the friction was almost unbearable. But he was touching her deep inside in a way that made her cling to him and cry out in a pleasure so strong she couldn't control it. It spiraled inside her, growing stronger and stronger, and when it finally shattered, she arched wildly beneath him, her slender body shuddering as her hips undulated, working herself on his invading shaft. She heard herself screaming, and didn't care.

His heavy weight crushed her into the mattress. His hands pushed beneath her and gripped her buttocks, hard. His hips pistoned back and forth between her widespread, straining thighs. Then he convulsed, slamming into her again and again while harsh sounds tore from his throat, and she felt the wetness of his release.

In the silence afterward, Roanna lay limply beneath him. She was exhausted, her body so heavy and weak that all she could do was breathe. She lapsed into a doze, barely aware of when he carefully separated their bodies and moved to lie beside her. Sometime later the light blinked off, and she was aware of cool darkness, of him stripping the bedspread down and positioning her between the sheets.

She turned instinctively into his arms, and felt them close around her. Her head settled into the hollow of his shoulder, and her hand rested on his chest, feeling the crisp hair beneath her fingers. For the first time in ten years she felt a small measure of peace, of rightness.

She had no idea how long it was before she became aware of his hands moving on her with increasing purpose. "Can you do it again?" he asked, the words low and intense.

"Yes, please," she said politely, and heard a low chuckle as he rolled atop her.

Roanna.

Webb lay in the darkness, feeling her slight weight nestled against his left side. She was asleep, her head on his shoulder, her breath sighing across his chest. Her breasts, small and perfectly shaped, pressed firmly against his ribs. Gently, unable to resist, he rubbed the back of one finger over the satiny outer curve of the breast he could reach. Oh, God, Roanna.

He hadn't recognized her at first. Though ten years had

passed and logically he knew she had grown up, in his mind's eye she had still been the skinny, underdeveloped, immature teenager with the urchin's grin. He hadn't seen any trace of her in the woman who had approached him in the grubby little bar. Instead he'd seen a woman who looked so buttoned-down he'd been surprised that she'd spoken to him. Women like her might go to a bar if they were looking for revenge against a straying husband, but that was about the only reason he could think of.

But there she'd been, too thin for his taste, but severely stylish in an expensive silk camp shirt and tailored slacks. Her thick hair, dark in the uncertain light, was cut in a stylish bob that swung just below chin length. Her mouth, though . . . he'd liked her mouth, wide and full, and had the thought that it would feel good to kiss her and feel the softness of those lips.

She'd looked totally out of place, a country-club woman lost in a low-rent district. But she'd been reaching out to touch him, and when he'd turned, she had dropped her hand and looked at him, her face still and strangely sad, her wide mouth unsmiling, and her brown eyes so solemn he wondered if she ever smiled.

And then she'd said, "Hello, Webb. May I talk to you?" and the shock had nearly felled him. For a split second he wondered if he'd had more to drink than he'd thought, because not only had she called him by name when he would have sworn he'd never seen her before, but she had used Roanna's voice, and the brown eyes were suddenly Roanna's whiskey-colored eyes.

Reality had shifted and adjusted, and he'd seen the girl in the woman.

Odd. He hadn't spent the past ten years sulking about what had happened. When he'd walked out of Davencourt that day, he'd intended it to be forever, and he'd gotten on with his life. He'd chosen southern Arizona because it was starkly beautiful, not because it was about as far as it could get from lush, green, northwestern Alabama and still be inhabitable. Ranching was hard, but he enjoyed the physical work as much as he'd enjoyed the cutthroat world of business and finance. Always a horseman, he'd made the transition easily. His family had narrowed to include only his mother and Aunt Sandra, but he was content with that.

At first he'd felt dead inside. Despite the imminent breakup, despite the fact that she'd cheated on him, he'd mourned Jessie with surprising depth. She'd been a part of his life for so long that he woke up mornings feeling strangely incomplete. Then, gradually, he had surprised himself by remembering what a bitch she had been and laughing fondly.

He could have let the uncertainty eat him alive, knowing that her killer was still out there and wasn't likely to be discovered, but in the end he'd accepted that there was nothing he could do about it. Her affair had been so secret that there had been no hints, no leads. It was a dead end. He could let it destroy his life or he could go on. Webb was a survivor. He'd gone on.

There had been days, even weeks, when he hadn't thought about his old life at all. He'd put Lucinda and the others behind him . . . all except for Roanna. Sometimes he'd hear something that sounded like her laugh, and instinctively turn to see what mischief she was in before he remembered she was no longer there. Or he'd be doctoring a cut on a horse's leg, and he'd remember the concern that had darkened her thin face whenever she'd tended a hurt mount.

Somehow she had wormed her way deeper into his heart than the others had, and it was harder to forget her. He'd catch himself worrying about her, wondering what latest trouble she had managed to get herself into. And over the years, it was the memory of her that still had the power to make him angry.

He couldn't forget Jessie's accusation that Roanna had deliberately made trouble between them that last night. Had Jessie lied? She certainly hadn't been above it, but Roanna's transparent face had clearly revealed her guilt. Over the years, given Jessie's pregnancy by another man, he'd come to the conclusion that Roanna hadn't had anything to do with Jessie's death and the murderer had instead been Jessie's unknown lover, but he still couldn't shake his anger. Somehow Roanna's behavior, though it paled in importance when compared with the other events of that night, retained the power to make him furious.

Maybe it was because he'd always been so dead certain of her love. Maybe it had stroked his ego to be worshipped so openly, so unconditionally. No one else on earth had loved him that way. Yvonne's mother-love was unyielding, but she was the woman who had spanked him when he misbehaved as a child, so she saw his flaws. In Roanna's eyes, he'd been perfect, or so he had thought until she had deliberately caused trouble just so she could get one up on Jessie. He wondered now if he'd ever been anything other than a symbol to her, a possession that Jessie had and she wanted.

He'd had women since Jessie's death. He'd even had one or two lengthy relationships, though he'd never been inclined to remarry. But no matter how hot the sex he enjoyed in other women's beds, it was dreams of Roanna that woke him in the cool early mornings before dawn, drenched in sweat and his dick standing up like an iron spike.

He was never able to remember the dreams clearly, just bits and pieces, like the way her bottom had rubbed against his erection, the way her nipples had pebbled just from kissing him, the way they'd felt when she pressed them against his chest. His lust for Jessie had been a boy's lust, a young man's hormone-crazed lust, a game of dominance. His lust for Roanna, disgusted as it made him with himself, always had an undertone of tenderness, at least in his dreams.

But she was no dream, standing there in the bar.

His first impulse had been to get her out of there, where she didn't belong. She had gone with him without protest or question, as silent now as she had once been mouthy. He was aware that he'd had too much to drink, known that he wasn't in complete control of himself, but putting her off until tomorrow hadn't seemed like a viable option.

At first he'd barely been able to concentrate on what she

was saying. She hadn't even wanted to look at him. She had sat there, shivering, looking every place but at him, and he hadn't been able to keep his eyes off her. She'd changed. God, how she'd changed. He didn't like it, didn't like her silence where once she'd been a chatterbox, didn't like the stillness of her expression where once every emotion she had felt had been written plainly on her little face. There was no mischief or laughter in her eyes, no vibrant energy in her movements. It was as if someone had stolen Roanna and left a doll in her place.

The ugly little girl had turned into a plain teenager, and the plain teenager into a woman who was, if not exactly pretty, striking in her own way. Her face had filled out so that her too-big features had assumed a more pleasing proportion. Her long, high-bridged, slightly crooked nose now looked aristocratic, and her too-wide mouth could only be described as lush. Complete maturity had refined her face so that high, chiseled cheekbones had been revealed, and her almond-shaped, whiskey-colored eyes were exotic. She had put on a little weight, maybe fifteen pounds, that softened her body and made her look less like a refugee from a World War II prison camp, though she could easily carry another fifteen pounds and still be slim.

Memories of the girl had haunted him. The reality of the woman had stirred his long-simmering lust to a hard boil.

But, on a personal level, she had seemed oblivious to him. She had asked him to return to Alabama because Lucinda needed him. Lucinda loved him, regretted their estrangement. Lucinda would give him back everything he'd lost. Lucinda was ill, dying. Lucinda, Lucinda, Lucinda. Every word out of her mouth had been about Lucinda. Nothing about herself, whether or not *she* wanted him to return, as if that long-ago hero worship had never existed.

That had made him even angrier, that he'd spent years dreaming about her while she seemed to have completely cut him out of her life. His temper had soared out of control, and the tequila had loosened any restraint he might have felt. He'd heard himself demand that she go to bed with him as the price for his return. He'd seen the shock on her face, seen it quickly controlled. He had waited for her rejection. And then she'd said yes.

He was angry enough, drunk enough, to follow through. By God, if she was willing to give herself to him for Lucinda's benefit, then he'd damn sure take her up on it. He cranked the truck and drove quickly to the nearest motel before she could change her mind.

Once inside the cheap little room, he had sprawled on the bed because his head had been spinning a little, and ordered her to strip. Once again he'd expected her to refuse. He'd waited for her to back out, or at least lose her temper and tell him to kiss her ass. He wanted to see fire break through the barrier of that blank doll's face, he wanted to see the old Roanna.

Instead she had silently begun to take off her clothes.

She did it neatly, without fuss, and from the moment the first button had slipped free he hadn't been able to think of anything else but the soft skin being revealed by each movement of her fingers. She hadn't tried to be coy; she hadn't needed to. His dick was pressing so hard against his fly that it probably had the imprint of his zipper running down it.

She had lovely skin, a little golden, with the faintest dusting of freckles across those classic cheekbones. She slipped out of her shirt, and her shoulders had a soft, mellow sheen to them. Then she had unhooked that plain, serviceable white bra and removed it, and her breasts had taken his breath. They didn't stick out a lot but were surprisingly round and upright, exquisitely formed, with her nipples drawn into tight, rosy buds that made his mouth water.

Silently she had removed her slacks and panties, standing naked before him. Her waist and hips were narrow, but the cheeks of her ass were as deliciously round as her breasts. The need to touch her was painful. Hoarsely he had ordered her to come to him, and she had silently obeyed, moving to stand beside the bed.

He'd touched her then, and felt her quiver under his hand. The column of her thigh was sleek and cool, her skin delicate in contrast with his tanned, work-roughened hand. Slowly, savoring the texture of her skin, he stroked upward and around to her buttocks; she had moved a little, rubbing herself against his hand, and mingled excitement and delight had roared through him. He had cupped the firm mounds and felt them flex, and she had begun to shake even harder. He teased her with a daring caress and sensed her shock, and he'd looked up to find that her eyes were tightly closed.

Somehow he couldn't quite believe it was Roanna who stood naked before him, yielding her body to his exploration, and yet everything about her was infinitely familiar, and far more exciting than ten years' worth of frustrating dreams.

He didn't have to imagine the physical details now; they were laid out before him. Her pubic hair was a neat, curly little triangle. It had drawn his gaze, and he'd been entranced by the delicate folds, shyly closed, that he could glimpse under the curls. The mysteries of her body had made him ache with need. Roughly he'd told her to spread her legs so he could touch her, and she had.

He'd put his hand on the most private part of her body, and felt her startled response. He'd petted her, stroked her, opened her, and eased one finger into her startlingly tight sheath. He was so hard he thought he might explode, but he held back, because here was the proof that the lust wasn't all on his part. She was slick and damp, and her soft, low moans of arousal had nearly driven him crazy. She seemed shyly bewildered by what he was doing, what she was feeling. Then he'd tried to slip another finger into her, and couldn't. He'd felt her instinctive withdrawal, and a sudden suspicion flared in his tequila-fogged brain.

She'd never done this before. He was abruptly certain of it.

Swiftly he tumbled her down onto the bed, dragging her body across his. With more deliberation he'd probed her body, watching her reaction, fighting the alcohol as he tried to think clearly. He'd been the first with a couple of girls, back in high school and college, and even once since he'd left Alabama, so he noticed the way she blushed, her slight flinch as he pushed his rough finger even deeper. If it hadn't been for her years of horseback riding, he doubted he would have been able to even get his finger inside her.

He should stop this, now. The knowledge seared him. His body damn near revolted. He hadn't meant to let it go this far anyway, but he'd been undone by the tequila, and by his own arousal. He'd had just the wrong amount to drink, enough to slow his thoughts and make him not give a damn, but not enough to soften his dick. He was disgusted with himself for making her do this, and he'd opened his mouth to tell her to put on her clothes when, for an instant, he saw how terribly vulnerable she was, and how he could destroy her with a careless word even if it was for her own good.

Roanna had grown up in Jessie's shadow. Jessie had been the pretty one, Roanna the plain one. Her physical self-confidence, except where horses were concerned, had always been close to zero. How could it not be, when rejection had been more the norm for her than acceptance? For a split second he saw the raw, desperate courage it had taken for her to do this. She had stripped naked for him, something he was certain she'd never done with any other man, and offered herself to him. He couldn't imagine what it had cost her. If he rejected her now, it would devastate her.

"You're a virgin," he'd said, his voice hard and flat with frustration.

She hadn't denied it. Instead she had blushed, a delicate rose tinting her breasts, and the delectable sight had been irresistible. He'd known he shouldn't do it, but he'd had to touch her nipple, and then he'd had to taste her, and he'd felt the answering need in her slender body as it arched to his touch.

He'd offered to stop. It took every ounce of willpower he

had to rein himself in and make that offer, but he'd done it. And Roanna had looked as if he'd slapped her in the face. She had gone white, and her lips had trembled. "Don't you want me?" she'd whispered, the plea so faint that his heart had squeezed. His own defenses, already weakened by the tequila, went down with a crash. Rather than answering, he had simply caught her hand and dragged it down to his groin, pressed it over his erection. He hadn't said anything even then, staying silent as he watched the sense of wonder creep into her eyes, chase away the pain. It was like watching a flower bloom.

Then she had turned her hand to hold him and had said, "Please," and he was lost.

Still, he had tried grimly for control. Even as he shucked off his clothes, he had been sucking in deep breaths, trying to cool the fire inside him. It hadn't worked. God, he was so ready he'd probably come as soon as he put it in her.

He had damn sure wanted to find out.

Somehow, he managed to hold himself back. His control hadn't extended to prolonged foreplay. He had simply mounted her, tucking her delicate body under his much more powerful one, and kissed her while he forced his erection in her to the hilt.

He'd known he was hurting her, but he couldn't stop. All he could do, once he was inside her, was make it good for her. "Ladies first" had always been his motto, and he had experience in achieving his objective. Roanna was startlingly, overwhelmingly responsive to his every touch, her hips moving, her back arching, hot little cries breaking from her lips. Jessie had always held back, but Roanna gave herself without restraint, without pretension. She had climaxed fast, and then his own orgasm had seized him and he had come violently, more violently than he'd ever experienced before, pounding into her and flooding her with semen.

She hadn't pulled away, hadn't jumped up to run into the bathroom and clean herself. She had simply dozed off with her arms still looped around his neck.

Maybe he had dozed, too. He didn't know. But eventually he had roused himself and slid off her, turned out the light, tucked her under the covers, and joined her there.

It hadn't been long before his cock had stirred insistently, lured by the silken body in his arms. And Roanna had welcomed him without hesitation, as she had every other time during the night that he'd reached for her.

It was almost dawn now.

The effects of the tequila had faded from his system, and he had to face the facts. Like it or not, he had blackmailed Roanna into this. The hell of it was, he hadn't needed to. She would have lain down for him without it being a condition for his return.

Something had happened to her, something that had robbed her of her zest, her spontaneity. It was as if she had finally been defeated by all the efforts to force her into a certain mold, and had surrendered herself.

He didn't like it. It made him furious.

He wanted to kick himself for becoming just one more person in a long line of people who had forced her to do something. It didn't matter that she had responded to him. He had to make it plain that his return didn't depend on her giving him the use of her body. He wanted her—hell, yes, he wanted her—but without any conditions or threats between them, and it was his own damn fault that he was in this situation.

He wanted to make his peace with Lucinda. It was time, and the thought of her dying made him regret the lost years. Davencourt and all the money didn't matter, not now. Mending fences mattered. Finding out what had extinguished the light in Roanna's eyes mattered.

He wondered if they were prepared for the man he'd become.

Yeah, he'd go back.

CHAPTER

10

*R*oanna seldom slept well, but she was so exhausted from the day of hard travel and emotional stress that when Webb finally let her sleep, she dropped immediately into a hard, deep slumber. She was groggy when she woke, unable for a moment to remember where she was, but over the years she had become accustomed to waking in places where she hadn't gone to sleep, so she didn't panic.

Instead she lay quietly while reality reassembled itself in her mind. She became aware of some unusual things: One, this wasn't Davencourt. Two, she was naked. Three, she was *very* sore in all her tender places.

It all clicked into place then, and she bolted upright in bed, looking for Webb. She knew immediately that he wasn't there.

He'd gotten up, dressed, and left her alone in this cheesy motel. During the night his heat had melted some of the ice that had encased her for so many years, but as she sat there naked in a tangle of dingy sheets, she felt the cold layer slowly solidify again.

It was the story of her life, it seemed. She had always felt that she could offer herself to him body and soul, and he still wouldn't love her. Now she knew for certain. Along with her body, she'd given him her heart, while he'd simply been screwing.

Had she really been silly enough to think he *cared* for her? Why should he? She'd done nothing but cause him trouble. He probably hadn't even been particularly attracted to her. Webb had always been able to get any woman he wanted, even the prettiest ones. She couldn't compare with the type he was accustomed to, in either face or body; she had simply been handy, and he'd been horny. He'd seen an opportunity to get his rocks off and taken it. Case closed.

Her face was expressionless as she slowly crawled out of bed, ignoring the discomfort between her legs. She noticed then the note on the other pillow, scribbled on the scratch pad stamped with the motel's name. She picked it up, recognizing the black slash of Webb's handwriting immediately. "Be back at ten," it read. The note wasn't signed, but then that wasn't necessary. Roanna smoothed her fingers over the writing, then tore the note from the pad and carefully folded it and slipped it into her purse.

She looked at her wristwatch: eight-thirty. An hour and a half to kill. An hour and a half of grace before she had to listen to him tell her that last night had been a mistake, one he didn't intend to repeat.

The least she could do was crawl back into her severely stylish shell, so she wouldn't look pitiful when he gave her the old heave-ho. She could bear a lot, but she didn't think she could stand it if he felt sorry for her.

Her clothes were as limp and wrinkled as she felt. First she washed out her underwear and draped it over the noisy climate control unit to dry, then turned the temperature control to heat and set the fan on high. She carried her slacks and blouse into the tiny bathroom with her, and hung them over the door while she took a shower in the minuscule stall that sported a cracked floor and yellowed water stains. The cubicle quickly filled with steam, and by the time she finished, both blouse and slacks looked fresher.

The climate control unit was a lot louder than it was efficient, but still the room quickly became stuffy. She shut it off and checked her panties; they were dry except for a lingering bit of dampness in the waistband. She pulled them on anyway, then quickly dressed in case Webb came back earlier than he'd said. Not that he hadn't already seen everything she had, she thought, and touched it as well, but that was last night. By leaving the way he had, he'd made it plain that last night hadn't meant anything to him beyond physical release.

She combed her straight, heavy hair back and left it to dry. That was the major benefit of a good cut: it didn't require much maintenance. The small amount of luggage she'd brought was locked in the trunk of her rental car, which was presumably still parked outside that grimy little bar just off the highway, but she wasn't certain exactly where she was in relation to it. The only makeup she had in her purse was a powder compact and a neutral-colored lipstick. She made quick use of it, not looking at her reflection in the mirror any longer than was required to get the lipstick on straight.

She opened the door to let in the freshness of the dry desert morning, turned on the small television that was bolted to the wall, and sat down in the lone chair in the room, an uncomfortable number with a torn vinyl seat, which looked as if it had been stolen from a hospital waiting room.

She didn't pay much attention to what was on, some morning talk show. It was noise, and that was all she required. Sometimes when she couldn't sleep, she would turn her own television on so the voices could give her the illusion of not being utterly alone in the night.

She was still sitting there when a vehicle pulled up right outside the door. The motor cut off as a cloud of dust blew in. Then a door opened and was slammed shut, there was the sound of booted feet on the concrete walk, and Webb filled the doorway. He was silhouetted against the bright sunlight, his broad shoulders almost stretching from one side of the door frame to the other.

He didn't come any farther inside. All he said was, "Are

you ready?" and she silently got up, turned off the light and the television, and picked up her purse.

He opened the truck door for her, his southern manners still holding sway despite a decade of self-imposed exile. Roanna climbed inside, concentrating on not giving any flinches that betrayed her physical discomfort, and settled herself. Now that it was daylight, she could tell that the truck was gunmetal gray, with a gray interior, and was fairly new. There was an extra stick shift on the floor, meaning it was four-wheel drive, probably a necessity for taking it across the range.

As Webb slid behind the wheel, he slanted her an unreadable glance. She wondered if he expected her to either start planning a wedding or pitch a fit because he'd left her alone this morning. She did neither. She sat silently.

"Hungry?"

She shook her head, then remembered that he liked verbal answers. "No, thank you."

His lips thinned as he started the motor and reversed out of the parking spot. "You're going to eat. You've gained a little weight, and it looks good on you. I'm not going to let you catch your flight without eating."

She hadn't booked a return flight, because she hadn't known how long she would be staying. She opened her mouth to say so, then caught the flinty expression in his eyes and realized he had booked one for her.

"When am I leaving?"

"One o'clock. I managed to get you on a direct flight from Tucson to Dallas. Your connection in Dallas is a bit tight, forty-five minutes, but it'll get you into Huntsville at a reasonable hour. You should get home around ten, ten-thirty tonight. Do you have to call anyone to pick you up in Huntsville?"

"No." She had driven herself to the airport, because no one else had been willing to get up at three-thirty to perform the service. No, that wasn't fair. She hadn't asked anyone to do it. She never asked anyone to do anything for her.

By the time she ate, as he seemed determined for her to

do, she would have to leave almost immediately in order to turn in her rental car at the airport and make it to the gate in time to board. He hadn't left her any breathing space, probably by design. He didn't want to talk to her, didn't want to spend any more time in her company than necessary.

"There's a little place not far from here that serves breakfast until eleven. The food's plain, but good."

"Just drop me off at the bar so I can pick up my car," she said as she looked out the window, anywhere but at him. "I'll stop at a fast-food place."

"I doubt it," he said grimly. "I'm going to watch every bite go into your mouth."

"I eat now and then," she replied in a mild tone. "I learned how."

"Then you won't mind if I watch."

She recognized that tone, the one he used when he'd made up his mind that you were going to do something, so you might as well not argue. When she'd been younger, that tone had been of infinite comfort, symbolizing the rock steadiness and security she had so desperately needed after her parents' death. In an odd way it was still comforting; he might not like her, might not desire her, but at least he didn't want her to starve to death.

The little restaurant he took her to wasn't much bigger than the kitchen at Davencourt, with a couple of booths, a couple of tiny tables, and four stools lined up at the counter. The rich scent of frying bacon and sausage was in the air, underlaid with that of coffee and the spiciness of chili peppers. Two sun-baked old men were in the back booth, and they both looked up with interest as Webb escorted Roanna to the other booth.

A thin woman of indeterminate age, her skin baked as hard and brown as that of the two old men, approached the booth. She pulled a green order pad out of the hip pocket of her jeans and held a stubby pencil at the ready.

Evidently there was no menu. Roanna looked at Webb in question. "I'll have the short stack, ham and eggs on the side, sunny side up," he said, "and she'll have an egg, plain scrambled, with dry toast, bacon, and hash browns. Coffee for both of us."

"We can't do eggs sunny side up no more. Health Department rules," the waitress said.

"Then I want them well done but take them up early."

"Gotcha." The waitress tore the top sheet off the pad as she walked over to an opening cut out in the wall. She laid the ticket on the sill. "Betts! Got an order."

"You must eat here often," Roanna said.

"I usually stop by whenever I'm in town."

"What does plain scrambled mean?"

"No peppers."

It was on the tip of her tongue to ask if they called that fancy scrambled but bit the comment back. How easy it would be to fall into the old habits with him! she thought sadly. But she had learned to curb her quips, because most people didn't appreciate even the milder ones. Webb had once seemed to, but perhaps he'd been kind.

The waitress set two steaming cups of coffee in front of them. "Cream?" she asked, and Webb said, "No," answering for both of them.

"It'll take me at least a week, maybe two, to get things squared away here," he said abruptly. "I'm keeping my ranch, so I'll be flying back and forth. Davencourt won't be my sole concern."

She sipped her coffee to hide her relief. He was still coming home! He'd said he would if she'd sleep with him, but until now she hadn't been certain he'd meant it. It wouldn't have made any difference if she'd known for sure he was lying; no matter what the day had brought, last night had been a dream come true for her, and she had grabbed at it with both hands.

"Lucinda wouldn't expect you to sell the ranch," she said.

"Bullshit. She thinks the universe revolves around Davencourt. There's nothing she wouldn't do to safeguard it." He leaned back and stretched out his long legs, carefully avoiding contact with hers. "Tell me what's been going on there. Mother tells me some of the news, and so does Aunt Sandra, but neither of them know anything about the day-to-day operations. I do know that Gloria has managed to move her entire family into Davencourt."

"Not *all* of them. Baron and his family still live in Charlotte."

"Being under the same roof with Lanette and Corliss is enough to make me think about buying my own place in town."

Roanna didn't voice her agreement, but she knew exactly what he meant.

"What about you?" he continued. "I know you went to college in Tuscaloosa. What changed your mind? I thought you wanted to attend college locally."

She had gone away because for a long time that had been easier than staying home. Her sleeping problems hadn't been as bad while she was away, the memories hadn't been as acute. But it had been over a year after he'd left before she had started college, and it had been a year of hell.

She didn't tell him any of that. Instead she shrugged and said, "You know how it is. A person can get along without it, but to have all the *right* contacts you have to attend the university." She didn't have to elaborate on which university, because Webb had gone to the same one.

"Did you do the sorority bit?"

"It was expected."

A reluctant grin tugged at his mouth. "I can't see you as a Greek. How did you get along with the little society snobs?"

"Fine." They had, in fact, been kind to her. It was they who had taught her how to dress, how to apply makeup, how to make social chitchat. She rather thought they had seen her as a challenge and taken her on as a makeover project.

The waitress approached with three plates of steaming hot food. She slid two plates in front of Webb and the remaining one in front of Roanna. "Yell when you need a refill," she said comfortably, and left them alone.

Webb applied himself to his food, buttering the pancakes

and soaking them in syrup, then liberally salting and peppering his eggs. The slab of ham covered half the plate. Roanna looked at the mountain of food, then at his steely body. She tried to imagine the amount of physical labor that required that many calories, and felt an even deeper sense of respect for him.

"Eat," he growled.

She picked up her fork and obeyed. Once she couldn't have managed it, but keeping her emotions controlled had allowed her stomach to settle down. The trick was to take her time and take tiny bites. Usually, by the time everyone else had finished their meal she had managed to eat half of hers, and that was enough.

That was the case this time, too. When Webb leaned back, replete, Roanna laid her fork aside. He gave her plate a long, hard look as if calculating exactly how much she'd eaten, but to her relief he decided not to push it.

Breakfast taken care of, he drove her to the bar. The rental car sat forlornly in the parking lot, looking abandoned and out of place. A CLOSED sign hung lopsidedly on the front door of the bar. In daylight, the building was even more ramshackle than it had appeared the night before.

Dust flew around the truck as he braked to a stop, and Roanna allowed the gritty cloud to settle while she fished the ignition key out of her purse. "Thanks for breakfast," she said as she opened the door and slid out. "I'll tell Lucinda to expect you."

He got out of the truck and walked over to the rental car with her, standing right beside the door so she couldn't open it. "About last night," he said.

Dread filled her. God, she couldn't listen to this. She put the key in the lock and turned it, hoping he would take the hint and move. He didn't.

"What about it?" she managed to say without any expression in her voice.

"It shouldn't have happened."

She bent her head. It was the best thing that had ever happened to her, and he wished it hadn't.

"God damn it, look at me!" Just as he had the night before, he cupped her chin in his hand and lifted her head so that she faced him. His hat was pulled low on his forehead, shadowing his eyes, but she could still see the grimness in them and in the line of his mouth. Very gently, he touched her lips with his thumb. "I wasn't exactly drunk, but I'd had too much to drink. You were a virgin. I shouldn't have made that a condition to going back, and I regret what I did to you."

Roanna held her spine very straight and still. "It was as much my responsibility as yours."

"Not quite. You didn't know exactly what you were getting into. On the other hand, I did know that you wouldn't turn me down."

She couldn't escape that hard, green gaze. This was very like the night before when she had stripped herself naked in front of him, except now she was emotionally naked. Her lower lip trembled, and she quickly controlled it. There was no point in denying what he'd said, because her actions had already proved him right. When he had given her the opportunity to call a stop to what was happening, she had begged him to continue.

"It's never been a secret how I feel about you," she finally said. "All you had to do at any time was snap your fingers, and I'd have come running and let you do anything you wanted to me." She managed a smile. It wasn't much of one, but it was better than weeping. "That hasn't changed."

He searched her face, trying to pierce the remoteness of her expression. A kind of angry frustration flashed in his eyes. "I just wanted you to know that my return doesn't depend on your sleeping with me. You don't have to turn yourself into a whore to make sure Lucinda gets what she wants."

This time she couldn't control her flinch. She pulled away from him and gave him another smile, this one even more strained than the first one. "I understand," she forced herself to say with fragile calm. "I won't bother you."

"The hell you won't," he snapped. "You've been bothering me for most of your life." He leaned forward, scowling at her. "You bother me by being in the same room. You bother me by breathing." Furiously he pulled her against him and ground his mouth down on hers. Roanna was too startled to react. All she could do was hang there in his hard grasp and open her mouth to the demand of his. The kiss was deep and intimate, his tongue moving against hers, and down below she could feel the iron ridge of his erection pressing into her belly.

He pushed her away as suddenly as he had grabbed her. "Now trot on back to Lucinda and tell her mission accomplished. Whether or not you tell her how you did it is up to you." He opened the car door and ushered her inside, then stood for a moment looking down at her. "And you don't understand a damn thing," he said evenly, before closing the door and striding back to his truck.

CHAPTER

11

When Roanna reached the long driveway to Davencourt that night, as exhausted from the second day of hard travel as she had been from the first, she groaned aloud at the lights still shining like a beacon from the big house. She'd hoped everyone would have gone to bed, so she could regroup before having to face the inquisition she knew was coming. She'd even hoped she could manage to get as much sleep as she had the night before, though that was unlikely. If she couldn't sleep, then at least she could relive those tumultuous hours, savor the memory of his naked body against hers, the kisses, the touches, the shattering, unending moments when he'd actually been inside her. And when she felt calmer, she would think about the rest of it, the hurtful things he'd said and the fact that he didn't want her again . . . But then why had he kissed her? She was too tired to think straight, so the analysis could wait.

She used the automatic opener for the garage, then braked when her headlights swept across a car already parked in her space. She sighed. Corliss again, taking advantage of Roanna's absence to park her own car inside. The detached garage had only five bays, and those bays were allotted to Lucinda, though she no longer drove herself, Roanna,

Gloria and Harlan, and Lanette and Greg, who each had a car. Brock and Corliss were supposed to park their cars outside, but Corliss had a habit of ignoring that and parking her car in any empty space.

Roanna parked her car beside Brock's and wearily climbed out, hauling her small overnight case with her. She thought about slipping up the outside stairway and around the balcony to her room on the back, but she had locked the French doors before leaving and couldn't get in that way. Instead she would go in through the kitchen and hope she could make it to the stairs unnoticed.

Luck wasn't with her. When she unlocked the kitchen door and opened it, Harlan and Gloria were both sitting at the kitchen table, demolishing thick slices of Tansy's coconut cake. Neither of them were in their nightclothes yet, which meant they had been watching television on the large set in the den.

Gloria hastily swallowed. "You couldn't find him!" she exclaimed, openly gleeful of the fact that Roanna was alone. Then she gave Roanna a sly, conspiratorial look. "Not that you tried very hard, did you? Well, *I* won't say anything. I thought Lucinda had lost her mind anyway. Why on earth would she want to bring him back here? I know Booley didn't arrest him, but everyone knew he was guilty, there was just no way to prove it—"

"I found him," Roanna interrupted. She felt fuzzy headed with fatigue, and wanted to cut the interrogation short. "He had some business to take care of, but he'll be coming home within the next two weeks."

Gloria's color faded, and she gaped openmouthed at Roanna. The cake crumbs thus revealed were unappetizing. Then she said, "Roanna, how could you be so *stupid?*" Each word rose until she was fairly shrieking. "Don't you know what you stand to lose? All of this could have been yours, but Lucinda will give it back to him, you mark my words! And what about us? Why, we could all be murdered in our beds, the way poor Jessie—"

"Jessie wasn't murdered in her bed," Roanna said tiredly.

"Don't split hairs with me, you know what I mean!"

"Webb didn't kill her."

"Well, the sheriff thought he did, and I'm sure he knows more about it than you do! We all heard him say he'd do anything to get rid of her."

"We all heard him tell her to get a divorce, too."

"Gloria's right," Harlan weighed in, knitting his bushy brows with concern. "There's no telling what he's capable of doing."

Normally Roanna didn't argue, but she was exhausted, and every nerve in her body felt raw from her encounter with Webb. "What you're really worried about," she said in a colorless voice, "is that he'll remember how you turned your backs on him when he needed our support, and tell you to find somewhere else to live."

"Roanna!" Gloria gasped, outraged. "How can you say such a thing to us? What were we supposed to do, shelter a killer from the law?"

There was nothing she could say to alter their position, and she was too tired to try any longer. Let Webb handle it when he got back. She had just enough energy to feel a flicker of interest at the prospect. If they thought he'd been intimidating before, wait until they saw what they had to deal with now. He was much harder and more forceful.

Leaving Gloria and Harlan still sputtering their rage into the coconut cake, Roanna dragged herself up the stairs. Lucinda was already in bed; she tired easily these days, another indication of her failing health, and was often asleep by nine. Morning would be plenty of time to tell her that Webb was coming home.

Roanna hoped that she would be able to get some sleep herself.

If wishes were horses . . . Several hours later, she glanced at the lighted dial of her clock and saw the hour hand creeping toward the two. Her eyes felt grainy from lack of sleep, and her mind was so dulled by fatigue she could barely think, but sleep was as far away as it had ever been.

She'd endured a lot of nights like this, waiting through the endless darkness for morning to come. All of the books on insomnia advised the sufferer to get out of bed, not to make the bed the site of their frustration. Roanna had already developed that habit, so the book hadn't helped any. Sometimes she read to pass the hours, sometimes she played endless card games for one, but for the most part she would sit in the darkness and wait.

That was what she was doing now, because she was too tired for anything else. She sat curled in a huge, overstuffed easy chair, large enough for two. The chair had been a Christmas present to herself five years ago, and she didn't know what she would do without it. When she did manage to doze off, as likely or not it was in the chair. In winter she would wrap up in her softest, thickest afghan and watch the night slowly creep past her windows, but this was summer and she wore only a thin, sleeveless nightgown, though the hem was tucked over her bare feet. She'd opened the French doors so she could hear the comforting sounds of the warm night. A thunderstorm was passing by in the distance; she could see the flashes of lightning, revealing dark purple clouds, but the storm was so far away that the thunder, when she heard it, was only a faint rumble.

If she had to be awake, summer nights were the best. And between insomnia and the other, she preferred insomnia.

When she slept, she never knew where she would wake up.

She didn't think she'd ever left the house. She'd always been inside, and her feet were never dirty, but still it frightened her to think of herself roaming around unknowing. She'd read about sleepwalkers, too. People could evidently negotiate stairs, drive, even carry on a conversation while still asleep. That wasn't much comfort, because she didn't want to do any of that. She wanted to wake up exactly where she'd been when she went to sleep.

If anyone had ever seen her on her nocturnal strolls, they hadn't mentioned it. She didn't think she did it every time she slept, but of course she had no way of knowing and she didn't want to alert the family to her problem. They did know she was troubled with insomnia, so perhaps if anyone did see her outside her room in the middle of the night, apparently perfectly awake, they assumed she was having trouble sleeping and forgot about it.

If it became known that she walked in her sleep . . . She didn't like to think ill of people without proof, but she didn't think she would trust several members of the household if they knew she was so vulnerable. The possibility for mischief was too great, especially with Corliss. In some ways Corliss reminded Roanna a lot of Jessie, though the relationship was only that of second cousin, which meant they didn't share a lot of genetic material. Jessie had been cooler of thought but hotter of temper. Corliss didn't plan, she acted on impulse, and she wasn't prone to temper tantrums. For the most part she seemed restless and unhappy, and liked to make other people unhappy. Whatever it was she wanted out of life, she hadn't gotten it.

Roanna didn't think Webb would get along with Corliss at all.

Thinking of Webb brought her back full circle to how she had begun the day, not that her thoughts had been off of him for long at any one time.

She didn't know what to think. She was no good at analyzing a man–woman relationship, because she'd never had one. All she knew was that Webb had been angry, and a little drunk. If he hadn't been drinking he probably wouldn't have put the pressure on her that he had, but the fact remained that she had fallen into bed with him without the slightest resistance. The circumstances had been humiliating, but that secret little part of her had reveled in the opportunity.

She wasn't sorry she'd done it. If nothing good ever happened to her for the rest of her life, at least she'd lain in Webb's arms and known what it was like to make love with him. The pain had been more severe than she'd imagined, but it hadn't been able to overshadow the joy she'd felt, and ultimately the satisfaction.

The tequila might account for the first time, and maybe the second, but what about the other times? Surely he'd sobered by the third time he'd reached for her, in the middle of the night, and the fourth, just before dawn. She still ached from his lovemaking, with a tenderness deep inside her body that she cherished because it reminded her of those moments.

He hadn't been a selfish lover. He might have been angry, but still he had satisfied her, sometimes more than once, before allowing himself release. His hands and mouth had been tender on her body, careful not to add to the pain she'd already experienced just in accepting him.

But then he'd slipped out of bed and left her alone in the cheap little motel, as if she were a coyote woman. Wasn't that what the wild, drinking crowd called a woman who was so ugly that, when a man woke up and looked over at her asleep on his arm, he gnawed off his own arm rather than wake her up? At least Webb had left a note. At least he *had* come back, and she hadn't been forced to get back to her rental car as best she could.

He'd said she acted like a whore for Lucinda. He'd said that she'd been a bother to him all her life, and that hurt more than the other comment. No matter what, she had always managed to hold on to the thought of those years before Jessie's death as the sweet years, because she'd had him as a friend and hero. The awful night Jessie had been killed, she'd realized that he felt sorry for her and that had nearly killed her, but still the sweet memories had been there. Now she was mortified to think she'd been fooling herself from the beginning. Kindness wasn't the same as love, patience wasn't the same as caring.

He'd made it plain that she shouldn't expect any continuance of their lovemaking when he returned to Davencourt. It had been a one-night stand, pure and simple. There was no ongoing relationship between them, except that of distant cousins.

But then he'd kissed her, and told her she didn't understand anything. He'd been unmistakably aroused; after the night she'd just spent, she was very familiar with his erections. If he didn't want her, why had he been hard?

One thing was for certain though: he'd still been angry.

She sat curled in her chair, watching the lightning and thinking of Webb, and sometime close to dawn she finally dropped into a doze.

Gloria marshaled her entire family to the breakfast table at the same time, a rare happening, but evidently she thought she needed reinforcements. After a restless night in which sleep had been as elusive as ever, Roanna had gone to Lucinda's room and given her the good news. Buoyed by that, there was more energy in Lucinda's movements that morning, more color in her face, than there had been in a long time. She lifted her eyebrows in surprise at the crowd seated at the table, then grinned and gave Roanna an I-know-what-they're-up-to wink.

Breakfast was a buffet, an efficient setup since more than two of them eating at the same time was pure chance. Roanna filled plates for Lucinda and herself and took her place at the table.

Gloria waited until they had food in their mouths before launching the beginning salvo. "Lucinda, we've all talked about it, and we wish you would reconsider this hare-brained idea to put Webb in charge of the business concerns again. Roanna has been doing a fine job, and we really don't need him."

"We?" Lucinda queried, staring down the table at her sister. "Gloria, I've been grateful for and enjoyed your company for the past ten years, but I think I need to remind you that this is Davenport business, and Roanna and I are the only Davenports here. We talked it over and agreed that we want Webb to resume his rightful place in the family."

"Webb isn't a Davenport," Gloria pointed out, pouncing on this detail. "He's a Tallant, one of *our* family. Davencourt and the Davenport money should be Roanna's. Why, it's only right that it go to her."

Anything to keep Webb out of the picture, Roanna

thought. Gloria would much prefer that her immediate family have the inheritance, but Roanna was evidently the second-best choice. Gloria figured she could manipulate and dominate Roanna, but Webb was a different story. That was the crux of the matter, she realized, not any exaggerated fear that Webb was a killer. It all came down to money, and comfort.

"As I said," Lucinda repeated, "Roanna and I are in agreement on this."

"Roanna's never been logical where Webb's concerned." Harlan weighed in on his wife's side. "We all know you can't trust her judgment in this."

Corliss leaned forward, her eyes bright as she scented trouble. "Why, that's right. Don't I remember something about Jessie catching them canoodling in the kitchen?"

Brock looked up from his breakfast and frowned at his sister. Roanna liked him best of all Gloria's brood. Brock was generally good-natured and was a steady worker. He didn't intend to stay at Davencourt forever but was using the opportunity to save as much money as he could so he could build his own house. He and his long-time girlfriend were planning to marry within the year. He was more forceful than his father, Greg, who let Lanette set the agenda for the family.

"I think that was blown all out of proportion," Brock said.

"What makes you think so?" Lanette asked, leaning forward to look at her son. Corliss smiled with satisfaction at having stirred up the waters.

"Because Webb wasn't a cheater, and I'm glad he's coming back."

Gloria and Lanette both glared at this traitor in their midst. Brock ignored them and returned to his meal.

Roanna concentrated on her own breakfast and did her best to tune out the conversation. Nothing would please Corliss more than provoking her into a response or to see her visibly upset. Corliss lacked Jessie's genius for cutting remarks, or perhaps it was Roanna's reaction that had changed, but she found Corliss merely annoying.

The verbal battering went on the entire meal, with Gloria and Harlan and Lanette taking turns coming up with what they obviously thought were good arguments against Webb's return. Greg frankly wasn't interested and left the protests to Lanette. Brock finished eating and excused himself to go to work.

Roanna concentrated on the chore of eating, saying little, and Lucinda was as immovable as a mountain. Having Webb home was more important to her than anything her sister could say, so Roanna didn't have any worries that Lucinda would change her mind.

Lucinda had lit up like a Christmas tree that morning when Roanna had given her the good news. She had asked question after question about him, how he looked, if he'd changed, what he'd said.

She had seemed undisturbed when Roanna told her that he still bore a grudge.

"Well, of course he does," Lucinda had said readily. "Webb's never been anyone's lapdog. I imagine he'll have plenty to say to me when he gets here, and it'll stick in my craw, but I guess I'll have to listen. I'm really surprised he gave in so easily, though. I *knew* you were the one who could make him listen."

He hadn't listened as much as he'd made a deal with her, and when she had followed through, he'd felt bound to do the same. For the first time, she wondered if he had expected her to flatly refuse, if he'd offered the deal without any expectation of having to keep it.

"Tell me how he looked," Lucinda said again, and Roanna described him as best she could. Was it accurate, when she saw him through eyes of love? Would others find him less dominant, less powerful? She didn't think so.

Certainly Gloria wasn't sanguine about his return. It was hypocritical of her, Roanna thought, because before Jessie's death Gloria had always made a point of fussing over Webb, declaring him her favorite nephew. But then she'd made the mistake of turning on him instead of defending him, and she knew he hadn't forgotten it.

"Where will he sleep?" Corliss drawled, interrupting her grandmother to throw another firebomb into the already volatile conversation. "I'm not giving up the suite, even if it did used to be his."

It had the opposite effect of what she'd expected. Silence fell around the table. After Jessie's death, Lucinda had eventually roused herself to have the suite completely redone, from the carpets to the ceilings. When Lanette and her family moved in, Corliss had immediately claimed the suite as her own, carelessly remarking that it didn't bother her at all to sleep there. It was typical of her callousness that she could even think of Webb reclaiming his old quarters.

Nevertheless, Lucinda's suite was the only one that equaled it in size. Gloria and Harlan occupied a smaller set of rooms, as did Lanette and Greg. Roanna's room was just one room, a spacious one, but not a suite. Brock's room was the same. There were four remaining single bedrooms. It was a picayune problem, but status was a subtle thing. Roanna knew Webb wasn't fixated on it, but he did realize the implications and how to use the symbols of status in order to dominate.

"Even if he doesn't want it, he may not like anyone else sleeping there," Lanette said, eyeing her daughter with a troubled expression.

Corliss scowled. "I'm not giving up my suite!"

"You will if Webb says you will," Lucinda said firmly. "I doubt he'll care, but I want it understood that what he says goes, without any argument. Is that clear?"

"No!" Corliss said petulantly, flinging her napkin to the table. "He killed his wife! It isn't fair that he can just waltz back in here and take over—"

Lucinda's voice cracked like a whip. "Another thing I want understood is that Webb did *not* kill Jessie. If I hear such a thing mentioned again, I will ask the person who said it to leave this house immediately. We didn't support him when he needed it most, and I'm deeply ashamed of myself. He *will* be welcomed back into his home, or I'll know why."

Silence followed this flat statement. To Roanna's sure knowledge, this was the first time Lucinda had ever said anything about evicting any of the current residents of Davencourt. Family was so important to her that her threat demonstrated how strongly she felt about Webb's return. For guilt or for love, or for both, Webb had her unqualified support.

Satisfied that her point had been taken, Lucinda daintily patted her napkin to her mouth. "The bedroom situation is difficult. What do you think, Roanna?"

"Let Webb decide when he gets here," Roanna replied. "We can't anticipate what he'll want."

"That's true. It's just that I want everything to be perfect for him."

"I don't think that's possible. He would probably prefer that we carry on as normal and not make a fuss."

"We're hardly likely to throw a party," Gloria sniped. "I can't think what everyone in town is going to say."

"Nothing, if they know what side their bread is buttered on," Lucinda said. "I'll begin immediately making it clear to our friends and associates that if they value our continued friendship, they'll make certain Webb is treated politely."

"Webb, Webb, Webb," Corliss said violently. "What makes him so special? What about *us?* Why don't you leave everything to Brock, if you're so certain that Roanna can't handle things? We're just as much kin to you as Webb is!"

She jumped up and ran from the room, leaving silence behind. Even Gloria, who generally had the hide of a rhinoceros, looked uncomfortable at such a blatantly materialistic outburst.

Roanna forced herself to eat one more bite before giving up the effort. It looked as if Webb's "welcome" was going to be even more strained than his departure had been.

CHAPTER

12

*T*en days later, Webb walked in the front door as if he owned the place, which to all intents and purposes he did.

It was eight o'clock in the morning, and the sunlight poured brilliantly through the windows, giving the cream-colored tiles in the foyer a mellow golden glow. Roanna was just coming down the stairs. She had a nine o'clock meeting with their broker, who was driving in from Huntsville, and was going to go over the particulars with Lucinda prior to the broker's arrival. She had already dressed for the meeting, in a summer-weight peach silk sheath with a matching tunic jacket, and afterward she was scheduled for a county commissioner's meeting. Beige snakeskin pumps were on her feet, and creamy pearl earrings dangled from her ears. She seldom wore jewelry other than her wristwatch, but her sorority sisters had taught her the value of wearing good, understated pieces for business occasions.

The front door opened, and she paused on the stairs, momentarily blinded by the dazzling sunlight reflected on the polished tiles. She blinked at the dark figure whose wide shoulders and wide-brimmed hat filled most of the doorway. Then he stepped inside and closed the door, letting a leather satchel drop to the floor, and her heart nearly stopped as realization dawned.

It had been ten days since he'd sent her home, and he hadn't sent advance word of his arrival. She had begun to fear that he wouldn't come after all, though Webb had always kept his word before. Maybe he'd decided the Davenports weren't worth the trouble; she wouldn't have blamed him if he had.

But he was here, taking off his hat and looking around with narrowed eyes as if assessing the changes made during the gap of ten years. They were few, but she had the feeling he noted every one. His gaze even lingered momentarily on the carpet that covered the stairs. When he'd left, it had been beige; now it was oatmeal, with a thicker and tighter weave.

The physical impact of his presence nearly staggered her. To see him standing there with the same natural assumption of authority, as if he'd never left, gave her an eerie sense of time having stood still.

But the differences in him were sharp. It wasn't just that he was older or that he was dressed in jeans and boots instead of linen slacks and loafers. Before, he had tempered the force of his personality with southern good-old-boy geniality, the way business was done down here. Now, however, he tempered it with nothing. It was there, sharp and hard, and he didn't give a damn if anyone didn't like it.

Her chest felt oddly restricted, and she struggled to breathe. She had seen him naked, had lain naked in his arms. He'd sucked her nipples, penetrated her. The sense of unreality made her dizzy again. In the week and a half since she had seen him, their lovemaking had begun to seem like a dream, but at the sight of him, her body began throbbing anew as if he had just withdrawn from her and her flesh still tingled from the contact.

She found her voice. "Why didn't you call? Someone would have met you at the airport. You did fly in, didn't you?"

"Yesterday. I rented a car at the airport. Mother and I spent the night in Huntsville with Aunt Sandra, then drove back this morning."

The intense green gaze was on her now, taking inventory of the suit and pearls, perhaps comparing the sleek stylishness of her clothes with the fashion failure she'd been as a teenager. Or perhaps he was comparing her now to the naked woman who had writhed beneath him, screaming as he brought her to climax. He'd rejected her fast enough, so the vision couldn't have been an enticing one.

She flushed hotly, then felt the color fade as fast as it had come.

She couldn't continue to stand there like an idiot. Carefully regulating her breathing, Roanna came down the last few steps to pause at his side. "Lucinda's in the study. We were going to go over some papers, but I'm sure she'll want to talk to you instead."

"I came back to take care of business," he said briefly, already striding down the hall to the study. "Bring me up to speed. The homecoming party can wait."

Somehow she kept her unruffled facade in place as she followed him. She didn't throw her arms around him, brokenly crying, "You're home, you're home," though that had been her first impulse. She didn't shriek with joy or cry. She merely said to his back, "I'm glad you came. Welcome home."

Lucinda seldom sat at the huge desk that had been her husband's, finding the overstuffed sofa more comfortable to her old bones. She was there now, leafing through several printouts of recent stock performances. She looked up when Webb entered, and Roanna, right behind him, saw the bewilderment in the faded blue eyes as she stared at this big, rough stranger who had invaded her domain. Then she blinked, and recognition dawned as brilliantly as the sunrise, bringing with it a flush of excitement that chased away the grayness of ill health. She struggled to her feet, printouts scattering across the thick Aubusson rug.

"Webb! Webb!"

This was the enthusiastic, tearfully gleeful welcome Roanna had been longing to give him and couldn't. Lucinda rushed toward him with her hands outheld, either not seeing or ignoring his shuttered expression. He didn't open his arms to her, but that didn't stop her from throwing her own arms around him and hugging him tightly, her eyes swimming with tears.

Roanna turned toward the door, intending to give them some privacy; if she and Webb had had a special relationship when she was younger, at least in her own mind, he had definitely had a strong, special relationship with Lucinda that rivaled his feelings for his mother. Even though Webb had come back for Lucinda's sake, there were hard feelings between them that needed to be settled.

"No, stay," Webb said when he noticed Roanna's movement. He put gentle hands on Lucinda's fragile old arms and eased her away but continued to hold her as he looked down at her. "We'll talk later," he promised. "For now, I have a lot of catching up to do. We can start with those." He nodded to the papers on the carpet.

If there was anything Lucinda understood, it was the concept of taking care of business. She wiped her eyes and nodded briskly. "Of course. Our broker will be here at nine for a meeting. Roanna and I have made it a practice of going over our stock performances beforehand, so we are in agreement on any actions before he arrives."

He nodded and bent down to pick up the papers. "Are we still using Lipscomb?"

"No, dear, he died, about . . . oh, three years ago, wasn't it, Roanna? Heart trouble ran in his family, you know. Our broker now is Sage Whitten, of the Birmingham Whittens. We've been pleased with him, for the most part, but he does tend to be conservative."

Roanna saw the wry expression cross Webb's face as he readjusted to the nuances of southern business, where everything was tinged with personal information and family relationships. Probably he had become accustomed to a much more straightforward method of doing things.

He was already studying the papers in his hand as he strolled over to the desk and started to drop into the massive leather chair. He halted and gave Roanna an inquiring glance, as if checking her reaction to this abrupt takeover of both territory and authority.

She didn't know whether to cry or shout. She had never really enjoyed business but had nevertheless staked out her own territory. Because this was the only thing in her life for which she had ever been needed, by Lucinda or anyone else, she had worked doggedly to understand and master the concepts and applications. With Webb's return she was losing that territory, and her usefulness. On the other hand, it would be a relief not to have to sit through any more interminable meetings or deal with businessmen and politicians who questioned her decisions with barely veiled condescension. She was glad to be rid of the duty but had no idea how she was going to replace it.

She allowed none of her ambivalence to show in her expression, however, maintaining the blank wall of indifference she presented to the world. Lucinda resumed her seat on the sofa and Roanna walked over to one of the file cabinets to extract a thick folder.

The fax machine beeped and began to whir as a document printed. Webb glanced at it, then at the rest of the electronic equipment that had been installed since he'd left. "Looks like we're on the information highway."

"It was either that or spend most of my time traveling," Roanna replied. She indicated the computer on the desk. "We have two discrete systems. This computer and printer are for our private records. The other one"—she pointed to the electronic setup in the corner, arranged on a custom-built oak computer desk—"is for communication." The second computer was hooked up to a modem. "We have the dedicated fax line, e-mail, and two laser printers. I'll show you the programs any time you want. There's also a laptop for traveling."

"Even Loyal is on computer now," Lucinda said, smiling. "The bloodlines are thoroughly cross-referenced, and his files include breeding times, results, medical history, and identification tattoos. He'd as proud of the system as he would be if it had four legs and neighed."

He glanced at Roanna. "Do you still ride as much as before?"

"There isn't time."

"You'll have more time now."

She hadn't thought of this benefit to Webb's return, and her heart gave an excited leap. She missed the horses with painful intensity, but her statement had been the flat truth: there simply hadn't been time. She rode when she could, which was enough to keep her muscles accustomed to the exercise, but not nearly enough to satisfy her. For now she had to devote herself to the intricacies of handing over the reins to Webb, but soon—soon!—she would be able to begin helping Loyal again.

"If I know you," Webb said lazily, "you're already planning to spend your days in the stable. Don't think you're going to dump everything in my lap and play hooky. I'll have my hands full with all this and my Arizona properties too, so you're still going to have to handle some of the work."

Work with Webb? She hadn't considered that he'd want her around, or that she would still be of any use. Her heart gave that little leap again at the prospect of being with him every day.

He concentrated then on studying the diagrams and analysis of stock performances and considering the projections. By the time Sage Whitten arrived, Webb knew exactly where they stood in the stock market.

Mr. Whitten had never met Webb before, but by his startled expression when he was introduced, he'd heard the gossip. If he was dismayed by Lucinda's explanation that Webb would henceforth be handling all the Davenport concerns, he hid it well. But no matter what people suspected, Webb Tallant had never been charged with the murder of his wife, and business was business.

The meeting was concluded faster than usual. Scarcely

had Mr. Whitten left than Lanette breezed into the study. "Aunt Lucinda, there's a bag of some sort in the foyer. Did Mr. Whitten—?" She stopped dead, staring at Webb seated behind the desk.

"The bag belongs to me." He scarcely glanced up from the computer, where he was reviewing the history of a stock's dividends. "I'll take it up later."

Lanette's cheeks were blanched, but she rallied with a forced laugh. "Webb! I didn't know you'd arrived. No one told us you were expected today."

"I wasn't."

"Oh. Well, welcome home." Her tone was as false as her laugh. "I'll tell Mama and Daddy. They've just finished breakfast, and I know they'll want to welcome you themselves."

Webb's eyebrows lifted sardonically. "Is that so?"

"I'll get them," she said, and fled.

"About the bag." Webb leaned back in the chair and swiveled so he was facing Lucinda, who was still on the sofa. "Where do I put it?"

"Wherever you want," Lucinda firmly replied. "Your old suite has been completely redecorated. Corliss has taken it over, but if you want it she can move into another room."

He rejected the offer with a slight shake of his head. "I suppose Gloria and Harlan have one of the other suites, and Lanette and Greg the fourth one." He slanted an unreadable look at Roanna. "You, of course, are still in your old room on the back."

He seemed to disapprove of that, but Roanna couldn't imagine why. Left uncertain of what to say, she said nothing.

"And Brock has one of the regular bedrooms on the left side," Lucinda said, confirming his supposition. "It isn't a problem, though. I've been considering what can be done, and it would be a simple matter to connect two of the remaining bedrooms by opening a door between them, and converting one of the rooms into a sitting room. The remodeling could be done within a week."

"That isn't necessary. I'll take one of the bedrooms on the back. The one next to Roanna will do fine. It still has a king-size bed, doesn't it?"

"All of the rooms have king beds now, except Roanna's."

He gave her a hooded look. "Don't you like big beds?"

The motel bed where they'd made love had been a double. It should have been too small for the two of them, but when one person was lying on top of the other it reduced the need for space. Roanna barely controlled a blush. "I don't need anything bigger." She glanced at her watch and gratefully got to her feet when she saw the time. "I have to go to the county commissioner's meeting, then I'm having lunch with the hospital administrator in Florence. I'll be back by three."

She leaned over to kiss the wrinkled cheek Lucinda presented to her. "Drive carefully," Lucinda said, as she always did.

"I will." There was an element of escape in her departure, and from the way Webb was looking at her, she was sure he'd noticed it as well.

After lunch, Webb and Lucinda returned to the study. He had endured Gloria and Harlan's effusive, embarrassingly false welcomes, ignored Corliss's sulky bad manners, and been fussed over by Tansy and Bessie. It was plain as hell that only Roanna and Lucinda had wanted him back; the rest of his family obviously wished he'd stayed in Arizona. The reason for that was pretty plain, too: they'd been mooching off Lucinda for years and were afraid he'd boot them out on their asses. It was a thought. Oh, not Gloria and Harlan. As much as he knew he'd dislike having them around, they were in their seventies, and the reasons he'd given Roanna ten years ago for their moving in were even more valid now. But as for the others . . .

He didn't plan to do anything right away. He didn't know the details of their individual situations, and it was a lot easier to get his facts straight before he acted than it would be to repair the damage done by a wrong decision.

"I suppose you want to have your say," Lucinda said

183

crisply, taking her seat on the sofa. "God knows you deserve it. This is your chance to get it off your chest, so go to it. I'll sit here, listen, and keep my mouth shut."

She was as indomitable as ever in spirit, he thought, but dangerously frail. When she'd hugged him, he'd felt the fragility of her brittle bones, seen the crepey thinness of her skin. Her color wasn't good, and her energy level was low. He'd known, from his letters from Yvonne, that Lucinda's health wasn't good these days, but he hadn't realized the imminence of her death. It was a matter of months; he doubted she would even see spring.

She'd been a cornerstone of his life. She had let him down when he'd needed her, but now she was willing to face his ire. It was a measure of her strength that he had tested his budding manhood against her, measured his growth by how well he held his own with her. Damn her, he wasn't ready to let her go.

He hitched one hip onto the edge of the desk. "I'll get to that," he said evenly, then continued with soft violence: "But first I want to know what in *hell* y'all have done to Roanna."

Lucinda sat in silence for a long time, Webb's accusation hovering in the air between them. She stared out the window, looking out over the sweep of sundrenched land, dotted here and there with the shadows of the fat, fluffy clouds drifting overhead. Davenport land, as far as she could see. She had always taken comfort in this vista, and she still loved to see it, but now that her life was nearing an end she was finding other things of far more importance.

"I didn't notice at first," she finally said, her gaze still far away. "Jessie's death was—well, we'll talk about that later. I was so preoccupied with my own grief that I didn't notice Roanna until she'd almost drifted away."

"Drifted away, how?" His tone was hard, sharp.

"She nearly died," Lucinda said baldly. Her chin trembled, and she sternly controlled it. "I'd always thought Jessie was the one who so desperately needed to be loved, to make up for her circumstances . . . I didn't see that Roanna needed love even more, but she didn't demand it the way Jessie did. Strange, isn't it? I loved Jessie from the cradle, but she would never have helped me the way Roanna has, or become as important to me. Roanna's more than my right hand; these past few years, I couldn't have managed without her."

Webb waved all of that away, focusing on the one statement that had his attention. "How did she nearly die?" The thought of Roanna dying shocked him to the bone, and he felt a cold sense of dread when he remembered her guilty, miserable expression the day of Jessie's funeral. She hadn't tried to kill herself, had she?

"She stopped eating. She never ate much anyway, so I didn't notice for a long time, almost too long. Everything was so disrupted, there were seldom any routine meals, and I suppose I thought she was snacking at odd hours the way we all were. She stayed in her room a lot, too. She didn't do it deliberately," Lucinda explained softly. "She just . . . lost interest. When you left, she totally withdrew. She blames herself for everything, you know."

"Why?" Webb asked. Roanna had told him she hadn't deliberately caused trouble, but maybe she really had, and confessed to Lucinda.

"It was a long time before she could talk about it, but several years ago she told me what happened in the kitchen, that she caught you by surprise when she impulsively kissed you. She didn't know Jessie was coming down, and of course, it was just like Jessie to make a huge scene, but to Roanna's way of thinking she caused all the trouble with that kiss. If she hadn't kissed you, you and Jessie wouldn't have argued, you wouldn't have been blamed for Jessie's death, and you wouldn't have left town. With you gone . . ." Lucinda shook her head. "She's always loved you so much. We laughed about it when she was little, thought it was hero worship and puppy love, but it wasn't, was it?"

"I don't know." But he did, he thought. Roanna had never had any self-protection where he was concerned. Hell, she'd never been good at any kind of subterfuge. Her feelings had been right out in the open, her pride as totally vulnerable as her heart. Her adoration had always been there, like a piece of sunshine in his life, and he'd depended on its being there though he seldom paid much attention to it. Like the sunshine, it was something he'd taken for granted. That was why he'd been so damn mad when he thought she had betrayed him just to get back at Jessie.

Lucinda gave him a shrewd look that told him she wasn't taken in by his denial. "After David and Karen died, you and I became the centerposts of Roanna's life. She needed our love and support, but for the most part we didn't give it to her. No, let me rephrase that, because most of the blame is mine: *I* didn't give her my love and support. As long as you were here to love her, though, she got by. When you left, there was no one here for her, and she gave up. She was almost gone before I noticed," Lucinda said sadly. A tear rolled down her wrinkled cheek, and she wiped it away. "She was down to eighty pounds. Eighty pounds! She's five-seven; she should weigh at least a hundred and thirty. I can't describe to you how pitiful she looked. But one day I saw her, really *saw* her, and realized that I had to do something or I'd lose her, too."

Webb couldn't say anything. He stood up and walked over to the window, his fists jammed deep into his pockets. His shoulders were rigid as he stood with his back to Lucinda, and it was hard for him to breathe. Waves of panic washed over him. My God, she'd almost died, and he hadn't known anything about it.

"Just saying 'You need to eat' wouldn't have done the trick," Lucinda continued, the words spilling out of her as if she'd held them in for too long, and she had to share the pain. "She needed a reason for living, something to hold on to. So I told her I needed her help."

She stopped and swallowed hard before resuming. "No one had ever said they needed her. I hadn't realized . . . Anyway, I told her I couldn't manage without her, that everything was too much for me to handle by myself. I didn't realize how true that was," Lucinda said wryly. "She pulled herself back. It was a long fight, and for a while I was terrified that I'd left it too late, but she did it. It was a year before her health recovered enough that she could go to college, a year before she stopped waking us up at night with her screams."

"Screams?" Webb asked. "Nightmares?"

"About Jessie." Lucinda's voice was soft, shredded with pain. "She found her, you know. And that was the way she screamed, the same sound, as if she'd just walked in and—and stepped in Jessie's blood." The words trembled, then firmed as if Lucinda wouldn't allow that weakness in herself. "The nightmares developed into insomnia, as if staying awake was the only way she could escape them. She still suffers from it, and some nights she doesn't sleep at all. She catnaps, for the most part. If you see her dozing during the day, whatever you do, don't wake her up because that's probably the only sleep she's had. I've made it a rule that no one wakes her, for any reason. Corliss is the only one who does. She'll drop something or let a door slam, and she always pretends it's an accident."

Webb turned from the window. His eyes were like green frost. "She might do it once more, but that'll be the last time," he said flatly.

Lucinda gave a faint smile. "Good. I hate to say it of my own family, but Corliss has a mean, trashy streak in her. It'll be good for Roanna, having you here again."

But he hadn't been here when she'd needed him most, Webb thought. He'd walked out, leaving her to face the horror, and the nightmares, alone. What was it Lucinda had said? Roanna had stepped in Jessie's blood. He hadn't known, hadn't thought about the strain she must have been under. His wife had been murdered and he'd been accused of the crime; he'd been undergoing his own crisis, and he'd assigned her stress to guilt. He should have known better, because he'd been closer to Roanna than anyone else.

He remembered the way she had ignored the united condemnation of the town and slipped her little hand into

187

his at Jessie's funeral, to give him comfort and support. Considering the wild tales that had been going around about Jessie catching him screwing Roanna, it had taken a great deal of courage for her to approach him. But she'd done it, not counting the cost to her reputation, because she'd thought he needed her. Instead of squeezing her hand, doing any little thing at all to show his trust in her, he'd rebuffed her.

She'd been there for him, but he hadn't be there for her.

She had survived, but at what cost?

"I didn't recognize her at first," he mused almost absently. His gaze never left Lucinda's. "It isn't just that she's older. She's all shut down inside."

"That was how she coped. She's stronger; I think it frightened her when she realized how weak and ill she had become. She's never let herself get in that condition again. But she coped by shutting everything out, and holding herself in. It's as if she's afraid to feel too much, so she doesn't let herself feel anything. I can't reach her, and God knows I've tried, but that's my fault, too."

Lucinda squared her shoulders as if settling an old burden, one she had become so used to that she seldom noticed it now. "When she found Jessie and screamed, we all went running into the bedroom and found her standing over the body. Gloria jumped to the conclusion that Roanna had killed Jessie, and that's what she and Harlan told the sheriff. Booley had a deputy guarding her while he checked it out. We were all on one side of the room, and Roanna was on the other, all by herself except for the deputy. I'll never forget the way she looked at us, as if we had walked up and stabbed her. I should have gone to her, the way I should have gone to you, but I didn't. She hasn't called me Grandmother since," Lucinda said softly. "I can't reach her. She goes through the motions, but she doesn't even care about Davencourt. When I told her I was going to change my will to benefit you, if she could get you to come home, she didn't even blink. I wanted her to argue, to get angry, to *care,* but she doesn't." The incomprehensibility of it rang in Lucinda's voice, for how could anyone not care about her beloved Davencourt?

Then she sighed. "Do you remember how she was always like a windup toy that never wound down? Running up and down the stairs, banging doors, yelling . . . I swear, she had no sense of decorum at all. Well, now I'd give anything to see her skip, just once. She was always saying the wrong thing at the wrong time, and now she hardly talks at all. It's impossible to tell what she's thinking."

"Does she laugh?" he asked in a rough tone. He missed her laughter, the infectious giggle when she was up to some mischief, the belly laughs when he told her jokes, the joyous chuckle as she watched foals romping in the pastures.

Lucinda's eyes were sad. "No. She almost never smiles, and she doesn't laugh at all. She hasn't laughed in ten years."

CHAPTER
13

*R*oanna glanced at her watch. The county commissioner's meeting was taking longer than usual, and she
would have to leave soon or be late for her lunch in
Florence. The Davenports had no official authority in
county matters, but it was almost traditional that a family
representative attend the meetings. Davenport support, or
lack of it, often meant life or death to county projects.

When Roanna had first begun attending the meetings in
Lucinda's stead, she had been largely ignored, or at best
treated to a figurative pat on the head. She had merely
listened, and reported to Lucinda; to a large degree, that
was still what she did. But Lucinda, when she had taken
action on the matters that interested her, had made a point
of saying, "Roanna thinks" or "Roanna's impression was,"
and soon the commissioners had realized that they had
better pay attention to the solemn young woman who
seldom spoke. Lucinda hadn't lied; Roanna did relay her
thoughts and impressions. She had always been observant
but so active that she had often missed details, much as a
speeder can see a highway sign but pass it too fast to read
the message. Now Roanna was still and silent, and her
brown eyes roamed from face to face, absorbing nuances of

expression, tones, reactions. All of this went straight back to Lucinda, who then made her decisions based on Roanna's impressions.

Now that Webb had returned, he would be attending the meetings just as he had used to do. This was likely the last time she would be sitting here, listening and assessing, another place where her usefulness was at an end. In some distant part of her psyche she was aware of hurt, and fear, but she refused to allow them to surface.

The meeting was finally dawdling to an end. She checked her watch once again and saw that she had perhaps five minutes before she *had* to leave or be late. Normally she took the time to chat with everyone, but today she had time only for a quick word with the commissioner.

He was coming toward her, a short, stocky, balding man with a deeply lined face. The creases rearranged themselves into a smile as he approached her in her usual position close to the back of the room. "How are you today, Roanna?"

"Fine, thank you, Chet," Roanna replied, thinking that she might as well tell him about Webb's return. "And you?"

"Can't complain. Well, I could, but my wife tells me no one's interested in listening." He laughed at his own joke, his eyes twinkling. "And how's Miss Lucinda feeling?"

"Much better, now that Webb's home," she said calmly.

He gaped at her in astonishment, and for a second, dismay was written plainly on his face. He blurted, "My God, what are ya'll going to do?" before the rest of her statement sank in and he realized that commiseration wasn't appropriate. He turned beet red and started to sputter in his attempt to retrench. "I—ah, that is—"

Roanna lifted her hand to stop his verbal stumbling. "He'll be taking up the reins again, of course," she said as if Webb's return was the most natural thing in the world. "It will take him a few weeks to review everything, but I'm certain he'll be contacting you soon."

The commissioner sucked in a deep breath. He looked faintly ill, but he had recovered his composure. "Roanna, I don't think that's such a good idea. You've been handling things just fine for Miss Lucinda, and folks around here will be more comfortable with you—"

Roanna's eyes were very clear and direct. "Webb is taking over again," she said softly. "It would distress Lucinda if anyone chose not to do business with us, but of course that's their choice."

His windpipe bobbed as he swallowed. Roanna had just made it very plain that anyone who didn't accept Webb would find themselves without Davenport support or patronization. She never got angry, never yelled, never insisted on a point, and seldom even voiced an opinion, but folks in the county had learned not to discount the influence this somber-eyed woman had with Lucinda Davenport. Moreover, most people liked Roanna; it was as simple as that. No one would want an open rift with the Davenports.

"This will probably be the last monthly meeting that I'll attend," she continued.

"Don't be too sure of that," a deep, lazy voice said from the doorway just behind her.

Startled, Roanna turned to face Webb as he stepped into the room. "What?" she said. What was he doing here? He hadn't even changed clothes. Had he been so afraid she would mess up something that he'd rushed down to the commissioner's meeting without even taking the time to unpack?

"Hello, Chet," Webb was saying easily, holding out his hand to the commissioner.

The commissioner's face turned red. He hesitated, then his politician's instincts took over and he shook Webb's hand. "Webb! Speak of the devil! Roanna was just telling me you were back at Davencourt. You're looking good, real good."

"Thanks. You're looking prosperous yourself."

Chet patted his belly and gave a hearty laugh. "Too prosperous! Willadean says I'm on a seafood diet—I eat everything I see!"

People milling about in the room had noticed Webb, and

an agitated buzz was growing in volume. Roanna glanced at Webb, and the glint in his green eyes told her that he was well aware of the stir his presence was causing and wasn't the least concerned about it.

"Don't think you're off the hook," he said to Roanna, turning a smile on her. "Just because I'm home doesn't mean you get to goof off from now on. We'll probably come to the meetings together."

Despite her shock, Roanna nodded gravely.

Webb looked at his watch. "Don't you have a lunch engagement in Florence? You're going to be late if you don't hurry."

"I'm on my way. 'Bye, Chet."

"See you at the next meeting," the commissioner said, still in that falsely jovial tone as she maneuvered past him and into the hallway.

"I'll walk you to your car." Webb nodded at the commissioner and turned to fall into step with Roanna.

She was acutely aware of him just at her elbow as they walked down the hall. His tall form easily dominated her even though she was wearing high heels. She didn't know what to think about what had just happened, so she didn't let herself jump to any conclusions. Maybe he truly intended they should work together, maybe he'd just been saying that to smooth the way. Only time would tell, and she wouldn't let herself hope. If she didn't hope, then she couldn't be disappointed.

A wave of double takes followed them down the hall as people recognized Webb and turned to stare. Roanna walked faster, wanting to get out of the building before a confrontation could develop. She reached the end of the hall, and Webb's arm extended in front of her to open the door. She felt the brush of his body against her back.

They exited into the glare and sticky humidity of the hot summer morning. Roanna fished her keys out of purse and slipped her sunglasses on her nose. "What made you come to town?" she asked. "I wasn't expecting you."

"I figured now was as good a time to break the ice as any."

His long legs easily kept up with her hurried pace. "Slow down, it's too hot for a race."

Obediently she slacked her pace. Her car was parked close to the end of a row, and if she hurried all that distance, she would be drenched in sweat by the time she got to it. "Were you serious about the meetings?" she asked.

"Dead serious." He had put on his own sunglasses, and the dark lenses kept her from reading his expression. "Lucinda has been singing your praises. You already know what's going on, so I'd be a fool if I didn't use you."

One thing Webb wasn't, particularly where business was concerned, was a fool. Roanna felt a wave of dizziness at the thought of actually working with him. She had been prepared for anything, she'd thought, from being ignored to being evicted, but she hadn't considered that he would want her help.

They reached her car, and Webb plucked the keys from her hand. He unlocked the door and opened it, then handed the keys back. She waited a moment for the wave of pent-up heat in the car to dissipate, then slipped behind the wheel. "Be careful," he said, and closed the door.

Roanna glanced in the rearview mirror as she pulled out of the parking lot. He was striding back toward the building; perhaps he was parked up that way, or he was going back inside. She let her gaze move hungrily over that wide, muscled back and long legs, just for a second's delight, then she forced her attention back to her driving and merged into traffic.

Webb unlocked his own car and got inside. The impulse that had sent him into town had been a simple one, but strong. He had wanted to see Roanna. That was all, just see her. After the disturbing things Lucinda had told him, the old protective instincts had taken over and he'd wanted to see for himself that she was all right.

She was, of course, more than all right. He had seen for himself how deftly she had handled Chet Forrister, her composure unruffled by the commissioner's opposition—

and on Webb's own behalf. Now he understood exactly what Lucinda had been telling him when she'd said Roanna was stronger, that she'd changed. Roanna no longer needed him to fight her battles.

The realization left him feeling oddly bereft.

He should have been glad, for her sake. The young Roanna had been so painfully vulnerable, an easy target for anyone who wanted to take a verbal potshot at her tender emotions. He had constantly been stepping in to shield her, and his reward had been her unflagging adoration.

Now she had forged her own armor. She was cool and self-contained, almost emotionless, keeping people at a distance so their slings and arrows couldn't reach her. She had paid for that armor with pain and despair, almost with her own life, but the steel was strong. She still suffered, in the form of insomnia and nightmares when she did manage to sleep, but she handled her own problems now.

When he had walked into Davencourt today and seen her standing there on the stairs, wearing that elegantly under-stated silk dress and creamy pearls, with her dark chestnut hair in a sleek, sophisticated style, he had been rendered almost speechless at the contrast between the rowdy, untidy girl she had been and the classy, classic woman she was now.

She was still Roanna, but she was different. When he looked at her now, he didn't see the urchin with the unruly tongue, the awkward teenager. He looked at her and thought of the slender body beneath the silk dress, the texture of her skin that rivaled the dress in luxurious silkiness, the way her nipples had peaked at his slightest touch during those long hours in the motel in Nogales.

He had covered her naked body with his own, pulled her legs wide open, and taken her virginity. Even now, sitting in the contained, roasting heat of the car, he shivered with the power of the memory. God, he remembered every little detail—how it had felt pushing into her, the hot, soft tightness of her body as he sheathed himself inside her. He remembered how delicate she had felt beneath him, her smaller body dominated by his size, his weight, his strength. He had wanted to cradle her in his arms, protect her, soothe her, pleasure her—everything but stop. There was no way he could have stopped.

Those memories had been driving him crazy for the past ten days, depriving him of sleep, interrupting his work. When he'd seen her again today, he had been shaken by a wave of pure possessiveness. She was his. She was his, and he wanted her. He wanted her so much that his hands had started shaking. It had taken all of his self-control not to climb the stairs to where she stood, take her arm, and march her the rest of the way upstairs to one of the bedrooms, any bedroom, where he could lift her skirt and bury himself inside her once more.

He had restrained himself for one reason, and one reason only. Roanna had carefully built her inner fortress, but every fortress had a weakness, and he knew exactly what her weakness was.

Him.

She could protect herself against everyone but him.

She hadn't tried to hide it, or deny it. She had told him with devastating honesty that all he had to do was snap his fingers and she would come running. She would have gone up those stairs with him and let him do anything he wanted to her.

Webb drummed his fingers on the hot steering wheel. It seemed there was one more dragon Roanna needed him to fight, and that was his own sexual desire for her.

He had told her that he would come home if she would let him use her sexually, and she hadn't hesitated. If that was what he wanted, then she would do it. If he needed a sexual outlet, she would be available. She would do it for Lucinda, for Davencourt, for him—but what about herself?

He knew he could walk into Roanna's bedroom at any time and have her, and the temptation was already eating at him. But he didn't want Roanna to give herself to him out of guilt, or duty, or even because of her misguided hero worship. He was no hero, damn it, he was a man. He wanted

her to want him as a man, male to her female. If she slipped
into his bed merely because she was horny and wanted the
relief he could give her, he would be delighted even by that,
because it was simple and uncomplicated by other people's
motives, or even her own.

God, what about his own motives?

Sweat dripped into his eye, stinging, and with a muffled
curse he turned the ignition switch, starting the motor so
the air conditioner would blast into life. He was going to
give himself a heat stroke, sitting in a closed car in the
middle of summer while he tried to sort through a tangle of
emotions.

He loved Roanna; he'd loved her all her life, but as a
sister, with an amused, protective indulgence.

He hadn't been prepared for the force and heat of the
physical desire that had flared when she had thrown her
arms around his neck and kissed him, ten long years ago. It
had come from nowhere, like swirling gases that had been
compressed until they reached critical mass, then exploded
into a white hot star. It had shaken him, made him feel
guilty. Everything about it had felt wrong. She'd been too
young; he'd always thought of her as a sister; he'd been
married, for God's sake. The guilt in that situation had been
all his. Even though his marriage had been collapsing, he
had still been married. He'd been the experienced one; he
should have gently turned the kiss into a gesture of impulsive affection, something that wouldn't have embarrassed
her. Instead, he'd pulled her tighter and turned the kiss into
something quite different, a deeper, adult kiss, laden with
sexuality. What had happened had been his fault, not
Roanna's, but she was still trying to pay the price.

Most of the original barriers to a sexual relationship
between them were gone. Roanna was a woman now, he
wasn't married, and he didn't feel at all brotherly toward
her. But other barriers remained: the pressures of family,
Roanna's own sense of duty, his pride.

He snorted at himself as he put the car in gear. God, yes,
let's not forget his male pride. He didn't want her to give

herself to him for Davencourt, family, any of those unimportant reasons. He wanted her to lie hot and panting beneath him for no other reason than she wanted *him*. Nothing else would do.

The bastard was back. The news was all over the county and reached the bars that night. Harper Neeley shook with rage every time Webb Tallant's name was mentioned. Tallant had gotten away with killing Jessie, and now he was back to start lording it over everyone again as if nothing had ever happened. Oh, that stupid fat-ass sheriff hadn't arrested him, said there wasn't enough evidence for a conviction, but everyone knew he'd been bought off. The Davenports and the Tallants of this world never had to pay for the shit they committed. It was the ordinary people who did time, not the la-di-dah rich folks who lived in their big, fancy house and thought the rules didn't apply to them.

Webb Tallant had bashed Jessie's head in with an andiron. He still wept when he thought about it, his beautiful Jessie with her hair all matted with blood and brains, one side of her head flattened. Somehow the bastard had found out about him and Jessie, and killed her for it. Or maybe Tallant found out that the little bun in the oven hadn't been his. Jessie had said she'd handle it, and she was a slick one if he'd ever seen one, but this time she hadn't been slick enough.

No one had ever belonged to him the way Jessie had. She'd been wild, that girl, wild and wicked, and it had excited him so much he'd nearly creamed his pants the first time she'd come on to him. She'd been excited, too, her eyes bright and hot. She'd loved the danger of it, the thrill of doing the forbidden. That first time she had been like an animal, clawing and bucking, but she hadn't come. It had taken him a while to figure it out. Jessie had liked to screw for a lot of reasons, but pleasure hadn't been one of them. She'd used her body to mess with men's heads, to gain power over them. She'd fucked him to get back at her son-of-a-bitch husband, to get back at everyone and show them she didn't give a damn. She'd never meant for anyone else to know, but *she* knew, and that was how she got her rocks off.

But once he'd figured it out, he hadn't let her get away with it. Nobody used him, not even Jessie. Especially not Jessie. He knew her the way no one else ever had or ever would, because inside she was like him.

He started her out with kinky little games, never pushing her too far at once. She'd taken to it like a cat to cream, something even a little more forbidden for her to gloat over when she was sitting up at the big house, acting like a perfect lady and laughing at how easily she fooled everybody because she'd just spent the afternoon screwing her brains out with the one man guaranteed to make them all piss in their lace drawers.

They'd had to be careful; they couldn't go to any local motel, and it wasn't always possible for her to come up with an excuse for being absent and unreachable for several hours at a time. Usually they'd just meet in the woods somewhere. They'd been in the woods when he'd decided he'd had enough of her game playing and finally showed her who was boss.

By the time he'd let her go, she'd been covered with bruises and bites, but she'd come so many times she'd barely been able to sit her horse. She'd complained bitterly about having to be careful and not let anyone see the marks on her body, but her eyes had been shining. He'd fucked her so long and so hard that he'd been pumped dry and she'd been raw, and she had loved it. Always before women had whined and blubbered when he got rough with them, but not Jessie. She came back for more, and dished out her own medicine. He'd gone home with his back clawed bloody more times than once, and every burning weal had reminded him of her and fed his hunger for more.

There'd never been another woman like his girl. She'd come back for more, too, and pushed for rougher and more kinky games, the dirtier the better. They'd gone on to butt fucking, and that had given her a real thrill, the most forbidden thing she could do with the most forbidden man. Wicked, wicked Jessie. He'd loved her so much.

There wasn't a day that had gone by that he hadn't thought about her, missed her. No other woman could turn him on the way she had.

That goddamn Webb Tallant had killed her, killed both her and the kid. Then he'd waltzed away, free as a jaybird, and left town before he could be made to pay.

But he was back.

And this time, he was going to pay.

He'd have to be careful not to be seen, but he'd sneaked around out at Davencourt enough, back when he was meeting Jessie, that he knew his way around on the property. It was big enough, hundreds of acres, that he could approach the house from any angle he chose. It had been a while since he'd been there; ten years, as a matter of fact. He'd have to make sure the old lady hadn't gotten a guard dog and that no alarm system had been installed. He knew there hadn't been one before, because Jessie had tried more than once to talk him into sneaking into her bedroom while her husband was away on a trip. She'd liked the idea of screwing him under her grandmother's roof and in her husband's bed. He'd had sense enough to refuse, but damn, it had been tempting.

Assuming there was no alarm system, there were a hundred ways to get into that old house. All those doors and windows . . . It would be child's play. He'd gotten into houses a lot better guarded than Davencourt. The fools probably felt safe, as far out of town as they were. Country folks just never got in the habit of taking the precautions that townspeople did automatically.

Oh, yes. Webb Tallant was going to pay.

CHAPTER

14

I think we'll have a welcome-home party for Webb,"
Lucinda mused the next day, tapping her teeth with one
fingernail. "No one would dare not accept, because then I'd
know exactly who they were. That way they'd be forced to
be polite to him, and it would get all those uncomfortable
first meetings over with at the same time."

There were moments when Roanna was forcibly reminded that, though Lucinda had married into the Davenport family over sixty years before and had, in her own
mind, thoroughly become a Davenport, if you scratched the
surface you found a Tallant. The Tallants were nothing if
not strong-willed and audacious. They might not always be
right, but it didn't always matter, either. Put them on a path
and point them at a target, and they rolled over every
obstacle you put in their way. Lucinda's goal was to
reinstate Webb's standing in the county, and she didn't
mind twisting arms to achieve that goal.

Belonging to the best circles in the Quad Cities didn't
necessarily depend on how much money you had, though it
helped. Some families of very modest means were acknowledged as belonging to that select social strata, by dint of
having an ancestor who had actually fought in The War, and

it wasn't either of the World Wars that was meant. Some of the younger set actually referred to it as the Civil War, but the more genteel called it the War of Northern Aggression, and the most genteel of all would delicately refer to the Late Unpleasantness.

Business associates would immediately see how things stood with the Davenports and would treat Webb as if nothing had ever happened. After all, he'd never been arrested, so why should his wife's death be allowed to cut into the bottom line?

Those who ruled the social calendar, however, adhered to a stricter standard. Webb would find himself uninvited to the dinners and parties where so much business was discussed, which would be a disadvantage for the Davenport interests. Lucinda cared about the money, but she cared about Webb even more, and she was determined that he wouldn't be shunned. She would invite everyone to her home, and they would come because they were her friends. She was ill, and it might be the last party she ever gave. Leave it to Lucinda to use her own approaching death as a means of getting her way. Her friends might not like it, but they would come. They would also be polite to Webb under his own roof; though it was technically still Lucinda's roof, everyone would assume that Webb had returned home to claim his inheritance, which he had, so it would soon be his. And having accepted *his* hospitality, they would then be obliged to extend their own to him.

Once that had happened, they would pretend they'd never had any doubts about him at all, and he would be welcome everywhere. After all, you could hardly vilify someone you had invited into your home. That just wasn't done.

"Are you out of your mind?" Gloria demanded. "No one will come. We'll be humiliated."

"Don't be silly. Of course people will come, they wouldn't dare not to. It went well yesterday with Mr. Whitten, didn't it, Roanna?"

"Mr. Whitten lives in *Huntsville*," Gloria replied, saving Roanna the necessity of a reply. "What would he know?"

"He knew what happened, that much was obvious from his face. But being an intelligent man, he decided that if *we* have faith in Webb, then those horrible accusations couldn't be true. Which they weren't," Lucinda said firmly.

"I agree with Mother," Lanette said. "Think of the embarrassment."

"You always agree with her," Lucinda replied, her eyes glittering with the light of battle. She had set her course and wasn't about to be swayed from it. "If you ever disagreed, then your opinion would carry more weight, my dear. Now, if Roanna told me my party was a bad idea, I'd be a lot more likely to listen."

Gloria snorted. "As if Roanna ever disagrees with *you*."

"Well, she does, on a regular basis. We seldom see eye to eye on every detail of a business decision. It pains me to admit that she's right more often than not."

That wasn't perhaps a blatant lie, Roanna thought, but it wasn't exactly the truth either. She never argued with Lucinda; she occasionally saw things differently, but she would simply present her case and Lucinda would make the final decision. That was a far cry from open disagreement.

The three of them turned to her, Lucinda with open triumph, Gloria and Lanette disgruntled at having her opinion valued over theirs.

"I think it should be Webb's decision," she said quietly. "He's the one who'll have to be on display."

Lucinda scowled. "True. If he isn't willing, there's no point in even talking about it. Why don't you ask him, dear. Maybe you can get his attention off that computer screen for five minutes."

They had taken a break for lunch and had finished eating but were now lingering over their iced tea. Webb had requested a couple of sandwiches and coffee while he continued to work. He'd been in the study until eleven the night before and had gotten up at six to resume his reading. Roanna knew because she had been awake at both times, silently curled in her big chair and counting down the hours. It had been a particularly bad night; she hadn't slept at all, and she was so tired now she was afraid she would fall into a deep sleep when she did go to bed. Those were the times when she was most likely to wake up somewhere else in the house and not remember how she'd gotten there.

It was Webb's presence that had unsettled her to the point she couldn't even doze. Both she and Lucinda had worked with him last night, going over reports, until Lucinda had become tired and gone to bed. After that, alone with him in the study, Roanna had become increasingly uneasy. Did he prefer not being alone with her, after what had happened? Did he think she was pushing herself at him, by staying there without Lucinda's buffering presence?

After less than an hour she had excused herself and gone to her room. She'd taken a bath to calm her frazzled nerves, then settled in her chair to read. The words on the page hadn't made sense, though; she couldn't concentrate on them. Webb was in the house. He'd moved his clothes into the room next to hers. Why had he done that? He'd made it plain, back in Nogales, that he wasn't interested in having an affair with her. There were three other bedrooms he could have used, but he'd chosen that one. The only explanation she could think of was that it simply didn't matter to him if she was next door; her proximity was of no interest, one way or the other.

She would try to stay out of his way as much as possible, she'd thought. Show him all the current files, answer any questions he had, but otherwise she wouldn't bother him.

At eleven she heard him in the room next door, saw the spill of light onto the veranda. She had reached up and turned off her lamp so he wouldn't see her own light and know she was still awake after pleading fatigue an hour and a half before. In the darkness she had leaned her head back, closed her eyes, and listened to him moving around, picturing in her mind what he was doing.

She heard the shower, and knew he was naked. Her heart thumped at the thought of his tall, steely muscled body, and her breasts tightened. She could scarcely believe that she'd actually made love with him, that she'd lost her virginity in a cheap motel room on the Mexican border, and that it was the closest to heaven she was ever likely to get. She thought of the crisp hair on his chest and the tightness of his buttocks. She remembered how his hard, hair-roughened thighs had held her own thighs spread wide, how she had dug her fingers into the deep valley of muscle down the middle of his back. For one wonderful night she'd lain in his arms and known both desire and fulfillment.

The shower cut off, and about ten minutes later the splash of light on the veranda was extinguished. Through her own open veranda doors she had heard the click as he opened his doors to let in the fresh night air. Was he still naked? Did he sleep raw, or in his underwear? Maybe he wore pajama bottoms. It struck her as odd that she had lived in the same house with him from age seven to seventeen, and didn't know if he wore anything to bed.

Then there was silence. Was he in bed, or was he standing there looking out at the peaceful night? Had he stepped out onto the veranda? He would be barefoot; she wouldn't be able to hear him. Was he standing there even now? Had he glanced to the right and noticed that her doors were open?

Finally, her nerves raw, Roanna had crept to the window and peeked out. No one, naked or otherwise, stood on the veranda enjoying the night. As quietly as possible she had closed her doors and gone back to her chair. Sleep had escaped her, though, and once again she had endured the slow passage of time.

"Roanna?" Lucinda prodded, and Roanna realized she'd been sitting there daydreaming.

Murmuring a vague apology, Roanna pushed back her chair. She had a meeting at two with the organizers of this year's W. C. Handy Festival in August, so she would just stick her head in the study door, ask Webb his opinion of Lucinda's plan, then escape upstairs to change clothes. Perhaps, by the time she returned, he would have tired of paperwork and she wouldn't have to endure another evening of exquisite torture, sitting at his elbow, listening to his deep voice, marveling at the speed with which he assimilated information—in short, reveling in his presence—while at the same time wondering if he thought she was sitting too close, or making too much of every opportunity to bend over him. Even worse, had he wished she would simply go away and get out of his hair?

When she opened the door, he looked up inquiringly from the papers in his hand. He was leaned back in his chair, the master of his space, his booted feet propped comfortably on the desk.

"I'm sorry," she blurted. "I should have knocked."

He stared at her in silence for a long moment, his dark brows drawing together over his nose. "Why?" he finally asked.

"This is yours now." Her reply was simply made, without inflection.

He took his feet off the desk. "Come in and close the door."

She did but remained standing there by the door. Webb stood and came around the desk, then leaned against the edge of it with his arms crossed over his chest and his legs stretched out. It was a negligent position, but if his body was relaxed, his gaze was sharp as it raked over her.

"You don't ever have to knock on that door," he finally said. "And let's get one thing straight right now: I'm not taking your place, I'm taking Lucinda's. You've done a good job, Ro. I told you yesterday that I'd be a fool if I shut you out of the decision-making process. Maybe you thought you'd get to spend your days with the horses now that I'm back, and you will have more time for yourself, I promise, but you're still needed here, too."

Roanna blinked, dazed by this turn of events. Despite what he'd said to her after the commissioner's meeting, she hadn't thought he had really meant it. A part of her had automatically dismissed it as the type of thing Webb had done when she was little, reassuring her to keep her from being upset, pretending that she was important to anything or anyone. She had stopped letting herself believe in fairy tales on the night she had stumbled into a pool of blood. Very likely, she had thought, she would bring Webb up to speed, and then her usefulness would be at an end. He'd handled everything by himself before—

Her mind stopped, startled. No, that wasn't true. He had taken *most* of the work on his shoulders, but Lucinda had still been involved. And that was before he'd had his property in Arizona to oversee as well. Silent joy spread through her, warming the corners of her heart that had already begun to chill as she prepared herself for being replaced. He really *did* need her.

He'd said she had done a good job. And he'd called her Ro.

He was watching her with a sharply intent gaze. "If you don't smile," he said softly, "then I can't tell if you're pleased or not."

She stared at him, perplexed, searching his face for a clue to what he really meant. Smile? Why would he want her to smile?

"Smile," he prompted. "You remember what a smile is, don't you? The corners of your mouth turn up, like this." He pushed the corners of his mouth up with his fingers, demonstrating. "It's what people do when they're happy. Do you hate paperwork, is that it? Don't you want to help me?"

Tentatively she stretched the corners of her mouth, curling them upward. It was a hesitant, fleeting little smile, barely forming before it was gone and she was regarding him solemnly once more.

But evidently that was what he'd wanted. "Good," he said, straightening from his relaxed perch on the desk. "Are you ready to get back to work?"

"I have a meeting at two. I'm sorry."

"What kind of meeting?"

"With the organizers of the Handy Festival."

He shrugged, losing interest. Webb wasn't a jazz fan.

Roanna remembered why she was there. "Lucinda sent me to ask what you think of having a welcome-home party."

He gave a short laugh, immediately realizing the implications. "She's going on the attack, huh? Are Gloria and Lanette trying to talk her out of it?"

He didn't seem to need an answer, either that or her silence was answer enough. He thought it over for all of five seconds. "Sure, why the hell not? I don't give a damn if it makes everyone uncomfortable. I stopped caring ten years ago what people think of me. If anyone thinks I'm not good enough to deal with them, then I'll take Davencourt's business elsewhere; it's up to them."

She nodded and reached for the door handle, slipping out before he could make any more strange demands that she smile.

Webb returned to his chair, but he didn't immediately pick up the file he'd been studying before Roanna's entrance. He stared at where she'd been standing, poised like a doe on the verge of fleeing. His chest still hurt as he remembered that pathetic excuse for a smile, and the look almost of fright that had been in her eyes. It was difficult to read her now, she kept so much hidden and gave so little response to the world around her. It grated at him, because the Roanna he remembered had been as open as anyone he'd ever known. If he wanted to know how she felt about anything now, he had to pay intensely close attention to every nuance of her expression and body language, before she managed to stifle them.

She had been stunned when he'd told her that he still needed her help. He silently thanked Lucinda for giving him the key to handling Roanna. The idea of anyone needing her got to her faster than anything else, and she couldn't help responding to it. For a split second he'd seen the wonder, the pure joy, that had lit the depths of her eyes, and then it had been so quickly hidden that if he hadn't been deliberately watching her he wouldn't have seen it at all.

He'd lied. He could handle everything without her help,

even with the added burden of his properties in Arizona. He thrived on pressure, his energy level seeming to increase with the demands made on his time. But she needed to feel needed, and he needed her to be close by.

He wanted her.

The phrase beat like a refrain through his mind, his veins, every cell of his body. Want. He hadn't taken her in Nogales out of revenge or because of that damned bargain he'd made with her, or even to keep from hurting her feelings by pulling back after going that far. The simple fact was he'd taken her because he wanted her and was ruthless enough to use whatever means necessary to get her. The tequila was no excuse, though it had relaxed his control over his more uncivilized instincts.

He'd lain awake in his bed last night, thinking of her in the next room, wondering if she was awake, his damned imagination driving him crazy.

Knowing that he could have Roanna any time he wanted was more powerful than any chemical aphrodisiac ever discovered or invented. All he had to do was get out of bed and walk out onto the veranda, then slip through the French doors into her room. She had insomnia; she would be awake, watching him come toward her. He could simply get into bed with her and she would take him into her arms, her body, without question or hesitation.

Erotic dreams of that one kiss they'd shared so long ago had haunted his sleep for years. That had been bad enough, but the dreams had been only imagination. Now that he *knew* exactly how it felt to make love to her, now that reality had taken the place of imagination, the temptation was a constant, gnawing hunger that threatened to shred his self-control.

God, she'd been so sweet, so shy, and so damn tight he broke out in a sweat remembering how it had felt when he'd entered her. He had looked down at her as he made love to her and watched the expression on her face, watched the delicate pink of her nipples darken with arousal. Even though he'd hurt her, she had clung to him, arching her hips up to take him even deeper. It had been so easy to bring her to climax that he'd been enchanted, wanting to do it time and again so he could watch her face as she convulsed, feel her body flexing and throbbing around him.

The night had been exquisite torture, and he knew he would be fighting the same battle every night, with his frustration growing by the minute. He didn't know how long he could endure it before his self-control broke, but for Roanna's sake he had to try.

He'd been back at Davencourt a little over twenty-four hours, and he'd had a hard-on for what seemed like most of that time, certainly for the hours he'd spent in her company. If she'd seemed even the least inclined to flirt with him, in any way signal that she wanted him, too, he probably couldn't have withstood the temptation. But Roanna seemed totally unaware of him as a man, despite the hours they had spent in bed together. The idea was infuriating, but it seemed likely that she had indeed slept with him just to get him to come back to Davencourt.

Even that thought, instead of dampening his ardor, only intensified it. He wanted to toss her over his shoulder and carry her away for some hot, lazy sex on a sun-drenched bed, *prove* to her that she wanted him, that Davencourt and Lucinda had nothing to do with it. The fact was, where Roanna was concerned, his sexual instincts were so damn primitive he expected to start grunting and swinging clubs any minute now.

And that was after only one day.

The grudge he'd held against her all those years was gone. Maybe it had been destroyed during the night they'd spent together, and he just hadn't noticed it at the time. Habit was a powerful thing; you got so used to something that you expected it to be there even when it wasn't. If any vestige had been left, she had demolished it the next morning with her quiet dignity and the utter defenselessness with which she had said, "All you had to do was snap your fingers, and I'd have come running." Not many women would have laid themselves on the line like that; none that he knew, in fact, except for Roanna. He'd been staggered by the courage it had taken for her to say that, knowing what a weapon she had put in his hands if he'd been inclined to use it.

He wasn't. He lifted his hand and snapped his fingers, watching the motion. Like that. He could have her just like that. He wanted her, God knows he wanted her so much he ached. But what he wanted more than anything, even more than he wanted to make love to her, was to see her smile again.

By the time she drove home late that afternoon, Roanna was aching with fatigue. She usually found organizational meetings deadly dull anyway, and this one had dragged on with hours of debate on insignificant details. As usual, she had sat quietly, though this time she had been concentrating more on holding her head upright and her eyes open than she had been on what people were saying.

By the time she turned south onto Highway 43, the sun and heat were almost more than she could fight. She blinked drowsily, glad that she was so close to home. It was almost time for supper, but she planned to lie down for a nap instead. She could eat whenever she chose, but sleep was a lot harder to achieve and far more precious.

She made a right turn off the highway onto a secondary road, and a mile or so after that she turned left onto Davencourt's private road. If she hadn't been so sleepy, she would have been driving faster, and she might have missed the blur of motion in her peripheral vision. She slowed even more, turning her head to see what had caught her attention.

At first she saw only the horse, plunging and rearing, and her first thought was that it had lost its rider and bolted, and now the trailing reins were caught on some underbrush. She forgot her tiredness as urgency flooded her muscles. She slammed on the brakes, shoved the gear shift into park, and jumped out of the car, leaving the motor running and the door open. She could hear the horse's squeals of fear and pain as it reared again.

Roanna didn't think about her expensive shoes or her silk dress. She didn't think of anything except reaching the horse before it hurt itself. She leaped the shallow ditch on the opposite side of the road, then ran awkwardly across the small field toward the trees, her high heels sinking into the earth with each step. She plunged through knee-high weeds that stung her legs, snagged her hosiery on some green briers, turned her ankle when she stepped in a hole. She ignored all of that as she ran as fast as she could, intent only on getting to the horse.

Then the horse sidled sideways, and she saw the man.

She hadn't noticed him before because he'd been on the other side of the horse, and the undergrowth had partially blocked her view.

The horse's reins weren't caught on anything. The man was holding them in one fist, and in the other fist he held a small tree limb that he was using to beat the horse.

Fury roared through her, pumping strength into her muscles. She heard herself yell, saw the man look in her direction with a startled expression on his face, then she surged through the undergrowth and threw her weight against him, knocking him to the side. She couldn't have done it if he'd been expecting it and braced himself, but she caught him by surprise. "Stop it!" she stormed, placing herself between him and the frightened horse. "Don't you dare hit this animal again!"

He regained his balance and swung toward her, gripping the limb as if he would use it on her. Roanna registered the danger in his face, the venomous anger in his eyes, but she stood her ground. Her detachment didn't include standing by and watching any animal in general, but horses in particular, being abused. She braced herself, waiting for him to swing at her. If she charged him, she could get inside the blow and maybe knock him off balance again. If she could, she wouldn't waste any more time but get on the horse and get away from him as fast as she could.

His eyes were a hot electric blue as he advanced a step toward her, his arm drawn back ready to strike. His face was dark red, his lips drawn back over his teeth in a snarl. "You damn little bitch—"

"Who are you?" Roanna demanded, taking a half step toward him herself to show that she wasn't afraid. It was a bluff—she was suddenly very much afraid—but the anger inside her was still so strong she stood her ground. "What are you doing on our land?"

Maybe he thought better of hitting her. For whatever reason, he halted, though he was slow to let his arm drop. He stood a few feet away, breathing hard and glaring at her.

"Who are you?" she demanded again. Something about him was eerily familiar, as if she'd seen that expression before. But she knew she'd never seen *him* before, and she thought she would remember if she had, because those vivid blue eyes and thick shock of gray hair were very distinctive. He was a thickly built man, probably in his fifties, whose wide shoulders and barrel chest gave the impression of an almost brutish strength. What disturbed her the most, though, was the sense almost of evil that emanated from him. No, not evil. It was more impersonal than that, a simple and total lack of conscience or morals. That was it. His eyes, for all their hot color, were cold and flat.

"Who I am ain't none of your business," he sneered. "And neither is what I'm doing."

"When you do it on Davenport land, it is. Don't you dare hit this horse again, do you hear?"

"It's my horse, and I'll do whatever I damn well please to it. The bastard threw me."

"Then maybe you should learn how to ride better," she retorted hotly. She turned to catch the dangling reins and murmur soothingly to the horse, then patted its neck. It snorted nervously but calmed down as she continued to gently stroke it. The horse wasn't a valuable purebred like Lucinda's babied darlings; it was of an indeterminate breed with indifferent formation, but Roanna couldn't see any reason why it should be mistreated.

"Why don't you just go about your own business, missy, and I'll forget about teaching you some manners."

The menacing voice made her whirl. He was closer, and there was a feral look in his expression now. Swiftly Roanna stepped back, maneuvering so that the horse was between her and the man.

"Get off our land," she said coldly. "Or I'll have you arrested."

His heavily sensual mouth twisted in another sneer. "I guess you would. The sheriff's an ass-licker, especially when it comes to a Davenport ass. It wouldn't make any difference to you that I didn't know I was on your precious property, would it?"

"Not when you're beating your horse," Roanna replied, her tone still cold. "Now leave."

He smirked. "I can't. You're holding my horse."

Roanna dropped the reins and took another cautious step back. "There. Now get off our property, and if I ever see you mistreating an animal again, I'll have you brought up on charges of cruelty. Maybe I don't know your name, but I can describe you, and probably not too many people look the way you do." None that she knew of; his eyes were very distinctive.

He turned dark with temper again, and violence moved in those eyes, but he evidently thought better once more of what he had been about to do and merely reached for the reins. He swung himself into the saddle with the minimum of effort that revealed him to be an experienced rider. "I'll see you again some day," he mocked, and dug his heels into the horse's sides. The startled animal leaped forward, brushing by her so closely that its massive shoulder would have knocked her down if she hadn't jumped aside.

He rode in the direction of the highway, leaning down to avoid low-hanging branches. He was out of sight in only a moment, though it took longer than that for the thud of the horse's hooves to fade from her hearing.

Roanna made her way over to a sturdy oak and leaned against it, closing her eyes and shaking.

That had been one of the most foolish, foolhardy things she'd ever done. She had been extremely lucky and she knew it. That man could have seriously hurt her, raped her, maybe even killed her—anything. She had charged head-long into a dangerous situation without stopping to think. Such impulsiveness had been the main cause of trouble in her childhood and had been the trigger for the tragedy of Jessie's death and Webb's leaving.

She had thought that the reckless streak had been de-stroyed forever, but now she found, to her distress, that it still lurked deep inside, ready to leap to the fore. She probably would have found it before, if anything had made her angry. But horses weren't abused at Davencourt, and it had been a long time since she had allowed herself to care about much of anything at all. Webb had been gone, and the endless procession of days had all been flat and dreary.

She was still shaking in the aftermath of fear and rage, and her legs wobbled beneath her. She drew in deep breaths, trying to will herself to calmness. She couldn't go home like this, with her self-control so paper-thin. Anyone who saw her would know that something had happened, and she didn't want to rehash the whole thing and listen to the recriminations. She *knew* she'd been stupid, and lucky.

But more than that, she didn't want anyone to see the break in her composure. She was embarrassed and terrified by this unexpected vulnerability. She had to protect herself better than that. She couldn't do anything about her perma-nent weakness where Webb was concerned, but neither could her internal wall withstand any additional weak-nesses.

When her legs felt steady enough, she left the woods and waded back across the field of weeds, this time taking care to avoid the briers. Her right ankle twinged with pain, reminding her that she had twisted it.

When she reached her car, she sat down sideways in the driver's seat, with her legs outside. Bending down, she took off her shoes and shook the dirt out of them. After a quick look around assured her that there were no cars on the road, she swiftly reached under her skirt and peeled off her shredded panty hose. She used the ruined garment to wipe off her shoes as best she could, then slipped them back on her bare feet.

There were tissues in her purse. She got one, wet it with her tongue, and rubbed at the scratches on her legs until the tiny beads of blood were gone. That, and a passage of a brush through her hair, was the best she could do. To be on the safe side, however, she would use her old childhood trick of going up the outside stairs to the second floor and circling around to her room.

She didn't know who that man was, but she hoped she never saw him again.

CHAPTER
15

*I*t was just like old times, trying to slip into her room without anyone seeing her. Back then, though, she had usually been trying to hide after committing some mischief or social *faux pas*. The confrontation with that unknown brute was far more serious. There was also the difference that now she was mature enough to admit her foolishness rather than tell whoppers to try to hide it. She wouldn't lie if asked, but still she had no intention of blurting out what had happened.

Roanna made it into her room without incident. Quickly she stripped and stepped into the shower, wincing as the water stung the scratches on her legs. After thoroughly washing, the best protection against any possible encounter with poison ivy that might have been lurking in the weeds and among the trees, she dabbed the scratches with an antiseptic, then followed that with a soothing application of pure aloe gel. The stinging stopped almost immediately, and without that constant reminder of the unsettling encounter, her nerves began to calm.

A few flips of the brush restored her hair to order, and three minutes spent applying an array of cosmetics hid any lingering sign of upset. Roanna stared in the mirror at the sophisticated reflection; sometimes she was surprised by the image that looked back, as if it wasn't really her. Thank God for her sorority sisters, she thought. Most of the passages of her life had been marked by loss: the death of her parents, Jessie's murder, Webb's departure. College had been one passage, however, that had been good, and the credit for that belonged solely to those drawling, sharp-eyed, and saber-tongued young women who had taken the misfit under their protection and used their expertise in things social and cosmetic to turn her into an acceptable debutante. Funny how the competent application of mascara had translated itself into a smidgen of self-confidence, how the mastering of a graceful dance step had somehow untied her tongue and allowed her to carry on a social conversation.

She slipped the wires of plain gold hoops into her pierced ears, turning her head to check her appearance. She liked the way they looked, the way the ends of her slightly, purposely tousled hair curled through the hoops, as if her hair had been specifically cut to do so. That was another thing the sorority sisters had taught her, how to appreciate certain things about her own appearance. The greatest gift they had given her was constructed out of the small accomplishments of learning to dance, to apply makeup, to dress well, to function socially. The foundation had taken shape so slowly that she hadn't noticed it, a brick going into place every so often, but now it was suddenly large enough for her to *see* it, and she was puzzled by it.

Self-confidence.

How she had always envied people who had it! Webb and Lucinda both had dynamic, aggressive self-confidence, the type that founded nations and built empires. Gloria was frequently blind to anything but herself, but certain in any case that she knew better than anyone else. Jessie's self-confidence had been monumental. Loyal was confident in his dealings with the animals in his care, and Tansy ruled the kitchen. Even the mechanics at the dealership where she'd bought her car were certain of their ability to fix any mechanical problem.

That slow-forming structure was her own self-confidence. The realization made her eyes widen with mild surprise. She was sure of herself when it came to horses; that had always been true. She'd had the self-confidence, or pure foolhardiness, to confront that awful man in the woods today and force him to stop mistreating that horse.

The sheer force of shock and anger had propelled her into action, a spirit she hadn't realized still lived inside her. The horse had been the catalyst, of course; she loved the animals so much, and it had always sent her into pure rage to see any one of them mistreated. Even so, her own actions shocked her, bringing her face-to-face with a part of herself she had thought long dead, or at least safely dormant. She no longer threw temper tantrums or insisted on having her way about things, but she *did* make her opinions known when it suited her. She kept a great deal of herself private, but that was her own decision, her own way of dealing with heartbreak and keeping pain at bay. She protected herself by not letting herself care, or at least not letting anyone *know* that she cared, and most of the time the appearance of indifference was enough.

She continued staring into the mirror at the face she knew so well, and yet the things she saw beyond it were new, as if she had just opened a door to a different outlook.

People in town treated her with respect, listening when she spoke, however seldom that was. There was even a group of young businesswomen in the Shoals area who regularly invited her for Saturday lunches at Callahan's, not to talk business, but to laugh and joke and . . . be friends. Friends. They didn't ask her to go with them because she was Lucinda's stand-in, or because they wanted to pitch ideas or ask favors of her. They asked her simply because they liked her.

She hadn't realized. Roanna's lips parted in surprise. She was so accustomed to thinking of herself as Lucinda's proxy that she hadn't considered she could be invited somewhere on her own account.

When had this happened? She thought, but couldn't

pinpoint a time. The process had been so gradual that there was no single outstanding incident to mark the occasion.

A sense of peace began to glow deep inside. Webb was going to have Davencourt, just as Lucinda had always planned, but the deep-seated fear Roanna had felt at having to leave its sheltering confines began to fade. She would still leave; she loved him so much that she wasn't sure of her own control where he was concerned. If she stayed, she would likely end up creeping into his bed some night and begging him to take her again.

She didn't want that. She didn't want to embarrass him, or herself. This newfound sense of worth was too new, too fragile, to survive another devastating rejection.

She began to think of where she would go, what she would do. She wanted to stay in the Shoals area, of course; her roots were generations deep, centuries strong. She had money of her own, inherited from her parents, and she would still inherit part of Lucinda's estate even though the bulk of it would go to Webb. She could do anything she wanted. The thought was liberating.

She wanted to raise and train horses.

When Lucinda died, the debt of gratitude that had been incurred when a terrified, grief-stricken seven-year-old had heard her grandmother say that she could come live with her would be paid. It was a debt of love, too, as strong as that of gratitude. It had kept her at her grandmother's side, gradually becoming Lucinda's legs and ears and eyes as her health grew fragile with age. But when Lucinda was gone, and Davencourt safely in Webb's capable hands, Roanna would be free.

Free. The word whispered through her, as gossamer as a butterfly's wing when it is newly emerged from the cocoon.

She could have her own home, something that was solely hers, and she would never again be dependent on anyone else for the roof over her head. Thanks to Lucinda's training, she now understood investments and finances; she felt confident that she was capable of managing her own money, so that she would always be secure. She would raise her own horses, but that would only be a sideline. She would go into business for herself as a trainer; people would bring their horses to her for schooling. Even Loyal said that he'd never seen anyone better able to gentle a frightened or misused animal, or even one that was just plain cussed.

She could do it. She could make a go of it. And for the first time in her life, she would be living for herself.

The grandfather clock in the foyer gonged softly, the sound barely audible here at the back of the huge house. Startled, she glanced at her own clock and saw that it was supper time, and she still wasn't dressed. The nap she had planned to take was impossible now with adrenaline still humming through her veins, so she might as well eat.

Hurriedly she went to her closet and took out the first outfit that came to hand, silk slacks and a matching sleeveless tunic. The pants would hide the scratches on her legs, and that was all she cared about. She knew how to choose flattering and appropriate clothes now, but had never learned to take pleasure in clothing.

"I'm sorry I'm late," she said as she entered the dining room. Everyone was already seated; Brock and Corliss were the only ones absent, but then they seldom ate supper at home. Brock spent what time he could with his fiancée, and God only knew where Corliss spent her time.

"What time did you get home?" Webb asked. "I didn't hear you come in." His eyes were narrowed on her just the way he'd looked at her when she was a kid and he'd caught her trying to slip in unnoticed.

"About five-thirty, I think." She hadn't noted the exact time, because she had still been so upset. "I went straight upstairs to take a shower before supper."

"The heat is so sticky, I have to shower twice a day," Lanette agreed. "Greg's company wanted to transfer him to Tampa. Can you imagine how much worse the humidity is down there? I simply couldn't face it."

Greg glanced briefly at his wife, then returned his attention to his plate. He was a tall, spare man who seldom spoke, wore his graying hair in a crew cut, and to Roanna's knowledge did nothing for fun or relaxation. Greg went to work, came home with more work in his bulging briefcase, and spent the hours between supper and bedtime hunched over paperwork. So far as she knew, he was one of a horde of pencil pushers in middle management, but suddenly she realized that she didn't really know what he did at work. Greg never talked about his job, never related funny stories about his co-workers. He was simply there, a dinghy dragged along in Lanette's wake.

"A lateral transfer?" Webb asked, his cool green gaze flicking from Greg to Lanette and back again. "Or a promotion?"

"Promotion," Greg said briefly.

"But it meant moving," Lanette explained. "And the living expenses would be so much higher that we'd have been *losing* money on that so-called promotion. He turned it down, of course."

Meaning she had flatly refused to move, Roanna thought as she methodically applied herself to the chore of eating. Living here at Davencourt, they had no housing expenses, and Lanette used the extra money to swan around in the best social circles. If they moved, they would then have to provide their own roof, and Lanette's standard of living would suffer.

Greg should have gone and left Lanette to follow or not, Roanna thought. Like herself, he needed to break away from Davencourt and have a place of his own. Maybe Davencourt was *too* beautiful; it was more than just a house to the people who lived here, it was almost a being in and of itself. They wanted to possess it, and instead it possessed them, holding them captive with the knowledge that, after Davencourt, no other home could be as grand.

But she would break away, she promised herself. She had never thought she could possess Davencourt, so she wasn't bound here by envy's chains. Fear had held her here, and duty, and love. The first reason was already gone, and the remaining two would soon follow, and she would be free.

After supper, Webb said to Lucinda, "If you aren't too

tired, I want to talk to you about an investment I've been considering."

"Of course," she said, and they walked together to the dining room door.

Roanna remained at the table, her expression blank. She forked up one last bite of the strawberry shortcake Tansy had served for dessert, forcing herself to eat that one even though she wanted it no more than she had the ones preceding it.

Webb paused at the door and looked around, a slight frown pulling his dark brows together as if he'd just realized she wasn't with them. "Aren't you coming?"

Silently she got up and followed them, wondering if he'd really expected her to automatically assume she was included, or if she was an afterthought. Probably the latter; Webb had always been accustomed to discussing his business decisions with Lucinda, but for all the things he'd said about wanting Roanna to continue with her present responsibilities, he didn't think of her as having any authority.

He was right, she thought, ruthlessly facing the truth. She had no authority beyond what either he or Lucinda granted her, which wasn't true authority. Either of them could pull her up short at any time, divest her of even the semblance of power.

They entered the study and took their accustomed seats: Webb at the desk that had so recently been hers, Roanna in one of the wing chairs, Lucinda on the sofa. Roanna felt jittery inside, as if everything had been jostled, switched around. The past couple of hours had been filled with a series of insights into her own character, nothing great and dramatic but nevertheless small explosions that left her feeling as if nothing was the same, and hadn't even been as she had always perceived it.

Webb was talking, but for the first time in her life Roanna wasn't hanging on his every word as if it came from the lips of God Almighty himself. She barely even heard him. Today she had faced down a brute, and realized that people liked her for herself. She had made a decision concerning the rest of her life. As a child she had been helpless to control her life, and for the past ten long years she had let life pass her by, withdrawing to a safe place where she couldn't be hurt. But now she *could* control her life; she didn't have to let things happen as other people dictated, she could set her own course, make her own rules. The feeling of power was both heady and frightening, but the excitement of it was undeniable.

"—a sizable investment on our part," Webb was saying, "but Mayfield has always been reliable."

Roanna's interest suddenly focused, caught by the name Webb had just mentioned, and she remembered the gossip she had heard just that afternoon.

Lucinda nodded. "It sounds interesting, though of course—"

"No," Roanna said.

Silence settled over the room, complete except for the muted ticking of the old mantel clock.

It was difficult to tell who was the most startled, Lucinda, Webb, or Roanna herself. She had sometimes thought Lucinda should rethink a decision, and quietly given her reasoning, but she had never openly, flatly disagreed. The no had just popped out. She hadn't even couched it in let's-think-it-over terms, but stated it definitely, firmly.

Lucinda sat back on the sofa, blinking a little in surprise. Webb swiveled his chair a little so he was looking directly at Roanna and merely stared at her for a long moment that strained every nerve in her body. There was a strange glitter in his eyes, bright and hot. "Why?" he finally asked, his tone soft.

Roanna desperately wished that she'd kept her mouth shut. That impulsive no had been based on gossip she'd heard that afternoon at the music festival organizational meeting. What if Webb listened to her, then gave her the condescending smile of an adult listening to a child's improbable but amusing scenario, and turned back to his discussion with Lucinda? The precious new sense of confidence would wither inside her.

Lucinda had grown accustomed to listening to Roanna's observations, but Roanna had always offered them as simply that, and left the final decision to her grandmother. Never before had she flatly said, "No."

"Come on, Ro," Webb coaxed. "You watch people, you notice things we don't. What do you know about Mayfield?"

She took a deep breath and squared her shoulders. "It's just what I heard today. Mayfield desperately needs money. Naomi left him yesterday, and the word is she's asking for a huge settlement, because she caught him in the laundry room with one of Amelia's college friends who's been visiting for a couple of weeks. Moreover, according to gossip, the hanky-panky has been going on since Christmas, and it appears that the college friend, who is all of nineteen, is four months pregnant."

There was an oasis of silence, then Lucinda said, "As I remember, Amelia did have her friend over for the Easter holidays."

Webb snorted, a grin widening his mouth. "Sounds as if Mayfield had his own personal arising, doesn't it?"

"Webb! Don't be blasphemous!" But for all her genuine shock at the comment, Lucinda's sense of humor had a bawdy streak, and she fought a smile as she cast a quick, concerned glance at Roanna.

"Sorry," Webb promptly apologized, though his eyes continued to sparkle. He had caught the look Lucinda gave Roanna, as if she were alarmed that Roanna should hear something off-color. It was an old-fashioned attitude, that a virgin, no matter what her age, should be shielded from sexual innuendo. That Lucinda still considered Roanna a virgin meant that there hadn't been any romantic interests at all in Roanna's life, even in college.

Lucinda had been absolutely correct, Webb thought, his heart beating fast as an image of that night in Nogales flashed through his mind. Roanna *had* been a virgin, until roughly one hour after she had walked up to him in that bar. It had taken him about that long to have her stripped, spread, and penetrated.

The memory shimmered through him like soft lightning, heating every nerve ending, making him ache. The feel of her soft, slender body beneath him had been . . . perfect. Her breasts, round and delicious and so delicately formed . . . perfect. The hot, tight sheathing of his cock . . . perfect. And the way her arms had wound so trustingly around his neck, the way her back had arched, the blind, exalted expression on her face as she came . . . God, it had been so perfect it left him breathless.

His dick was hard as a spike. He shifted uncomfortably in the chair, glad that he was sitting behind the desk. That's what he got for letting himself think of that night, of the utter ecstasy of coming inside her. Which he had, he realized. Several times, in fact. And not once had he used a rubber.

He'd never before in his life been so careless, no matter how much he'd had to drink. The fine hairs stood up on his body as an almost electrical thrill ran through him. The thought of birth control hadn't once entered his mind that night; with primal male instinct he had taken her time and again, imprinting himself on her flesh, and in the most primitive claiming he had spurted his semen into her. During those long hours, his body had taken control from his mind, not that his mind had been in top form anyway. The flesh had no conscience; with instincts formed over thousands of years, he had claimed her as his own and sought to forge an unbreakable bond by making her pregnant, so that their two selves would mingle into one.

It was an effort to keep his face impassive, not to leap up and grab her, demand to know if she carried his child. Hell, it hadn't even been two weeks yet; how could she know?

"Webb?"

Lucinda's voice intruded on his consciousness, and he wrested his thoughts from the shattering direction they had taken. Both Lucinda and Roanna were watching him. Roanna's expression was as calm and remote as usual, but at that moment he was so acutely attuned to her that he thought he could see a hint of anxiety in her eyes. Did she expect him to dismiss what she'd said as mere gossip? Was she waiting so impassively for one more blow to her self-esteem?

He rubbed his chin as he regarded her. "What you're saying is that Mayfield's personal life is a mess, and you think he's so desperate for money that he isn't using good judgment."

She held his gaze. "That's right."

"And you heard all this at your meeting today?"

Solemnly she nodded.

He grinned. "Then thank God for gossip. You've probably saved us from a big loss—Mayfield, too, come to that, because he needs our backing to swing the deal."

Lucinda sniffed. "I doubt Burt Mayfield will feel very grateful, but his personal mess is his own fault."

Roanna sat back, a little dizzy at the ease with which they had both accepted her analysis. Her emotions were so unsteady that she didn't know how to act, what to do, so she sat quietly and did nothing. Occasionally she could feel Webb look at her, but she didn't let herself meet his gaze. Her feelings were too close to the surface right now, her control too tenuous; she didn't want to harass him and embarrass herself by staring at him with doglike devotion. The stress of the past few hours was taking its toll on her anyway; the adrenaline high had faded, and she was dreadfully tired. She didn't know if she could sleep; in fact she was so tired that she was afraid she *would* sleep, because it was when she was most exhausted and finally fell into a deep sleep that the sleepwalking episodes occurred. But sleep or not, she very much wanted to lie down, just for a while.

Then suddenly Webb was beside her, his hand on her arm as he lifted her to her feet. "You're so tired you're wobbling in your chair," he said in an abrupt tone. "Go on up to bed. Mayfield's proposal was all we needed to discuss."

Just that small touch was enough to make Roanna want to lean into him, rest against his strength, feel the heat and hardness of his body against her one more time. To keep from giving in to the impulse, she made herself move away from him. "I am tired," she admitted quietly. "If you're sure that's all, I'll go upstairs now."

"That's all," Webb said, a frown pulling his eyebrows together.

Roanna murmured a good-night to Lucinda and left the room. Webb watched her go with narrowed eyes. She had pulled away from him. For the first time in his memory, Roanna had avoided his touch.

"Will she sleep?" he asked aloud, not looking at Lucinda.

"Probably not." She sighed. "Not much, anyway. She seems . . . oh, I don't know, a bit edgy. That's the most she's put herself forward in years. I'm glad you listened to her instead of just shrugging it off. I had to teach myself to pay attention to what she says. It's just that she notices so much about people, because they do all the talking and she just listens. Roanna picks up on the little things."

They chatted for a few minutes longer, then Lucinda carefully rose from the couch, proudly refusing to reveal the difficulty of the movement. "I'm a bit tired, too," she said. "My days of dancing 'til dawn are over."

"I never had any," Webb replied wryly. "There was always work to be done."

She paused, watching him with a troubled look. "Was it too much?" she asked suddenly. "You were so young when I gave Davencourt to you. You didn't have time to just be a boy."

"It was hard work," he said, shrugging. "But it was what I wanted. I don't regret it." He had never regretted the work. He'd regretted a lot of other things but never the sheer exhilaration of pushing himself, learning, accomplishing. He hadn't done it just for Davencourt, he'd done it for himself, because he'd gotten off on the power and excitement of it. He'd been the golden boy, the crown prince, and he'd reveled in the role. He'd even married the princess, and what a disaster that had turned out to be. He couldn't blame Lucinda for that even though she had happily promoted his and Jessie's marriage. It was his own blind ambition that had led him willingly to the altar.

Lucinda patted his arm as she passed, and he watched her, too, as she left the room, noting the care with which she took each step. She was either in pain or far weaker than she wanted anyone to guess. Because she wouldn't want anyone to fuss over her, he let her go without comment.

He sighed, the sound soft in the quiet of the room. Once this room had been his own domain, and bore the uncompromising signs of purely masculine use. Not much had been changed other than the addition of the computers and fax, because Davencourt wasn't a house given to swift or dramatic changes. It aged subtly, with small and gradual differences. This room, however, now seemed softer, more feminine. The curtains were different, lighter in color, but it was more than that. The very scent of the room had changed, as if it had absorbed the inherent sweetness of female flesh, the perfumes and lotions Lucinda and Roanna had used. He could detect very plainly Lucinda's Chanel; it was all she had worn in his entire memory. Roanna's scent was lighter, sweeter, and was strongest when he was sitting at the desk.

The faint perfume lured him. He resumed his seat at the desk and shuffled through some papers but after a few minutes gave up the pretense and instead leaned back, frowning as his thoughts settled on Roanna.

She had never pulled away from him before. He couldn't get that out of his mind. It disturbed him deep inside, as if he'd lost something precious. He'd sworn he wouldn't take advantage of her; hell, he'd even felt a bit noble about it, because he'd been denying himself something he really wanted: her. But she was so damn *remote,* as if that night in Nogales had never happened, as if she hadn't spent her childhood years tagging along at his heels and beaming worshipfully up at him.

She was so self-contained, so closed in on herself. He kept looking at her with a grin, expecting her to grin back in one of those moments of humor they had always shared, but her smooth, still face remained as solemn as always, as if she had no more laughter in her.

His thoughts moved back to their lovemaking. He wanted to see Roanna smile again, but even more than that, he wanted to know if his baby was inside her. As soon as he could manage it, he was going to have a private conversation with her—something that might prove to be more difficult than he'd ever imagined, given the way she'd begun avoiding him.

The next afternoon, Roanna sighed as she leaned back in the big leather chair, massaging her neck to relieve the stiffness. A neat stack of addressed invitations was on one corner of the desk, but a glance at the guest list told her that there was at least a third of the envelopes still to be addressed.

Once Lucinda had gotten Webb's okay for the party, she had begun making her battle plans. Everyone who was anyone had to be invited, which put the guest list at a staggering five hundred people. A crowd that size simply wouldn't fit into the house, not even a house as large as Davencourt, unless they wanted to open up the bedrooms. Lucinda had been unfazed; they would simply throw open the French doors onto the patio, string lights in the trees and shrubbery, and let people wander in and out as they chose. The patio was better for dancing anyway.

Roanna had begun work immediately. There was no way Tansy could handle preparing food for that many people, so she had set herself to locating a caterer who could handle that size party on such short notice, because the date Lucinda had selected was less than two weeks away. She had chosen that date intentionally, not wanting to give people time to deliberate too much, but time enough to buy new dresses and schedule appointments with hairdressers. The few caterers in the Shoals area were already booked for that date, so Roanna had been forced to hire a firm from

Huntsville that she'd never dealt with before. She only hoped everything worked out okay.

There was a ton of decorations stored in the attic and hundreds of strands of lights, but Lucinda had decided that only peach-colored lights would do because it would be such a mellow, flattering color for everyone. There were no peach lights in the attic. After a dozen phone calls, Roanna had tracked some down at a specialty store in Birmingham, and they were shipping the lights overnight.

There weren't enough chairs, even allowing for the people who would be dancing or milling around rather than sitting. More chairs had to be brought in, a band had to be hired, flowers had to be ordered, and a printer had to be found who could print the invitations *immediately*. That last accomplished, Roanna was now occupied with addressing the envelopes. She had been doing it for the past three hours, and she was exhausted.

She could remember Lucinda doing this chore years ago. Once she had asked why Lucinda didn't hire someone to do it, because it had seemed so horribly boring, having to sit for hours and address hundreds of envelopes. Lucinda had replied haughtily that a lady took the trouble to personally invite her guests, which Roanna had taken to mean it was one of those old southern customs that would continue no matter how illogical. She had promised herself at the time that *she* would never do something so boring.

Now she patiently worked through the guest list. The job was still boring, but she understood now why customs continued; it gave one a sense of continuity, of kinship with those who had gone before. Her grandmother had done this, as had her great-grandmother, her great-great-grandmother, going back an unknown number of generations. Those women were a part of her, their genes still living in her, though it looked as if she would be the end of the line. There had only ever been one man for her, and he wasn't interested. End of story, end of family.

Roanna resolutely pushed all thoughts of Webb out of her

mind so she could concentrate on the job at hand. She was accustomed to doing any paperwork at the desk, but Webb had been working there that morning. She still felt a tiny shock whenever she saw him sitting in the chair she had come to regard as *hers,* a shock that had nothing to do with the surge of joy she always felt at the very sight of him.

She had retreated to the small, sunny sitting room at the back of the house, because it was the most private, and began writing at the escritoire there. The chair had proven to be an instrument of torture to one sitting in it for longer than fifteen minutes, so she had gotten a lap desk and moved to the sofa. Her legs had gone to sleep. When Webb had left after lunch to visit Yvonne, with relief Roanna had taken advantage of his absence to work in the study. She settled into the chair, and everything felt just right. The desk was the right height, the chair was comfortable and familiar.

She had *belonged* in this chair, she thought. She refused to let herself feel resentment, however. She had felt needed here for the first time in her life, but soon she would have something that belonged solely to her. Lucinda's death would be the end of one part of her life and the beginning of another. Why fret over this symbol of power when she would soon be moving on anyway? Only to Webb could she have given it up without heartbreak, she thought, because all of this had been promised to him long before she assumed, by default, the stewardship of Davencourt.

There was a great deal of difference between handling financial paperwork and addressing envelopes, at least in the significance of it, but the physical requirements were the same. Working at last in relative comfort, she let her mind slip into neutral as she worked through the invitations.

At first she was scarcely aware of the fatigue creeping through her body, she was so accustomed to it. She forced herself to ignore it and carefully wrote out a few more addresses, but suddenly her eyelids were so heavy she could barely hold them open. Her fears for the past two nights that she would fall deeply asleep and sleepwalk had been groundless; despite the fatigue that dragged at her, she had merely dozed in fits and starts, managing to get perhaps a total of two hours' sleep each night. Last night, again, she had been almost painfully aware of Webb's presence next door, and she had awakened herself several times listening for his movements.

Now she became aware of how quiet the house was. Webb was gone, and Lucinda was napping. Greg and Brock were both at work. Gloria and Lanette might be against having the party, but they had both gone shopping for new dresses, and Harlan had gone with them. Corliss had left right after breakfast, with a careless "I'll be back later," and no indication where she was going.

Despite the efforts of the air-conditioning, the study was warm from the fierce summer sunlight pouring through the windows. Roanna's eyelids drooped even more and closed completely. She always tried not to nap during the day because that only made it more difficult for her to sleep at night, but sometimes the fatigue was overpowering. Sitting there in the warm, quiet room, she lost the battle to stay awake.

Webb noticed when he pulled into the garage that Roanna's car was in its bay, and Corliss had returned as well, but Gloria and Lanette were still out shopping. It was the presence of Roanna's car, however, that caused a hot little thrill of anticipation to shoot through him. She'd had afternoon meetings both days since he'd come home, and he had half-expected her to be gone this afternoon, too, even though she hadn't said anything about an appointment. In the tightly knit structure of small towns, business and social obligations often overlapped, with the former being conducted at the latter. Until he was fully integrated into county society again, Roanna would have to fulfill those obligations by herself.

Somehow he hadn't expected that he would see so little of her. In the past, Roanna had always been right on his heels no matter what he was doing. When she'd been seven or eight, he'd actually had to keep her from following him into the bathroom, and even then she had huddled in the hallway waiting for him. Back then, of course, she had just lost her parents and he had been her only security; the frantic clinging had gradually ceased as she adjusted. But even when she'd been a teenager, she'd always been right there, her homely little face turned up to him like a sunflower to the sun.

But she wasn't homely now; she had grown into a striking woman with the sort of strong, chiseled bone structure that wouldn't yield much to age. He'd braced himself to resist constant temptation; he couldn't take advantage of her heartbreaking vulnerability just to satisfy his lust. Damn it all to hell, though, instead of being vulnerable she was downright remote with him, and most of the time she wasn't even around. It was as if she actively avoided him, and the realization jolted him deep inside. Was she embarrassed because she'd slept with him? He remembered how closed her expression had been the next morning. Or did she resent it because he was going to inherit Davencourt instead of her?

Lucinda said Roanna had no interest in running Davencourt, but what if she was wrong? Roanna hid so much behind that calm, remote face. Once he'd been able to read her like a book, and now he found himself watching her whenever he could, trying to decipher any flicker of expression that might hint at her feelings. For the most part, though, all he saw was the fatigue that drained her, and the mute patience with which she endured it.

If he'd realized how much trouble this damn party would be for her, he never would have agreed to it. If she was still working on it when he got inside, he was going to put his foot down. Her face had been drawn and wan, and dark circles lay under her eyes, evidence that she hadn't been sleeping. Insomnia was one thing; staying awake at night and working incessantly during the day was something else. She needed to do something she enjoyed, and he thought a long, leisurely ride was just the ticket. Not only did she love riding, but the physical exercise might force her body into sleep that night. He was getting antsy himself; he'd gotten accustomed to spending long hours in the saddle almost every day, and he missed the exercise as well as the soothing company of the horses.

He entered the kitchen and smiled at Tansy, who was humming happily as she meandered around the kitchen, never getting in a hurry or seeming to have any design in her movements, but nevertheless putting together huge, scrumptious meals. Tansy hadn't changed much in all the years he'd known her, he thought. She had to be in her sixties, but her hair was still the same salt and pepper it had been since he'd come to live at Davencourt. She was short and plump, and her kindhearted nature shone out of her blue eyes.

"Lemon icebox pie for dessert tonight," she said, grinning, knowing that it was his favorite. "Be sure you save enough room for it."

"I'll make a point of it." Tansy's icebox pie was so good he could make a meal of it by itself. "Do you know where Roanna is?"

"Sure do. Bessie was just here, and she said Miss Roanna's asleep in the study. I'm not surprised, I'll say that. You could tell just by looking at the poor child that the last few nights have been bad, even worse than usual."

She was asleep. Relief warred with disappointment, because he'd been looking forward to that ride with her. "I won't disturb her," he promised. "Is Lucinda awake from *her* nap yet?"

"I imagine so, but she hasn't come downstairs." Tansy sadly shook her head. "Time's weighing heavy on Miss Lucinda. You can always tell when old folks start going, 'cause they stop eating food they used to love. It's nature's way of winding down, I guess. My mama, rest her soul, loved kraut and wienies better'n anything, but a few months before she passed on she said they just didn't taste good no more, and she wouldn't eat 'em."

Lucinda's all-time favorite food was okra. She loved it

fried, boiled, pickled, any way it could be prepared. "Is Lucinda still eating her okra?" he asked quietly.

Tansy shook her head, her eyes sad. "Said it don't have much taste this year."

Webb left the kitchen and walked silently down the hall. He turned the corner and stopped when he saw Corliss with her back to him, opening the study door and peeking inside. He knew immediately what she was about to do; the little bitch was going to slam the door and awaken Roanna. Fury shot through him, and he was already moving as she stepped back and opened the door wide, as wide as her arm would allow. He saw the muscles in her forearm tighten as she prepared to slam the door with all her strength, and then he was on her, his steely fingers biting into the nape of her neck. She gave a stifled little squeak and froze.

Webb eased the door shut, then dragged her away from the study, still holding her neck in a tight grip. He hauled her head around so that she was looking at him. He'd seldom in his life been more angry, and he wanted to shake her as if she were a rag. On the scale of things, waking Roanna from a nap was nothing more than petty and spiteful, no matter how desperately she needed the sleep. But he didn't give a damn about the scale of things, because Roanna *did* need that nap, and the spitefulness angered him all the more because it was so senseless. Corliss wouldn't accomplish or gain a damn thing by disturbing Roanna; she was simply a bitch, and he wasn't going to put up with it.

Her face was a picture of alarm as she stared up at him, still with her neck arched back in an uncomfortable position. Her blue eyes were rounded with startlement at being caught when she had thought herself alone, but already a sly look was creeping into them as she began trying to figure out a way to slither out of this predicament.

"Don't bother with the excuses," he said bluntly, keeping his voice low so Roanna wouldn't be disturbed. "Maybe I'd better spell things out, so you'll know exactly where you stand. You'd better pray that the wind never catches a door and slams it while Roanna's asleep, or that a stray cat never knocks anything over, and God forbid you should actually forget to be quiet. Because no matter what happens, if you're anywhere on the property, I'm going to blame it on you. And do you know what will happen then?"

Her face twisted as she realized he wasn't going to listen to any of her excuses. "What?" she taunted. "You'll get out your trusty andiron?"

His hand tightened on her neck, making her wince. "Worse than that," he said in a silky tone. "At least from your point of view. I'll throw you out of this house so fast your ass will leave skid marks on the stairs. Is that clear? I have a real low tolerance for parasites, and you're so close to the limit that I'm already reaching for the flea powder."

She flushed a dark, ugly color and tried to jerk away from him. Webb held her, lifting his eyebrows at her as he waited for a response.

"You bastard," she spat. "Aunt Lucinda thinks she can force people to accept you, but they won't ever. They'll be nice to you for her sake, but as soon as she's dead, you'll find out what they think of you. You only came back because you know she's dying, and you want Davencourt and all the money."

"I'll have it, too," he said, and smiled. It wasn't a nice smile, but he didn't feel nice. Contemptuously he released her. "Lucinda said she would change her will if I'd come back. Davencourt will belong to me, and you'll be out on your ass. But you're not only a bitch, you're a stupid one. As it stood before, Roanna was going to inherit instead of me, but you've acted like a malicious spoiled brat to her. Do you think she'd have let you go on living here, either?"

Corliss tossed her head. "Roanna's a wimp. I can handle her."

"Like I said: stupid. She doesn't say anything now because Lucinda's important to her, and she doesn't want her upset. But one way or the other, you'd better be looking for somewhere else to live."

"Grandmother won't *let* you throw me out."

Webb snorted. "Davencourt doesn't belong to Gloria. It isn't her decision."

"It doesn't belong to you yet, either! There's a lot that can happen between now and when Aunt Lucinda dies." She made the words sound like a threat, and he wondered what mischief she was considering.

He was tired of dealing with the little bitch. "Then maybe I'd better add another condition: If you start shooting off your mouth and causing trouble, you're outta here. Now get out of my sight before I decide you're already more trouble than you're worth."

She flounced away from him, sashaying her ass to show him she wasn't scared. Maybe she wasn't, but she should damn sure take him at his word.

He quietly opened the study door to make certain they hadn't awakened Roanna with their argument. He'd tried to keep his voice low, but Corliss hadn't had any such concern, and grimly he promised himself that she'd be out on the street tonight if Roanna's eyes were open.

But she still slept, curled in the big office chair with her head tucked into the wing. He stood in the doorway, watching her. Her dark chestnut hair was tousled around her face, and sleep had brought a delicate flush to her cheeks. Her breasts moved up and down in a slow, deep rhythm.

She had slept like that the night they'd spent together—what time he'd let her sleep. If he'd know then how rare real, restful sleep was for her, he wouldn't have awakened her all those times. But afterward, each time, she had curled in his arms just that way, with her head pillowed on his shoulder.

A sharp pang of longing went through him. He'd like to hold her that way again, he thought. She could sleep in his arms for as long as she wanted.

CHAPTER

16

Corliss was shaking as she climbed the stairs, but the trembling was as much inside as out. She needed something, fast. She hurried into her suite and locked the door, then began to frenziedly search all of her favorite hiding places: inside the tiny rip in the lining on the bottom of the sofa, the empty cold cream jar, the bottom of the lamp, the toe-shapers for her shoes. She found exactly what she'd known she would find, nothing, but she needed a fix bad enough that she looked anyway.

How dare he talk to her like that? She'd always hated him, hated Jessie, hated Roanna. It simply wasn't fair! Why should they get to live at Davencourt while she had to live in that stupid little house? All of her life she'd been looked down on at school as the Davenports' poor relation. But sometimes good things did happen, like when Jessie was killed and Webb blamed for it. Corliss had silently celebrated; God, it had been so hard to keep from laughing at that turn of events! But she had made all the proper noises, looked properly sad, and when Webb had left, pretty soon things had fallen into place and her family had moved into Davencourt, where they should have been all those years anyway.

She'd had a lot of friends then, people who knew how to really party, not the snooty my-great-great-granddaddy-fought-in-the-War crowd, the ones who wore pearls and the men didn't cuss in the ladies' presence. What bullshit. Her friends knew how to have *fun*.

She'd been smart, she'd stayed away from the hard drugs. No mainlining for her, no sirree. That shit would kill you. She liked booze, but she *loooved* that sweet white powder. One snort, and no worries; she felt on top of the world, the best, the prettiest, the sexiest. Once she'd been so damn sexy that she'd taken on three guys, one after the other, then all three together, and worn them all out. It'd been great, she'd been fantastic, she'd never had sex like that since. She'd like to do it again, but it took more to fly now, and really she'd rather enjoy that than concentrate on screwing. Besides, a couple of times she'd had a little problem a month or so later, and she'd had to go to Memphis where no one knew her to have it taken care of. Wouldn't do to have a bun in the oven ruining her fun.

But all of her little hiding places were empty. She didn't have any coke, and she didn't have any money. Desperately she roamed the suite, trying to think. Aunt Lucinda always kept a good bit of money in her purse, but the purse was in her bedroom and the old lady was still in her suite, so she couldn't get at it. Grandmother and Mama had gone shopping, so they would have taken all their cash with them. But Roanna was asleep in the study . . . Corliss laughed to herself as she slipped from her rooms and hurried down the hallway to Roanna's room. Guess it was a good thing Webb had kept her from slamming that door after all. Let dear little Roanna sleep, the stupid bitch.

Silently she entered Roanna's bedroom. Roanna always put her purses away in the closet like a good little girl. It took Corliss only a moment to filch Roanna's wallet and count the money. Only eighty-three bucks, damn it. Even someone as dense as Roanna would notice if a couple of twenties went missing. She seldom bothered searching

Roanna's purse for that reason, because Roanna didn't normally carry much cash.

She eyed the credit cards but resisted the temptation. She would have to sign for a cash advance on them, and anyway the bank teller might know she wasn't Roanna. That was the trouble with hick towns, too many people knew your business.

The automatic teller bank card was something else, though. If she could just find Roanna's PIN . . . Swiftly she began pulling scraps of paper out of the little pockets of the wallet. No one was supposed to write down their PIN, but everyone did. She found a slip of paper, neatly folded, with four numbers on it. She snickered to herself as she took an ink pen from the bottom of Roanna's purse and scribbled the numbers on her palm. Maybe it wasn't the PIN, but so what? All the machine would do was not give her the money, it wasn't as if it would call Roanna and tell on her.

Smiling, she slipped the bank card into her pocket. This was better than sneaking a twenty here and a twenty there. She'd get a couple of hundred, put the card back before Roanna missed it, and have some fun tonight. Hell, she'd even put the transaction slip in the folder where Roanna kept things like that; that way, there wouldn't be a discrepancy when the bank statement came out. This was a good plan; she'd have to use it again, though it would be smart to use Aunt Lucinda's card occasionally, if she could get it, and alternate rather than using the same one all the time. Variety was the spice of life. It also cut down on her chances of getting caught, which was the most important thing; that, and getting money.

By eight o'clock that night, Corliss felt much better. After hitting the automatic bank machine, it had taken her some time to find her regular supplier, but at last she had located him. The white powder beckoned, and she wanted to sniff it all up at once, but she knew it would be smarter if she rationed it, because there was no telling how often she would be able to sneak a bank card. She allowed herself just a single line, enough to take the edge off.

Then she was in the mood for fun. She hit her favorite bar, but none of her friends were there, and she sat by herself, humming a little. She ordered her favorite drink, a strawberry daiquiri, which she liked because it packed quite a punch the way the bartender made them for her but still looked like one of those cute drinks it was okay for a nice girl to drink.

The longer she sat there, though, the more her mood darkened. She tried to hang on to the drug-induced euphoria, but it faded as it always did, and she wanted to cry. The daiquiri was good, but the alcohol didn't work the same way coke did. Maybe if she got a real buzz on, it would help.

The hour dragged past, and still none of her friends came in. Had they gone somewhere else tonight and not told her? She felt a sense of panic at being abandoned. Surely no one had heard that Webb had threatened to throw her out of Davencourt, not yet.

Desperately she sipped the daiquiri, trying not to stick herself in the eye with the stupid little turquoise paper parasol. Either the straw was shorter than usual, or that damn parasol had grown. She hadn't had this kind of trouble with the first two drinks. She glared at the bartender, wondering if he was playing a practical joke on her, but he wasn't even looking at her, so she decided he wasn't.

The carcasses of the other two little paper parasols lay in front of her. One was yellow, the other was pink. Put them all together and she'd have a pretty little parasol bouquet. Whoopee. Maybe she'd save them to put on Aunt Lucinda's grave. That was a thought; by the time the old bat kicked off, she should have enough little parasols collected to make a real pretty wreath.

Or maybe she could stuff them down Webb Tallant's throat. Death by parasol; that had a nice ring to it.

The bastard had scared her half to death this afternoon when he'd grabbed her like that. And the look in his eyes— God! That was the coldest, meanest look she'd ever seen, and for nothing! Little Miss Mealy-Mouth's beauty sleep hadn't been disturbed, and God knows she needed all she could get. Corliss snickered, but her mirth died when she remembered the threats Webb had made.

She *hated* him. Why did he have everything? He didn't deserve it. It had always galled her that he was the chosen favorite when he wasn't any closer kin to Aunt Lucinda than she was. He was mean and selfish, the old bitch was going to give Davencourt to him, and he wasn't going to let her live there after Aunt Lucinda died. It just wasn't fair!

As much as she disliked Roanna, at least Roanna was a real Davenport, and she wouldn't feel as bad if Davencourt went to her. Like hell, she wouldn't. Roanna was a stupid wimp, and she didn't deserve Davencourt either. The only good thing about Roanna having the house was that Corliss knew she could handle Roanna with one hand tied behind her back. She'd have that little mouse so buffaloed Roanna would be handing over money instead of forcing Corliss to sneak it.

But if Aunt Lucinda wasn't going to leave Davencourt to Roanna, then it just wasn't fair that Webb should get it! Aunt Lucinda might not think that Webb had killed Jessie, but Corliss had her own opinion, and it was even stronger after the look she'd seen on his face that afternoon. She had no doubts that he could kill. Why, for a minute she'd thought he was going to kill *her,* and over a little joke she'd been about to play. She'd only been thinking about slamming the door, she hadn't actually done it. But he'd grabbed her and hurt her neck, the bastard.

Someone slid onto the stool beside her. "You look like you need another drink," a smooth masculine voice purred in her ear.

Corliss cast a dismissive glance at the man beside her. He was good-looking enough, she supposed, but way too old. "Get lost, Pops."

He chuckled. "Don't let the gray hair fool you. Just because there's snow on the roof doesn't mean there's no fire in the furnace."

"Yeah, yeah, I've heard it all before," she said, bored. She took another draw on the daiquiri. "You may be too old to cut the mustard, but you can still spread the mayonnaise. Big deal. Beat it—and you can take that any way you like."

"I'm not interested in fucking you," he said, sounding as bored as she had.

She was so shocked by the bluntness that she looked at him then, really looked at him. She saw the thick hair that had gone mostly gray, and a body that was still powerful and in shape even though he had to be in his fifties. It was his eyes that riveted her, though; they were the bluest eyes she'd ever seen, and looking into them was like looking into a snake's eyes: flat, totally devoid of feeling. Corliss shivered, but couldn't help feeling fascinated.

He nodded at the parasols littering the bar. "You've been pouring the booze down pretty fast. Have a bad day?"

"You don't know the half of it," she said, but then laughed. "Things are looking up, though."

"So why don't you tell me about it," he invited. "You're Corliss Spence, aren't you? Don't you live out at Davencourt?"

That was often one of the first questions people asked when meeting her for the first time. Corliss loved the distinction it gave her, the sense of being someone special. Webb was going to take that away from her, and she hated him for it. "Yeah, I live there," she said. "For a while longer, anyway."

The man lifted his glass to his mouth. From the color of the liquid, it looked like straight bourbon. He sipped it as he stared at her with those cold blue eyes. "Looks to me like you'd already be hauling ass out of there. It must be pretty uncomfortable living with a killer."

Corliss thought of Webb's hand biting into the back of her neck, and she shivered. "He's a bastard," she said. "I'll be moving out soon. He attacked me today for no reason!"

"Tell me about it," he urged again, and held out his hand. "By the way, my name's Harper Neeley."

Corliss shook hands with him and felt a little thrill of

fascination. He might be an old guy, but there was something about him that gave her the shivers. For now, though, she was more than willing to tell her new friend anything he wanted to know about how hateful Webb Tallant was.

Roanna wished she hadn't succumbed to the nap that afternoon. It had helped immeasurably at the time, but now she faced another long night. She had come upstairs at ten and gone through the ritual of showering, putting on her nightgown, brushing her teeth, getting in bed, all for nothing. She had known immediately that sleep would be a long time coming, if at all, so she had gotten out of bed and curled up in her chair. She picked up the book she'd been trying to read for the past two nights and finally managed to get interested in it.

Webb came up at eleven, and she snapped off her reading light while she listened to him showering. She watched the splash of light from his room, wondering if he would back between it and the windows so she could see his shadow on the veranda. He didn't; his light went out, and there was silence from the other room.

The light from her lamp attracted mosquitoes, so Roanna always kept her veranda doors closed while she was reading, and she wasn't able to hear if he opened his own doors that night. She sat quietly in the dark, waiting until he'd had time to fall asleep, hoping she might become sleepy herself. She watched the fluorescent hands of her clock move past midnight; only then did she turn her lamp back on and resume reading.

An hour later she yawned and let the book drop into her lap. Even if she couldn't actually sleep, she was so tired that she wanted to lie down. She glanced outside and saw that an evening storm was building; she could see the red arc of lightning, but it was so far away she couldn't hear any thunder. Perhaps if she opened her doors and got into bed, the storm would sweep nearer, bringing the sweet rain with it. Rain was the best sedative, soothing her into what was usually her most restful sleep.

She was so tired that it was a long moment before she realized that lightning wasn't red. There was no storm.

Someone was on the balcony, his darker form barely discernible in the shadows.

He was watching her.

Webb.

She recognized him immediately, so swiftly that she didn't have time to panic at the thought of a stranger on the veranda. He was smoking, and the cigarette glowed in a red arc as he lifted it to his lips. The fiery end burned even brighter when he inhaled, and in the brief flare she could make out the hard outline of his face, the slash of his high cheekbones.

He was leaning against the veranda railing, just outside the frame of light from her windows. A faint, silver light gleamed on his naked shoulders, cast from the stars dotting the night sky. He was wearing dark pants, perhaps jeans, but nothing else.

She had no idea how long he'd been out there, smoking and silently watching her through the glass French doors. She inhaled deeply, her physical awareness of him suddenly so intense that she ached with the force of it. Slowly she nestled her head against the back of the chair and stared back at him. She was acutely aware of her bare flesh beneath the fabric of the modest nightgown: the breasts he had kissed, the thighs he had parted. Was he remembering that night, too?

Why wasn't he asleep? It was almost one-thirty.

He turned and flicked the cigarette over the railing, into the dew-wet grass below. Roanna's gaze automatically followed the movement, the arc of fire, and when she looked back, he was gone.

She didn't hear his doors close. Had he gone back inside, or was he strolling around on the veranda? With her own doors closed, she wouldn't have heard his open or close. She reached up and turned off the lamp, plunging her room into darkness again. Without the light on she could clearly see the balcony, bathed in that faint, silvery starlight. He wasn't there.

She was shaking a little as she crawled into bed. Why had he been watching her? Had there been any intent to it, or had he simply been outside smoking and looked through her windows because her light was on?

Her body ached, and she hugged her arms over her throbbing breasts. It had been two weeks since that night in Nogales, and she yearned to feel his hot, naked flesh against her again, his weight pressing her down into the mattress, moving over her, into her. The soreness left by the loss of her virginity had long since faded, and she wanted to feel him there again. She wanted to go to him in the silence of the night, slip into bed beside him, give him the gift of her own flesh.

Sleep had never been further away.

He gave her a sharp glance when she entered the study the next morning. She had used makeup to mask the dark circles beneath her eyes, but he immediately noted the effort. "It was a bad night for you, wasn't it?" he asked brusquely. "Did you get any sleep at all?"

She shook her head but kept her expression blank so he wouldn't guess at her physical torment. "No, but eventually I'll get tired enough to sleep. I'm used to it."

He closed the file that had been open on the desk, punched the exit key on the keyboard, and turned off the computer. He got to his feet with an air of decision.

"Go change clothes," he ordered. "Jeans and boots. We're going for a ride."

At the word *ride* her whole body was consumed with eagerness and renewed energy. Even as tired as she was, a ride sounded like heaven. A horse moving smoothly beneath her, the breeze flowing over her face, the fresh, heated air soothing her lungs. No meetings, no schedule, no pressure. But then she remembered that there *was* a schedule, and a meeting, and she sighed. "I can't. There's a—"

"I don't care what kind of meeting you have," he interrupted. "Call and tell them you won't be there. Today, you're going to do nothing but relax, and that's an order."

Still she hesitated. For ten years her entire existence had been focused on duty, on taking care of business, on helping fill the gap left by his departure. It was difficult to abruptly turn her back on the foundation of those ten years.

He put his hands on her shoulders and turned her toward the door. "That's an order," he repeated firmly, and gave her a light swat on the rump to send her on her way. It was supposed to be a swat, but instead his touch gentled the motion to a pat. He drew his hand back before it could linger, before his fingers could cup the firm buttock he had just touched.

She stopped at the door and looked back at him. He noted that she was blushing a little. Because he'd patted her ass? "I didn't know you smoked," she said.

"I usually don't. A pack lasts me a month or longer. I end up throwing most of them away because they've gone stale."

She started to ask him why he'd been smoking last night if he didn't normally smoke any more than that but held the words back. She didn't want to pester him with personal questions the way she had when she was a kid. He'd had a lot of patience with her, but now she knew that she'd been a bother to him.

Instead she quietly went upstairs to change clothes, and her heart lifted as she did. An entire day to herself with nothing to do but ride! Pure heaven.

Webb must have called down to the stable, because Loyal was waiting with two horses already saddled. Roanna gave him a shocked look. She'd always taken care of her own horse from the time she'd been big enough to lift a saddle. "I would have saddled him myself," she protested.

Loyal grinned at her. "I know you would, but I thought I'd save you some time. You don't get to ride nearly enough, so I wanted you to have a few extra minutes."

Buckley, her old favorite, was fifteen years old now, and she rode him only on more leisurely trails, over easy terrain.

The horse Loyal had chosen for her today was a sturdy bay, not a streak of lightning, but with legs like iron and a lot of stamina. Webb's horse, she noticed, had much the same characteristics. Loyal evidently figured they were going out for more than a Sunday trot.

Webb came out of one of the stalls where he'd been patting the inhabitant, a frisky yearling who had gotten into rough play with some other yearlings and a kick had opened up a cut on his leg. "Your salve still works magic," he said to Loyal. "That cut looks like it's a week old instead of just two days."

He took the reins from Loyal, and they swung into their saddles. Roanna felt her body change, the old magic sweeping over her muscles the way it always had. Instinctively she aligned herself with the horse's rhythm from the first step he took, his strength flowing upward into her lithe, graceful limbs.

Webb held his horse a pace back from hers, mainly for the pleasure of watching her. She was the best rider he'd ever seen, period. His own horsemanship was of the quality that, had he had the desire, he could have competed successfully in either of the opposing equestrian poles, show jumping or rodeo, but Roanna was better. Sometimes, every decade or so, there would be an athlete on the scene whose grace of movement transcended the sport, turning every meet, game, or competition into a work of art, and that was what it was like to watch Roanna ride. Even when the pace was easy, as it was now, and they were riding simply for the pleasure of it, her body was fluid as she adjusted to and controlled every nuance of the animal's motion beneath her.

Would she look like that if she were riding him? Webb's breath caught. Would her sleek thighs tighten and relax, lifting her, then letting her slide down onto his erection, so that she enveloped him with one smooth motion while her torso moved in that graceful sway—

He cut the thought off as blood rushed to his loins, and he shifted uncomfortably. Getting a hard-on while horseback riding wasn't a good idea, but it was difficult to dispel the image. Every time he looked at her he saw the curve of her buttocks, and he remembered touching them, caressing her, driving deep and hard, and coming inside her with a force that made him feel as if he were exploding.

He was going to do himself a serious injury if he didn't stop thinking about it. He wiped the beads of sweat from his brow and deliberately wrenched his gaze away from her bottom. He looked instead at the trees, the horse's ears, anything except her, until his erection had subsided and he was comfortable again.

They didn't talk. Roanna was so often silent anyway, and now she seemed totally absorbed in the pleasure of the ride and he didn't want to disturb her. He enjoyed the freedom himself. He'd been working almost from the minute he set foot back on Davencourt land, and he hadn't taken the time to acclimate himself. His eyes were accustomed to stark, dramatic mountains and an endless sweep of sky, to cactus and scrub bushes, to clouds of dust and air so clear you could see for fifty miles. He was used to dry, searing heat, to arroyos that would abruptly flood from a rain the day before, far upstream.

He'd forgotten how damn *green* this place was, every shade of green in creation. It soaked into his eyes, into the pores of his skin. The air was thick and hazy with humidity. Hardwoods and evergreens rustled softly in a breeze so slight he couldn't feel it, wildflowers nodded their technicolor heads, birds darted and soared and sang, insects buzzed.

It hit him hard, low down in the gut. He'd developed a real love for Arizona and would never give up that part of his life, but this was *home*. This was where his roots were, sunk generations deep into the rich soil. Tallants had lived here for almost two hundred years, and hundreds of years longer than that if you counted the Cherokee and Choctaw heritage that ran in his family.

He hadn't let himself miss Alabama when he left. He had concentrated solely on the future and what he could build with his own two hands in the new home he'd chosen. But now that he was back, it was as if his soul had revived. He'd handle his family, ill-tempered and ungrateful as some of them were. He didn't like having so many Tallants living off the Davenports and not doing a damn thing to earn their keep. Lucinda was the tie between the Davenports and the Tallants, and when she died . . . He looked at the slim figure riding in front of him. The family hadn't been prolific, and untimely deaths had decimated their ranks. Roanna would be the only surviving Davenport, the last of the line.

No matter what he had to do, he would hold the Davenport legacy intact for her.

They rode for hours, even skipping lunch. He didn't like for her to miss any meals, but she looked so relaxed, with a flush on her cheeks, that he decided it was an acceptable trade-off. He would make certain from now on that she had time for a ride every day if she wanted, and it wouldn't be a bad idea if he applied the same decision to himself.

She didn't bubble over with enthusiasm the way she once would have done, talking nonstop and making him laugh with her quirky, sometimes rowdy observations. That Roanna would never return, he thought with a pang. It wasn't just trauma that had changed her into this controlled, reserved woman; she had grown up. She would have changed anyway, though not to this extent; time and responsibility had a way of transforming people. He missed the mischievous imp, but the woman got to him in a way no one else ever had. This volatile mixture of lust and protectiveness was driving him crazy, the two instincts warring with each other.

He'd stood on the balcony the night before and watched her through the windows while she read. She'd been isolated in a soft pool of light, curled in a huge chair that dwarfed her slender body. The light had picked up the red in her chestnut hair, making it gleam with rich, dark tones. A modest white nightgown had swathed her to her ankles, but he could see the faint shadow of her nipples beneath the cloth, the darkness at the junction of her thighs, and he knew that the gown was all she wore.

He'd known that he could go into her room and kneel down in front of that chair, and she wouldn't protest. He could slide his hands under the gown to cup her bottom and pull her forward. He'd been hard as rock, thinking of it, imagining the feel of her sliding down onto him.

Then she had looked up, as if she'd felt the heat of his thoughts. Her whiskey-brown eyes had been mysterious, shadowed pools as she stared back at him through the glass. Beneath the white cloth, her nipples had hardened into tiny peaks.

Just like that, her body had responded to him. A look. A memory. He could have had her then. He could have her now, he thought, watching her.

Was she pregnant?

It was too soon for her body to show any sign, but he wanted to strip her naked anyway, turn her this way and that with his big hands so he could minutely examine every inch of her in the bright sun, memorize her so that in the future he would be able to tell even the smallest change in her.

He was going to go out of his mind.

Roanna reined in. She felt exhilarated from the ride, but her muscles were telling her that it had been a while since she'd been in the saddle for such a long time. "I need to walk for a while," she said, dismounting. "I'm getting a little stiff. You can go on if you want."

She almost hoped that he would; it was a strain, being alone with him, riding with him in such perfect accord, the way they had before. Relaxed, with her guard down, several times she had almost turned to him with a teasing comment. She had caught herself each time, but the close calls made her nervous. It would be a relief to be alone.

But he dismounted as well and fell into step beside her. Roanna glanced at his expression and just as quickly looked away. His jaw was set, and he was staring straight ahead as if he couldn't bear to even look at her.

Stricken, she wondered what she had done wrong. They walked in silence, the horses clopping along behind them.

She hadn't done *anything* wrong, she realized. They had barely spoken. She had no idea what was bothering him, but she refused to automatically take the blame on herself the way she had always done before.

He put his hand on her arm and drew her to a halt.

The horses stopped, shifting behind them. She gave him a questioning look and went still. His eyes were a deep, intense green, glittering with a heat that had nothing to do with anger. He stood very close to her, so close that she could feel the damp heat of his sweaty body, and his broad chest was rising and falling with hard, deep breaths.

The impact of male lust hit her like a blow, and she swayed. Dazedly she tried to think, to pull back, but something inside her responded of its own volition. *He wanted her!* Happiness bloomed inside her, an internal golden glow that blotted out years of sadness. The reins dropped from her limp fingers, and she surged forward as if pulled by an invisible chain, rising on tiptoe as her arms went around his neck and her soft mouth lifted to his.

He stiffened in her embrace, just for a second, then he too dropped his reins, and his arms went around her, crushing her hard against him. His mouth was just as hard on hers, his tongue plunging deep. He was almost savaging her, the pressure of the kiss bruising her lips, his grip compressing her ribs. She could feel the ridge of his erection grinding against the soft juncture of her thighs.

She couldn't breathe; a giddy blackness began to creep over her consciousness. Desperately she wrenched her mouth away from him, her head falling back like a flower too heavy for its fragile stem. Her body was on fire and she didn't care, didn't care what he did to her, let him take her here, now, on the ground without even a blanket to cover the earth. She had craved his touch, ached for him—

"No!" he said hoarsely, putting his hands on her hips and forcing her away from him. "God damn it, no!"

The shock was as staggering as that blatant look of lust had been. Roanna stumbled, her knees too wobbly to hold her upright. She grabbed her horse's mane, clenching her fingers on the coarse hair and letting the big animal take her weight as she leaned against him. All color washed out of her face as she stared at Webb. "What?" she gasped.

"I told you," he said in a savage tone. "What happened in Nogales won't happen again."

An icy hollow formed in the pit of her stomach. My God, she had misunderstood. She'd misread that expression on his face. He hadn't wanted her at all, he'd been angry about something. She had wanted so desperately for him to want her that she had ignored everything he'd said and listened only to her own eternal, hopeless longing. She had just made a colossal fool of herself, and she thought she would die of shame.

"I'm sorry," she managed to choke out, backing away from him. The well-trained horse backed up, too, keeping pace with her. "I didn't mean—I know I promised—Oh, *God!*" With that despairing wail, she threw herself onto the horse's back and kicked him into a gallop.

She heard him yell something, but she didn't stop. Tears blurred her eyes as she bent over the horse's neck. She didn't think she would ever be able to face him again, and she didn't know if she would ever be able to recover from this final rejection.

Webb stared after her, his own face white, his hands knotted into fists at his side. He cursed himself, using every vicious term he'd ever heard. God, he couldn't have handled that any worse! But he'd been in an agony of desire all day, and when she had thrown herself against him like that, he'd lost it. The red tide of lust had swamped him, and he'd stopped thinking, plain and simply. He'd have pushed her to the ground and taken her right there, pounded her into the dirt, but she had pulled away from him and her head had fallen back as limply as any rag doll's, and he'd realized how roughly he was treating her.

He'd forced her into bed with him in Nogales, using blackmail as a means of slaking his lust for her. This time he'd been about to use brute force. He'd hauled himself back from the edge, but just barely. God, just barely. He had only kissed her, hadn't even touched her breasts or taken off any of her clothes, and he'd been on the verge of orgasm. He could feel the dampness of preliminary semen on his underwear.

And then he'd pushed her away—Roanna, who had already suffered so much rejection that she had withdrawn from everyone rather than give them the power to hurt her again. Only he retained that power, he was her only vulnerability, and with raw, savage frustration blinding him, he had pushed her away. He'd wanted to explain, to say that he didn't want to take advantage of her the way he had in Nogales. He wanted to talk to her about that night; he wanted to ask when her period was due, if she was already late. But the clumsy words that had come out of his mouth had been like a blow to her, and she had fled before he could say anything else.

There was no point in trying to catch her. Her horse wasn't the fastest thing on four legs, but then neither was his. She had the advantage of weighing about half what he did, and being the better rider to boot. Chasing after her would be a wasted effort, and hard on his mount in this heat.

But he had to talk to her, had to say something, anything, that would chase the haunted, empty look from her eyes.

Roanna didn't go back to the house. She wanted only to hide and never have to face Webb again. She felt shredded inside, and the pain was so new and raw that she simply couldn't face anyone.

She knew she couldn't avoid him forever. She was bound to Davencourt for as long as Lucinda lived. Somehow, tomorrow, she would find the strength to see him and pretend that nothing had ever happened, that she hadn't literally thrown herself at him again. Tomorrow she would have her protective shell rebuilt; maybe some cracks would show where she had mended it, but the walls would hold. She would apologize, pretend it hadn't been important. And she would endure.

She stayed away for the rest of the afternoon, stopping at a shady creek to water the horse and let him graze on the soft, fresh grasses nearby. She sat in the shade and blanked her mind, letting the time drip away as she did at night when she was alone and the sleepless hours stretched before her. Anything could be gotten through, one second at a time, if she refused to let herself feel.

But when the purple and lavender shades of twilight began to darken the world around her, she knew she couldn't delay any longer and reluctantly mounted the horse and turned his head toward Davencourt. An anxious Loyal came out to meet her.

"Are you all right?" he asked. Webb must have been in a black mood when he returned, but Loyal didn't ask what had happened; that was her business, and she'd tell him if she wanted. But he did want to know if she was physically okay, and Roanna managed to nod.

"I'm fine," she said, and her voice was steady, if a trifle husky sounding. Odd; she hadn't cried, but still the strain was evident in her tone.

"You go on up to the house," he said, his brow still furrowed with concern. "I'll take care of the horse."

Well, that was twice in one day. Her protective shell must not be as far along in reconstruction as she'd hoped. She was tired enough, devastated enough, that she simply said, "Thanks," and dragged herself toward the house.

She thought about sneaking up the outside stairs again, but somehow that seemed like too much effort. She had sneaked up those stairs too often in her life, she thought, instead of facing things. So she walked up the front steps, opened the front door, took the main stairs. She was halfway up them when she heard the thud of boot heels and Webb said from the foyer, "Roanna, we need to talk."

It took every ounce of strength she had, but she turned to face him. If anything, he looked as strained as she felt. He was standing at the foot of the stairs, his hand on the newel post and one foot on the first step, as if prepared to come after her if she didn't obey. His eyes were hooded, his mouth a grim line.

"Tomorrow," she said, her voice soft, and turned away . . . and he let her go. With every step she expected to hear him coming after her, but she reached the top of the stairs and then her room, unhindered.

She took a shower, dressed, went down for supper. Her instinct was to hide away in her room, just as it had been to take the back stairs, but the time for that was past. No more hiding, she thought. She would face what she had to face, handle what she had to handle, and soon she would be free.

Webb watched her broodingly during supper, but afterward he didn't try to maneuver her into a private conversation. She was tired, more exhausted than she thought she'd ever been before, and though with what had happened weighing on her mind she doubted she would even doze that night, still she wanted to lie down, had to lie down. She said good-night to everyone and returned to her room.

As soon as she stretched out in her comfortable bed, she felt the odd, limp weightiness of drowsiness come over her. Whether it was the ride, the accumulated lack of sleep, the stress, or a combination of all of it, she fell deeply asleep.

She didn't know when Webb silently entered the room through the balcony doors and checked on her, listening to her deep, even breathing to make certain she was asleep, watching her for a while, then leaving as quietly as he had entered. On this night, she wasn't awake to watch the hands on the clock sweep inexorably around.

She didn't remember dreaming; she never did.

In the deepest hour of the night she left her bed. Her eyes were open but strangely unseeing. She walked without haste, without hesitation, to her door and opened it. Her bare feet were sure and silent on the carpet as she drifted down the hall, ghostly in her white nightgown.

She wasn't aware of anything until a sudden bursting pain shot through her head. She heard a strangely distant cry, and then there was only darkness.

CHAPTER

17

Webb bolted out of bed, instantly awake and horribly certain that he'd heard Roanna crying out, but the sound hadn't come from her room. He grabbed up his pants and jerked them on, fastening them as he ran out the door. The cry had sounded as if it came from the direction of the stairs. God, what if she'd fallen down them—

The rest of the family had been awakened, too. He heard a babble of voices, saw lights coming on, doors opening. Gloria poked her head out just as he ran past. "What's going on?" she asked fretfully.

He didn't bother to answer, all his attention focused on getting to the stairs. Then he saw her, lying crumpled like a broken doll in the front hall that ran at a right angle to the stairs. He turned on the overhead light, the chandelier almost blinding in its brilliance, and his heart almost stopped. Blood, wet and dark, matted her hair and stained the carpet beneath her head.

He heard a clatter downstairs, as if someone had stumbled into something.

Webb looked up and saw Brock standing there blinking sleep from his eyes, not quite understanding what was going on. "Brock," he snapped. "There's someone downstairs."

His cousin blinked again, then comprehension cleared his gaze. Without a word he ran down the stairs. Greg didn't hesitate as he followed his son.

Webb knelt beside Roanna and gently pressed his fingers to her neck, hardly daring to breathe. Panic swelled in him like a balloon, suffocating him. Then he felt her pulse throbbing under his fingertips, reassuringly strong, and he went weak with relief. He ignored the rising crescendo of voices around him and gently turned her over. Harlan was blustering, Gloria and Lanette were clinging to each other and making moaning sounds. Corliss stood frozen just outside her bedroom door, her eyes wide with terror as she stared down at Roanna's limp form.

Lucinda struggled through the press of bodies and sank heavily to her knees beside him. Her color was pasty, and her trembling hand dug into his arm. "Roanna," she whispered, her voice catching. "Webb, is she—?"

"No, she's alive." He wanted to say she'd just been knocked out, but her injury could be more serious than that. She hadn't regained consciousness, and the fear was growing in him again. Impatiently he looked at Gloria and Lanette, driving each other into higher levels of hysteria, and dismissed them as useless. His gaze snapped over to Corliss.

"Corliss! Call 911. Get the paramedics out here, and the sheriff." She just stared at him, not moving, and he barked, *"Now!"* She swallowed convulsively and darted back into her suite. Webb heard her voice, high and trembling, as she talked to the 911 operator.

"What happened?" Lucinda moaned, stroking Roanna's face with shaking fingers. "Did she fall?"

"I think she surprised a burglar," Webb said, his voice tight with anger and anxiety, and the fear he was barely holding at bay. He wanted to pick Roanna up in his arms, cradle her against his chest, but common sense told him to let her lie still.

She was still bleeding, her blood soaking into the carpet. A dark red stain was spreading out from where her head lay.

"Corliss!" he yelled. "Bring a blanket and a clean towel!"

She was there in just a moment, stumbling over the blanket she was dragging, and simultaneously struggling to pull on a robe over her rather skimpy silk sleepshirt. Webb took the blanket and carefully tucked it around Roanna, then folded the towel and as gently as possible slipped it under her head, cushioning it from the floor and positioning the pad so that it pressed against the bleeding wound.

"W-will she be all right?" Corliss asked, her teeth chattering from shock.

"I hope so," he said grimly. There was a savage pain in his chest. What if she *wasn't* all right? What would he do?

Lucinda collapsed backward, her legs folding under her. She buried her face in her hands and began sobbing brokenly.

Gloria stopped wailing, the sound ceasing as if it had been cut with a knife. She dropped to her knees beside her sister and put her arms around her. "She'll be all right, she'll be fine," she crooned in reassurance, smoothing Lucinda's white hair.

Roanna stirred, moaning a little as she tried to lift her hand to her head. She didn't have the strength or the coordination, and her arm fell limply back to the carpet. Webb's heart leaped wildly. He picked up her hand and cradled it in his. "Roanna?"

At his tone, Lucinda pulled away from Gloria, frantically scrambling closer. Her expression was both terrified and hopeful.

Roanna took two deep breaths, and her eyelids fluttered open. Her gaze was unfocused, confused, but she was regaining consciousness, and that was what mattered.

Webb had to swallow a lump in his throat. "Roanna," he said again, leaning over her, and with an obvious effort she looked at him, blinking as she tried to clear her vision.

"You're fuzzy," she mumbled.

He could hardly breathe, his heart was pounding so violently. He placed her fingers against his rough cheek. "Yeah, I need to shave."

"Not that," she said, her words slurred. She took another deep breath, as if exhausted. "Four eyes."

Lucinda gulped back her sobs, choked laughter mingling with the tears as she reached for Roanna's other hand.

A tiny frown pulled at Roanna's brow. "My head hurts," she announced in confusion, and closed her eyes again. Her speech was clearer. She tried again to touch her head, but Webb and Lucinda were each holding a hand, and neither of them was inclined to let go.

"I imagine it does," Webb said, forcing himself to speak calmly. "You've got a hell of a bump back there."

"Did I fall?" she murmured.

"I guess so," he replied, not wanting to alarm her until he knew something for certain.

Brock and Greg came panting back up the stairs. Brock was wearing only a pair of jeans, zipped but not snapped, and his sturdy chest gleamed with sweat. He had picked up a poker from somewhere, and Greg had taken the time to get the .22 squirrel rifle from its rack over the fireplace in the den. Webb looked inquiringly at them, and they shook their heads. "He got away," Greg mouthed silently.

Sirens were wailing in the distance. Greg said, "I'd better put this up before the sheriff gets here. I'll let them in." He went back downstairs to return the rifle to its rack, lest he alarm a deputy already on edge with adrenaline.

Roanna tried to sit up. Webb put his hand on her shoulder and pressed her back down, alarmed at how little effort it took to do so. "No you don't. You're going to stay right here until a medic says it's all right for you to move."

"My head hurts," she said again, a bit truculently.

It had been so long since he'd heard that tone in her voice that he couldn't help grinning, despite the terror that had been clawing at his insides and was only now beginning to truly subside. "I know it does, honey. Sitting up will only make it worse. Just lie still."

"I want to get up."

"In a minute. Let the paramedics take a look at you first."

She gave an impatient sigh. "All right." But before the

sirens had wound to a stop outside, she was trying again to sit up, and he knew she was disoriented. He'd seen it before in injured people; the instinct was a primitive one, to get up, keep moving, put distance between yourself and whatever had caused the injury.

He could hear Greg explaining as he led a veritable parade of people up the stairs. There were six paramedics and at least that many deputies, with more arriving, from the sound of the sirens as additional vehicles speeded up the road.

Webb and Lucinda were shouldered to the side as the paramedics, four men and two women, gathered around Roanna. Webb backed against the wall. Lucinda clung weakly to him, trembling, and he put a supporting arm around her. She leaned heavily against him, using his strength, and with dismay he felt how fragile her once strong body felt in his grip.

More deputies arrived, and the sheriff. Booley Watts was retired now, but the new sheriff, Carl Beshears, had been Booley's chief deputy for nine years before being elected sheriff, and he had worked on Jessie's case. He was a compactly muscular man with iron gray hair and cold, suspicious eyes. Booley had operated with a sort of good-old-boy Andy Taylor kind of manner; Beshears was more brusque, straight to the point, though he had learned to temper the bulldog, straight-ahead tactics he'd learned in the marines. He began gathering the family together, ushering them to the side. "Folks, let's get out of the medics' way now, and let them take care of Miss Roanna." His steely gaze lit on Webb. "Now, what happened here?"

Until then, Webb hadn't realized the similarities between what had happened to Roanna tonight and Jessie's death ten years earlier. He had been concentrating on Roanna, terrified for her, taking care of her. The old, cold fury began to build in him as he realized Beshears suspected him of attacking Roanna, perhaps trying to kill her.

He ruthlessly suppressed his anger, though, because now wasn't the time for it. "I heard Roanna scream," he said in as even a tone as he could manage. "The sound came from the front of the house, and I was afraid she'd gotten up without turning on any lights and fallen down the stairs. But when I got here, I saw her lying just where she is now."

"How did you know it was Roanna screaming?"

"I just did," he said flatly.

"You didn't think it could be anyone else in the house who'd gotten up?"

Lucinda gathered herself, galvanized by the obvious suspicion in Beshears's voice. "Not usually," she said in a firm tone. "Roanna suffers from insomnia. If anyone is wandering around the house at night, it's likely to be her."

"But you were awake," Beshears said to Webb.

"No. I woke up when I heard her scream."

"We all did," Gloria put in. "Roanna used to have nightmares, you know, and that's what *I* thought was happening. Webb ran past my door just as I opened it."

"You're sure it was Webb."

"I know it was," Brock put in, squarely facing the sheriff. "I was right behind him."

Beshears looked frustrated, then shrugged, evidently deciding he didn't have a tie between the two events after all. "So, did she fall or what? The dispatcher said it was a call for the paramedics *and* the sheriff's department."

"Just as I got to her," Webb said, "I heard something downstairs."

"Like what?" Beshears's eyes sharpened again.

"I don't know. A crash." Webb looked at Brock and Greg.

"Brock and I went downstairs to take a look," Greg said. "A lamp had been knocked over in the den. I went outside while Brock checked the rest of the house." He hesitated. "I *think* I saw someone running, but I couldn't swear to it. My eyes hadn't adjusted to the dark."

"What direction?" Beshears asked briefly, already beckoning to one of his deputies.

"To the right, toward the highway."

The deputy approached, and Beshears turned to him. "Y'all get some lights and check the yard on the other side of the driveway. There's a heavy dew tonight, so if anybody's been through there, it'll show on the grass. There may have been an intruder in the house." The deputy nodded and departed, taking several of his fellows with him.

One of the paramedics came over. He had obviously leaped out of bed to answer the call; a ball cap covered his uncombed hair, and his eyes were puffy from sleep. But he was alert, his gaze sharp. "I'm pretty sure she's going to be all right, but I want to transport her to the hospital to be checked out and to have that cut in her head stitched up. Looks like she's got a mild concussion, too. They'll probably want to keep her for twenty-four hours, just to make certain she's okay."

"I'll go with her," Lucinda said, but suddenly staggered. Webb grabbed her.

"Lay her down on the floor," the paramedic said, reaching for her, too.

But Lucinda batted their hands away and pulled herself erect once more. Her color still wasn't good, but she glared fiercely at them. "Young man, I will not lie down on the floor. I'm old and upset, that's all. You tend to Roanna and don't pay any attention to me."

He couldn't treat her without her permission, and she knew it. Webb looked down at her and thought about picking her up and carrying her to the hospital himself, bullying her into letting a doctor check her. She must have known what he was thinking, because she looked up and managed a smile. "It's nothing to fret about," she said. "Roanna's the one who needs seeing to."

"I'll go with her to the hospital, Aunt Lucinda," Lanette said, surprising everyone. "You need to rest. You and Mama stay here. I'll go put on some clothes if y'all will gather up the things she'll need."

"I'll drive," Webb said. Lucinda started to protest again, but Webb put his arm around her. "Lanette's right, you need to rest. You heard what the paramedic said, Roanna will be all right. It would be different if she were in danger, but she isn't. Lanette and I will be there with her."

Lucinda clutched his hand. "You'll call me from the hospital, let me talk to her?"

"Just as soon as she's settled," he promised. "They'll have to do X-rays first, I imagine, so it could take a while. And she might not feel like talking," he warned. "She'll have a hell of a headache."

"Just let me know she's all right."

With that, Lucinda and Gloria went down the long hall to the back bedrooms, to gather the personal items Roanna would need for even a short stay in the hospital. Webb and Lanette went to their own rooms to dress. It took him less than two minutes, and he reached Roanna's side just as they were transferring her to a stretcher to carry her downstairs.

She was fully conscious now, and her eyes were wide with alarm as she looked up at him. He took her hand again, folding her cold, slender fingers against his rough, warm palm. "I don't like this," she said fretfully. "If I need stitches, why can't I just drive to the emergency room? I don't want to be *carried.*"

"You have a concussion," he replied. "It's not safe for you to drive."

She sighed and gave in. He squeezed her hand. "Lanette and I are going to be with you. We'll be right behind the ambulance."

She didn't protest again, and he almost wished she had. Every time he looked at her, he was hit by another wave of panic. She was paper white, what part of her face that wasn't covered by blood. The dark, rusty stain was spread over her face and neck, where it had run down from the laceration on her scalp.

Lanette came hurrying down, carrying a small overnight case, just as they were sliding the stretcher into the ambulance. "I'm ready," she said to Webb, already moving past him toward the garage.

Sheriff Beshears fell into step beside Webb. "The boys

found marks in the dew," he said. "Looks like someone took out running across the yard. Somebody's been messing with the lock on the kitchen door, too, there's some scratches on the metal. Miss Roanna's lucky, if she came face-to-face with a burglar and a bump on the head's all she got."

Remembering how she had looked like a crumpled little doll lying in the hall, with blood spreading around her, Webb thought Beshears's definition of *lucky* was different from his own.

"I'll be at the hospital later on to ask her some questions," the sheriff continued. "We'll do some more checking around here."

The ambulance was pulling out. Webb turned away and strode to the garage, where Lanette was waiting for him.

It took several hours and a shift change at Helen Keller Hospital before Roanna had been scanned, stitched, and settled into a private room. Webb impatiently waited in the hallway while Lanette helped her to clean up and get dressed in a fresh nightgown.

The bright morning sun was shining through the windows when he was finally allowed to reenter the room. She was lying in bed, looking almost normal now that most of the blood had been washed away. Her hair was still matted with it, but that would have to be taken care of later. A white pad covered the stitches in the back of her head, and stretchy gauze had been wrapped around her head to hold the bandage in place. She was very pale, but all in all she looked much better.

He eased down on the side of the bed, careful not to jar her. "The doctor told us to wake you up every hour. That's a helluva thing to do to an insomniac, isn't it?" he teased.

She didn't smile as he'd hoped. "I think I'll save you the trouble and just stay awake."

"Do you feel like talking on the phone? Lucinda was frantic."

Carefully she pushed herself higher in the bed. "I'm okay, it's just a headache. Will you dial the number for me?"

Just a headache from a bruised brain, he thought grimly as he picked up the receiver and punched the number for an outside line, then the number at Davencourt. She still thought she'd fallen, and no one had told her any differently. Sheriff Beshears wasn't going to get a lot of information from her.

Roanna talked briefly to Lucinda, just long enough to reassure her that she felt all right, a blatant lie, then gave the phone back to Webb. He was going to give Lucinda his own reassurances, but to his surprise it was Gloria who came on the line.

"Lucinda had another spell after y'all left," she said. "She's too stubborn to go to the hospital, but I've called her doctor and he's going to stop by this morning."

He glanced at Roanna; the last thing she needed to hear right now was that Lucinda was ill. "Keep her in line," he said briefly, and lowered his voice as he turned away so Roanna wouldn't be able to hear him. "I'm not going to say anything to the others now, so don't mention it to them just yet. I'll call in a couple of hours and check on her."

He got off the phone just as Sheriff Beshears came in and tiredly settled himself into one of the two chairs in the room. Lanette was in the other, but Webb wasn't inclined to sit anyway. He wanted to be closer to Roanna's side.

"Well, you're looking better than the last time I saw you," Beshears said to Roanna. "How do you feel?"

"I don't believe I'll go dancing tonight," she said in that solemn way of hers, and he laughed.

"Don't guess you will. I want to ask you a few questions if you feel up to it."

A puzzled look crossed her face. "Of course."

"What do you remember about last night?"

"When I fell? Nothing. I don't know how it happened."

Beshears shot a quick look at Webb, who gave a tiny shake of his head. The sheriff cleared his throat. "The thing is, you didn't fall. It looks like someone broke into Davencourt last night, and we figure you walked right up on him."

If Roanna had been pale before, now she was absolutely

white. Her face took on a pinched, frightened expression. "Someone hit me," she murmured. She didn't say anything else, didn't move. Webb, watching her closely, had the distinct impression she was drawing in on herself, holding everything inside, and he didn't like it. Deliberately he reached out and took her hand, squeezing it to let her know she wasn't alone, and he didn't give a damn what conclusions Beshears drew about his action.

"You don't remember *anything?*" the sheriff persisted, though his gaze flickered briefly to their clasped hands. "I know everything's confused now, but maybe you caught a glimpse of him and you just haven't realized it yet. Let's take it step by step. Do you remember leaving your room?"

"No," she said tonelessly. Her hand was motionless in Webb's grip. Once she would have been clinging to him, but now she didn't hold on to him at all. It wasn't just that she didn't seem to need him anymore, but that she didn't want to even be around him. For a while, when she had been so confused, all the barriers had been down and she had seemed to be comforted by his presence, to need him. But now she was pulling away from him again, putting emotional distance between them even though she made no effort to physically pull away. Because of what had happened between them yesterday, or was it something else, a detail about her injury? Did she remember something after all? Why didn't she want to tell the sheriff?

"What's the last thing you remember?" Beshears asked.

"Going to bed."

"Your folks say you have insomnia. Maybe you were awake, and you heard something and went to see what it was."

"I don't remember," she said. The pinched look was more pronounced.

He sighed and got to his feet. "Well, don't fret about it. A lot of folks don't remember at first what happened right before they took a bump on the noggin, but sometimes it comes back to them after a while. I'll be checking back with you, Miss Roanna. Webb, come on out in the hall with me, and I'll tell you what we've done so far."

Webb went with him, and Beshears strolled down the hall toward the elevators. "We followed the trail through the weeds all the way to that pasture road that cuts off from the highway, just past the turnoff going up to Davencourt," he said. "I figure he left his car parked there, but it's been a couple of weeks since we've had any rain and the ground was too hard for us to get any tread marks. Just to be sure, we brought in a couple of dogs, and they followed the trail as far as the pasture road, too, but nothing after that. It's a good place to hide a car; the brush is so thick anything parked even twenty yards up the road would be damn hard to see even in the daylight, much less at night."

"He got in through the kitchen door?"

"That's what it looks like. We couldn't find any other sign of entry." Beshears snorted. "I thought he was a fool at first, for not going in through some of those fancy glass doors y'all got all over the house, but maybe he was pretty smart. You think about it, the kitchen is the best place. Everyone should be upstairs in bed at that time of night, so he don't want to risk waking anyone by going through any of the upper veranda doors. The doors on the patio are on the side of the house, visible from the stables. But the kitchen door is on the back, and you can't see it from the driveway, the stables, or anywhere else."

They had reached the elevators, but Beshears didn't stop to punch the button to call it. He and Webb strolled on to the end of the hall, out of earshot of anyone getting off the elevator on that floor.

"Was anything taken?" Webb asked.

"Not that anyone can tell. That lamp's knocked over in the den, but except for that and the lock on the kitchen door nothing looks like it was touched. Don't know what he was doing in the den, unless he got rattled when Miss Roanna screamed. I suppose he ran back downstairs, looking for a quick way out, but the front door has a double lock on it and he couldn't figure it out in the dark. He ran into the den, saw it doesn't have an outside door, and accidentally blundered into the lamp. Looks like he finally went out the kitchen door, same as he got in."

Webb roughly ran his hand through his hair. "This won't happen again," he said. "I'll have a security system installed this week."

"Y'all should already have had one." Beshears gave him a look of disapproval. "Booley used to go on and on about how easy it would be to break into that house, but he never could talk Miss Lucinda into doing anything about it. You know how old folks are. With the house so far out of town, she felt safe."

"She didn't want to feel like she was in a fortress," Webb said, remembering the comments Lucinda had made over the years.

"This will probably change her mind. Don't bother with one of the systems that automatically call for help, because y'all are so far out of town it would be a waste of money. Put in a loud alarm that'll wake everyone up, if you want, but remember that wires can be cut. Your best bet is to put good locks on the doors and windows, and get a dog. Everybody should have a dog."

"Lucinda's allergic to dogs," Webb said wryly. He wasn't about to get one now and make her miserable for the few remaining months of her life.

Beshears sighed. "Guess that's why you never had one. Well, forget that idea." They turned and walked back toward the elevators. "Miss Lucinda had another spell after y'all left."

"I know. Gloria told me."

"Stubborn old woman," Beshears commented. They reached the elevators, and this time he punched the button. "Call me if Roanna remembers anything, 'cause otherwise we don't have jack shit."

Roanna rested quietly the remainder of the day, though she was troubled by nausea. The doctor ordered a mild medication to remedy that, and she ate most of her lunch, a light meal of soup and fruit. Lanette was surprisingly good in a sickroom, making sure Roanna had plenty of ice water in the bedside pitcher where she could reach it, and helping her to the bathroom when she needed to go. Otherwise she sat patiently, reading a magazine she'd bought in the gift shop, or watching television with the sound turned low.

Webb was restless. He wandered in and out of the room, moodily watching Roanna's face whenever he was there. Something about her manner bothered him more and more. She was *too* quiet. She had reason to be upset and alarmed, but instead she was showing very little response to anything. She avoided meeting his gaze and pleaded a headache when he tried to talk to her. The nurses checked on her regularly and said she was doing okay, her pupil responses were normal, but still he was uneasy.

He called back twice to check on Lucinda, but both times Lucinda answered the phone herself and wouldn't let him talk to Gloria. "I'm fine," she said crossly. "Don't you think the doctor would have put me in the hospital if anything serious was wrong? I'm old, I have cancer, and my heart isn't what it used to be. What else do you think could be wrong? Frankly, I can't think why I'd bother even taking medicine for a cold."

Both times she asked to talk to Roanna, and both times Roanna insisted that she felt well enough to talk. Webb listened to her side of the conversation and realized how guarded she sounded, as if she were trying to hide something.

Had she seen her assailant after all?

If so, why hadn't she told Beshears? There was no reason he could think of for her to keep something like that secret, no one she would be protecting. She was definitely hiding something, though, and he was determined to find out what. Not right now, not while she was still rocky, but as soon as she was home, he was going to sit her down in a private place for a little talk.

Lanette said she would stay overnight, and Webb finally

left at nine that night. He was back at six-thirty the next morning, though, ready to take Roanna home as soon as she was released. She was ready, already dressed in street clothes and looking much better than she had the day before. Twenty-four hours of enforced rest had done her a lot of good, even under the circumstances.

"Did you sleep any?" he asked.

She shrugged. "As much as anyone does in a hospital, I suppose."

Behind her, Lanette met his eyes and shook her head.

It was after eight when the doctor came in and checked her pupil responses, then smiled and told her to go home. "Take it easy for about a week," he said, "then see your family doctor for a checkup."

Webb drove them home then, easing over every bump and railroad track in an effort not to jar her head. Everyone at home at the time came out to meet her, and his plan to have a private talk with her was soon demolished. He didn't have a chance to be alone with her all day long. She was promptly put to bed, though she complained a bit irritably that she would rather be in her chair, but nothing would satisfy Lucinda except bed rest. Lucinda and Gloria fussed over her, Bessie was in and out at least ten times asking if she was comfortable, and Tansy left her kitchen domain to personally bring up the meal trays she had prepared with Roanna's favorites. Even Corliss stirred herself to visit and uncomfortably ask if she was all right.

Webb kept watch, knowing he'd get his chance.

It didn't come until late that night, when everyone else had gone to bed. He waited in the darkness, watching the veranda, and as he had expected, it wasn't long before a light came on in the next room.

He knew her veranda doors were locked, because he'd locked them himself before leaving her room the last time. He went out into the hallway, where the lights had been left burning at night since Roanna had been hurt, and quietly entered her room.

She had gotten out of bed and was once again ensconced

in that huge, soft-looking chair, though she wasn't reading. He supposed her head still hurt too much for her to do any reading. Instead she'd turned on her television, with the sound so low he could barely hear it.

She looked around with a guilty expression when the door opened. "Caught you," he said softly, shutting the door behind him.

Immediately he caught a hint of uneasiness in her face, before she smoothed her expression to blankness. "I'm tired of being in bed," she explained. "I've rested so much I'm not in the least bit sleepy."

"I understand," he said. She'd been in bed for two days, no wonder she was sick of it. "That isn't what I wanted to talk about."

"I know." She looked down at her hands. "I made a fool of myself day before yesterday. It won't happen again."

So much had happened since then that for a moment he stared blankly at her, then realized she was talking about what had happened when they were riding. He'd been a clumsy idiot, and typically, Roanna was taking the blame for it.

"You didn't make a fool of yourself," he said harshly, walking over to the veranda doors to check them again, just to make certain they were locked. "I didn't want to take advantage of you, and I handled it all wrong." He stood there, watching her reflection in the glass. "But that's something we'll talk about later. Right now, I want to know what it is you aren't telling the sheriff."

She kept her gaze on her hands, but he saw how still she went. "Nothing." He could see the guilt, the discomfort, even in the reflection.

"Roanna." He turned around and went over to her, squatting down in front of the chair and taking her hands in his. She was sitting in what was evidently her favorite position, with her feet pulled up onto the seat and tucked her under nightgown. He looked at the bandage on her head rather than the shadowy peaks of her nipples poking against the white cloth, because he didn't want anything to distract him from what he wanted to find out, and just being close to her was bad enough. "You can fool the others, but they don't know you the way I do. I can tell when you're hiding something. Did you see who hit you? Do you remember more than you're telling?"

"No," she said miserably.

"Then what is it?"

"Nothing—"

"Ro," he said warningly. "Don't lie to me. I know you too well. What are you hiding?"

She bit her lip, worrying it between her teeth, and her golden brown eyes lifted to him, filled with a distress so intense he almost reached out for her in comfort. "I walk in my sleep," she said.

He stared at her, astounded. Whatever he'd been expecting, that wasn't it. "What?"

"I'm a sleepwalker. I guess that's part of the reason I have insomnia," she explained in a soft tone, looking down again. "I *hate* waking up in strange places, not knowing how I got there, what I've done, if anyone has seen me. I only do it when I'm in a deep sleep, so—"

"So you don't sleep," he finished. He felt himself shattering inside as he realized the sheer enormity of the burden she carried, the pressure under which she lived. God, how did she stand it? How did she function? For the first time, he sensed the slender core of pure steel in her. She wasn't little, needy, insecure Roanna any longer. She was a woman, a Davenport, Lucinda's granddaughter, with her share of the Davenport strength. "You were sleepwalking night before last."

She inhaled deeply. "I must have been. I was so tired, I went to sleep as soon as I got in bed. I don't remember anything until I woke up in the hall with a splitting headache and you and Lucinda leaning over me. I thought I *had* fallen, though I've never had any accidents before when I was sleepwalking."

"Jesus." He stared at her, shaken by the image that came to mind. She had walked up to the burglar like a lamb to slaughter, not seeing him even though her eyes had been open. Sleepwalkers *looked* awake, but they weren't. Possibly the burglar even thought she could identify him. Attempted burglary and assault weren't crimes that warranted murder to avoid arrest, but she could be in danger anyway. Not only were new locks going on everywhere, as well as an alarm system that would wake the dead if there was an unauthorized intrusion, but he would make damn certain everyone in the county knew she had a concussion and didn't remember anything about the incident. An article about the attempted burglary had been in the paper, and as a follow-up, he would have that information printed as well.

"Why didn't you tell the sheriff that you walk in your sleep?"

"Lanette was there," she said, as if that were reason enough.

It was, but it took him a moment to think it through. "No one knows, do they?"

She gave a slight shake of her head, then winced and stopped the motion. "It's embarrassing, knowing that I wander around in my nightgown, but it's more than that. If anyone knew . . ."

Again, it didn't take a genius to follow her thoughts. "Corliss," he said grimly. "You're afraid the little bitch would play nasty tricks on you." He rubbed his thumbs over the backs of her hands, feeling the slender, elegant bones just under the skin.

She didn't respond to that, just said, "It's better if no one knows."

"She won't be here much longer." He was glad he could make that promise.

Roanna looked startled. "She won't? Why?"

"Because I told her she'd have to move out. She can stay until Lucinda . . . She can stay for a few more months if she behaves herself. If she doesn't, she'll have to leave before then. Lanette and Greg will have to find another place to live, too. Greg makes good money, there's no excuse for them to be sponging off Lucinda the way they have."

"I think living here was Lanette's decision, hers and Gloria's."

"Probably, but Greg could have said no. I don't know about Brock. I've always liked him, but I didn't expect him to be a moocher."

"Brock has a plan," Roanna explained, and unexpectedly a faint smile touched her pale lips. "He's living here so he can save as much money as possible before he gets married. He's going to build his own house. He and his fiancée have already had an architect draw up the blueprints."

Webb stared at her mouth, enchanted by that tiny, spontaneous smile. He hadn't had to coax that one out of her. "Well, at least that's a plan," he grumbled to hide his reaction. "Gloria and Harlan are in their seventies; I'm not going to make them move. They can live here the rest of their lives if they want."

"I know you don't want the house crammed with relatives," she said. "I'll be moving out, too—"

"You aren't going anywhere," he interrupted harshly, rising to his feet.

She looked at him in bewilderment.

"This is your home, damn it. Did you think I was trying to tell *you* to get out?" He couldn't keep the anger out of his voice, not just at the thought of her leaving, but that she had thought he would want her to.

"I'm just a distant cousin, too," she reminded him. "How would it look for us to be living here together, even with Gloria and Harlan here? It's different now, because the house is so full, but when the others move out people will gossip if I don't, too. You'll want to get married again someday, and—"

"This is your home," he repeated, grinding his teeth together in an effort to keep his voice down. "If one of us has to move out, I will."

"You can't do that," she said, shocked. "Davencourt will be yours. It wouldn't be right for you to leave just so I'll have a place to stay."

"Haven't you ever thought that it should be yours?" he

snapped, goaded beyond endurance. "You're the Davenport. Don't you resent the hell out of me for being here?"

"No. Yes." She watched him for a moment, her eyes shadowed and unreadable as the words lay between them. "I don't resent you, but I envy you, because Davencourt is going to be yours. You were raised with that promise. You shaped your life around taking care of this family, this house. Because of that, you've earned it, and it should be yours. I knew when I went to find you in Arizona that Lucinda would change her will, giving everything to you again; we discussed it beforehand. But even though I envy you, I've never thought of Davencourt as mine. It's been home since I was seven years old, but it wasn't *mine*. It was Lucinda's, and soon it'll be yours."

She sighed, and gingerly rested her head back against the chair. "I have a degree in business administration, but I got it only because Lucinda needed help. I've never been interested in business and finance, while you thrive on it. The only kind of work I've ever wanted to do is train horses. I don't want to spend the rest of my life in business meetings; *you* take that part of it, and welcome to it. I won't be left destitute, and you know it. I have my own inheritance."

He opened his mouth and she held up her hand to stop him. "I'm not finished. When I'm no longer needed here —" She paused, and he knew she was thinking of Lucinda's death, as he did. It was always there, looming in their future whether they could bring themselves to speak openly of it or not. "When it's over, I'm going to set up my own stables, my own house. For the first time something will belong to *me*, and no one else will ever be able to take it away."

Webb's fists clenched. Her gaze was very clear, yet somehow distant, as if she looked back at all the things and people that *had* been taken from her when she'd been too young and helpless to have any control over her life: her parents, her home, the very center of her existence. Her self-esteem had been systematically stripped from her by Jessie, with Lucinda's unknowing assistance. But she had had him as her bulwark until he, too, had turned from her, and since then Roanna had allowed herself to have no one, to care for nothing. She had in effect put herself in dormancy. While her life was on hold she had devoted herself to Lucinda, but that time was coming to an end.

When Lucinda died, Roanna planned to leave.

He glared down at her. Everyone else wanted Davencourt, and they weren't entitled to it. Roanna was legitimately entitled to it, and she didn't want it. *She wanted to leave.*

He was so pissed off that he decided he'd better go back to his room before he really lost his temper, something she wasn't in any shape to endure and that he didn't want to do anyway. He stalked to the door, but paused there for the last word. "We'll work all that out later," he said. "But you are *not* moving out of this house."

CHAPTER
18

*I*t was the day of Lucinda's welcome-home party for him, and as Webb drove home he wondered how big of a disaster it would be. He didn't care, but it would disturb Lucinda a great deal if things didn't go exactly as she had planned. From what he'd experienced that afternoon, things weren't looking good.

It hadn't been much, not even a confrontation, but as a barometer of public sentiment it had been fairly accurate. He'd had lunch at the Painted Lady with the chairman of the agricultural commission, and the comments of the two women behind him had been easily overheard.

"He certainly has a lot of brass on his face," one of the women had said. She hadn't raised her voice, but neither had she lowered it enough to ensure she couldn't be heard. "If he thinks ten years is long enough for us to forget what happened . . . Well, he has another think coming."

"Lucinda Davenport never could see any fault in her favorites," the other woman commented.

Webb had looked across at the commissioner's face, which was turning dark red as the man studiously applied himself to his lunch and pretended he couldn't hear a thing.

"You'd think even the Davenports would balk at trying to force a murderer down our throats," the first woman said.

Webb's eyes had narrowed, but he hadn't turned around and confronted the women. Suspected murderer or not, he'd been raised to be a southern gentleman, and that meant he wouldn't deliberately embarrass the ladies in public. If men had been saying the same things he would have reacted differently, but not only were the two verbal snipers female, they were rather elderly, from the sound of their voices. Let them talk; his hide was tough enough to take it.

But the social matriarchs wielded a lot of power, and if they all felt the same way, Lucinda's party would be ruined. He didn't care for himself; if people didn't want to do business with him, fine, he'd find someone who did. But Lucinda would be both hurt and disappointed, and blame herself for not defending him ten years ago. For her sake, he hoped—

The windshield shattered, spraying Webb with tiny bits of glass. Something hot hummed by his ear, but he didn't have time to worry about it. His reflexive dodge had jerked the steering wheel in his hand, and the right wheels of the car bumped violently as the car veered onto the shoulder of the road. Grimly he fought for control, trying to ease the car back onto the pavement before he hit a hole or a culvert that would send him careening into the ditch. He was effectively blinded by the shattered windshield, which had held together but turned white with a thick webbing of fractures. A rock, he thought, though the truck in front of him had been far enough away that he wouldn't have expected the tires to throw a rock that far. Maybe a bird, but he would have seen something that big.

He got all four wheels back onto the pavement, and the car's handling smoothed. Automatically he braked, looking out the relatively undamaged right side of the windshield in an effort to judge his distance to the shoulder of the road and whether or not he would have enough room to pull off. He was almost to the side road that led to Davencourt's private road. If he could reach the turn off, there wouldn't be as much traffic—

The windshield shattered again, this time farther to the right. Part of the broken glass sagged from the frame, little diamond bits held together by the safety film that prevented the glass from splintering. *Rock, hell,* he thought violently.

Someone was shooting at him.

Quickly he leaned forward and punched the safety film with his fist, tearing it down so he could see in front of him, then he pushed the gas pedal to the floor. The car rocketed forward, the force jerking him back in the seat. If he stopped and gave the shooter a stationary target, he'd be dead, but it was damn hard to make an accurate shot at someone going eighty-five miles an hour.

Remembering that hot humming he'd heard just beside his right ear after the first shot, he made a rough estimate of the trajectory of the first bullet and mentally placed the gunman on a high bank just past the cutoff for the side road. He was almost to the road now, and if he turned onto it, the gunman would have a broadside shot at him. Webb kept the gas pedal down and roared past the cutoff, then past the thickly wooded pasture road where Beshears thought the burglar had hidden his car—

Webb narrowed his eyes against the whistling wind and stood on the brakes, spinning the steering wheel as he threw the car into a state-trooper-turnaround, a maneuver he'd mastered when he'd been a wild-ass teenager running this same road, with its long, flat straightaway. Smoke boiled from his tires as they left rubber on the pavement. Another car blew past him, horn blaring. His car rocked and skidded, then straightened out with its hood pointing back in the direction from which he'd come. This was a four-lane divided highway, so that meant he was going the wrong way, against traffic. Two cars were headed straight toward him. He hit the gas again.

He reached the pasture road just before he would have collided head-on with one of those cars, and took the turn on two wheels. He braked immediately and threw the transmission into park. He jumped out of the car before it stopped rocking, dodging into the thick cover to the side and leaving the car to block the exit from the pasture road, just in case this was where the shooter had left his car. Was it the same man who had broken into the house, or coincidence? Anyone who used this highway on a regular basis, which was thousands of people, could have noticed the pasture road. It looked like it was a hunting road leading up into the woods, but the trees and bushes cleared out after about a quarter of a mile and opened up onto a wide field that butted up against Davencourt land.

"Fuck coincidence," he whispered to himself as he weaved his way silently through the trees, taking advantage of the natural cover to keep anyone from getting a clear shot at him.

He didn't know what he'd do if he came face-to-face with someone carrying a hunting rifle while he himself was barehanded, but he didn't intend for that to happen. His had been a fairly typical rural upbringing in spite of, or perhaps because of, the advantage of living at Davencourt. Lucinda and Yvonne had made certain he fit in with his classmates, and the people he'd be dealing with the rest of his life. He'd hunted squirrel and deer and possum, learning early how to slip through thick woods without making a sound, how to stalk game that had eyes and ears a lot better than his. The rustlers who had taken his cattle and high-tailed it into Mexico had found out how good he was at tracking and at not being seen if he didn't want to be. If the gunman was in here, he'd find him, and the man wouldn't know he was anywhere around until it was too late.

There was no other vehicle parked on the pasture road. Once he'd established that, Webb hunkered down and listened to the sounds around him. Five minutes later, he knew that he was stalking the wind. No one was there. If he'd figured the trajectory correctly, then the shooter had taken another route off that high bank.

He stood up and walked back to his car. He looked at the demolished windshield, with those two small holes punched in it, and got seriously pissed off. Those had been good shots; either one or both of them could have killed him if the angle of fire had been corrected just a hair. He opened the door and leaned in, examining the seats. There was a ragged hole in the back of the driver's headrest, just about an inch from where his right ear had been. The bullet had had enough power, even after going through the windshield, to completely pierce the seat and make an exit hole in the back windshield. The second bullet had torn a hole in the back seat where it entered.

He picked up the cellular phone, flipped it open, and called Carl Beshears.

Carl drove out without lights or sirens, at Webb's request. He didn't even bring a deputy with him. "Keep it quiet," Webb had said. "The fewer people who know about this, the better."

Now Carl walked around the car, looking at every detail. "Damn, Webb," he finally said. "Someone's got a real hard-on for you."

"Tough. I'm not in the mood to get fucked."

Carl cast a quick look at Webb. There was a cold, dangerous look on his face, an expression that boded ill for anyone who crossed him. Everyone knew Webb Tallant had a temper, but this wasn't temper: this was something else, something deliberate and ruthless.

"Got any ideas?" he asked. "You've been back in town— what, a week and a half? You're making enemies real fast, serious ones."

"I think it's the same man who broke into the house," Webb said.

"Interesting theory." Carl thought about it, stroking his jaw. "So you don't think it was just a burglar?"

"Not now, I don't. Nothing has happened at Davencourt for the past ten years, until I came home."

Carl grunted, and stroked his jaw some more as he studied Webb. "Are you saying what I think you're saying?"

"I didn't kill Jessie," Webb growled. "That means someone else did, someone who was in our rooms. Normally, I would have been there. I never did go in for the late-night bar scene, and I didn't fool around with other women. Maybe Jessie surprised him, the way Roanna did. Roanna met up with him in the front hall; mine and Jessie's rooms were on the front left side, remember? Corliss has the rooms now, I sleep in a bedroom on the back. But the so-called burglar wouldn't have known that, would he?"

Carl whistled softly between his teeth. "That would make you the intended victim all along, which means this is the third attempt to kill you. I tend to believe you, son, mainly because there wasn't a reason for you to kill Miss Jessie. That's what had us so buffaloed ten years ago. Whoever did it must have thought it was real funny, you being blamed for killing her. That would be better than killing you himself. Now, who hated you enough to try to kill you ten years ago, and stay mad this long?"

"Damn if I know," Webb said softly. For years he'd thought Jessie's secret lover must have killed her, but with these new developments that didn't make sense. It would have made sense for the murderer to try to kill him, but not for him to kill Jessie. It would even have been reasonable, if he wanted to think of murder as reasonable, for the two of them to plot to kill him. That would get him out of the way, and Jessie would have inherited more of the Davenport fortune. If she had simply divorced him, her inheritance wouldn't have been as much, because despite Jessie's threats she had to have known that Lucinda wouldn't have disinherited him just because they'd divorced. To her credit, he didn't think Jessie had been involved in a plot to murder him. Like Roanna, she had simply been in the wrong place at the wrong time, but for Jessie the bad timing had been fatal.

Carl took a length of string from his pocket and tied one end of it around a pen. "Come hold this windshield up as straight as you can," he said, and Webb complied. Carl passed the free end of the string through the first bullet hole, threading it through until the pen caught on the outside and held. Then he tied the other end around another pen, this time securing the string under the pen's clip, and passed that pen through the holes in the back of the headrest.

He looked at the trajectory and whistled softly again. "At the distance he was shooting from, if he'd adjusted his sights just a teeny bit to the right, that bullet would have caught you smack between the eyes."

"I noticed it was a fine shot," Webb said sarcastically.

Carl grinned. "Thought you might be a man who appreciated good marksmanship. How about the second bullet?"

"It went on through the trunk."

"Well, any good deer rifle would shoot a bullet with that much power over that distance. No way of tracing it, even if we could have found one of the slugs." He eyed Webb. "You took a chance, stopping here like this."

"I was mad."

"Yeah, well, if there's a next time, cool off before you decide to go after someone who's armed. I'll have the car towed in, and my boys will go over it, but I don't think we'll find anything that will help us."

"In that case, I'd just as soon no one else knows about this. I'll take care of the car."

"Mind telling me why you want to keep it quiet?"

"Number one, I don't want him on guard. If he's relaxed, maybe he'll make a mistake. Number two, you can't do a whole hell of a lot anyway. You can't give me an escort everywhere I go, and you can't keep a twenty-four-hour watch on Davencourt. Number three, if Lucinda finds out, it just might kill her."

Carl grunted. "Webb, your folks need to know to be careful."

"They do. The so-called burglar spooked them. We have new deadbolt locks now, more secure windows, and we're wired to an alarm that, if it goes off, will set every dog inside a thirty-mile radius to howling. It's not any secret in Tuscumbia that we've done this, either."

"So you think he knows, and isn't likely to try getting into the house again?"

"He's gotten in twice before without any trouble. Instead of trying it again, this time he tried to shoot me off the road. Sounds as if he heard the news."

Carl crossed his arms and stared at him. "Miss Lucinda's big party is tonight."

"You think he could be among the guests," Webb said. He'd already thought of that himself.

"I'd say there's a good chance. You might want to take a look at the guest list and see if you recognize the name of someone you didn't get along with, somebody who came out on the short end of some business deal. Hell, he wouldn't even have to be invited; from what I hear, so many people will be there that he could waltz right in and no one would notice."

"You were invited, Carl. Are you coming?"

"Couldn't keep me away. Booley will be there, too. Is it okay if I run all of this by him? That old dog is still pretty sly, and if he knows to be watching, he might see something."

"Sure, tell Booley. But no one else, you hear?"

"All right, all right," Carl grumbled. He looked at Webb's car again. "You want me to give you a ride up to the house?"

"No, everyone would ask questions. Take me back to town. I have to get something else to drive anyway, and I'll arrange to have this one taken care of. As far as anyone is concerned, I had car trouble." He looked at his watch. "I'll be pushing it to get home in time for the party."

The guests were due to arrive in only half an hour, and Webb was nowhere around. All of the family was already there, including his mother and Aunt Sandra. Yvonne was beginning to pace, because it wasn't like Webb to be late to anything, and Lucinda was growing increasingly fretful.

Roanna sat very still, holding her own worry inside. She didn't let herself think about car accidents, because she couldn't bear it. Her own parents had died that way, and since then she shrank from the very idea of an automobile accident. If she passed one on the highway, she never rubbernecked but carefully kept her gaze averted and got past the accident site as soon as she could. Webb couldn't have been in an accident, he simply couldn't

Then they heard the front door open, and Yvonne rushed to the door. "Where have you *been?*" Roanna heard her demand with a mother's asperity.

"I had car trouble," Webb replied as he took the stairs two at a time. He was back downstairs in fifteen minutes, freshly shaved and wearing the black-tie apparel on which Lucinda had insisted.

"Sorry I'm late," he said to everyone as he crossed to the liquor cabinet and opened the doors. He poured himself a shot of tequila and tossed it back, then set the glass down and gave them a reckless grin. "Let the games begin."

Roanna couldn't take her eyes off him. He looked like a buccaneer despite the fineness of his clothes. His thick dark hair was still black with dampness and brushed into a severe style. He moved with the lithe grace of a man accustomed to formal clothes, without a trace of self-consciousness. The jacket sat perfectly on his broad shoulders, and the trousers were just snug enough to look trim without being binding. Webb had always worn his clothes well, no matter what they were. She had thought no one could look better than he did in jeans and boots and chambray work shirt, and now she thought no one looked better in black tie. Jet studs marched down the front of his snow white shirt, which had rows of tiny tucks, and matching jet cuff links gleamed darkly at his thick wrists.

She hadn't talked privately with him since the night he'd come to her room, and she had told him why she hadn't seen the burglar. Webb had forbidden her to work at all until the family doctor had checked her and given her the all clear, which he'd done just the day before. Truth to tell, for the first several days after she'd gotten home from the hospital, she hadn't felt like working or doing anything except sitting very still. The headache had been persistent, and if she had moved around much, she suffered a recurrence of that nausea that went with concussion. It was only in the past two days that the headache had gone away, and the nausea with it. She didn't think she would risk dancing tonight, though.

Webb had been busy, and not just with work. He had overseen the installation of steel-reinforced doors on the main entrances, dead-bolt locks on even the French doors, and an alarm system that had made her pull a pillow over her head to buffer the sound when it was tested. If she couldn't sleep and wanted the veranda doors open so she could enjoy the fresh air, first she had to punch in a code on a small box installed by the window of every room. If she opened the doors without entering the code, the resulting blast would jolt everyone out of their beds.

Between her headache and his work, there simply hadn't been time for a private talk. In the drama of her injury, most of her embarrassment had faded away. After his midnight visit to her room, the subject hadn't come up again, as if they both wanted to avoid it.

"My, you look handsome," Lucinda said now, eyeing Webb up and down. "Better than you did before, if you don't mind my saying so. Wrestling cows, or whatever it was you did in Arizona, certainly kept you in shape."

"Steers," he corrected, his eyes gleaming with amusement. "And, yes, I wrestled a few of them."

"You said you had car trouble," Yvonne said. "What's wrong with it?"

"The transmission went out," he said smoothly. "I had to have it towed."

"What are you driving then?"

"A pickup truck." His eyes gleamed greenly as he said it, and Roanna saw the fine tension in him, a sort of heightened state of alertness, as if he were poised for some sort of crisis that only he anticipated. At the same time there was an obvious amusement in the line of his mouth, and she saw him glance expectantly at Gloria.

"A truck," Gloria said with disdain. "I hope it doesn't take long to get your car repaired."

The amusement became even more pronounced, though Roanna wondered if she was the only one who saw it. "Doesn't matter," he said, and grinned in wicked relish. "I bought the truck."

If he'd expected a tirade, Gloria didn't disappoint him. She launched into a lecture on "how it looks for one of *our* family to drive such a *common* vehicle."

When she segued into the part about the image they had to uphold, Webb's eyes gleamed even brighter. He said, "It's four-wheel drive, too. Big tires, like the kind bootleggers use so they can get into the woods." Gloria stared at him, aghast and momentarily silenced, as her face turned red.

Lucinda was hiding her smile behind her hand. Greg coughed and turned away to look out the window.

Corliss was also looking out the window. She said, "My God, it looks like that scene in *Field of Dreams.*"

Lucinda, understanding exactly what she meant, stood up and said with evident satisfaction, "Of course it does. If I give a party, they will come."

That remark elicited laughter from everyone except Roanna, but Webb noticed that a smile briefly touched her lips. That was the third one, he thought.

Soon the house was brimming over with laughing, chattering people. Some of the men wore black tie, but most of them were in dark suits. The women were arrayed in a variety of styles ranging from above-the-knee cocktail dresses to tea length to more formal long gowns. Everyone in the Davenport and Tallant families wore long gowns, again at Lucinda's direction. She knew exactly how to make an impression and set the tone.

Lucinda looked good, better than she had in a long time. Her white hair was in a queenly twist on the back of her head, and her pale peach gown, aided by a skillful application of cosmetics, lent its delicate color to her face. She had known what she was doing by insisting on peach-colored lights.

While Lucinda held court with her friends, Roanna

quietly saw to it that everything ran smoothly. The caterer was very efficient, but disaster had been known to strike even the most rigidly organized of parties. Waiters hired for the evening moved through the crowd with trays laden with glasses of pale gold champagne or with a dazzling array of hors d'oeuvres. For those who had heartier appetites, a huge buffet had been set up. Out on the patio, the band had already begun playing old standards, luring people outside to dance under the peach fairy lights.

Roanna noticed Webb moving through the crowd, talking easily with people, stopping to tell a joke or make a few remarks about politics, then going on to another group. He seemed perfectly relaxed, as if it hadn't occurred to him that anyone might look askance at him, but still she could see his increased tension in the hard, bright glitter of his eyes. No one would say anything derogatory about him in his presence, she realized. There was a power about him that made him stand out even in this crowd of social elites, a personal assurance that not many people had. He really didn't give a damn what any of them thought. Not for his own sake, at least. He came across as both relaxed and self-assured but ready to act if necessary.

Around ten o'clock, when the party had been going strong for over two hours, he came up behind her as she was surveying the buffet table to make certain nothing needed replenishing. He stood so close that she felt the heat of his big body, and he rested his right hand on her waist. "Are you feeling all right?" he asked in a low voice.

"Yes, I'm fine," she said automatically as she turned to face him, repeating the same words she had used at least a hundred times that night in answer to the same question. Everyone had heard about the burglar, and her concussion, and wanted to know about it.

"You look fine," everyone else had said, but Webb didn't. Instead he was looking at her hair.

The stitches in her scalp had been removed just the day before when she had gone to the family doctor. Today, in preparation for the party, she had gone to her hairdresser, who had gently arranged her hair in a sophisticated twist that concealed the small shaved patch.

"Can you tell?" she asked anxiously.

He knew what she meant. "No, not at all. Is your head still sore?"

"Just a little. It's tender rather than actually sore."

He lifted his hand from her waist and flicked one of her dangling earrings, setting the gold stars to dancing. "You look good enough to eat," he said quietly.

She blushed, because she had hoped she looked attractive tonight. The creamy gold of her gown complemented her warm complexion and the dark chestnut of her hair.

She looked up at him, and her breath caught in her chest. He was looking down at her with a hard, intense, *hungry* cast on his face. Time suddenly seemed to stand still around them, people fading from her consciousness, the noise and music muted. Her blood throbbed through her veins, slowly, powerfully.

This was the way he had looked the day they'd gone riding together. She had mistaken it for lust . . . or *had* she been mistaken?

They were utterly alone there in the middle of the crowd. Her body quickened, her breath coming fast and shallow, her breasts rising as if to his touch. The ache of wanting him was so intense that she thought she would die. "Don't," she whispered. "If you don't mean it . . . don't."

He didn't reply. Instead his gaze moved slowly down to her breasts, lingered, and she knew her nipples were visibly erect. A muscle twitched in his jaw.

"I want to make a toast."

Lucinda knew how to make herself heard in a crowd without appearing to raise her voice. Slowly the chatter of hundreds of voices stilled, and everyone turned toward her as she stood slightly alone, frail but still queen.

The spell that had held Roanna and Webb in its grip was shattered, and Roanna shuddered in reaction as they both turned to face Lucinda.

"To my grand-nephew, Webb Tallant," Lucinda said

clearly, and lifted her glass of champagne to Webb. "I missed you desperately while you were away, and I'm the happiest old lady in Colbert County now that you're back."

It was another of her masterful strokes, forcing people to toast him, acknowledge him, accept him. All over the room glasses were lifted to Webb, champagne was drunk to his return, and a chorus of "Welcome home" filled the room. Roanna, whose hands were empty, gave him a fleeting, rueful smile.

Number four, he thought. That was two in one night.

Her nerves felt raw from the silently charged interval that had passed between them. She slipped away into the crowd and worked her way outside to make certain everything was okay on the patio. Couples strolled over the grounds, their way lit by the thousands of lights woven into the trees and bushes, the maze of electrical cords carefully covered with foam stripping and taped over so no one would trip over them. The band had moved out of old standards, having sufficiently warmed up the dancing crowd, and was now playing more lively tunes, specifically "Rock Around the Clock." At least fifty people were bopping their hearts out on the dance floor.

The tune ended to applause and laughter, and then there was one of those errant little pockets of silence in which the words "killed his wife" were clearly heard.

Roanna stopped, her expression freezing. The silence spread as people looked uncomfortably at her. Even the band members stood still, not knowing what was going on but aware that something had happened. The woman who had been talking turned around, her face dark red with embarrassment.

Roanna stared steadily at the woman, who was a Cofelt, a member of one of the oldest families in the county. Then she looked around at all the other faces, frozen in the lovely peach light as they watched her. These people had come to Webb's home, enjoyed his hospitality, and still talked about him behind his back. It wasn't just Cora Cofelt, who had been unlucky enough to be heard. All of these faces were guilty because they too had been saying the same thing she had. If they had possessed any good judgment to begin with, she thought with growing fury, they would have realized ten years ago that Webb couldn't possibly have killed his wife.

It was common courtesy that a hostess do nothing to embarrass one of her guests, but Roanna felt anger move through her. She trembled with the rush of emotion, the sheer energy. It flowed through her until even her fingertips tingled.

She had endured a lot on her own account. But, by God, she wasn't going to stand there and let them slander Webb.

"You people were supposed to have been Webb's friends," she said in a clear, strong voice. She had seldom in her life been angrier, except at Jessie, but this was a different kind of anger. She felt cool, perfectly in control of herself. "You should have known ten years ago that he would never have harmed Jessie, you should have supported him instead of putting your heads together and whispering about him. Not one of you—*not one*—expressed any sympathy to him at Jessie's funeral. Not one of you spoke up in his behalf. But you've come to his house tonight as guests, you've eaten his food, you've danced . . . and you're still talking about him."

She paused, looking from face to face, then continued. "Perhaps I should make my family's position clear to everyone, in case there's been any misunderstanding. We support Webb. Full stop, period. If anyone of you here feels you can't associate with him, then please leave now, and your association with the Davenports and the Tallants will be at an end."

The silence on the patio was thick, embarrassed. No one moved. Roanna turned to the band. "Play—"

"—something slow," Webb said from behind her. His hand, hard and warm, curled around her elbow. "I want to dance with my cousin, and her head is still too sore for bopping."

A spatter of self-conscious laughter ran around the patio. The band began playing "Blue Moon," and Webb turned her into his arms. Other couples moved together and began swaying to the music, and the crisis was over.

He held her with the distance of cousins, not the closeness of a man and a woman who had lain naked together amid tangled sheets. Roanna stared at his throat as they danced. "How much did you hear?" she asked, her voice quiet and level once more.

"Everything," he said carelessly. "You were wrong about one thing, though."

"What was that?"

A rumble of thunder sounded in the distance, and he looked up at the dark sky as a sudden cool breeze arrived with the promise of rain. After days of teasing, it looked as if a storm was finally coming. When he glanced back down at her, his green eyes were glittering. "There was one person who offered me sympathy at Jessie's funeral."

CHAPTER
19

*T*he party was over, the guests gone home. The band had unplugged and loaded up, and they, too, were gone. The caterer and her staff had cleaned, washed, and efficiently stored everything in two vans and driven away, tired but well paid.

Lucinda, exhausted by the superhuman effort she had made that night, had gone immediately up to bed, and everyone else had soon followed.

The storm had lived up to its promise, arriving with great sheets of lightning, window-rattling thunder, and torrents of rain. Roanna watched all the drama from the dark safety of her room, snugly curled in her chair. The veranda doors were thrown open so she could get the full effect of it, smell the freshness of the rain and watch the wind sweep it across the land in battering waves. She was cuddled under a light, baby-soft afghan, deliciously chilled by the dampness in the air. She was relaxed and a little drowsy, hypnotized by the rain, her body sinking into the chair's comforting depths in utter relaxation.

The worst of the storm had already passed, and the rain had settled down into a steady, heavy downpour accompanied by an occasional flash of lightning. She was content to sit there, remembering—not the scene on the patio, but that moment before Lucinda's toast when she and Webb had been caught in a private bubble of suspended time, desire pulsing thickly between them.

It *had* been desire, hadn't it? Sweet, hot. His gaze had drifted, as heated as a torch, down to her breasts. They had throbbed, her nipples lifting to him. She hadn't been mistaken in his intent, she couldn't have been. Webb had wanted her.

Once she would have gone to him, heedless of everything except her desire to be with him. Now she remained in her own room, watching the rain. She wouldn't chase after him again. He knew that she loved him, he'd known it all her life. The ball was now in his court, for him to hit it back or let it go by. She didn't know what he would do or if he would do anything at all, but she had meant what she'd told him at the party. If he wasn't serious in his attentions, then she didn't want them.

Her eyes drifted shut as she listened to the rain. It was so soothing, so peaceful; she felt at rest, whether or not she slept that night.

A faint scent of cigarette smoke came to her. She opened her eyes, and he was there, standing in the open doors, watching her. His gaze bored through the darkness of the room. The sporadic flashes of lightning revealed her to him, her eyes shadowed and calm, her body relaxed and waiting . . . waiting.

In the same brief moments of illumination she could see the way he lounged there with one shoulder against the door frame, a negligent posture that in no way concealed the tension in his coiled muscles, the intensity of the way he watched her, like a predator focusing on its prey.

He had partially undressed. His coat was gone and his black tie. The snowy white shirt was unbuttoned and pulled free of his pants, and it hung open across his broad chest. A half-smoked cigarette was in his hand. He turned and flicked it over the veranda railing, out into the rain, and then he was silently crossing the room to her, his tread lithe and pantherish.

Roanna didn't move, didn't say anything in either welcome or rejection. This move was his.

He knelt in front of the chair and put his hands on her legs, smoothing the afghan across her knees. The heat of his touch burned her through the covering.

"God knows, I've tried to stay away from you," he muttered.

"Why?" she asked, her voice low, the question simple.

He gave a rough laugh. "God knows," he said again.

Then he tugged gently on the afghan, pulling it away from her and dropping it to the floor beside the chair. Just as gently he slipped his hands under the hem of her nightgown and caught her ankles. He pulled her legs out of their tucked position, straightening them, and spread them so that he was between them.

Roanna caught a deep, shuddering breath.

"Are your nipples hard?" he whispered.

She could barely speak. "I don't know . . ."

"Let me see." And he slid his hands all the way up her body, under the nightgown, and closed his fingers over her breasts. Until he touched them, she hadn't realized how desperate she had been for this. She moaned aloud at the relief, the pleasure. Her nipples stabbed his palms. He rubbed his thumbs over them and laughed softly. "I do believe they are," he whispered. "I remember the way they taste, the way they feel in my mouth."

Her breasts lifted into his hands with every quick, sighing breath. Desire was coiling hotly in her loins, loosening her, turning her flesh warm and pliable to his touch.

He lifted the nightgown up and over her head, pulling it away and dropping it to the floor as he had the afghan. She sat naked before him in the huge chair, her slender body dwarfed by its bulk. Lightning flickered again, briefly revealing the details of breast and loin, tightly puckered nipples and opened thighs. His breath hissed through his teeth, his broad chest expanding. Slowly he stroked his hands up her legs, pushing her thighs wider and wider apart until she was fully exposed to him.

The damp night air washed over her, the breeze cooling the heated flesh between her legs. The feeling of exposure, of vulnerability, was too sharp to be borne, and with a soft, panicked sound she tried to close her legs.

His hands tightened on her thighs. "No," he said. Slowly he leaned forward, letting his body touch her, lightly press down on her, and his mouth closed over hers with a sweetness, a tenderness, that was devastating. The kiss was as gentle as a butterfly's wings, as leisurely as summer. With the utmost delicacy he cherished her mouth, lingered over the kiss. At the same time his wicked fingers moved boldly between her legs, opening the secret folds that protected the soft opening of her body. One big finger probed at her, making her squirm, then it pushed deep inside. Roanna arched helplessly, moaning into his mouth, overcome by the startling sense of being penetrated.

He kept on kissing her, the sweetness of his mouth gentling her for the marauding thrust of his fingers. It was almost diabolical, that contrast of intensity, arousing every aspect of her sensuality. She was both seduced and ravished, enticed and taken.

His lips left her mouth, slid hotly down her throat, then were at her breasts. He sipped delicately, sucked hard. Roanna sank into a dark, whirling storm of pure desire, trembling with need. She put her hands on his head, feeling the thick, cool silk of his hair between her fingers. She felt dizzy, drunk with arousal, with the heated musky scent of his skin. He was hot, so hot, his body heat burning through his shirt.

His mouth moved downward, over her trembling stomach muscles. His tongue probed her shallow navel, making her loins clench wildly as a bolt of pleasure shot through her. Down, down . . .

He gripped her buttocks hard, pulling them forward so that her bottom was right on the edge of the chair, then draped her legs over his shoulders. She made an incoherent sound of panic, of helpless anticipation.

"I told you," he muttered. "Good enough to eat."

Then he kissed her, his mouth hot and wet, his tongue swirling around her straining, yearning nub. Her hips lifted wildly, her heels digging into his back. She cried out, muffling the sound with her own hand. She couldn't stand it, it was too intense, it was torture and ecstasy all at once, and her hips bucked in an effort to escape the sensation. He gripped her bottom tighter, pulling her harder against his mouth, and his tongue stabbed deep into her. She climaxed violently, shuddering, biting her hand to keep from screaming from the force of it.

When the sensations finally ebbed and released her from their dark whirlpool, she lay sprawled limply in the chair with her legs still spread on his wide shoulders. She couldn't move. She had no strength, not even enough to open her eyes. Whatever he wanted to do to her now, she was open, compliant, completely vulnerable to his desire.

He lifted her thighs off his shoulders and she felt him moving, felt the brush of bare skin against her as he stripped out of his shirt. She forced her heavy eyelids open as he undid his pants and pushed them down. His urgency was a hot, wild thing. He hooked one arm around her bottom and dragged her forward even more, off the chair and onto his thighs, onto his thick, thrusting penis. It speared upward into her, so hard that she felt bruised, so hot that she felt burned. Her weight aided in her own penetration, pushing her down so that he went even deeper, and she choked on a soft scream.

Webb groaned, leaning back on his hands so that his body arched powerfully beneath her. "You know what to do," he said from between clenched teeth. "Ride."

She did. Automatically her body responded, rising and falling, her thighs clasping his hips, flexing as she lifted herself almost completely off him only to slide back down. She rode him slowly, so that she took him by increments.

Her body was magic, moving with the fluid grace that had always captivated him; she enveloped him with a downward glide, then tormented him with the threat of release as she moved upward again, almost off of him . . . *no, no* . . . then back down, and he groaned at the wet heated relief of being surrounded by her flesh, held, caressed. He was stallion-hard inside her, and finally she rode him hard, moving fast, slamming herself down onto him. Sensation built unbearably, and he thrust upward, hard. Helplessly she cried out, her sweet inner flesh pulsing and hugging him as she came again.

A harsh cry tore out of his throat and he reared up, throwing her back against the chair. He pinned her to it with his weight as he plunged and bucked, spurting hotly into her.

He lay heavily on her, trembling and sweating. His release had been so powerful that he couldn't speak, couldn't think. Sometime later a measure of strength returned to his muscles and he withdrew from her, bringing a wordless murmur of protest from her lips. He stood and kicked his pants off, then lifted her up into his arms and carried her to the bed. He stretched out on the bed beside her, and she curled into his embrace and went to sleep. Webb buried his face against her hair and let the darkness claim him, too.

Some unknown time later she moved out of his arms and got up from the bed. Webb awoke at once, disturbed by her absence. He blinked sleepily at the pale form of her naked body. "Ro?" he murmured.

She didn't answer but walked calmly, deliberately toward the door. Her bare feet were silent. It almost looked as if she were drifting over the floor.

The hair stood up on the back of his neck and he shot out of bed. His hand slapped against the door just as she reached out for the doorknob. He peered at her face. Her eyes were open, her expression as serene as a statue's.

"Ro," he said, his voice rough. He put his arms around her and pulled her against him. "Wake up, darlin'. Come on, baby, wake up." He shook her a little.

She blinked once or twice and yawned as she cuddled closer. He held her tighter and felt tension slowly rob her body of pliancy as she realized that she was out of bed, standing at the door.

"Webb?" Her voice was choked, shaken. She shivered, her skin roughening with a chill. He picked her up and carried her back to the bed, sliding her beneath the warm covers and getting in beside her. He held her close to the warmth of his own body, held her as the shivers became shudders.

"Oh, my God," she said against his shoulder, the words almost toneless with strain. "I did it again. I don't have any clothes on. I almost walked out of here *naked."* She began pushing against him, trying to squirm away. "I need my nightgown," she said frantically. "I can't sleep like this."

He controlled her struggles, pressing her down into the mattress. "Listen to me," he said, but she kept trying to pull away from him, and finally he rolled on top of her, ruthlessly controlling her delicate body with his much bigger, stronger one.

"Shh, shh," he murmured against her ear. "You're safe with me, baby. I woke up as soon as you moved away from me. You don't have to worry; I won't let you leave this room."

Her breath was coming in gasps, and two tears rolled out of the corners of her eyes into the hair at her temple. He rubbed the wet tracks with his beard-stubbled cheek, then kissed the last traces away. She was soft beneath him; his penis was stiff and urgent. He tugged her thighs apart. "Hush, now," he said, and stabbed deeply into her.

She gasped again, but stilled at his penetration. He lay on her and felt her slowly calm. It was a gradual process, her body changing beneath him, around him, as her distress faded and her physical awareness of him, and what he was doing, increased. "I won't let you leave," he whispered in reassurance as he began to move inside her.

At first she was simply quiescent, accepting his possession, and that was enough. Then his hunger grew and he wanted more than her compliance, and he began stroking her in ways that made her cry out, made her flesh heat and begin to press urgently against him. She began to climax and he pressed deep into her, pulsing with his own release.

Afterward she tried again to get up, to put on her nightgown, but he held her tightly. She needed to trust him, to be able to fall asleep knowing that he would wake up if she tried to leave, that he wouldn't let her roam the house in defenseless sleep. Until she had that assurance, sleep would remain difficult for her.

Roanna huddled against him, devastated by what had almost happened. She began to cry again, choked sobs that she tried to stifle. She hadn't cried in years, but she was helpless to stop, as if the very fierceness of the pleasure she received from his lovemaking had battered down the walls of her defenses, so that she couldn't hold *any* emotion at bay.

It was too much, all of it, everything that had happened since Lucinda had sent her to Arizona in search of Webb. Within an hour of finding him, she had been lying beneath him, and nothing had been the same since. How long had it been? Three weeks? Three weeks that comprised shattering ecstasy and devastating pain, three weeks of tension and sleepless nights and fear, and the more recent days when she had felt herself changing inside, facing life and in the process beginning to live again.

She loved Webb, loved him so much that she felt it in every pore of her body, every particle of her soul. Tonight he had made love to her, not with anger, but with a breath-taking possessiveness and sensuality. She hadn't gone to him, he had come to her, and he was holding her as if he never intended to let her go.

But if he did—if, when morning came, he said it had been a mistake—she would survive. It would hurt, but she would go on. She had learned that she could endure almost anything, that her future was still out there.

Oddly, realizing that she could live without him made his presence all the sweeter. She cried until she couldn't anymore, and he held her the entire time, stroking her hair, murmuring to her. Exhausted both emotionally and physically, she slept.

It was six o'clock when she woke, the morning already bright and sweet, the storm long gone and the birds singing with mad abandon. The veranda doors were still standing open, and Webb was leaning over her.

"Thank God," he muttered roughly as he saw her eyes flutter open. "I don't know how much longer I could have waited." Then he mounted her, and she forgot about the morning, about the household awakening around them. For all his impatience, he made love to her with a lingering enjoyment they hadn't been able to savor the night before.

When it was over, he gathered her trembling body close and wiped the tears, this time of ecstasy, from her eyes. "I think we've found the cure for your insomnia," he teased, his voice still hoarse and strained from his own climax.

She gave a hiccupping little laugh and buried her face against his shoulder.

Webb closed his eyes, that small, happy sound reverberating through his entire body. His throat clogged, and his eyes burned. She had laughed. Roanna had laughed.

Her small laugh died away. She kept her face pressed to him, and her fingers moved along his ribcage. "I can handle not sleeping," she said quietly. "But knowing that I walk in my sleep . . . terrifies me."

He moved his hand down her spine, stroking each vertebrae. "I promise you," he said, "that if you're in bed with me, I won't let you leave the room."

She shivered, but it was from the delicious sensations his stroking fingers were causing as they moved along her spine, probing and caressing. She arched inward, the movement pressing her body more firmly against him. "Don't try to distract me," she said. "I really would feel more secure if I wore my nightgown."

He shifted so that he was lying to face her, gathering her in. "But I don't want a nightgown between us," he murmured, coaxing her. "I want to feel your skin, your breasts. I want you to go to sleep and know that I won't let anything happen to you—unless I'm the one doing it."

She was silent, and he knew that he hadn't convinced her, but for now she wasn't going to argue the point. Slowly he combed his fingers through her tangled curls, letting the strands drift down so that the sunlight caught them, highlighting the reds and golds and richest browns. He thought of the night he had first taken her, and damned himself for his callousness. He thought of the empty nights since then, when he could have been making love to her, and damned himself for his stupidity.

"I thought I was being noble by not taking advantage of you," he said in lazy amusement.

"Stupid," she said, rubbing her cheek against his hairy chest. She nuzzled one of his flat nipples and caught it with her teeth, lightly biting. He sucked in his breath, undone by her uncomplicated sensuality.

He tried to explain further. "I blackmailed you into that first night. I didn't want you to think you had no choice."

"Dumb." She tilted her head back and looked up at him, whiskey eyes drowsy with sensual completion. "I thought you didn't want me."

"Ye gods," he muttered. "And you called *me* dumb."

She smiled and returned her head to its resting place on his chest. Number five. They were coming more often now, he thought, but were just as precious.

He thought of the shots that someone had taken at him the day before, of the danger she had already faced because of him. He should get the hell away from Davencourt, out of her life, for her safety and that of everyone else in the house. But he couldn't, because he had already been careless of her safety even before returning to Davencourt.

He put his hand on her belly, spanning the narrow distance between her hipbones. For a moment he studied the contrast between his big, rough, sun-browned hand and the silky smoothness of her stomach. He had made it a principle all his life to protect a woman from pregnancy, and AIDS had made the practice even more sensible. All his fine principles had flown out the window when he'd had Roanna beneath him; not once had he worn a rubber when he was making love to her, not in Nogales and not last night. He flattened his palm on her belly. "Have you had a period since that night in Nogales?"

His tone was soft, even, but the words hung between them as if he had shouted. She went very still in that way of hers, motionless except for her breathing. Finally she replied with caution, "No, but I've never been regular. A lot of times I'll completely skip a month."

He'd wanted certainty but realized he wasn't going to find it yet. He rubbed his hand over her stomach, then up to lightly cup a breast. He loved her breasts, so firm and high and elegantly shaped. He watched in sensual delight as the nipple immediately began to pucker, standing up as if begging for attention. Were her nipples slightly darker than they had been that first night? God, he loved her reaction, the immediate response to him. "Have your breasts always been this sensitive?"

"Yes," she whispered, her breath catching as pleasure flooded through her. At least they were whenever *he* looked at them, or touched them. She could no more stop her reaction to him than she could halt the tides.

He wasn't immune himself. Though it hadn't been long since they'd made love, his sex stirred as he watched color flush her breasts and cheeks. "How did you manage to stay virgin for twenty-seven years?" he marveled, thrusting himself against the cleft of her bare thighs.

"You weren't here," she said simply, and the open honesty of her love humbled him.

He nuzzled her hair, feeling himself grow more urgent. "Can you take me again?" To make his meaning plain, he pushed his erection even harder against her.

For answer she lifted her thigh, sliding it along his hip, up to his waist. Webb reached down and guided himself to the soft, swollen opening and pushed inside.

He didn't feel any urgent need for orgasm, just the need for *her*. They lay together, gently rocking to keep the level of sensation. The morning was getting older, and the chances were increasing that they would be caught naked in bed together. Of course, everyone was more likely to sleep late today after the party last night, so he judged it fairly safe to indulge themselves for a while longer. He didn't want to embarrass her, but neither did he want to let her go.

He loved being inside her, loved the tight clasp of her body. They began to slip apart, and he put his hand on her bottom to anchor her to him. She might not think so, but he'd bet the ranch that she was pregnant, and the thought of her carrying his baby at once thrilled him to his bones and scared him half to death.

Maybe it wasn't the most romantic conversation to be having while they were making love, but he tilted her chin up and looked square into her eyes, so she would know he meant it. "You have to eat more. I want you to put on another fifteen pounds, minimum."

A shadow of insecurity darkened her eyes, and he cursed aloud even as he thrust deeper into her. "Don't look like that, damn it. After last night, there's no way you can doubt how much you turn me on. Hell, what about right *now?* I wanted you when you were seventeen, and I sure as hell want you now. But I also want you strong and healthy enough to carry my baby."

It took her a moment to catch her breath after that strong thrust. She moved against him, an enticing wiggle to make herself more comfortable. "I don't think I'm—" she began, then stopped, and her whiskey eyes widened. "You wanted me then?" she whispered.

"You were sitting on my lap," he said wryly. "What did you think, that I was carrying a lead pipe around in my pocket?" He thrust again, letting her feel every inch of him. "And after the way I kissed you—"

"I kissed you," she corrected. Her face was growing flushed, and she clung tighter to him.

"You started it, but I didn't push you away, did I? As I remember, it took about five seconds before I had my tongue halfway down your throat."

She made a little hum of pleasure, perhaps at the memory, more likely at what he was doing to her now. A hard surge of sensation brought him to the realization that the need for orgasm was abruptly urgent, for both of them. He stroked her bottom, trailing his fingers down the cleft until he reached the point of their union. Gently he rubbed her, feeling how stretched and tight her soft flesh was around him. She whimpered, arched, and dissolved. It took only two thrusts for him to join her, and they strained together in completion.

He was still sweating a long time later, when he maneuvered out of her arms and out of bed. "We have to stop before someone comes looking for us," he muttered. Swiftly he dressed, stepping into wrinkled black pants and picking up his equally wrinkled shirt. He leaned down to kiss her. "I'll be back tonight." He kissed her again, then straightened, winked at her, and sauntered out onto the veranda as casually as if it were perfectly natural for him to be leaving her room, half naked, at eight o'clock in the morning. She didn't know if anyone saw him or not because she jumped up, grabbed her nightgown, and darted into the bathroom.

She was still quivering with excitement and pleasure as she showered. Her skin was so sensitive from his lovemaking that even the act of bathing felt sexual. She couldn't believe the raw sexuality of the night, but her body had no such difficulty.

Her hands moved over her wet abdomen. Was she pregnant? It had been three weeks since Nogales. She didn't feel any different, she didn't think, but then it had been an eventful three weeks and her attention hadn't been on her menses. Her periods were so irregular anyway that she never paid much attention to the calendar or how she felt. He seemed oddly certain, though, and she closed her eyes as sweet weakness made her tremble.

She was glowing when she went down to breakfast. Webb was already there, halfway finished with his usual hefty meal, but he paused with his fork in midair when she entered the room. She saw his eyes linger on her face, then slip down her body. Tonight, she thought. Tonight, he'd promised. She filled her plate with more than she usually took and made an effort to eat most of it.

It was Saturday, but there was still work to be done. Webb had already gone into the study, and Roanna was lingering over her second cup of coffee when Gloria came down. "Lucinda isn't feeling well," she said fretfully as she began dipping scrambled eggs onto a plate. "Last night was too hard on her."

"She wanted to do it," Roanna said. "It was important to her."

Gloria looked up, and her eyes were sheened with tears. Her chin wobbled a bit before she controlled it. "It was silly," she grumbled. "All that trouble for a party."

But Gloria knew, as they all did: that had been Lucinda's last party, and she had wanted to make it memorable. It had been her effort to set aright the wrong she felt she had done to Webb ten years ago by not standing up for him.

Lucinda had been holding her decline at bay by sheer willpower, because there had still been things she wanted to accomplish. Those things were done now, and she had no more reason to fight. The snowball was rolling downhill now, picking up speed and hurtling toward its inevitable end. From long, quiet talks with Lucinda, Roanna knew this was what she wanted, but it wasn't easy to let go of the woman who had been the family's bulwark for so long.

Booley Watts called Webb that afternoon. "Carl told me what happened," he drawled. "Interesting as hell."

"Thanks," Webb said.

Booley chuckled, the sound ending in a wheeze. "Carl and I both watched the crowd last night, but we didn't see anything out of the way except for that little scene on the patio. Roanna was something, wasn't she?"

"She took my breath away," Webb murmured, and he wasn't thinking just of the lovemaking that had happened later. She had been standing in the middle of the crowd like a pure, golden candle, her head high, her voice loud and clear. She hadn't hesitated to wade into battle on his behalf, and the last part of him that had held on to the image of "little Roanna" had faded away. She was a woman, stronger than she knew and perhaps beginning to realize that strength. She was a Davenport and, in her own way, every bit as queenly as Lucinda.

Booley's voice intruded into his thoughts. "Have you thought of anybody who would carry a grudge against you for that long, a grudge serious enough that Jessie was killed because of it?"

Webb sighed tiredly. "No, and I've wracked my brain trying to come up with something. I've even gone over old files, hoping I'll notice a detail, remember something that would make sense out of all this."

"Well, keep thinking. That's what bothered me about Jessie's murder from the beginning: there just didn't seem to be any sense to it, no reason that I could see. Hell, even drive-by shootings have a reason behind them. So whoever killed Jessie—and I'm saying now that I don't believe you did it—killed her for a reason no one else knows. If your theory's right, then the reason didn't apply to her anyway. Someone was after you, and she got in the way."

"Come up with the motive," Webb said, "and we come up with the killer."

"That's the way it's always worked for me."

"Then let's hope we can figure it out before he takes another shot at me . . . or someone else gets in his way."

He hung up and rubbed his eyes, trying to put the pieces of the puzzle together but they simply refused to fit. He stretched and stood up. He had to go into town on an errand, so he had a decision to make: play it safe and take a roundabout route, or drive his usual route and hope he got shot at so he'd have another chance at catching the gunman—assuming the shot missed. Some choice.

Lucinda came down for supper that evening, the first time all day she'd been out of her room. Her color was waxy, and the palsy in her hands was worse than it had been before, but she was jubilant over the success of the party. Several of her friends had called her during the course of the day and told her it had been simply wonderful, which meant she had accomplished her aim.

They were all at the table except for Corliss, who had gone out earlier in the day and hadn't yet returned. After chattering excitedly for several minutes, Lucinda looked at Roanna and said, "Dear, I'm so proud of you. What you said last night really made a difference."

Everyone else, except for Webb and Roanna, looked confused. Lucinda had never missed much that was going on, though probably it was one or more of her cronies who had filled her in on what had happened on the patio.

"What?" Gloria asked, looking from Lucinda to Roanna and back.

"Oh, Cora Cofelt made a snide remark about Webb, and Roanna took up for him. She managed to make everyone feel ashamed of themselves."

"Cora Cofelt?" Lanette was aghast. "Oh, no! She'll never forgive Roanna for embarrassing her."

"On the contrary, Cora herself called me today and apologized for her own bad manners. Admitting when you're wrong is the mark of a lady."

Roanna didn't know if that was a dig at Gloria or not, for Gloria had certainly never admitted being wrong about anything. Lucinda and Gloria loved each other, and in a crisis they could each be relied on to support the other, but their relationship had its sharp edges.

Webb's eyes met hers, and he smiled. Slowly, blushing a little, she smiled in return.

Number six, he thought triumphantly.

The front door slammed, and heels clattered unsteadily across the foyer tile. "Yoo-hoo!" Corliss yelled. "Where is everybody? Yoo—"

"Damn it!" Webb said violently, shoving his chair back from the table. The alarm went off, shrieking like all the fiends in hell. Everyone jumped and covered their ears. Webb ran from the room, and after a second Brock followed him.

"Oh, no, the horses," Roanna cried, and darted for the door. When the alarm had been tested, the horses had all panicked. Webb had debated changing the alarm to one less shrill but had opted for the safety of his family over the nervousness of the horses.

The godawful racket stopped as she reached the hall, and instead she heard Corliss whooping with uncontrollable laughter and Webb cussing with every breath he drew. Brock turned on Corliss and yelled, "Shut up!"

Everyone else piled into the hall behind Roanna as Corliss straightened from where she was clinging to the huge, carved newel post at the bottom of the stairway. Corliss's face twisted with fury. She worked her mouth and spat a gob of saliva at her brother. "Don't tell me to shut up," she sneered. The spit missed Brock, but he looked down at the wet splatter on the floor with disgust etched on his face.

Lanette stared at her daughter in horror. "You're drunk!" she gasped.

"So?" Corliss demanded belligerently. "Just having a li'l fun, nothin' wrong with that."

Webb gave her a look that would have frozen antifreeze. "Then you can have your fun somewhere else. I warned you, Corliss. You have a week to find somewhere else to live, then I want you out."

"Oh, yeah?" She laughed. "You can't throw me out, big boy. Aunt Lucinda might have one foot in the grave, but until they're both there, this place isn't yours."

Lanette covered her mouth with her hand, staring at Corliss as if she didn't recognize her. Greg took a threatening step forward, but Webb stopped him with a look. Lucinda drew herself up, her expression hardening as she waited for Webb to handle the situation.

"Three days," he grimly said to Corliss. "And if you open

your mouth again, the deadline will be tomorrow morning." He glanced at Roanna. "Come on, we'd better go help get the horses settled down."

They went out the front door and around the house; they could hear the horses' frightened whinnies as soon as they stepped outside, and the thuds as the ones in the stable kicked frantically at their stalls. Webb's long legs made one stride for every two of hers, and Roanna was practically running to keep up with him. Loyal and the few stable hands who were still at work at that hour were doing their best to soothe the terrified animals, crooning to them, trying to hold them still. True, most of the words they were using were lurid curse words, but they were uttered in the softest of tones.

Roanna ran into the stable and added her own special croon to the lullaby. The horses outside were just as frightened as the animals in the stable, but they weren't as likely to hurt themselves because they had room to run. The horses in the stable were mostly animals with injuries or illnesses, and they could damage themselves even more in their panic to escape.

"Hush," Loyal said to the hands, and they fell silent, letting Roanna sing. They all continued their petting, but Roanna's voice had a unique quality to it that caught the attention of every animal in the stable. She'd had the gift from childhood, and Loyal had used it more than once to settle a frightened, nervous horse.

Webb moved down the rows of stalls, stroking sleek, sweating necks, just as they all were doing. Roanna sang softly, going from stall to stall, her voice pitched at just the right tone so that the horses' ears pricked forward as if trying to catch every note. Within five minutes, all the occupants of the stalls were calm, if still sweating.

"Get some cloths, boys," Loyal murmured. "Let's get my babies dried off."

Roanna and Webb helped with that, too, while Loyal checked each animal for any new injury. They all seemed to be all right, except for their original ailments, but Loyal shook his head at Webb. "I don't like that damn squeal," he said flatly. "And the horses ain't going to get used to it, it's too high pitched. Hurts their ears. Hurts mine too, come to that. What the hell happened?"

"Corliss," Webb said disgustedly. "She's shit faced and didn't enter the code when she came in."

Loyal scowled. "What Miss Lucinda was thinking to let that little bitch, pardon my French, move into Davencourt, I don't know."

"Neither do I, but she's moving out within three days."

"Not soon enough if you ask me."

Webb looked around and located Roanna at the far end of the stable. "There's some trouble going on, Loyal. Until it's settled, I'm keeping the alarm because it's loud enough to wake you even down here, and we may need your help."

"What kind of trouble, boss?"

"Someone shot at me yesterday. I think it's the same person who broke into the house last week and maybe even the same person who killed Jessie. After Corliss leaves, if that alarm goes off, then it's a real emergency. In a worse-case scenario, you may be the only one who can help us."

Loyal eyed him consideringly, then gave one abbreviated nod. "Reckon I'll make sure my rifle's cleaned and loaded," he said.

"I'd appreciate it."

"Miss Roanna doesn't know, does she?"

"No one does except for me, Sheriff Beshears, and Booley Watts. And now you. It's hard to catch someone if they're looking for the trap."

"Well, I hope this varmint gets caught real soon, because I'm not going to rest easy as long as I know that damn siren can go off at any time and make every horse here go wild."

CHAPTER

20

*T*he house was still in an uproar when Webb and Roanna returned to it, with Corliss now sitting on the stairs weeping hysterically and begging Lucinda not to let Webb throw her out. Not even her own mother was taking her side this time; drunkenness was bad enough, but to *spit* at her brother was totally unacceptable.

Brock was nowhere in sight, probably having removed himself from the temptation to do physical damage to his sister.

To Corliss's sobbing entreaties, Lucinda merely gave her a cold look. "You're right, Corliss. Despite my own foot in the grave, I *am* still the owner of this house. And as the owner, I give Webb full authority to act on my behalf, no questions asked."

"No, no," Corliss moaned. "I can't leave, you don't understand—"

"I understand that you're leaving," Lucinda replied, not bending an inch. "You're disgusting. I suggest you go to your room now, before Webb's threat to make you leave in the morning begins to sound even more delightful than it already does."

"Mama!" Corliss turned to Lanette, a pleading expression on her tear-blotched face. "Tell her to let me stay!"

"I'm very disappointed in you," Lanette said softly and stepped past her daughter on her way upstairs.

Greg leaned down and hauled Corliss to her feet. "Upstairs," he said sternly, turning her around and bodily forcing her upward. They all watched until the pair reached the top of the stairs and turned toward Corliss's suite. They could hear her sobbing until a door closed firmly behind her.

Lucinda sagged. "The ungrateful little wretch," she muttered. Her skin tone was even more waxy than before. "Are the horses all right?" she asked Roanna.

"None of them were injured, and they're quiet now."

"Good." Lucinda put a trembling hand to her eyes, then took a deep breath and straightened her shoulders once more. "Webb, could I talk to you, please? We need to go over some details."

"Of course." He put a supporting hand under her arm to steady her as they walked to the study. He glanced over his shoulder at Roanna, and their eyes met. His were steady and warm with promise. "Go finish your supper," he said.

When he and Lucinda were alone in the study, she dropped heavily onto the couch. She was breathing hard and perspiring. "The doctor said that my heart's giving out, too, damn it," she muttered. "There, I've used a cuss word." She peeped up at Webb to see his reaction.

He couldn't help grinning at her. "You've used them before, Lucinda. I've heard you cuss that roan mare you used to ride until it was a wonder her ears didn't singe and drop off."

"She was a bitch, wasn't she?" The words were fondly uttered. As hardheaded as the mare had been, Lucinda had always gotten the best of her. Until just a few years before, Lucinda had been strong enough to handle almost any horse she straddled.

"Now, what details do you want to discuss?"

"My will," she said baldly. "I'm having the lawyer in tomorrow. I'd better get that chore taken care of, because it's beginning to look like my time's a bit shorter than I expected."

Webb sat down beside her and took her frail, palsied hand in his. She was too shrewd and mentally tough for him to even consider trying to comfort her with platitudes, but damn it, he hated to let her go. "I love you," he said. "I was damn mad at you for not defending me after Jessie was killed. It hurt like hell that you thought I could have done it. I still hold a grudge about that, but I love you anyway."

Tears swam briefly in her eyes, then she blinked them away. "Of course you hold a grudge. I never thought you'd totally forgive me, God knows I don't deserve that consideration. But I love you, too, Webb. I always knew you were the best choice for Davencourt."

"Leave it to Roanna," he said. His own words took him by surprise. He'd always thought of Davencourt as his, always expected to have it. He'd worked hard for it. But as soon as the words were out of his mouth he knew they were right. Davencourt should be Roanna's. Despite what Lucinda thought, despite even what Roanna thought, she was more than capable of handling it.

Roanna was tougher and smarter than any of them knew, even including herself. Webb was only now beginning to understand the strength of her character. For years everyone had thought of her as fragile, irreparably damaged emotionally by the trauma of Jessie's death, but instead Roanna had been protecting herself, and enduring. It took a special kind of strength to endure, to accept what couldn't be changed and simply hunker down and wait it out. More and more lately Roanna was coming out of her shell, showing her strength, standing up for herself with a quiet maturity that didn't attract much attention, but was there.

Startled, Lucinda blinked several times. "Roanna? Don't you think I've talked this over with her? She doesn't want it."

"She doesn't want to spend her life reading financial

statements and watching stock reports," he corrected. "But she loves Davencourt. Give it to her."

"You mean split the inheritance?" Lucinda asked in bewilderment. "Give the house to her and the financial holdings to you?" She sounded shocked; that had never been done. Davencourt and all it entailed had always been kept intact.

"No, I mean leave it all to her. It should be hers anyway." Roanna needed a home. She had told him so herself; she needed something that was *hers,* that could never be taken away from her. "She's never really felt as if she belonged anywhere, and if you leave everything to me, she'll feel as if she wasn't good enough to have Davencourt, even if she did agree to the terms of the will. She needs her home, Lucinda. Davencourt should have Davenports living here, and she's the last one."

"But . . . of course she would live here." Lucinda looked at him uncertainly. "I never thought that you would make her leave. Oh, dear. That would look funny, wouldn't it? People would talk."

"She told me that she plans to buy her own place."

"Leave Davencourt?" The very idea shocked Lucinda. "But this is her home."

"Exactly," Webb said softly.

"Well." Lucinda sat back, mulling over this change in her plans. Except it wasn't a change, she realized. It was simply leaving everything as it already stood, with Roanna as her heir. "But . . . what will you do?"

He smiled, a slow smile that lit his entire face. "She can hire me to handle the financial dealings for her," he said lightly. Suddenly he knew exactly what he wanted, and it was like a light being turned on inside him. "Better yet, I'm going to marry her."

Lucinda was truly speechless now. It was an entire minute before she could manage a squeaky "What?"

"I'm going to marry her," Webb repeated with growing determination. "I haven't asked her yet, so keep it quiet." Yes, he was going to marry her, one way or the other. It felt as if a piece of the puzzle had suddenly been placed in its correct position. It felt right. Nothing else would ever be as right. Roanna had always been his—and he had always been Roanna's.

"Webb, are you sure?" Lucinda asked anxiously. "Roanna loves you, but she deserves to be loved in return—"

He gave her a level look, his eyes very green, and she fell silent in astonishment. "Well," she said again.

He tried to explain. "Jessie—I was obsessed with her, I suppose, and in a way I loved her because we grew up together, but it was mostly ego on my part. I never should have married her, but I was so locked into the idea of inheriting Davencourt and marrying the crown princess that I didn't realize what a disaster our marriage would be. Roanna, now . . . I've loved her for as long as she's been alive, I reckon. When she was little I loved her like a brother, but now she's all grown up, and I'm damn sure not her brother." He sighed, looking back over the years at how relationships had gotten tangled up with inheritances. "If Jessie hadn't been killed, we'd have gotten divorced. I meant what I said that night. I was fed up, through with her. And if we'd been divorced, instead of things happening the way they did, I'd have been married to Roanna for a long time now. The way Jessie died split us all apart, and I've wasted ten years because of a grudge."

Lucinda searched his face, looking for the truth, and what she found made her sigh with relief. "You really do love her."

"So much it hurts." Gently he squeezed Lucinda's fingers, taking care not to hurt her. "She's smiled at me six times," he confided. "And laughed once."

"Laughed!" Tears welled again in Lucinda's eyes, and this time she let them fall. Her lips trembled. "I'd like to hear her laugh again, just once more."

"I'm going to try real hard to make her happy," Webb said.

"When do you plan to get married?"

"As soon as possible, if I can talk her into it." He knew Roanna loved him, but convincing her that he loved her in return might take some doing. Once she would have married him under any circumstances, but now she would quietly turn stubborn if she thought something wasn't right. On the other hand, he wanted Lucinda to be at their wedding, so that meant it had to happen quickly, while she was still able to attend. And there might be another, more private reason for a quick wedding.

"Oh, posh!" Lucinda scoffed. "You know she would walk through fire to marry you!"

"I know she loves me, but I've learned not to think she'll automatically do anything I ask. Those days are long gone. I wouldn't like having a doormat for a wife anyway. I want her to have the confidence to stand up for what *she* wants."

"The way she stood up for you."

"The way she's always stood up for me." When no one else had been there, Roanna had been at his side, slipping her little hand into his and offering what comfort she could. She had been far stronger than he, strong enough to make the first move, to reach out. "She deserves the inheritance," he said. "But besides that, I don't want her to ever feel that she had to please me in order to stay in her home."

"She might feel the same way about you," Lucinda pointed out. "Whenever you're nice to her, she might think it's only because she holds the purse strings. I've been in that situation," she added dryly, no doubt thinking of Corliss.

Webb shrugged. "I'm not a pauper, Lucinda, as you know damned well, since you had me investigated. I have my Arizona holdings, and they're going to be worth a good-sized fortune before I get through with them. I assume Roanna read the same report you did, so she knows my financial situation. We'll be equals, and she'll know that I'm with her because I love her. I'll take care of the financial dealings if she really isn't interested; I don't know if she'll want to stay involved with that part of it or not. She says she doesn't like it, but she has the Davenport knack, doesn't she?"

"In a different way." Lucinda smiled. "She pays more attention to people than she does to numbers on a sheet of paper."

"You know what she really wants to do, don't you?"

"No, what?"

"Train horses."

She laughed softly. "I might have known! Loyal has been using some of her training ideas for years now, and I have to say we have some of the best-behaved horses I've ever been around."

"She's magic with a horse. They're where her heart is, so that's what I want her to do. You've always had horses just for the pleasure of it, because you love them, but Roanna wants to get into it as a business."

"You have it all planned out, don't you?" She smiled fondly at him, because even as a boy Webb had mapped out his strategy, then followed through on it. "No one else around here knows about your properties out west. People will talk, you know."

"That I married Roanna for her money? That I was determined to get Davencourt any way I could? That I'd married Jessie for it and then, when she died, moved on to Roanna?"

"I see you've thought of all the angles."

He shrugged. "I don't give a damn about the angles as long as Roanna doesn't believe any of them."

"She won't. She's loved you for twenty years, and she'll love you for another twenty."

"Longer than that, I hope."

"Do you know how lucky you are?"

"Oh, I've got an idea," he said softly. He was surprised it had taken him so long to get that idea, though. Even though he'd *known* that he loved Roanna, he hadn't thought of it as a romantic, erotic love; he'd been stuck in the big-brother mode even after they had kissed the first time and he'd almost lost control. He hadn't been jolted out of it until she had walked up to him in the bar in Nogales, a woman, with a gap of ten years between their meetings so he hadn't *seen* her grow up. That night was burned in his memory, and still he'd struggled with the misapprehension that he had to protect Roanna from his own lust. God, what a dope. She positively reveled in his lust, which made him about the luckiest man alive.

Now, all he had to do was convince her to marry him, and clear up the small matter of attempted murder—his own.

Roanna was standing out on the veranda watching the sunset when he entered her room. She turned and glanced over her shoulder when she heard the door open. She was gilded by the last rays of the sun, turning her skin golden, her hair glinting red and gold. He came on through and out onto the veranda with her, turning to lean against the railing so that he faced the house, and her. Looking at her was so damn easy. He kept rediscovering the angles of those chiseled cheekbones, seeing anew the golden lights in her whiskey-colored eyes. The open collar of her shirt let him see enough of her silken skin to remind him how silky she was all over.

He felt the beginning twinges of lust in his groin but nevertheless asked an utterly prosaic question. "Did you finish your supper?"

She wrinkled her nose. "No, it was cold, so I ate a slice of lemon icebox pie instead."

He scowled. "Tansy made another pie? She didn't tell me."

"I'm sure there's some left," she said comfortingly. She looked up at the vermillion streaks in the sky. "Are you really going to make Corliss leave?"

"Oh, yes." He let both his satisfaction and determination come through in those two words.

She started to speak, then hesitated.

"Go on," he urged. "Tell me, even if you think I'm wrong."

"I don't think you're wrong. Lucinda needs peace now, not constant turmoil." Her expression was distant, somber. "It's just that I remember what it's like to be terrified of having nowhere to live."

He reached out and caught a tendril of her hair, winding it around his finger. "When your parents died?"

"Then, and later, until—until I was seventeen." Until Jessie died, she meant, but she didn't say it. "I was always afraid that if I didn't measure up, I'd be sent away."

"That would never have happened," he said firmly. "This is your home. Lucinda wouldn't have made you leave."

She shrugged. "They were talking about it. Lucinda and Jessie, that is. They were going to send me away to college. Not just to Tuscaloosa; they wanted me to go to some women's college, in Virginia, I think. It was someplace far enough away that I couldn't come home regularly."

"That wasn't why." He sounded shocked. He remembered the arguments. Lucinda had thought it would be good for Roanna to be away from them, force her to mature, and Jessie, of course, had egged her on. He saw now that, to Roanna, it must have seemed that they didn't want her around.

"That's what it sounded like to me," she said.

"Why did it change when you were seventeen? Was it because Jessie was dead and wasn't there to keep bringing up the subject?"

"No." That remote look was still in her eyes. "It was because I didn't care anymore. Going away seemed like the best thing to do. I wanted to get away from Davencourt, from people who knew me and felt sorry for me because I wasn't pretty, because I was clumsy, because I was so socially graceless." Her tone was matter-of-fact, as if she were discussing a menu.

"Hell," he said wearily. "Jessie made a career out of making you miserable, didn't she? Damn her. It should be against the law for people under the age of twenty-five to get married. I thought I was king of the mountain when I was in my early twenties, so damn sure I could tame Jessie and turn her into a suitable wife—my idea of suitable, of course. But there was something missing in Jessie, maybe the ability to love, because she didn't love anyone. Not me, not Lucinda, not even herself. I was too young to see it, though." He rubbed his forehead, remembering those last horrible days after her murder. "Maybe she did love *someone,* though. Maybe she loved the man whose baby she carried. I'll never know."

Roanna gasped, shock running through her. She turned to face him. "You knew about him?" she asked incredulously.

Webb straightened away from the railing, his gaze sharpening. "I found out after she was killed." He caught her shoulders, his grip urgent. "How did you know?"

"I—I saw them together in the woods." She wished she had controlled her reaction to finding out he knew about Jessie's lover, but it had been such a shock. She had protected that secret all these years, and he'd known anyway. But she hadn't known that Jessie was pregnant when she was killed, and that made her feel sick.

"Who was it?" His tone was hard.

"I don't know, I'd never seen him before."

"Can you describe him?"

"Not really." She bit her lip, remembering that day. "I only saw him once, the afternoon of the day Jessie was killed, and I didn't get a good look at him. I didn't tell you then because I was afraid . . ." She paused, a look of unutterable sadness crossing her face. "I was afraid you'd fly off the handle and do something dumb and get in trouble. So I kept quiet."

"And after Jessie was killed, you didn't say anything because you thought I would be arrested, that they'd say I killed her because I'd found out she was cheating on me." He'd kept his silence on the same subject and nearly choked on his bitterness. It made him ache inside to know that Roanna had kept the same secret and for the same reason. She had been so young, already traumatized by finding Jessie's body and briefly being suspected of murder herself, hurt by his own rejection of her, and still she'd kept quiet.

Roanna nodded, searching his face. The sunlight was fading fast, and the shades of twilight were veiling them in mysteriously shadowed blues and purples, wrapping them in that brief moment when the earth hovered between day and night, when time seems to stop and everything seems richer, sweeter. His expression was guarded, and she couldn't tell what he was thinking or feeling.

"So you kept it to yourself," he said softly. "To protect me. I'll bet you nearly choked on it, with Jessie accusing us of sleeping together when you'd just seen her with another man."

"Yes," she said, her voice strained as she remembered that horrible day and night.

"Did she know you'd seen her."

"No, I was quiet. In those days I was good at sneaking around." The glance she gave him was full of wry acknowledgment of what an undisciplined handful she had been.

"I know," he said, his tone as wry as her look. "Do you remember where they met?"

"It was just a clearing in the woods. I could take you to the area but not to the exact spot. It's been ten years; it's probably grown over by now."

"If it was a clearing, why couldn't you see the man?"

"I didn't say I couldn't see him." Feeling uncomfortable, Roanna moved restlessly under his hands. "I said I couldn't describe him."

Webb frowned. "But if you saw him, why can't you describe him?"

"Because they were having sex!" she said in stifled exasperation. "He was naked. I'd never seen a naked man before. Frankly, I didn't look at his face!"

Webb dropped his hands in astonishment, peering at her through the fading twilight. Then he began to laugh. He didn't just chuckle, he roared with mirth, his entire frame shaking. He tried to stop, took one look at her, and started again.

She punched him on the shoulder. "Hush," she muttered.

"I can just hear you telling Booley about it," he chortled,

almost choking with laughter. "S-sorry, Sheriff, I didn't notice his f-face because I was looking at his—Woof!" This time she punched him in the belly. The breath rushed out of him and he bent over, clutching his stomach and still laughing.

Roanna lifted her chin. "I was not," she said with dignity, "looking at his woof." She strode into her room and started to close the veranda doors in his face. He barely slipped through the rapidly shrinking opening. Roanna set the alarm for the doors, then pulled the curtains closed over them.

He slipped his arms around her before she could move away, pulling her snugly back against him. "I'm sorry," he apologized. "I know you were upset."

"It made me *sick*," she said fiercely. "I hated her for cheating on you."

He bent to rub his cheek against her hair. "I think she must have been planning to have the baby and pretend it was mine. But first she had to get me to have sex with her, and I hadn't touched her in four months. There was no way in hell she could pass it off as mine as things stood. When she caught us kissing, she probably thought all her plans had gone up in smoke. She knew damn well I wouldn't pretend the baby was mine just to prevent a scandal. I'd have divorced her so fast her head would spin. She was crazy jealous of you anyway. She wouldn't have been nearly as furious if she had caught me with anyone else."

"Me?" Roanna asked incredulously, turning her head to stare at him. "She was jealous of *me?* Why? She had everything."

"But you were the one I protected—from her, most of the time. I took your side, and she couldn't stand that. She had to be first in everything and with everybody."

"No wonder she was always trying to talk Lucinda into sending me away to college!"

"She wanted you out of the way." He brushed her hair to one side and lightly kissed her neck. "Are you certain you can't describe the man you saw her with?"

"I'd never seen him before. And since they were lying down, I couldn't really see his face. I got the impression that he was older, but I was only seventeen. Thirty seemed old to me then." His teeth nipped at her neck, and she shivered. She could feel him losing interest in his questions; quite literally, in fact. His growing erection pushed at her bottom, and she leaned back against him, closing her eyes as warm pleasure began to fill her.

Slowly he slid his hands up her body and put his palms over her breasts. "Just what I thought," he murmured, moving his love bites to her earlobe.

"What?" she gasped, reaching back to brace her hands on his thighs.

"Your nipples are already hard."

"Are you fixated on my breasts?"

"I must be," he murmured. "And assorted other body parts, too."

He was very hard now. Roanna turned into his arms, and he walked her backward to the bed. They fell down upon it, Webb bracing his weight on his arms to keep from crushing her, and in the cool darkness their bodies came together with a fire and intensity that left her weak and shaking in his arms.

He held her close to his side, her head cradled on his shoulder. Left weak and boneless, utterly relaxed, Roanna felt drowsiness begin to ease over her. Evidently he was right about her insomnia: tension had kept her sleepless for ten years, but after his lovemaking she was too relaxed to resist. But sleep was one thing; the sleepwalking was something else entirely and disturbed her on a much deeper level. She said, "I need to put on my nightgown."

"No." His refusal was instant and emphatic. His arms tightened around her as if he would prevent her from moving.

"But if I walk in my sleep—"

"You won't. I'm going to hold you all night long. You won't be able to get out of bed without waking me up." He kissed her long and slow. "Go to sleep, sweetheart. I'll watch over you."

But she couldn't. She could feel the tension coming back, invading her muscles. A habit of ten years' duration couldn't be broken in a single night, or even two. Webb might understand the dread she felt at the thought of walking through the night so defenselessly, but he couldn't *feel* the panic and helplessness of not waking up in the same place where she'd gone to sleep, not knowing how she'd gotten there or anything that had happened.

He felt the tension that kept her from relaxing. He held her closer, tried to soothe her with reassurances, but finally he evidently came to the conclusion that nothing would help except complete exhaustion.

She had thought she was accustomed to his lovemaking, that she already knew the extent of his sensuality. She found that she was wrong.

He brought her to climax with his hands, with his mouth. He put her astride his hard, muscled thigh and rocked her to completion, though she clutched at him and begged him to fill her. Finally he did, pulling her off the bed and turning her so that she was on her knees, bent over with her face buried in the covers. He drove into her from behind, slamming into her buttocks with the force of his thrusts, reaching around to the front of her sex to caress her at the same time. She cried out hoarsely and stifled the sound against the mattress as she climaxed a fourth time, and still he wasn't finished. She was dissolving, going beyond peaks to a state where the pleasure simply went on and on, like the waves of the tide. It happened again, fast, and she reached back to grab his hips and pull him hard into her as she pulsed around him. Her action caught him by surprise and with a low, savage cry he joined her, shuddering and jerking as he came.

They were both shaking violently, so weak they could barely crawl back onto the bed. Sweat dripped from their bodies, and they clung together like shipwreck survivors.

This time there was no way to fight off the sleep that claimed her as surely as he had.

She woke once, only enough to be aware that he was still holding her, just as he had promised, and she drifted back to sleep.

The next time she awoke she was sitting up in bed, and Webb's fingers were hard around her wrist. "No," he said softly, implacably. "You aren't going anywhere."

She went back into his arms, and began to believe.

She woke for the last time at dawn, when he got out of bed. "Where are you going?" she asked, yawning and sitting up.

"To my room," he replied, pulling on his pants. He smiled at her, and she felt herself melting inside all over again. He looked tough and sexy, with his dark hair tousled and his jaw darkened with beard stubble. His voice was still rough with sleep, and his eyelids were a little puffy, giving him a heavy-lidded, just-had-sex look. "I have to get something," he said. "Stay right there, and I mean *right there*. Don't get out of bed."

"All right, I won't." He left by the hallway door, and she lay back down and cuddled under the sheet. She wasn't certain she *could* get out of bed. She remembered the night that had just passed, the things that had happened between them. She ached deep inside, and her thighs felt weak, sore. That hadn't been mere lovemaking, that had been a melding that went beyond the mere physical. There were deeper levels of intimacy than she had ever imagined, and yet she knew there were still delights as yet untasted.

He was back in only a moment, carrying a plastic bag with a pharmacist's name on it. He placed the bag on the bedside table.

"What's that?" she asked.

He shucked off his pants again and got into bed beside her, tucking her close to his side. "An early pregnancy test."

She stiffened. "Webb, I really don't think—"

"It's possible," he interrupted. "Why don't you want to know for certain?"

"Because I—" She stopped herself that time, and her eyes were somber when she looked up at him. "Because I don't want you to feel obligated."

He went still. "Obligated?" he asked carefully.

"If I'm pregnant, you'll feel responsible."

He snorted. "Damn right. I'd *be* responsible."

"I know, but I don't want . . . I want you to want me for myself," she said softly, trying to hide the longing but knowing that she hadn't quite succeeded. "Not because we were careless and made a baby."

"Want you for yourself," he repeated just as softly. "Haven't the last two nights given you an idea about that?"

"I know you want me physically."

"I want *you,* period." He cupped her face in his hand, stroking his thumb over the soft curve of her mouth. His eyes were very serious. "I love you, Roanna Frances. Will you marry me?"

Her lips trembled under his touch. When she'd been seventeen, she had loved him so desperately that she would have jumped at any chance to marry him, under any conditions. She was twenty-seven now, and she still loved him desperately—loved him enough that she didn't want to trap him into another marriage in which he would be miserable. She knew Webb, knew the depths of his sense of responsibility. If she were pregnant, he would do anything to take care of his child, and that included lying to the mother about his feelings for her.

"No," she said, her voice almost soundless as she refused what she wanted most on this earth. A tear slipped from the corner of her eye.

He didn't insist, didn't lose his temper, though she had halfway expected that. His expression remained serious, intent, as he caught the tear with a gentle thumb. "Why not?"

"Because you're asking in case I'm pregnant."

"Wrong. I'm asking because I love you."

"You're just saying that." And she wished he would stop saying it. In how many dreams had she heard him whisper those words? It wasn't fair that now he should say it, now when she didn't dare let herself believe him. Oh, God, she loved him, but she deserved to be loved for herself. At last she knew the truth of that, and she couldn't cheat herself of that final dream.

"I'm not 'just' saying anything. I love you, Ro, and you have to marry me."

Under the serious expression was a certain smugness. She studied him, looking beneath the surface with her somber brown gaze that saw so much. There was a self-satisfied glint deep in his green eyes, a fierce triumph, the way he had always looked when he'd pulled off a difficult deal.

"What have you done?" she asked, her eyes widening with alarm.

Amusement curled the edges of his mouth. "When Lucinda and I talked last night, we agreed that it would be better to leave the terms of her will as they stand. Davencourt will be better off in your hands."

She went white. "What?" she whispered, something almost like panic edging into her tone. She tried to pull away from him but he forestalled the movement, cuddling her even closer so that her next protest was muffled against his neck.

"But it's been promised to you since you were fourteen! You worked for it, you even—"

"I even married Jessie for it," he finished calmly. "I know."

"That was the bargain. You'd come back if Lucinda changed her will in your favor again." She felt a great hollow fear growing in the pit of her stomach. Davencourt was the lure that had brought him back, but she and Lucinda had both been aware that he had built his own life in Arizona. Maybe he preferred Arizona to Alabama. Without Davencourt to keep him here, after Lucinda died he would leave again, and after these past two nights she didn't know if she could stand it.

"That's not quite true. I didn't come back because of the bargain. I came back because I needed to tie up old loose ends. I needed to make my peace with Lucinda; she was a big part of my life, and I owe her a lot. I didn't want her to die before we cleared the air between us. Davencourt is special, but I've done all right in Arizona," he said in calm understatement. "I don't need Davencourt, and Lucinda thought you didn't want it—"

"I don't," she said firmly. "I told you, I don't want to spend my life in business meetings and studying stock reports."

He gave her a lazy smile. "Pity, when you're so good at it. I guess you'll have to marry me, and I'll do it for you. Unlike you, I get my kicks making money. If you marry me, you can very happily spend your time raising kids and training horses, which is what you would have been doing even if Lucinda had left Davencourt to me. The only difference now is that it will all belong to you, lock, stock, and barrel, and you'll be the boss."

Her head was whirling. She wasn't quite certain that she'd heard what she thought she'd heard. Davencourt was going to be hers, and he was staying anyway? Davencourt was going to be hers . . .

"I can hear those wheels turning," he murmured. He tilted her head up so that she was looking at him. "I came back for one final reason, the most important one. I came back because of you."

She swallowed. "Me?"

"You." Very gently he stroked one finger down her spine to the cleft of her buttocks, then retraced the caress up her back. She shivered delicately, melting against him. He knew what he was doing with that small, delicate touch. His purpose wasn't to arouse her but to soothe her, reassure her, reestablish the trust with which she gave her body over to him during lovemaking. The very fact that he *wasn't* making love to her now was proof of how intent he was on accomplishing his aim.

"Let me see if I can make this any clearer," he mused softly, brushing his lips against her forehead. "I loved you when you were a snot-nosed kid, into so much mischief it's a wonder my hair didn't turn prematurely gray. I loved you when you were a teenager with long, skinny legs and eyes that broke my heart every time I looked at you. I love you now that you're a woman who makes my brain go soft, my legs go weak, and my dick get hard. When you walk into a room, my heart damn near jumps out of my chest. When you smile, I feel as if I've won a Nobel Prize. And your eyes still break my heart."

The soft litany washed over like the sweetest of songs, soaking into her flesh, her soul, her very being. She wanted so much to believe him, and that was why she was afraid to, afraid she would let her own desires convince her.

When she didn't speak, he began those gentling caresses again. "Jessie really did a number on you, didn't she? She made you feel so unloved and unwanted that you still haven't gotten over it. Haven't you figured out yet that *Jessie lied?* Her whole life was a lie. Don't you know that Lucinda dotes on you? With Jessie dead, she was finally able to get to know you without Jessie's poison ruining everything, and she adores you." He picked up her hand and carried it to his lips, where he kissed each fingertip, then began nibbling on the sensitive pads. "Jessie's been dead ten years. How long are you going to continue letting her ruin things for you?"

Roanna tilted her head back, searching his expression with solemn, wondering eyes. With a sense of amazement, she realized she had never seen him look more determined, or more intent. That hard face looking back at her was the face of a man who had made up his mind and was damn sure going to get what he wanted. He meant it. He didn't want to marry her because she would have Davencourt, because *he* could have had it without any strings. Lucinda would have honored her bargain. He didn't want to marry her because she might be pregnant—

As if he were reading her mind, and perhaps he was, he said, "I love you. I can't tell you how much, because the words don't exist. I've tried to count the ways, but I'm no

Browning. It doesn't matter if you're pregnant or not, I want to marry you *because I love you*. Period."

"All right," she whispered, and trembled at the enormity of the step she was taking, and from the joy that was blooming inside her.

Her breath whooshed out of her as he crushed her to his chest. "You know how to make a man sweat," he said fiercely. "I was getting desperate. What do you think about getting married next week?"

"Next week?" She all but shouted the words, at least as much as she was able to, crushed against his chest the way she was.

"You didn't think I was going to give you time to change your mind, did you?" She could hear the smile in his voice. "If you have your heart set on a big church wedding, I suppose I can wait if it doesn't take too long to arrange. Lucinda . . . Well, I think we should be married within a month, at the most."

Tears sprang to her eyes. "That soon? I hoped she . . . I hoped she would last through the winter, maybe see another spring."

"I don't think so. The doctor told her that her heart is failing, too." He rubbed his face against her hair, seeking comfort. "She's a tough old bird," he said roughly. "But she's ready to go. You can see it in her eyes."

They held each other quietly for a moment, already grieving for the woman around whom the entire family revolved. But Webb wasn't a man to be deterred for long from his set course, and he leaned back from her, giving her an inquiring look. "About that wedding—"

"I don't want a big church wedding," she said forcefully, shuddering at the idea. "You did that with Jessie, and I don't want to repeat it. I was miserable that day."

"Then what kind of wedding do you want? We could have it here, in the garden, or at the country club. Do you want just family present, or invite our friends, too? I know *you* have some, and maybe I can scare up a couple."

She pinched him for that remark. "You know darn well you have friends, if you can bring yourself to forgive them and *let* them be friends again. I want to get married in the garden. I want our friends to be here. And I want Lucinda to walk with me down the aisle, if she's able. A big wedding would be too much for her, too."

One corner of his lip quirked at all of those decisive "I wants." He suspected that before long, even though she professed not to be interested in Davencourt's business concerns, she would be poking her nose into it, butting heads with him over some of his decisions. He couldn't wait. The thought of Roanna arguing with him made him weak with delight. Roanna had always been stubborn, and she still was, even though her methods had changed. "We'll work out the details," he said. "We'll get married next week if we can, two weeks max, all right?"

She nodded, smiling a little mistily.

Number seven, he thought triumphantly. And this one had been open, natural, as if she were no longer wary about showing joy.

Twisting, he reached for the plastic bag on the bedside table and withdrew the contents. He opened the box, read the instructions, then gave her the small plastic wand with a wide slot on the side. "Now," he said, with a determined glint in his green eyes, "go pee-pee on the stick."

Ten minutes later he knocked on the bathroom door. "What are you doing?" he asked impatiently. "Are you all right?"

"Yes," she said in a muffled voice.

He opened the door. She was standing nude in front of the sink, her face blank with shock. The plastic stick lay on the rim of the bowl.

Webb looked at the stick. The slot had been white; now it was blue. It was a simple test: if the color of the slot changed, the test was positive. He eased his arms around her, pulling her into the comforting warmth of his body. She was pregnant. She was going to have his baby. "You really didn't think you were, did you?" he asked curiously.

She shook her head, her expression still stunned. "I don't—I don't feel any different."

"I imagine that will start changing soon." His big hands slid down to her flat belly, gently massaging. She could feel his heart thumping hard and fast against her back. His penis rose to jut insistently against her hip.

He was excited. He was aroused. She was stunned at the realization. She had been thinking he would feel only responsibility for the baby; she hadn't considered that he would be excited at the prospect of being a father. "You want the baby," she said, her amazement plain in both face and voice. "You *wanted* me to be pregnant."

"I sure as hell did." His voice was rough, and he tightened his arms around her. "Don't *you* want it?"

Her hand drifted downward, lightly settling over the place where her child, his child, was forming inside her. Radiant wonder lit her face, and her gaze met Webb's in the mirror. "Oh, yes," she said softly.

CHAPTER
21

Corliss slipped into Roanna's bedroom. She was alone upstairs, because all the others had either gone to work or were downstairs at breakfast. She had been trying to eat, but with her pounding headache and upset stomach, it had been more of a pretense than anything else. She needed some coke, just a little of it to make her feel better, but all the money she'd gotten before was already gone.

When Webb and Roanna had entered the breakfast room, she had made a point of getting up and leaving in dignified, offended silence, but they hadn't cared, the bastards. She had stopped just outside the door and listened, waiting to hear what they said about her. They hadn't mentioned her at all, as if she weren't important enough for discussion. Webb had told her to leave Davencourt and *poof!* just like that she didn't matter any more. Instead, Webb had announced that he and Roanna were getting married.

Married! Corliss couldn't believe it. The thought made her mind fog with rage. Why would anyone, especially someone like Webb, want to marry a mealymouth like Roanna? Corliss hated the bastard, but she didn't underestimate him. Despite what he'd said, she could have handled Roanna, she was sure of it. She couldn't handle Webb, though. He was too hard, too mean. He was going to throw her out of Davencourt. And that's why she had to get rid of him.

She couldn't leave Davencourt. She felt sick with panic at the prospect. Nobody seemed to care that she *needed* to live here. She couldn't go back to that dinky little house in Sheffield, back to being just a poor relation to the rich Davenports. She was somebody now, Miss Corliss Spence, of Davencourt. If Webb threw her out, she'd become a nobody again. She wouldn't have any means of getting money for her expensive little habit. The thought was unbearable. She had to get rid of Webb.

She prowled through Roanna's room. She'd get to the money, but first she wanted to poke around a little. She'd gone first into Webb's room, hoping to find something of *his* she could use, but—surprise, surprise! It didn't look as if he'd slept there. His bed was perfectly made, not a wrinkle in it. Somehow she couldn't see him making his own bed, not the arrogant Webb Tallant.

Well, wasn't he the sly one? No wonder he hadn't wanted his old suite. He'd chosen this room beside Roanna's so they would have a cozy little arrangement, alone here at the back of the house.

She'd gone then into Roanna's room, and sure enough, the bed was a wreck, and both pillows bore the imprint of a head. Who ever would have thought it of prissy Roanna, who didn't even date? But she sure didn't mind screwing, from the looks of that bed. Smart of her, too. Corliss hated to admit it, but this was one time Roanna had been the smart one. She'd made certain Webb wouldn't tell *her* to leave, by setting herself up as a convenient source of sex, and somehow she'd convinced him to marry her. Maybe she was better in bed than she looked. Corliss would have slept with him herself if she'd thought of it. It pissed her off that she hadn't.

She wandered into the bathroom and opened the mirrored door to the medicine cabinet. Roanna never kept anything interesting in there, no birth control pills or condoms, no diaphragm, just toothpaste and boring shit like that. She didn't even have any good cosmetics Corliss could borrow.

She glanced down at the small trash can and went still. "Well, well," she said softly, bending down to pick up the box. A do-it-yourself pregnancy test.

So that was how Roanna had done it.

She was a fast worker, Corliss had to give her that. She must have made her plans and gotten in bed with him first thing, when she'd gone to Arizona. She probably hadn't expected to get pregnant so fast, but what the hell, sometimes you took a chance and hit the jackpot.

Wouldn't Harper Neeley be interested in hearing about this?

She didn't bother with the money after all. This was too good to wait. Quickly she slipped out of Roanna's room and went back to her own. Harper was her only hope. He was one strange dude; he scared her, but he excited her, too. He looked like there was nothing too low or raunchy for him to do, nothing he would balk at. It was weird the way he hated Webb, almost to the point he couldn't think about anything else, but that was to her advantage. Harper had messed up twice, but he would keep trying. He was like a gun; all she had to do was point him and fire.

She called him to set up a meeting.

Harper's eyes gleamed with a cold, feral light that made Corliss shiver inside with both fear and satisfaction. His reaction had been more than she'd expected.

"Are you sure she's pregnant?" he asked softly, leaning back in his chair so that the front legs came off the floor. He was poised on the back legs of the chair like an animal preparing to spring.

"I saw the damn test," Corliss replied. "It was on top in the trash can, so she must have done it just this morning. Then they came downstairs all smiley-faced and Webb said they're getting married. What about my money?"

Harper smiled at her, his eyes so very blue and empty. "Money?"

Panic nibbled at her nerves. She needed some money; she'd been in too much of a hurry to get out of Roanna's room, and now she really needed a line or two to hold her steady. She was really on edge; she only had two days left before Webb made her move. Harper had to do something, but the waiting was killing her. She wouldn't be able to hold it together unless she could get just a little coke to tide her over.

"You never said anything about money," he drawled, and his smile made cold shivers go over her again. Nervously she looked around. She didn't like this place. She met Harper at a different place every time, but always before, the locations had been public: a truck stop, a bar, places like that. After the first time, they'd always met out of town, too.

This time he'd given her directions to a ratty little trailer out in the middle of nowhere. There were junk cars in the yard and discarded carcasses of old chairs and box springs piled haphazardly against the trailer, as if they'd just been tossed outside and never thought of again. The trailer was tiny, consisting of a cramped little kitchen with a cramped little table and two chairs as the dining area, a cracked Naugahyde couch and a nineteen-inch television sitting on a rickety end table, and beyond that she could see a closet-sized bathroom and a bedroom in which the double bed took up most of the floor space. Dirty dishes, beer bottles, crumpled cigarette packs, overflowing ashtrays, and dirty clothes littered every surface.

This wasn't where Harper lived. There had been a different name, crudely lettered, on the mailbox, but she couldn't remember what it was. He'd said the trailer belonged to a friend. Now she wondered if the "friend" had ever heard of Harper Neeley.

"I've got to have money," she blurted. "That was the deal."

"Nope. The deal was you'd pass along information about Tallant, and I'd take care of your problem for you."

"Well, you've done a piss-poor job of it!" she snapped.

He blinked slowly, his cold blue gaze growing even colder, and belatedly she wished she'd kept her mouth shut.

"It's taking longer than I expected," she said, moderating her tone to a plea. "I'm broke, and I need things. You know how girls are—"

"I know how cokeheads are," he said indifferently.

"I'm not a cokehead!" she flared. "I just use a little every now and then to settle my nerves."

"Sure, and your shit don't stink either."

She flushed, but something in the way he was looking at her made her afraid to push him any further. Nervously she got up from the couch, peeling her thighs from the Naugahyde where sweat had made her stick to the damn thing. She saw his gaze drop down to her legs, and she wished she hadn't worn shorts. It was just so damn hot, and she hadn't expected to be sitting on Naugahyde, for God's sake. She wished she hadn't worn these shorts especially, but they were her favorites because they were so short and tight, and they were white besides, which really showed off her tan.

"I got to go," she said, trying to hide her agitation. Harper had never tried anything with her, but then they'd never been in a place where he could. It wasn't that he was ugly, far from it, for an old dude, but he scared the living shit out of her. Maybe if they'd been someplace where she wasn't so alone, like a motel, where someone would hear if she screamed, because Harper looked like a man who made women scream.

"You ain't wearing any panties," he observed, never moving from his balanced position on the back legs of the chair. "I can see your pussy hair through your shorts."

She knew that; that was one reason she liked the shorts so much. She loved the way men glanced at her, then did a double take and looked again, with their eyes all bugged out and their tongues all but flapping like a dog's. It made her feel sexy, hot. But when Harper looked at her, she didn't feel hot, she felt scared.

He tilted even further back in the chair and reached into

the right pocket of his jeans. He pulled out a Baggie filled with about an ounce of white powder, twisted into a little pouch and secured with red yarn tied around the neck of the pouch. The yarn drew her gaze, held it. She'd never seen a cocaine bag tied up with red yarn before. It looked exotic, unreal.

He swung the little bag back and forth. "Would you rather have this, or money?"

Money, she tried to say, but her lips wouldn't form the words. Back and forth the little bag went, back and forth. She stared at it, hypnotized, fascinated. There was snow in that little bag, a Christmas present all tied up with red yarn.

"M-maybe just a taste," she whispered. Just a taste. That was all she needed. A little snort to chase away the edginess.

Carelessly he turned and swiped everything off the surface of the dirty little table, knocking newspapers and ashtrays and dirty dishes to the floor where it joined the rest of the litter and looked right at home. The owner of the trailer might not even notice. Then he untied the red yarn and carefully poured a portion of the white powder onto the table. Eagerly Corliss started forward, but he gave her a cold look that stopped her in her tracks. "Just wait," he said. "It's not ready for you yet."

A magazine insert, one of the stupid little cards that magazines stuck all through the pages, giving the reader an opportunity to become a subscriber, was lying on the floor. Harper picked it up and began to divide the tiny white mound into uniform lines on the table. Corliss watched his quick, sure movements. He'd done this before, many times. That puzzled her, because she thought she knew how to spot the cokers, and Harper didn't have any of the signs.

The little lines were perfect now, four of them. They weren't very long, but they would do. She quivered, staring at them, waiting for the word that would release her from her position.

Harper took a piece of straw from his pocket. It was a regular soda straw, cut down to not much longer than an inch. It was shorter than she liked, so short she'd have to bend down right over the table and take care that her hand didn't brush the lines and disturb them. But it was a straw, and when he held it out to her, she eagerly took it.

He pointed to a place on the floor. "You can stand there."

The trailer was so tiny that it was only one step forward. She took it, then looked at the table and back at him. She would have to bend all the way forward and stretch to reach the lines. "That's too far," she said.

He shrugged. "You'll manage."

She reached out and braced her left hand on the table and carefully held the little straw in her right. She bent forward, inching, hoping she wouldn't fall and turn the table over. The lines came closer and she lifted the straw to her nose, already anticipating the rush, the sizzle of ecstasy as her head expanded, the glow—

"You're not doing it right," he said.

She froze, her gaze still on those sweet little lines. She had to have them. She couldn't wait much longer. But she was afraid to move, afraid of what would happen if she moved before Harper said she could.

"You have to drop your drawers first."

His voice was expressionless, as if they were playing May I? But now she knew what he wanted, and relief almost made her knees sag. It was just screwing, nothing important. So what if he was older than anyone else she'd ever screwed? The little lines beckoned, and how old he was didn't matter.

Hastily she straightened and unbuttoned her shorts, let them drop to her ankles. She started to step out of them, but he stopped her again. "Leave them there. I don't want your legs spread, it's tighter when they're together."

She shrugged. "Whatever cranks your tractor."

She didn't pay any more attention to him as he moved behind her. She bent forward, eagerly focused on the cocaine, left hand braced on the table, right hand holding the straw. The tip of the straw touched the white powder, and she inhaled sharply just as he shoved into her, driving deep, the force of his thrust making the straw skid across the table and knock the cocaine out of its neat lines. She was dry, and he hurt her. She chased after the coke with the straw and he shoved again, making her miss. She whimpered, frantically adjusting her position and inhaling as hard as she could to suck up any particle the tip of the straw might touch.

The coke was scattered all over the table. There was no point in trying to aim, only to time her inhalations as his thrusts rhythmically pushed her forward. Corliss held the short straw to her nose, avidly sweeping the tip across the table, sucking hard through her nose as she went back and forth, back and forth, and it didn't matter any more that he was hurting her, damn him, because she was managing to inhale enough, and the glow, the rush, was spreading through her. She didn't care what he did as long as he could get the coke for her, and as long as he took care of Webb Tallant before the bastard kicked her out of Davencourt.

That afternoon when Roanna returned from a meeting of the Historical Society, she opened the garage door and saw that Corliss had returned before her and taken advantage of her absence to take her parking slot again. Sighing, she pressed the button on the remote control to lower the garage door again, and parked her car to the side. Corliss would be gone in two days; she could be patient that long. If she said anything about the parking space, there would be another big scene that would upset Lucinda, something she wanted to avoid.

She was walking across the yard to the back door when something moved softly in her heart, and she stopped and looked around. It was one of the most beautiful days she'd ever seen. The sky was a deep, pure blue and the air was unusually clear, without the usual haze of humidity. The heat was so intense it was like a touch, releasing the rich, heavy fragrance from the rose bushes, which had been carefully cultivated over decades and were laden with blooms. Down at the stables, the horses were prancing around and tossing their glossy heads, full of energy. That morning, Webb had asked her to marry him. And above all that, she was carrying his child.

Pregnant. She was actually pregnant. She was still a little stunned, as if it couldn't possibly be happening to her, and she had been so distracted she had no idea what had been discussed at the Historical Society meeting. She was accustomed to being the only person inhabiting her body. How did she get used to the concept of someone else living inside her? It was alien, and it was frightening. How could something so strange be so precious? She was so happy she wanted to weep.

That, too, felt alien. She was happy. She examined the emotion cautiously. She was going to marry Webb. She was going to raise kids and horses. She looked up at the huge old house and felt a wave of pure elation and possessiveness sweep over her. Davencourt was *hers*. It was her home now, truly and for real. Yes, she was happy. Even with Lucinda's inevitable passing coming closer and closer, she was filled with a rich contentment.

Webb was right; Jessie had poisoned enough of her life, convinced her that she was too ugly and clumsy for anyone to love her. Well, Jessie had been a spiteful bitch, and she'd been lying. Roanna felt the knowledge seep into her pores. She was a capable, likable human being, and she had a special talent with horses. She *was* loved; Lucinda loved her, Loyal loved her, Bessie and Tansy loved her. Gloria and Lanette had been concerned when she'd been injured, and Lanette had been surprisingly helpful. Brock and Greg liked her. Harlan—well, who knew about Harlan? But most of all, Webb loved her. Sometime during the day, the certainty of that had penetrated the layers of her soul. Webb loved her. He'd loved her all her life, just as he'd said. He was certainly aroused by her, which meant that her looks weren't all that odd either.

She smiled a private little smile as she remembered how he'd made love to her the night before, and again that morning, after the pregnancy test had shown positive. There was no doubting his physical reaction to her, any more than he could doubt her desire for him.

"I saw that," he said from where he lounged in the kitchen doorway. She hadn't heard him open the door. "You've been standing there daydreaming for five minutes, and you just got a mysterious little smile on your face. What are you thinking about?"

Still smiling, Roanna walked toward him, her brown eyes heavy lidded and filled with an expression that made him catch his breath. "Riding," she murmured as she walked past, deliberately brushing her body against his. "And woofs."

His own eyes grew heavy, and color stained his cheekbones. It was the first seductive move Roanna had made toward him, and it had brought him to a full, immediate erection. Tansy was behind him in the kitchen, cheerfully going about her daily baking and concocting. He didn't care if she noticed his aroused state. He turned around and silently, purposefully followed Roanna.

She glanced over her shoulder at him as they went up the stairs, her face glowing with promise. She walked faster.

The bedroom door was barely closed behind them before Webb had her in his arms.

Getting married involved running a lot of errands, Roanna thought the next morning as she drove down the long, winding private road. The guest list for the wedding was much smaller than the one for Lucinda's party had been, with a total of forty people, including family, but there were still details to be taken care of.

She and Webb were to have their blood tests later that afternoon. This morning, she had arranged for the flowers and the caterer and the wedding cake. Normally wedding cakes took weeks to prepare, but Mrs. Turner, who specialized in wedding cakes, had said she could do an "elegantly simple" one in the eleven days left until the chosen wedding date. Roanna understood that "elegantly simple" was a tactful way of saying less elaborate, but that was what she preferred anyway. She had to stop by Mrs. Turner's house and pick out the design she liked best.

She also had to shop for a wedding gown. If she couldn't find anything she liked in the Quad Cities on such short notice, she would have to go to Huntsville or Birmingham.

Fortunately, Yvonne had been ecstatic about the prospect of Webb's second marriage. She had tolerated Jessie but never really liked her. Roanna suited her to a T, and she had even said that she'd always wished Webb had waited for Roanna to grow up rather than marrying Jessie. Yvonne had thrown herself into the preparations, taking over the onerous chore of invitations and volunteering to handle the logistics of everything else once Roanna had made her choices.

Roanna reached the side road and stopped, waiting for an oncoming car to pass. Her brakes felt mushy when she applied them, and she frowned, experimentally pumping the pedal again. This time it felt fine. Perhaps the level of brake fluid was low, though she kept the car well maintained. She made a mental note to stop at a service station and have it checked.

She turned right onto the side road, traveling toward the highway. The car that had just passed was at least a hundred yards ahead of her. Roanna gradually accelerated, her thoughts drifting to the style of gown she wanted: something simple, in ivory rather than pure white. She had some gold-hued pearls that would look gorgeous with an ivory gown. And a fairly slim skirt in the Empire style would suit her far better than a full-skirted, fairy princess gown.

There was a curve in the road, then a stop sign where the road intersected with Highway 43, a busy four-lane highway, with traffic continually zooming past. Roanna rounded the curve and saw the car ahead of her halted at the stop sign, left turn signal blinking, waiting for an opening in the traffic to enter the highway.

A car turned onto the side road, coming toward her, but

the traffic was too heavy for the car stopped at the intersection to make it across to the other side. Roanna put her foot on the brake pedal to slow down, and the pedal went to the floorboard without any resistance at all.

Alarm shot through her. She pumped the pedal again, but there was no response the way there had been the first time. If anything, the car seemed to pick up speed. She had no brakes, and both lanes of the road were occupied.

Time warped, stretching like elastic. The road elongated in front of her, while the oncoming car loomed twice its normal size. Thoughts flashed through her mind, lightning fast: Webb, the baby. A deep ditch was to the right, and the shoulder was narrow; there was no room for her to swing past the car stopped at the intersection, even if there hadn't been the danger of shooting across four lanes of traffic.

Webb! Dear God, Webb. She gripped the steering wheel, anguish almost choking her as the seconds churned past and she ran out of time. She couldn't die now, not now when she had Webb, when his child was just beginning its life inside her. She had to do something . . .

But she already knew what to do, she realized, memory gleaming like a bright thread through the terror that threatened to engulf her. She'd been a terrible driver, so she had taken a driving course when she was in college. She knew how to handle skids and lousy road conditions; she knew what to do in case of brake failure.

She knew what to do!

The car was shooting forward, as if it were on a downhill course and the roadway was greased.

The driving instructor's voice sounded in her head, calm and prosaic: *Don't take a solid hit if you can help it. Don't let yourself hit anything head on, that's when the worst damage occurs. Turn the car, slide into a collision, dissipate the force.*

She reached for the gear shift. Don't try to put it into park, she thought, remembering those long-ago lessons. The instructor had said it likely wouldn't go into park anyway. She could hear his voice as clearly as if he was sitting beside her: *Put the gear into low range and pull the emergency brakes. The emergency brakes work on a cable, not on pneumatic pressure. A loss of brake fluid won't affect them.*

The stopped car was just fifty yards ahead now. The oncoming car was less than that.

She pulled the gear shift into low and reached for the emergency brake lever, pulling it with all her strength. Metal shrieked as the transmission ground down, and black smoke boiled up from her tires. The stench of burning rubber filled the car.

The rear end of the car will likely come around. Steer out of the skid if you can. If you don't have room, and you see you're going to hit someone or be hit, try to maneuver so it's an indirect collision. Both of you will be more likely to walk away.

The rear end swung into the other lane, in front of the oncoming car. A horn blared, and Roanna caught a glimpse of a furious, terrified face, just a blur in the windshield. She turned into the skid, felt the car began to slide in the other direction, and quickly spun the steering wheel to correct that skid, too.

The oncoming car swept past with inches to spare, horn still blaring. That left only the car in her lane, still sitting patiently at the stop sign, turn signal blinking.

Twenty yards. No more room, no more time. With the left lane clear now, Roanna sent the car into a spinning slide across it. A cornfield stretched out on the other side of the road, nice and flat. She left the road and plunged across the shoulder, the car still skidding sideways. She crashed into the fencing, wood splintering, and a whole section came down. The car plowed down head-high stalks of corn as it bumped and thudded across the furrows, clods of dirt flying in all directions. She was thrown forward, and the seat belt bit hard into her hips and torso, jerking her back as the car shuddered to a stop.

She sat there with her head resting on the steering wheel, too weak and dazed to get out of the car. Numbly she took stock of herself. Everything seemed to be all right.

She became aware that she was trembling uncontrollably. She'd done it!

She heard someone yelling, then there was a tapping on the window beside her. "Ma'am? Ma'am? Are you all right?"

Roanna lifted her head and stared into the scared face of a teenage girl. Willing her shaking limbs to obey, she unclipped the seat belt and tried to get out. The door didn't want to open. She shoved, and the girl pulled from the outside, and together they forced it open enough for Roanna to climb out. "I'm okay," she managed to say.

"I saw you run off the road. Are you sure you're okay? You hit that fence pretty hard."

"The fence got the worst of it." Roanna's teeth began chattering, and she had to lean against the car or sink to the ground. "My brakes failed."

The girl's eyes widened. "Oh, gosh! You ran off the road to keep from hitting me, didn't you?"

"It seemed like a better idea," she said, and her knees sagged.

The girl sprang forward, sliding an arm around her. "You *are* hurt!"

Roanna shook her head, forcing her knees to stiffen as the girl showed signs of bursting into tears. "No, I'm just scared, that's all. My legs feel like limp noodles." She took a few deep, steadying breaths. "I have a cell phone in the car, I'll just call someone to come—"

"I'll get it for you," the girl said, wrenching the door open wider and scrambling inside to find the cellular phone. After a brief search she located it under the right front seat.

Roanna took some more calming breaths before she called home. The last thing she wanted to do was unduly alarm Webb or Lucinda, so that meant she had to steady her voice.

Bessie answered the phone, and Roanna asked for Webb. He came on the line a moment later. "You haven't been gone five minutes," he teased. "What else have you thought of?"

"Nothing," she said, and was proud of how calm she sounded. "Come down to the intersection and get me. I had trouble with the brakes on my car and ran off the road."

He didn't reply. She heard a violent, muffled curse, then there was a clatter and the phone went dead. "He's on his way," she said to the girl, and pressed the END button on the phone.

Webb bundled Roanna into his truck, thanked the teenager for checking on her, and drove back to Davencourt so fast that Roanna clung to the overhead strap to steady herself. When they reached the house, he insisted on carrying her inside.

"Put me down!" she hissed as he swung her up into his arms. "You'll have everyone worried to death."

"Hush," he said, and kissed her, hard. "I love you and you're pregnant. Carrying you makes *me* feel better."

She looped her arm around his neck and hushed. She had to admit, the warmth and strength of his big body was very soothing, as if she were absorbing some of it through her skin. But as she had predicted, the fact that she wasn't walking on her own brought everyone scurrying, frightened questions on their lips.

Webb carried her into the living room and placed her on one of the couches as carefully as if she were made of fine crystal. "I'm all right, I'm all right," she kept saying to the chorus of questions. "I'm not even bruised."

"Get her something hot and sweet to drink," Webb said to Tansy, who rushed to obey.

"Decaffeinated!" Roanna called after her, thinking of the baby.

After assuring himself for the tenth time that she was unhurt, Webb stood up and told her he was going out to have a look at her car. "I'll go with you," she said in relief at the prospect of escaping from all the cosseting, getting up, but she was immediately drowned out by a chorus of protests from the women in the household.

"You most certainly will not, young lady," Lucinda said, at her most autocratic. "You've had a shock to your system, and you need to rest."

"I'm not hurt," Roanna said again, wondering if anyone was actually listening to what she said.

"Then *I* need for you to rest. It would fret me no end if you went off gallivanting, when common sense says you should give yourself time to get over the shock."

Roanna gave Webb a speaking glance. He lifted one eyebrow and shrugged, not at all sympathetically. "Can't have you gallivanting," he murmured, and dropped his gaze lower, to her belly.

Roanna sat back down, warmed by the silent communication, the shared thought about their child. And while Lucinda was blatantly using emotional blackmail to get her way, it was done out of genuine concern, and Roanna decided there wouldn't be any harm in letting herself be fussed over for the rest of the day.

Webb went outside to get into his truck, and stared thoughtfully at the spot where Roanna's car had been parked. There was a dark, wet stain on the ground, visible even from where he was. He walked over and hunkered down, examining the stain for a moment before touching it with his finger, then sniffing the oily residue. Definitely brake fluid, a lot of it. She must have had only a little fluid left in the lines, and it would have been pumped out the first time she used her brakes.

She could have been killed. If she had gone across the highway instead of into a cornfield, she very likely would have been seriously injured, at the least, if not killed outright.

A cold sense of dread touched him. The shadowy, unknown assailant could have struck again, but this time at Roanna. Why not? Hadn't he done it before with Jessie? And with more success, too.

He didn't use the cellular phone, with its insecure channels, or go back inside to face the inevitable questions.

Instead he walked down to the stables and used Loyal's phone. The trainer listened to the conversation, his thick, graying brows pulling together as his eyes began to snap with anger.

"You think somebody tried to hurt Miss Roanna?" he demanded as soon as Webb hung up.

"I don't know. It's possible."

"The same person who broke into the house?"

"If her brakes have been sabotaged, then I'd have to say yes."

"That would mean he was here last night, messing around with her car."

Webb nodded, his expression stony. He tried not to let his imagination run away with him until he knew for certain if Roanna's car had been tampered with, but he couldn't stop the stomach-tightening panic and anger at the thought of the man being so close.

He drove out to the intersection, all the while carefully scanning around him. He didn't think this would be a trap designed to get him out in the open, because there was no way to predict exactly where Roanna's accident would happen. Though he was acutely aware that this was roughly the same location where he had been shot at from ambush, he was more afraid that this hadn't been aimed at him, but specifically at Roanna. Maybe she hadn't simply been in the wrong place at the wrong time the night she'd been hit on the head. Maybe she'd been lucky instead, that she'd managed to scream and alert the household before the bastard had been able to finish the job.

Jessie had been killed, but by God, he wouldn't let anything happen to Roanna. No matter what he had to do, he'd keep her safe.

He parked the truck on the shoulder next to the downed section of fencing and waited for the sheriff. It wasn't long before Beshears drove up, and Booley was riding in the front seat with him. The two men got out and joined Webb, and together they waded through the flattened cornstalks to where the car sat. They were all grim and silent. After the other two incidents, it was asking a bit much to believe that Roanna's brakes had failed on their own, and they all knew it.

Webb lay down on his back and wormed his way under the car. Broken corn stalks scraped his back, and tiny insects buzzed around his ears. The smell of grease and brake fluid filled his nostrils. "Carl, hand me your flashlight," he said, and the big flashlight was passed under the car to him.

He turned it on and directed the beam to the brake line. He spotted the cut almost immediately. "Y'all want to take a look at this?" he invited.

Carl lay down and grunted as he squirmed under the car to join Webb, cussing as the cornstalks gouged his skin. "I'm too old for this," he muttered. "Ouch!" Booley declined to join them, as the weight he'd added since retirement would have made it a tight fit for him.

Carl hauled himself into position next to Webb and scowled when he saw the line. "The son of a bitch," he growled, lifting his head to examine the line as close as he could without touching it. "Cut almost through. A nice fresh, clean cut. Even if she'd managed to make it onto the highway okay, she'd have wrecked when she got to the stop light on 157. Guess it was pure luck she ran into this field the way she did."

"Skill, not luck," Webb said. "She took some driving courses in college."

"No fooling. Wish more folks would take something like that, then we wouldn't have to pick pieces of them off the highway." He glanced at Webb, saw the tightening of his mouth, and said, "Sorry."

Carefully they wormed their way out from under the car, though Carl cussed again when a stalk caught his shirt and tore a small hole in it.

"Did you check the other cars at the house?" Booley asked.

"I took a quick look under all of them. Roanna's was the only one touched. She usually parks in the garage, but she left her car outside last night."

"Now, that's a bit coincidental." Carl scratched his chin, a sign that he was thinking. "Why didn't she park in the garage?"

"Corliss was parked in her slot. We've had some trouble with Corliss lately, and I told her she had to move out. I started to make her move her car, but Ro told me to leave it alone and not cause a fuss that would upset Lucinda."

"Maybe you should've made that fuss anyway. You reckon Corliss would do something like this?"

"I'd be surprised if she knew a brake line from a fishing line."

"She got any friends who would do it for her?"

"I've been away for ten years," Webb replied. "I don't know who she hangs out with. But if she had anyone tamper with a brake line, it would be mine, not Roanna's."

"But yours was in the garage."

"Corliss has a control for the doors. We all do. If she was behind it, it wouldn't matter if the car was inside the garage or not."

Carl scratched his chin again. "None of this ties together, does it? It's like we've got pieces from ten different puzzles, and nothing goes together. It just don't make a lick of sense."

"Oh, it all fits," Booley said grimly. "We just don't know how."

CHAPTER
22

The house was quiet that night when Webb finally entered Roanna's room. As usual, she was curled up in her chair with a book in her lap, but she looked around with a warm welcome in her eyes. "What took you so long?"

"I had some last-minute paperwork I needed to do. With all the excitement today, I'd forgotten about it." He knelt in front of her, searching her eyes with his. "Are you honestly okay? You aren't hiding anything from me?"

"I'm *fine*. Not a single bruise. Do you want me to pull off my clothes and show you?"

His eyes turned smoky, and his gaze dropped to her breasts. "Yes."

She felt herself begin to warm and soften inside, and her nipples beaded the way they always did when he looked at her. He laughed softly, but got to his feet and caught her hands, pulling her up. "Come on."

She thought they were going to the bed, but instead he directed her to the door. She gave him a confused look. "Where are we going?"

"To another bedroom."

"Why?" she asked, bewildered. "What's wrong with this one?"

"Because I want to try another bed."

"Yours?"

"No," he said briefly.

Roanna resisted the pressure on her back as he urged her toward the door. She turned and gave him a long, steady regard. "Something's wrong." She said it as a statement, not a question. She knew Webb too well; she'd seen him angry and she'd seen him amused. She knew when he was tired, when he was worried, when he was aggravated as all hell. She thought she'd seen him in all his moods, but this one was new. His eyes were hard and cool, with an alertness that made her think of a hungry cat stalking prey.

"Let's just say I'd feel better if you were in a different room tonight."

"*If* I go, will you tell me why?"

That bladelike gaze sharpened even more. "Oh, you'll go," he said softly.

She drew herself up and faced him, not backing down an inch. "You can reason with me, Webb Tallant, but you can't order me around. I'm not a fool or a child. Tell me what's going on." Just because she loved him to distraction didn't mean she couldn't think for herself.

He looked briefly frustrated, because once she wouldn't have balked at doing anything he told her. But she'd been a child then, and now she was a woman; he needed to be reminded of that every so often. He made a rapid decision. "All right, but come on. And be as quiet as you can; I don't want to wake anyone. When we get to the other room, don't turn on any lights either."

"The bed won't have any sheets on it," she warned.

"Then bring something to put around you in case you get cold."

She picked up her afghan and went quietly with him down the hall to one of the unoccupied bedrooms, the last one on the left side. The curtains were open, letting in enough light from the quarter moon that they could see how to maneuver. Webb went over to the windows and looked out, while Roanna sat down on the bed.

"Tell me," she said.

He didn't turn away from the windows. "I suspect we might have a visitor tonight."

She thought about it for a few seconds, and her stomach knotted at the obvious answer. "You think the burglar will come back?"

He gave her a brief glance. "You're quick, you know that? I don't think he was a burglar. But, yes, I think he'll come."

He could see the side lawn from this room, she realized, while from either of their rooms he could have seen only the back. "If he isn't a burglar, why would he come back?"

Webb was silent a moment, then said, "Jessie's killer was never caught."

She was suddenly chilled, and pulled the afghan around her shoulders. "You think . . . you think whoever killed Jessie was in the house again that night, and hit me?"

"I think it's possible. Your accident today wasn't an accident, Ro. Your brake line had been cut. And someone took a couple of shots at me the other day when I was late getting here for the party. I didn't have car trouble; my windshield was shot out."

Roanna sucked in a deep, shocked breath, her mind reeling. She wanted to jump up and yell at him for not having said something before, she wanted to throw something, she wanted to get her hands on whoever had tried to shoot him. She couldn't do any of that, however. If she wanted him to finish telling her what was going on, she had to sit there and not make a lot of noise. She pulled herself together and tried to reason it out. "But . . . why would whoever killed Jessie want to kill you? And me?"

"I don't know," he said in frustration. "I've gone over and over everything that happened before Jessie died, and I can't think of anything. I didn't know she had a lover until Booley told me she was pregnant when she died, but why would he have killed Jessie? It would have made sense if he'd tried to kill me, but not Jessie. And if Jessie was killed because of something else she was doing, there wouldn't be a reason for the killer to come after you and me. We don't know who he is, and after ten years he should feel safe from discovery, so why take the risk of starting it all again?"

"So you don't think her lover is the one?"

"I don't know. There's no reason for it. On the other hand, if *I'm* the real target and have been all along, that means Jessie died because she was my wife. I thought she might have surprised the killer, the same way you did, and he killed her so she couldn't identify him. I made sure it's common knowledge that you can't remember anything about the night you were attacked, so he wouldn't have that as a reason for coming back. But when your brake line was cut, I knew it had to be more than that. Tampering with your car was directed specifically at you."

"Because we're getting married," she said, feeling sick inside. "But how could he have found out so fast? We just decided yesterday morning!"

"You started making arrangements yesterday," Webb said, shrugging. "Think of the people you called, all the people they must have told. News travels. Whoever it is must hate me a lot, to go after first Jessie, then you."

"But Jessie's death had to be unplanned," Roanna argued. "No one could have known that y'all would argue that night or that you would have gone to a bar. Normally you would have been at home."

"I know," he said, exhaling hard in frustration. "I can't think of a reason for any of it. No matter how I look at it, some of the details don't fit."

She got up from the bed and went over to him, needing his closeness. He put his arms around her and hugged her to him, tucking the afghan more securely around her shoulders. She laid her head on his chest, softly breathing in the warm, musky scent of his skin. It was unthinkable that anything should happen to him.

"Why do you think he'll come back tonight?"

"Because he's made several attempts in a short period of time. He keeps coming back, trying something different. Loyal is watching from the stables. If he sees anything, he'll call me on the cellular phone, then notify the sheriff."

"Are you armed?"

He tilted his head toward the dresser. "There."

She turned her head and in the dimness could see a darker shape lying on top of the dresser. Abruptly she knew what was different about his mood. This was how he must have been when he'd tracked the rustlers into Mexico: the hunter, the predator. Webb was a man not normally inclined to violence, but he would kill to protect his own. He wasn't excited or on edge; the thud of his heart beneath her head was steady. He was coolly, ruthlessly determined.

"What if nothing happens tonight?" she asked.

"Then we'll watch again tomorrow night. Eventually, we'll get him."

She stood with him for a long time, staring out at the moonlit night until her eyes ached. Nothing moved, and the crickets chirped undisturbed.

"You're sure the alarm is on?"

He pointed to the code box beside the veranda doors. A tiny green light was steadily shining. A red light flashed if a door was opened, and if the code wasn't entered within fifteen seconds, the alarm sounded.

Webb appeared to have the patience of Job and the stamina of a marathoner. He stood unmoving, keeping watch, but Roanna couldn't manage to stand still for that length of time. She paced slowly around the dark bedroom, hugging the afghan around her, until Webb said softly, "Why don't you lie down and get some sleep?"

"I have insomnia, remember?" she shot back. "I only sleep after—"

She stopped, and he chuckled. "I could say something crude, but I won't. I kind of like this strange type of insomnia," he teased. "It gives me incentive."

"I haven't noticed that you needed any."

"After we've been married thirty years or so, I might—"

He broke off, every line of his big body tensing.

Roanna didn't hurry to the window, though that was her first urge. She was wearing a white nightgown; her appearance at the window might be spotted. Instead she whispered, "Do you see someone?"

"The son of a bitch is slipping up the outside stairs," he murmured. "I didn't see him until just now. Probably Loyal didn't either." He took the cellular phone from his pocket and punched the numbers for Loyal's private line. A few seconds later he said quietly, "He's here, coming up to the veranda by the outside stairs." That was all. He closed the phone and returned it to his pocket.

"What do we do?" she whispered.

"Wait and see what he does. Loyal is calling the sheriff, then he's coming over as backup." He shifted his position a little, so he had a better angle to watch the silent intruder. The moonlight slanted across his face. " He's going around to the front . . . He's out of sight now."

A red light blinked, catching Roanna's attention. She stared at the code box. "Webb, he's in the house! The light's blinking."

He swore softly and moved across the room to get the pistol from the top of the dresser.

Still watching the light, Roanna said, startled, "It's stopped blinking. It's green again."

He swung around and stared at the code box. "Someone let him in." His voice was almost soundless, but laden with a quiet menace that didn't bode well for someone. *"Corliss."*

He kicked off his shoes and silently went to the door.

"What are you going to do?" Roanna asked fiercely, trying to keep her voice down. It was difficult, with anger and fear rushing through her veins with every beat of her heart. She trembled with the need to go with him, but she forced herself to stand still. She had no means of protecting herself, and the last thing he needed was to have to worry about her.

"Try to get behind him." He opened the door the tiniest crack, looking down the hallway for the intruder. He couldn't see anything. He decided to wait, hoping the man would give away his position. He thought he heard a faint whisper of sound but couldn't be certain.

Seconds ticked past, and Webb took the risk of opening the door a bit more. He could see all the way to the front of the house now, on this side of the house, and the hallway was empty. He slipped out of the room and down the back hallway, his bare feet soundless on the carpet, keeping close to the wall. When he approached the corner he slowed, lifting the pistol and pulling the hammer back. With his back flattened against the wall, he took a quick look around the corner. A dark figure loomed at the other end of the hallway. Webb jerked back, but not in time—he'd been seen. A thunderous shot reverberated through the house, and plaster flew from the wall.

Webb swore viciously even as he threw himself into the open, rolling, bringing his own weapon around. He squeezed off a shot, the heavy pistol bucking in his hand, but the dark figure at the other end darted toward Lucinda's door. Smoke filled the hallway, and the stench of cordite burned in his nostrils as Webb scrambled to his feet and threw himself forward.

As he'd expected, the shots had the entire family opening their doors, poking their heads out. "God damn it, get back in your rooms," he yelled furiously.

Gloria ignored him and stepped completely out into the hallway. "Don't swear at me!" she snapped. "What on earth is going on?"

Behind her, the assailant stepped out into the hallway, but Gloria was between them and Webb couldn't get off a shot. Roughly he shoved her, and with a cry she sprawled to the floor.

And he froze, suddenly helpless. The man had one arm hooked around Lucinda's neck, holding the frail old woman in front of him as a shield. The gun was steady in his other hand, the barrel laid against Lucinda's temple, and a savage grin was on his face.

"Unload the gun real slow," he ordered, backing toward the front hallway. Webb didn't hesitate. There was an expression on the man's face that told him Lucinda would be dead if he didn't obey. With deliberate movements he flipped open the cylinder and removed all the bullets.

"Throw them behind you," the man said, and Webb obeyed, tossing the bullets down the hallway. "Now kick the gun toward me."

Carefully he bent and placed the empty weapon on the carpet, then took his foot and shoved it toward the man, who made no move to pick it up. He didn't have to; he had separated the bullets from the weapon, so there was no way anyone could pick up a bullet, get to the pistol and reload it, then fire, before he could shoot them.

Lucinda was standing very still in his grip, as colorless as her nightgown. Her white hair was rumpled as if he had dragged her from her bed, and perhaps he had, though more likely she had jumped up at the first shot and was coming to see what had happened when he grabbed her.

The man looked around, his savage grin growing even bigger as he saw all the people standing frozen in their bedroom doors, except for Gloria, who was still lying on the carpet and whimpering softly.

"Everybody!" he suddenly bellowed. "I want to see everybody! I know who you all are, so if anybody tries to hide, I'll put a bullet in the old biddy's head. You got five seconds! One—two—three—"

Harlan stepped out of the bedroom and bent to help Gloria to her feet. She clung to him, still whimpering. Greg and Lanette came out of their rooms, ashen faced.

"—four—"

Webb saw Corliss and Brock appear from the other hallway.

The man looked around. "There's one more," he said, sneering. "We're missing your little brood mare, Tallant. Where is she? You think I'm fooling around about killing this old bitch?"

No, Webb thought. No. As much as he loved Lucinda, he couldn't bear the thought of risking Roanna. Run, he silently pleaded with her. Run, darling. Get help. *Run!*

The man looked to the left and gave a pleased laugh. "There she is. Come on out, darlin'. Join the happy crowd."

Roanna slipped forward, moving to stand between Corliss and the front double doors of the veranda. She was as pale as Lucinda, her slender figure almost insubstantial. She stared at the man and gasped, going even whiter.

"Well, ain't this nice?" the man crowed, grinning at Roanna. "I see you remember me."

"Yes," she said faintly.

"That's good, because I remember you real well. Me and you got some unfinished business. You gave me a scare when you walked up on me here in the hall that night, but I heard tell that little bump on the head gave you a concussion, and you don't remember nothing about it. That right?"

"Yes," she said again, her eyes huge and dark in her white face.

He laughed, evidently pleased by the irony. His cold eyes swept over them all. "A real family reunion. All of you get together, over here in the front hall, under the light so I can see all of you real good." He moved back, out of reach, holding Lucinda's head arched back as Webb silently shepherded the others forward, grouping them together with Corliss, Brock, and Roanna.

Webb spared a single murderous look at Corliss. She was watching the man as if fascinated, but there wasn't a single flicker of fear on her face. She had let him in, and she was too stupid to realize he would kill her, too. All of them were dead, unless he did something.

He tried to move closer to Roanna, hoping that perhaps he could shield her with his body, that somehow she might survive. "Uh-uh," the man said, shaking his head. "You stand still, you bastard."

"Who *are* you?" Gloria shrilled. "Turn loose of my sister!"

"Shut up, bitch, or I'll feed the first bullet to you."

"It's a good question," Webb said. He stared at the man with a cool, hard gaze. "Who the hell are you?"

Lucinda spoke, her bloodless lips moving. "His name," she said clearly, "is Harper Neeley."

The man gave a rough, feral laugh. "I see you've heard of me."

"I know who you are. I made it a point to find out."

"Did you, now? That's real interesting. Wonder why you never visited. We're family, after all." He laughed again.

Webb didn't want his attention on Lucinda, didn't want him watching any of them except himself. "Why, God damn it?" he snarled. "What do you want? I don't know you, I've never even heard of you." If he could stall long enough, Loyal might be able to work himself into position and do something, or the sheriff would arrive. All he had to do was stall.

"Because you killed her," Neeley said viciously. "You killed my girl, you fucking bastard."

"Jessie?" Webb stared at him, astonished. "I didn't kill Jessie."

"God damn you, don't lie!" Neeley roared, jerking the pistol from Lucinda's temple to point it at Webb. "You found out about us, and you killed her!"

"No," Webb said sharply. "I didn't. I didn't have any idea she was cheating on me. I didn't know until after the autopsy when the sheriff told me she was pregnant. I knew it couldn't be mine."

"You knew! You knew and you killed her! You killed my girl and you killed my baby, and I'm going to make you watch while I kill *your* baby. I'm going to shoot this little bitch right in the stomach and you're going to stand there and watch her die, and then I'm going to do you—"

"He didn't kill Jessie!" Lucinda's voice rang out over Neeley's. She lifted her white head high. "I did."

The pistol wavered slightly. "Don't try to mess with me, old woman," Neeley panted.

Webb kept his attention glued to Neeley; the man's eyes were gleaming hotly, sweat beading on his face as he worked himself into a frenzy. He was planning to kill nine people. He'd already wasted one shot. The pistol was an automatic;

how many bullets did it have in the clip? Some carried as many as seventeen, but still, after the first shot he could hardly expect them all to stand there like sheep waiting for the slaughter. He had to realize that he was in an almost impossible situation, but that made him all the more unstable. He had nothing to lose.

"I killed her," Lucinda repeated.

"You're lying. It was him, everybody knows it was him."

"I didn't mean to kill her," Lucinda said calmly. "It was an accident. I was scared, I didn't know what to do. If Webb had actually been arrested, I would have confessed, but Booley couldn't find any evidence because there wasn't any. Webb didn't do it." She gave Webb a look of sorrow, of love, of regret. "I'm sorry," she whispered.

"You're lying!" Neeley howled, jerking her hard against him and tightening his arm around her throat. "I'll break your goddamn neck if you don't shut up!"

Greg jumped for him. Quiet, unassuming Greg, who had let Lanette run their lives without even opening his mouth to give an opinion. Lanette screamed, and Neeley jerked back, firing once. Greg stumbled and fell forward, all of his coordination suddenly gone, his legs and arms moving spasmodically. He sprawled on the floor, his chest heaving and his eyes wide with surprise. Then he gave a funny little cough that turned into a moan, as blood slowly spread beneath him.

Lanette stuffed her fingers into her mouth, staring in horror at her husband. She started forward, instinctively going to him.

"Don't move!" Neeley screamed, waving the pistol erratically. "I'll kill the next one who moves!"

Corliss was staring down at her father, her mouth open, her expression stunned. "You shot my daddy," she said in amazement.

"Shut up, you fucking bitch. Stupid," he sneered. "You're so fucking stupid."

Webb caught the faintest movement out of the corner of his eyes. He didn't dare move, didn't dare turn his head, as terror seized him. Roanna shifted again, just the slightest of movements, taking her a fraction of an inch closer to the doors.

On the code box to the left of the doors, Webb saw the green light change to red.

Roanna had opened the door.

Fifteen seconds. The deafening blare would be all the diversion he would get. He began counting, hoping he could time it right.

Tears streamed down Corliss's face as she stared down at Greg, feebly writhing on the floor. "Daddy," she said. She looked back at Neeley and her face twisted with rage, and something else. *"You shot my daddy!"* she screamed, lunging at Neeley, her hands extended like claws.

He pulled the trigger again.

Corliss skidded, her torso jerked backward even as her feet tried to keep moving. Lanette screamed hoarsely, and the pistol swung unevenly toward her.

The alarm went off, the shrill, deafening sound painful in its intensity. Neeley's finger tightened on the trigger even as Webb was moving, and the bullet plowed into the wall right over Lanette's head. Neeley shoved Lucinda to the side, his free hand coming up to cover one ear as he tried to bring the pistol around. Webb hit him, driving one shoulder hard into the man's stomach, slamming him back against the wall. With his left hand he grabbed Neeley's right wrist, holding it up so he couldn't shoot anyone else even if he pulled the trigger.

Neeley shoved back, gathering himself. He was enraged, and as strong as an ox. Brock threw himself into the fray, adding his strength to Webb's as they both forced Neeley's arm back, pinning it to the wall, but still the man pushed back against them. Webb drove his knee upward, slamming it into Neeley's groin. A choked, guttural sound exploded from him, then he gasped soundlessly, his mouth working. He began sliding down the wall, taking them with him, and the movement wrenched his arm free of their grasp.

Webb grabbed for the gun as the three of them sprawled on the floor in a tangle. Neeley got his breath back with a high-pitched shriek of laughter, and only then did Webb realize that the shriek of the alarm had stopped, that Roanna had silenced it as quickly as she had set it off.

Neeley was scrabbling around, turning his body, still laughing in that shrill, maniacal tone that made the hair stand up on Webb's neck. He was staring at something, and laughing as he struggled, squirming on the floor, trying to bring the pistol around one more time—

Roanna.

She was kneeling beside Lucinda, tears running down her face as she looked from her grandmother to where Webb was struggling with Neeley, obviously torn between the two of them.

Roanna.

She was a perfect target, a little isolated from everyone else because Lanette, Gloria, and Harlan had rushed to Greg and Corliss. Her nightgown was a pristine white, perfect, impossible to miss at this range.

The gray metal of the barrel inched around, despite his and Brock's best efforts to hold Neeley's arm still, to wrestle the gun away from him.

Webb roared with fury, a great rush of it that surged through his muscles, his brain, obscuring everything in a red tide. He lunged forward that extra inch, his hand clamping down on Neeley's, slowly forcing the gun back, back, until he literally broke it free as the bones in Neeley's thick fingers popped under the pressure.

He screamed, writhing on the floor, his eyes going blank with pain.

Webb staggered to his feet, still holding the gun. "Brock," he said in a low, harsh voice. "Move."

Brock scrambled away from Neeley.

Webb's face was cold, and Neeley must have read his death there. He tried to surge upward, reaching for the gun, and Webb pulled the trigger.

At almost point blank range, one shot was all he needed.

The reverberation faded away, and in the distance he could hear the faint wail of sirens.

Lucinda was trying feebly to sit up. Roanna helped her, bracing the old woman with her own body. Lucinda was gasping for breath, her color absolutely gray as she pressed her hand to her chest. "He—he was her father," she gasped desperately, reaching out to Webb, trying to make him understand. "I couldn't—I couldn't let her h-have that baby." She choked and grimaced, pressing harder on her chest with her other hand. She collapsed back against Roanna, her body going limp and sagging to the floor.

Webb looked around at his family, at the blood and destruction and grief. Over the groans of pain, the sobs, he said in a steely voice, "This stays in the family, do you understand? I'll do the talking. Neeley was Jessie's father. He thought I killed her, and he was out for revenge. That's it, do you understand? All of you, *do you understand?* No one knows who really killed Jessie."

They looked back at him, the survivors, and they understood. Lucinda's terrible secret remained just that, a secret.

Three days later, Roanna sat by Lucinda's bed in the cardiac intensive care unit, holding the old lady's hand and gently stroking it as she talked to her. Her grandmother had suffered a massive heart attack, and her body was already so frail that the doctors hadn't expected her to live through the night.

Roanna had been by her bedside all that night, whispering to her, telling her of the great-grandchild that was on its way, and despite all logic and medical knowledge, Lucinda had rallied. Roanna stayed until Webb had forced her to go home and rest, but was back as soon as he would allow it.

They all marched to Webb's orders, the family closing ranks behind him. There was so much to get through that they were all numb. They had buried Corliss the day before. Greg was in intensive care in Birmingham. The bullet had clipped his spine and the doctors expected him to have some paralysis, but they thought he would be able to walk with the aid of a cane. Only time would tell.

Lanette was like a zombie, moving silently between her daughter's funeral and her husband's hospital bed. Gloria and Harlan were in almost the same state, shocked and bewildered. Brock handled the funeral arrangements and took care of the others, his good-looking face lined with grief and fatigue, but his fiancée was at his side the entire time, and he took comfort from her.

Roanna looked up when Webb came into the small cubicle. Lucinda's eyes brightened when she saw him, then filmed with tears. It was the first time she had been awake when he'd been to visit. She groped for his hand, and he reached out to gently take her fingers in his.

"So sorry," she whispered, gasping for breath. "I should have . . . said something. I never meant for you . . . to take the blame."

"I know," he murmured.

"I was so scared," she continued, determined to get it said now after all the years of silence. "I went to your rooms . . . after you left . . . try to talk some sense into her. She was . . . wild. Wouldn't listen. Said she was . . . going to teach you . . . a lesson." The confession came hard. She had to gasp for breath between every few words, and the effort was making perspiration shine on her face, but she focused her gaze on Webb's face and refused to rest. "She said she would . . . have Harper Neeley's baby . . . and pass it off . . . as yours. I couldn't . . . let her do it. Knew who he was . . . her own father . . . abomination."

She drew a deep breath, shuddering with the effort. On her other side, Roanna held tightly to her hand.

"I told her . . . no. Told her she had to . . . get rid of it. Abortion. She laughed . . . and I slapped her. She went wild . . . knocked me down . . . kicked me. I think . . . trying to kill me. I got away . . . picked up the andiron . . . She came at me again. I hit her," she said, tears rolling down her face.

"I . . . loved her," she said weakly, closing her eyes. "But I couldn't . . . let her have that baby."

There was a soft scraping sound at the sliding glass doors. Webb turned his head to see Booley standing there, his expression weary. He gave Booley a hard stare and turned back to Lucinda.

"I know," he murmured as he bent over her. "I understand. You just get well now. You have to be at our wedding, or I'll be mighty disappointed, and I won't forgive you for *that.*"

He glanced at Roanna. She too was staring at Booley, a cool look in those brown eyes that dared him to do or say anything that would upset Lucinda.

Booley jerked his head at Webb, indicating that he wanted to talk to him outside. Webb patted Lucinda's hand, carefully placed it on the bed, and joined the former sheriff.

Silently they walked out of the CICU and down the long hall, past the waiting room where relatives kept endless vigils. Booley glanced into the crowded room and continued strolling.

"Guess it all makes sense now," he finally said.

Webb remained silent.

"No point in it going any further," Booley mused. "Neeley's dead, and there wouldn't be any use in pressing any sort of charges against Lucinda. No evidence anyway, just the ramblings of a dying old woman. No point in stirring up a lot of talk, all for nothing."

"I appreciate it, Booley," said Webb.

The old man clapped him on the back and gave him a level, knowing look. "It's over, son," he said. "Get on with your life." Then he turned and walked slowly to the elevator, and Webb retraced his steps to the CICU. He knew what Booley had been telling him. Beshears hadn't asked too many questions about Neeley's death, had in fact skirted around some things that were fairly obvious.

Beshears had been around. He knew an execution when he saw one.

Webb quietly reentered the cubicle, where Roanna was once again talking softly to Lucinda, who seemed to be dozing. She looked up, and he felt his breath catch in his chest as he stared at her. He wanted to grab her in his arms and never let her go, because he had come so close to losing her. When she had explained about her confrontation with Neeley over his treatment of his horse, Webb's blood had run cold. It had been just after that when Neeley had broken into the house for the first time, and when Roanna walked up on him, he had to have thought she would recognize him. He would have killed her then, Webb was certain, if Roanna hadn't awakened enough to scream when Neeley hit her. His idea of putting it about that the concussion had caused her to lose her memory about that night, just as a precaution, had undoubtedly saved her life, because otherwise Neeley would have tried to get to her sooner, before Webb managed to have the alarm installed.

As it was, Neeley had been within a hair's breadth of settling that pistol sight on her, and that had signed his death warrant.

Webb went to her, gently touching her chestnut hair, stroking one finger down her cheek. She rested her head on him, sighing as she rubbed her cheek against his shirt. She knew. She had been watching. And as she had knelt beside Lucinda, when he had turned back to her after pulling the trigger, she had given him a tiny nod.

"She's asleep," Roanna said now, keeping her voice to a whisper. "But she's going to come home again. I know it." She paused. "I told her about the baby."

Webb knelt on the floor and put his arms around her, and she bent her head down to him, and he knew that he held his entire world there in his arms.

Their wedding was very quiet, very small, and took place over a month later than they had originally planned.

It was held in the garden, just after sunset. The gentle shades of twilight lay softly over the land. Peach lights glowed in the arbor where Webb waited beside the minister.

A few rows of white chairs had been set up on each side of

the aisle, and every face was turned toward Roanna as she walked down the carpet laid out on the grass. Every face was beaming.

Greg and Lanette sat in the first row; Greg was in a wheelchair, but his prognosis was good. With physical therapy, the doctors said, he would likely regain most of the use of his left leg, though he would always limp. Lanette had cared for her husband with a fierce devotion that refused to let him give up, even when his grief over Corliss had almost defeated him.

Gloria and Harlan were also in the first row, both of them looking much older as they held hands, but they too were smiling.

Brock pushed Lucinda's wheelchair to keep pace with Roanna's stately stride. Lucinda was dressed in her favorite peach, and she wore her pearls and makeup. She smiled at everyone as they passed. Her frail, gnarled fingers were linked with the slender ones of her granddaughter, and they went together up the aisle, just as Roanna had wanted.

They reached the arbor and Webb reached out for Roanna's hand, drawing her to his side. Brock positioned Lucinda's wheelchair so that she was in the traditional place as matron of honor, then took up his own position as best man.

Webb's gaze briefly met Lucinda's. There was a serene, almost translucent quality to her. The doctors had said she wouldn't have long, but she had confounded them once again, and it was beginning to look as if she might make it through the winter after all. She was saying now that she wanted to wait until she knew if her great-grandchild was a boy or a girl. Roanna had immediately stated that she had no intention of letting the doctor or ultrasound technician tell her the baby's sex before its birth, and Lucinda had laughed.

Forgive me, she had said, and he had. He couldn't hold on to anger, to hurt, when he had so much to look forward to.

Roanna turned her radiant face up to him, and he almost kissed her right then, before the ceremony even started.

"Woof," he whispered, so low that only she could hear him, and he felt her stifle a giggle at what had turned into their private code for "I want you."

She smiled more readily these days. He'd lost count, at least in his mind. His heart still noted each and every curve of her lips.

Their fingers twined together, and he lost himself in her whiskey-colored eyes as the words began, washing over them in the soft purple twilight: "Dearly beloved, we are gathered here together . . ."

Son of the Morning

To Susan Bailey, my friendly banker who answered all my questions about ATMs, and didn't accuse me of planning a robbery—thanks.

"How art thou fallen from heaven, O Lucifer, son of the morning!"

—*Isaiah, 14:12*

Part One

Grace

Prologue

December 1307
France

THE STONE WALLS OF THE SECRET UNDERGROUND CHAMBER were cold and dank, the chill penetrating wool and linen and leather, going straight to the bone. Two smoking torches provided the only illumination, and too little heat to make any difference. The pair of men revealed by the flickering light paid no attention to the cold, however, for such discomfort was of small matter.

The first man was standing, the other kneeling before him in a posture that should have been submissive, had it not been obvious that such an attitude was alien to that proud head, those broad shoulders. The man who was standing looked frail in contrast with the vitality of the other, and in fact the kneeling man's head was level with the chest of the first. Valcour was, indeed, frail in comparison to the warrior he had once been, and to the man who knelt before him, but age and despair had taken their toll. He was fifty-one, long past the age of vigor. His hair and beard were more gray than brown, his thin face lined from the burdens he had endured. It was time to pass along the responsibility, the duty, that had been his for all these long years. They would be safe with this fierce young lion, he thought. There was no better warrior in the Order, which was the same as saying there was no better warrior in Christendom, for they were—had been—a brotherhood of warriors, the best of the best, the cream skimmed from Europe's battlefields and tourneys.

No more.

Just two months past, on Friday, the thirteenth of October in this year of Our Lord 1307, a day that would surely be remembered through the ages as a day of darkness, Philip IV of France and his puppet, Pope Clement V, had given in to their greed and in one fell swoop effected the destruction of the greatest military order ever to exist: the Knights of the Temple. Some of the brethren had escaped, but others had already died horrible deaths, and more deaths would follow as those captured refused to recant their beliefs.

The Grand Master had received mere moments of warning, and had chosen to use those moments to secure the safety of the Treasure rather than of himself. Perhaps Jacques de Molay had sensed the approach of catastrophe, for he had already spoken with Valcour several times about keeping their enormous fleet of ships out of Philip's hands, but above all his concern, and that of the great warrior Geoffroy de Charnay, had been the safekeeping of the Treasure. After long hours of consideration the Guardian had been chosen: the true and fierce warrior, Niall of Scotland. He had been chosen very carefully, not just for his prowess with a sword, which was unrivaled, but for the protection that came with his very name. The Treasure would be safe in Scotland.

The Grand Master hadn't been certain his choice was the correct one, even given Niall's connections. There was something untamed and ruthless about the Scot, despite his unswerving loyalty to God and the Brotherhood, and the oaths he had sworn to both. Some of those oaths had been given unwillingly, the Grand Master was certain, especially the oath of chastity. Niall had been forced into the Brotherhood, for of course a monk could never be king; a king must have at least the possibility of children, for kingdoms were built on continuity. His illegitimacy should have been an unsurmountable barrier, but even at a young age Niall had been tall and proud, intelligent, cunning, ruthless, a born leader; in short, he had all the characteristics of a great king. The choices had been simple: kill him, or make it impossible for him to be king. Niall was loved by his father and half-brother, so there had really been no choice. The young man would be a servant of God.

It was a master stroke. Should Niall renounce his vows to the Temple, that too would render him unacceptable for the crown, for he would be dishonored. No, putting young Niall into the protection of the Temple had at once saved his life and now and forever removed him from consideration for the Scots throne—such as it was.

But if Niall had been unsuited for the life of a monk, he had been perfectly suited for that of a warrior. He had taken his lust for female flesh and turned it into fierceness on the battlefield, and if his eyes sometimes lingered overlong on that which was forbidden to him, still, to the Grand Master's sure knowledge he had never broken his vows. He was a man of his word.

That, and his fighting ability, was what had finally convinced de Charnay to choose Niall as the next Guardian, and though the Grand Master was the head of the Order, de Charnay was undoubtedly the most powerful Knight. Moreover, de Charnay had borne the responsibility for the safety of the Treasure for many years, and his was the final say. His choice was Niall of Scotland, and Valcour agreed wholeheartedly. The Scot would safeguard the Treasure with his life.

"Take them," Valcour whispered now to that bent black head, feeling the younger man's bitter rage and knowing no way to ease it. "No matter what happens, the Treasure must never fall into the hands of others. The Brotherhood has devoted itself to the protection of our God and His followers, and we must not falter in our duty."

The cold stone floor was hard beneath Niall's knees, but he scarcely noticed it. His thick black hair, cut short as was required, gleamed with sweat despite the chill of the underground chamber. Steam drifted from his body. Slowly he lifted his head, his eyes stark, and as black as night with bitterness. "Even now?" he asked, the bite of betrayal in the deep, softly burred tones of his voice.

Valcour smiled thinly. "Especially now. We serve God, not Rome. Methinks the Holy Father has forgotten there is a difference."

"The concept should come easily to him," Niall all but snarled. "He does not serve God, but rather licks Philip's arse every time the king presents it." His night-dark gaze wandered over the collection of artifacts that had been spirited out of the Temple in Jerusalem more than a century before. He studied them, and felt his bitterness growing. Good men had died horrible deaths protecting these . . . things. The King of France and the Holy Father were so intent on stripping the Order of its more earthly treasures, of gold and silver, but the Brotherhood's secretiveness centered around these things rather than mere gold. Oh, there was gold aplenty—Niall had it. But its only purpose was to provide for the safekeeping of the real Treasure, this disturbing and powerful group of–

Things. A cup, plain and scarred. A shroud, with its secrets embedded in the very fabric. A throne, unsettling and pagan—or was it? A banner, rich and compelling despite its age, reputed to hold strange powers in its frayed threads. And an ancient text, written in a mixture of Hebrew and Greek, which told of a secret, and of a power beyond belief.

"I could go back," Niall said, thinking of the text. He lifted his merciless warrior's gaze to Valcour. "Both Philip and Clement could fall under my sword, and this could be undone as if it never was, and our brothers would live."

"Nay," said Valcour. His face had the drawn, exalted look of someone who has gone beyond horror, beyond fatigue. "We must not risk discovery for our own sakes. *Only for the sake of God* may the secret be used."

"Is there a God?" Niall asked bitterly. "Or are we but fools?"

Valcour's thin, bloodless hand lifted, gently touched Niall's head in both a benediction and a restraint. He felt the steamy heat emanating from the warrior's muscled body, for Niall had just discarded his helm and still wore heavy armor. Would that he had a fraction of Niall's great strength, Valcour thought tiredly. The Scot was like iron, neither breaking nor wearing down no matter the hardships he faced. His sword arm was tireless, his will unswerving. There was no greater warrior in the Lord's service than this formidable Scot with royal blood running through his bastard veins. Not just noble, but *royal*. 'Twas that blood that had won him entrance into the Order, for legitimacy was a requirement. Wisely, the Grand Master had decided that, in this case, blood ties were more important than rules.

And because of that blood, Niall would be protected. Clement would not be able to lay his bloody, greedy hands on the Scot, for he would be safe in his homeland, among the craggy mountains of the Highlands.

"We believe," Valcour finally said, in simple response to Niall's question. "And, believing, we've sworn our lives to protect. You are released from all your other vows, but on the blood of your brothers, you must swear to devote your life to the guardianship of these holy relics."

"I swear," Niall said fiercely. "But for *them*. Never again for *Him*."

Valcour's eyes were troubled. Loss of faith was a terrible thing—and a common one, in these days of horror. More men would lose their faith, or their lives. Not all Brothers had remained true; some of them had turned their backs on the Order, and the God, they had served so faithfully but who had allowed this ungodly thing to happen to them. Friends, brothers, had been tortured, dismembered, burned at the stake, the Order shattered—all for the love of gold. It was difficult to believe in anything except betrayal, and vengeance.

And yet Valcour tried to keep a small, central part of himself pure, to keep his belief enshrined there, for without belief there was nothing. If he didn't believe, then he had to accept that so many good men had died in vain, and that he could not do, could not live with. So, because the alternative was so unbearable, he believed. He wished Niall could have that comfort, but the Scot was too uncompromising, his warrior's heart seeing only black and white. He had been on too many battlefields where the choices were simple: kill, or be killed. Valcour had fought for the Lord, but he had never been the soldier Niall was. The heat of battle did tend to make one's vision very clear, to distill life down to the simplest of choices.

The Order needed Niall, to fulfill its greatest, most secret vow. The Brotherhood was at an end, at least in this incarnation, but its sacred duty would continue, and Niall was the chosen protector.

"For whatever reason, then," Valcour murmured. "Guard them well, for they are the true treasures of our Lord. Should they fall into the hands of evil, then the blood of our brothers will have been shed in vain. So shall it be, then: if not for *Him,* for *them.*"

"With my life," said Niall of Scotland.

December 1309
Creag Dhu, Scotland

"Three more Knights have found their way here since last you visited," Niall murmured to his brother as the two men sat before a crackling fire in Niall's private chamber. A tall, thick tallow candle sat on the table where they had recently filled their bellies, its flame adding to the golden glow of the hearth fire. Except for that, the chamber was in shadows, and delightfully warm. No drafts crept through the stone walls to stir the air with icy breaths; the cracks and crevices had been carefully daubed with clay, and the tapestries were thick and heavy. The door to Niall's chamber was stout, and securely barred. For all that, the two men kept their voices low, and spoke in French, so that if they were somehow overheard they wouldn't be understood. None of the Scots servants spoke the language; most of the nobility did, but here in this impregnable fortress, in a remote corner of the Highlands, they had only the servants and men-at-arms with whom they had to concern themselves.

Both held heavy goblets filled with fine French wine, and now Robert sipped his in contemplation. He had seated himself in a huge, carved wooden chair, while Niall had drawn up a heavy bench and placed it at an angle to the fire, so that he faced his visitor rather than the flames. Robert watched the dancing flames as he drank his wine; when he glanced back at Niall, it took a moment for his vision to adjust, and suddenly he realized that was why Niall had placed the bench as he had. Even here, in his own castle, secure in his own chamber with his brother, Niall's instincts were those of a warrior and he had protected his vision. Should an enemy somehow take him unawares, he would not be hampered by limited sight.

The realization made Robert's mouth curl wryly. After years of battle with the English, he too had learned to protect his night vision, but here in this safe place he had allowed himself to relax. Not so Niall. He never relaxed; he was eternally vigilant.

"Have any of the Knights sought other refuge?"

"Nay. They remain here, for there is no other certain refuge. Yet they know they must go, soon, or by their very number they could bring to Creag Dhu the attention they wish to avoid." Niall's black gaze was piercing as he stared at his brother. "I have not asked for myself, for I have no wish to add to your troubles, but for them I must know: do you intend to enforce Clement's edict against us?"

Stung, Robert drew back. "Ye ask that!" he growled, angered enough to speak in Gaelic, but Niall's gaze didn't waver and after a moment he reined in his temper.

"You need the alliance with France," Niall said calmly. "Should Philip discover my identity, he would stop at nothing to capture me, including joining his forces to Edward's. You cannot risk that." What he didn't say was, *Scotland* needed the alliance; the distinction wasn't needed, for his brother *was* Scotland, all her hopes and dreams personified.

Robert drew in a deep, calming breath. "Aye," he admitted, returning to French. "It would be a crippling blow. But already I've lost three brothers to England's butchery; my wife and daughter, and our sisters, have been captives for three years already and I know not if I'll ever see them alive again. I'll not lose you, too."

"You scarcely know me."

" 'Tis true that we were not much in each other's company, but I *do* know you," Robert disagreed. Know him, and love him. It was that simple. None of his other brothers could have challenged him for the crown, but he and his father had known from the time Niall had been a tall, sturdy lad of ten that this illegitimate half-brother had the stuff of kings, uncommonly gifted with the boldness and intelligence that were Robert's own characteristics. For Scotland's sake, they could not risk an internal struggle between the brothers, and even had Niall grown up to prove loyal, such was his personality that folk would have flocked to him anyway. The circumstances of his birth had been kept secret, but secrets had a way of outing, as Niall himself had proven at that time by boldly approaching Robert and asking if 'twas true they were brothers.

It wasn't unusual for aspirants to the throne to clear the way by killing those who might challenge them, but neither Robert nor his father, the Earl of Carrick, had been able to tolerate the thought. It would have been like extinguishing a bright flame, leaving them in darkness. Niall burned with life's force, full of joy and deviltry, drawing people to him like a lodestone. He had always been the leader among the younger lads, fearlessly taking his followers into mischief and then just as fearlessly taking the blame onto his own shoulders whenever they were caught.

By the time he was fourteen, the lasses had begun following him, too, with their bright eyes and lissome bodies. Already his voice had deepened, his shoulders widened, his chest broadened as manhood settled easily on his tall frame. He had proven himself unusually adept at arms, and the constant practice with heavy swords had further strengthened him. Robert doubted the lad had spent many nights alone, for it wasn't just the young lasses who had pursued him, but the older ones as well, including some who were wed.

He had changed, though. Robert wasn't surprised, given the treachery that had befallen the Templars. His magnetism hadn't lessened, but it was harsher now, his black eyes remaining grim even if his lips smiled. As a lad he had been restless with inexhaustible energy, but now he was a man grown, and a fearsome warrior. He had learned the art of patience, and his stillness was like that of a predator waiting for its next meal.

Now Robert said deliberately, "Scotland will not join in the persecution of the Templars."

Again Niall's gaze bored into him, like a black sword in its sharpness. "You have my gratitude . . . and more, should you care to use it."

What Niall had left unspoken hung heavily in the shadowed room. The watchful black gaze never wavered, and Robert lifted his eyebrows. "More?" he asked, sipping again at the wine. He was curious about what "more" would entail. He scarcely dared to hope . . . perhaps Niall was offering *gold*. More than anything, Scotland needed gold to finance its battle to resist English domination.

"The Brethren are the best soldiers in the world. They must not gather here, yet I see no need for their skills to go unused."

"Ah." Thoughtfully, Robert stared into the fire again. Now he knew Niall's goal, and it was tempting indeed. Not gold, but something almost as valuable: training, and experience. The arrogant, excommunicated Knights no longer wore their red crosses, but essentially they were still exactly what they had been before the Pope and the King of France had conspired to destroy them: the best military men in the world. This endless war with England was stretching Scotland's poor resources so thin that they were, at times, literally fighting with their bare hands. As gallant as his people were, especially the wild Highlanders, Robert knew they indeed needed more: more funds, more weapons, more training.

"Blend them in with your armies," Niall murmured. "Give them the responsibility of training your men. Consult with them in strategy. Use them. In repayment, they will become Scots. They will fight to the death for you, and for Scotland."

The Templars! The very idea was dizzying. Robert's fighting blood sang through his veins at the idea of having such soldiers under his command. Still, how much could a handful of men do, no matter how well trained? "How many are there?" he asked doubtfully. "Five?"

"Five here," Niall said. "But hundreds in need of refuge."

Hundreds. Niall was proposing to make Scotland a place of sanctuary for the Knights who had escaped and gone into hiding all over Europe. If they were caught, they had the choice of betraying their Brethren, or enduring torture before being burned at the stake. Some had cooperated and lost their lives anyway.

"You can bring them here?"

"I can." Niall rose from the bench and stood with his broad back to the fire, his massive shoulders throwing a huge shadow across the floor. His thick black hair flowed over his shoulders, and in the Celtic fashion he had plaited a small braid to hang on each side of his face. In his hunting-plaid kilt and white shirt, with a knife thrust in his wide belt, he looked every inch the wild Highlander. His expression was grim. "What I cannot do is join them."

"I know," Robert said softly. "Nor would I ask it of you. I seek no details, yet I know that you are in greater danger than those you wish to aid, and not just because you are my brother. Whatever mission the Temple has charged you with is one no lesser man could accomplish. If ever you need my aid, or that of the Knights you wish to put at my service, you have only to send word."

Niall inclined his head with a motion that conveyed acceptance, and yet Robert knew that day would never come. Niall had forged a stronghold here in the wildest, most remote part of the Highlands, the rugged northwest mountains, and he would defend it against all threats. He had gathered about him a strong force of disciplined knights and men-at-arms, and turned Creag Dhu into an impregnable fortress.

Already the country folk whispered about him, even as they gathered closer to Creag Dhu for his protection. They called him Black Niall. The Scots tended to name as black anyone with dark coloring, but the whispers about Niall said that it was his heart so described, not just his mane of hair and midnight eyes.

Robert, who knew Niall's ancestry, could see the resemblance between his half-brother and his own best friend, Jamie Douglas, the infamous Black Douglas, and the coincidence of coloring and name made him uneasy. Niall's mother had been a Douglas; he and Jamie were first cousins. Jamie was tall and broad-shouldered, though not as tall or strongly built as Niall. Should anyone see them together, would the resemblance be noted? Would it then also be noticed that Niall had the great physical strength of the Bruces, as well as the almost unholy handsomeness for which Nigel, another of Niall's half-brothers, had been so famous? Bruce and Douglas blood had combined in Niall to form a man of unusual looks and force, the type of man who strode the earth only once every hundred years or so. He did not go unnoticed. For his own safety, and for the sake of the mission charged to him by the ravaged Order, no one must ever know that the infamous Black Niall was the beloved half-brother of the King of Scotland, and the bastard son of the lovely Catriona Douglas, for Catriona's husband still lived and would stop at nothing to kill the result of his wife's infidelity.

Niall was also a Templar, excommunicated, and by order of the Pope under a penalty of death should he ever be captured. On the surface, his existence was precarious indeed.

On the other hand, it would take a fool to try to breach Creag Dhu's defenses. The Order had chosen its champion well.

Robert sighed. There was naught he could do for his brother except respect his secrecy, and offer his kingdom as sanctuary to the scattered, persecuted Knights. Little enough, given what Scotland would gain in return.

" 'Tis time I take my leave," he said, draining his goblet and setting it aside. "The hour grows late, and the lovely wench waiting for you below may become impatient, and seek another's bed." Niall had completely discarded his Templar's vows of poverty, chastity, and obedience, but most particularly chastity. Robert wondered now how his brother had ever endured eight years without a woman, for even though he was a man himself, he could still see the burning, intense sexuality of Niall's nature. If there had ever been a man less suited to monkhood, Robert couldn't imagine it.

Niall's mouth quirked. "Perhaps," he said placidly, without a shred of either jealousy or doubt, for there was no likelihood Meg would do so; she was thoroughly enjoying her current status as his favorite, though by no means only, bedmate.

Robert laughed and clapped his hand to the broad shoulder. "As I ride through the cold night, I will envy you *your* ride between warm thighs. God be with you."

Niall's expression didn't change, but Robert was instantly aware of a sudden coldness, and intuitively he knew his last remark was what had elicited that reaction. Troubled, he tightened his hand on his brother's shoulder. Sometimes faith was all folk, be they common or king, had to sustain them, and Niall had turned his back on that bulwark as the Church had turned her back on him.

But there was nothing to be said, no comfort to be offered except the promise he had already made. "Bring them here," he said softly. "I will make them welcome." Then Robert the Bruce, King of the Scots, pressed on a certain stone to the left of the great hearth, and a whole section opened inward. He took up the torch he had left just inside the hidden way, and held it into the fire until it was once more flaring brightly. He left Creag Dhu as he had entered it, in secret.

Niall watched as the door closed, immediately becoming invisible within the stonework. His face was impassive as he took the goblet his brother had used and wiped the rim clean, then filled it again with the fine wine. His own goblet was still nearly full; he set both of them beside the bed, then unbarred his door and went in search of Meg. His mood had darkened, despite the sanctuary Robert had offered to the fugitive Templars. The rage was always there, controlled after two years but never weakening. Damn Clement, damn Philip, and most of all, damn the God whom the Knights had served so faithfully, but who had abandoned them when they needed Him most. If he went to hell for such blasphemy, so be it, but Niall no longer believed in hell; he didn't believe in anything.

He would work out his black mood on Meg's lush, willing body, wrapped tight by her arms and legs. The rougher the love play, the more she liked it.

Finding Meg was no effort; she was lurking near the bottom of the huge, curving stone stairway, and came forward with a smile when he appeared at the top. Niall halted, merely standing there, waiting. Meg lifted her skirts and hurried up the stairs, the flickering torchlight intensifying the flush in her cheeks. Niall turned before she reached him, striding back to his chamber. Her quick, light footsteps followed, and he could hear her breathing as it too quickened, both from her exertion and from anticipation.

She was already shrugging out of her shawl, tugging at the laces to her bodice, as she followed him through the door to his chamber. He shut it and watched as she feverishly shed her clothes, revealing the lushness of her body to him. His shaft rose hard and pulsing, tenting the front of his kilt.

She spied the two wine goblets and a pleased smile curved her lips. He'd known she would take it as an expression of his besottedness with her, but let her think what she liked, rather than suspect he'd had a secret visitor, or that it was none other than the King himself. Though he was willing to soothe her ego with small gestures, and more than willing to return twofold the physical ease she gave him, his only interest in her was for the pleasure he found in her soft, bountiful body.

Naked, she took up one of the goblets and sipped the wine, doubly gratified to find it contained a fine vintage rather than the sour, watery ones to which she was more accustomed. The firelight played over the full curves of her bosom, turning her dark nipples to the color of fine wine themselves, deepening the shadows of her navel and the full nest of curls between her thighs.

He didn't want to wait. He approached and took the goblet from her hand, setting it down with a thud that sloshed some of the red liquid over the rim. She gave a little squeal of surprise as he lifted her and tossed her onto the big bed, but the squeal turned into laughter as he landed on top of her.

He kneed her thighs apart. "Are ye no going to remove yer boots, at least?" she asked, giggling. She reached up to tug at the laces of his shirt.

The smell of her was dark and rich, female. His thin nostrils flared, drinking in the scent. "Why?" he asked in a reasonable tone. "They're on my feet, not my cock." The giggles turned into full-scale laughter. Niall reached beneath his kilt and grasped his erect rod, guiding it to her wet cleft.

15

He surged forward, sheathing himself, shuddering with relief, and Meg's laughter died a quick, strangled death as her body absorbed the force of the thrust.

The darkness within him receded, pushed back by sheer delight. So long as he had a woman in his arms, he could forget the betrayal, and the crushing burden of responsibility that weighed on his shoulders.

Chapter 1

April 27, 1996

A LOW, COUGHING RUMBLE ANNOUNCED TO THE NEIGHBORHOOD that Kristian Sieber was home from school. He drove a 1966 Chevelle, lovingly restored to all its original gas-guzzling, eight-cylinder power. The body was a patchwork of different colors, as the parts had been taken from the corpses of other Chevelles, but whenever someone commented on the multicolored car, Kristian would grumpily say that he was "working on it." The truth was, the exterior didn't bother him. He cared only that the car ran the way it had when it was new, when some lucky, macho guy had thrilled every girl around with its growling power. In the instinctive, primal, murky way of males, he was certain all that horsepower would overcome his image as a nerd, and all the girls would flock to his side, wanting to ride in his supercar.

So far it hadn't happened, but Kristian hadn't given up hope.

As the rumbling car passed her house and turned at the corner, Grace St. John hastily took one last bite of the stew

17

she had prepared for supper. "Kristian's home," she said, jumping up from the table.

"No kidding," Ford teased. He winked at her as she grabbed up the case that contained her laptop computer and the multitude of papers she had been translating. The sides of the supple leather case bulged outward, so crammed was it with notes and disks. She had unplugged her modem earlier, wrapped the cords around it, and placed it on top of the case. She cradled case and modem in her arms as she leaned over to reach Ford's mouth. Their kiss was brief, but warm.

"It'll probably take a couple of hours, at least," she said. "After he finds out what the problem is, he wants to show me a few new programs he has."

"It used to be etchings," her brother Bryant murmured. "Now it's programs." The three of them took most of their meals together, a convenience they all liked. When Bryant and Grace had inherited the house from their parents, they turned it into a duplex; Grace and Ford lived in one side, and Bryant in the other. The three of them not only worked for the same archaeological foundation, but Ford and Bryant had been best friends since college. Bryant had introduced Ford and Grace, and still patted himself on the back for the outcome of that introduction.

"You're just jealous because you can't hack it," Grace said, poker-faced, and Bryant groaned at the pun.

Her hands were full, so Ford got up to open the kitchen door for her. He leaned down to kiss her again. "Don't get lost in Kristian's programs and lose track of time," he cautioned, his hazel eyes sending her a very private message that, after almost eight years of marriage, still thrilled her to her toes.

"I won't," she promised, and started out the door, only to halt on the top step. "I forgot my purse."

Ford picked it up from the cabinet and looped the strap over her head. "Why do you need your purse?"

"The checkbook's in it," she said, blowing a strand of hair out of her eyes. She always paid Kristian for his repair services, though he would gladly have done it for free just for the joy of fooling around with someone else's computer.

His equipment was expensive, and his skill better than any she had seen at computer or software companies. He deserved to be paid. "Plus I'll probably buy him a pizza."

"As much as that kid eats, he should weigh four hundred pounds," Bryant observed.

"He's nineteen. Of course he eats a lot."

"I don't think I ever ate that much. What do you think, Ford? When we were in college, did we eat as much as Kristian?"

Ford gave him a disbelieving look. "You actually asking *me*, when you're the guy who once ate thirteen pancakes and a pound of sausage for breakfast?"

"I did?" Bryant frowned. "I don't remember that. And what about you? I've seen you down four Big Macs and four large fries at one sitting."

"Both of you ate as if you had tapeworms," Grace said, settling the discussion as she went down the steps. Ford closed the door behind her, his chuckle rich in her ears.

Thick, resilient grass cushioned her steps as she walked across their backyard, then angled her steps in a shortcut through the Murchisons' overgrown lawn. They had taken a month's vacation in South Carolina, and weren't due to return until the end of the week. It was a shame; in seeking warm weather, and spring, they had missed it at home.

It had been an unusually warm April, and spring had exploded in Minneapolis. The grass was green and lush, the trees leafed out, flowers were in bloom. Even though the sun had set and only the last bits of twilight remained, the evening air was warm and fragrant. Grace inhaled with deep delight. She loved spring. Actually, she loved every season, for they all had their joys.

Kristian stood in the Siebers' back door, waiting for her. "Hi," he said in cheerful greeting. He was always cheerful at the prospect of getting his hands on her laptop.

He hadn't turned on a light. Grace entered through the dark laundry room, passing through the kitchen. Audra Sieber, Kristian's mother, was sliding a tray of rolls into the oven. She looked up with a smile. "Hello, Grace. We're having lamb chops tonight; would you like to join us?"

"Thanks, but I've just finished eating." She liked Audra,

who was comfortably fifty, slightly overweight, and completely understanding of her son's obsession with gigabytes and motherboards. Physically, Kristian was just like his father, Errol: tall, thin, with dark hair, myopic blue eyes, and a prominent Adam's apple bobbing in his throat. Kristian couldn't have looked more like the prototypical computer nerd if he'd had the words stenciled on his forehead.

Remembering his appetite, Grace said, "Kris, this can wait until after you eat."

"I'll fix a plate and carry it up," he said, taking the case from her arms and cradling it lovingly in his. "That's okay with you, isn't it, Mom?"

"Of course. Go on and have fun." Audra aimed her serene smile between the two of them, and Kristian immediately loped out of the kitchen and up the stairs, carrying his prize to his electronics-laden lair.

Grace followed him at a slower pace, thinking as she climbed the stairs that she really needed to shed the twenty extra pounds she'd gained since she and Ford had married. The problem was, her work was so sedentary; a specialist and translator of old languages, she spent a lot of her time with a magnifying glass going over photos of old documents, and very occasionally the actual papers themselves, but for the most part they were too fragile to be handled. The rest of the time she was working on the computer, using a translation program that she and Kristian had enhanced. It was difficult to burn many calories doing brain work.

Earlier that day she had been doing just that, trying to access the university's library to download some information, but the computer hadn't obeyed her commands. She wasn't certain if it was a problem with the laptop itself, or with the modem. She had caught Kristian at home for lunch, and arranged for him to take a look at it when his classes were finished for the day.

The delay had almost driven her mad with frustration. She was fascinated by the batch of documents she'd been translating for her employer, the Amaranthine Potere Foundation, a huge archaeological and antiquities foundation. She loved her work anyway, but this was special, so special that she was almost afraid to believe her translations were correct. She felt almost . . . *pulled,* drawn into the documents in a way that had never happened before. The night before, Ford had asked her what the documents contained, and she had reluctantly told him a little about them—just the topic. Usually she talked freely with Ford about her work, but this time it was different. She felt so strongly about these strange old documents that it was difficult to put it into words, and so she had been rather casual about the whole thing, as if it wasn't even particularly interesting.

Instead, it was . . . special, in ways she didn't fully understand yet. She had translated less than a tenth of the whole, and already the possibilities were driving her half mad with anticipation, swirling just beyond comprehension, like a jigsaw puzzle with only the border assembled. In this case, though, she had no idea what the finished product would look like, only that she couldn't stop until she knew.

She reached the top of the stairs and entered Kristian's bedroom. It was a maze of electronic equipment and cords, with just enough room for his bed. He had four separate phone lines, one each to the one laptop and two desktop computers he owned, and another to a fax machine. Two printers shared the duty among the three computers. One of the desktops was on, with a chess game displayed on the monitor. Kristian glanced at it, grunted, and used the mouse to move a bishop. He studied the results for a moment, before clicking the mouse and turning back to the puzzle at hand. He pushed a stack of papers to one side and moved another onto the bed. "What's it doing?" he asked as he opened the case and removed her laptop.

"Nothing," Grace said, taking another chair and watching as he swiftly unhooked the other desktop's electrical umbilical cords from power port and modem, and plugged in hers. He turned it on and it whirred to life, the screen flickering to a pale blue. "I tried to get into the university's library this morning, and nothing happened. I don't know if it's the unit or the modem."

"We'll find out right now." He knew his way around her menu as well as she did; he clicked onto the one he wanted, then double-clicked on the telephone icon. He dialed the number for the university's electronic library, and ten seconds later was in. "Modem," he announced. His fingers were practically quivering as they hovered over the keys. "What did you want?"

She leaned closer. "Medieval history. The Crusades, specifically."

He scrolled down the list of offerings. "That one," Grace said, and he clicked the mouse. The table of contents filled the screen.

He scooted away. "Here, you take over while I try to find out what's wrong with the modem."

She took his place in front of the computer, and he switched on a lamp on the desk, automatically pushing his glasses up on his nose before he began dismantling the modem.

There were several references to the military religious orders of the time, the Knights Hospitaller and the Knights Templar. It was the Templars she wanted. She clicked onto the appropriate chapter, and lines of information filled the screen.

She read intently, looking for one certain name. It didn't appear. The text was a chronicle and analysis of the Templars' contribution to the Crusades, but except for a few grand masters none was mentioned by name.

They were interrupted briefly when Audra brought a filled plate up to Kristian. He positioned it next to the disassembled modem and happily munched as he worked. Grace went back to the main list and chose another text.

Sometime later she became aware that Kristian had evidently either repaired her modem or given up on it, for he was reading over her shoulder. It was difficult to pull herself out of medieval intrigue and danger, and back into the modern world of computers. She blinked to orient herself, aware of the strangely potent lure of that long-ago time. "Could you fix it?"

"Sure," he replied absently, still reading. "It was just a loose connection. Who were these Templar guys?"

"They were a military religious order in the Middle Ages; don't you know your history?"

He pushed his glasses up on his nose and flashed her an unrepentant grin. "Time began in nineteen forty-six."

"There *was* life before computers."

"Analog life, you mean. Prehistoric."

"What kind of gauges are in that muscle-bound thing you call a car?"

He looked chagrined, caught in the shameful knowledge that his beloved chariot was hopelessly old-fashioned, with analog gauges instead of digital readouts. "I'm working on it," he mumbled, hunching his thin shoulders. "Anyway, about these Templar guys. If they were so religious, why were they burned at the stake like witches or something?"

"Heresy," she murmured, turning her attention back to the screen. "Fire was the punishment for a lot of crimes, not just for witchcraft."

"Guess people back then took their religion seriously." Kristian wrinkled his nose at the electronic display of a crude drawing of three men bound to a center pole while flames licked around their knees. All three men were dressed in white tunics with crosses emblazoned on their chests. Their mouths were little black holes, opened in screams of agony.

"People are still executed because of religion today," Grace said, shuddering a little as she stared at the small drawing, imagining the sheer horror of being burned alive. "In the Middle Ages, religion was the center of people's lives, and anyone who went against it was a threat to them. Religion gave them the rules of civilization, but it was more than that. There was so much that wasn't known, or understood; they were terrified by eclipses, by comets, by sicknesses that struck without warning, by things we know now are normal but which they had no way of understanding. Imagine how frightening, and deadly, appendicitis must have been to them, or a stroke or heart attack. They didn't know what was happening, what caused it, or how to prevent it. Magic was very real to them, and religion gave them a sort of protection against these unknown, frightening forces. Even if they died, God was still taking care of them, and the evil spirits didn't win."

His brow furrowed as he tried to imagine living in such ignorance. It was almost beyond him, this child of the computer age. "I guess television would've given them a real spasm, huh?"

"Especially if they saw a talk show," she muttered. "Now *there* are some evil spirits."

Kristian giggled, sending his glasses slipping down his nose. He pushed them up again and squinted at the screen. "Did you find what you want?"

"No. I'm looking for mention of one particular Templar—at least, I think he was a Templar."

"Any cross-references you can check?"

She shook her head. "I don't know his last name." *Niall of Scotland.* She had already found his name several times in the portion of the documents written in Old French. Why wasn't his surname recorded, in a time when family and heritage were so important? From what she had gleaned from her translations so far, he'd been a man of immense importance to the Templars, a Knight himself, which meant he was well born and not a serf. Part of the documents were also in Gaelic, strengthening the unknown tie with Scotland. She'd read up on Scotland's history in her encyclopedia, but there hadn't been any mention of a mysterious Niall at all, much less one in the time frame of the Templars' existence.

"Dead end, then," Kristian said cheerfully, evidently deciding they had wasted enough time on someone who had died even before the age of analog. His blue eyes sparkled as he moved his chair a little closer. "Want to see this cool accounting program I've worked up?"

"I don't think the words *cool* and *accounting* go together," Grace observed, keeping her expression deadpan.

Shocked, Kristian stared at her. He blinked several times, making him look like a myopic crane. "Are you kidding?" he blurted. "It's the greatest! Wait until you see—wait. You *are* kidding. I can tell."

Grace's lips curved as she deftly tapped keys, backing out of the university's library system. "Oh, yeah? How?"

"You always tighten your mouth to keep from smiling." He glanced at her mouth, then quickly looked away, blushing a little.

Grace felt her own cheeks heating and carefully glued her eyes to the screen. Kristian had a tiny crush on her, based mostly on his enthusiasm for her expensive, powerful laptop, but on a few rare occasions he had said or done something that bespoke a physical awareness of her as well.

It always disconcerted her; she was thirty years old, for heaven's sake, and was certainly not a femme fatale by any stretch of the imagination. She considered herself very ordinary, with nothing about her to inspire lust in a nineteen-year-old—though God knows, almost anything female and breathing could inspire lust in a nineteen-year-old boy. If Kristian was the stereotypical image of a computer nerd, she'd always thought she looked the typical shy academic type: dark brown hair, impossibly straight, which she had long ago given up trying to coax into curls and now wore pulled back into a single thick braid; light blue eyes, almost gray, usually framed by reading glasses; no makeup, because she didn't know how to apply it; sensible clothes, tending toward corduroy slacks and denim skirts. She was hardly the stuff of an erotic dream.

But Ford had always said she had the most kissable mouth he'd ever seen, and it flustered her that Kristian had looked so pointedly at her lips. To distract him, she said, "Okay, let's see this hotshot program." She hoped the Chevelle would work its macho magic soon, and lure into Kristian's orbit some smart girl who appreciated both horsepower and multitasking.

Looking grateful for the change of subject, he opened a plastic case and removed the diskette, then inserted it into the disk drive. Grace scooted to the side, giving him better access to the keys. He directed the computer to access the disk in the A drive, there was some electronic whirring, and a menu appeared on the screen.

"What bank do you use?" Kristian asked.

Grace told him, frowning as she scanned down the menu. Kristian zipped the cursor to the item he wanted, clicked on it, and the screen changed again. "Bingo," he crowed as a new menu appeared, this time of bank services. "Am I slick, or what?"

"You're illegal, is what you are!" Appalled, Grace watched as he chose another item, clicked on it, then typed "St. John, Grace." Instantly a record of her checking account transactions appeared on the screen. "You've hacked into the bank's computers! Get out of there before you get in big trouble. I mean it, Kris! This is a felony. You told me you had an accounting program, not a back door into every bank in the area."

"Don't you want to know how I did it?" he asked, clearly disappointed that she didn't share his enthusiasm for the deed. "I'm not stealing or anything. This lets you see how long it takes each check to clear, so you can establish a pattern. Some places only deposit once a week. You can get a better handle on your cash flow if you know how long it takes for a particular check to clear. That way, if you have an interest-bearing checking account, you can time your payments so your average balance doesn't dip below the minimum."

Grace simply stared at him, amazed at the wiring of his brain. To her, money matters were a straightforward affair: you had X amount of money coming in, and you had to keep your expenses below that amount. Simple. She had long ago decided there were two types of people on earth: math people, and non-math people. She was an intelligent woman; she had a doctoral degree. But the intricacies of math, whether it dealt with finance or quantum physics, had simply never appealed to her. Words, now . . . she reveled in words, wallowed deliriously in the nuances of meaning, delighted in the magic of them. Ford was even less interested in math than she was, which was why she took care of the checkbook. Bryant tried; he read the financial section of the newspaper, subscribed to investment magazines—in case he ever had enough money to invest—but he didn't have a real grasp of the dynamics. After fifteen minutes of wading through one of his investment magazines, he was tossing it aside and reaching for something, anything, on archaeology.

But Kristian was a math person. Grace had no doubt he'd be a billionaire by the time he was thirty. He would write some brilliant computer program, wisely invest the profits, and retire happily to tinker away at more innovative programs.

"I'm sure it's a real boon to depositors," she said dryly, "but it's still illegal. You can't market it."

"Oh, it's not for public knowledge, it's just goofing

around. You'd think banks would have better security programs, but I haven't found one yet that's much of a challenge."

Grace propped her chin on her hand and eyed him. "My boy, you're either going to be famous, or in jail."

He ducked his head, grinning. "I've got something else to show you," he said enthusiastically, his fingers darting over the keyboard as he exited the bank's accounting records.

Grace watched as the screen changed rapidly, flickering from one display to another. "Won't they be able to tell you've been in their files?"

"Not with this baby. See, I got in through a legitimate password. Basically, I put on an electronic sheepskin, and they never knew a wolf was prowling around."

"How did you get the password?"

"Snooping. No matter how coded the info, there's always a back door. Not that your bank has very good computer security," he said with obvious disapproval. "If I were you, I'd consider moving my account."

"I'll think about it," she assured him, with a baleful glare that had him grinning again.

"That's just part of the program. Here's the accounting system." He pulled up another screen and motioned Grace closer. She obligingly scooted her chair forward an inch or so, and he launched into the intricacies of his digitalized baby. Grace paid attention, because she could easily see it *was* a good system, deceptively simple to execute. He had programmed it to compare the current entry against past entries in the same account, so if anyone accidentally typed in, say, "$115.00" instead of "$15.00," the program alerted the user that the amount wasn't within the previously established range, and to check for an input error.

"I like that," she mused. She had always paid bills and done her bookkeeping the old-fashioned way, by hand and on paper. However, she was completely at home with computers, so there was no reason for her not to do their household finances electronically.

Kristian beamed. "I knew you would." His long fingers stroked the keys, downloading the program into her hard disk. "Its name is Go Figure."

She groaned at the sly corniness of it, the groan changing

midway into a laugh. "Do me a favor. When you get busted for playing around in the bank's computers, don't tell the feds that I have a copy of the program, okay?"

"I'm telling you, it's safe, at least until the banks change all their passwords. Then you simply won't be able to get in. *I* could get in," he boasted, "but most people couldn't. Here, let me give you a list of the passwords."

"I don't want it," she said quickly, but Kristian ignored her. He rifled through a stack of papers and plucked out three sheets of closely printed material, which he stuck in her computer case.

"There. Now you'll have it if you need it." He paused, staring at the computer with the ongoing chess game. His opponent had made a move. He studied the board, head cocked slightly to one side, then he chortled. "Aha! I know that gambit, and it won't work." Gleefully he moved a knight and clicked the mouse.

"Who are you playing with?"

"I dunno," he said absently. "He calls himself the Fishman."

Grace blinked, staring at the screen. Naw, it couldn't be. Kristian was playing with someone who had probably chosen that Net name with malice aforethought, to trick people into making just that assumption. The real Bobby Fischer wouldn't be surfing the Net looking for games; he could play anyone, anywhere, and get paid huge amounts of money for doing it.

"Who usually wins?"

"We're about even. He's good," Kristian allowed as he rehooked his other desktop.

Grace opened her purse and pulled out her checkbook. "Want a pizza?" she asked.

His head cocked as he pulled his mind back from cyberspace to check the status of his stomach. "Boy, do I ever," he declared. "I'm starving."

"Then call it in; this one's on me."

"Are you going to stay and split it with me?"

She shook her head. "I can't. I have things waiting for me at home." She barely controlled a blush. Ford would have roared with laughter if he'd heard her.

She wrote out a check for fifty dollars, then pulled out a

twenty to pay for the pizza. "Thanks, buddy. You're a lifesaver."

Kristian took the check and tip, grinning as he looked at it. "This is going to be a good career, isn't it?" he asked, beaming.

Grace had to laugh. "If you can stay out of jail." She placed the laptop in the case and balanced the repaired modem on top of her unzipped purse. Kristian gallantly took the heavy case from her and carried it downstairs for her. Neither of his parents was in sight, but the sounds of gunshots and a car chase drifted from the den and pinpointed their location; both of the older Siebers unabashedly loved Arnold Schwarzenegger's action movies.

Kristian's gallantry lasted only as far as the kitchen, where the proximity to food reminded him of the pizza he hadn't yet ordered. Grace retrieved the computer case from him as he halted at the wall phone. "Thanks, Kris," she said, and left the same way she had entered, through the darkened laundry room and out the back door.

She paused for a moment to let her eyes adjust to the darkness. During the time she had been with Kristian, clouds had rolled in to block most of the starlight, though here and there was a clear patch of sky. Crickets chirped, and a cool breeze stirred around her, bringing with it the scent of rain.

The light from her kitchen window, fifty yards to the right, was like a beacon. Ford was there, waiting for her. Warmth filled her and she smiled, thinking of him. She began walking toward her home, stepping carefully in the darkness so she wouldn't stumble over some unevenness in the ground, the soft spring grass cushioning her movements in silence.

She was in the Murchisons' backyard when she saw someone in her kitchen, briefly framed by the window as he moved past it. Grace paused, frowning a little; that hadn't looked like either Ford or Bryant.

Oh, Lord, they had company. Her frown deepened. It was probably someone interested in archaeology or associated with the Foundation. College kids pondering a career in archaeology sometimes dropped by to talk, and sometimes she was the one they wanted to see, if they were having a problem with Latin or Greek terms. It didn't matter. She didn't want to talk shop, she wanted to go to bed with her husband.

She was reluctant to go in, though of course she would have to; she couldn't stand out there in the dark waiting for whoever it was to leave, which could be hours. She edged to the right, trying to see if she recognized the visitor's car, hoping that it belonged to one of Bryant's friends. If so, she could signal her brother to take his friend into his side of the house.

Her familiar Buick sat in the carport, and beside it was Bryant's black Jeep Cherokee. Ford's scratched and dented Chevrolet four-wheel-drive pickup, which was used for field work, was parked off to the side. No other vehicle occupied their driveway.

That was strange. She knew they had company, because the man she'd so briefly glimpsed had had sandy-colored hair, and both Ford and Bryant were dark-haired. But unless it was a neighbor who had walked over, she had no idea how he had arrived. She knew most of their neighbors, though, and none of them fit the description of the man she'd seen.

Well, she wouldn't find out who he was until she went inside. She took a step toward the house and suddenly stopped again, squinting through the darkness. Something had moved between her and the house, something dark and furtive.

A chill ran down her spine. Icy shards of alarm ran through her veins, freezing her in place. Wild possibilities darted through her mind: a gorilla had escaped from a zoo . . . or there was a really, really big dog in her backyard.

Then it moved again, ghosting silently up to her back door. It was a man. She blinked in astonishment, wondering why someone was skulking around in her yard, and going to the back door instead of the front. A robbery? Why would any thief with half a brain break into a house where the lights were still on and the occupants were obviously at home?

Then the back door opened, and she realized the man must have knocked on it, though softly, because she hadn't heard anything. Another man stood in the door, a man she knew. There was a pistol, the barrel long and curiously thickened, in his hand.

"Nothing," the first man said, his voice low, but the night air carried the sound.

"God damn it," the other man muttered, stepping aside to let the first man enter. "I can't stop now. We'll have to go ahead and do it."

The door closed behind them. Grace stared across the dark yard at the blank expanse of her back door. Why was Parrish Sawyer there, and why did he have a pistol? He was their boss, and if he'd called to let them know he was coming over, for whatever reason, Ford would have called her to come home. They were on cordial terms with Parrish, but they had never socialized; Parrish played in the more rarefied stratosphere of the rich and well connected, qualifications Grace's family didn't have.

"Do it"—that was what he'd said. Do what? And why couldn't he stop?

Puzzled and uneasy, Grace left the shadows of the Murchisons' yard and walked across her own. She didn't know what was going on, but she was definitely going to find out.

While she had been cooking earlier she had opened the kitchen window so she could enjoy the freshness of the spring day, and it was still raised. She plainly heard Ford say, "Damn it, Parrish, what's this about?"

Ford's voice was rough, angry, with a tone in it she'd never heard before. Grace froze again with one foot lifted to the first step.

"Where is she?" Parrish asked, ignoring Ford's question. His voice was indifferent and cold, and the sound of it made the hairs lift on the back of her neck.

"I told you, the library."

A lie. Ford was deliberately lying. Grace stood still, staring at the open window and trying to picture what was happening on the other side of the wall. She couldn't see anyone, but she knew there were at least four people inside. Where was Bryant, and the man she'd seen enter the kitchen?

"Don't give me that shit. Her car's here."

"She went with a friend."

"What's this friend's name?"

"Serena, Sabrina, something like that. Tonight's the first time I've met her."

Ford had always thought fast on his feet. The names were enough out of the ordinary that it gave the lie a bit of credence, where a plain Sally wouldn't. She didn't know why Ford was lying, but the fact that he was doing it was enough for Grace. Parrish had a pistol, and Ford didn't want him to know where Grace was; something was very wrong.

"All right." It sounded as if Parrish exhaled through his teeth. "What time will she be back?"

"She didn't know. She said they had a lot of work to do. When the library closes, I guess."

"And she carried all of the documents with her."

"They were in her computer case."

"Does this Serena-Sabrina know about the documents?"

"I don't know."

"It doesn't matter." Now Parrish sounded a little bored. "I can't take the chance. All right, stand up, both of you."

She heard chairs being scraped back, and she moved silently to the right, so she could see inside the window. She was careful to stand back, so if anyone glanced out the window she wouldn't be framed in the pool of light.

She saw Bryant, shirtless, his hair damp; he must have just gotten out of the shower, which told her that Parrish and the other man had arrived not long before. Her brother's face was drawn and pale, his eyes curiously blank. Grace moved another step, and saw four more people.

There was Ford, as pale as Bryant, though his eyes glittered with a kind of anger she'd never seen before. Parrish, tall and sophisticated, his blond hair expensively styled, stood with his back to the window. The man she'd seen earlier stood beside him, and another man stood just inside the interior kitchen doorway. The man at the doorway was armed; his pistol, like Parrish's, was silenced. The third man would also be armed, Grace thought, since the other two were.

She didn't know what was going on, but she was sure of one thing: she needed the police. She would call them from the Siebers' house. She took a cautious step backward.

"Go into the bedroom, both of you," she heard Parrish say. "And don't do anything stupid, like trying to jump one of us. I can't tell you how very painful it is to be shot, but I'll be forced to demonstrate if you don't cooperate."

Why was he making them go to the bedroom? She had heard enough to know that she was the one he really wanted, and he seemed to be concerned about the documents she carried.

If Parrish wanted the documents, all he had to do was say so; he was her boss, and she worked on the assignments he gave her. It would break her heart to give up the tantalizing papers, but she couldn't stop him from taking them. Why hadn't he just called, and told her to turn them over tomorrow morning? Why had he come to her house with a gun in his hand, and brought two armed thugs with him? None of this made sense.

She started to walk quickly back to the Siebers' house, but impulse led her around the corner of the house to where she could look into the bedroom window. She waited for the light to come on, waited to hear voices in the room, but nothing happened, and abruptly she realized Parrish had taken them to Bryant's bedroom, on the other side of the house. Given the configuration of the house when they had divided it, Bryant's bedroom was at the back of the house with the kitchen. Parrish would have had to take them up the hallway to the front of the house, then through the connecting door into Bryant's part of the house and back to the bedroom.

As quickly as possible Grace retraced her steps, taking care to remain in the deepest shadows. A water hose was curled like a long, skinny snake around the protruding outside faucet; she skirted it, and also sidestepped a big sifting board one of the men had propped against the house. This was her home; she knew all its idiosyncrasies, the little traps for the unwary. She knew where the squeaks in the floor were, the cracks in the ceiling, the ruts in the yard.

Light was already shining from Bryant's window. She pressed her back against the wall and sidestepped until she was right beside it. She moved her head around, slowly, trying to move just enough that she could see inside.

One of the men stepped to the window. Grace jerked her

head back and stood rigidly still, not even daring to breathe. He jerked the curtains together, shielding the window and darkening the spill of light.

Blood thundered in her ears, and sheer terror made her weak. She still couldn't breathe; her heart felt as if it were literally in her throat, suffocating her. If the man had seen her she would have been caught, for she couldn't possibly have moved.

"Sit on the bed," she heard Parrish say over her pounding heartbeat.

Grace's lungs were finally working again. She gulped in deep breaths to steady her nerves, then once again shifted position.

The curtain hadn't quite fallen together. She moved so she could see through the slit, see Ford and Bryant—

Parrish calmly lifted his silenced pistol and shot Ford in the head, then quickly shifted his aim and shot Bryant. Her brother was dead before her husband's body had toppled to the side.

No. *No!* She hung there, paralyzed. Somehow her body was gone, vanished; she couldn't feel anything, couldn't think. A dark mist swam over her vision and the unbelievable scene receded until it was as if she saw it at the end of a long tunnel. She heard them talking, their voices oddly distorted.

"Shouldn't you have waited? There'll be a discrepancy in the times of death."

"That isn't a concern." Parrish's voice; she knew it. "In a murder-suicide, sometimes the killer waits awhile before killing himself—or herself, in this case. The shock, you understand. Such a pity, her husband and brother conducting a homosexual affair right under her nose. No wonder the poor dear got upset and went a little berserk."

"What about the friend?"

"Ah, yes. Serena-Sabrina. Bad luck for her; she'll have an unfortunate accident on the way home. I'll wait here for Grace, and you two wait in the car, follow Serena-Sabrina."

Slowly the mist cleared from Grace's vision. She wished it hadn't. She wished she had died right there, wished her heart had stopped. Through the gap in the curtains she could see her husband sprawled on his back, his eyes open and unseeing, his dark hair matted with . . . with—

The sound rose from her chest, an almost silent keening that reverberated in her throat. It was like the distant howl of the wind, dark and soulless. The pain ripped out of her. She tried to hold it back with her teeth, but it boiled out anyway, primitive, wild. Parrish's head snapped around. For a tenth of a second—no more—she thought that their gazes met, that somehow he could see through that small gap into the night. He said something, sharply, and lunged for the window.

Grace plunged into the night.

Chapter 2

SHE NEEDED MONEY.

Grace stared through the rainy night at the ATM; it was lit like a shrine, inviting her to cross the street and perform its electronic ritual. It was thirty yards away, at most. It would take her only a couple of minutes to reach it, punch in the necessary numbers, and she would have cash in her hand.

She needed to empty out the checking account, and probably a single ATM wouldn't have enough cash on hand to give her that amount, which meant she would have to find another ATM, then another, and every time she did the odds that she would be spotted would increase—as well as the odds of being mugged.

The ATM cameras would all film her, and the police would know where she had been, and when. A sudden image of Ford blasted into her brain, paralyzing her anew with shattering pain. *God, oh God.* The inhuman, involuntary keen rose in her throat again, rattled eerily against her clenched teeth. The sound that leaked out made a prowling cat freeze with one paw uplifted, its hair standing out. Then the animal turned and leaped and vanished into the rain-washed darkness, away from the crouched creature who emitted such a ghostly, anguished sound.

Grace rocked back and forth, pushing the pain deep inside, forcing herself to *think*. Ford had bought her safety with his life, and it would be a betrayal beyond bearing if she wasted his sacrifice by making bad decisions.

A slew of late-night withdrawals, all *after* the estimated times of death, would cement her appearance of guilt. Kristian would know what time she had left the Siebers' house, and Ford and Bryant had been killed at roughly that time. They had both been partially undressed, and in Bryant's bedroom. Parrish had set up the situation with his usual thoroughness; any cop alive would believe she had walked in on a homosexual encounter between her husband and her brother, and killed them both. Her subsequent disappearance was another point against her.

The men with Parrish had been professional in their manner; they wouldn't have done anything sloppy like leave fingerprints. No neighbors would have seen strange cars parked at the house, because they had parked elsewhere and walked to the house. There were no witnesses, no evidence to point to anyone except her.

And even if by some miracle she convinced the police she was innocent, she had no proof Parrish had killed them. She had *seen* him do it, but she couldn't prove she had. Moreover, to the cops' way of thinking, he wouldn't have had a motive, while she obviously had plenty of motive. What could she offer as proof? A batch of papers written in a tangle of ancient languages, which she hadn't even deciphered yet, and which Parrish could have gotten from her at any time simply by telling her to turn them over to him?

There was no motive, at least none she could prove. And if she turned herself in, Parrish would get the papers, and she would end up dead. He would make certain of it. It would be made to look as if she'd hung herself, or perhaps a drug overdose would cause a brief scandal about the presence of drugs in jails and prisons, but the end result would be the same.

She had to stay alive, and out of police hands. It was the

only chance she had of finding out *why* Parrish had killed Ford and Bryant—and avenging them.

To stay alive, to stay free, she had to have money. To get money, she had to use the ATMs no matter how guilty it made her look.

Would the police freeze her bank account? She didn't know, but if they did they would probably need a court order to do it. That should give her a little time—time she was wasting by huddling behind a trash bin, instead of walking across the street to the ATM and getting out what she could, while she could.

But she felt numb, almost incapable of functioning. The thirty yards might as well have been a hundred miles.

The shiny black surface of the wet pavement reflected the distorted, surreal image of the lights: the brightly colored hues of neon, the stark white of the streetlights, the never-ending, monotonous progression of the traffic light through green, yellow, red, over and over, exerting its control over nonexistent traffic. At two A.M. there was only an occasional car, and none at all for the past five minutes. No one was in sight. Now was the time to approach the ATM.

But still she crouched there, hidden from view and partially protected from the rain by the overhang of the building and the bulk of the trash bin. Her hair was plastered to her head, her sodden braid hanging limp and rain-heavy down her back. Her clothes were soaked, and even though the night was still unusually warm by Minneapolis standards, the dampness had leached the heat from her body so that she shivered with cold.

She clutched a garbage bag to her chest; it was a small bag, the type sometimes used to line the trash cans in public buildings. She had liberated it from just such a can in the ladies' rest room of the public library. The computer and the precious papers were protected inside the case, but when it had started raining she had panicked at the possibility of them getting wet, and all she could think of using to protect them was a plastic bag.

Maybe it hadn't been smart, going to the library. It was, after all, a public place, and one she frequented. On the other hand, how often did the police search libraries for suspected murderers? It was impossible for Parrish to have gotten a good look at her through that tiny slit in the bedroom curtains, but he certainly guessed she was the one lurking outside the window and had seen everything. He and his men were searching for her, but even though Ford had told them she'd gone to the library she doubted they would think she had gone *back* to one to hide.

The police might not even have been notified of the murders yet. Parrish couldn't report them without bringing himself into the picture, which he wouldn't want to do. The neighbors wouldn't have heard anything, since the shots had been silenced.

No. The police knew. Parrish wouldn't take the chance of letting days go by before the bodies—her mind stumbled on the word, but she forced herself to finish the thought—were discovered. Was there any way for forensics to tell if the pistol had been fitted with a silencer? She didn't think so. All Parrish would have to do would be to call in a "suspicious noise, like gunshots," at their address, and use a pay phone so nothing would show up on the 911 records.

Both Parrish and his henchmen, and the police, were looking for her. Still, she had gone to the main branch of the library. Instinct had led her there. She was numb with shock and horror, and the library, as familiar to her as her own house, had seemed like a haven. The smell of books, that wonderful mingling of paper and leather and ink, had been the scent of sanctuary. Dazed, at first she had simply wandered among the shelves, looking at the books that had defined the boundaries of her life until a few short hours ago, trying to recapture that sense of safety, of normalcy.

It hadn't worked. Nothing would ever be normal again.

Finally she had gone into the rest room, and stared in bewilderment at the reflection in the mirror. That white-faced, blank-eyed woman wasn't *her,* couldn't possibly be Grace St. John, who had spent her life in academia and who specialized in deciphering and translating ancient languages. The Grace St. John she was familiar with, the one whose face she had seen countless times in other mirrors, had happy blue eyes and a cheerful expression, the face of a woman who loved and was loved in return. Content. Yes, she had been content. So what if she was just a little too plump, so what if she could have been the poster girl for

Bookworms Anonymous? Ford had loved her, and that was what had counted in her life.

Ford was dead.

It couldn't be. It wasn't real. Nothing that had happened was real. Maybe if she closed her eyes, when she opened them she would find herself in her own bed, and realize it had only been a ghastly nightmare, or that she was having some sort of mental breakdown. That would be a good trade, she thought as she squeezed her eyes shut. Her sanity for Ford's life. She'd go for that any day of the week.

She tried it. She squeezed her eyes really tight, concentrated on the idea that it was just a nightmare and that she was about to wake up, and everything would be all right. But when she opened her eyes, everything was the same. She still stared back at herself in the stark fluorescent light, and Ford was still dead. Ford and Bryant. Husband and brother, the only two people on earth whom she loved, and who loved her in return. They were both gone, irrevocably, finally, definitely gone. Nothing would bring them back, and she felt as if the essence of her own being had died with them. She was only a shell, and she wondered why the framework of bone and skin that she saw in the mirror didn't collapse from its own emptiness.

Then, looking into her own eyes, she'd known why she didn't collapse. She wasn't empty, as she'd thought. There was something inside after all, something wild and bottomless, a feral tangle of terror and rage and hate. She had to fight Parrish, somehow. If either he or the police caught her, then he would have won, and she couldn't bear that.

He wanted the papers. She had only begun to translate them; she didn't know what they contained, or what Parrish thought they contained. She didn't know what was so important about them that he had killed Ford and Bryant, and intended to kill her, merely because they knew these particular papers existed. Maybe Parrish thought she had deciphered more than she actually had. He didn't just want physical possession of the papers; he wanted to erase all knowledge of their existence, and their content. What was in them that her husband and brother had died because of them?

That was why she had to protect the laptop. Her computer held all her notes, her journal entries, her language programs that aided her in her work. Give her access to a modem, and she could connect to any resource on-line that she needed in her work, and she could continue her translations. She would find out why. *Why.*

To have any chance of successfully hiding, she had to have cash. Good, untraceable cash.

She had to make herself walk to that ATM. And when she'd emptied it—assuming there was any cash left in it, given the hour—she would have to find another one.

Her fingers were numb, and bloodless. The temperature had remained in the sixties, but she had been wet for hours.

She didn't know where she found the surge of energy that carried her to her feet. Perhaps it wasn't energy at all, but desperation. But suddenly she was standing, even though her knees were so stiff and weak she had to lean against the wet wall for support. She pushed away from the wall, and momentum propelled her several unsteady steps before panic and fatigue dragged at her again, slowing her to a standstill. She clutched the garbage bag to her chest, feeling the reassuring weight of the laptop within the plastic. Rain dripped down her face, and a massive black weight pressed on her chest. *Ford. Bryant.*

Damn everything.

Somehow her feet were moving again, clumsily shuffling, but moving. That was all she required, that they move.

Her purse swung awkwardly from her shoulder, banging against her hip. Her steps slowed, stopped. *Stupid!* It was a miracle she hadn't already been mugged, wandering back alleys at this time of night with her purse plainly in sight.

She edged back into the shadows, her heart thumping from a surge of panic. For a moment she stood paralyzed, afraid to move as her gaze darted around the dark alley, searching for any of the night predators who prowled the city. The narrow alley remained silent, and her breath sighed out of her. She was alone. Perhaps the rain had worked in her favor, and the homeless, the druggies, the hoodlums, had decided to take shelter somewhere.

She laughed in the darkness, the sound small and humorless. She had grown up in Minneapolis, and she had no real idea which sections of the city she should avoid. She knew her neighborhood, her routes to the university, the libraries, the post office and grocery, doctor and dentist. In the course of her work, and Ford's, she had traveled to six continents and God knows how many countries; she had thought herself well traveled, but suddenly she realized how little she knew of her own city because she had been encapsulated in her own little safe, familiar world.

To survive, she would have to be a lot smarter, a lot more aware. Street smarts meant a lot more than locking your car doors as soon as you were inside. She would have to be ready for anything, an attack from any quarter, and she would have to be ready to fight. She would have to learn to think like the night predators, or she wouldn't make it a week on the street.

Carefully she slipped the ATM card into her pocket, then huddled once again under the overhanging roof. After depositing the precious, plastic-wrapped computer on her feet, she opened her purse and began ruthlessly sorting through the contents. She took out what cash she had, stuffing it into a pocket of the computer case without bothering to count it; she knew it wasn't much, maybe forty or fifty dollars, because she didn't normally carry much cash. She hesitated over the checkbook, but decided to take it; she might be able to use it, though a paper trail was dangerous. Ditto for the American Express card. She dropped both of them into the plastic bag. Any use they had, though, would be immediate and short-term. She would have to leave Minneapolis, and after she did, using either checks or a credit card would lead the police right to her.

There were several photos in the plastic pockets. She didn't have to see them to know what they were. Her fingers trembling, she pulled the entire photo protector out of her wallet and slipped it too into the bag.

Okay, what else? There were her driver's license and social security card, but what good were they now? The license would only identify her, which she wanted to avoid, and as for the social security card—a hollow laugh escaped her. She didn't think she had much chance of living to collect social security.

Any identification she left behind would undoubtedly be

found and used by the street scavengers, which might help dilute the police search for her if they had to run down leads that had nothing to do with her. She left the cards, and on impulse dug the checkbook out of the plastic bag. After carefully tearing out one check and storing it in the same pocket with her cash, she dropped the checkbook back into her purse.

She left the tube of lip balm, but couldn't bear not having a comb. Another eerie, hollow laugh sounded in her throat; her husband and brother had just been murdered, the police were after her, and she was worried about being *unkempt?* Nevertheless, the comb went into the bag.

Her scrabbling fingers touched several pens and mechanical pencils, and without thought she took two of them. They were as essential to her work as the computer, because sometimes, when she was stumped on deciphering a particularly obscure passage or word, actually rewriting the words in her own hand would form a link of recognition between her brain and her eyes, and suddenly she would understand at least some of the words as she saw similarities to other languages, other alphabets. She had to have the pens.

There was her bulky appointment book. She ignored it, shutting it out of her thoughts. It held the minutiae of a life that no longer existed: the appointments and lists and reminders. She didn't want to see the scribbled notation for Ford's next dental cleaning, or the sappy heart he'd drawn on the calendar on her birthdate.

She left her business cards—she'd never used them much, anyway. She left the small pack of tissues, the spray bottle of eyeglass cleaner, the roll of antacid tablets, the breath mints. She took the metal nail file, tucking it into her pocket. It wasn't much, but it was the only thing she possessed in the way of a weapon. She hesitated over her car keys, wondering if perhaps she could sneak back and get either her car or Ford's truck. No. That was stupid. She left the keys. With both the keys and her address, perhaps whoever found the purse would steal either the car or the truck, or both, and lead the police astray even more.

Chewing gum, rubber bands, a magnifying glass . . . she identified all of those by feel, and removed only the magnifying glass, which she needed for work. Why had she been carrying so much *junk* around? A flicker of impatience licked at her, the first emotion other than grief and despair that had seeped through the numbness that surrounded her. It wasn't just her purse; she couldn't afford to make any mistakes, carry any excess baggage, let anything interfere with her focus. From this second forward, she would have to do whatever was necessary. There couldn't be any more wasting of precious time and energy because she was paralyzed by fear. She had to *act,* without hesitation, or Parrish would win.

Grimly she tossed the purse on top of the trash bin, and heard a faint squeak and scrabble as a scavenging rat was disturbed. Somehow she made her feet begin moving again, shuffling across the littered alley, painfully inching from safety to exposure.

The headlights of an approaching car made her freeze just before stepping onto the sidewalk. It passed, tires swishing on the wet pavement, the driver not even bothering to glance at the bedraggled figure standing between two buildings.

The car turned right at the next intersection, and disappeared from view. Grace focused on the ATM, took a deep breath, and walked. She was staring so hard at the brightly lit machine that she missed the curb and stumbled, twisting her right ankle. She ignored the pain, not letting herself stop. Athletes walked off pain all the time; she could do the same.

The ATM loomed closer and closer, brighter and brighter. She wanted to run, to return to the safety of the trash bin. She might as well have been naked; the sensation of being exposed was so powerful that she shuddered, fighting for control. Anyone could be watching her, waiting for her to finish the transaction before mugging her, taking the money, and perhaps killing her in the process. The ATM camera would be watching her now, recording every move.

She tried to recall how much money was in the checking account. Damn it, she'd thrown away the checkbook without looking at the balance! There was no way she was going to go back to that alley and climb into the trash bin to search for her purse, even assuming she could manage the exertion. She would simply withdraw money until the machine stopped her.

The machine stopped her at three hundred dollars.

She stared at the computer screen in bewilderment. "Transaction Denied." She *knew* there was more than that in the account, there was more than two thousand—not a great amount, but it could mean the difference between death and survival for her. She knew there was a limit on what she could withdraw in a single transaction, but why had the machine balked at the second one?

Maybe there wasn't enough cash left in the ATM to fill the request. She started over, punching in her code, and this time she requested only one hundred.

"Transaction Denied."

Panic shot through her stomach, twisting it into knots. Oh, God, the police couldn't have frozen the account so soon, could they?

No. *No.* It was impossible. The banks were closed. Something might be done first thing in the morning, but nothing could have happened yet. The machine was just out of money. That was all it was.

Hurriedly, she stuffed the three hundred dollars into her pockets, dividing it up so that if she were mugged, she might be able to get away with emptying out only one pocket. She only hoped nothing would happen to the computer; she would hand over the money without argument, but she would fight for the computer and those precious files. Without them, she would never know why Ford and Bryant had died, and she had to know. It wouldn't be enough to avenge them; she had to know *why.*

She began walking hurriedly, desperation driving her numb feet. She had to find another ATM, get more money. But where *was* another one? Until now, she had used only the one located at her local bank branch, but she knew she had seen others. They were located at malls, but malls were closed at this hour. She tried to think of places that were open twenty-four hours a day, and also had ATMs. Grocery stores, maybe? She remembered when she had opened the account, the bank had given her a booklet listing all its ATM "convenient locations," but she wasn't finding them all that damn convenient.

"Gimme the money."

They materialized in front of her, lunging out of an alley

so fast she had no time to react. There were two of them, one white, one black, both feral. The white guy jabbed a knife at her, the blade glinting ghostly pale in the rain-filtered streetlight. "Don't fuck wi' me, bitch," he breathed, his breath more lethal than the weapon. "Just gimme the money." He was short a few teeth and a lot of intelligence.

Wordlessly she stuck her hand into her pocket and took out the fold of money. She knew she should be scared, but evidently the human mind could sustain fear only to a certain level, and anything after that simply didn't register.

The black guy grabbed the money, and the other one jabbed the knife closer, this time at her face. Grace jerked her head back just in time to keep the blade from slicing across her chin. "I saw you, bitch. Gimme the rest of it."

So much for her grand scheme; they had probably been watching her from the time she crossed the street. She reached into her other pocket, and managed to wedge her fingers inside the fold so that she brought out only half of it. The black guy snatched it, too.

Then they were gone, pelting back into the alley, melting into the darkness. They hadn't even asked about the plastic bag she carried. They'd been after cash, not something that required extra trouble. At least she still had the computer. Grace closed her eyes, and fought to keep her knees from buckling under the crushing weight of despair. At least she still had the computer. She didn't have her husband, or her brother, but at least she still had . . . the . . . *damn* . . . computer.

The harsh, howling sound startled her. It was a moment before she realized it came from her own throat, another moment before she realized that she was walking again, somehow, somewhere. Rain dripped down at her face, or at least she thought it was rain. She couldn't feel herself crying, but then she couldn't feel herself walking, either; she was simply moving. Maybe she *was* crying, useless as that would be. Rain, tears, what difference did it make?

She still had the computer.

Computer. Kristian.

Oh, God. Kristian.

She had to warn him. If Parrish had any inkling Kristian

knew about the files, much less part of their content, he wouldn't hesitate to kill the boy.

Pay telephones, thank God, were far more plentiful and convenient than ATMs. She fished some change out of the bag, desperately clutching the coins in her wet palm as she crossed one corner and hurried up the block, then turned at another street, wanting to put plenty of distance between her and the two muggers before she stopped. God, the streets were so deserted, something she would never have imagined in a metro area the size of Minneapolis–St. Paul. Her footsteps echoed; her breathing sounded ragged and uneven, unnaturally loud. The rain dripped from eaves and awnings, and the buildings towered high and close over her, with the occasional lighted window indicating some poor office prisoner pulling an all-nighter. She was a world removed from them, all dry and warm in their steel and glass cocoons, while she hurried through the rain and tried to be invisible.

Finally, panting, she stopped at a pay phone. It wasn't in a booth, they seldom were now, just a phone with three small pieces of clear plastic forming shelters on each side and overhead. At least it had a shelf for her to rest the bag on, propping it in place with her body while she held the receiver between her head and shoulder and fumbled a quarter into the slot. She couldn't remember Kristian's number but her fingers did, dancing in the familiar pattern without direction from her brain.

The first ring was still buzzing in her ear when it abruptly stopped and Kristian's voice said, "Hello?" He sounded tense, unusually alert for this time of night—or rather, morning.

"Kris." The word was nothing more than a croak. She cleared her throat and tried again. "Kris, it's Grace."

"Grace, my God! Cops are everywhere, and they said—" He stopped suddenly and lowered his voice, his whisper forceful and almost fierce. "Are you all right? Where are you?"

All right? How could she be all right? Ford and Bryant were dead, and there was a great empty hole in her chest. She would never be all right again. She was, however, physically unharmed, and she knew that was what he was asking. From his question, she also knew that Parrish had indeed called the police; the quiet neighborhood must be in a turmoil.

"I saw it happen," she said, her throat so constricted that her voice sounded like a stranger's, flat and empty. "They're going to say I did it, but I didn't, I swear. Parrish did. I saw him."

"Parrish? Parrish Sawyer, your boss? That Parrish? Are you sure? What happened?"

She waited until the barrage of questions had halted. "I *saw* him," she repeated. "Listen, have they questioned you yet?"

"A little. They wanted to know what time you left here."

"Did you mention the documents I'm working on?"

"No." His voice was positive. "They asked why you were here, and I said you brought your modem over for me to repair. That's it."

"Good. Whatever you do, don't mention the documents. If anyone asks, just say you didn't see any papers at all."

"Okay, but why?"

"So Parrish won't kill you, too." Her teeth began to chatter. Oh, God, she was so cold, the light wind cutting through her wet clothes. "I'm not kidding. Promise me you won't let anyone know you have any idea I was working on anything. I don't know what's in these papers, but he intends to get rid of everyone who knows of their existence."

There was silence on the line, then Kristian said in bewilderment, "You mean he doesn't want us to know about that Knight Templar guy you were trying to track down? He lived seven centuries ago, if he existed at all! Who the hell cares?"

"Parrish does." She didn't know why, but she intended to find out. "Parrish does," she repeated, her voice trailing off.

She listened to his breathing, the sound quick and shallow, amplified by the phone. "Okay, I'll keep my mouth shut. I promise." He paused. "Do you need any help? You can borrow my car—"

She almost laughed. Despite everything, the sound bubbled up in her throat and hung there, unable to work its way past restricted muscles. Kristian's mechanical monument to testosterone was a sure attention-getter, the one thing she most wanted to avoid. "No, thanks," she managed to say. "What I need is money, but the ATM I just tried ran out of cash, and I was mugged as soon as I walked away from it anyway."

"I doubt it," he said.

He doubted that she was mugged? "What?" She was so tired she could barely move or think, but surely he couldn't mean that.

"I doubt it was out of money," he said. Suddenly his voice sounded older, taking on the cool intensity that meant he was thinking of computers. "How much did you take out?"

"Three hundred. Isn't that the limit for each transaction? I remember the banker said something about three hundred dollars when we set up our account."

"Not three hundred per transaction," Kristian patiently explained. "Three hundred per *day*. You could make as many transactions as you wanted, until the total reached three hundred for that twenty-four-hour period. Each bank sets its own limit, and the limit for your bank is three hundred."

His explanation fell on her like words of doom. Even if she found another ATM, she wouldn't be able to get more money until this time tomorrow morning. She couldn't wait that long. If the police could freeze her account, they would definitely have it done by then. And she needed to get out of Minneapolis, to find some safe hiding place where she could work on the documents and find out just why Parrish had killed Ford and Bryant. To do that, she had to have money; she had to have access to a phone, to resource material.

"I'm sunk," she said, her tone leaden.

"No!" He almost yelled the word. More softly he repeated, "No. I can fix that. How much is your balance?"

"I don't know exactly. A couple of thousand."

"Find another ATM," he instructed. "I'll get into your bank's computer, change the limit to . . . say, five thousand. Empty out your account, then I'll change the limit back to the original amount. They'll never know how it happened, I promise."

Hope bloomed inside her, a strange sensation after those past nightmare hours. All she had to do was find another ATM, something easier said than done when she was on foot.

"Look in the phone directory," he was saying. "Every

branch of your bank will have an ATM. Pick the closest one and go there."

Of course. How simple. Normally she would have thought of that herself, and the fact that she hadn't was a measure of her shock and exhaustion.

"Okay." Thank heavens, there was still a directory chained to the shelf. She opened the protective cover. Well, there was part of a directory, at least, and it contained the most important part, the Yellow Pages. She thumbed through them until she reached "Banks," and located her own bank, which had sixteen of those so-called convenient locations.

She estimated it would take her half an hour to get to the nearest one. "I'm going now," she said. "I'll be there in thirty to forty-five minutes, unless something happens." She could be picked up by the police, or mugged again, or Parrish and his goons might be out cruising the city, looking for her. None of the things that could happen to her would be pleasant.

"Call me," Kristian said urgently. "I'll get into the bank's computer now, but call me and let me know if everything went okay."

"I will," she promised.

The thirty-minute walk took almost an hour. She was exhausted, and the laptop gained weight with each step she took. She had to hide every time a car went past, and once a patrol car sped through an intersection just ahead of her, lights whirring in eerie silence. The spurt of panic left her weak and shaking, her heart pounding.

Her familiarity with the downtown area was limited to specific destinations. She had lived, gone to school, and shopped in the suburbs. She took a wrong turn and went several blocks out of her way before she realized what she had done, and had to backtrack. She was acutely aware of the seconds ticking away toward dawn, when people would be getting up and turning on their televisions, and learning about the double murder in her quiet neighborhood. The police would have photographs of her, taken from the house, and her face might be on hundreds of thousands of screens. She needed to be somewhere safe before then.

Finally she reached the branch bank, with the lovely ATM on the front of it, all lit up and watched over by the security camera, so if someone got killed right there they'd have a tape of the murder to show on the evening news.

She was too tired to worry about the camera, or the possibility that another couple of jerks might be watching her. Just let someone else try to mug her. The next time, she would fight; she had nothing to lose, because the money meant her life. She walked right up to the machine, took out her bank card, and followed the instructions, asking for a full two thousand.

The obedient machine began regurgitating twenty-dollar bills. It coughed up a hundred of them before it stopped. Oh, blessed automation!

What with the three hundred she had already withdrawn, she didn't think there could be much left. She didn't try to find out the exact amount, not with two thousand dollars in her hand and time pressing hard on her. She darted around the corner and hid herself in the shadows, hunkering down against the wall and hurriedly stuffing bills inside the computer case, in her pockets, in the cups of her bra, inside her shoes. All the while she scanned the area for movement, but the streets were quiet and empty. The night predators would be heading for their lairs now, turning the city back over to the day denizens.

Maybe. She couldn't afford to take any chances now. She needed some kind of weapon, anything, no matter how primitive, with which she could protect herself. She looked around, hoping to find a sturdy stick, but the only things littering the ground were small pieces of glass and a few rocks.

Well, weapons didn't get much more primitive than rocks, did they?

She picked up the biggest ones, slipping all but one into her pocket. That one, the biggest one, she kept clutched in her hand. She was aware of how pitiful this defense was, but at the same time she felt oddly comforted. Any defense was better than none.

She had to call Kristian, and she had to get out of Minneapolis. She wanted nothing more than to lie down and sleep, to be able to forget for just a few hours, but the luxury of rest would have to wait. Instead Grace hurried through the streets as the sky began to lighten, and the sun began to rise on her first day as a widow.

Chapter 3

"IT SHOULDN'T BE DIFFICULT TO FIND HER," PARRISH SAWYER murmured, leaning back in his chair and tapping his immaculately manicured nails against the wooden arm. "I'm sadly disappointed in the Minneapolis Police Department. Little Grace has no car, no survival skills, yet still she's managed to elude them. That really surprises me; I expected her to run screaming to a neighbor, or to the first policeman she could find, but no, instead she's gone to earth somewhere. Annoying of her, but all she's doing is delaying the inevitable. If the police can't find her, I'm confident you can."

"Yes," Conrad said. He didn't elaborate. He was a man of few words, but over the years Parrish had found him extremely reliable. Conrad could have been either his first or last name; no one knew. He was stocky and muscular and didn't look very bright; his bullet-shaped head was covered by short dark hair that grew low on his forehead, an unfortunate apelike resemblance that was only heightened by his small dark eyes and prominent brow ridges. His appearance, however, was deceiving. His chunky body could move with amazing speed and finesse, and behind his stolid expression was a brain that was both astute and concise. Best of all, Parrish had never seen Conrad exhibit any distressing signs of conscience. He carried out orders with admirable, machinelike precision, and what he thought of them no one but himself ever knew.

"When you find her," Parrish continued, "bring the computer and the papers to me immediately." He didn't give any instructions on how to deal with Grace St. John; Conrad wouldn't need direction on anything that simple.

There was a sharp, slight incline of the bullet head, and Conrad silently left the room. Alone, Parrish sighed, his fingers still drumming out his frustration with the situation.

It had turned unaccountably messy. Nothing had gone as planned. They should have been there, all three of them; he had made certain all three vehicles had been present before going in. But Grace hadn't been there, and neither had her computer or the documents. Moreover, Ford and Bryant had been remarkably good liars; Parrish hadn't expected it of them, and he didn't like being surprised. Who would have thought two nerdish archaeologists would have sized up the situation so accurately, and in an instant formulated a very believable lie?

But they had, and he'd made a very bad mistake in believing them. Such gullibility wasn't at all like him, and the sense of having been made a fool of was irritating.

Unfortunately, it seemed Grace had been just outside the house, watching and listening. That strange little sound he'd heard outside the window had probably been her; leaving a gap in the curtains, even a tiny one, had been another uncharacteristic mistake. Some days were just a *bitch*.

He and Conrad's team had quickly withdrawn, leaving no fingerprints or other sign of their presence behind, and the scene in the bedroom had looked pretty much as they had planned. Any cop walking in on that, two men half-naked together in a bedroom, both of them shot in the head, and one's wife missing—well, it wouldn't take a genius to figure it out. Minneapolis's finest had reacted just as he had expected; they were being circumspect, keeping details from the media, but Grace was their prime suspect.

He had thought she would seek help immediately, so he had returned to his luxurious home in Wayzata to wait. He wasn't worried about her accusations; after all, why would he kill two people in order to steal some documents he could obtain by simply asking for them? He was a respected and well-connected member of the community. He was on two hospital boards, he gave regularly and generously to all the politically correct charities, and several of the richest families in Minnesota had hopes—useless ones, of course—of enticing him into the fold by way of marriage. Moreover, he had an alibi in the form of his housekeeper, Antonetta Dolk. She would swear he had been working in his study all evening, that she had even taken coffee to him. Antonetta could pass any lie-detector test devised by man, a useful ability in a housekeeper, and one he valued far more than dusting. She worked, of course, for the Foundation; he had surrounded himself with people loyal only to him.

To think that the documents had surfaced after so long! They had come out of an insignificant dig in southern France, a dig that had produced so little, and nothing that appeared of any great age, that the documents hadn't drawn any attention. Certainly no one whose job it was to evaluate all finds and report anything interesting to him had found anything intriguing in documents that seemed to be only a few centuries old. He would have to take care of the bungler—another job for Conrad. If the documents had been correctly evaluated, they would never have been photographed, stored, and the photographs sent to Grace St. John for routine translation. None of this would have happened, and the information would be in his hands instead of Grace's.

It was Ford who had alerted him to the content of the obscure documents, and therefore caused his own death. Life could be so ironic, Parrish thought. Ford's chance comment about Grace's latest project, something about the Knights Templar, had set events into motion.

Parrish had quickly checked the assignment records and traced the original documents to their storage location in Paris. The French could be so difficult about allowing artifacts, even not-so-old ones, out of the country. Parrish had sent his people in to retrieve the papers, only to find that they had been destroyed, apparently by fire—though nothing else in the vault had been damaged. Nothing remained of the documents except a fine, white ash.

Grace St. John had the only existing copies. And according to the assignment record, she had been working on the translation for three days. Grace was good at her job; in fact, she was the best language expert on staff. He couldn't take the chance that she had already deciphered enough of the documents to know what she had; she, and everyone else who knew what she'd been working on, had to be eliminated.

Strange that Grace should prove more difficult than either Ford or Bryant. How long had he known her? Almost ten years? She had always seemed such a shy, mousy type, no makeup, her hair scraped back in an unflattering braid, slightly overweight. Her complete lack of style was an affront to his sensibilities. For all that, several times over the years he had been tempted to seduce her. Likely he had been bored, between women; little Grace presented something of a challenge, with her ridiculous middle-class morals. She "loved" her husband, and was faithful to him. But she had perfect skin, like translucent porcelain, and the most astonishingly carnal mouth he'd ever seen. Parrish smiled, feeling the blood pool in his groin as he considered the uses to which he could put that mouth, so wide and soft and pouty. Poor old Ford had certainly lacked the imagination to enjoy her as he could have!

She would be as helpless in the streets as any child. Anything could have happened to her during the night. She might already be dead.

If so, one problem would be conveniently solved, but he sincerely hoped she was still alive. She would keep the papers with her, and when Conrad found her, he would find the papers. If any of the human trash that prowled the streets at night killed her, however, her computer would be taken and fenced, and the papers thrown away. Once the copied documents disappeared into the maw of the night world, they would likely never surface again. They would be gone, and with them the long-searched-for, critical information. There would no longer be a purpose in the Foundation, and his plans would be reduced to so much ash, just like the original documents.

That couldn't be allowed to happen. One way or another, he would get those papers.

Grace couldn't sleep. She was exhausted, but every time she closed her eyes she saw Ford, the sudden, horrible blankness of his eyes as the bullet snuffed out his life, saw him toppling over on the bed.

It was still raining. She sat huddled in a metal storage building, hidden behind a lawn mower that was missing a wheel, a greasy tool box, some rusting cans of paint, and several moldy cardboard boxes marked "Xmas Decorations." The eight-by-ten building hadn't been locked, but then there wasn't anything in it worth stealing, except for a few wrenches and screwdrivers.

She wasn't certain exactly where she was. She had simply walked north until she was too tired to walk any farther, then taken refuge in the storage building behind a 'fifties-style ranch house. The neighborhood was showing signs of raggedness as its lower-middle-class respectability slowly deteriorated. No cars were parked in the carport, so she had taken the chance that no one was there. If any neighbors were at home, the rain had kept them indoors, and no one shouted at her as she walked slowly across the backyard and opened the flimsy metal door.

She had scrambled over the clutter until she reached a back corner, then settled down on the dirty cement. She had sat in a stupor, staring at nothing. Time passed, but she had no grasp of it. After a while she heard a car drive up, and several car doors slammed. Kids yelled and argued, and a woman's voice irritably told them to shut up. There was the squeak of a storm door opening, then the slam of another door, and the human clatter was silenced behind walls that held warmth and normalcy.

Grace leaned her head on her knees. She was so tired, and so hungry. She didn't know what to do next.

Ford and Bryant would be buried, and she wouldn't be there to see them one last time, to touch them, to put flowers on their graves.

Her throat worked, closing tight on the surge of grief that made her rock back and forth. She felt herself flying apart, felt her control shredding, and she hugged her arms tightly as if she could hold everything together that way.

She had never even taken Ford's name, Wessner, as her own. She had kept her maiden name, St. John. The reasons had been so practical, so modern; her degree had been awarded to Grace St. John, and there was her driver's license, her social security, so much paperwork to be changed if she changed her name. And, of course, Minneapolis was in the vanguard of political correctness; it would have been considered hopelessly gauche by the academic crowd if she had taken Ford's name.

The pain was almost unbearable. Ford had been willing to die for her, but she hadn't been willing to use his surname as her own. He'd never asked, never even mentioned it; knowing Ford, it hadn't been important to him. He'd been so *grounded;* their marriage had mattered to him, not what name she used. But suddenly, to her, it mattered. She yearned for that link to him, a link she would never have now, any more than she would ever have his children.

They had planned to have two. They had talked about it, but put parenthood off while they both built their careers. After this past Christmas, they had decided to wait another year, and Grace had continued taking her birth control pills.

Now Ford was dead, and the useless pills had been left behind in a house to which she would never return.

Oh, God, Ford!

She couldn't bear this. The pain was too great. She had to do something or she would lose her mind, run screaming from this filthy little metal building and stand in the middle of the street until she was either arrested or killed.

Jerkily she pulled the computer case from the plastic bag. The light in the building was a dim, muted green, too poor to do any translation work off the copies themselves, but she had already had some of them transferred to disk and she could work on the computer. She was too tired to get much accomplished, but she desperately needed a few minutes of distraction. She had always been able to lose herself in her work; maybe this time it would save her sanity.

She didn't have much room, crammed in the corner the way she was. She repositioned the boxes of Christmas decorations, sliding one in front of her to use as a desk; she knew from experience that the laptop generated too much heat to rest it on her legs. She slapped down the mouse pad, then opened the top of the computer and pushed the switch on the side. The screen lit and the machine made its musical electronic noises as it went through the booting process. When the menu appeared on the screen, she moved the cursor down to the program she wanted and clicked the mouse. She already knew which disk she wanted, and had it ready to slide into the A drive.

The disk contained the section she had been working on before, when curiosity had led her to do more research on the Knights Templar. The language was Old French, something she was so familiar with that she should be able to work even with her mind so numb.

She accessed the file, and the words filled the screen. The letters were indistinct with age, strangely formed, and medieval people had been very creative spellers. There hadn't been any standardized spellings back then, so people had used whatever sounded right to them.

Grace stared at the screen, slowly scrolling as she read and reestablished herself in the work. Despite everything, she could feel her concentration gathering, her focus narrowing as the documents pulled her into their power. The name popped out at her again, "Niall of Scotland," and she took a deep breath. She eased down into a cross-legged position on the concrete, moving closer to the computer as she automatically fished out a pen and the pad that was always in the computer case for taking notes.

Whoever this Niall of Scotland had been before joining the Order, he had quickly become renowned as its greatest warrior. She skimmed over the cramped lines on the screen, jotting down notes on sections she couldn't quite make out, or on words that were unfamiliar to her. She didn't notice her heartbeat speeding, or feel the increased oxygen boosting her concentration. Instead she felt as if she were being sucked into the screen, into the epic account of a monk who had lived and died almost seven hundred years before.

Niall had been "of great size, three *elnes* and five more." Since this document was in French, Grace decided the measurement would more likely have been a Flemish *ell,* twenty-seven inches, rather than an English one of thirty-seven inches. And though Niall had been Scots, the Scots *ell* was something like forty-five inches, which meant that by Scots measurement three *ells* and five inches would have placed him close to twelve feet tall. The Flemish *ell* was more reasonable, making the man stand about six feet four, tall for his time but not freakishly so. Medieval people had been of varying sizes, depending on their nutrition during childhood. Some knights had been ridiculously small, their suits of armor looking as if they had been made for children, while others had been big even by modern standards.

According to this paean, Niall had been unsurpassed in swordsmanship and the other arts of war. There was account after account of battles he had fought, Saracens he had killed, fellow Knights he had saved. Grace felt as if she were reading a tale of a mythical hero along the lines of Hercules, rather than a Middle Ages record of an actual Templar. Granted, the Templars had been superb soldiers, the best of their time and the equivalent of modern-day special forces. But if the Templars had been such good soldiers, why had Niall of Scotland been singled out for excessive praise? She assumed she was reading actual records of the Knights Templar, and while outsiders would understandably be impressed by the great Knights, the Knights themselves would take such exploits for granted. It seemed unlikely they would aggrandize the accomplishments of one.

She scrolled down, and there was a break in the narrative. The text picked up on what seemed to be a letter, signed by someone named Valcour. He expressed concerns about the safety of "the Treasure," and the importance of protecting this, which had worth "greater than gold."

Treasure. Grace stretched her back, rotating her shoulders to ease the kinks. She didn't know how long she had been staring at the computer, but her feet were asleep and her neck and shoulder muscles tight with strain. There had been something about a treasure in the material she had read on Kristian's computer, but she had been skimming, looking for any mention of Niall of Scotland, and she hadn't read it closely. She did remember that the Knights Templar had been an extremely wealthy order, so much so that kings and popes had borrowed gold from them. Their treasure had been gold, so how could its worth be "greater than gold"?

She had been holding fatigue at bay by the sheer force of her concentration, but now it hit her again, pulling at her limbs and eyelids. Her hands were suddenly clumsy as she exited the program and removed the disk, fumbling it back into its protective sleeve. She turned off the computer and scooted back, almost groaning aloud as she stretched out her numb legs and renewed blood flow surged painfully through her veins.

Clumsily she edged herself around, propping herself up against the boxes of decorations. She could feel sleep coming, rushing toward her like a black tide of unconsciousness. She welcomed it, desperately needing the surcease. Her eyelids were too heavy to remain open a second longer. Her last thought was "Niall," and she had a brief picture of him, tall and powerful, swinging a six-foot sword with one iron-hewn arm while enemies fell dead all about him, before she slipped completely beneath the tide.

1322

Six hundred and seventy-five years away, Niall awoke with every nerve alert, his head lifting from his pillow. A single candle guttered in its holder, and the fire in the hearth had almost burned out. He had been asleep for almost an hour, he estimated, relaxed by some energetic love play. He had heard—what? Only the slightest whisper of sound, different but somehow nonthreatening. Normally, if he was awakened suddenly he had a dagger in one hand and a sword in the other even before his eyes were fully opened. He hadn't reached for his weapons, which meant his battle-trained senses hadn't detected any danger.

But something had awakened him, and the sound had

been near. He looked at the woman sleeping beside him, softly snoring, the noise little more than a snuffle. That wasn't what had disturbed him.

They were alone in the chamber, the thick door securely barred, and the secret door beside the hearth was closed. Robert never came without first sending a message. But Niall felt as if someone had been there, and the sudden presence of a stranger had jerked him awake.

He got out of bed, his movements so silent and controlled that Eara slept on undisturbed. Though he could *see* no one was in the chamber with him except for the woman in bed, still he prowled the perimeter, trying to detect a scent, a whisper of sound, anything.

There was nothing. Finally he went back to bed and lay awake, staring into the night. Eara still snored beside him, and he began to feel irritated. He should have sent her to her own pallet after they had finished. He liked sleeping with women, liked the warmth and softness of their bodies beside him, but tonight he would have preferred being alone. He felt a vague need to concentrate on the elusive sound that had awakened him, and Eara's presence was distracting.

He tried to remember exactly how the noise had sounded. It had been soft, almost like a sigh.

Someone had called his name.

1996

Conrad gripped the punk's greasy hair, jerking his lolling head back. He studied the effects of his work. Both of the punk's eyes were swollen nearly shut, his nose was a bleeding mass of crushed cartilage, and instead of missing just a few teeth he now had few left. That had been nothing more than the softening up, though. The real persuasion had taken the form of broken ribs and fingers.

"You saw her," he said softly. "You robbed her."

"No, man—" The words were mushy, almost unintelligible.

That wasn't the answer Conrad wanted. He sighed, and twisted one of the broken fingers. The punk screamed, his body arching against the tape that held his ankles strapped to the chair legs and his wrists lashed to the wooden arms.

"You saw her," he repeated patiently.

"We don' have the money no more!" the punk sobbed, his minuscule store of courage already depleted.

"I am not interested in the money. Where did the woman go?"

"We got th' hell outta there, man! We din' hang around, y'know?"

Conrad thought about it. The punk was probably telling the truth. He glanced at the crumpled body behind the chair. Too bad the young black man had used very bad judgment and pulled a knife on him. Perhaps he would have noticed something this cretin hadn't.

To be certain, he twisted another finger, and waited until the screams subsided. "Where did the woman go?" he asked again.

"I don' know, I don' know, I don' know!"

Satisfied, Conrad nodded. "What was she wearing?"

"I don' know—"

Conrad reached for a finger, and the punk shrieked. "No, don't, stop!" he screamed, blood and mucus streaming from his broken nose. "It was rainin', all her clothes was dark—"

"Pants or a dress?" Conrad asked. It *had* been raining, and if the woman had been out in it all the time she would have been soaked. He wasn't unreasonable; he didn't expect this idiot to notice colors at night, and in the rain.

"I don'—pants. Yeah. Maybe jeans, I dunno."

"Did she have a coat, a jacket?" The weather had turned colder, which wasn't unexpected. It was the warmth that had been unusual for Minneapolis, not this more seasonable chill.

"I don' think so."

"Short sleeves or long?"

"Sh-short, I think. Not sure." He gulped in air through his mouth. "She was carryin' a garbage bag, kinda hid her arms."

No jacket, and short sleeves. She had been wet to the skin, and she would now be very cold. Conrad didn't wonder what was in the garbage bag; it was a commonsense solution to keeping papers dry. Mr. Sawyer would be pleased.

She had gotten money from an ATM, and this piece of excrement had promptly robbed her. She was without funds, without any means of coping. Conrad thought he should be able to find her within a day, if she hadn't sought out the police by then. Though Mr. Sawyer had everything under control even if she made accusations against him, Conrad preferred to find her himself. It would be easier that way.

He looked at the human trash in the chair. The punk had no redeeming qualities. He had no skills, no morals, no value.

A bullet was too expensive for exterminating vermin, and too quick. Conrad reached out his gloved hand and closed it on the punk's throat, and expertly crushed his trachea. Leaving him suffocating in the chair, Conrad walked out of the abandoned house in the worst part of the city. He moved silently, unhurriedly. Screams were common in the neighborhood. No one paid him any attention.

Chapter 4

DISTANCE, GRACE LEARNED, WAS RELATIVE. EAU CLAIRE, WIS-consin, wasn't all that far from Minneapolis if you were driving, a matter of an hour or two, depending on where you were in Minneapolis when you began and how fast you drove. In a plane, it was nothing more than a hop. On foot, and having to hide during the day, it took her three days.

She didn't dare take a bus; with her long hair and carrying a computer case she would be too easily recognized. She didn't know, but she thought it would only be common sense for the police, knowing she didn't have her car, to check all public transportation leaving the city. Parrish would likely be hunting her, too, and he wouldn't have to compare her appearance to a photo in order to recognize her.

She operated in a vacuum, because that was the only way she could manage. Things she had always taken for granted, basics such as food, water, warmth, a toilet, were now an effort to obtain. At least she had money, and there were always convenience stores, though she knew she should avoid them because of their surveillance cameras. Food wasn't much of a problem; she simply wasn't hungry.

She looked homeless; she *was* homeless. She walked north for a while, then cut east, paralleling state roads whenever she could rather than walking on the shoulder where she would more easily be seen. She hadn't realized before how little human presence there was between Minneapolis and Eau Claire; if she had been on the interstate, there would at least have been a motel or truck stop every few exits, but away from the interstate there was nothing but a few houses and the occasional service station.

At ten-thirty on her second night on the run, she went into a service station and asked for the key to the rest room. The attendant looked up with bored, hostile eyes and said, "Get lost." It took her more than an hour to find another station. The second attendant wasn't as polite, and threatened to call the cops if she didn't leave.

The need to urinate was excruciating, exacerbated by her constant shivering. Grace's face was blank as she silently turned and left the station. She walked across the parking lot, aware of the attendant watching every step she made. Just as she was about to step onto the shoulder of the highway, she looked back and saw that the man had returned to the magazine he'd been reading when she went in to ask for the key. She made a sharp turn, skirting the edge of the parking lot, and circled around behind the station. She *had* to relieve herself, and she wasn't about to do it on the side of the road.

Gravel crunched as a customer drove up, and she heard a man saying something to the attendant, then the answer, but she couldn't understand what they were saying. Sheltered by the back wall, she carefully placed her precious trash bag out of the splash area, and unzipped her jeans.

Footsteps approached, scraping on the gravel.

There was no place to hide. A dim bulb over each of the rest-room doors stole even the advantage of darkness from her. There was nothing to do but run, and hope the approaching customer wouldn't get too good a look at her.

She grabbed for the trash bag and her gaze swept over the rest-room door, the one with "Ladies" painted on it in big block letters. There was a hasp attached to the door, and an open padlock hung from it. The door wasn't even locked!

The footsteps were close, almost to the corner. She didn't hesitate. Leaving the trash bag where it was, she darted into the dark little room, and pressed herself against the painted block wall. She didn't even have time to close the door. The customer walked past, and a second later a brighter light came on as he flipped the switch in the other rest room. The door slammed.

Grace sagged against the wall. The rest room was nothing more than a tiny cubicle, just large enough to accommodate a toilet and a washbasin. The walls were concrete block, the floor was cement. The smell wasn't pleasant.

She didn't dare turn on the light, though she closed the door until only a two-inch crack remained. Jerking down her jeans, she perched over the stained porcelain toilet just as her mother had taught her to do, and then she couldn't hold back any longer. Crouched there like an awkward bird, her legs aching from the unnatural position, tears of relief sprang into her eyes and she stifled a humorless laugh at the ridiculousness of what she was doing.

In the rest room next door there was a long, explosive sound of gas releasing, then a contented "Ahhh." Grace clapped a hand over her mouth to hold back the hysterical giggle that rose in her throat. She had to finish before he did, or he might hear her. The competition was the strangest in which she'd ever engaged, and no less stressful because she was the only one who knew it was in progress.

She finished just as a loud, gurgling flush sounded. Quickly she reached for the handle and pushed it down, the noise of the second covered by that of the first. Then she didn't dare move, because the man didn't pause to wash his hands but immediately left the rest room. She froze, not even daring to take a breath. He walked right by without noticing that the door that had been standing open when he'd gone into the rest room was now almost closed.

Grace inhaled a shaky breath and stood for a moment in the dark, smelly little rest room, trying to calm her nerves.

The rest room wasn't the only thing that smelled. She could smell herself, the stink of fear added to almost three days without a shower. Her clothes were sour, the effect of being rain-soaked and drying on her body.

Her stomach rolled. She didn't mind being dirty; she did mind being unclean, which was something else entirely. She was an archaeologist's wife—*widow,* an insidious little voice whispered before she could silence the thought—and had often accompanied him on digs, where dust and sweat had ruled the day. They had always cleaned up at night, however. She didn't think she had ever before gone so long without bathing, and she couldn't bear it.

She opened the rest-room door another inch or so, letting in more light. The sink was as stained as the toilet, but above the basin hung a towel dispenser, and beside the faucet sat a pump bottle of liquid soap.

The temptation was irresistible. Perhaps she couldn't do anything about the smell of her clothes, but she could do something about the smell of her body. Turning the faucet so a small stream of water came out, being as quiet as possible, she washed as best she could. She didn't dare undress, and she had only the rough brown paper towels to use for both washing and drying, but she felt much fresher when she had finished. Now that her hands were clean, she cupped them and filled them with water, and bent over to drink. The water was cold and fresh on her tongue, sliding down her dry throat and soothing the parched tissues.

"What's this shit?"

The irritable words speared her with shards of panic. Grace whirled, forgetting to turn off the water. It was the attendant's voice, and next she heard the unmistakable rustle of plastic as he picked up the trash bag containing her computer and all the documents.

A low growl sounded in her throat and she jerked the door open. He was standing with his back to her, holding the bag open as he looked inside it, but at her movement he turned. A mean look entered his eyes as he recognized her.

"I told you to get the fuck off this propitty." He reached out and grabbed her arm, roughly hauling her out of the rest-room doorway and shoving her several feet forward. Grace stumbled and almost fell, going down hard on one knee before she regained her balance. A rock dug sharply into her knee, making her gasp with pain. Another hard shove in the middle of her back sent her sprawling on the ground.

"Worthless piece of shit," the man said, drawing back his booted foot. "You won't leave when you're told, I'll kick your ass off."

He was skinny, but with the wiry, hardscrabble strength and meanness of a junkyard dog. Grace scrambled away from the swinging boot, knowing that it would break her ribs if the kick landed. He missed and staggered, and that made him even angrier. She crawled frantically to the side and he followed, drawing back his leg for another kick.

He was too close; she knew she couldn't move fast enough to escape this time. Desperately she lashed out with her own foot, catching him on the knee. He was standing on one leg, the other drawn back, and the blow sent him lurching off balance. He fell heavily on his side, and he dropped the plastic bag with a thud.

Grace bounced to her feet but she wasn't fast enough; cursing, he regained his own feet, looming over her and the bag between them. She spared a quick look at the bag, gauging her distance to it.

"You little bitch," he spat, his face drawn tight with rage. "I'll kill you for this."

He lunged forward, his hands outstretched to grab her. Desperately Grace tried what had worked before: she dropped to the ground and kicked with both feet. One foot landed harmlessly on his thigh, but the other connected solidly with the spongy tissue of his testicles. He stopped as if he'd hit a wall, a strange, high-pitched wheezing sound escaping from his throat as he folded over, both hands clasping his crotch. She grabbed the plastic bag, scrambling away even before she was upright, and then she ran. Her feet pounded on the hard parking lot as she circled the building and raced across the highway. She didn't stop even when darkness swallowed her and the gas station was nothing more than a pinpoint of light far behind.

Gradually she slowed, her heart pounding in her chest, her breath rasping painfully in her throat. She had to assume the attendant would call the cops, but she doubted they would look very hard for a vagrant, since nothing had been taken and the only damage was to the man's family jewels. Still, if a county deputy was cruising the highway and saw her, he wouldn't just drive on by. She would have to leave the highway whenever she saw a car coming, and hide until it was gone.

She had been relatively clean. Now dirt smeared her hands and face again, and her clothes were coated with it. She stopped, dusting herself off as best she could, but she was aware that, if anything, she looked even worse than before.

The situation had to be corrected. She didn't need a public rest room as much for the toilet as she did for water, and the opportunity to clean herself up, though she hadn't yet been able to bring herself to squat in a field or a ditch to relieve herself. That time would probably come, she thought numbly. The next time she had the opportunity she would steal some toilet paper, just in case. Still, if she wasn't to encounter over and over the same reaction she'd met with tonight, she would have to look, if not respectable, at least as if she had a place to live. The plastic trash bag was great for protecting the computer from rain, but it marked her as a homeless person, a vagrant, and store owners wouldn't want her on their property.

She would have to find another place to wash off, to make herself as presentable as possible, and then she would brave a discount store to buy a few clothes and a cheap bag of some sort. Simple things, but they would make life much easier; she would be able to use public rest rooms without attracting notice, for one thing. What she really needed was a car, but that was out of the question unless she stole one, and common sense said that stealing a car would attract just the kind of attention she most wanted to avoid. No, for right now she was better off walking.

The struggle and flight had sent adrenaline pumping through her system, warming her, but she felt shaky in the aftermath. Her knees wobbled as she marched along the dark highway, carefully holding the bag to her chest with both arms. She couldn't believe what she'd done. She had never hit another person before in her life, never even considered fighting. But she had not only fought, she had won. Dark, feral triumph filled her. She had won purely by luck, but she'd learned something tonight: how to use whatever weapon was available, and that she could win. The boundary she'd crossed had been a subtle, internal one, but she could feel the change deep inside, a strength growing where there had been only numbness, and fear.

Light shifted in the leaves of the trees ahead, signaling the approach of a car around a curve. Grace made a sharp turn away from the highway, unable to run because the darkness kept her from seeing the unevenness of the ground, and even a sprained ankle now could mean the difference between living and dying. She hurried toward the shelter of the tree line, but it was farther away than she'd thought, and the car was moving fast. The lights became brighter and brighter. The ground rose sharply, unexpectedly, and her feet slipped on the wet weeds. She fell facedown, landing hard on the computer case, jarring her shoulder. She glanced to her right, urgency pumping through her, and the car rushed into sight.

Grace dropped her head to the ground and lay still, hoping the sparse weeds were enough to hide her.

She felt as if the headlights pinned her to the earth like spotlights, so bright were they. But the car sped past without even slowing, and she was left behind in the blessed darkness, her clothes growing cold and wet, weeds stinging her face, her chest hurting from hard contact with the computer case. Once again she climbed to her feet, her movements clumsy as the various hurts she'd absorbed began to make themselves felt.

But every step took her farther from Minneapolis, from her home, her life—no, she had no home, no life. Every step was taking her closer to safety, away from Parrish. She would come back and face him, but on her own terms, when she was better able to fight him.

She ignored the cold, and the aches. She ignored the bruises, the strained muscles, the great empty place where her heart had once been.

She walked.

Scanners were wonderful inventions. Conrad learned a great deal from listening to the police bands. He knew all the codes, understood the cop slang. It was to his advantage to understand how cops think, so he had invested a great deal of time in studying them. Beyond that, a well-informed person had to know what was happening in the law-enforcement world, for so much of what happened in any given day was never reported by the media, which went after only the dramatic or the weird, or whatever bolstered the current politically correct causes. He recognized addresses of trouble spots to which the cops returned time and again to referee domestic problems, he knew where the drug deals went down, which street corners the whores worked. He also listened, with increased attention, whenever they answered calls to places that were out of the ordinary; their voices would be tighter, the adrenaline pumping because this was *different*.

The metro area was never quiet, never still. There was always trouble working. It was more peaceful out in the rural areas, and the county scanners picked up much more routine radio messages. Those scanners had to reach out for greater distances, and even though the payback in information was much less than what he gleaned from the city scanner, he was a prudent man, and had invested in more powerful scanners with special boosters for the rural areas. If anything happened within a sixty-mile radius, he wanted to know about it.

Conrad liked to lie in bed with all the scanners on, listening to the flow of information. The constant sound was soothing, connecting him to the dark underbelly of life that he'd deliberately chosen. He left the scanners on all night, and sometimes he thought he absorbed the crackle of words even in his sleep, because any urgent code would bring him immediately awake.

Not that he slept a lot, anyway. He rested, in a sort of suspended twilight state, but he didn't need much real sleep. He found physical rest more satisfying than mere unconsciousness; half dozing, he could enjoy his own total relaxation, the feel of the sheets beneath him, the gentle stirring of air on his hairy body. That was the only caress he enjoyed, perhaps because it wasn't sexual. Conrad was totally uninterested in sex; he didn't like waking with erections, didn't like feeling as if his body was not under his control. He considered sexual activity a weakness; neither women nor men appealed to him, and he disliked the sleazy promiscuity that seemed to pervade society. He never watched sexy thrillers on television, though he very much enjoyed reruns of *The Andy Griffith Show.* It was good, clean entertainment. Perhaps there were still places like Mayberry in the world; he would like to visit one someday, though of course he could never live there. Mayberrys were not for him; he just wanted perhaps to sit on a bench on the courthouse square, and breathe the air of goodness for a minute or two.

Conrad closed his eyes, and routed his thoughts from Mayberry to Grace St. John. *She* belonged in a Mayberry. Poor woman, she had no idea how to function in the world he listened to on the scanners, night after night. Where had she gone, after that witless vermin had robbed her? Had she found a hiding place, or had she fallen victim to someone else? He hadn't been able to pick up the thread of her movements, but he had no doubt that he would eventually succeed. He had feelers out all over Minneapolis, and he *would* find her. Conrad had no doubt in his ability; sooner or later, all those he sought fell into his hands.

He was surprised by a slight sense of concern for her. She was just an ordinary woman, like millions of other women; she had lived quietly, loved her husband and her job, done the laundry, the grocery shopping. She should have no problems too serious to be solved with anything more than a dose of Mayberry common sense. Unfortunately, she had become involved in something that was far outside her experience, and she would die. Conrad regretted it, but there was no alternative.

One of the county scanners crackled to life. "Ah, attendant at Brasher's service station reports a vagrant who refused to leave the premises and attacked him when he tried to make her leave."

Her? Conrad's attention perked.

After a moment, a county deputy somewhere in the night clicked his radio. "This is one-twelve, I'm in the area. Is the vagrant still there?"

"Negative. The guy isn't hurt much, didn't want any medics."

"Ah, did he give a description?"

"Female, dark-haired, approximate age twenty-five. Dark pants, blue shirt. Height five-ten, weight one-eighty."

"Big woman," the deputy commented. "I'll swing by Brasher's and take his statement, but it's probably nothing more than a scuffle."

And the attendant had probably lied, Conrad thought, throwing back the sheet and getting out of bed. He switched on a lamp, the light mellow and soothing, and unhurriedly began dressing. He wanted to give the deputy plenty of time to dutifully take the attendant's statement and leave.

Five-ten, one-eighty? Possible, but it was equally likely the attendant had been the loser in the encounter, and he didn't want to admit he'd been bested by a woman who wasn't quite five-foot-four, and who weighed a hundred thirty-five pounds. It looked better if he added six inches and forty-five pounds to her size. The hair, the age, the clothes, were about right, so it was worth checking out.

He arrived at the service station an hour later. It was quiet, well after midnight, no other customers. Conrad pulled up to the gas pump with the sign "Pay Before Pumping" posted on the side, and walked toward the small, well-lit office. The attendant was on his feet, watching, the expression on his thin, ferrety face an incongruous mixture of suspicion and anticipation. He didn't like Conrad's looks, few people did, but at the same time he wanted an audience to listen to a retelling of his adventure.

Conrad took out his wallet as he walked, fishing out a twenty. He wanted information, not gas.

Seeing the money come out, the attendant relaxed.

Conrad stepped inside and laid the twenty on the counter, but kept his hand on the bill when the attendant reached for it. "A woman was here tonight," he said. "The twenty is for answers to a few questions."

The attendant eyed the bill, then darted a glance back up at Conrad. "A twenty ain't much."

"Neither are my questions."

Another glance, and the attendant decided it wouldn't be smart to try to get more out of this ape. "What about her?" he mumbled sullenly.

"Describe her hair."

"Her hair?" He shrugged. "It was dark. I already told the deputy all this."

"How long?"

"About an hour ago, I guess."

Conrad controlled an impulse to crush another trachea. Unfortunately, this idiot wasn't street trash; if he were killed, questions would definitely be asked, and Conrad didn't want to lead the cops in Grace St. John's direction. "Her hair. How long was her hair?"

"Oh. Well, it was in one of them twisted things, you know, whaddaya call it?"

"A braid?" Conrad offered helpfully.

"Yeah, that's the word."

"Thank you." Taking his hand off the twenty, Conrad left the office and walked calmly back to his car. No other questions were needed. The woman had definitely been Grace St. John. She needed to get out of Minneapolis, out of the state. She was headed east, probably to Eau Claire. It was the next city of any size in that direction. She would feel more anonymous in a city, attract less attention.

He might be able to find her en route, but at night she would have the advantage of being better able to hide when a car approached. Perhaps she was moving during the day, too, but he thought not. She had to rest, and she would be afraid to go out in the daylight. Would she try to hitch a ride to Eau Claire? Again, he didn't think so. She was middle-class, suburban cautious, taught from childhood how dangerous it was to pick up a hitcher or thumb a ride herself. She was also smart; a hitcher was noticeable, and being noticed was the last thing she would want.

The gas station attendant must have hassled her in some way, or she would never have risked drawing attention by scuffling with him. She would be cold, upset, possibly hurt. Perhaps she had gone to ground somewhere nearby, trying to get warm, crying a little, too discouraged to go on. She was close, he knew, but he had no way of finding her right now short of bringing in tracking dogs, and wouldn't *that* draw attention! He wanted this kept as quiet as she did. It would be better all around if no cops or media were involved beyond the present level.

He estimated how long it would take her to reach Eau Claire. At least two more days, and that was if nothing else happened to her. She was staying off the interstate highway, and secondary roads would give her more points of entry into the city. That made his job more difficult, but not impossible. He could narrow down her most likely routes to two, and two was a very manageable number. He would need backup, though. He wanted someone who wasn't trigger-happy, someone who could adjust without panic if things didn't go according to plan. He thought over the men who were available, and settled on Paglione. He could be a bit thickheaded, but he was steady, and Conrad would be doing all the thinking anyway.

Poor Ms. St. John. Poor little woman.

Chapter 5

By the time she reached the outskirts of Eau Claire, Grace knew she had to find something to eat. She wasn't hungry, hadn't been hungry, but she could feel herself getting increasingly weaker.

The cold wasn't helping. Spring had flipped her skirts to show her petticoats of flowers and greenery, luring everyone into a giddy hope they had seen the last of winter, but as usual she had just been teasing, the bitch. Grace couldn't look at weather's vagaries with her usual complacency. She shivered constantly, though now her shivers were weakening, another indication of her body's need for fuel. At least it wasn't snowing. She had fought off hypothermia the way all the street people did, with newspapers and plastic bags, anything to hold in her lessening output of body heat. Evidently the pitful measures weren't so pitiful, because they had worked; she was still alive.

Alive, but increasingly uneasy. She couldn't go on like this. Even more than her precarious survival, a lack of opportunity to work was gnawing at her. If she couldn't work, she couldn't learn for what Parrish had been willing to kill them all. She had always believed the old adage that knowledge was power, and in this case knowledge was also her best path to vengeance. She needed a stable base, long hours without interruption, electricity. Her computer batteries were good for about four hours, and she had already used them for two. She craved work, craved the one part of her former life she had brought with her. To get that, she had to reenter the civilized world, or at least the fringes of it. It was time to put her strategy into effect.

She needed to clean up again before appearing in any store. She sought out another service station, but she'd learned to bypass the attendant altogether. Instead she left the road and approached from the back; if the rest-room doors were padlocked, she moved on until she found a station where they weren't. At least half of them were left unlocked, perhaps because the attendants didn't want to be bothered with having to keep track of the keys. Of course, most of the rest rooms left unlocked were incredibly grungy, but that no longer bothered her. All she needed was a flushing toilet and a sink with running water.

Finding such a station didn't take long. She stepped into the dank little cubicle and turned on the light, a low-watt naked bulb hanging from the ceiling, out of reach of anyone inclined to steal the bulb unless they brought a ladder with them into the rest room. Her image floated in the streaked, spotted mirror, and she stared dispassionately at the unkempt, hollow-eyed woman who bore so little resemblance to the real person. After taking care of necessities, she took off her clothes and washed. The rest room had no towels or soap, but after encountering that lack of amenities the first time she had solved the problem by taking a supply of paper towels from the next station, and lifting a half-used bar of soap from another. Most places used liquid soap in a dispenser attached to the wall, to prevent what was evidently rampant soap theft, so she felt lucky to have found the bar.

She neatened her hair, undoing the braid and vigorously combing the long length, almost shuddering with relief as the teeth dug into her scalp. Her hair was so dirty she hated to touch it, but washing it would have to wait until another day. She rebraided it with the speed of experience, securing the end with a clip and tossing the thick rope of hair over her shoulder to bang against her back.

There wasn't much she could do with her clothes. She wet a paper towel and sponged the dirtiest places, but the results were minimal. Shrugging mentally in a way she couldn't have done three days before, she tossed the paper towel into the overflowing trash can. She had done what she could. There were worse things in life than dirty clothes, like being mugged, or a snarly man trying to kick in her ribs, or being chased by neighborhood dogs—or watching her husband and brother being shot to death.

Grace had learned how to shut off those last memories whenever they sneaked in and threatened to destroy her, and she did so now, turning her thoughts to practical matters. What would be the best place to buy a change of clothes? A Kmart or a Wal-Mart, maybe; they would still be open, and no one would notice what she bought.

The problem was, she knew absolutely nothing about Eau Claire, and even if she had the address of a store she wouldn't know how to get there.

She dismissed taking a cab as too expensive. The only other alternative was to ask directions. The idea made her stomach tighten with panic. She hadn't had any contact with people since her encounter with the service station attendant. Alone, concentrating on survival, she hadn't spoken a word in two days. There wasn't anyone to speak to, and she'd never been one to talk to herself.

Time to break the silence, though. She worked her way around the station, watched the attendant for a while, and decided that he wouldn't be the one with whom the silence was broken. She didn't like his looks. Though pudgy where the other man had been lean, there was something about him that reminded her of the look in the man's eyes when he'd tried to kick her. Birds of a feather, perhaps. She wasn't going to take the chance.

Instead she cut across a field toward another road, taking care in the darkness. She ran into a wire fence, but she was lucky: it was neither barbed nor electrified. It was falling down, and wobbled precariously under her weight when she scrambled over it. The condition of the fence meant there were no cattle in the field, though she really wouldn't have expected cattle so close to town. Still, it was reassuring to know she wouldn't suddenly find herself facing an irritated bull.

As she climbed the fence on the other side of the field, a dog began barking off to her right. As soon as her feet hit the ground she immediately angled to the left, because sometimes dogs shut up and lost interest if she moved away from their territory. The maneuver didn't work this time. The dog barked even more frantically, and the sound came closer.

She leaned down and swept her hand over the ground until she located a few rocks. The dog was innocent, performing its instinctual duties by barking at an intruder; she didn't intend to hurt the animal, but neither did she want to be bitten. A rock bouncing nearby was usually enough to send the animal in retreat. She threw one at the sound and said "Git!" in a voice as low and fierce as she could make it, stomping her foot for added emphasis.

She could barely make out the movement in the dark as the animal skittered back, away from the abruptly aggressive motion she had made. She took another step and said "Git!" again, and the dog evidently decided retreat was the best course of action. It went one way, and Grace went the other.

Well, at least she had broken her silence, even if it had been to a dog.

"I think I saw her," Paglione reported by cellular phone. "I'm pretty sure it was her. I just caught a glimpse of someone kinda slipping around behind a service station, you know?"

"Did you see where she went?" Conrad started his car. He had chosen highways 12 and 40 as the most likely for her to enter Eau Claire; he had elected to watch highway 12 because it was the busiest, leaving Paglione to cover 40. The two highways would intersect only a few miles from his present position.

"I lost her. I think she cut through a field. I haven't been able to pick her up again."

"She's headed for Eau Claire. Work in that direction. She has to hit a highway or street again somewhere."

Conrad folded the phone and laid it beside him on the car seat. Excitement hummed through him. He was close to her, he knew it. He could feel her, an interesting prey because her elusiveness was so unexpected. But soon he would have her, and his job would be done. He would have triumphed once again. He let himself feel the thrill for a sweet moment, then firmly put the emotion aside. He didn't let anything interfere with the job.

A Kmart sign soared into the night sky, drawing Grace toward it. She had crossed fields and vacant lots, negotiated backyards, and faced down several more dogs. The animals had been pets, rather than watchdogs, but still it had been tricky to work her way through the ever-thickening maze of houses without drawing undue attention to herself.

At the back of the Kmart parking lot loomed a Salvation Army collection container, piled around with discarded furniture and broken odds and ends. She skirted the container, having learned that a surprising number of people routinely went through the donations and took the best of the discards, leaving only the junk. She needed a safe place to stash her bag, but hiding it in the heap of donations was out of the question.

She walked around to the back of the building, taking care to stay in the darkest shadows. Beside the shipping and receiving bay was a pile of empty cardboard boxes, but the area was brightly lit with vapor lights. That would be an ideal hiding place, except for the lights. She continued on around the building to the lawn and garden section, with flowerpots and bags of grass seed stacked high against a chain-link fence. The exit gate was closed for the night, but a few people still braved the chill to pick out the latest in imitation earthenware plastic pots.

Ducking down behind a stack of grass seed, Grace carefully placed the plastic bag against the fence. The pavement was black, and the shadows dense enough that the bag was virtually invisible unless someone stumbled over it. Panic twisted her insides at the thought of letting her computer out of her possession, and she crouched there, taking another long look around to make sure no one was watching her. There was a small copse of trees behind her, and the crickets were setting up their usual racket, which told her no one was moving about in the trees.

Eau Claire wasn't Minneapolis, she told herself. It was less than one-sixth the size of Minneapolis–St. Paul. The city would have its share of bums, drug addicts, and homeless, but she was far less likely to be observed here. The Kmart parking lot wasn't exactly a hotbed of intrigue, especially this close to closing time.

She couldn't wait any longer. She got up and walked purposefully around the fenced-in area, not looking back, taking strong strides as if she had every right in the world to be there, which she did. She wasn't going to steal anything, she was going to pay for it with the cash she had in her pocket.

An employee had been stationed at the doors to watch the customers as they entered. He gave Grace a hard look and turned to the service desk, and she suspected he would have her followed by another employee to make certain she didn't steal anything.

She pulled a shopping cart free of the line. Let someone follow her; she didn't care.

"Attention, shoppers." The announcement rang out over the loudspeakers. "The store will close in fifteen minutes."

Walking as fast as she could, she pushed the cart toward women's clothing. She grabbed a pair of jeans in her size, a sweatshirt, a denim jacket, then darted over to the under-wear section. A pack of panties went into the cart, followed by a pack of socks. Looking at the overhead signs in the store, she located the shoe department, and set off for the back of the store; on the way she passed through the men's clothing section, and she grabbed a baseball cap as she went by. When she reached the shoe department, she swiftly selected a pair of white athletic shoes. They would be better for walking than her loafers, which were much the worse for wear.

Okay, now for a bag. Luggage was at the front of the store, sandwiched between the sports department and the phar-macy. Grace gave the selection a quick survey and chose the cheapest of the medium-sized duffel bags offered. On her way to the checkout counters, she also tossed in a tooth-brush, toothpaste, and shampoo.

Five minutes after entering the store, she wheeled the cart up to a checkout counter. She didn't look around to see if anyone was watching. The counter was lined with boxes of chewing gum and candy bars. Her stomach growled, and she stared at the selection. She had to eat something, and she loved chocolate, but somehow the thought of candy was sickening. Nausea twisted her stomach, making her swallow the mini-flood of saliva that threatened to overflow.

Peanuts weren't sweet. Peanuts were nice and salty. The customer ahead of her finished checking out, and Grace shoved the cart forward. She grabbed a pack of peanuts and tossed it onto the counter, then began unloading her selections.

The bored, sleepy-looking cashier rang up the items, stuffing them in crinkly plastic bags. "One thirty-two seventeen," she muttered.

Grace gulped. A hundred and thirty-two dollars! She looked at the two plastic bags and the duffel. If she were to be more efficient in hiding, in traveling, she needed every item there. Grimly she dug in her pocket and pulled out the wad of bills, counting out seven twenties. When her change was returned, she took the duffel in one hand and the two plastic bags in the other, and used her body to nudge the cart toward the lines of nested carts waiting for another day's flood of shoppers.

There was a vending machine in front of the store. Grace got a soft drink from it and dropped it into one of the bags.

Her heart was pounding as she strode back around the lawn and garden section. It was empty now, except for an employee covering plants for the night. When his back was turned she quickly ducked down behind the stacked bags of seed. Releasing the duffel, she swept her free hand over the dark, cold pavement, searching for her trash bag. Her fingers encountered only grit and dampness. Sheer horror immobilized her. Had someone been watching her after all, and stolen the bag as soon as she'd disappeared into the store? She crouched in the shadows, eyes dilated, her breathing hard and fast as she tried to think. If someone *had* been watching her, he must have been hidden in the woods.

Had he gone back there? Could she manage to find him? What would she do, attack anyone she saw carrying a bag? The answer was yes, if she had to. She couldn't give up now.

But had she come far enough down the fence? Was she in the right location? The store's bright lights had ruined her night vision, and perhaps she had underestimated how far from the corner she'd left the bag. Carefully setting aside the rustly Kmart bag containing her new clothes, she crawled along the fence, not really daring to hope she had simply miscalculated the distance but making the effort anyway.

Her outstretched hand touched plastic.

Relief poured through her, making her weak. She sank down on the pavement, gathering the reassuring weight into her arms. Everything was still there, the computer, the disks, the papers. She hadn't lost them, after all.

She shook the weakness away. Hastily she collected the duffel and unzipped it, stuffing both her new clothes and the computer into it. Then she melted into the trees, losing herself in the night before she dared stop to eat the bag of peanuts and drink the soft drink.

After she'd eaten and rested, she stared through the trees at the bright signs that beckoned her. Kmart had closed, but down the street shone the lights of a fast-food joint and a grocery store. The thought of a hamburger made her feel queasy, but a grocery store . . . she could buy a loaf of bread and a jar of peanut butter, the makings of many meals, the purchases themselves so ordinary no one would remember her or what she'd bought.

Do it all tonight, she thought. She had already done so much: spoken, if only to a dog, gone among people again, bought clothes. The customers who frequented grocery stores at night were stranger on average than the day crowd; she'd often heard cashiers talking about the weird things that happened at night. She would be just another of the weirdos, and no one would pay much attention to her. Resolutely Grace lifted the duffel and began walking up the street to the grocery store.

Obviously she couldn't enter the store carrying the bag, though. She stood across the street and surveyed the situation. The street behind the store was residential, lined with houses and cars. A ten-foot-high chain-link fence ran around three sides of the store. On the left side of the store was a receiving bay and a huge, jumbled stack of empty cardboard boxes, prefab housing for a wino, or for a woman on the run. Even a cardboard shelter felt good during the cold nights.

She thought of the denim jacket in the suitcase, and laughed silently, humorlessly, at herself. She was cold; why hadn't she put on the jacket? A silly reason came to mind. She was dirty, and the jacket was new. She didn't want to put it on until she'd had a bath and changed into her new, clean clothes. The teachings of a lifetime were holding sway even though she'd been shivering for three days.

Tomorrow, she told herself. Somehow she would manage a bath, a real bath, and wash her hair. Tomorrow she would put on her new clothes.

For tonight, she just had to buy sandwich makings, and be on her way.

Some odd caution kept her from crossing the street right then; instead she went up to the corner, crossed with the light, then worked her way back. She kept to the back edge of parking lots, worming her way around smelly trash bins, slipping into the shadows of trees whenever she could. Finally she was behind the grocery store, but something about it made her uneasy. Maybe it was the fence, restricting her choice of escape direction, if escape became necessary. She had planned to leave the bag there but changed her mind, instead carrying it toward the front. There weren't any cars parked in back, which meant the employees all parked in front too, probably along one side of the lot in order to leave the most desirable center-aisle spots for the customers.

Grace lurked at the side of the building, waiting until the lot was momentarily empty of customers either arriving or leaving, before bending down until her head was just below the level of a car hood and darting to the side row of parked cars. Crouched in front of the first car, she put her hand on the hood and found it cold; the vehicle had been there for hours, so she'd guessed right about where the employees would park. She slid the bag beneath the car, between the front tires. The store hadn't closed at nine so it should be open at least until ten, if not all night, and the employees would stay later than that. She would be back long before the owner of the car.

As an added caution, she didn't immediately straighten up and walk toward the store. Instead she crab-walked down the line of cars until she reached the last two. Then she moved between them, stood, took a deep breath, and braved the public exposure of a grocery store.

"Got her," Paglione reported. "I thought I spotted her walking down the street, but then I lost sight and all of a sudden she popped up in a grocery store parking lot. She's in there now."

"Give me the directions," Conrad said calmly. By this time, he and Paglione knew Eau Claire fairly well, having spent more than a day simply driving the streets, studying maps, memorizing the layout of the city. As he listened to Paglione's voice in his ear, he realized he was less than a minute from the grocery store.

He smiled.

Grace moved swiftly through the brightly lit aisles, focused on two things and two things only: bread and peanut butter. Her appetite was nonexistent, and none of the calculated displays caught her attention. She would buy food because she had to eat, but that was the only reason.

The peanut butter was, as always, on the same aisle with the ketchup and mustard. She grabbed the biggest jar available, then set out for the bakery section, only to be sidetracked by a sudden realization that she needed a knife to spread the peanut butter. A box of plastic utensils sprang to mind; that's what she would have bought before, but fragile plastic, designed to be disposable, would soon break and she would have to buy more. It would be cheaper simply to buy a real knife. She backtracked to the previous aisle, where she found the kitchen supplies. There was a row of plastic-sealed knives hanging from hooks. She took the first one she came to that wasn't serrated, because cleaning peanut butter from all the little teeth would be a pain. Her choice was a paring knife with a four-inch blade, and the print on the cardboard backing guaranteed its sharpness.

Knife and peanut butter in hand, she hurried to the bakery section and grabbed a giant-size loaf of bread.

Looking at her watch, she saw that she had been in the store for one minute and twenty seconds, a personal record for her, but that was eighty seconds her computer had been left unguarded.

There were two checkout counters open. At one, a bachelor was unloading a couple of microwave dinners, a six-pack of beer, and an economy-size bag of potato chips, standard fare for the unclaimed male. At the other, a bent old gent was carefully counting out his money for a bottle of aspirin. Grace chose the second counter, placing her items on the belt just as the clerk gave the receipt to the old guy, who smiled sweetly.

"Wife's got a headache," he explained, a product of an earlier age when friendliness to strangers was something to be expected, not feared. "Not an aspirin in the house. Can't understand it, she's usually got a bottle for this and a bottle for that, something for any ailment a body could produce, but tonight there's not a single aspirin." He turned his head and winked at Grace, his eyes twinkling cheerfully. He didn't mind the errand, the usefulness.

The swift-moving clerk rang up Grace's three items while the old man fumbled his wallet into his pocket. "Twelve thirty-seven. Kill a tree or choke a bird?"

Grace blinked. "I—what?" She handed over thirteen dollars.

"Paper or plastic?" the clerk translated, grinning a little, and the old man chuckled as he toddled off.

"Plastic," Grace said. The night shift was definitely a little off kilter. She felt a tiny spurt of amusement, a hint of life in the desolation of her heart and mind like a faint, fragile heartbeat to show she still lived, after a fashion. Her lips curved involuntarily, the elusive smile fading almost as soon as it had formed, but for a moment the life had been there. She turned her head to watch the old gentleman as he approached the automatic doors, and through the big plate-glass windows she saw two men getting out of a beige Dodge sedan parked in the center of the lot.

The man nearest the store paused and waited for the other to come around the car, then they walked together toward the store. One was dark, powerfully built, vaguely simian in the shape of his head; the other was of medium height and build, ordinary brown hair, just . . . ordinary. Slacks and jackets, neither natty nor threadbare. Neither of them would stand out in a crowd, not even the ape-man. He was just another guy who was a little too hairy, a little too bulky, nothing unusual.

But they were walking together in a subtle sort of lock-step, as if they had a definite goal, a mission.

"Your change is sixty-three cents."

Absently Grace took the change and slid it into her pocket. Archaeologists picked up a lot of anthropology stuff, because the two went hand-in-hand in understanding how people had lived, and Grace had lived with two archaeologists, brother and husband, absorbing a lot of their conversations over the years.

Two men, walking together in a purposeful manner. Men didn't do that unless they were working together as a team, to some definite end. This was different from the more casual, walking-in-company-but-not-*together* gait of males who didn't want to send the wrong signal to any watching females.

She grabbed the bag from the startled clerk and darted back into the store. The clerk said "Hey!" but Grace didn't hesitate, merely took a quick glance not at the clerk but at the two men, who must have been watching her, because they broke into a run.

She dropped to the floor and scrambled down an aisle, knowing the two men couldn't see directly down it from their angle of approach. Her heart rate increased, but oddly she didn't feel panic, only an elevated state of urgency. She was caught in an enclosed area, stalked by two men who could catch her in a pincers movement unless she moved fast. Her chances of outrunning them were small, because they had to be Parrish's men, and Parrish wouldn't hesitate at giving the order to shoot her in the back.

A woman pushed a shopping cart into the aisle at the far end, her attention focused on the stacks of soft drinks. Her purse was unguarded in the cart's child seat, a red sweater draped over it.

Grace moved down the aisle, not running but walking

fast. The woman wasn't paying any attention; she turned to pick up a carton of soft drinks, and as Grace walked by she snagged the red sweater from its resting place.

Quickly she turned the corner into the next aisle and pulled on the sweater, leaving her hair caught beneath the fabric. Her long braid was too identifiable, but the red sweater worked in reverse, because she hadn't been wearing one and the men's gazes would, she hoped, slide over anything so attention-getting.

She hooked the plastic bag over her arm like a purse and walked calmly toward the front of the store. She schooled her expression to the absorbed passivity of the grocery shopper, seeming to examine the contents of the shelves as she walked past them.

Up front, she could hear the checker telling someone, probably the night supervisor, that a woman had gone back into the store instead of out as shoppers were expected to do.

A man, the average-looking, brown-haired one, crossed in front of the aisle. His gaze barely touched on Grace, sliding right past the red sweater. Her heart jumped into her throat, but she kept a steady, unhurried pace. Her skin felt tight, fragile, no barrier at all to a bullet. The man had crossed out of sight but perhaps he was sharp, perhaps he had seen through her improvised disguise and was simply waiting for her at the front of the aisle, just out of sight. Perhaps she was walking right into a death trap.

Her legs felt weak; her knees shook. Three more steps took her out of the aisle, into the front checkout area. She didn't turn her head, but her peripheral vision caught the movement of the man, walking away from her as he looked down every aisle.

Run! Her instinct was to bolt, but her legs were too shaky. Her mind held her back, whispering to hold on, that every second without being noticed was an extra second for hiding. Shopping carts had been pushed up to block the entrances to the checkout counters that weren't open, and she nudged one aside, slipping into the narrow space that funneled customers to the exit. She angled to the left, to the set of doors nearest the line of cars where she'd left the computer. The automatic doors opened with a pneumatic sigh and she walked out into the night chill, heart pounding, unable to believe it had worked. But she had gained, at best, only a minute.

She ran for the row of employees' cars, diving for their shelter. Lying down on the pavement, she crawled under the car, wedging herself with her computer between the front wheels.

Sharp, loose gravel bit into her, even through her clothes. The smell of oil and gasoline, of things mechanical, seemed to coat her nostrils with a greasy film. She lay very still, listening for two pairs of footsteps.

They came within ten seconds, moving a bit fast, but the men were professional. They weren't doing anything to attract undue attention. They weren't yelling, they apparently didn't have weapons drawn, they were simply searching. Grace listened to the steps coming close and then retreating, and she huddled closer to the wheel, tucked into as small a ball as she could manage. They were quartering the parking lot, she realized, trying to spot her among the scattered cars.

"I can't believe she slipped past us," one voice said, the tone rather aggrieved.

"She has proven surprisingly elusive," a second, deeper voice replied. There was a subtle formality to the phrasing, a mild deliberateness as if the speaker thought of every word he spoke.

Something else was said but the words were indistinct, as if the speaker were walking away from her. After a few moments the voices grew plainer.

"She made us. Man, I can't believe that. She took one look and bolted. She musta slipped out through the receiving bay, no matter what that kid said about nobody coming by."

"Perhaps, perhaps not." The second voice was still mild, almost indifferent. "You said she had a suitcase when you saw her on the street."

"Yeah."

"She didn't have it just now."

"She must've stashed it somewhere. You figure she's gone back for it?"

"Undoubtedly. She would have hidden it fairly close by,

but the location would be secure enough that she felt safe leaving it while she went into the store."

"Whadda we do now?"

"Fall back to our observation points, and refrain from discussing our plans in public."

"Uh, yeah."

A car started close by, presumably the beige Dodge, but Grace didn't move. Their withdrawal could be a trick; they could park somewhere close by and return on foot, waiting for her to show herself. She lay on the cold pavement, listening to the sporadic comings and goings of customers. The adrenaline level in her body began to drop, leaving her lethargic. The sweater was a thick one; she felt warmer now than she had in three days, and with warmth came drowsiness. Her eyelids were heavy, a heaviness that she fought. She could afford rest, but not inattention.

Her body had its own agenda. Three days and nights of struggle, of little or no rest, no food, and moments of sheer terror that overlaid a base of profound despair, had taken their toll on her. She was exhausted and weak, strained to the breaking point. One moment she was awake, fighting sleep, and in the next moment the fight was lost.

The grocery store closed at midnight, and it was the sudden dousing of the parking lot lights that woke her. She lay very still, jolted from sleep but unaware of where she was. Her surroundings were totally alien, she was crowded against something massive and dark and the smell was awful, like motor oil . . . she was under a car. Awareness hit her and in panic she looked around, but no one was leaving the store. The employees would have to close up, perhaps do some cleaning, before they would leave.

Though a peek at her watch told her the time, she had no idea how long she'd slept, because she didn't know how long she'd lain there before dozing. Her carelessness frightened her. What if whoever owned the car had left work early?

Don't borrow trouble, she told herself as she gathered her possessions and inched out from under the car. She had enough problems without worrying about something that hadn't happened.

She hoped that while she had slept, enough time had lapsed that her two pursuers had given up hope of spotting her in this area. She didn't dare stay any longer; she had to risk being seen. But the night was darker now as fewer cars were on the street, houses had darkened, stores had closed.

She was stiff from the cold and her cramped position under the car. She moved slowly, staying in a crouch to keep out of sight behind the parked cars. But finally there were no more cars, only a naked expanse of parking lot. She moved fast, then, almost running as she scuttled along the edge of the pavement, the duffel banging against her left hip and her food supply bouncing against her right. As soon as she cleared the fence she swerved into deeper shadows, and was swallowed by the night.

Chapter 6

GRACE BROKE INTO A HOUSE.

She had chosen a hiding place well before dawn, in a lower-middle-class neighborhood where there weren't likely to be security systems, only nosy neighbors. She had watched the houses, picking out the ones that didn't have toys, bicycles, or swing sets in the yards. She wanted a house without children, a house where both husband and wife worked and no one was at home during the day. Children would complicate the issue; they got sick at inconvenient times and disrupted schedules.

The darkness had barely begun to lessen when the houses began coming alive, windows brightening with lights, the muted sounds of radios and televisions seeping through the walls. The scents of coffee and bacon teased her. She didn't know what day it was, weekday or weekend, if children would be going to school or playing in the yards and street all day. She prayed for a weekday.

People began leaving, the exhaust of cars and pickup trucks leaving plumes behind in the chill morning air.

Carefully Grace took note of how many people left each house.

Finally she selected her target. The husband left first, and about twenty minutes later the wife drove off with a clatter of lifters marking her progress.

Still Grace waited, and her prayers were answered. Children began appearing, carrying books and backpacks, their voices loud with a shrill giddiness induced by the approaching summer vacation. These past few days of chilly weather hadn't cooled their enthusiasm. Soon school would be out, the weather would be warm, and a long summer stretched before them. Grace envied them the simplicity of their joy.

The bus arrived, the street emptied. Silence ruled the neighborhood again, except for the occasional departure of a few whose workdays didn't start until at least eight o'clock.

Now was the time, when the street was mostly empty but there was still enough customary noise in the neighborhood that people were less likely to notice the little extra noise made by the breaking of glass.

Grace slipped around to the back of her targeted house, concealed by the neatly clipped hedgerow that separated the property from its neighbors.

As she'd hoped, the upper half of the back door was glass panes. Someone was still home in the house on the left, but the curtains were drawn so no one from that side was likely to see her. The house on the right was a 'fifties-style ranch, with a longer length but shallower depth than this one; anyone looking out a window wouldn't be able to see the back of this house.

Hoping for an easy way in, she looked around for a convenient place to hide a key. There weren't any flowerpots, and the doormat yielded nothing. Breaking the glass was more difficult than she'd expected. Television and the movies made it look so easy, panes shattering at a tap from a pistol or a blow from an elbow. It didn't work that way in real life. After bruising her elbow, she looked around for a harder weapon, but the yard was neatly kept and no handy rocks were left lying around. There were bricks, however, carefully laid to form the border of a flower bed.

With the red sweater held over the glass to muffle the

noise, Grace pounded the brick against the pane until it shattered. After replacing the brick, she took a deep breath, then reached in and unlocked the door.

It took every nerve she had. Walking into that strange, silent house shook her. When she put her foot over that threshold, she officially became guilty of breaking and entering, she who had always been so conscientious that she'd actually obeyed the speed limit.

She wasn't there to steal anything, except hot water and a little electricity. The close call in the grocery store had made it imperative that she begin blending in with the population, and also work up some disguises. She could no longer look homeless; she had to look . . . homogeneous. Blend in or die.

Her heart pounded as she stripped out of her filthy clothes and put them in the unknown lady's washing machine. What if she had miscalculated, what if either the lady or her husband *hadn't* left for the day, hadn't gone to jobs, but instead one of them was just on an errand and would return any minute? At the very least the cops would be called, if a strange woman was found naked, and showering, in their house.

But she hadn't dared try to rent a motel room, assuming no one would let her take a room the way she looked and smelled, even if she paid cash. And perhaps Parrish's men were checking motels; a clerk would definitely remember her. Just this once she needed to take a bath and wash her clothes where she couldn't be seen, where no one would notice her, and after this she would look more respectable. She would be able to go into a laundromat and wash her clothes, to go into stores and buy the things she needed to disguise her appearance, to lose herself in the immense sea of respectability.

She should have hurried through the shower. She knew she should, but she didn't. She stood under the spray of water, feeling the grit wash off her skin, feeling her greasy hair soak up the moisture. She shampooed twice, and scrubbed herself until her skin was bright pink all over, and still she didn't want to get out of the shower. She stood there even when the hot water began to go and the spray grew chilly. She didn't turn off the water until it was so cold she'd begun shivering, and she did so then only because she'd been cold for three days and she was tired of it.

It was such a relief to feel clean again that she almost wept. Almost, because somehow the tears wouldn't quite come. Had she cried for Ford, for Bryant? She couldn't remember. She had crystal-clear memories of a lot of things about that horrible night, but she couldn't remember tears. Surely she had cried. But if she hadn't . . . if she hadn't cried for them, then she couldn't cry for something as ultimately mundane as being clean. Crying for less would minimize them, and that she couldn't bear.

Roughly she rubbed the towel over her bare skin, then wrapped the damp fabric around her head. She didn't want to abuse the owners' unknowing hospitality any more than necessary, and using two towels instead of one was a definite luxury.

Then, almost trembling with eagerness, she unzipped the duffel and took out her new clothes. The jeans and sweatshirt were very wrinkled, the denim jacket less so. Grace peeled the hard plastic bubble away from her kitchen knife and tested its sharpness by cutting the tags off her purchases. The knife easily sliced through the plastic loops and she thoughtfully regarded the shiny blade. Not bad.

She tossed the garments into the clothes dryer to get out the wrinkles, and brushed her teeth while the dryer did its thing. She eyed her reflection in the mirror, a little puzzled. She looked different, somehow, and it wasn't just the exhausted starkness of her expression. The pallor was expected, as were the circles under her eyes. No, it was something else, something elusive.

Shrugging aside her puzzlement, she turned her attention to more practical matters. Her long hair took forever to dry on its own, so she used the blow dryer lying next to the sink.

Her thick braid was too identifiable. She should cut her hair. She thought of looking for scissors, but the thought didn't transfer itself into action. Ford had loved her long hair, he had played with it—

The pain was like a mule kick in the chest, destroying her. She sagged against the wall, her teeth clenched against a keening wail as her body doubled over from the impact. *Oh God oh God.*

She could feel herself shattering inside, the enormity of loss so overwhelming that surely she couldn't keep living, surely her heart would simply stop beating from the stress. Except for the savage need for vengeance against Parrish, she had no reason to live. But her heart, that sturdy, oblivious muscle, didn't feel her grief and continued without pause its preordained pumping mission.

No. No. She couldn't do this. Grieving was a luxury she couldn't afford; she had known from the beginning it would tear her apart. She had to put it away until after she had taken care of Parrish, when she could approach Ford's memory, and Bryant's, and say, "I didn't let him get away with it."

Drawing in deep, shuddering breaths, she straightened her aching body. The pain was real, so intense it actually permeated her muscles. With shaking hands she finished drying her hair, though she was at a loss what to do with the thick mass except rebraid it. For the time being she left it loose, hanging down her back, and retrieved her clothes from the dryer.

The garments were hot, almost too hot, but she relished the heat. Quickly she pulled on clean panties and socks, then dressed before all the heat could dissipate. The sweatshirt felt like heaven; she sighed as the warmth enfolded her. Her bra was in the washer, but she didn't really need one. She'd never been bosomy, and the sweatshirt was thick.

The jeans were loose, almost too loose to stay up. She'd chosen her usual size, but perhaps the label was wrong. Frowning, she unzipped the fly to check the inside tag. Nope, the size was right. The cut must be unusually large, unless she'd somehow lost about ten pounds. Realization dawned. After four days without food, without much sleep, walking all night long, under constant stress, of course she had lost weight.

Reminded of the need to eat, she got her loaf of bread, now sadly mashed, and the jar of peanut butter. After resetting the washer to put her filthy clothes through one more sudsing, she sat down at the battered kitchen table and smeared the peanut butter on one slice of bread. An entire sandwich would probably be wasteful, because her throat was closing up at the prospect of eating half of one.

With the help of a glass of water, she doggedly began eating. Swallowing was an effort, and her stomach, accustomed to emptiness, lurched in sudden nausea. Grace sat very still and concentrated on not vomiting. She had to eat or she wouldn't be able to function, period.

After a minute or so she took a sip of water, and another small bite.

By the time the washer had gone through its cycle again, she had managed to eat the half sandwich.

She washed the glass and returned it to the cabinet, cleaned the table of any crumbs, washed her knife, and put the bread and peanut butter back into the duffel. The knife . . . she tried putting it in her belt loop, but the handle wasn't big enough to prevent it from sliding through. She didn't want to put a naked blade in her pocket, but neither did she want to wrap it up so securely that she'd have to waste precious time unwrapping it if she needed the knife in an emergency, such as fighting for her life.

She needed one of those knife scabbards, the kind that slipped over a belt. Come to that, she needed a belt with or without a scabbard, because the jeans were seriously loose.

What she *really* needed was a switchblade, so she wouldn't have to worry about belts or scabbards.

It struck her that she had come a long way in four days, and not just the distance between Minneapolis and Eau Claire. Four days ago she couldn't even have thought of using a knife on anyone, even to defend herself. Today she wouldn't hesitate.

Going back into the kitchen, she unrolled a couple of paper towels and folded them twice before wrapping the bulk around the knife blade and sliding it into her front right pocket, leaving the handle sticking out and covered by the sweatshirt. If she needed the knife, it would slide right out. She'd have to be careful and not puncture herself before she could get something safer, but for now she felt better.

That done, she put her clothes in the dryer along with the bath towel she had used, threw in a sheet of fabric softener, then returned to the bathroom to do something with her hair. As she passed the open duffel she automatically glanced at it to reassure herself of the computer's safety, and the sight of the bulging bag stopped her cold. A hunger grew in her, a need that had nothing to do with food or warmth. It wasn't physical at all, but it gnawed at her just the same. She wanted to *work*. She wanted to sit for hours poring over text, making notes, referring to her language programs, tapping in information. She wanted to find out what had happened to Niall of Scotland, all those centuries ago.

The battery pack was weak, almost depleted. She could have been recharging it while she showered, but she'd let an hour go by. Still, she could set up the computer and work on the household current, just until her clothes were dry.

She resisted the urge. She might have to leave in a hurry, and she didn't want to make things more difficult by having her belongings scattered about. If she began working she might lose track of time, which had happened more than once, and she had things to do today. She had been traveling at night and hiding during the day, but that had to change. They were hunting her at night, they knew that was when she'd been moving, so she had to alter her habits as well as her appearance.

Using some bobby pins she found in the bathroom, she twisted her hair up and pinned it on top of her head. Knowing from experience that the slippery strands would soon slide right out of the pins, she jammed the baseball cap on her head to hold everything in place.

It wasn't much of a disguise, but added to the change of clothes it just might do. She needed sunglasses and a wig, two items she intended to acquire as soon as possible, and she would be able to vary her appearance. She made a mental note to look for a knife scabbard, too.

The men following her would expect her to keep moving, to follow her previous pattern. She didn't intend to do so. After bettering her disguise with a wig, she would rent a cheap motel room there in Eau Claire and stay for a couple of days. She needed to rest, she needed to stabilize, and she needed to work. More than anything, she needed to lose herself in work.

The plan worked. After tidying the house, removing all signs of her invasion, she let herself out and locked the door, then tossed a rock through the window to provide an explanation for the broken glass. It took her a while to find a store that sold cheap wigs, and an equally long time trying them on before she managed to slip the frizzy blond one under her sweatshirt. She bought one, a dark red pageboy, and while the clerk was ringing up the sale she slid the money for the blond wig under the edge of the cash register. If the men following her were really good, they might connect her to the red wig, but no one would know about the blond one.

She was wearing the blond wig when she rented a room. The motel was only a step above sleazy, officially in the run-down category, but the plumbing worked and the bed, though the mattress was lumpy and the sheets dingy, was still a bed. Except for her nap under the car she hadn't had any sleep, but she resisted the urge to lie down. Instead she took off the itchy wig and set up the laptop on the rickety table and forced herself to stay awake by plunging into the intricacies of language use that had died out before Christopher Columbus was born.

Grace loved her work. She loved losing herself in the challenge of accurately putting together the torn or shattered remnants of early man's painstaking efforts to communicate thoughts, customs, dreams—reaching out to the future with hammer and chisel, or with quills dipped in dye, and in the act of creation going beyond the forever *now* of time, setting down the past for the sake of the future, uniting the three dimensions of existence. Writing had begun when mankind began thinking in abstracts, rather than just physically existing. Whenever she studied a worn, broken piece of stone, puzzling over the figures so roughly etched into the surface and almost worn away by time and the elements, she always wondered about the writers: who had they been, what had they been thinking that was important enough for them to crouch for hours over a bit of stone, legs cramping, back and arms aching, as they cut the images into the stone with little more than the sharpened edge of another piece of stone?

These documents about the mysterious Niall of Scotland were much more sophisticated than that. They had been written with ink on parchment, parchment that had survived the centuries remarkably intact, though not unscathed. She would love to get her hands on the originals, she thought. Not because they would be any plainer; no, it was always best to work with reproductions, to avoid additional damage to the ancient parchment. There was just something unusual about these papers, though in archaeological terms they were far too recent to be of interest. Seven hundred years was nothing to a science devoted to deciphering life from millions of years ago.

There was such a hodgepodge of languages here! Latin, Greek, Old French, Old English, Hebrew, even Gaelic, yet the documents all seemed to be connected in some way. She wasn't proficient in Gaelic, and deciphering the documents written in that language would take considerable research and study on her part. She was better in Hebrew, better still in Greek, and completely at ease in the other three languages.

She had worked before in the Old French sections; this time, after inserting the CD, she pulled up a section in Latin. Latin was such a tidy, structured language, extremely efficient; easy reading, for her.

Five minutes later she was rapidly making notes, her brow furrowed in concentration.

She had underestimated the age of the documents by about two centuries. The oldest of the Latin papers seemed to have been written in the twelfth century, which would make them almost nine hundred years old. She whispered a phrase, testing it on her tongue: "Pauperes Commilitones Christi Templique Salomonis." The syllables rolled with a measured cadence, and a chill ran up her back. *The Poor Fellow-Soldiers of Christ and the Temple of Solomon.* The Knights of the Temple. Templars.

What she'd read in the library's files came back to her. The Templars had been the richest organization in medieval society. Their wealth had exceeded that of kings and popes; they had, indeed, operated the first rudimentary banking system in Europe, handling the transfer of funds and extending loans to kings. Their original reason for existence had been to protect the Christian pilgrims on their way to the Holy Lands, and the warrior monks had become the best-trained, best-equipped fighting force of their time. They had been so feared and respected on the battlefield that they were never ransomed when taken prisoner by the Muslims, but put to death immediately.

They had, for a time, been quartered on the site of King Solomon's Temple in Jerusalem. During that time, they had evidently done extensive excavation on the site, and from that time until the Order had been destroyed, they had been the most powerful and wealthy force in Europe. Their treasure, supposedly taken from the ruins of the great Temple, had been rumored to be enormous.

Their treasure had been their downfall. Philip of France, in debt to the Templars, had devised a unique way of repaying the debt: he and Pope Clement V conspired to have all the Templars arrested and condemned for heresy, a charge that allowed the property of the charged to be confiscated. In a surprise move against the Knights on Friday the thirteenth, in October of 1307, thousands of Knights and their retainers had been arrested, but no treasure was found—or had ever been found. Moreover, shortly before that, the Grand Master of the Knights had ordered many of their records destroyed.

Or had he? She seemed to be looking at some of them right now.

The name jumped at her again. Niall of Scotland. Her pen dug into the paper as she wrote out the translation. "It has been ordained that Niall of Scotland, of Royal blood, shall be the Guardian."

Of royal blood? She hadn't been able to find a Niall in Scotland's history, so how could he be of royal blood? And what had he been guardian *of?* Had it been a political position or a military one?

She needed a library. She would prefer the Library of Congress. She could get into it with her modem and computer if the motel room had a phone, which it didn't. Tomorrow she would find a library in Eau Claire and do what research she could, make notes of the books she would need. She would like to find a Gaelic/English dictionary, because the papers written in Gaelic would likely be the most informative about this Niall of Scotland, but the Eau Claire public library might not have such an exotic item in its inventory.

The Chicago library system probably would, though,

given the Irish heritage of such a large part of the city's population. New York, Boston . . . those were other likely places accessible by computer.

She ejected the CD and carefully stored it, then exited the program. The computer was great, but she wanted the feel of paper in her hands, to give her the illusion of handling the originals. She pulled out the thick sheaf of copies, tracing her finger over the slick, smooth texture of modern paper. These too would fade over the centuries; sometime in the future other people would puzzle over the remaining scraps, trying to piece together what twentieth-century life had been like. They would try to restore videotape and retrieve the images from it, they would have CDs, books, disks, but only portions of the vast number would survive the centuries. Languages would have changed, and technology would be vastly different. Who knew what present time would look like from a distance of seven hundred years?

She stopped at a sheet written in Old French. Taking her magnifying glass to help her see the faded marks more clearly, she began reading. This page was an account of a battle; the handwriting was thin, spidery, the words crammed together as if the writer had wanted to make use of every inch of paper.

"Though the enemy numbered five and Brother Niall was but one, yet he slew them all. His mastery of the sword is unequaled among the Brethren. He fought his way to the side of Brother Ambrose, who lay sorely wounded, and lifted his fallen fellow Knight onto his shoulder. Burdened by Brother Ambrose, he slew three more of the enemy before escaping, and bearing the wounded Knight to a place of safety."

Grace sat back, restlessly running her fingers through her freed hair. Her heart was pounding. How could an ordinary man have done that? Outnumbered five to one, Niall had nevertheless killed all five opponents and rescued his fellow Knight. Then, carrying a grown man who had been wearing chain mail and probably weighed, armor and all, more than two hundred fifty pounds, he had still managed to kill three more opponents and escape with his burden.

What kind of man had he been? A powerful one, both in battle and in authority, but had he been mean-spirited or generous, jolly or dour, quiet or boisterous? How had he died, and, more important, how had he lived? What had led him to become a warrior monk, and had he survived the destruction of his Order?

She wanted to keep reading but a yawn took her by surprise, and weariness swamped her. She checked her watch, expecting to see that about an hour had elapsed, but instead more than three hours had gone by. It was late afternoon, and she didn't know how much longer she could stay awake.

Why should she? This was the safest she had been in four days, hidden behind the disguise of a blond wig and a fake name. She was clean and warm; there was water to drink, food to eat, and a working bathroom. There was a bolted door between her and the rest of the world. The sheer luxury of it made her almost boneless with relief.

The temptation was more than she could withstand. After carefully repacking the laptop and the papers, and making certain her money was secure, she turned out the lights and slipped off her shoes. She couldn't relax her guard more than that, not after four days of only fitful naps, but that was enough.

A sigh shuddered from her lips as she stretched out on the bed. Every muscle in her body ached from the release of tension, the chance to relax and rest. Turning on her side, she curled into a ball and hugged the pillow to her, and then she slept.

She dreamed of Niall. The dreams were chaotic, turbulent, full of swords and battlefields. She dreamed of a castle, a great dark one, and the sight of it sent shivers of dread through her. The people whispered about the castle, and about the lord who lived there. He was a ruthless, brutal warrior who slew all who dared cross him. Decent folk kept their daughters away from the castle, for otherwise the lasses lost their virtue to him, and he wed none of them.

She dreamed of him sitting sprawled before the huge fire in the great central hall, black eyes narrowed and unreadable as he watched his men drink and eat. His hair was long and thick, braided at the temples.

A saucy wench plopped herself in his lap, and in her dream Grace held her breath, afraid of what this dream

Niall might do. He merely smiled at the serving wench, a slow curve of his mouth that made Grace's breath catch yet again. Then, in the way of dreams, the image shifted and moved on, and she slept more peacefully.

He felt it again, that sensation of being watched.

Niall lifted the wench from his lap with a promise of more attention when they were abed that night, but his alert gaze was moving around the hall. Who watched him, and why? He was lord of this castle and as such was accustomed to people looking to him for answers, for approval, or just to measure his mood. A lot of people looked at him, and to him, but this was different.

This was . . . watching.

There seemed nothing amiss in the hall. The air was smoky, the men loud. Laughter spilled from one bench and others turned to hear the jest. The serving wenches moved about, filling cups, fielding advances, bestowing smiles or frowns depending on how welcome was each advance. All was normal.

But still he felt that presence, the same one that had pulled him from his bed a few nights past. There was a softness that made him think it was a woman who watched him. Perhaps she found him to her liking, but she was shy. She couldn't come to him boldly as most of the wenches did when they wanted a night of hard riding. She merely watched, and yearned.

But, looking around, he could find no lass who fit that description, and he scowled in frustration. If indeed a woman watched him, he would know her identity. Perhaps she had no reason other than a lass's soft feelings, but Niall never forgot the Treasure he had sworn to protect. Any unusual occurrence heightened his alertness, and his hand unconsciously sought the blade at his belt. His black eyes narrowed as they swept the smoky hall, probing the shadows, reading men's expressions in an instant, and passing on if nothing was amiss. The women, too, were carefully judged.

Again, he found nothing unusual.

But twice now he had felt himself watched, felt that other presence. He did not think it mere imagination. Niall had fought too many battles against foes both open and unseen, and he trusted his warrior's instincts which had grown even more acute over the years.

His probing regard of the hall had been noticed, and the noise of many voices was quieting, uneasy glances sliding his way. Niall was aware of the whispered tales that had spread over the years. He was Black Niall, a warrior so fearsome he'd never been defeated in open fight, so canny he'd never been taken unawares. His own men trained with him, knew he bruised when hit, bled when cut, knew he sweated and groaned and cursed just as they did, but still . . . why was he so vigorous at an age when most men were losing their teeth and becoming graybeards? It was as if the hand of time had left him untouched. His hair remained black, his body strong, and illness didn't touch him.

He sometimes wondered, uneasily, if Valcour had damned him to immortality by appointing him Guardian of the Treasure for which so many of his brothers-in-arms had died.

He didn't like to think so. He would do his duty, uphold his vow, but he did it with bitterness. He guarded God's treasures, but God had not guarded the guardians. Niall had not prayed, had not been to mass or confession, in more than thirteen years. His belief had died on a black night in October, along with so many of his friends, his brethren. It was for them he remained on guard, for otherwise they would have died in vain.

But he did not want to spend eternity guarding the secrets of a God whom he no longer worshipped. What a bitter joke that would be!

His mouth twisted with cold amusement, and restlessly he rose from his chair. His gaze sought and found the wench who had whispered so naughtily in his ear, and with a motion of his head he directed her toward the stair, and his chamber. As always, when the blackness of spirit was upon him, the relief he sought was in a woman's body.

As soon as he'd stood, a woman had moved forward to remove his cup, and now he heard a hissing sound from her.

"What ails you, Alice?" he asked without looking around.

"Have a care with that lass," she grumbled, earning an amused glance from him.

"Why is that?" He was fond of Alice. She had worked in the castle from the time of his return, a widow who had desperately needed even the most sinister of shelters for herself and her bairns. She was roughly his age, but was now a grandmother. Having been blessed with rather stringent common sense, over the years she had gradually assumed responsibility for household matters, and he was pleased with the situation.

She settled her cap more firmly over her springy gray hair. "She says ye'll wed 'er, if she catches yer bairn in her belly."

Niall's eyes grew cold. Marriage and children were not for him, not with his life dedicated to guarding the Treasure. The women who shared his bed knew from the outset that he would not wed them, that he was interested only in bed sport, and he had always taken care that they were experienced in the ways of avoiding conception. It annoyed him that a woman, no matter how saucy or pretty, should try to trap him in such a way. With Alice's warning, however, he wouldn't let it happen.

He nodded briefly, then took himself up the stairs to rid his bedchamber of the untrustworthy wench. Before he left the hall, however, he took one last look around, hoping to espy the woman who had been watching him, whose feminine concentration he had felt.

There was nothing, but he knew she had been there. He had felt her. He would find her.

Chapter 7

THERE WAS NOTHING UNUSUAL ABOUT THE WOMAN WHO GOT OFF the bus in Chicago. No one had paid her any attention, not the agent who had sold her the ticket, not the driver, not the other passengers who sat absorbed in their own lives, their own troubles, their own reasons for being on the bus.

Her hair was blond and curly, one of those frizz jobs that didn't look good on anyone but required no maintenance beyond washing. Her clothes were clean but nondescript, the kind that could be bought at any discount store: baggy jeans, inexpensive athletic shoes, a navy blue sweatshirt. Nothing about her luggage attracted attention, either. It was a cheap nylon model, in a particularly unappealing shade of brown that the designer had tried to brighten by adding a red stripe down one side. It hadn't worked.

Maybe it was a little unusual that she'd worn sunglasses the entire trip, because, after all, the bus windows were tinted, but there was one other passenger who also wore sunglasses, so overall there was nothing about her that would make anyone look twice.

When the bus lurched to a stop at the depot in Chicago, Grace silently produced her luggage receipt and took possession of the ugly brown duffel. She would have preferred keeping the laptop with her, but people tended to notice if someone carried a computer everywhere. With that in mind, she had packed the computer in its protective case, then further buffered it in the duffel with her meager supply of clothing.

It had been a week since her world had shattered, a week exactly.

Her life then had ended, and another had begun. She didn't feel the same, didn't look the same, didn't think the same way she had before she had lost everything and been thrown into a life in the streets and on the run. The sharp paring knife rode in a scabbard on her belt, and was covered by the sweatshirt. The screwdriver she had taken from the storage building on that horrible first day was tucked into her right sock; it wasn't as good a weapon as the knife, but she had honed it against a rock until she was satisfied with its sharpness.

She had exhausted the Eau Claire library's fund of knowledge about the Templars. She had learned a lot, including the significance of the date on which the Order had been destroyed: Friday the thirteenth, giving birth to the superstition about the combination of day and date. Interesting, but not what she had wanted. She had searched in vain for any reference, in either the Templars' recorded history or in Scotland's history, to Niall of Scotland.

She had to dig deeper, and Chicago, with its vast library on things Gaelic, was a good place to start. Remaining another day in Eau Claire would have been risky, anyway. Parrish's men would have tried to pick up her trail outside Eau Claire, but when they didn't find anything they would return to the town. Any halfway competent goon would begin checking the motels, and though she'd been careful to alter her appearance by either wearing the blond wig or tucking her hair up under the baseball cap, eventually they would find her.

She felt stronger now, no longer operating in a barely controlled panic, but at the same time she was alert. She had slept, and she had forced herself to eat a peanut butter sandwich at least once a day. Eating was still difficult, and her jeans were even looser now than they had been before. The belt she wore, bought at another Kmart, was a necessity. She had even washed the jeans in hot water in an effort to shrink them, but any shrinkage must have been in length instead of width, because they still hung on her. If she lost much more weight, even the belt wouldn't help. She didn't intend to spend any more of her precious store of money on new clothes, so what she already had would have to do.

She had formulated a plan. Rather than living off her cash until it was all gone, she had to have a job. There were underground jobs in Chicago, washing dishes or cleaning houses, and those suited her perfectly. No one would become concerned if one day she didn't show. On the other hand, those types of jobs would be low-paying, and while they would tide her over for now, she would soon need something better. For that, she would need to develop another identity, and back it up with documentation.

Being what she was, a researcher, that was the approach she had used to find out how to establish a new identity. In this instance, the Eau Claire library had provided her with the information she needed.

It seemed relatively simple, though it would take time. First she would need a dead person, someone who had been born about the same time she had, but who had died young enough that there wouldn't be a job history, school records, or traffic violations to follow Grace around after she assumed the girl's identity. Once she had a name, she could write to the proper department at the state capital and get a copy of the birth certificate. With the birth certificate, she could get a social security number; with that, she could get a driver's license, establish credit, become a new person.

She stored the duffel in a locker and carefully tucked the key in her front pants pocket. Then she located a phone book and flipped through the directory until she found the listing for cemeteries. After jotting down the names, she stopped a maintenance worker and asked which cemetery was the nearest, then went to someone else, a ticket agent, and asked for directions.

Two hours later, after having ridden on five different buses, she arrived back at the bus depot.

She bought a newspaper, found a seat, put on her glasses, and began looking through the tiny, densely printed classifieds for a place to stay. She didn't want crummy and couldn't afford comfortable, so run-down was the best alternative. By comparing prices, she eliminated both ends of the scale, and that left several places that fell in the middle. Two were boardinghouses, and she put those at the top of her list. Two phone calls later, she had a place to stay and directions on how to get there, including which El train and buses to take.

The best thing about a large city, she thought as she walked toward the El station, was the intracity transportation system. The buses had made getting to the cemetery easy enough. She could have walked to the boardinghouse; a week ago the distance would have daunted her, but now five miles seemed like nothing. She could easily walk five miles in an hour and a half. But the trains and buses were cheap and fast, so why should she? Half an hour later she got off the train, walked a block just in time to get on the bus she needed, and five minutes after that was walking down the street looking at house numbers.

The boardinghouse was a square, lumpish three-story building that hadn't seen a new coat of pain in several years. A three-foot-high picket fence, sagging in places, separated the scraggly, minuscule patch of lawn from the broken sidewalk. There was no gate. Grace walked up to the door and pushed the buzzer.

"Yeah." The voice was the same one that had answered the telephone: deep and raspy, but somehow female.

"I called about the room for rent—"

"Yeah, okay," the voice interrupted brusquely. Grace waited, and heard heavy steps clomping toward the door.

Grace had put on her sunglasses again as soon as she'd finished reading the classifieds, and was deeply grateful for that protection when the door was unlocked and swung open to reveal one of the most astonishing creatures she'd ever seen. At least the woman couldn't see her gawking.

"Well, don't just stand there," the landlady said impatiently, and in silence Grace entered the house. Without another word the woman—and now Grace wasn't so certain of the gender—closed and locked the door, then clomped back the way she'd come. Grace followed, bag in hand.

The woman was easily six feet tall, rangy and loose-limbed. Her hair was bleached lemony white, and cut in short spikes. Her skin was a smooth, pale brown, like heavily creamed coffee, hinting at some exotic ancestry. A huge sunflower earring dangled from one ear, while a row of studs marched up the outer rim of the other. Her shoulders were broad and bony, her feet and hands big. Her feet looked bigger than they probably were because she was wearing hiking boots and thick socks. Her ensemble was completed by a black T-shirt with a loose yellow tank top layered over it, and tight black bicycle shorts with narrow lime-green stripes on the sides. She managed to look both ominous and festive.

"You a working girl?"

The question was fired at her as the landlady led her into an office so tiny it had to be a converted closet. There was a small, scarred wooden desk, an ancient office chair behind it, a two-drawer filing cabinet, and what looked like a kitchen chair. It was scrupulously neat, the two pens, stapler, receipt book, and telephone lined up like soldiers for inspection. The woman took a seat behind the desk.

"Not yet," Grace replied, taking off her sunglasses now that she had her reaction under control. She would have preferred leaving them on, but that would look suspicious. She sat in the other chair, and placed the bag beside her. "I just got into town, but I intend to look for a job tomorrow."

The landlady lit a long, thin cigarette and eyed Grace through the billow of blue smoke. Every finger was decorated with an ornate ring, and Grace found herself watching the movements of those big, oddly graceful hands.

Suddenly the woman snorted. "I guess not," she said shrewdly. "Honey, a working girl is a whore. Didn't think you looked the type, despite the cheap wig. No makeup, and you're wearing a wedding ring. You on the run from your old man?"

Grace looked down at her hands, and gently turned the plain gold band Ford had given her when they married. "No," she murmured.

"He's dead, huh?"

Surprised, Grace looked up.

"You ain't divorced, or you wouldn't be wearing the ring. First thing, you split from an asshole, the ring comes off." Sharp green eyes flicked over Grace's clothes. "Your clothes are too big, too; looks like you've lost some weight. Misery takes away the appetite, don't it?"

She understood, Grace realized, both terrified and comforted. In less than two minutes this strange, tough, disturbingly astute woman had sized her up and accurately read details no one else had even noticed. "Yes," she said, because some answer seemed indicated.

Whatever she saw in Grace's face, whatever deductions she drew from it, the woman abruptly seemed to make up her mind. "M'name's Harmony," she said, leaning over the desk and holding out her hand. "Harmony Johnson. More people named Johnson than Smith or Brown or Jones, you know that?"

Grace shook it; it was like shaking a man's bigger, rougher hand. "Julia Wynne," she said, using the name she'd taken from a small marker on an unkempt grave. The girl, born five years before Grace, had died just after her eleventh birthday. The marker had read: "Our Angel."

"Rooms are seventy a week," Harmony Johnson said. "They're damn clean. I don't allow no drugs, no parties, no whores. I got outta that, and I don't want it in my house. You clean up after yourself in the bathroom. I'll clean your room if you want, but that's another ten bucks a week. Most people do for themselves."

"I'll do the cleaning," Grace said.

"Thought so. You can have a hot plate, coffeemaker in your room, but no major cooking. I like to cook a big breakfast. Most of my people eat breakfast with me. How you feed yourself the rest of the time is your problem." She gave Grace another once-over. "Don't guess you're too worried about food right now, but time'll take care of that."

"Are there phones in the rooms?"

"Get a grip. Do I look like a fool?"

"No," Grace said, and had to stifle a sudden urge to laugh. Harmony Johnson looked like a lot of things, but fool wasn't on the list. "Do you mind if I have my own line installed? I do some computer work, and use a modem sometimes."

Harmony shrugged. "It's your money."

"When can I move in?"

"As soon as you pay me a deposit and haul your bag upstairs."

"Tell me, Conrad," Parrish said lazily, tipping his chair back. "How can Grace St. John, of all people, elude you for a week?" He wasn't at all pleased. Conrad had never failed him before, and though the Minneapolis police had bought the setup with a gratifying completeness and issued warrants for her arrest, no one had managed to find her. A nerd, an *ancient languages specialist,* of all people, had somehow managed to outsmart them all. "Mind, I don't give a shit about Grace, but she has the papers and I really do want them, Conrad. I really do."

Conrad's face was impassive. "She managed to empty out their bank account, so she has cash. The police figure she overrode the bank's computer system, but the bank's systems analyst hasn't determined how."

Parrish waved that aside with a languid movement of his hand. "The how doesn't matter. All that matters is finding her, and you haven't accomplished that."

Fool, Conrad thought dispassionately. The how always mattered, because when something worked once, people invariably repeated it. That was how patterns were established, and patterns were detectable.

"She had been traveling at night, but I think that's changed now. She had a bag when Paglione saw her in Eau Claire, so it follows that she has accumulated more clothing and now we have no idea what she's wearing." There were notes in his thick, brutish hand, but he didn't need to consult them. "A woman roughly answering her description bought a red wig in Eau Claire."

"A redhead should be easy to find."

"Unless it was a decoy." Conrad was of the opinion that the red wig was exactly that, and his admiration for Ms. St.

John had risen sharply. She was proving to be very interesting quarry. "There haven't been any leads on a redhead. She could have stolen another wig, one the proprietor didn't know anything about. She could also have cut her hair, colored it, done any number of things to change her appearance."

"Well then, damn it, how do you intend to find her?" Parrish snapped, his patience at an end.

"Her most likely destination, after Eau Claire, would be Chicago. A big city would give her a sense of security. Even though she has money, she's cautious; she will try to save that money in case she has to run again. She'll get a job, but it will have to be off the books, because she can't use her social security number. The kind of job she will be able to get will be low-skill, low-paying. I will put men in the streets, put out the word that there is a cash reward for information on her. I will find her."

"See that you do." Parrish rose and walked to the window, indicating the interview was ended. Conrad left, his movements as noiseless as always.

The garden was looking good, Parrish thought, eyeing the prize-winning roses beneath his window. The cold snap hadn't been a severe one; the temperature had remained above freezing. The days were growing warmer as spring settled in again, perhaps for good this time. The cold had to have been a trial for poor little Grace, though she had some extra padding on her bones for warmth. How soft she had looked! A man on top of her wouldn't feel as if he were lying on a skeleton.

What a strange attraction, he mused, setting his fingertips against the cool panes. He'd always preferred sleek women, but little Gracie was so unconsciously, unaccountably sensual, despite her weight. She wasn't much overweight, just enough to look rounded.

Perhaps he should instruct Conrad to keep her alive, just for a while. One day, perhaps, long enough for him to satisfy a particular fantasy.

He smiled, thinking about it.

Chapter 8

WEARILY GRACE UNTIED THE APRON FROM HER WAIST AND tossed it into the hamper. This was her sixth day on the job, as part-time dishwasher and general slave in Orel Hector's pizza and pasta restaurant. Sometimes she thought she'd never get the smell of garlic out of her hair, off her skin. The constant exposure to spicy food had, if anything, depressed her appetite even more. The workers were allowed to have anything in the restaurant for lunch, free, but so far she hadn't eaten anything. Just the thought of sitting down to a hearty pasta meal made her stomach clench.

"You comin' back tomorrow?" Orel asked as he took the cash box out of a locked drawer and opened it to pay her. There were three part-time workers in the restaurant, and none of them was on a payroll list. About a third of each day's take went into the cash box instead of being rung up on the cash register. He paid them in cash at the end of each day, and if one of them didn't show up the next day, he'd find someone else. Cut way down on the damn federal paperwork, he said.

"I'll be here," she said. It was exhausting work, but it suited her to be part of the underground economy. Orel handed over three tens, thirty dollars for seven hours of work, but it worked out to a hundred eighty dollars for the six days she'd been working. After paying Harmony seventy dollars a week, she'd have a hundred and ten left over. Her expenses were minimal, just the bus fare to work every day, and a few more clothes. She had bought two more pairs of cheap jeans, a size smaller this time, and a couple of T-shirts. Washing dishes was hot work. The new jeans were loose, too, and growing baggier by the day.

She folded the bills and slid them into her front pocket, then retrieved her computer case from under the cabinet where she'd stored it safely away from spills and drips. She'd told Orel she was going to school nights, and everyone accepted the explanation. Her coworkers didn't ask many personal questions, content to go their own way and not get involved with anyone. She preferred it that way, too.

She left through the back door, stepping out into a littered alley. The wind wound its way even down this narrow little space, freshening the air. She inhaled deeply, thankful for a breath that didn't bring the scent of garlic with it.

Cautiously she looked both left and right, the computer case clutched tightly in one hand and her other hand on her knife. So far she hadn't had any trouble, but she was prepared.

She walked two blocks to a bus stop, where the next bus was due in about ten minutes. The late-afternoon sky was a clear, dark blue; the day was fresh and sweet, and there was a jauntiness to everyone's step even this late in the day. Spring had definitely arrived, sending the temperature into the high seventies. Grace remembered her joy in the spring as she had walked across the Murchisons' backyard—how long ago had it been? Two weeks? Three? Closer to three, she thought. It had been the twenty-seventh of April, the last day she had felt joy in life. She could see the clearness of the day, but it didn't touch her heart. Inside, everything was bleak and barren, colorless.

The bus arrived and she got on, paid her fare. The bus driver nodded to her. This was the sixth day in a row she'd gotten on at that stop, and he had learned her face. She would have to take a different bus for a while.

She got off at the Newberry Library, one of the world's foremost historical research libraries. She had waded through text after text of medieval history, in both books and computer files, looking for some mention of Niall of Scotland. So far she had learned a lot about medieval times, but hadn't turned up one iota of information on the warrior Knight. She wasn't discouraged, though, because she had barely scratched the surface of the available material.

She went straight to the appropriate aisle and picked up where she had left off the night before, selecting several books and carrying them to an isolated table. Then she put on her glasses and began skimming, page by page, looking for any mention of anyone named Niall who had been connected to the Templars.

She almost missed it. She had been reading for more than two hours and her mind had gone on automatic. The reference didn't register for a moment, and she continued down the page. Then the similarity between the names caught her attention and she reread the paragraph:

"Chosen as Guardian was a Knight proude and fierse, a Scot of Royal blude, Niel Robertsoune."

Excitement flared, and her heartbeat kicked into a faster rhythm. It had to be Niall! The names were too similar, and the reference to the Guardian was the clincher.

Had she read anything before about a Niel, and passed over it because she hadn't connected the names? She knew how erratic spelling had been; she should have paid particular attention to any name that began with an *N*. And at last she had a surname! Robertsoune, or Robertson. Quickly she began rechecking the references for any variation of Niall, such as Niel, Neil, Neal, and also for anything remotely close to Robertson.

There was nothing. There were Robertses and Robertsons, even a couple of Neals, but nothing within the time frame she needed. Her hands trembled as she closed the book, and she had to restrain herself from pounding on the table in frustration. The wildness of her disappointment took her aback. She had been thwarted in her studies before, and taken it in stride. This fierce sense of desperation burned through her protective numbness, frightening her with its intensity. She didn't want to feel anything except rage and the unquenchable thirst for revenge, because she was afraid she would shatter if she ever began feeling again. The few times grief had managed to leak past the numbness had almost destroyed her.

But she *did* feel, she realized, had felt this intense interest in Niall of Scotland from the first moment she'd received the copies of old parchments and glanced through them. All that had happened to her since hadn't changed that, or even lessened it. If anything, her fascination grew with each day, with every page she read.

She had begun to think Niall of Scotland only a myth, though why his fictional exploits should be included in a history of the Knights Templar was something she couldn't fathom. This one mention of "Niel Robertsoune" being chosen as Guardian was the only confirmation of his existence she'd been able to find, but it was enough. He had existed, had been a real man who lived and breathed and ate and slept as all men did. Perhaps, after the Order had been destroyed, he had escaped persecution and had lived a normal life, had found happiness with a wife, had children, died an old man. The real Niall of Scotland had likely been nothing similar to the black-haired warrior who haunted her dreams, but the fantasy was one she needed emotionally, so she couldn't regret it. The dreams were proof that her inner self hadn't completely died; shreds of Grace St. John still existed deep inside her.

And Niall of Scotland had existed. Briskly, with renewed determination, she pushed the heavy reference books aside. She wouldn't find him there. As one of the notorious Knights, his life would have depended on remaining as anonymous as possible. Anything she discovered about him would be in the pages of documents to be deciphered, the exquisite photographed copies—

Copies.

Her mind stumbled to a halt for a moment, then began racing. Why did Parrish want this copy of the documents, when he could have the real McCoy? Why was he so desperate to get his hands on this copy that he would kill Ford and Bryant, and try to kill her?

Logically, there were only two explanations, both of them requiring a degree of coincidence that strained her credulity. One was that he didn't know where the originals were now, but obviously they had been recorded and photographed, and the copies sent to her. Could someone have stolen the originals, for some unfathomable reason—the same reason Parrish wanted them? If so, what about the negatives? Other copies could be made from them. The other explanation was that the originals had somehow been destroyed; accidents happened. Again, what about the film negatives?

That led her to two other possibilities. One was that the negatives had also been destroyed or stolen, and the other was that Parrish not only wanted this copy, he wanted to erase all knowledge of its contents, which would mean killing anyone who knew about it.

Her reasoning brought her full circle, back to what she had known from the beginning: Parrish meant to kill her. And the why of it was hidden in the mystery of those pages.

She had been wasting her time looking through reference books. From now on, she had to concentrate on translating the crabbed, tightly crowded text of the documents, and that was a task better accomplished in the privacy of her room at Harmony's rather than in a public library.

Quickly she returned the books to the shelves and gathered her things. By habit she carefully looked around for anyone unusual, or anyone watching her, but the people seated at the desks and tables seemed to be lost in their own studies. The Newberry attracted serious scholars more than the average high-schooler researching a term paper.

When carrying the computer, she looped the strap of the carrying case around her neck and over her shoulder, and also clutched the handle tightly in her left hand. When she walked, her right hand was always on the knife at her belt. The bus fare was in her right jeans pocket, so she never had to release the computer to fish out money.

It was almost dark when she left the library and hurried to the bus stop. That wasn't unusual; several times she had stayed much later. A cool evening breeze fanned her face as she joined the two people waiting at the corner, a plump young black woman with a round, pleasant face, who clutched the hand of a wide-eyed and energetic two-year-old. The little boy repeatedly climbed on and off the bench, not much hampered by his mother's determined grip on him. He crawled over and under and between her legs, and she merely adjusted her hold to whatever part of him she could reach. Grace thought that being a mother must be something akin to wrestling an octopus, but the young woman rode herd on her rambunctious offspring with remarkable calmness.

There was no warning, no sudden footsteps behind her. Someone slammed into her, hard, and Grace stumbled off balance. Her neck wrenched to the left as violent hands jerked at the computer case. The young woman uttered a startled scream, grabbed her child into her arms, and began running. The attacker, frustrated when the case didn't come free, uttered a foul curse on a cloud of equally foul breath. Desperately Grace tightened her grip on the handle and managed to get her feet under her, letting the man's own tugging efforts pull her upright. He cursed again and slashed a knife at her, trying to slice the strap around her neck. She twisted, protecting the strap, and cold fire burned along her forearm. She saw his eyes, narrow and vicious under a grimy fall of hair, as he jabbed the knife at her again.

In sheer reaction Grace swung the heavy case at him. Startled, he jerked back and the case caught him on the arm, jarring the knife free. It sailed through the air and clattered on the sidewalk. "Shit!" he said between clenched teeth, and turned to run.

And then fury arrived, surging through her veins like a flash flood. He hadn't even completed his turn to escape before she was on him, a foot thrust between his ankles to trip him. He yelled as he sprawled on the rough sidewalk, taking Grace down with him in a furious, punching tangle. Her hands were balled into fists and she used them, going for his eyes, his nose, his ears, any part of him that was momentarily unprotected as he tried to shove her away. Remembering the service station attendant, she tried to jab a knee into his groin, but he rolled aside. Growling in frustration, Grace grabbed his greasy hair with both hands and jerked as hard as she could. He howled with pain and struck back, punching her in the belly. Her breath exploded out of her and she gagged, momentarily paralyzed, but somehow she hung on. He hit her again, and one of her hands loosened. His fist jabbed at her face, caught her a glancing blow on the chin. The blow jarred her, made her eyes water, and he took advantage of her momentary weakness to shove free of her and lurch to his feet. Grace scrambled onto her hands and knees but he was already gone, running down the sidewalk, shoving his way past pedestrians who paid him little attention.

Groaning, Grace got to her own feet and stood swaying. The computer case still hung around her neck. The battle fury left as suddenly as it had arrived and almost unbearable fatigue dragged at her. A small crowd of about ten people had gathered, watching, and their faces swam before her like balloons. She took a deep breath, then another, then still another when the first two didn't work.

The mugger's knife still lay on the sidewalk. The handle was black, wrapped in electrician's tape, and the blade was a good six inches long. It looked much more lethal than her kitchen paring knife. She hobbled over to it, abruptly aware of bruises and scrapes she hadn't noticed during the heat of struggle. Bending over with effort, she picked it up and stared with some surprise at the red stain on the blade. Only then did she notice the blood dripping down her arm to splash scarlet dots on the sidewalk, and feel the burn of the two-inch gash that slanted across her forearm.

The wound needed stitches, she thought rather dispassionately, examining it as best she could for the welling blood. Tough. She wasn't inclined to spend two or three hundred dollars of her precious cash for emergency room care, in addition to probably being questioned by the cops. So long as she didn't get an infection, she could take care of the cut herself. Shrugging, she slipped the knife into one of the outside pockets of the case.

At least the mugger had been only that, a mugger. Probably he made a good living, or at least supported a drug habit, by snatching laptop computers. If he had been one of Parrish's men he would have sliced her throat first, then made off with the computer. But she had attracted attention, even if none of the bystanders had been inclined to help her, so the first thing she had to do now was get out of sight. The bus she had intended to take turned the corner then and stopped with a wheeze of hydraulics, but Grace didn't board it. The bus driver would be too likely to remember the passenger with the bleeding arm, and the stop where she got off, which would lead any followers that much closer to Harmony's house. Instead Grace quickly crossed the street and walked in the opposite direction.

Her arm began to ache, and blood was dripping on the computer case. Scowling, Grace pressed her right hand over the wound. She had acted with a disgusting lack of presence of mind, she thought as she strode along. She had felt so tough and well prepared because she'd had a kitchen paring knife on her belt, and instead she was so far from being street smart she hadn't even thought of the knife.

Look at me now, she thought furiously. She was walking openly down a busy sidewalk, dripping blood marking her every step. She could walk smack into a cop at any second, and that was only the most immediate danger. Any number of people were taking note of her, and Parrish was capable of putting a small army on the streets to locate her. Surely the search had moved to Chicago by now, it being the most logical place for her to hide, not to mention affording her the resources she needed to work. She had to assume the worst, and that meant she had to get off the street and change her appearance, immediately.

Just ahead of her, a couple entered a busy bar and grill. Grace barely slowed down, darting through the closing door. She stood close to them, angled so that the man's body hid her bleeding arm from the hostess, who smiled as she asked, "Smoking or non?" and plucked three menus from a stack.

"Non," replied the man. The hostess checked her seating chart, made a notation, then led them through the maze of close-crowded tables and booths. Grace spied the sign indicating the location of the rest rooms down a narrow hall, and she walked swiftly in that direction.

The ladies' room was small, dark, and empty. The decor

didn't invite people to linger. The lighting was dim, and swallowed by the dark glazed tiles of the floor and walls. A pink and purple neon flamingo was poised over the upper right corner of the mirror, casting a decidedly unnatural tint on the face of anyone repairing her makeup or admiring herself. Grace did neither. Instead she pulled several paper towels out of the holder and swiftly washed her hands and arm. Blood welled from the cut as fast as the water rinsed it away.

"Damn, damn, damn," she whispered. Glancing in the mirror, she saw that the blond wig was askew. Hastily, using one hand, she removed the pins that still halfway anchored the wig in place, then snatched it from her head. Her long, matted hair tumbled down her back.

She needed the use of both hands, if only for a minute. Taking one of the folded brown paper towels, she pressed it over the bleeding wound, holding it until the paper adhered to her arm. The red stain immediately began spreading, but for the moment she wasn't dripping. She stuffed the wig into the computer case, wound her hair into a knot on top of her head, and pinned it in place. Pulling out her baseball cap, she jammed it on and pulled the bill down low over her eyes.

Using her arm made it ache even worse. The makeshift pad was soaked with blood already, and coming loose. She peeled it off and tossed it into the trash, then pressed another towel over the wound. Gritting her teeth against the pain, she stared at her pale, sickly reflection in the mirror. Essentially the wound was negligible; she wasn't likely to bleed to death, and she still had the use of her arm. Niall wouldn't even have paused for so paltry a wound, but continued the battle.

And so had she, Grace realized with a spurt of surprise. Granted, her counterattack hadn't been well thought out, but she hadn't even realized she'd been cut until the fight was over. Niall would be proud of her, after he got over his murderous rage that she'd been hurt at all—

"I'm losing it," Grace said aloud, blinking. She must have lost more blood than she had realized, to be thinking of Niall as if he were someone she actually knew, instead of an obscure medieval warrior who had been dead for hundreds of years. She would be better off figuring out how to bandage her arm, and with what.

The answer followed on the heels of the thought. Holding the pad of towels in place with her right hand, she used her left to untie her shoe. Slipping out of it, she removed her sock, then shoved her bare foot back into the shoe. The sock had considerable stretch in the fabric. She laid the sock on the vanity top, then positioned her arm across it. Using her teeth and her free hand, she knotted the sock around her arm, pulling it as tight as possible over the pad of towels and then knotting it again for security.

The makeshift bandage wouldn't last long, but it should do to get her home. The effect was pretty noticeable, so she pulled off her other shoe and sock, and tied the remaining sock around her right arm. At least now it looked as if she'd done it for some reason other than necessity, maybe insanity, or membership in a gang. Socks around the arms weren't exactly in the same class as 'do rags, but there were a lot of crazies in Chicago.

An hour later, Grace let herself into the boardinghouse. She intended to slip quietly up the stairs, but as luck would have it she met Harmony herself in the hallway.

"That's some getup," Harmony drawled, taking in the baseball cap, the absence of the blond wig, and the socks tied around Grace's arms.

"Thanks," Grace muttered.

"Arm's bleeding," Harmony observed.

"I know." Grace started up the stairs.

"No point in running. Anybody in my house gets in trouble, I want to know what it's about, in case the cops gonna beat my door down in the middle of the night." Her green eyes narrowed, Harmony was right on Grace's heels as they climbed the stairs.

"I was mugged," Grace briefly explained. "Or rather, someone tried to mug me."

"No shit. Whadja do, scare 'im off with that wussy little knife you carry?"

"I didn't even think about it," she confessed ruefully, wondering how Harmony knew about the knife.

"Good thing. Any self-respecting mugger would've

laughed, then made you eat it." Harmony waited while Grace unlocked the door, then followed her inside. After eyeing the spartan neatness of the room, the tall woman turned her attention back to Grace. "Okay, Wynne, let's see the arm."

After two weeks, Grace had accustomed herself to her pseudonym enough that she no longer hesitated at the name. Two weeks was also long enough for her to learn that Harmony Johnson considered her home her castle, over which she had a dictator's authority, and anything that went on in her house was her business.

Silently she untied the bloodstained sock. Beneath it, the pad of paper towel was completely soaked. She removed that, too, and Harmony studied the sullenly oozing cut.

"Needs stitches," she pronounced. "And when was your last tetanus shot?"

"Not quite two years ago," Grace replied after a little thought, and with some relief. She hadn't even considered tetanus. Fortunately she'd updated all her vaccinations before going with Ford on a dig in Mexico. "No stitches, though. I can't afford an emergency room."

"Sure you can't," Harmony said shrewdly. "Any street bum can see a doctor for a cut, but you can't? More likely you don't want to answer no questions. Anyway, forget about a hospital. You want, I can sew that up for you, if you don't mind not having nothing for pain."

"You can?" Grace asked, astonished.

"Sure. I useta do it for the other girls all the time. Wait here while I get my kit."

While Harmony was gone, Grace pondered her landlady's undoubtedly colorful past. She wondered how successful a streetwalker Harmony would have been, with her brusque manner, unusual height, and equally unusual looks. Today she was wearing scarlet leotards and a sleeveless scarlet T-shirt, which revealed remarkably well-muscled legs and arms. Men who frequented prostitutes were looking for sexual gratification rather than sexual attraction, but still, how many would choose a woman who was not only taller than most men, but more masculine? Grace would have thought Harmony a cross-dresser or even a transsexual, if it hadn't been for a throwaway comment she had once made about having a miscarriage when she was fifteen and never getting pregnant again. Modern surgical procedure could outwardly change someone's sex, but it couldn't retain fertility for the patient.

Awkwardly, because her left arm was really aching now and she used only her right hand, she retrieved the tangled wig and bloodstained knife from the computer case. She laid the knife on the tiny round table she used for eating, and gave the frizzy wig a shake before placing it on the bed. Remembering it was supposed to be bad luck to put a hat on a bed, she wondered wryly if a wig qualified for equal status in the superstition.

Harmony returned, carrying a bottle of whiskey, a small black box, and an aerosol can. A clean white towel was draped over her arm. She set the first three items on the table, and eyed the bloody knife before pushing it aside and placing the towel over the clear space. "Yours?" she asked, nodding toward the knife.

"I guess it is now. I knocked it out of his hand." Exhausted, Grace sank into one of the chairs and laid her left arm across the towel.

Harmony's eyebrows rose. "No shit? He musta been surprised." Taking the other chair, she opened the bottle of whiskey and shoved it toward Grace. "Take a few good swallows. Won't stop it from hurting as bad, but you won't care as much."

Grace warily eyed the bottle. It was an expensive Scotch whiskey, but she had never drunk whiskey before and had no idea how it would sit. Given her exhaustion, and the fact she hadn't eaten since breakfast, it was likely to knock her on her butt. Shrugging, she seized the bottle and tipped it to her mouth. She could get her arm stitched while on her butt as well as she could sitting in a chair.

The smoky taste of the whiskey lay smooth and rich on her tongue, but when she swallowed, it was like swallowing fire. The liquid flame seared its way down her esophagus and into her stomach, stealing her breath along the way. Her face turned red and she began gasping and wheezing, trying to draw enough oxygen into her lungs to cough. Everything inside her was in revolt. Her eyes watered; her nose ran. She coughed violently, bent over at the waist while spasms wracked her. Finally, when she could breathe half normally again, she tilted the bottle and took another healthy swallow.

When the second bout had ended, she straightened to find Harmony watching and waiting with unruffled patience. "Not much of a drinker, are you?" she observed neutrally.

"No," Grace said, and drank again. Perhaps the nerves in her esophagus had already been burned out, or perhaps they were merely numb. For whatever reason, this time she didn't choke. The fire was spreading through her entire body, making her head swim. She broke out in a sweat. "Should I take another one?"

No smile cracked Harmony's angular face, but the corners of her green eyes crinkled in a subtle expression of amusement. "Depends on whether or not you want to be conscious."

Suspecting that she had only begun to feel the effects of the whiskey, Grace pushed the bottle aside and capped it. "Okay, I'm ready."

"Let's wait another few minutes." Harmony leaned back in the chair and crossed her long legs. "Guess the guy was after that computer you tote around like it was a baby."

Grace nodded, unaware that her head bobbed unsteadily. "Right outside the library. People saw what was happening, but no one did anything."

"Guess not. He'd already proved he meant business with the knife."

"But even after I'd knocked the knife out of his hand, and tripped him, and was punching him in the face, no one tried to help." Grace's voice rose indignantly.

Harmony blinked, and blinked again. She threw her head back and a deep, full-bodied laugh erupted from her throat. Rocking back and forth, she whooped until tears ran down her face and she was gasping for breath, much as if she had been into the whiskey bottle herself. When she could breathe, she hunched first one shoulder and then the other to dry her wet cheeks on her shirt. "Hell, girl!" she said, still giggling a little. "By that time they were probably more scared of you than they were of that stupid son of a bitch!"

Startled, Grace considered that. She was much taken by the possibility. Her face brightened. "I did good, didn't I?"

"You did good to come out of it alive," Harmony scolded, despite the grin on her face. "Girl, if you're gonna get in fights, somebody's gotta teach you *how* to fight. I would, but I ain't got time. Tell you what. I'll fix you up with this guy I know, meanest little greaser son of a bitch on God's green earth. He'll teach you how to fight dirty, and that's what you need. Somebody as little as you don't need to be doing something as dumb as fighting fair."

Maybe it was the whiskey thinking for her, but that sounded like a fine idea to Grace. "No more fighting fair," she agreed. Parrish certainly wouldn't fight fair, and neither did the street scum she would have to deal with. She needed to learn how to stay alive, by whatever means possible.

Harmony tore open another antiseptic pad and carefully washed Grace's arm, examining the cut from every angle. "Not too deep," she finally said. She opened a small brown bottle of antiseptic and poured it directly into the wound. Grace caught her breath, expecting it to burn like the whiskey, but all it did was sting a little. Then Harmony took up the aerosol can and sprayed a cold mist on the wound. "Topical analgesic," she muttered, the medical terminology somehow fitting right in with her street slang. Grace wouldn't have been surprised if her landlady had begun quoting Shakespeare, or conjugating Latin verbs. Whatever Harmony was now or had been in the past, she certainly was not ordinary.

With perfect calm she watched Harmony thread a small, curved suturing needle and bend over her arm. Delicately squeezing with her left hand, Harmony held the edges of the wound together and deftly began stitching with her right. Each puncture stung, but the pain was endurable, thanks to the whiskey and the analgesic spray. Grace's eyelids drooped as she fought the fatigue dragging at her. All she wanted was to lie down and sleep.

"There," Harmony announced, tying off the last stitch. "Keep it dry, and take some aspirin if it hurts."

Grace studied the neat row of tiny stitches, counting ten of them. "You should have been a doctor."

"Don't have the patience for dealing with nitwits." She began repacking her small first aid kit, then slid a sideways glance at Grace. "You gonna tell me why you don't want nothing to do with the cops? You kill somebody or something?"

"No," Grace said, shaking her head, which was a mistake. She waited a minute for the world to stop spinning. "No, I haven't killed anyone."

"But you're running."

It was a statement, not a question. Denying it would be a waste of her breath. Other people might be fooled, but Harmony knew too much about people who were running from something, whether the law or their past or themselves. "I'm running," she finally said, her voice soft. "And if they find me, they'll kill me."

"Who's this 'they'?"

Grace hesitated; not even the stout whiskey was enough to loosen her tongue to that extent. "The less you know about it, the safer *you'll* be," she finally said. "If anyone asks, you don't know much about me. You never saw a computer, didn't know I was working on anything. Okay?"

Harmony's eyes narrowed, a spark of anger lighting them. Grace sat very still, waiting for this newfound friend to become an ex-friend, and wondering if she would have to find a new place to live. Harmony didn't like being thwarted, and she hated, with reason, being left in the dark about anything concerning herself and the sanctity of her home. She pondered the situation in silence for a very long minute, before finally making a decision and giving one brisk nod of her lemony-white head. "Okay. I don't like it, but okay. You don't trust me, or anyone else, that much. Right?"

"I can't," Grace said softly. "It could mean your life, too, if Pa—if he even suspected you knew anything about me."

"So you're gonna protect me, huh? Girl, I think you got that backwards, because if I've ever seen a babe in the woods, you're it. The average eight-year-old here is tougher than you are. You look like you lived your whole life in a convent or something. Know it's not your style, but you'd make a helluva lot of money on the street, with looks like yours."

Grace blinked, startled by the abrupt, and ridiculous,

change of subject. Her, a successful prostitute? Plain, quiet, nerdy Grace St. John? She almost laughed in Harmony's face, which would never do.

"Yeah, I know," Harmony said, evidently reading her mind. "You got no sense of style, you don't wear makeup. Stuff like that's easy to change. Wear clothes that fit, instead of hanging on you like a bag. You don't want loose clothes no way, gives people something to grab, understand? And your face looks so damn innocent it probably drives a lot of men crazy, thinking how much they'd like to be the one to teach you all the nasty stuff. Men are simple sons of bitches about stuff like that. A little makeup would throw them off, make 'em think you're not so innocent after all. Plus you got one of those pouty mouths all the models pay good money for, having fat or silicone shots in their lips. Damn idiots. And that hair of yours. Men like long hair. I guess I know why you're wearin' that tacky wig, though."

Harmony's speech was a fast-moving mix of accents and vocabulary, from Chicago street to Southern drawl, with the occasional flash of higher education. It was impossible to tell her origin, but no one listening to her for more than thirty seconds would have any doubts about her mental acuity. Sprinkled among the comments on Grace's appearance had been a nugget or two of sharp advice.

"Is the wig that noticeable?" she asked.

"Not to most men, I don't guess. But it's blond. Blond and red stand out. Get a brown wig, light brown, in a medium length and a so-so style. And get one that's better quality. It'll last longer and look more natural." Abruptly she got to her feet, first aid kit in hand, and walked to the door. "Get some sleep, girl. You look like you about to fall outta that chair."

As exhausted as she was, and with the effects of the whiskey thrown in, Grace expected sleep was all she would be able to manage. She was wrong. Several hours later, her head finally clear of alcohol but her body still heavy with fatigue, she still hadn't managed to doze. She sat propped against the headboard, her left arm dully throbbing, with the laptop balanced on her blanket-covered legs. She had tried to work, but the intricacies of ancient languages, written in an archaic penmanship style, seemed to be beyond her. Instead she logged on to her personal journal and read her past entries. She couldn't remember some of the entries, and that disturbed her. It was as if she were reading someone else's diary, about someone else's life. Was that life so completely gone? She didn't want it to be, and yet she was afraid that she couldn't survive if she held on to it.

The loving but casual references to Ford and their life together, to Bryant, almost undid her. She felt the rush of pain and hastily scrolled down, closing her mind to the memories. She reached the last entry, made April twenty-sixth, and with relief saw that the entire entry was about the intriguing documents she'd been deciphering and translating. She had typed "NIALL OF SCOTLAND" in capital letters, and followed it with "real or myth?"

She knew the answer to that. He'd been real, a man who strode boldly through history, but behind the scenes, so that few traces remained of his passing. He'd been entrusted with the enormous Treasure of the Templars, but what had he done with it? With the means at his disposal, he could have accomplished anything, toppled kings, but instead he'd vanished.

Her fingers moved over the keys. "What were you, Niall? Where did you go, what did you do? What is so special about these papers that men have died just for knowing they existed? Why can't I stop thinking about you, dreaming about you? What would you do if you were here?"

A strange question, she thought, looking at what she had typed. Why would she even think of him in modern times? Dreaming about him was at least understandable, because immersing herself in her research, trying so hard to find any mention of him, had indelibly imprinted him in her mind. Because of Ford's and Bryant's deaths, there was nothing more important to her now than finding out *why,* so naturally she dreamed about the research.

But she hadn't, she realized. She hadn't dreamed about the Templars, about ancient documents, or even about libraries or computers. She had dreamed only of Niall, her imagination assigning him a face, a form, a voice, a presence. Since the murders she hadn't dreamed much at all, as if her subconscious tried to give her a respite from the terrible reality she faced every day, but when she had dreamed it had been of Niall.

What *would* he do if he were there? He'd been a highly trained warrior, the medieval equivalent of the modern military's special forces. Would he have run and hidden, or would he have stood his ground and fought?

Whatever was best to achieve my goal.

Her head snapped around, her heart racing. Someone had spoken, someone in the room. Her panicked gaze searched out every corner of the small room, and though her eyes told her she was alone, her instincts didn't believe it. Her body felt electrified, every nerve alert and tingling. She breathed shallowly, her head cocked as she sat very still and listened, straining to hear a faint rustle of fabric, a scrape of a shoe, an indrawn breath. Nothing. The room was silent. She was alone.

But she'd *heard* it, a deep, slightly raspy voice with a burred inflection. It hadn't been in her head, but something external.

She shivered, her skin roughening with chill bumps. Beneath her T-shirt, her nipples were tight and hard.

"Niall?" she whispered into the empty room, but there was only silence, and she felt foolish.

It had been only her imagination, after all, producing yet another manifestation of her obsession with those papers.

Still, her fingers tapped on the keys again, the words spilling out of her: "I'll learn how to fight. I can't be passive about this, I can't merely react to what others do. I have to make things happen, have to take the initiative away from Parrish. That's what you would do, Niall. It's what I will do."

Chapter 9

PARRISH SIPPED THE MERLOT, AND GAVE A BRIEF NOD OF appreciation. Though merlot usually wasn't to his taste, this one was unexpectedly fine, very dark and dry. Bayard "Skip" Saunders, his host, considered himself a connoisseur of wine and had gone to great lengths to impress Parrish by trotting out his best and rarest vintages. Parrish was accustomed to members of the Foundation becoming slightly giddy whenever he visited; though he would have preferred a fine champagne or a biting martini, or even a properly aged bourbon, he was publicly never less than gracious about his underlings' efforts.

Skip—a ridiculous nickname for a grown man—was one of the more wealthy and influential members of the Foundation. He also lived in Chicago, which was the sole reason for Parrish's presence. Though Conrad had been unable to find a definite trail, he was nevertheless certain Grace had made her way to Chicago, and Parrish had faith in his henchman. Skip Saunders would be able to provide support in the search, in the form of both logistics and influence. Should

Grace's capture be too messy—in other words, too public—Skip would be able to whisper a few words into an ear or two and the matter would simply go away, as if it had never existed. Parrish appreciated the convenience.

What he would appreciate more, he thought idly as his gaze briefly met that of Saunders's wife, Calla, was half an hour alone with the lovely Mrs. Saunders. What a superb trophy she was, a glorious testament to the seductiveness of money and power. Wife number one, the recipient of Saunders's youthful seed and vigor and the bearer of his two exceedingly spoiled children, was unfortunately fifty and therefore no longer young enough or glamorous enough to satisfy his ego. Parrish had met the first Mrs. Saunders, when she had still been Mrs. Saunders, and had been charmed by her wit. At any dull social affair he would have much preferred to have number one beside him—but if the position were changed to *under* him, he would definitely choose the lovely Calla. Saunders was a fool. He should have kept the wonderful companion as his wife, the main course, and enjoyed Calla as a side dish. Ah, well. Men who thought with their genitals often made poor choices.

Calla was certainly tempting. Parrish's manners were too polished to allow him to stare openly at her, but nevertheless each look was thoroughly assessing. She was about five-six, willowy, impeccably dressed in a simple, midnight-blue sheath that lovingly hugged every siliconed and liposuctioned curve and provided ample bare flesh on which to display the multitude of diamonds and sapphires she wore. She was a striking woman, with warmly golden skin and big, china-blue eyes, but what interested him most was her long, straight swath of hair, which she let hang freely down her back. Smart woman. She knew her hair was a magnet for male attention, the way it lifted and swung with every graceful movement she made. It wasn't as long as Grace's, he thought dispassionately, or as dark, but still . . .

She was taller than Grace, and more slender. She probably hadn't blushed with shyness since the age of eight, and the expression in her eyes was knowing, completely lacking Grace's innocence and trust. Her mouth wasn't thin, but neither did it have the lush, unconscious sexuality of Grace's lips. Her hair, though . . . he wanted to wrap his fist in that hair, hold it tight while he used her. He would close his eyes and pretend she was shorter, softer, that the hair he gripped was as sleek and thick as dark mink.

Perhaps later, he thought, and gave her a long, cool, deliberate look he knew she wouldn't misunderstand. One elegantly arched brow lifted as she caught his intent, and her lips curved in both invitation and satisfaction. Once again she had attracted the most powerful male present, and she was obviously pleased.

That minor detail taken care of, Parrish turned his attention back to her husband. "Very good," he said, seeing that Skip was anxiously awaiting verbal approval of his choice of wine. "I don't usually care for merlot, but this is exceptional."

A flush of pleasure warmed Skip's tanned face. "There are only three bottles of that particular vintage left in the world. I have two of them," he couldn't resist adding.

"Excellent. Perhaps you should acquire the third bottle as well," Parrish suggested, and hid his perverse amusement at the knowledge that Skip would now spend an untold amount of time and money trying to do just that. The three bottles could turn to vinegar for all Parrish cared.

He clapped a friendly hand to Skip's shoulder. "I want to have a private word with you, if I may, whenever you are free from playing host."

As he'd expected, Skip immediately straightened. "We can go to my study now. Calla won't mind, will you, darling?"

"Of course not," she calmly replied, knowing her role and in truth not giving a damn where her husband was or what he did. She immediately turned away to see to the needs of her other guests, a select fifty or so of Chicago's wealthiest citizens.

Skip led the way down a wide corridor to a set of double doors which he opened inward, admitting them into a mahogany-paneled office with a huge expanse of window overlooking Lake Michigan. "Magnificent view, isn't it?" Skip asked with obvious pleasure, crossing to the window.

"Magnificent," Parrish agreed. The view was more spectacular than his view of Lake Minnetonka, but he wasn't envious. He could have had such a view, had he chosen.

Instead he was well pleased with the more staid but equally moneyed Wayzata; it suited him to be slightly out of the mainstream of the larger cities, tucked away in Minnesota. His neighbors were incurious, and so long as he gave the impression of being socially and politically correct, no one ever looked beneath the surface.

The two men stepped out onto the balcony, and the brisk wind off the lake still carried a chill even though summer had truly arrived. Parrish looked both left and right to make certain they were completely alone. "We're searching for a woman, Grace St. John. She's been accused of murdering her husband." He didn't bother to explain that he himself was responsible for both the accusation and the murder. "I believe she has information we would find of vital importance, so of course I would prefer finding her before the police do."

"Of course," Skip murmured. "Anything I can do—"

"My men have the search operation in hand, but should things go wrong, I want you on hand to turn any interest away. I hope requiring your presence here won't interfere with any vacation plans you've made." Parrish said it knowing Skip and Calla were scheduled to leave shortly for a month-long stay in Europe, not that it mattered; Skip would cancel an audience with the Pope to be of service to the Foundation. Of the two, the Foundation was more powerful, though its power and influence were far less noticeable.

"No problem," Skip hastily assured him.

"Good. I'll call you if I need you."

As Parrish turned to enter the study he saw Calla standing just inside the doors, and he paused, wondering what she knew and how much she'd overheard. It would be a pity if she fell over the balcony; such a tragic accident, but accidents happened.

"Dear," Calla said to Skip as she glided onto the balcony. "I'm sorry to disturb you, but Senator Trikoris has just arrived, and you know how he is."

The senator was notorious for expecting a great deal of ass-licking in exchange for legislative favors. The Foundation was working to develop a file on the senator, one that would bring him in line so that the favors he did were for the Foundation's benefit. When that happened, the senator would be the one doing the ass-licking, and Parrish's would be the ass being licked. The senator wasn't yet aware of the future direction of his legislative efforts, and until he was, Parrish was content to let Skip keep him happy. He nodded a dismissal, and Skip hastily left.

Calla leaned against the wall, her gaze cool and brilliant and calculating as she watched him. The wind lifted the silky ends of her hair, playing with it. Out here in the night, her hair looked dark, as dark as Grace's. Perhaps he would fuck her before assisting her over the balcony, Parrish thought, and felt his body respond to the excitement of the idea.

"Yes, I know about the Foundation," Calla murmured, her gaze never wavering from his face. "Skip's a fool. He leaves paperwork lying around in his office where anyone can see it. You would be better off to get rid of him and work with me."

Parrish lifted his eyebrows. She was right; Skip was a fool, and an unforgivably careless one. He would have to be taken care of. Dear Calla wasn't a fool, however, and the problem of what to do about her was one that demanded an immediate decision.

He leaned against the balcony railing, slim and elegant in his black silk trousers and white evening coat. His debonair image was both carefully cultivated and entirely natural to him, blinding people to the cold reality that lay beneath the silk. He sensed that Calla, unlike most people, had read him correctly and knew how close she was to death. Instead of being dismayed, she was excited by the danger. Beneath the clingy midnight fabric of her dress, her nipples were erect.

"It's Skip who has the contacts, the money," he said neutrally, but he was becoming more excited, too. Grace was the only other woman who had instinctively sensed the reality of him, and she had resisted his charm. Calla made no effort to resist him, but the similarity was enough to make him hot. It wouldn't be like having Grace; Grace had an innocence, a shining incorruptibility, that would drive him to new heights in his efforts to sully her. He doubted there was any sullying in which Calla had not already indulged. But in a way Calla was a twisted, corrupted version of Grace, and he wanted her.

Calla grimaced at his statement. "He has the power, you mean, because he controls the money. But does the true power lie with the man who controls the money, or with the woman who controls the man? What I know about the movers and shakers in this city is ten times more useful than Skip's social contacts."

"You use the word *know* in the biblical sense, I presume?"

Her lips curved in a slight smile but she didn't answer the charge. "The Foundation is real power. Forget the trade unions, the political parties; they all have ties to the Foundation, don't they? No matter which party is in the White House, you have a private line to the Oval Office."

In most cases, he thought, but not all. The Foundation hadn't had good luck with the past two Republican presidents, or the Democratic one before them. Their luck had changed four years earlier, however, and he had moved swiftly to make the gains denied the Foundation for sixteen long years. He was also working hard to make certain he maintained guaranteed access for another four years, at least. Politics was boring, but necessary, at least for now. If he could get his hands on the documents Grace held, he wouldn't have to bother with manipulating politics to try and ensure a reasonable occupant of the White House; the president would be coming to him, as would all the world's ostensible leaders.

The Foundation had been poised for centuries, ready to act when the papers were found. How wonderful that the discovery had been made on *his* watch, Parrish thought, but less wonderful that a bungling fool in France had let the documents slip out of his hands. Those papers meant power. Unimaginable power. The world would be in the palm of his hand, to be manipulated as he willed. Oh, the money and the power would *technically* belong to the Foundation, to be passed on to his successor, but his to use as he wished for his lifetime. A man of limited imagination wouldn't see the possibilities, but Parrish had no such limitations.

He had no interest in holding any office, whether president or prime minister, or in waging war. War was so gauche, so much effort for so little gain. The time had passed when nations could be won; now war meant little but destruction. Real power lay in money, as Calla had observed, and whoever controlled the money controlled the world as well as the puppets who stood onstage, in the limelight, and pretended to be the ones in power.

The documents in Grace's possession led to such power, to unlimited wealth. Over the centuries legends and superstitions had formed about some magical source of power the Templars had controlled, much like the ridiculous claims about the Ark of the Covenant, but unlike some in the Foundation, Parrish secretly scoffed at the idea. If the Templars had controlled some magical power, how could they have been so easily destroyed by treachery? Obviously the only power they had possessed had been a material one, an enormous treasury that had attracted the envy of a king and caused their downfall. No, the Templars' power had been wealth, more than could be imagined. There was nothing magical about it, though to the fourteenth-century mind the sheer magnitude of the treasury must have been beyond comprehension, and thus had to be magic. They had been nothing but superstitious fools. Parrish, however, was not.

Nor was he sentimental. If Calla thought to enslave him with her considerable charm, she was doomed to disappointment.

"I'm interested in working with the Foundation," Calla said when he remained silent, his cold gaze fixed on her face. "My assets are considerably more useful than Skip's."

"No one works *with* the Foundation," Parrish corrected. "The proper term is *for.*"

"Not even you?" she delicately needled.

He shrugged. For his lifetime he *was* the Foundation, but it wasn't necessary for her to know that. It wasn't necessary to talk to her at all. As delightful as it would undoubtedly be to let her into the Foundation, to have her at his beck and call until he was bored with her, he wasn't about to let someone of her intellect and daring, as well as complete lack of scruples, get that close to the center of power. He would have to watch his back every minute.

She moistened her lips, staring at him. "Do you know what I think?" Her voice was a purr. "I think you're the center of it all. A man with your kind of power—why, you can do anything, have anything you want. And I can help you get it."

Oh, she was definitely too smart for her own good.

He reached her in three steps, smiling slightly in the semidarkness as he looked down at her. Calla stood very still, her perfectly chiseled face illuminated by the light from the study behind her. She licked her lips again, the action unconscious, feline.

"Here?" she whispered. "People with telescopes watch, you know."

He paused. If he were merely going to screw her, he wouldn't care who watched. But since she would be going for a long, vertical walk afterward, he didn't want witnesses.

Smiling, he stepped back and gestured to the door. She laughed as she walked ahead of him into the study. "Somehow I expected you to be more adventurous."

"There's a difference, my dear, between adventurous and stupid." He went to the wall switch and turned out the lights, then locked the door. Calla stood calmly waiting for him, the city lights spilling through the windows, glittering on the jewels at her ears and throat.

He took off his dinner jacket and draped it over the back of a chair, not caring to have it smeared with telltale makeup. His shirt would likely bear the marks, but it would be covered by the jacket, and he would dispose of it as soon as he returned to his own hotel. As a last precaution he took his handkerchief from the jacket and put it in his pants pocket.

Arousal coursed through him as he stood in front of her and worked the tight sheath of her skirt up about her waist. She didn't have on any underwear, but then he hadn't expected any. He lifted her onto the desk and she leaned back until she was lying flat across the polished surface. They both knew what this was, and it wasn't lovemaking. She didn't pretend to have any romantic feelings, or demand foreplay. This was power sex, a gambit involving bodies, though she hadn't yet realized the true game or that she wouldn't survive it.

He unfastened his pants and stepped between her spread thighs, entering her with a smooth thrust that had her humming with pleasure. *Good,* he thought as he began thrusting. It would be nice if she enjoyed her last time.

Calla's long hair fanned across the desk. Parrish closed his eyes and thought of Grace, of her luscious mouth. He imagined that the heat surrounding him was Grace's heat, and he pumped steadily into it. She too would die afterward, but perhaps not immediately. Perhaps he would play with her for a while.

Calla gasped, arching. The response struck him as too theatrical, and he paused to consider her. Her eyes were half closed, her head tilted back, her lips open and moist. It was a lovely picture she made, and a totally false one. Why, she was faking, damn her, pandering to his ego. She probably faked it with all her rich lovers, twisting and moaning so they thought they were great in the sack, while all the time she was smirking inside and feeling nothing but contempt because men were so easily manipulated with sex.

Not this time.

He slipped one of her shoes off, dropping it to the floor. Deliberately he reached do vn between their bodies and pinched her clitoris, rubbing his thumb across it in a repeated motion. She gasped again, and tried to twist away from him. Parrish dragged her back, thrusting into her to the hilt and recapturing her hardened nub. "What's the matter?" he softly taunted, his voice coming in soft pants in rhythm with his thrusts. "Don't tell me you like faking it better than actually coming. Can't you feel superior if you let yourself enjoy being fucked?"

"Bastard," she hissed at him, digging her claws into his sleeved arms. Her breath was coming faster, her eyes furious and gleaming in the darkness.

"You like the power you have over men, don't you? You like knowing you can turn them into panting beasts. Is that what makes your nipples get so hard, or do you fake that too, pinching them when no one's looking?"

The glitter of her eyes almost matched that of her jewels. "I pinch them. Did you think a *man* could turn me on? Don't be funny!"

"What does turn you on? A woman?" He kept his rhythm

steady, his thumb moving ceaselessly back and forth while he thrust. Her hostility was far more exciting than her compliance had been; if it hadn't been for her superficial resemblance to Grace, he would simply have pushed her over the railing without giving her a tumble first. But he liked her venom, her contempt; at least she wasn't faking *that.*

"That would please your ego, wouldn't it, if I were a lesbian? No wonder you couldn't make me enjoy it, I'm a man-hater! No such luck," she jeered. "I please myself, a lot better than a man can."

"Until now." He openly gloated as he felt how wet she was getting. Her breath was getting faster and faster, her nipples standing upright without being pinched. He read the signs and thrust harder and deeper, driving into her, and with a choked cry she began climaxing. Triumphant, he rode her to the end, until his own climax began boiling upward. He snatched the handkerchief out of his pocket as he jerked out of her, coming into the silk square while he stroked himself in the final pleasure.

Her features twisted with rage as she sat up. It wasn't just that he'd made her climax, but that he had pulled away from her at the last and accomplished his own pleasure without her, taunting her with the reversal of her usual role with men.

Calmly Parrish folded the handkerchief and replaced it in his pocket, to be disposed of when he could safely do so. He straightened his clothing, tucking and zipping, then assisted her off the desk. She stood silently as he restored her dress to its proper position. "Don't sulk," he advised. "It isn't becoming. You should learn, my dear, to be a better loser. And to be a better judge of the men you play your power games with, because I fear you badly misjudged the situation this time."

She glared at him, not ready to give him any sort of victory, and bent down to retrieve her shoe. Parrish stayed her with a hand under her elbow. "Not yet," he said, smiling, and clipped her under the chin with his fist.

She obligingly sagged forward, and he lifted her in his arms. She wasn't unconscious, just stunned, and she blinked owlishly at him as he swiftly carried her out onto the balcony. "I would apologize for the little bruise you'll have," he told her as he stood her up at the waist-high wall, "but really, my dear, no one will notice." Then he bent and caught her ankles, and tipped her over.

She didn't scream at all, or if she did, the sound was stifled by terror. Parrish didn't linger to watch; after all, they were fifty-six stories up, and it would take her several seconds to hit the street. He went back into the study and picked up her shoe, then returned to the balcony. Crouching, he pressed the heel of the shoe against the polished marble until the high, sharp heel snapped off. He thought about tossing the shoe over too, but someone might notice its arrival on the street several seconds after its wearer, so instead he left it lying on the marble. All that remained to do was to retrieve his jacket and rejoin the guests, and wait for the cops to arrive and tell Skip his wife had apparently taken a header off the balcony. That should take long enough for everyone to be hazy about the time he rejoined them, especially since the wine and cocktails had been freely flowing for at least an hour now.

He did regret having to soil his handkerchief.

Chapter 10

GAELIC WAS A BITCH. GRACE HAD SPENT TWO WEEKS WORKING on the Gaelic section, and made very little headway. The language wasn't in her computer programs, so she had no electronic aid in deciphering the faint chicken scratches. Whoever had copied the originals had tried to darken the copy to bring out more detail, with little success. She could see the tattered edges of the originals on the copy, telling her that the Gaelic sections hadn't fared as well as those written in Latin. Perhaps the paper hadn't been of as good a quality, or the pages had gotten damp at some time. Not that a good, clear copy would have helped much.

She had bought a Gaelic/English dictionary, and several guides to speaking Gaelic to aid her in figuring out syntax. The problem, however, was that she hadn't been able to find any guides to Gaelic as it had been spoken in the fourteenth century. She thought she would go mad with frustration. There were only eighteen letters in the Gaelic alphabet, but the Scots and Irish had overcome that restriction by using wildly creative spelling. Add to that the archaic styles of handwriting, word usage, and no standard spelling anyway, and the effort involved in translating one sentence was twice what it would have taken her to do an entire page of Latin or Old English.

But even with all the difficulties, eventually she pieced together sentences that made sense. The Gaelic section detailed the exploits of a Highland renegade called Black Niall. Though the section's inclusion with the rest of the papers made it likely Black Niall was the same man as Niall of Scotland, Grace didn't automatically assume they were one. She had already dealt with the complication of different spellings of the same name, so it was just as possible that the spelling could be the same but refer to someone else. After all, any number of Nialls had lived in Scotland. *Her* Niall was Niall of Scotland, of royal blood; what connection would royalty have with a Highland renegade? These chronicles were different from the others; different handwriting, different paper. They could have been mixed by accident with the others, simply because of the name.

Black Niall was an entertaining rogue, though. Deciphering his exploits occupied all her free time, except for the hours she spent with Harmony's "mean little greaser son of a bitch," one Mateo Boyatzis, a delicate and deadly young man of Mexican and Polish heritage. Matty knew more dirty tricks than a political ad man, and as a favor to Harmony he had agreed to teach "Julia" a few basics of fighting to win. She had no illusions about her slowly growing skill; she was not and never would be anything approaching expert. All she hoped to do was to be able to use the advantage of surprise to protect herself and the papers.

Not that she had anything to worry about, she thought, rubbing eyes grown weary from hours of wading through incomprehensible spellings and unlikely pronunciations. Any minute now, Gaelic was going to reduce her to drooling insanity, and then she wouldn't care what happened.

To give herself a break, she put the Gaelic section aside and turned on the computer, then scrolled through until she came to a section in Old French. The papers weren't in any chronological order; putting the story together was like placing pieces of a puzzle, an ancient one in many languages.

She saw the name almost at once, so attuned to it that her eyes picked up the familiar pattern of letters almost before she'd brought the words into focus. *Black Niall.*

"Whaddaya know," she murmured, leaning forward. It looked as if Black Niall and Niall of Scotland were indeed one and the same. Why would papers written in French detail the exploits of an obscure Scots rogue, unless he wasn't so obscure after all? A Templar of royal blood, excommunicated, under the penalty of death should he ever be taken outside Scotland, and Guardian of the Treasure to boot—obscure perhaps by design, but certainly not unimportant. There had been people, perhaps remnants of the Order, who had known who and what Black Niall was, and made a point to keep track of where.

But royal? She had gone over and over the genealogical charts in the Newberry Library, and there hadn't been a Niall recorded during that era.

"Who *were* you?" she whispered, seeking that elusive wisp of contact, almost like touching the mind of a man who was centuries dead. She had never before realized how powerful her imagination could be, but she took comfort in the sense of connection. She didn't dare let anyone else too close, not even Harmony, but there were no limits with the man who lived now only in her dreams. She didn't have to be wary with him, didn't have to hide her identity, didn't have to disguise herself.

These papers were yet another account of his exploits, where he had searched out a band of raiders and destroyed them, leaving no man alive. Niall had evidently gone to a great deal of trouble to protect his stronghold, dealing swiftly and harshly with any threat. This was another sticking point: if he were royal, he would have a title, and legal claim to his stronghold. The Gaelic papers, however, called him a renegade, a man who had taken by force a remote castle in the western Highlands, and held it without title or deed, without anything except the power of his sword. Could a royal be a renegade, and if he had indeed been outcast from the family to such an extent that his name had been stricken from all records, would or could

Robert the Bruce have tolerated such insolence within his own borders?

The Gaelic papers would probably be more enlightening, but her brain simply couldn't absorb any more of it that night. Putting aside the French papers, she thumbed through until she found the pages in Old English.

Again, the name almost jumped off the page at her: Black Niall, a Scots warrior so bold and ruthless he was feared throughout the Highlands. His stronghold, Creag Dhu, was never breached, except once by "a layde who entered bye wicked trickery." Grace felt a tiny spurt of amusement when she read that, for of course a woman couldn't have accomplished the seemingly impossible without using "wicked trickery."

"She fooled you, didn't she, laddie?" she murmured to Niall, almost smiling as she imagined his disbelief, his outrage at finding his castle's protection breached by a lone woman. He would have been in an absolute fury, the kind that had the castle guards hiding from him— Grace stopped her thoughts, grimacing as she realized her imagination had kicked in again. She might dream about him, he might seem so real that sometimes she thought she could turn her head and actually see him standing there, but in reality he had turned to dust a good six centuries before she'd ever been born.

Reading on, she found that Black Niall had captured the woman, so the "layde"'s trickery had gained her nothing, except his attention, and perhaps that was what she had wanted. The papers didn't indicate what he had done with her after capturing her. Bedded her, probably, Grace thought. He'd been a lusty man, ill suited for monkhood.

Another account began: "Black Niall, the MacRobert—" and Grace sat upright as all the tumblers clicked into place.

Niel Robertsoune—son of Robert, and a great warrior in an order renowned for its warriors. Niall MacRobert— again, son of Robert, and a warrior so great his stronghold was never breached, save by that unnamed enterprising lady. "A Scot of Royal blude" . . . son of Robert . . . son of *Robert the Bruce?*

Electrified, she quickly checked the dates, only to sag back in disappointment. She could only guess at Black

Niall's age, since she knew neither his birthdate nor the date he had died, but he had been a grown man when the Order had been condemned in 1307. King Robert I of Scotland, the most famous Bruce, had been too young to be Black Niall's father. Quickly Grace rechecked her notes on the chronology of Scotland's royal line. Robert the Bruce's father, the Earl of Carrick, had also been named Robert.

Was Black Niall *brother* to Robert the Bruce? How? The Bruce's four brothers, Edward, Nigel, Thomas, and Alexander, had been well documented as they fought with their brother and king to push the English out of Scotland. The only way Niall could be connected, but left in obscurity, would be if he were illegitimate.

"That's it," Grace breathed, sitting back.

The ramifications, the possibilities, made sitting still impossible. She jumped up and began pacing the confines of her small room as detail after detail fell into place to complete the puzzle. A bastard half-brother, in medieval times, wouldn't have been that unusual or even that important—unless the legitimate heir happened to be aiming for a throne. Scotland had always been different from the rest of Europe in the way it looked at kinship, and while Niall's bastardy would normally have put him beyond the pale, in Scotland the crown had been up for grabs by the one who wielded the most power. The Bruce had been an undeniably powerful warrior and foe, but Niall's skills in warfare had been legendary. His very existence would have been a threat to Robert.

The wonder was that he hadn't been murdered, to remove that threat. The fact that he hadn't suggested that he had been held in some affection. Then, too, he had joined the Templars, so perhaps his ambitions had been churchly rather than political. No—remembering what she'd already read about Black Niall, he hadn't been the churchly sort at all. So why had he been a Templar? Adventure, wealth? She could see where the promise of both might have lured Black Niall to the Order, but overall his nature seemed far too fierce and earthy for him to accept the restrictions.

Whatever his reasons for becoming a Templar, his doing so had been convenient for the future King of Scotland. The Bruce wouldn't have had to worry about a monk gaining the crown, because his vows of chastity would have precluded heirs to the throne.

His chastity had ended with the destruction of the Order, Grace thought, if she had translated some of the passages correctly. The references to sexual activity hadn't been explicit, but fairly plain for all that. However Niall had honored his vows while a Templar, after the Order had been destroyed he had embraced life—and women—to the fullest. He still would not have been a threat to the throne, because as an ex-Templar he would have shunned exposure.

But it explained so much—why Niall had been able to take Creag Dhu and hold it without interference from the King, even why the Bruce had been the one European monarch who had not only not enforced the papal death sentence against the Templars, but whose country had become a sanctuary of sorts for the hunted men. Robert had refused to sign his half-brother's death sentence. It even explained why Niall had been chosen as Guardian; the Temple Masters had known his lineage, known he and the Treasure would be safer in Scotland than anywhere else in the world.

She inhaled suddenly, and the room turned dark around her as knowledge struck with the force of a blow. The Treasure. Ford and Bryant had died because these stupid papers told the location of the famed, lost Treasure of the Templars: Creag Dhu.

Money. That was what it came down to. They had died because of money, money that Parrish Sawyer wanted. Because she had the papers, he had either assumed she had already translated enough to know what they were about and also told Ford and Bryant, or he had wanted to wipe out all knowledge of them regardless.

She had thought the grief would be easier to bear if she just knew *why*.

It wasn't.

Conrad lay quietly in bed, lights off, but the city was never dark and the bland hotel walls were washed with muted, flickering colors from a plethora of neon. The latest computer list lay on the desk, put aside for now. Some things were best reserved for the night, but others had to wait for busy daylight and normal office hours. The delay didn't bother him; he was a patient man. Grace wasn't going anywhere, at least not yet. She had gone to ground somewhere in the massive urban sprawl, and she would stay there as long as she felt safe. She was a scholar, a researcher; she would research. The libraries in Chicago were very good. Yes, he was confident she would remain in Chicago for a while, and all the time he would be looking for her. She wouldn't know he was close until he was ready to pounce.

Mr. Sawyer had a small army of men out combing the streets, but Conrad didn't put any faith in that tactic. The people who operated in the underground economy weren't about to answer any questions truthfully, for one thing, and for another, Grace had proven herself capable of quite a few disguises. By now she could have shaven her head and dressed in leather, so relying on description was a waste of time.

Conrad preferred his own methods. To him it was simple: if anyone on the run remained in one place for long, he or she would have to establish an identity. For some it would be as uncomplicated as selecting a name. That worked so long as there was no need for credit, or a driver's license, or you didn't try to work in a legitimate place that demanded a social security number. In the long run it was smarter to establish a documented identity, and Grace St. John had impressed him with her intelligence.

The process was simple, but slow. To document an identity, one had to have a birth certificate. To get a birth certificate, one had to have a real name. Obviously, using a living person's name could be complicated when the two identities began colliding with each other, as would inevitably happen, so the best thing was to go to a cemetery and read tombstones. Find someone who had been born at approximately the same time as you were, within a couple of years either way, but who had died young. Sometimes the parents' names were on the tombstone, too: something along the lines of "Beloved Daughter of John and Jane Doe." Bingo, you had the information you needed to get a birth certificate.

Requests for birth certificates would go to the state capital, in this case Springfield. Getting a birth certificate was fairly easy; it was getting a full set of identification papers that would take time. Next she would have to get a social security number, and the federal government was slow. He had time to focus on the birth certificate requests.

With the Foundation's resources, gaining access to the Illinois state computer system had taken a mere phone call. He had been surprised, however, by the volume of requests. It was amazing how many people needed to prove their existence, whether for social security claims, passport applications, or whatever. The sheer numbers involved were what was slowing him down.

He could automatically delete those requests for men, but again there were a lot of people with ambiguous names. Shelley, for instance. Male or female? And what about Lynn, or Marion, or Terry? Those people had to remain on his list until he could check them out.

Nor did he have a specific date of request, which made his task more difficult. She couldn't have made a request any sooner than the day after he had almost caught her in Eau Claire, but what if she waited a few days, a week, maybe even a couple of weeks? That uncertainty added literally hundreds of people to the list, from all over the state. He narrowed the focus to the Chicago area, but that still left hundreds because he figured at least a fourth of the state's entire population lived in the metro area.

Checking out that many people took time, and the list grew every day. Some of the people who requested birth certificates had moved in the meantime; they had to be located, and sometimes they had moved out of state. Some had gone on vacation, but until he had traced them he didn't dare eliminate them from his list. Grace could be hiding behind any of those names, even the most improbable. He would not underestimate her again.

"Girl, you look like shit," Matty said genially, uncoiling his compact, graceful body from the tattered sofa in his apartment.

"Thanks," Grace muttered. She was tired from sitting up nights trying to decipher Gaelic. Her eyes felt gritty, she had the energy of a slug, and she had burned her hand that day when she picked up a pan to wash and discovered it had just been taken from the oven. Harmony had tended the burn, scowling the entire time, and then had insisted on accompanying Grace to Matty's for another "lesson," just to make certain something else didn't happen to her.

"Just skin hangin' on a rack of bones," Harmony pronounced, still scowling. "I can't get her to eat, no matter what I cook. She's done lost ten pounds or more since she's been living in my house, which ain't exactly the best advertisement I could have."

Grace looked down at herself. She was used to Harmony's complaints that she didn't eat enough, but still she was surprised now when she really *looked* at herself, and saw her bony wrists, her body lost within the baggy folds of clothes that had once been the right size. She knew she'd lost weight, a lot of weight, that first horrible week after the murders, but she hadn't realized she was still losing weight. She was *thin,* and verging on downright skinny. She had to use a safety pin to tighten the waistband of her jeans so that they didn't slide right off. Even her underwear was too big these days, and loose panties weren't comfortable.

"I told her she don't need to be wearing those baggy clothes," Harmony continued, folding bonelessly onto the couch and crossing her long legs. "But does she listen to me? You tell her."

"Harmony's right," Matty said, frowning at Grace. "Don't give no sumbitch nothing to grab. You ain't got no size to you, Julia, and you ain't got no meanness. You'll fight if you're cornered, but the thing is, you gotta keep from gettin' cornered, 'cause then your chances go way down. Are you listenin' to me?" It wasn't like him to give a shit about anybody, but he worried about Julia. Something bad had happened to her, and she was still on the run. She didn't talk about it, but he could see it in her eyes. Hell, he was used to shootings and stabbings, drug overdoses, gang violence, little kids with big, scared, uncomprehending eyes, so he didn't know exactly what it was about Julia that got to him, but something did. Maybe it was because she looked so frail, so that sometimes he thought he could almost see right through her, or maybe it was the sadness that wrapped around her like a coat. She never smiled, and her big blue eyes just looked . . . empty. The look in her eyes made him hurt inside, and Matty was a man who made a point of not letting people close enough to him that he'd be hurt if anything happened to them. He'd failed with Julia.

"I'm listening," Grace said obediently. "I listen to Harmony, too. I just can't afford a bunch of new clothes."

"You heard of yard sales?" Harmony asked. "Take your nose outta your books once in a while and look around. People sell old jeans for four or five dollars, and usually you can get 'em for a dollar if you stand around long enough complainin' that five bucks is too much."

"I'll look," Grace promised. Yard sales. She'd never been to one in her life, but if she could get jeans in her size for a dollar, she was about to become a yard-sale fanatic. She was getting tired of holding her clothes up with safety pins, and tired of her underwear wandering around inside her jeans.

"Okay, enough of shoppin'," Matty said impatiently. "I'm tryin' to teach you how to stay alive. Pay attention here."

Matty's method of teaching didn't involve gyms or dojos, because he said fights generally didn't happen there. They happened on the streets, in houses, where people went about their business and lived their lives. A couple of times he'd taken her down to an alley for her lesson, which involved him attacking her from a variety of directions, tackling her or simply wrapping his arms around her and throwing her to the ground, and she had to get away from him. He'd shown her where to kick, where to punch, and what items commonly found in an alley could be used as a weapon, from a wooden slat to a broken bottle. He'd taught her how to carry her knife, the one she'd taken from the mugger, how to hold it and how to use it.

Matty saw weapons everywhere. In his hands, a pencil was lethal, a book could do serious damage, and a salt or pepper shaker presented a priceless opportunity. Flashlights, paperweights, matches, pillows, a sheet, a jacket—all those could be used. Such a ridiculous notion as a fair fight never entered his head. Chairs were battering rams. A baseball bat or a golf club was for beating people in the head, ice skates were for slicing them open—the possibilities were endless. Grace didn't think she would ever be able to look at a room the same way again. Before, rooms had been just . . . rooms. Now they were weapons repositories.

He fell on her without warning, wrapping his surprisingly strong arms around her and dragging her to the floor. The fall stunned her, rattled her brain, but she remembered her earlier lessons and promptly raked the sole of her shoe down his shin, and simultaneously got enough leverage with one arm to hit him under the chin with the heel of her palm. His teeth snapped together with an audible pop, and he shook his head to clear it. Grace didn't stop. She wiggled, she butted him with her head, she tried to punch him in the testicles, she gouged for his eyes.

Matty didn't just let her beat up on him, because that wouldn't teach her much, he said. She had to work to get in her licks. He deftly turned aside most of her efforts, but he'd explained to her that he was expecting her to fight and had a good idea what she'd do; a stranger wouldn't have that advantage. Still, she landed some of her attempts, enough to make him grunt occasionally, or swear when she managed to hit him in the chin again an! he bit his tongue. Harmony sat on the couch and didn't exactly smile, but she looked pleased.

The effort quickly exhausted Grace. She collapsed on the floor, breathing heavily. Matty stood up and frowned down at her. "You're too weak," he pronounced. "Weaker than last week. I don't know what's eatin' at you, Julia, but you gotta eat, 'cause you ain't got no stamina." He wiped his mouth, and looked with interest at the blood that smeared his hand. "Guts, but no stamina."

Grace struggled to her feet. She truly hadn't realized how weak she had become; she had simply attributed her fatigue to staying up late trying to decipher all the papers. Once she had enjoyed food, but now she had no interest in it; everything was tasteless, as if her taste buds had been dulled by shock and never recovered.

"I'll eat," she said simply, realizing now that she didn't have a choice. Because it was such a struggle now to work up any appetite at all, what she did eat would have to be nutritious. She had no idea how long this time of sanctuary would last; she had to be ready to leave at any time, and she had to be healthy. Suddenly she felt a little edgy; perhaps she shouldn't wait until something happened, perhaps she should leave now, and find another brief sanctuary. She had Julia Wynne's birth certificate; she had filed for a social security number, and when she got that she would be able to get a driver's license. With a driver's license she could risk driving, and not worry if a cop stopped her for speeding, or for a blown taillight. She could buy a cheap car, risk driving, go anywhere she wished whether there was a bus route there or not.

Harmony stood and stretched. "I'll start feedin' her tonight," she told Matty. "Maybe some strengthening excercises, too, whaddaya think?"

"Food first," Matty said. "Poke some meat down her throat. You gotta have the brick before you can build the wall. A nice steak, or some spaghetti and meatballs, stuff like that."

Grace tried not to gag at the mention of spaghetti. After working at Hector's, she couldn't stand the smell of garlic and tomato sauce.

"I'll think of something," Harmony promised, noticing the look of revulsion on Grace's face. She understood, because she'd once worked three months at a seafood joint down south; she still couldn't stand the smell of hush puppies frying, but thank God she'd never even caught a whiff of one in Chicago. Pissed her off when she thought about it; she'd always liked hush puppies before, and now she'd lost that pleasure.

Grace and Harmony walked down three blocks to a bus stop. Grace had developed the habit of looking all around her, and Harmony watched with approval as she checked out her surroundings. "You learning," she said. "Now, what made you so uptight all of a sudden, there at Matty's?"

Harmony was the most observant person Grace had ever met. She didn't even try to blow smoke. "I was thinking of leaving."

Harmony's eyebrows slowly climbed toward her yellow-white hair. "Was it something I said? Maybe you don't like my cooking? Or maybe something's got you scared."

"Nothing has happened to make me nervous," Grace tried to explain. "It's just . . . I don't know. Intuition, maybe."

"Then I guess you'd better be packing," Harmony said calmly. "It don't pay to go against your gut feeling." She looked up the street. "Here comes the bus."

Grace bit her lip. Though Harmony hadn't asked her to stay, and wouldn't, suddenly she felt the other woman's loneliness. They hadn't been intimates; both of them had too much to hide. But they had been friends, and Grace realized that she would miss Harmony's tough unconventionality.

"You need to stay a couple more days, if you can," Harmony continued, still watching the bus. "Let me get some food in you, build up your strength a little. And get you some clothes that fit, damn it. Plus I got a few things I can show you, too, things that might come in handy."

She could live with the edginess for a day or two, Grace thought. Anything Harmony wanted to teach her was bound to be worth the stress. "Okay. I'll stay until the weekend."

Harmony's only reaction was a brief nod, but again Grace felt her pleasure.

That night, sitting in the kitchen while Harmony worked a small miracle with a wok, Grace idly leafed through an impressive stack of newspapers. Harmony read the morning paper while sitting at the kitchen table and methodically emptying a pot of coffee, and tended to toss the paper onto an unused chair rather than into the trash. It had been so long since Grace had read a paper or listened to the news that she had no idea what was happening on a national level, and it felt strange to read the headlines and peek into an unknown past.

She had flipped through about half the stack when a grainy newsprint photograph caught her attention, and her gaze flew back to it. Suddenly she couldn't breathe, her lungs stilled in her chest, and her ears buzzed. *Parrish.* Parrish was one of the men in that photo.

Dimly she heard Harmony say something, then a hand was on the back of her neck, pushing her head down until it rested on her knees. Gradually the buzzing in her ears began to fade, and her lungs began working again. "I'm all right," she said, the words muffled against her knees.

"Izzat so? Coulda fooled me," Harmony said sarcastically, but she released Grace's neck and plucked the newspaper from her nerveless fingers. "Let's see. What did you read that made you keel over? 'Peace Talks Resume'? Don't think so. How 'bout this: 'Graft in City Hall Costs City Millions.' Makes *my* blood pressure go up, but it ain't never made me faint. Maybe it was 'Industrialist's Wife Dies.' There's even a picture of the poor grievin' husband to tweak your emotions. Yep, that looks like something would hit you hard." She slapped the paper down on the table, staring at the photo. "So, which one of these guys do you know?"

Still breathing deeply, Grace looked again at the photo. It was still a shock to see Parrish's handsome face, but now she noticed there were other people there as well. The husband, for one, his face stark with grief. Beside him stood a man who looked vaguely familiar, and a quick look at the caption beneath the photo identified them as Bayard "Skip" Saunders, wealthy industrialist, and Senator Trikoris. Three other men were in the background, Parrish among them, none of them identified by name. Parrish's expression was suitably somber, but knowing what she did about him, she didn't trust the impression he gave.

Swiftly she read the four inches of column space. Calla Saunders had apparently fallen to her death from her penthouse balcony. There was no evidence of foul play. One of Mrs. Saunders's high-heeled shoes, with the heel broken off, had been found on the balcony. Investigators surmised she had fallen off balance when the heel broke, and gone over the railing; flecks of white paint from the railing had been found on her evening dress. She had evidently been alone on the balcony.

The investigators didn't know Parrish Sawyer the way she did, Grace thought, shivering. If he was anywhere near a death scene, she doubted the death was accidental.

She had forgotten how handsome he was. In her mind he had taken on a demonic aspect, his features shaped by the evil within, but the black-and-white photo captured his smooth, blond good looks, the chiseled face and slim, athletic body. As usual, he was impeccably attired. He looked completely civilized and cosmopolitan, a gentleman to his manicured fingertips.

His expression had been just as pleasant when he shot Ford in the head.

He was in Chicago. She checked the date on the newspaper, saw that it was almost two weeks old. Parrish was *here*. She wasn't safe, as she'd thought. Her instincts were right; it was time to leave.

"Let's see," Harmony mused when Grace didn't answer. "Wouldn't be the senator; he's all bullshit. Forget that Saunders guy; he's a complete wuss, just look at him. The other three . . . hmm . . . one looks like a cop, see the bad suit?"

Harmony was systematically, and with irritating accuracy, summing up every person in the photo. In another few seconds she would arrive unerringly at the correct conclusion. To save her the time and trouble, Grace tapped her fingernail once on Parrish's face.

"Now forget you ever saw him," she advised, her face and voice tense. "If he even thinks you might know something about me, he'll kill you."

Harmony's lashes shielded her eyes as she studied the photo. When she finally looked up at Grace, her green gaze was hard and clear. "That man's evil," she said flatly. "You gotta get out of here."

The next two days were a flurry of activity. Grace worked furiously on translating as much of the Gaelic as possible, because she wouldn't have time to work while she was traveling. Harmony made the rounds of yard sales, and came up with some jeans that actually fit Grace, as well as some tight knit tops and a pair of sturdy hiking boots. When they were together, Harmony talked. Grace felt like Luke Skywalker listening to Yoda, but instead of imparting pearls of mystical wisdom Harmony discussed ways of losing a tail, how to travel without leaving tracks, how to get a fake driver's license and even a fake passport if she didn't have time or it was too dangerous to acquire the real thing. Harmony knew a lot about how to survive on the streets, and on the run, and that was her gift to Grace.

Her final gift was borrowing a car and driving Grace to Michigan City, Indiana, where she planned to catch a bus. Grace didn't tell Harmony her intended destination, and Harmony didn't ask; it was safer for both of them.

"Watch your back," Harmony said gruffly, hugging Grace to her. "And remember everything Matty and I showed you."

"I will," Grace said. "I do." She hugged Harmony in return, then gathered her bags and trudged into the bus station. Harmony watched the slight figure disappear inside, and blinked twice to dispel the blur from her eyes.

"God, you watch over her," she whispered, giving her orders to the Almighty, then Harmony Johnson got back into the borrowed Pontiac and drove away.

Grace watched from the window, her eyes dry despite the tight ache in her chest. She didn't know how many more good-byes she could say; maybe it would be best to stay on the go, not staying in any one place long enough to get attached to people.

But she still had a lot of work to do on the papers, and she needed a safe place in which to do it. She studied a map of the bus routes, then bought a ticket to Indianapolis. Once there, she would decide her next destination, but it had to be something totally unexpected. Parrish hadn't been in Chicago by accident, she was certain. Somehow, he'd known she was there. His men had been searching for her. She must have been utterly predictable, and soon they would have found her.

That wouldn't happen again, she promised herself. She was going to ground, in a place where they would never expect to find her, and suddenly she knew exactly where she was going. It was the one place they wouldn't think to look, the one place where she could keep tabs on Parrish and his movements: Minneapolis.

Chapter 11

THE NAME GRACE TOOK FROM THE CEMETERY IN MINNEAPOLIS was Louisa Patricia Croley. This time she didn't get a birth certificate. Instead, armed with Harmony's pearls of illegal wisdom, by that afternoon she had a social security number, an address, and a driver's license. The last two were fake. The social security number was real, because it had belonged to the real Louisa Patricia Croley. Getting the number had been a snap, and she didn't need an actual card, just the number.

The next morning she was the owner of a pickup truck, a beige, rusted-out Dodge that nevertheless shifted gears smoothly and did not emit either any strange noises or telltale puffs of smoke. By paying cash, she got the owner to knock four hundred off his asking price. With the title and bill of sale in her possession, she then stood in line to get the title switched to her name—or rather, to Louisa Croley's name.

Grace was grimly satisfied as she walked back out to the truck. She had wheels now. She could leave any time she wished, and she didn't have to buy a ticket to do so, or worry about disguising herself in case the ticket agent remembered her if anyone came around asking questions. The truck meant liberation.

She rented a cheap room close to downtown, and after a little research applied for a job with the cleaning service that cleaned some of the lavish homes in Wayzata. There was no better pipeline of information than a cleaning service, because no one paid any attention to the cleaners. She knew that Parrish employed a full-time housekeeper, as did some of the other home owners on the lake, but enough of them used an outside service to make the business very lucrative. Not enough of the lucre made it down to the hands of those who did the cleaning, however, so the turnover was fairly high. She was hired immediately.

That night, in her drab little room, she lay in the lumpy bed and thought drowsily of the papers she had just finished translating. In 1321, a man named Morvan of Hay had tried to kill Black Niall, but lost his own head. His father, a clan chieftain whose lands lay to the east, had then launched the entire clan into open warfare with the renegades of Creag Dhu. Niall had been captured during one battle and locked in the Hays' dungeon, but escaped by unknown means that same night.

Niall. Grace kept her thoughts focused on him, afraid to let them wander. Being in Minneapolis was more difficult than she'd thought—not because of the danger, but because this was the city where she had lived with Ford, the city where her husband and brother were buried. She wanted desperately to go to their graves, but knew she didn't dare. Not only would it be an extremely risky move on her part, but she didn't think she could bear it. Seeing their graves would destroy her, shred the paper-thin wall she had built around her emotions. How long had it been now? Two months? Yes, two months and three days, almost to the hour. Not long enough. Not nearly long enough.

She would think of Niall instead. Concentrating on him was what kept her sane.

* * *

He was loving her.

On the periphery of her consciousness, Grace knew she was dreaming, but that awareness wasn't enough to stop the images. Always before when she had dreamed of Niall she had been an observer, but that night she was a participant.

The dream was vague, shifting, but she knew she was in bed with him. The bed was huge, piled high with furs; she would have felt lost and insignificant in such a bed, but with *him* there she was only vaguely aware of the vast expanse on which they lay. He mounted her, and the intense heat of his body startled her. Surprised, she realized they were both naked, his bare skin scorching hers. He was heavy, and the pressure of his weight almost crushed her, but it felt so wonderful to have a man on top of her again that she held him close. She had missed that so much, the weight of a man on her, the strength of a man's arms around her, his smell in her nostrils, his taste on her mouth.

She ran her hands over his back, feeling the layers of hard muscle under his taut skin. His mane of black hair was damp with sweat, his body was sheened with it. His scent was raw and hot and wild, that of a man aroused beyond control. She had caused this wildness in him and she loved it, she reveled in it, she wanted everything he could give her.

Then he entered her, and in her dream she cried out from the unbearable pleasure of it. He was so big she felt stretched, so hot she felt seared. Her body gathered and focused and tightened, and she began climaxing.

The spasms awoke her and at first she lay there awash in voluptuous sensation, breathing deeply and feeling the tremors subside. Niall must have just left her, she thought sleepily, because she could still feel in her loins the lingering throb caused by his thrusts. She wanted to curl in his arms, and she reached out her hand and touched—

Nothing.

Grace came sharply awake, her breath suddenly harsh in her lungs. She sat up, staring wildly around the dark, empty room. Horror filled her at what she had done, and she clenched her teeth against a howl of rage, of despair, of violent rejection.

No.

She hated herself, hated her stupid hungry body for

letting a figment of her imagination tempt it to pleasure. How dare she dream of Niall, how dare she let the dream Niall invade her body, give her pleasure? He wasn't Ford. Only Ford had ever touched her, made love to her, explored with her the intense sexuality of her nature. She had lain naked only with Ford, loved only Ford, yet only two months after his death she dreamed of another man, a *dead* man, and found sexual pleasure in the dream.

She huddled on the bed, keening softly to herself. She had betrayed Ford. It didn't matter that she had done so only in imagination, in her subconscious. Betrayal was betrayal. It should have been Ford she'd been dreaming about, Ford who had died protecting her.

But if her dreams were of Ford . . . she would have gone insane by now. His death, Bryant's death, was a great internal wound she didn't dare touch because it was still bleeding, still too painful to bear. She had focused on studying the documents about Black Niall because that was the only way she could function, and her subconscious had thrown her a curve ball by continuing to focus on him during her sleep.

Damn her body, damn her own nature. When she was awake it was as if her sensuality had died with Ford; she felt no desire, no frustration, no attraction. But when she slept, her body remembered, and yearned. She had loved making love, loved everything about it—the smells, the sounds, the delicious rub of his body against hers, the way he had stroked her while she arched and purred, the sweet, startling moment of entry when their bodies linked. When Ford was off on a dig and she hadn't been able to join him, she had been tormented by sexual frustration until he returned. He had always walked into the house grinning, because he knew that within five minutes they would be locked in their bedroom.

Grace locked her arms around her knees and stared at nothing. Perhaps, now that she had calmed down, she could understand how she had come to dream about Niall, but she didn't want it to happen again. She wouldn't think about the papers when she was in bed. Instead she would think about Parrish. That would be safe, because she didn't find him remotely attractive; she could see the evil beneath the beauty of his form. She would try to devise some means of revenge. She didn't just want him dead, she wanted justice, she wanted the world to know the truth about him. She wanted it known he had killed two wonderful men, and why. But if justice eluded her, she would settle for vengeance.

Finally she lay back down, half afraid to sleep again but knowing she had to try; she started work at seven in the morning, and cleaning houses was hard work. She needed to sleep, she needed to remember to eat, she needed . . . oh, God, she needed Ford, and Bryant, she needed everything to be the way it was before.

Instead she lay alone in a narrow, lumpy bed, and watched the night pass while she tried to think of some way to use the papers against Parrish.

Niall jerked himself out of sleep, cursing as he carefully rolled onto his back and pushed the bedcovers away from his straining, jutting penis, unable to tolerate even the slightest touch lest he spill his seed in the bed. He hadn't done such a thing since he was an untried lad of thirteen, not even during his eight years of sexual deprivation as a Knight.

He had dreamed of a woman, dreamed he was plowing deep into her belly. He couldn't fathom why he should be dreaming of such, when only a few hours earlier he had enjoyed a lusty encounter with Jean, a widow who had sought the safety of living within castle walls and traded her skills in the kitchen for a pallet in Creag Dhu.

He hadn't dreamed of Jean, or of any other woman he knew. But the woman in his dreams had been familiar, somehow, though in his dream they had coupled in darkness and he hadn't been able to see her face. She was small in his arms, as most women were, but there had also been a certain frailty, a slightness that made him want to take care with her. She hadn't wanted careful tenderness, however; she had been hot and wanton, clinging to him, her hunger as fierce as his. Her hips had lifted to meet him and as soon as he had entered her, groaning at the perfect, silky tightness that gloved him, her spasms of pleasure had begun. The intensity of her response to him had made him burn hotter and faster than he ever had before, and he'd been on the verge of joining her in climax when he abruptly woke to an empty bed, empty arms, and furious frustration.

He judged the hour to be near dawn, too near to seek sleep again. Scowling, he groped for flint and lit a candle, then strode to the fireplace to stir the banked embers and add a few small sticks to catch fire. The chill air washed around his naked body, but he didn't feel cold; he was hot, almost steaming from the force of his arousal. His penis was still thick and erect, aching from the loss of that tight internal clasp. He could feel her on his flesh as vividly as if he had indeed just left her body.

She had smelled . . . sweet. The memory was elusive, fleeting, but his thin nostrils flared as he instinctively tried to catch it again. Clean and sweet, not the overpowering sweetness of a flowery perfume but something light, tantalizing, and underlying it had been the exciting muskiness that signaled her arousal.

Ah, it had been a great dream, despite the frustrating aftermath. He seldom laughed, for life did not much amuse him, but his lips curved upward as he stared down at his rebellious manly parts. The dream woman had aroused him more than any real woman ever had, and he had greatly enjoyed many women. If he should ever truly lay his hands on one such as his dream woman, he would no doubt kill himself rutting on her. Even now, when he remembered how it had felt to enter her, the heat and wetness and tight, perfect fit—

The throb in his loins intensified, and his smile grew to a grin, one that none of his people had ever seen, for it was free and lighthearted, and he hadn't been that since the age of sixteen. He grinned at his own foolishness, and at remembered pleasure, real or not. He tormented himself by letting his thoughts linger on the dream, yet it was too arousing to forget.

Small tongues of flame were licking at the sticks now, so he added a larger log, and pulled his shirt on over his head. After wrapping his plaid about his hips and belting it, then draping the excess around his shoulders, he put on his thick wool stockings and shoved his feet into the soft leather boots that he preferred over the short, rough *brogaich* worn by his men. He never went unarmed, even in his own castle, so next he slipped a slender dagger into his boot, a larger one into his belt, then buckled on his sword. He had just finished when a hard knock sounded on his door.

His dark brows snapped together. It wasn't yet dawn; a knock at this hour could mean only trouble. "Come," he barked.

The door opened and Eilig Wishart, captain of the night guards, poked his ugly head inside the chamber. He looked relieved at seeing Niall already dressed.

"Raiders," he said briefly, in Scots. He was a broken man from Clan Keith, a man separated from his clan by will or by expulsion, and the Lowlanders more normally spoke Scots than Gaelic. Eilig always did so when he was excited.

"Where?"

"T' the east. 'Twill like be the Hays."

Niall grunted as he strode from the chamber. "Rouse the men," he ordered. He agreed with Eilig; over the years Huwe of Hay had come to bitterly hate the renegades of Creag Dhu, for they controlled a large area he had previously regarded as his to plunder. He had made bleating protests to the Bruce, for such a large gathering of broken men from all over Scotland could only mean trouble. Robert, during one of his midnight visits, had warned Niall to be wary of his neighbor to the east. The warning had been unnecessary. Niall was wary of everyone.

He himself saw to having the horses readied, and invaded the kitchens to have provisions gathered for himself and the men. Big loaves of coarse bread were already baking in the ovens for the evening meal, and a huge pot of porridge was beginning to bubble over the fire.

He tore off a hunk of stale bread from yesterday's loaf, and washed it down with ale. Between bites, he gave orders. Jean and the others scurried around, gathering bags of oats and wrapping bread, cheese, and smoked fish in cloth. The women's eyes were large and frightened, but they regarded him with confidence, trusting him to see to the matter as he'd done for the past fourteen years.

When he went down into the inner bailey he found it

teeming with terrified crofters who had been allowed into the castle for protection. Torches burned brightly on the turmoil, as the horses were brought around and his men descended to take their bags of food and make the many small preparations for going to war. The wounded lay where they had fallen, and others scurried around them, sometimes stepping over them. One sturdy old woman was making an effort to gather the wounded into one area so they could be cared for. Men cursed and snarled, and some women wept inconsolably for loved ones they had lost, husbands and children, and perhaps for what they had endured at the hands of the raiders. Some women were silent, closed in on themselves, their torn clothing telling the tale that their closed lips refused to speak. Children huddled close to their mothers, or stood alone and wailed.

It was war. Niall had seen its image many times, been hardened to it. That did not mean he would ignore such an attack on what was his. He strode over to the old woman who was trying to bring order to chaos, recognizing in her the hallmarks of a leader. He put his hand on her plump arm and pulled her aside. "How many hours have passed?" he asked curtly. "How many were they?"

She gaped up at the big man who towered over her, his black mane swirling about his broad shoulders, his eyes as cold and black as the gates of hell. She knew immediately who he was. "It canna ha' been more than an hour or twa. 'Twas a fair party, thirty or more."

Thirty. That was a large raiding party, for raiding was something best accomplished by stealth. In fourteen years he had never left Creag Dhu guarded by fewer than half his men-at-arms, but if he pursued and engaged that many men he would need more than his usual force.

Such a large raiding party was a challenge, an affront, that couldn't be ignored. Huwe of Hay must know that Niall would retaliate immediately, so it followed that he would have prepared for such an event. Perhaps he had even planned it deliberately, to draw Niall and most of his men away from the castle.

Niall beckoned to Artair, who left his horse with a lad and obeyed the summons immediately. The two men walked a little away from the noise and chaos. Artair was the only other former Templar left at Creag Dhu, a solitary and devout man who had never lost faith even when the Grand Master had gone to his fiery death seven years before. Artair was forty-eight and gray-haired, but his shoulders were still straight and, like Niall, he trained every day with the men. He'd forgotten none of the battle strategies they had learned in the Order.

"I suspect this to be a ruse to draw most of the men away from the castle," Niall said quietly. His mouth was a grim, thin line, his eyes narrowed and cold. "The Hay will likely attack as soon as he thinks us well away. I canna think he's close enough to watch, nor do I think the clumsy oaf that canny. I will take fifteen with me; the others will remain here, under your command. Be watchful."

Artair nodded, but his gaze was worried. "Only fifteen? I heard the woman say thirty—"

"Aye, but we've had the training of these lads, have we not? Two to one are not fair odds, for we've still the advantage."

Artair smiled wryly. The Hay clansmen would be fighting against unknowing, unsworn Templars, for Niall, with his help, had trained them well. Most Scots roared into battle with little thought other than to slash or stab whoever was in front of them, but the clanless men at Creag Dhu attacked with a discipline that would have done a Roman legion proud. They had been taught strategy and technique, had it hammered into them by the most fearsome warrior in Christendom, if they but knew it. They knew only that since he had appeared in the Highlands none had defeated Black Niall, and they were proud to serve under him. All their clan loyalty, their sense of kinship and belonging, had been transferred to him, and they would unhesitatingly fight to the death for him.

Satisfied that Creag Dhu was well defended, Niall chose fifteen of his men and led them out of the gates, then rode hard into the dawn. He pushed both man and beast hard to overtake the raiders, for he suspected their intent was to lead him as far away from Creag Dhu as possible. His face was grim and hard as he rode. The Hay clansmen had made a fatal mistake by committing their thieving, raping, and

murdering on land Niall considered his own. He had taken
Creag Dhu, fortified it, remade it for his purposes; the
Treasure was safe there, and no one was going to take it
from him.

Huwe was a fool, but a dangerous one. He was a blustering bull of a man, quick to take offense and too stubborn to
admit when he was outmatched. Niall was a soldier by both
nature and training, and despised the heedlessness that cost
unnecessary clan lives. Though he usually tried not to cause
such an uproar in the Highlands that Robert would be
called upon to intervene, for he knew it would mean trouble
for his brother when he refused to oust the renegades and
broken men from Creag Dhu, Niall's patience was at an
end. By threatening Creag Dhu, the Hay now threatened the
Treasure—and he would die because of his foolishness.

A good horse could make the difference between victory
and defeat, and Niall had made a point over the years of
providing the best mounts possible for his men. By stopping
only to water the sturdy beasts and allow them a moment's
rest, he overtook the raiders at mid-morning.

The raiders were in the middle of a glen, laden with the
goods they had stolen and driving a straggling herd of stolen
kine before them. The morning sun glittered on the mist
that still hung overhead like a veil. There was no place for
them to take shelter, and when Niall and his men first
thundered out of the wood toward them the raiders milled
about in a moment of panicked confusion.

The old granny had guessed aright, Niall saw; the enemy
numbered more than forty, making the odds close to three
to one, but almost half the forty were on foot. His teeth
bared in a savage grin. Seeing the relatively small number of
pursuers, the raiders would no doubt turn to meet them—a
move they would have leisure to regret for only a short time.

As he had expected, there was a flurry of shouts and the
company gathered, then charged across the glen, shouting
and waving a variety of weapons, claymores and axes and
hammers, even a scythe.

"Hold," Niall said. "Let them come to us."

His men ranged on either side of him, spreading out so
that they weren't clumped together and thus couldn't be

flanked. They held, the horses stamping restlessly and tossing their heads, while the screaming attackers poured across the misty, sun-dappled glen.

But a good three hundred yards had separated the two groups, and three hundred yards is a long way for a weary man to charge, especially when he has been about the tiring business of raiding all night and has not slept, and has been traveling hard to evade pursuers. Those on foot soon slowed, and some stopped altogether. Those who pushed stubbornly on were no longer shouting, no longer borne onward by battle fever.

So the host of horsemen who charged ahead of the stragglers barely outnumbered Niall and his men. Niall's gaze targeted a bullish young man who rode in front, his wild tangle of sandy hair flying behind him. That would be Morvan, the Hay's ill-tempered, brutish elder son, and the spit of his father. Morvan's small, mean eyes were likewise locked on Niall.

Niall raised his sword. The claymore was, for most men, a two-handed weapon, but his strength and size gave him the power to swing the six-foot blade one-handed, freeing his left hand for yet another blade, or a Lochaber axe. Seizing the reins with his teeth, he took up an axe. His well-trained horse quivered beneath him, muscles bunching. When Morvan and his men were a mere thirty yards away, Niall and his men charged.

The impact was swift and staggering. Once he had fought with shield and armor, a hundred pounds of mail weighing him down, but now Niall fought free and wild and savage, his eyes burning with a fierce light as he blocked a sword with his axe and then went in under the man's defenses with his own sword, spitting him. He always fought silently, without the yells and grunts of other men, instinctively sensing the next attack while he was still dealing with the present one.

Before his sword was free he turned, swinging the axe up to block another blow. Metal clanged as a sword struck the axe head, and the force of it jarred his arm. One powerful leg pressed and his horse turned, bringing him around to face this new challenge. Morvan of Hay pressed forward, using all his considerable weight in an effort to unhorse Niall.

Niall shifted his horse back, away from Morvan's weight. With a curse the younger man straightened, his yellowed teeth bared as he drew back the claymore for another attack. *"Diolain!"* Morvan hissed.

Niall didn't even blink at being called a bastard. He simply swung his own sword to parry, then buried his axe in the oaf's head, cleaving it almost in two. With a jerk he freed his weapon and turned for another adversary, but there was none. His men had worked as efficiently as he, and the Hay clansmen who had been mounted were no longer astride their horses, but lay sprawled in the indignity of death, limbs exposed, their blood turning the sweet earth to mud. The familiar stench of blood and waste marked their death.

Niall's black gaze swept over his men. Two were wounded, one seriously. "Clennan," he said sharply, drawing the attention of the man who had taken a wound in the thigh. "Care for Leod." Then he and his thirteen remaining men charged to meet the Hay clansmen who were on foot.

It was a rout, for a man on horseback had an enormous advantage over one afoot. The animals themselves were weapons, their steel-shod hooves and massive weight simply crushing those who could not move out of the way. Niall vaulted from his horse's back, the blood lust singing through him as he swung sword and axe, twisting, parrying, thrusting. He was a dark blade of death, unutterably graceful as he moved in his lethal dance. Five men fell before him, one beheaded by a massive sweep of the claymore, and Niall did not even feel the shock in his sword arm as the blade sliced through bone.

The carnage lasted two minutes, no more. Then quiet fell across the glen, the clash of swords replaced by an occasional moan. Swiftly Niall took stock, not expecting his men to have escaped unscathed. Young Odar was dead, lying sprawled beneath the body of a Hay clansman. His clear blue eyes stared sightlessly upward. Sim had taken a sword cut in the side and was cursing luridly as he tried to stanch the flow of blood. Niall judged him well enough to ride.

Goraidh, however, was unconscious, his forehead bloody. All suffered from small cuts and bruises, himself included, but those wounds were as nothing. With two wounded in the first attack, he had ten healthy men remaining, and two would have to stay behind to help with the wounded and herding the cattle back to Creag Dhu.

"Muir and Crannog, remain with Sim and Clennan to help with the wounded, and the cattle." The two he had named did not look pleased at having to remain behind, but knew it was necessary.

They could not ride as hard as they had before, for the horses were tired. Niall kept them to a steady pace, his warrior's heart beating fierce and wild in his chest as he rode to another fight. The wind lifted his long hair, drying the sweat of battle. His thighs were clamped to the powerful animal beneath him, heat meeting heat, flesh against flesh. The thick wool plaid kilted about his waist gave him a freedom that braies and hose and hot sheepskin undergarment had denied him, and he exulted in his unfettered wildness.

He had easily cast aside the physical accoutrements of the Knights, let his hair grow long, shaved his beard, discarded the hated sheepskin. Though he had become one of them, there had always been a place in his soul that yearned for Scotland, for the wildness and freedom, the mountains and mists, the sheer lustiness of youth. The life of warfare offered by the Knights had appealed to him, and as he had grown older he had learned what they did and accepted the burden, the sheer faith, but still Scotland had lived within him.

He was home, and though he reveled in his physical freedom he was bound now by a far heavier burden, one that ruled his life far more rigidly than before. Why had Valcour chosen him, an unwilling though faithful Knight? Had Valcour suspected how easily and eagerly he would rejoin his former land and life, giving no hint that he'd once been a Templar and thereby better protecting the Treasure? Had Valcour guessed the secret relief with which Niall had accepted his freedom from all his vows, save one? But that one was the greatest of all, and the most bitter, for it served to protect those who had destroyed the Order.

Why could not Artair have been chosen? Of necessity he had shaved his beard and grown his hair, for to do otherwise would have been courting death, but other than that he held still to the vows he had taken, to chastity and service. Artair never doubted, never cursed God for what had happened, never turned from the faith to which he had sworn. If he had hated, at first, he had long since found peace and released his hatred, finding solace in prayer and war. Artair was a good soldier, a good companion.

He would not have been a good Guardian.

Niall had not forgiven either the Church or God. He hated, he doubted, he cursed himself and Valcour and his own vow, but in the end he always came back to the same truth: he was the Guardian. Valcour had chosen well.

To protect the Treasure, Niall rode to face Huwe of Hay, well aware that a blood feud had started that day and determined that most of the blood would leak from Hay clansmen. Huwe wanted war? Very well, then, there would be war.

Part Two

Niall

Chapter 12

"FEAR-GLEIDHIDH," GRACE MUTTERED TO HERSELF, MOV-
ing the words around on the computer screen and trying to
make sense of the sentence. *Fear-gleidhidh* meant "guardian"; she was familiar enough with *that* word to recognize it
at a glance. Over the past several months she'd spent so
much time with these blasted Gaelic papers that she'd
learned to recognize a lot of the nouns, though sometimes
the spelling threw her off. Even with the help of a two-
hundred-dollar set of tapes that promised to teach her how
to speak Gaelic, and which she'd bought in a useless hope
that it would help clarify the murky medieval Gaelic syntax,
it could still take hours to translate a few sentences.

But what on earth did *cunhachd* mean? Running her
finger down the page of the Gaelic/English dictionary, she
couldn't find any such word. Could it be *cunbhalach,* which
meant "steady," or *cunbhalachd,* which was "judgment"?
No, it wouldn't be the first, for if she was reading it correctly
the sentence was "The Guardian has the Cunhachd." The
capitalization didn't necessarily mean anything, but the

sentence certainly wouldn't be "The Guardian has the Steady."

"The Guardian has the Judgment"? Grace rearranged the words on the screen once again, wondering if she had misread the verb or tangled the syntax for what seemed like the millionth time. Without the benefit of classes, it was taking her more time to learn Gaelic than any other language she had studied. She was getting better at it, though.

She rechecked the paper, bending close and using her magnifying glass to study the faded letters. No, the verb was definitely "has." *Cunhachd* was the stumbling block. She turned her attention to it, and noticed that the *n* was smeared. Could it be an *m* instead? Returning to the dictionary, she looked up *cumhachd,* and a surge of triumph went through her. *Cumhachd* meant "power."

"The Guardian has the Power."

She raked her hands through her hair, lifting the long strands and letting them sift through her fingers. What were some synonyms for *power? Authority, right, might, will.* All of those would fit, yet each differed somewhat in meaning. If she interpreted the sentence literally, then what power did the Guardian have? Power over the Treasure, absolute control of it? Money was power, as the old saying went, but the chronicles had also said that the Treasure was "greater than gold." It followed, then, that though there had likely been a monetary treasury, that wasn't the Treasure referred to so reverentially.

So what had the Treasure been, and what sort of power had the Guardian wielded because of it? If Black Niall had been the possessor of such mighty power, why had he spent his life as a renegade in the remote western Highlands? How had a Templar, supposedly a religious man, become a man as renowned for his sexual appetite as he was for his skill with a claymore?

Two more hours of work still left her in the dark. The Treasure was either "a knowing of God's will," something that was certainly ambiguous enough, or "proof of God's will," which was equally unenlightening. It possessed the power to "bow kings and nations before it," and "vanquish evil."

She read aloud the words on the screen. "The Guardian shall pass—or travel, or walk—beyond the bounds of time, or season—in the way of Our Lord Jesus Christ, to do His battle with the Serpent." That sounded as if the Guardian would emulate Jesus's struggle with Satan, which hardly translated into any great power, but rather an effort to live an honorable, blameless life—something difficult enough, and from what she'd read about Black Niall he hadn't even *tried.*

So what was the Treasure, and what was the Power? Religious myth? Parrish evidently believed the gold was real; on the surface that was motive enough, yet she kept coming back to the Treasure that was greater than gold, and wondering if more than wealth was involved. If so, what? No Templar had ever betrayed the secret of the Treasure, though some of them had been hideously tortured. Perhaps most of them hadn't known anything to tell, but certainly the Grand Master had known, and he had gone to the stake with the secret untold. Instead he had cursed the King of France and the Pope, and within a year both Philip and Clement had died, giving credence to the superstition of the time that the Templars had been in league with the devil.

Slowly Grace paraphrased the unwieldy sentence. "The Guardian shall walk beyond time to vanquish evil." Sometimes putting the words in a more modern context helped her see through the lapsed centuries to find the most logical translation. She tried again. "The Guardian shall pass the season in battle against evil." What season? The years following the destruction of the Order? Was the Guardian supposed to fight Philip and Clement on behalf of the Order? If so, Black Niall had instead fought his skirmishes in bed and in the mountains and moors of Scotland.

It didn't make sense, and she was too tired to keep at it. Grace saved the file, then turned off the computer. In six months she had translated all the tales of Black Niall's battles and conquests, the Latin and French and English, but parts of the Gaelic still defeated her. Come to that, some of the Latin didn't make sense, because for some reason a *diet* had been included. What did a carefully regulated consumption of salt have to do with a history of the Templars? And why was the amount of water they drank based on their weight? But there it was, right in the middle of a long passage on the duties of a Guardian: *Victus Rationem Temporis,* the diet of time, or for time.

She paused in the act of removing her sweatshirt. Time. What was this about time, that it cropped up in both Latin and Gaelic? Come to think of it, there had been something similar in the French documents. Swiftly she returned to the rickety table she used as a desk, flipping through the documents until she found the page she sought. "He shall be unbound by the chains of time."

Walking beyond time. Unbound by the chains of time. Diet for time. There was a common thread here, but she couldn't make sense of it. They had all been fixated on time, but was it in a metaphorical sense, or a conceptual thing? And what did time have to do with the Templars?

Well, it wasn't a puzzle she was going to solve by worrying at it; she would have to complete her translations, a project she could see the end of now. Another three weeks, perhaps a month, and she would have the Gaelic section completed. Gaelic was so difficult she'd saved it for last and she couldn't be certain of her translation, but she'd done the best she could. Whether it would tell her anything beyond the supposed location of the Templars' gold remained to be seen.

After undressing for bed, she neatly placed the computer and all her papers in the computer case, and set it within easy reach beside the bed. If she had to leave abruptly, she didn't want to waste time gathering everything together.

She turned out the light and lay on the narrow, lumpy bed, staring out the dingy window at the softly falling snow. The seasons had changed, summer giving way to fall, color dulling into the monochromatic shades of winter. It had been eight months since her old life had ended. She survived, but she couldn't say that she lived.

Her heart felt as bleak and stark as the winter. Her hatred for Parrish kept the pain at bay, untouched and undiminished. She knew it was there, knew she would someday lose control over it, but she would pay that price when the time came.

She blessed Harmony every day. She had a passport in Louisa Croley's name, in case she had to get out of the country in a hurry. After obtaining that, she had left Louisa behind and taken another name, as well as another job. Marjorie Flynn had existed for two months, then she'd moved on and become Paulette Bottoms. Another low-paying job, another cheap room. The Minneapolis–St. Paul area was large enough that she could lose herself in it, never meeting anyone she knew from before, so she had no difficulty in changing names. She made no friends, on Harmony's advice. She saved every penny she could and had amassed almost four thousand dollars, counting what she'd had left after buying the truck. She would never again be as helpless as she'd been after the murders.

Not that she ever *could* be, even without the assets of cash and transportation. Part of her helplessness had been her own total lack of knowledge about survival on the streets, and she was no longer ignorant. Her face was a cool, expressionless mask, and she walked with an alertness, a readiness, that told seasoned street predators she wouldn't be easy prey. At night, alone, she practiced the moves Mateo had taught her, and she carefully arranged her grim little rooms to provide the maximum in protection and opportunity for herself.

She was never unarmed. She had bought a cheap revolver and kept it with her, but she also had the knife in its sheath, tucked out of sight under her shirt. She had a sharpened screwdriver in her boot, a hatpin threaded in her shirt cuff, a pencil in her pocket. Finding a place to practice her nonexistent marksmanship hadn't been easy; she'd had to drive far out into the country, but she had achieved, if not true skill, at least a degree of efficiency and familiarity with the weapon, so she could carry it with some confidence.

She doubted anyone from her former life would recognize her now, even if she came face-to-face with a friend. Her long, thick hair was let down only in the privacy of her room; she wore a cheap, light brown wig to work, and at other times she twisted her hair into a knot on top of her head and covered it with a baseball cap. She was thin, weighing barely a hundred pounds, her cheekbones prominent over hollow cheeks. She had managed not to lose any more weight, but she had to make a deliberate effort to eat, and she exercised faithfully to stay strong. She wore tight jeans and sturdy black boots, and a fur-lined denim jacket as protection against the frigid Minnesota winter. On Harmony's excellent advice she'd bought some cheap cosmetics and learned how to use mascara, blusher, and lipstick so she didn't look as if she were fresh out of a convent.

A couple of men had hit on her, but a blank, frozen expression and a terse "No" were enough to turn them away. She couldn't imagine even having a cup of coffee with a man. Only in her dreams did her sexuality reawaken, and she couldn't control that. Black Niall was so firmly in her thoughts, preoccupied her so many hours of the day, that she had found it impossible to shut him out of her subconscious. He was there, living in her dreams, fighting and loving, grim and beautiful and terrifyingly male, and so lethal she sometimes woke shivering with fear. She never dreamed that he threatened *her,* but the Black Niall of her imagination was not a man one crossed with impunity.

She felt alive, painfully so, when she dreamed of him. She couldn't preserve the vast emptiness that protected her when she was awake; she ached, and yearned, and trembled at his touch. Only twice more had she dreamed of actual lovemaking, but both times had been shattering.

It was a mistake to remember those dreams now, when she was trying to sleep. She knew that, and turned restlessly on her side. She was all but inviting a recurrence. But the dreams of lovemaking were more welcome than the dreams of battle, which had been occurring incessantly for the past four months. He hacked and slashed his way through her sleep, wading through blood and body parts, the images so intense she could hear the clang of swords striking together, see the men slip and stumble, hear them grunt with effort, hear the screams of pain and watch their faces distort in death throes. Given a choice between carnage and sex, she would definitely choose sex, were it not for the guilt that haunted her afterward.

After an hour of lying there she sighed, resigning herself to a sleepless night. She was tired but her brain refused to stop working, going over and over the papers, thinking about Niall, trying to piece together some feasible means of revenge against Parrish. She had hoped to find something in the papers to use against him, but if she'd been thinking

straight she would have realized there couldn't be anything
incriminating about him in papers that were almost seven
hundred years old. The papers fascinated her so much that
she hadn't been able to see past her own obsession. No, if
she could manage any sort of revenge against Parrish it
would have to be something much more straightforward,
like killing him herself.

She got out of bed and turned on the light, her eyes stark,
her soft mouth set in a grim line. Over the past eight months
she had learned she could fight to protect herself, perhaps
even kill in self-defense, but she didn't know if she could
kill in cold blood. She paced back and forth, hugging her
arms around her to ward off the night chill. Could she kill
Parrish? Could she walk up, stick the revolver to his head,
and pull the trigger?

She closed her eyes, but the vision that came to mind
wasn't of herself shooting Parrish, but of the utter disregard,
almost boredom, with which he had shot Ford and Bryant.
She saw the sudden blankness on Ford's face, the boneless-
ness of his body as he slumped over.

Her teeth clenched, her hands knotted into fists. Oh, yes,
she could kill Parrish.

Why didn't she just do it, then?

She had driven by his house a few times when she'd been
working for the cleaning service; she had never seen him or
his car, but then she hadn't expected to. If he were at home,
his car would be in the garage, and Parrish wasn't the type
of man who enjoyed gardening. She knew nothing of his
schedule, hadn't spent her days watching his house in order
to follow him. She had taken self-protective measures, but
in reality she had done nothing to avenge her family.
Instead she had concentrated on the papers, persuaded
herself that there could be something useful in them,
deluded herself so she could merely mark time and lose
herself in the translations.

But self-delusion was at an end. She needed either to do
something about Parrish or to go away quietly and spend
the rest of her life grieving and hiding.

All right. She would do it. She would track Parrish down,
and kill him.

Grace felt the weight of the decision settle on her. She

didn't have the stuff of which killers were made, and she knew it. On the other hand, she hadn't sought any of this; Parrish had begun the dance. The Old Testament said, "Thou shalt not kill," but it also said, "An eye for an eye." Perhaps she was rationalizing, but she took that to mean that once a murder was committed, society or the wronged family had a right to put an end to the murderer's existence.

No matter. Tomorrow she would begin tracking him down like the animal he was.

Morning, however, brought a new reality: she had to work. She couldn't spend all day sitting in some hidden place and watching Parrish's house. Her old truck would be out of place, and very noticeable, in any case. Physically watching for him, following him, seizing an opportunity, simply wasn't feasible. She had to know in advance where he would be, and be there before him.

For all she knew, he wasn't even in town. During the winter he often took long vacations in warmer climes, staying away for as long as a month at a stretch.

There was only one way to find out. During her lunch break with another cleaning service, she stopped at a fast-food joint and used a pay phone to call the Foundation.

Her fingers moved without volition, punching in the familiar numbers. It wasn't until the first ring buzzed in her ear that she realized what she was doing, and her heart thumped wildly in her chest. Before she could slam down the receiver the flat, impersonal voice of the receptionist answered. "Amaranthine Potere Foundation. How may I direct your call?"

Grace swallowed. "Is Mr. Sawyer in the office today?"

"One moment."

"No, don't ring—" she started to say, but the line had already clicked and another ring was sounding. She took a deep breath and prepared to ask the question again of Parrish's secretary; she would need to disguise her voice a little, because Annalise had once been fairly familiar with—

"Parrish Sawyer."

The smooth, cultured tones stunned her, panicked her. She froze in place, her mind going blank at actually hearing that hated voice again.

"Hello?" he said, more sharply.

Grace gasped.

"Is this an obscene call?" he asked, sounding both bored and annoyed. "I really don't—" Then he stopped, and she could hear his own breathing for a few endless seconds. "Gracie," he said, purring her name. "How nice of you to call."

She felt wrapped in ice, a coldness that had nothing to do with the fifteen-degree weather. She couldn't speak, couldn't move, could only clench the receiver with white, bloodless fingers.

"Can't you speak, darling? I want to talk to you, clear up this dreadful misunderstanding. You know I wouldn't let anything happen to you. There's always been something between us, but I didn't realize how potent it was until you ran away. Let me help you, darling. I'll take care of everything."

He was a wonderful liar, she thought dimly. His warm, seductive voice oozed sympathy, trustworthiness; if she hadn't *seen* him commit the murders, she would have believed every word out of his mouth.

"Gracie," he said, cajoling, whispering. "Tell me where to meet you. I'll take you away, just the two of us, to someplace safe. You won't have to worry about anything."

He *wasn't* lying. It was lust she heard in his voice. Horrified, sickened, she finally managed to hang up the phone and blindly made her way back to the truck. She felt filthy, as if he'd actually touched her.

My God, how could he have the utter gall, how could he possibly think she would let him touch her? But there wasn't any *letting* involved, she realized. She started the truck and drove carefully away, not doing anything to attract attention, but her heart was beating so rapidly she felt faint. He didn't know for certain she'd seen him that night, so he'd taken the chance that she hadn't and tried to talk her into coming to him. She had never had any doubts he would kill her; now she knew he would rape her first.

Wispy snowflakes drifted across her windshield, just a few at first, but by the time she got to the next house on her list the snow was coming down fast enough to begin collecting on the hood of the truck. This was one of her least favorite houses to clean; Mrs. Eriksson was always there, carefully watching every move Grace made as though she expected her to walk off with a television or something. But she didn't chatter, as some people did, and today Grace was grateful for the silence. She moved in a daze through the cleaning, her mind spinning while she carefully mopped and dusted and vacuumed.

Mrs. Eriksson dumped a load of clothing on the sofa. "My bridge club is coming over tonight and I have to bake a cake; it would help me a lot if you'd fold the laundry while I start the baking."

The woman was tireless in trying to get the cleaning service to perform extra, unpaid tasks. Grace made a show of looking at her watch. "I'm sorry," she said politely. "I have to be at another house in half an hour. I have just enough time to finish your floors." It was a lie; today was a light day for her, and she had only one more house to do, at four o'clock. But Mrs. Eriksson was probably lying about the bridge club, too, and perhaps even about the cake.

"You're very uncooperative," the woman said sharply. "You've refused my requests before, and I'm thinking of changing services. If your attitude doesn't change, I'm going to have to speak to your supervisor."

"I'm sure she'll be happy to schedule laundry services for you."

"Why should I use her service for that, when you've been so unsatisfactory in everything else?"

"She can assign someone else, if you like." Grace didn't look up, but stuffed her dusting cloth back into the canvas bag in which she carried all her cleaning products, then deftly plugged in the vacuum cleaner and turned it on. The noise drowned out anything Mrs. Eriksson might have said, and Grace industriously shoved the machine back and forth across the carpet. The service owner had Mrs. Eriksson's number; she might assign someone else to clean the house, but Mrs. Eriksson still wouldn't get her laundry folded or her dishes washed unless she paid for it.

Mrs. Eriksson sat down on the sofa and began folding clothes, snapping the garments and glaring all the while, but Grace's mind immediately went back to Parrish.

Everything inside her recoiled in revulsion. She couldn't

even imagine the horror of being in his hands. He wouldn't have to kill her, because she would go mad if he touched her, her mind would shut down completely.

How had he known? How had he guessed it was her on the phone? What kind of feral instincts did he have that had led him so swiftly and unerringly to her identity? More important, had he immediately phoned the Minneapolis police and told them she was in the area?

Parrish did place an immediate phone call, but it was to Conrad instead of the police department. "Ms. St. John just called my office," he said smoothly, pleasure and exhilaration in his voice. "Doubtless she only wanted to know if I am here, and she would have expected Annalise to answer the phone. Get to our source with the phone company immediately and find out where that call came from." He glanced at his Rolex. "The call came in to me at twelve twenty-three."

He hung up without waiting for Conrad's reply, if he had intended to make one. Parrish leaned back in his massive leather chair, breathing hard from the excitement pouring like water through him. Grace! After six damnably frustrating months, in which she had seemed simply to disappear from Chicago, who would have thought she would make contact herself?

Conrad was sure he'd found where she'd been working in Chicago, at an Italian dump where most of the employees were paid under the table. The woman had been thinner but she had sometimes carried a small case, had kept to herself, and had a blond, frizzy hairdo. The blond frizz job had also been reported involved in a peculiar altercation outside the Newberry Library. The Newberry happened to be one of the foremost research libraries in the country, something Grace would know, and a resource she would need. Parrish knew by that she was working on the papers, and Grace was very good at her work. She would have a very good idea of why he wanted the papers.

But then she'd vanished again, simply not returning to the restaurant, and no one there had known where she lived. Conrad had checked the bus lines, the trains, airlines, but no one had noticed a woman with frizzy blond hair carrying a computer case. She had disappeared, and not even Conrad had been able to find a trace of her.

Where was she now? In Minneapolis, or hiding in some backwater? Why had she called? She hadn't said anything but he was almost positive, just from that one tiny betraying gasp, that she was the caller.

Soon he would know, if not her present location, at least where she'd been when she made the call. The police had to have a court order to access those kinds of records at the phone company, but he wasn't hindered by their ridiculous regulations. Conrad would at least know where to begin searching for her, and his pride was at stake now; he was still smarting from letting a little nobody like Grace St. John escape from him.

Why would she want to know if he was in the office? He laughed softly to himself. Was little Grace planning some sort of revenge? What did she think she could do, walk into his office and point a pistol at him? She knew the security of the building, knew she wouldn't get past the lobby.

Perhaps he should let her, though, draw her to him. He could overpower her easily enough, and then he'd have her.

He could work late; the building would be deserted, and she would feel more confident. He could arrange for the guards to be looking conveniently the other way, but not make it so easy that she became suspicious. He would wait by the door for her, ready to disarm her of whatever weapon she carried; he wouldn't want to give her an opportunity for a lucky shot.

Perhaps he wouldn't wait for a more comfortable, convenient place in which to take her. Perhaps he would have her right on the desk, stretched across the glassy surface. She would struggle and kick and he would soothe her, whisper to her, and kiss her astonishingly carnal mouth. She would feel so soft beneath him, so helpless.

He was fully aroused, almost panting. Once wouldn't be enough, he knew that now. He wanted to come in her mouth, and he wanted to feel her come. He wanted to hear her cry out his name in pleasure.

Then he would kill her. What a waste, but it had to be done.

* * *

"She called from a pay phone at a McDonald's in Roseville," Conrad reported. "No one noticed her, but the only other calls received around that time originated from legitimate contacts."

"Roseville." Parrish considered the location. It was a suburb just northeast of downtown. "Do you have men watching the place in case she returns?"

"Yes." Conrad had taken care of that detail immediately. People were generally creatures of habit, adhering to the same routine for months, years. Grace had shown herself to be unusually unpredictable, but he couldn't afford to assume she would immediately take off for parts unknown. If she remained in the city, sooner or later she would at least pass by that McDonald's—if not today, then tomorrow. If not tomorrow, then perhaps on this same day next week. He was a patient man; he would wait.

"So she came back here," Parrish mused. "Gutsy of her, don't you think? I never would have expected it. Do you think she's going to try to kill me?"

"Yes," Conrad said impassively. Otherwise, there was no logical reason for her to return to Minneapolis. The danger was too great.

"Perhaps we should let her try." Parrish smiled, his eyes bright with anticipation. "Let her come to us, Conrad. We'll be ready."

Chapter 13

"Niall, I dreamed about you again last night. For once, you weren't either fighting or having sex, just sitting quietly in front of a fire, cleaning your sword. You looked—not sad, but grim, as if you carried a burden that would break most men. What were you thinking about? What makes you so alone? Do you think about the Templars, all the friends who died, or is there something else that made you so hard? Do you resent being a renegade, when your brother is a king?"

Grace lifted her hands from the keys, disturbed by what she had just typed. Dreaming about him was one thing, writing to him was another. It was unsettling, the way she felt as if she were truly communicating with him, as if he would read her words and reply. She knew the constant stress of the past eight months had taken a toll on her, but she hoped she hadn't totally flipped out.

She had tried to resume writing in her electronic journal, but somehow her brain refused to seize on the everyday detail that she had recorded before. For one thing, she had no routine life, and without a routine there couldn't be anything *un*routine. She would stare at the empty screen, her fingers poised over the keys, but in the end she had no comment to make about the day. She had no appointments to keep, no news to share, no one to share it with in any case. She went through the days silent and numb, coming alive only with hatred for Parrish or when she was translating the papers.

But however illusory Niall was, he was far more vivid than anything else in the grayness of her life. He *seemed* real, as if he were just on the other side of the door, unseen but undeniably there. His myth, his history, was her one bit of color. Through him, she still lived, still felt the hot rush of vitality and passion. She could talk to him as she would never again be able to talk to anyone living. The division between before and now was too deep, too drastic; there was too little left of the shy, bookish, rather innocent woman she had been. In her own way, she was as unreal as Niall.

She felt her aloneness all the way to the bone. Not loneliness; she didn't pine for company, for a sympathetic ear, for gossip and chatter and laughter. She was alone in a way she'd never before imagined, as solitary as if she were an astronaut come untethered from the mother ship, drifting unnoticed in an emptiness so vast it was beyond comprehension. She had found a whisper of companionship with Harmony Johnson, but remaining would have been too dangerous to Harmony, and during the six months she'd been back in Minneapolis she hadn't truly talked with anyone. She woke up alone, she worked in mental if not physical isolation, and she went to sleep alone. *Alone.* What a desolate, empty word.

In her dream, Niall had been alone. Alone inside, as she was. He could be surrounded by people and still be alone, because there was something untouchable in him, something no one else even knew existed. The golden glow of the fire had outlined the hard, pure lines of his face, shadowed the deep-set eyes and high cheekbones. His movements had been deft as he saw to the cleaning and repair of his weapon, his long fingers tracing over the razor edge to find any chips that dulled its effectiveness. His manner had been absorbed, deliberate, remote.

Once his head had lifted and he sat very still, as if listening for or to something that hadn't registered in the dream. Black mane flowing over his broad shoulders, his black eyes narrowed, he had been the picture of animal alertness, on guard and wary. No threat had materialized and gradually he had relaxed, but she had the impression of a man who could never truly ease his vigilance. He was the Guardian.

She had wanted to touch his shoulder, and sit silently beside him by the fire while he tended his tools of war, giving him the comfort of her warmth and presence so that he knew he wasn't alone after all—and perhaps, in doing so, she too would find comfort and companionship. But in this dream she had been locked into the role of observer, unable to go closer, and in the end she had awakened without touching him.

"If I were with you . . ."

Startled, she stared at what she had typed. The words hadn't been consciously planned; her fingers had simply moved on the keyboard and they had appeared. Suddenly frightened, she closed the file on her journal. Her hands were shaking. *She had to stop thinking of Niall as if he were alive.* The fixation on him was too vivid, too powerful. At first concentrating on him had seemed reasonable, a way of keeping herself sane, but what if it were having the opposite effect and she was losing herself in fantasy? After reading her journal entries, any psychiatrist would be forgiven for thinking she had lost contact with reality.

But reality was seeing her husband and brother murdered, crouching in a cold rain too terrified to cross a street, going hungry and being cold, sleeping in storage buildings and fighting off attackers. Reality was freezing in horror at the sound of Parrish's voice. What did she have left except the escape she found in her dreams?

She looked at the stack of documents, at the pages and pages of notes she had scribbled. "I have work," she murmured, and the sound of her own voice was reassuringly normal. She might feel as if she were coming apart at the seams, but she still had the work. It had saved her for eight months and would continue to save her for a few days yet, though that damn Gaelic had nearly defeated her.

Just another week or two of work, and then the tales of the Knights Templar and the Guardian, of Black Niall, would be ended. When she wasn't spending hours struggling with the translations every night before bed, the dreams of him would stop.

Unexpected desolation swamped her at the thought. Without Niall, the spark that made her feel alive, even if only in her dreams, would be extinguished. There would be no more translations, because she was too well known by sight in her field to get a job with another archaeological foundation, even under an assumed name. There would be no more intriguing puzzles, not that any other work she had done had come close to fascinating her as much as did Niall and the Templars.

She would have nothing but vengeance. The need for it burned inside her, but she sensed that beyond vengeance there was nothing but bleak, gray nothingness, assuming she survived. She would be on the run for the rest of her life, her identity gone, nothing to look forward to, and never knowing the joy of having Ford's children and growing old with him, cradling their grandchildren, perhaps watching Bryant succumb at last to love and matrimony.

Being insane was better.

She pulled the Gaelic papers to her, opened the Gaelic/English dictionary, and picked up her pen.

As usual, she was drawn almost immediately into the magic of the papers, the sense of reading something enormously compelling and important.

"Mankind shall not know the True Power," she read some minutes later. "The Cup and the Winding Cloth shall blind them to the sun, the Throne and Banner denied, but the True Power shall be used by the Guardian in the Lord's stead, to pass through the Veil of Time and protect the Treasure from Evil.

"None save the Treasure can defeat Evil, and none save the Guardian shall use the Power."

It read like a Bible passage, but she was certain nothing like this had ever been in the Bible. The Cup . . . that could refer to the Chalice, and the Winding Cloth could well be the shroud in which Jesus had been wrapped after the crucifixion. The Shroud of Turin was supposed to be Jesus's shroud, but it was surrounded by controversy; there were references to its existence long before the fourteenth century, which was when carbon dating had placed its origin. Of course, the earlier references could have been to another shroud, perhaps the real one . . . which did nothing to explain how a fourteenth-century forger could have created a cloth bearing an impregnable negative image of a crucified man, five centuries before photography had been invented.

"The Cup and the Winding Cloth shall blind them to the sun," she read again. If the Chalice still existed, it had never been found. But perhaps the arguments about the validity of the shroud did indeed blind people to the true nature of faith; they were so busy making points and counterpoints that the argument became the focus and they couldn't see the whole picture.

The Templars were irrevocably connected to the shroud. They had battled the Moors and won Jerusalem for the Crusaders for a time, and themselves occupied the Temple on the Mount for longer than that. During their occupation, they had determinedly excavated as much of the Temple as possible, perhaps finding many artifacts dating back to the early years of the Temple, to the very beginning of Judaism. What treasures indeed had they found . . . what Treasure?

One of the charges against the Templars was that they had worshipped false gods, for in every chapel the Templars had built after occupying the Temple on the Mount, there had been the face of a man, a stern, strong-boned face—the same face that had been revealed centuries later on the Shroud of Turin.

It followed that they had unearthed the shroud; it also followed that its location in the Temple gave it validity. But what else had they found? The "Cup" and the "Winding Cloth" were listed, as well as the "Throne" and the "Banner," but the "True Power" was something else, something so far left undescribed.

"The Guardian shall defend the world from the Foundation of Evil."

Grace sighed at the continued ambiguity. The Foundation of Evil was obviously Satan, but why hadn't the writer simply said so? Evidently even medieval scribes had been afflicted by wordiness.

Just the word *Foundation* made her think of better days, with Ford and Bryant delicately and happily sifting mounds of dirt through screens, looking for the smallest shard of pottery; or sitting on the ground whisking a small brush over a half-buried bone. The three of them had loved their work, and the Amaranthine Potere Foundation had been one of the few places in the world where an archaeologist could be permanently employed. Independently funded, the Foundation hadn't concentrated just on the hugely important digs, but on the smaller ones that would provide detail rather than drama. Bryant had once said that the Foundation seemed determined to leave no dirt in the world unsifted.

Grace stiffened, her pupils contracting with shock. Potere . . . Power. *Amaranthine Potere* Foundation, the Foundation of Unending Power.

Why hadn't she made the connection before? Languages and translations were her field of expertise. She should have seen it, should have realized—

It was a stretch, a real stretch. It was ridiculous. A huge foundation committed to unearthing the Templar Treasure? The money spent would surely far exceed the worth of any gold found.

"The Treasure's worth is greater than gold," she whispered. Not money, then; the documents had made that plain. Power. The Templars had possessed some mysterious power, had dedicated their lives to protecting it.

She got up and paced, mentally feeling her way through the puzzle. Was it possible the Foundation existed to *prevent* people from learning about the Power, whatever it was? Could Parrish, in some twisted way, think he had to kill everyone who learned of the papers in order to keep the Power secret? Was he acting as Guardian?

No, she could drive a truck through the holes in that theory. For one thing, the Foundation hadn't had anything to guard. The papers had disappeared centuries before and anyone who knew anything about archaeology could not have reasonably expected the documents would survive. Paper deteriorated rapidly; that was why there were relatively few original documents left from even two centuries before, much less almost seven.

No, forget about any mystic power, any great struggle between right and wrong. She was tired, and fatigue was fogging her brain. The most likely motive was money, pure and simple. Parrish must have reason to believe the Templars' Treasure was enormous beyond belief, and as director of the Foundation he could expend any amount of effort he wanted in finding it. He must have devised some way of appropriating the gold for his own use. The Foundation was probably exactly what it seemed, an archaeological foundation, without any sinister motive behind its existence. Parrish was the villain, not the Foundation itself.

But the Foundation had been founded in 1802, and named "Unending Power," long before Parrish's arrival on earth.

Where had the funding come from, all these decades? Who had originally founded Amaranthine Potere? How was it sustained now? As far as she knew, there hadn't been any fund-raisers.

She did know that the Foundation had a very sophisticated computer system, far more sophisticated than she might have expected an archaeological foundation to have; after all, why should a list of contributors, assuming there was one, be either secret or sensitive? The Foundation was supposed to be nonprofit; presumably donations would be tax-deductible, so any list of contributors would be public anyway.

It would be nice if she could get into the system, just to see what she could find.

Doing so would require a hacker's skills, though, and she wasn't that good.

Kristian Sieber was.

As soon as the idea registered she discarded it. Not only was it dangerous to let anyone know where she was, but to involve Kris again was dangerous to him.

What could she possibly learn, anyway? A list of contributors, that's all. That wouldn't help her. It would be nice if she could learn Parrish's schedule . . .

She bit her lip. No. She wasn't going to call Kris.

Grace sat down and forced herself to return to the documents. After a moment, she was engrossed again.

There had always come a time, while she was studying a language, when suddenly her brain seemed to "get" it. She would struggle with syntax and verbs for months, then the accumulated knowledge and familiarity would reach critical mass, the synapses would connect, and presto! From one moment to the next she would pass from struggling to *reading,* the language opening up to her as if the letters had rearranged themselves from gibberish into real words.

Three minutes after she sat down, the old language synapses connected.

"The Guardian holds the Knowledge to bring down the Mother Church, and he Shall hold it Close, for the Power of our Lord God is Greater than the thought of Man, and so he Shall serve our Lord God all his days.

"To this End Shall he Journey through Time, his body Prepared by food and drink, and the Years shall be as nothing to him. Be it a Thousand years, yea, still he Shall go forth to Battle the Foundation of Evil, for he alone may wield the Power."

Journey through time? Grace blinked at the words. What was the Guardian supposed to be, a time traveler? She hadn't realized that bit of silliness had existed for so long. Medieval scholars hadn't even been able to grasp the concept of a round earth; they had still pictured dragons lurking around the edges, waiting to devour anyone foolish enough to fall off.

But evidently the Templars had not only believed it, they had devised a special diet to prepare the body for the trip. What else could the Diet of Time be?

Curiously, she pulled out the sheet on which she had translated the diet. At first glance, or second or third, there wasn't anything magical about it. First one precisely calculated one's weight by sitting in a barrel of water; ingenious of them, using water displacement as a measure. Then, according to one's weight, there was a formula for working out how much salt, calf's liver, and various other foods one must consume, and exactly how much water to drink.

It was a diet rich in sodium, iron, and all the trace minerals, she noted. Not a bad diet, except for the liver; that would be hell on a time traveler's cholesterol level.

She kept that page in her hand, and returned to the Gaelic documents.

"His body Prepared, he will then by striking Steel to Stone find the Spark of Lightning that will Carry him to the Chosen Time."

Grace almost choked. "What were you idiots trying to do?" she blurted, staring at the page. "Electrocute yourselves?" They had deliberately flooded their bodies with iron and water, then worked up some source of electricity. Who had been the guinea pigs for this experiment, and had anyone survived?

The rest of the page was mathematical formulas. Evidently, they had thought to control the number of years traveled by the amount of water drunk and the force of electricity applied. Interesting concept, but what had they known about electricity, much less controlling it?

She turned to the next page, and her blood ran cold.

"And the Evil one shall be called Parrish."

"Oh, my God," she whispered.

"Kris, this is Grace."

There was silence on the end of the line, then he said explosively, "Grace!"

"Shh," she cautioned. Nervously she twisted the steel cord of the pay phone, wondering once again if she had any right to involve Kris in this mess. She had been up most of the night, reading and rereading the documents, trying to apply common sense to the situation, but finally coming to the conclusion that extraordinary events called for extraordinary actions. Nothing about her life in the past eight months had been ordinary. Perhaps she would find something in the Foundation's computers, perhaps not, but she couldn't afford to leave any avenue unexplored.

"It's okay. Mom and Dad are in Florida. Where are you? Are you okay?"

"I'm fine," she said automatically. *Fine* was a relative term. She wasn't dead, she wasn't injured, she wasn't hungry. Physically, she supposed she was fine; emotionally was another story. "Did you have any trouble . . . after talking to me that time? Did Parrish or any of his men question you?"

"Maybe. I don't know," he said. "A detective came to the house that day, but he wasn't the one I'd talked to before. He showed me a badge, y'know, but how would I know if it looked the way it should? He asked me a lot of questions I'd already answered, and I stuck to the story. I'd worked on your modem, showed you a program I was working on, you paid me and left. That was all. You didn't mention anything about your work."

She breathed a sigh of relief. The "detective" could have been legitimate, and could also have been one of Parrish's men rechecking Kris's story. Kristian had pulled it off, protected by his computer wonk persona. No one meeting him would think him involved in anything beyond bytes and programs.

"Where are you?" he asked again.

"It's safer for you if you don't know."

"Yeah, well, so what?" He sounded older than before, tougher and more assured. "I know you didn't do it, so if you need help, all you have to do is ask."

His unquestioning faith hit her so hard that it was a moment before she could speak past the knot that formed in her throat.

"You'll be breaking the law if you help me." She felt compelled to warn him, because her conscience was still nagging at her for calling.

"I know," he said calmly. "I broke the law by not telling them everything I knew about that night, and I broke the law when I got into the bank's computers so you could get your money out. What's one more felony between friends?"

She took a deep breath. "All right. Is there any way you can get into the Foundation's computer system without setting off any alarms?"

"Sure," he said, completely confident. "I told you, there's always a back door. All I have to do is find it. But if it's a closed system, I'll have to go on-site to get in. Any problem there?"

Grace took a deep breath, trying to remember what she'd seen of the computer system the times she'd been in the Foundation's offices, which actually hadn't been that often. "I think it's a closed system."

"Are we going to do some midnight breaking and entering?" He sounded eager; Kris was a true hacker, willing to go to any lengths to perform his illegal art.

"No." Harmony hadn't given her any advice on getting

into a secured professional building without setting off its alarm system, but she had given her some pointers about hiding in plain sight. "We'll go in during the day, as part of the maintenance crew. I don't know how we'll get onto the floor without being seen, but we'll think of something."

"I keep telling you," Kris said. "There's always a back door."

Chapter 14

When Niall rode in from patrol, Sim met him with a worried expression. "Artair and Tearlach havena returned from hunting," he reported.

Niall looked at the darkening sky. The short winter day was fading fast, and the lowering gray clouds promised more snow. The wind whipped at his hair, blowing it across his face, and impatiently he tossed it back as he jumped from the horse.

"Bring Cinnteach," he ordered. The gelding was as steady as his name, and had the stamina of two horses.

"Done." Sim nodded to a stable lad approaching with the big bay. "I've had the other lads make ready, should ye want them also."

"Only you and Iver," Niall said. The two men were Creag Dhu's best archers, save himself. Perhaps he was foolhardy to take only two with him, but he was always mindful of leaving the castle well protected. Winter had cooled the Hay's raging blood feud with Creag Dhu; over a month had passed without attack. Still, Artair and Tearlach were both accomplished hunters, and could read the weather well; if naught was amiss, they would have returned by now.

Artair and Tearlach had gone out with the dawn, intent on a *fiadh,* a deer, whose tracks they had cut in the snow twice before, but the wily beast had escaped each time. Tearlach had slowed with age but was still the castle's best tracker. Artair had a gift for silence, Tearlach one for patience; they worked well together. Niall suspected Artair liked to hunt in winter because the wild, empty, snow-dusted mountains somehow reminded him of a cathedral, vaulted and holy. Creag Dhu had a chapel but no priest, for holy men sought safer duty than being confessor to wild renegades, and the chapel had long stood empty. Niall preferred no reminder of the Church or God, but Artair deeply felt the absence and sought his sanctuary in nature. He had thought it safe enough to replenish the castle's larder.

Niall rode out again five minutes later, having taken only enough time to wolf down a bit of bread and meat, and drink a cup of hot ale. The cold snapped at his face, but he was warm enough in wool and fur.

They rode in a slow circle about the castle, picking up Artair's and Tearlach's tracks where they went into the wood. The tracks were plain enough in the snow, and were easily followed.

Niall's head lifted, his nostrils flaring and his mouth grim as he surveyed the stark black and white wood. The snow deadened sound, so that they were surrounded by a silence unbroken except by the noise of their own passing, and that was slight enough. He sensed trouble, and there was a prickling between his shoulder blades.

"Ware," he said softly, and Sim and Iver moved apart from him, spreading out so that an ambush would be less likely to trap all three of them, and also that they might better use the cover available to them.

The day's patrolling had not revealed the tracks of either man or Highland pony coming onto Creag Dhu land, but if the Hay were determined enough, and sly enough, he could have sent in his men a day or more before the snow, and had them wait for their best opportunity. Given a small cave, Highlanders could easily survive the cold and snow in relative comfort. Hiding their mounts would be more difficult, and not even the Hay was stupid enough to send out his men afoot. They would also need running water.

"If any Hays are aboot, they'll be hard by the burn." He kept his voice low, but pitched it so both Sim and Iver could hear. They both nodded, their eyes moving restlessly, not pausing on any detail for more than a split second.

But Niall didn't sense any presence in the wood, despite his feeling of danger. He knew well when someone watched him, for he'd felt it often enough these past months. At times the eyes on him belonged to a Hay; other times, he knew it was *she,* the woman, the spirit. He didn't know why she watched or what she wanted, but ofttimes he could feel her gaze on him as he fought, feel her anxiety at his danger and her relief when he emerged victorious, and unscathed. Be damned if that wasn't less unsettling than sensing her near while he was abed with, and most like atop, a warm, willing woman. He was growing more and more irritable with her; if he ever got his hands on the wench, he'd be tempted to throttle her.

She watched him at the most inconvenient times, but now he rode through the darkening wood alone. Snowflakes swirled downward, brushing his face with their icy kiss. He could barely make out the tracks in the snow.

Cinnteach's ears pricked forward, and Niall held up a warning hand, slowing their approach. Naught moved before them, but the wind brought a scent, faint and unmistakable. Sim's mount shifted restlessly, tossing his head.

Niall dismounted, his right hand closing around the hilt of his sword. His acute senses felt the sudden brush of a gaze upon him, as definite as a touch, and he whirled to the side just as his ears caught the singing whisper of an arrow and sharp metal bit into his left shoulder with solid force.

He went down on his knee behind cover of a large tree. Looking around, he saw both Sim and Iver also behind cover, their faces grim as they watched him. He signaled that he was all right and motioned for them to change positions, moving out and forward to catch the intruders between them.

His shoulder burned like seven hells, but he had taken the precaution of wearing a silk undertunic, something he insisted all his men do. An arrow couldn't pierce silk, something all Templars knew. The most damage from an arrow didn't occur on entry, but when it was removed. If one was wearing silk, the fabric went into the wound and twisted around the arrowhead, preventing debris from entering the wound and causing infection, and also allowing the arrow to be safely removed by covering the barbs.

He reached inside his shirt, grasped the silk around the arrow, and jerked. The weapon popped free of his flesh, though not without effort. He ground his teeth against the pain; silk might lessen the severity of an arrow wound, but he reflected that it still wasn't pleasant. Fresh blood streamed down his shoulder, wetting his shirt.

Pain had always made him angry. His eyes narrowed until they were nothing more than midnight slits as he slid to the ground and crawled forward behind a fallen log. Every move jarred his shoulder and he became even angrier.

The snow was falling faster, almost obliterating what little light remained. Both Sim and Iver were in position now, waiting for a target, but nothing moved. Niall dug his fingers under the snow, searching for a cone or rock. A pebble would suffice, for a subtle noise would be more effective than a great crashing.

Ah, there; a cone, mushy with wet and rot. Without rising from behind the log he tossed the cone in the direction from whence the arrow had come and it landed with a soft scraping noise, as if a careless shoulder had brushed against a snow-laden branch and caused it to spill its burden.

An archer rose swiftly from behind a rock, bow drawn, hunter's eyes locked on the target area. That singing whisper came again, and Iver's arrow pierced the archer's neck. His nerveless fingers released the bow tension and the arrow sank into the dirt before him. Eyes widened, teetering on tiptoe, he clawed at his throat. A choked, gurgling sound issued from his mouth, followed by a rush of blood, and he collapsed in the snow.

From the other side Sim released an arrow. He had no definite target so he sent it flying into a thick bush capable of providing concealment. His guess was correct, because a cry of pain split the cold air.

Niall took advantage of the distraction to move yet again,

sliding behind another tree, much closer than he had been when caught by the arrow. His white teeth gleamed as he tilted back his head and loosed a bloodcurdling roar. He erupted from his cover like a lion springing for its prey. Four men sprang from concealment, startled by the bloody apparition that was suddenly upon them, huge sword flashing. One man managed to get his own sword up and metal rang against metal, but he went down under Niall's greater weight.

Sim and Iver each loosed one more arrow, then sprang forward screaming their own cries. Niall thrust his dagger up under his man's ribs and slashed sideways until he hit bone. The man arched and convulsed and Niall swung away from him, dropping to one knee under the rushing attack of a second foe and jabbing upward with the bloody dagger. The sharp metal sliced into the soft belly and Niall held the dagger steady while the man's momentum hurled him forward, eviscerating himself with his own motion.

Niall surged to his feet, but Sim and Iver had taken down their own men and only the three of them remained standing, panting softly, wisps of steam rising from their heads.

"Yer shoulder?" Iver asked, nodding at the wound.

"'Tis minor enough." That was true, but it burned like hell for all that. Niall strode furiously to reclaim his horse. He was certain now that he'd not find Artair and Tearlach alive. The Hay clansmen had planned well, skulking close and hiding until they could ambush those fewer in number than they, the whoreson cowards.

He found his men a minute later. Artair lay on his back, his blue eyes open and empty as he stared sightlessly upward. Niall dismounted and knelt beside his old friend, touching his face, lifting his hand. He was already cold, his limbs stiffening. The arrow had entered his heart.

He had not suffered, Niall thought, drawing Artair's plaid up to cover his face. His expression was almost peaceful, as if he'd at last quit a life in which he had no place.

"Adieu, mon ami," he whispered. French was the language in which he had been schooled as a Templar, and it was in that tongue he bid good-bye to his last friend from that time. They were all gone now, all the Knights who had

sought sanctuary at Creag Dhu. Some had died on the battlefield for Scotland, some had died natural deaths, others lived on in quiet places. Some had taken wives, had children; some still held to their vows. But they were Knights no longer; only he remained in service to the Order. It had been so for fourteen years, and yet so long as Artair had been with him he had felt the kinship. Now there was no one left at Creag Dhu who had even a glimmer of understanding.

"Tearlach lives," Sim said, pressing his tough, blunt fingers deep into the wounded man's neck. Surveying the amount of blood on the snowy ground, he shook his shaggy head. "He's near bled out, though. He'll no last 'til morn."

Niall stood and lifted Artair's body over his shoulder. "Perhaps," he said. "But if he dies, 'twill be among friends."

He sat alone in his chamber that night, unable to sleep, drinking raw spirits that burned down his throat. He was drunk, but the raw ale had done nothing to lift his mood. His shoulder throbbed; it had been rinsed with the same ale he drank, and bound with a poultice to draw out any putrefaction. He was hot with fever, but he didn't fear it; the fever had come soon after each wound he'd ever received, and he had noted that he seemed to heal faster than those whose fevers came on later. The wound had been clean, the ale fierce; in two days, he'd scarce feel a twinge in the shoulder.

The heat from the fireplace washed his bare shoulders and back. His plaid was draped about his hips, but except for that he was naked.

He stared across the chamber at nothing, his expression grim. Damn the Hays; if he had to wipe out the entire clan, rid the Highlands of their stinking presence, he would have vengeance for Artair. The time would come soon enough, when winter lifted its icy hand from the mountains.

But for now he was drunk, feverish, and alone with his thoughts. There was no one watching, no one near, when he needed to feel her with him.

He closed his eyes, aching inside with the loneliness. For all his life he had been forced to hide parts of himself from the world. Always his kinship with the Bruce had been hidden, even before the Bruce was king. Later, with the Knights, he had been forced to deny his own nature, though he had gone to sleep every night with his arms and loins aching with need. Now he could give free rein to his lusts, but he must hold secret his years as a Knight, though those eight years had done much to shape him into the man he was now. Even from Robert, who knew all those things, he must conceal his true role as Guardian, and the cursed vow that ruled his life.

Only with *her* was there nothing to hide. Whoever and whatever she was, he sensed that she knew him as no one else had ever done, knew his body bone-deep and his mind even when he slept. When he took her in his arms, when she came to him in the dark silence of the night, she knew all of the man he was and still she clung to him, offering her body and herself.

Niall inhaled through his teeth as lust hit him hard. He wanted her, but not in a dream. He wanted her real and warm under his hands, her sweet scent fresh in his nostrils as he took her.

He could almost feel her, his longing was so sharp. His hands curled into fists, trying to capture the sensation of her silky skin under his palms.

The fever and ale and longing combined, and suddenly she was there, her hands sliding lightly over his bare shoulders. He felt her concern as she touched the pad covering his wound, but her concern wasn't what he wanted. Fiercely he caught her to him, and held her on his lap while he stripped away the small scraps of clothing that were all she wore. He couldn't quite see her face, but she was here and that was all that mattered. He put his hand on her cool belly, warming her with his touch, feeling the muscles beneath contract as she drew in her breath. Her small nipples beaded, as he had known they would. She responded to his slightest touch; he knew that if he slid his fingers between her legs to the delicate opening hidden there, he would find it wet, ready for him.

Instead he smoothed his hand up to her breasts, cupping them, rubbing his thumb over her nipples, then bending his dark head to take the tightened buds in his mouth and gently suck. She shivered in his arms, trying to press closer to him. Such lovely, plump little things her breasts were, small and delightfully round, so delicate and sensitive he knew it would pain her if he handled them roughly as some women liked. She was more finely made than any woman he had ever known, both fragile and strong, her skin like translucent silk.

He couldn't wait any longer. He needed her too much. Swiftly he turned her, laying her back on the bench. He shoved his plaid aside and straddled the bench, spreading her thighs open and moving between them. He watched as he entered her, his thick shaft too large, too brutish, for the soft flesh that stretched under his pressure, but she took him, her back arching, her cries those of pleasure. He gritted his teeth as the tightness of her sheath enveloped him and he crouched over her, thrusting long and slow and deep, almost delirious with fever and drink and the sensations boiling through him, but needing her so much he couldn't stop. Her arms curled around his neck and he felt her passion matching his, her need as great as his, her acceptance of everything he was; and he knew he wasn't alone anymore—

But he was.

His eyes opened and the fantasy shattered. He sat there, breathing hard as he silently cursed her. Damn her for taunting him like this, tantalizing him with a whisper of her presence, then disappearing when he needed her most. His aloneness crashed down on him and he hunched his shoulders against the burden. His head dropped down on his chest and he closed his eyes, trying to regain her presence, but it was gone as if she had never been there at all.

"So where are ye now, lass?" he murmured.

Grace bolted out of bed, grabbing for the pistol. Someone had spoken right beside her, the voice almost in her ear. She stood with her back against the wall and the pistol locked in a two-handed grip, swinging from point to point in search of a target, but nothing was there. The room was empty, dark, lit only by the streetlights filtering through the drawn curtains.

She sagged back, gasping. A dream. Only a dream, and for once not of Niall—or was it? The voice that had jerked her awake had been deep, burred, and she'd heard the word *lass.*

Yes. Niall. She closed her eyes, breathing deep and slow in an effort to calm her racing heart. After a few moments she was more relaxed, but far from drowsy, and she mentally replayed that voice in her ear.

Deep, whiskey-rough, burred. Not the smooth voice of a practiced seducer, but that of a man used to command: completely self-assured, determined. And yet he'd asked, very quietly, "So where are ye now, lass?" as if he truly needed her—

Grace's eyes opened again, widening. She had been dreaming, after all; she remembered a snippet now, of Black Niall sitting quietly before a fire. But something was different, as if it wasn't her dream at all, something outside herself that had drawn her in.

More and more of the dream unfolded itself. She saw him alone, half naked, with only his plaid draped loosely about his hips. He had evidently been injured, for a rough bandage was wrapped about his left shoulder, the linen pale against his olive-toned skin. Fear licked at her and she wanted to go to him, assure herself he was all right.

A metal cup was in his hand. He was drinking, staring at nothing, his expression somber. His loneliness, his absolute *aloneness,* made her ache inside. Then he closed his eyes and abruptly she was there, in his arms, lying naked on his lap while he fondled and sucked gently at her breasts.

Grace trembled at the memory that wasn't quite a memory, was more than a memory. Somehow she was lying on the bench and he was crouched over her, his face tense as he thrust again and again. The pleasure rose beating inside her, and she reached up to twine her arms around his strong neck, almost weeping with joy.

And then, nothing. He was gone, the dream ended, with only his murmured, "So where are ye now, lass?" echoing in her mind, as if she should have been there, tending his wound, offering him the comfort women have always offered warriors.

She felt a wrench of regret that she hadn't been there.

The image of him was sharp and clear in her mind. He sat with his back to the fire and the golden light had glistened on his bare shoulders, broad and powerful with muscle, and a halo limned his long black hair. Equally black hair spread across his chest, and a thin, silky line of it ran down his washboard stomach to the small, taut circle of his navel. His long legs were thick with muscle, the most powerful legs she had ever seen on a human, the delineation of his musculature built on the rock-solid strength produced by a lifetime of swordplay and battle, of controlling a huge stallion with the strength in his thighs, wearing more than a hundred pounds of armor and actually *fighting* in it. His was the body of a warrior, honed into a weapon, a tool.

But he was still just a man, she thought with aching tenderness. He bled, he ached, he sat alone and got drunk and grumpily wondered why some woman wasn't dancing attendance on him. It was her imagination that made her dream he'd been speaking only to her.

If he had been . . . if she were actually with him . . . She would get him to lie down in bed, make him more comfortable. He was probably a bit feverish; a cold cloth on his brow would make him feel better. She didn't doubt, however, that he would be a terrible patient. Instead of resting he would insist she lie down with him, and soon his hands would be roaming under her shirt—

"Damn it!" Grace moaned, pressing her hands to her eyes. Her breath was coming soft and fast, and she felt warm, liquid. Her nipples were tight and erect, pushing against the thin fabric of her T-shirt. It was bad enough that she sometimes had erotic dreams about him, but it was a far worse betrayal of Ford that she daydreamed about Black Niall, too.

The pistol was still in her hand, cold against her temple. Carefully she replaced it and thought about getting back into bed, but she was wide awake. She glanced at the clock. Why, it wasn't even eleven o'clock yet; she'd been asleep less than an hour. Long enough, however, for Niall to take over her subconscious.

For eight months she had been dead inside, and she wanted to remain that way. There hadn't been any laughter, any sunshine, any appreciation of a deep blue sky or the drama of a storm. It was safer that way, easier; if she hadn't been numb, she couldn't have survived. She didn't want any sign of returning life because it would only weaken her. In eight months she hadn't yet been able to weep, even tears held at bay by the bleak ice surrounding her. Niall was a crack in that wall of ice; one day it would collapse, and so would she.

She couldn't afford the weakness he represented. She had to hurry with those damn Gaelic papers, get them finished and out of her mind so Black Niall would cease to plague her. If she could get some measure of revenge against Parrish, perhaps her mind would ease and she could begin to heal, and her subconscious would then no longer need to cling to the dream image.

Well, sleep was definitely out of the question. Groaning, knowing she needed to rest because tomorrow she and Kris planned to break into the Foundation's computer system; instead she turned on a light. Her mind was racing; until she calmed, she might as well use the time to work.

She didn't bother getting out the laptop, just took her notepad and the remaining Gaelic papers and curled up in the room's one armchair, a cracked vinyl job she had made more comfortable by throwing a sheet over it. She could still hear the creaking and crackling of the vinyl, but at least now the chair didn't stick to her.

She picked up a page and groaned. More mathematical formulas, though, thank God, they were in Latin. Her brows rose in surprise. This was the first time two languages had been mixed in one section. The handwriting was different, too, heavier, plainer. She scribbled the formulas on her notepad, translating them into English. "For twenty years, the proportion of water to weight shall be . . ." On and on it went, giving the precise fractions for, supposedly, targeting the year to which one wanted to travel. Also included was the voltage of energy required, or at least she thought that was what it was; they hadn't had any knowledge of electricity other than watching lightning bolts, so what exactly had they been measuring? Energy, yes, but what kind?

Still, she copied it all down, yawning as she did so. It was like copying down a complicated recipe, though not half as interesting. If anything was going to put her to sleep, this would do it.

She began reading aloud to herself, droning the words.

" 'For DCLXXV years'—let's see, *D* is five hundred years, the *C* is after it so that adds another hundred, *L* is fifty, the two *X*'s after it add ten years each, and then a *V,* which is five. Six hundred and seventy-five years. Getting pretty precise there, aren't you?" she muttered to the long-ago writer.

Absently, she subtracted six hundred seventy-five from 1997, just to see what year a current time traveler would end up in, using this exact formula: 1322. "A wonderful year," she said, yawning. "I remember it well." What a coincidence; 1322 would have been in Black Niall's time.

She turned the page, ready for more math. She blinked at the words, wondering if she was sleepier than she had thought, or perhaps had somehow gotten a sheet that didn't belong mixed up with the Gaelic papers.

She read the words again, and chills ran over her entire body. "No," she said softly. "It's impossible."

But there it was, in Gaelic, and in the same heavy hand that had written the mathematical formulas:

"Require ye proof? In the Year of Our Lord 1945, the Guardian slew the German beast, and so came Grace to Creag Dhu. —Niall MacRobert, y. 1322."

She became aware she was panting, and a shudder wracked her. The page swam before her eyes, the words blurring. The term *German* hadn't existed in the thirteen hundreds.

How could someone who lived in the fourteenth century have knowledge of something that happened in the twentieth? It was impossible—unless the formula truly worked.

Unless they had known how to travel through time.

Chapter 15

KRIS DIDN'T RECOGNIZE HER. THEY HAD ARRANGED TO MEET outside a supermarket late the next afternoon, and Grace had arrived more than an hour early so she could watch for anything suspicious. She hated not feeling able to trust Kris completely, but there was too much at stake for her to take anything for granted.

She watched Kris arrive in his beloved '66 Chevelle, the engine rumbling with a muscular cough that had a couple of middle-aged men throwing envious glances his way. Poor Kris. He wanted female attention, but instead his car was attracting the male variety. At least he'd done some additional work on the Chevelle since she had last seen it; it was actually painted now, a bright fire-engine red.

He parked at the end of a lane and waited. There hadn't been any suspicious, repetitious traffic during the hour Grace had been watching, but still she waited. After fifteen more minutes had passed she slid out of the truck and crunched across the thin layer of snow that had fallen on the parking lot since she arrived. It was still snowing lightly, lacy flakes swirling and dancing in the wind. She went up to the Chevelle and tapped on the window.

Kris rolled the window down a couple of inches. "Yeah, what is it?" he asked, a little impatiently.

"Hi, Kris," she said, and his eyes widened with shock.

He scrambled out of the car, slipping a little and grabbing the door to right himself. "My God," he mumbled. "My God."

"It's a wig," she said. She wore a blond one, plus a baseball cap and sunglasses. Add losing more than thirty pounds, and no one who had known her before would have recognized her.

Kris's stupefied gaze started at her booted feet, went up her tight jeans, took in the denim jacket, and ended once again on her face. His mouth opened, but no sound came out. The tip of his nose turned red. "My God," he said again. Abruptly he lunged at her and wrapped both arms around her, holding her tight and rocking her back and forth. Grace's nerves had been on edge for too long; her first instinct, barely restrained, was to kick his feet out from under him. But then he made a strangled sound, his shoulders shook, and she realized he was crying.

"Shh," she said gently, putting her own arms around him. "It's all right." It felt odd to let someone touch her, and to touch someone in return. She had gone so long without physical contact that she felt both awkward and starved.

"I've been so scared," he said into her baseball cap, his voice shaking. "Not knowing if you were okay, if you had a place to stay—"

"Sometimes yes, sometimes no," she said, patting his back. "The first week was the worst. Do you think we can get in the car? I don't want to attract attention."

"What? Oh! Sure." He trudged around the car to open the passenger door for her, a courtesy that touched her. He was still thin and gangly, his glasses still slid toward the end of his nose, but in several small ways she could see the advance of maturity. His shoulders looked a tad heavier, his voice had lost some of its boyishness, even his stubble was a little thicker. Manhood would suit him a lot better than boyhood;

when other men his age were fighting middle-age spread, Kris would still be lean.

He slid under the wheel and slammed the door, then turned to survey her. His eyes were still wet, but now he shook his head in wonderment. "I wouldn't have known you," he admitted in awe. "You—you're *tiny.*"

"Thin," she corrected. "I'm as tall as I always was. Taller," she said, pointing at the inch-and-a-half heels of her boots.

"Cool," he said, eyeing them and blinking hard. He glanced at his own feet, and she thought he might soon become a boot man. There was nothing like boots to give a man attitude. Or a woman, come to that; she definitely walked with more authority when she wore the boots.

Then he looked back at her face, and she saw his lower lip wobble again. "You look tired," he blurted.

"I couldn't sleep last night." That was the unvarnished truth. She hadn't been able to close her eyes after reading that little note from Black Niall. Every time she thought of it she felt her spine prickle, and chills would roughen her skin. But after the initial shock, it wasn't the bit about 1945 that was so eerie, it was the phrase "and so came Grace to Creag Dhu." Surely he meant a state of grace, but it felt so—personal, somehow, something written specifically to *her.* She felt as if he were inviting her to use the formula, to step through the layers of time energy. His calculations had been very specific, for exactly six hundred seventy-five years; back to the year 1322, the year the message had been written.

Kris reached out and took her gloved hand, squeezed it. "Where have you been?"

"On the move. I haven't stayed in one place for long."

"The police—"

"It isn't the police I worry about so much as Parrish's men. At least the police aren't actively hunting me, not after this length of time. Sure, they'll follow a lead, but that's about it. Parrish's men nearly caught me once."

"It's so weird," he said, shaking his head. "Do you still think it's because of those papers you had?"

"I *know* it was." She stared out the window, which was

fogging up from their breathing. "I translated them. I know exactly why he wants them."

Kris clenched his hands into fists, staring at her delicate profile. He wanted to take her somewhere and feed her, he wanted to tuck a blanket around her, he wanted—he wanted to punch something. She looked so frail. Yeah, that was it. Frail.

Grace had always been a special person to him; he'd known her most of his life, had a crush on her since he was seventeen. She had always been so nice to him, treating him as an equal when most adults didn't. Grace was a genuinely good person, smart and kind, and her mouth, oh her mouth made him feel all hot and dizzy-headed. He'd dreamed of kissing her but never worked up the nerve. It was lousy of him, but when she had called the day before, he had thought again of kissing her, and even thought that it would be okay now because Ford was dead. But looking at her he knew it wasn't okay, might never be okay. She was quiet and sad and distant, and that mouth didn't look as if it ever smiled.

He pulled himself away from his thoughts and reached into the backseat to grab a computer printout. "Here," he said, placing it on her lap. He might not ever kiss her, but he would do what he could to help her. "It's a blueprint of the building where the Foundation is headquartered."

Grace pulled off her sunglasses and put them on the dash. "Where did you get this?" she asked in surprise, flipping through the pages.

"Well, it's a fairly new building," he explained. "A copy of the plans are on file with the city planners, I guess in case of emergencies and stuff."

She gave him a sideways glance. "So you went to city hall and got a copy?"

"Not exactly. I got it out of their computers," he said blithely.

"Without setting off any alarms, I hope."

"Oh, please," he scoffed. "It was a joke."

There was no point in scolding him about it; after all, she was asking him to commit a much more serious crime than computer hacking. "Getting into the Foundation's computers won't be as easy," she warned.

"No, but I've already got it figured out. Your idea about

the maintenance crew was great. We steal a couple of the uniforms, waltz right in. But all we need is to get into the building, we don't need to actually get into the Foundation's offices. Look," he said, pointing to the blueprint. "Here is the service elevator. We take it to the floor below, then use this access panel in the ceiling to get to the electronic panel. I tap into a line, pull up a file list, and we go from there."

"What about alarms?"

"Well, it's a self-contained system, so they don't have to worry about anyone hacking in; certain files may be security-coded, but not the system itself. My job is to get the coded files."

He made it sound so easy, but she didn't expect the Foundation's files to be as vulnerable as the city's. Parrish was too smart, too wily, and he had too much to hide. "There has to be a list of the passwords for any coded files, but it could be anywhere. Parrish may keep it in his house, or there could be a safe in the offices where it would be kept. Either way, we won't be able to get it."

He shook his head, grinning. "You'd be surprised how many people keep a list of passwords in their desk. It's worth a look, anyway, once we're certain everyone has gone home."

"I have some ideas about the passwords," she said. "We'll try those first." She shuddered at the idea of going into the empty offices and finding they weren't empty after all, but that Parrish had worked late. Hearing his voice on the telephone had been bad enough; she didn't think she could bear actually seeing him. Still, if it became necessary to break into his private office, she would do it. Kris would be willing, but she wasn't willing to let him; she had already involved him enough.

"Okay," he said, practically twitching in his enthusiasm. "Let's go."

"Now?"

"Why not?"

Why not, indeed. There was no reason to wait, not if they could manage to liberate a couple of uniforms from the maintenance service. "Do you have your laptop?" she asked.

"In the backseat."

She shrugged. "Then we might as well give it a try. We'll go in my truck."

"Why?" He looked a bit affronted at her reluctance to travel in the Chevelle.

"This car is a little noticeable," she pointed out, her tone dry.

A grin broke across his face. "Yeah, it is, isn't it?" he said, giving the dash a fond pat. "Okay." He got the laptop out of the backseat and took the keys from the ignition. Grace grabbed her sunglasses. They got out and locked the doors, and they trudged across the slippery parking lot to her pickup.

They were silent as Grace drove. She tried to come up with some feasible plan for getting the maintenance uniforms, but none occurred to her. And there was still security at the building after office hours; perhaps the maintenance service had a key to the rear service door, perhaps not. After cleaning houses for six months, she knew some people without thought turned over a spare key to the cleaning service so they wouldn't be inconvenienced by having to be at home when their houses were cleaned. Grace was always amazed at their lack of caution. Still, it happened. Unless Parrish owned the entire building, the chances were fifty-fifty the maintenance crew could enter without ringing for a guard. If Parrish owned the building, no way; he wouldn't care if the crew had to wait, or that a guard had to trudge from wherever he was in the building to let them in. He wouldn't even consider their inconvenience in the security scheme.

With what she had learned in the past eight months, Grace had to admit he was right. If you had something worth protecting, you protected it, and you didn't compromise security by fretting about whether or not the maintenance crew had to wait a couple of minutes. Of course, a sophisticated system would use closed-circuit cameras to identify the crew, and the door would be opened by remote control—

Cameras.

She drew in her breath with a hiss. "We're going about this all wrong."

"We are?" Kris asked blankly. "What do you mean?"

"There may be security cameras at the maintenance entrance. How are we going to waltz up to the truck and search it for extra uniforms?"

He rubbed his chin, his long, skinny fingers rasping over his beard stubble as he went into his thinking mode. "Let's see . . . okay. First thing, you let me out a block away and I'll check it out. If there *are* cameras, then we have to find out if they're closed-circuit and are being monitored, or if they're just the kind that tapes so someone can watch the tape after a crime has already been committed."

"Either way, if there are cameras, that means you need a disguise too," Grace said firmly.

He looked taken with that idea, and her heart ached at his youth.

"You'll have to take off your glasses," she decided. "I'll wear them instead. And we'll beef you up by stuffing towels in your uniform."

He looked doubtful. "I won't be able to see," he objected. "And neither will you."

That made sense. One of them had to be able to navigate. She plucked her sunglasses out of her pocket and handed them to him. "Pop the lenses." She had paid fifty cents for them at a yard sale, so she didn't hesitate to ruin them.

Kris obediently popped out the plastic lenses, and gave the frames back to her. Grace slid them on, and glanced at herself in the rearview mirror. At close range it was fairly obvious there was no glass in the frames, but a security camera wouldn't detect it.

"We really should have scouted this out and maybe taken the time to buy our own maintenance uniforms," she said, shrugging. "But it might work anyway."

It worked.

Kris came jogging back to the truck, his face red from both excitement and exposure to the cold. He climbed in, gasping, and his glasses immediately fogged up. He snatched them off and absently held them in front of the heat vent while he gave her a myopically triumphant smile. "There's a camera," he reported breathlessly. "But it isn't closed-circuit."

"How do you know?"

"I checked it out."

"Kris!"

"No problem. It's in a corner, aimed at the maintenance door. I slipped around the side of the building and stayed out of its range. I didn't see any cable wires running from the camera into the building. And even better—" He paused, grinning at her.

"What?" she demanded impatiently when he let the pause drag out, and he laughed delightedly.

"The door is propped open!"

It was obvious Parrish and the Foundation didn't own the building, Grace thought.

"It's the kind of door that locks every time it closes," Kris explained. "I guess the maintenance crew gets tired of having to unlock it every time, so they dragged one of those rubber-backed mats over the threshold, and it keeps the door from completely closing."

Oh, the simple, elegant ingenuity of people trying to get out of a little inconvenience. With that one act, they had negated the building's security.

"We still need uniforms."

He grinned triumphantly at her. "There's a big van parked there. I checked it out. The front doors are locked, and there's a steel screen separating the cab from the back of the van, I guess so they can leave the back doors open and not have to worry about the van being stolen. Anyway, there's lots of stuff in the back, and some dirty coveralls." He slid his glasses into place. "What more do we need?"

What more, indeed?

The camera outside the service door wasn't closed-circuit. The one in the hallway was.

Parrish watched as two more maintenance people entered the building. His eyebrows had lifted a fraction when the first crew had propped open the door. For now it suited his purposes to let it remain open, to give Grace an easy access should she take the bait, but as soon as he had her he would make certain the owners of the building found a new maintenance service. Of course, the Foundation's offices had far more stringent security measures, but that didn't excuse the sloppiness of the present crew.

These two latest arrivals carried tool boxes, and wore tool

belts strapped over their shapeless coveralls. One was a skinny woman, wearing an unattractive baseball cap over her unattractive frizzy hair. Oversized glasses dominated her face. The man was tall, pudgy, clumsy. He wore gloves and a weird fur hat with ear flaps, and he didn't seem to know where he was going. The woman led the way as they trudged down the short hall to the service elevator.

He wasn't interested in them. He watched carefully for the little mouse he hoped would nibble at his bait. Perhaps she wouldn't come; if she had seen him do the shooting, she wouldn't want to be anywhere near him, unless of course she planned to shoot him in revenge, but he was certain Grace wasn't a woman who could kill. He could recognize the killer instinct in certain people; Conrad, for instance. Grace didn't have it.

On the other hand, she had surprised him and everyone else by being able to elude both the cops and his best men for more than eight months. She had proven herself to be unusually resourceful. If she hadn't called the Foundation, no one would have had any idea she was back in Minneapolis. Shocking mistake. But then, felons often tripped themselves up by returning to the scene of their crime, perhaps to gloat at their own cleverness.

But Grace had called the Foundation, himself specifically, and since she hadn't spoken, the only reason would have been to find out if he was in town. Now that she knew he was, what would she do? Show up at his house to talk to him? She could have talked on the phone, unless she suddenly panicked at the thought of giving away her whereabouts.

So had she seen him or not? Did she want to talk or shoot? Perverse of him, but he rather hoped it was the latter. The thought of Grace with a gun in her hand was strangely exciting. She would never get to use it, of course, but he didn't want her weepy and weak in his arms; he wanted her furious, fighting, so that his victory was all the sweeter when, as with Calla, his skill overrode her anger. His little interlude with Calla had been unusually satisfying; surely with Grace his pleasure would be even more intense.

Would she come or not? The service door was conveniently propped open, but perhaps she would try to enter during the day, when she could more easily mix with the flow of people coming and going.

He waited patiently.

"Here we are," Kris whispered excitedly as he opened the access panel in the ceiling of the Foundation's main computer room. It was quiet, dim, with only the hum of electronics breaking the silence.

It had taken them an hour to work their way into place. Nothing was ever as easy as it looked on paper. First they had had to dodge the real maintenance crew, finally climbing seventeen flights of stairs instead of using the service elevator. After locating the access panel to the overhead heating ducts, they climbed onto a high stool and managed to hoist themselves inside, putting the panel back in place so no one would know they were there. Then, using a flashlight taken from her glove box, they navigated the miles of ductwork only to find they had to go into the Foundation's offices after all. They located the computer room and listened for a while, but the room seemed empty. Carefully they removed the ceiling access panel.

Kris leaned his head and shoulders out of the opening and looked around. "There aren't any cameras," he whispered. "But there's a window in the door, so we'll need to sit where anyone passing by can't see us."

"If we happen to be climbing in or out when someone walks by, we're sunk," Grace said. It couldn't be helped, though; they had no access through any of the doors, so it had to be the ceiling.

Kris braced his arms on each side of the opening and slowly lowered himself through it until he was hanging by his fingers. The ceilings were standard eight feet, for easy heating; with his arms outstretched, he had little more than a foot to drop. He landed quietly on the tile floor, then turned for Grace to hand down the laptop. With that safely stored, he held up his arms for her as she swung down from the ceiling, catching her around the waist and carefully setting her on the floor.

He looked swiftly around, sizing up the setup. This was his milieu, and his thin face glowed with eagerness. "Sit over there, behind that desk," he said, pointing. "Let me get this hooked up and I'll join you." As he spoke he was busy removing cords and wires from a terminal, and rehooking them to his laptop. That done, he repositioned some operating manuals to block any view of their heads, which would be sticking up above the edge of the desk.

He flopped down beside her and drew his long legs up, cradling the laptop between them. He fingered a switch and the powerful little machine began to hum and make discreet little chirps as it booted up. They had been crossing their fingers on this, because Kris used the Windows 95 operating system; if the Foundation used DOS, he wouldn't be able to use his laptop. Instead he would have to sit at a monitor, and given the window in the door that would be risky. But the Foundation used the same operating system, and the menu flashed on the screen.

"Okay, let's see the files," he murmured, rubbing his fingertip across the little mouse tucked in the middle of the keyboard and directing the cursor to the correct icon. He clicked once, and the screen filled with file names.

He scrolled down while they looked for something interesting. "Let's look at the financial statement and tax returns," she said, and he pulled up those files. They were incredibly complicated; they didn't have time to decipher everything, so he copied the files onto a floppy and returned to the list.

"Donor list," Grace directed, and he copied that file too.

There was little else that looked interesting; they looked into the payroll file, and Grace gasped at what Parrish was paid. Millions. The Foundation paid him *millions* every year. Just for directing the Foundation? She was certain the Foundation could find an able overseer for much less money, if that was all that was needed.

"Nothing much here," Kris said after an hour of pulling up individual files and checking their contents. "What were those ideas you had on passwords? Let's try a few of them and see what happens."

"Treasure," she directed, and he gave her a sharp glance as he obediently typed in the word and clicked on "Retrieve."

File Not Found.

"Temple."

File Not Found.

"Knight."

File Not Found.

"Templar."

"You mean those bad-ass monks you were reading about at my house that night?" Kris asked, typing the word.

"The very same."

File Not Found.

"Damn," she breathed. She was running out of likely passwords. "Guardian."

File Not Found.

"Niall . . . Pope . . . Temple Treasure. Whose bright idea was it to allow unlimited space in naming files? Let's see . . . he's egotistical enough to name a file after himself. Try Parrish and Sawyer."

File Not Found popped up on the screen after every entry. Kris had been silent except for asking her how to spell Niall.

"Power," she suggested.

He typed. "Nope."

"Shroud . . . Turin . . . Covenant . . . Ark."

He shook his head after each entry. "Nope."

Grace rubbed the back of her neck. The Ark of the Covenant had been way out in left field anyway. She had only thought of it because of the Indiana Jones movie, where the Nazis had been trying to find the Ark and conquer the world. There had been a seed of truth in the movie, because Hitler had indeed been obsessed with acquiring ancient religious artifacts.

"In the Year of Our Lord 1945, the Guardian slew the German beast, and so came Grace to Creag Dhu."

She remembered the entry, and once again chills roughened her skin. Creag Dhu couldn't be the password, because the location of the Treasure was what Parrish didn't know. "Hitler," she suggested.

Again Kris gave her a startled look, but he typed in the name.

The screen filled with words.

She sat back, stunned. It couldn't be. She hadn't even

considered a connection, despite the document's warnings about the Foundation of Evil.

"My God," Kris whispered. Hastily he shoved another floppy into the disk drive and copied the file without taking time to read it. Only when the file was copied and the disk safely stored did he slowly scroll downward.

"They really think they can rule the world if they find this so-called treasure," he whispered. What they were reading was nothing less than a manifesto, a declaration of intent. "The papers you have supposedly give the location of it, right? And he's actually killed Ford and Bryant just because they *knew* about the papers?" Outrage and disbelief warred in his tone.

She looked at him. Her gaze was glassy from shock. "They do," she said dazedly. "Give the location, that is."

"Holy shit," he whispered. Then his eyes widened and he looked nervously at the screen. "I guess I shouldn't say that, huh?"

A door closed in the hallway.

They froze. After a split second, Kris hurriedly pulled the lid down so the computer was almost closed, to hide the glow of the screen. There was only a whisper of sound outside the door; whoever it was moved very quietly. But the footsteps moved on without pause, and after a moment came the sound of another door closing in the hallway.

"We gotta get out of here," Kris muttered. "You got any more ideas on passwords?"

She shook her head. He swiftly exited the file, backed out of the program, and shut off the laptop. Within a minute he had reconnected the other terminal and replaced the manuals in their original position.

He crawled over to the door and poked his head up just enough to peer out the window, checking in both directions. "It's clear," he whispered, standing up and hurriedly crossing the room.

Grace dragged a chair beneath the access panel and climbed onto the seat. First she stowed the laptop and the disks in the duct, then she levered herself through the hole. Kris assisted with a boost from beneath.

She turned to reach down and grab the collar of his coveralls, half dragging him through the hole. They were both panting as they replaced the access panel and switched on the flashlight. In silence they retraced their path, both of them thinking about what they had read.

"She isn't coming tonight," Parrish told Conrad, disappointment evident in his tone. "It's midnight; she wouldn't expect me to work this late."

Conrad didn't reply. He watched the screen as two of the maintenance crew came down the hallway and left by the propped-open door. They appeared to be hurrying, and the woman was carrying some kind of satchel.

She was small, and had frizzy blond hair. The angle of the camera wasn't good, but something about her jawline was familiar.

A growl rumbled in his throat, and Parrish lifted questioning eyebrows. "That was her!" Conrad said, already running when he hit the door.

Parrish was right behind him when he burst out the service door and ran down the short alley to the street. He looked both ways, but the sidewalks were empty. A car went by; the driver was a suited young black man, probably a junior executive who had been burning the midnight oil.

A block or so away, an engine coughed to life. Conrad ran down the sidewalk toward the sound, his shoes slipping on the snowy sidewalk. His breath fogged in the frigid air. He reached the corner in time to see a set of taillights disappear around another corner.

"Did you see her?" Parrish gasped, coming to a stop beside him. "What kind of car was it?"

"I couldn't tell," Conrad said. "But the woman was Grace St. John. She was carrying a small satchel, perhaps a computer case."

"Computer!" Parrish felt his blood pressure rise. "God damn it, the bitch has been in our files!" He and Conrad hurried back to the office, shivering as the cold bit through their clothes. She wouldn't have been able to get into his password files, but it infuriated him that she had slipped past his guard, that she had been so close all that time and he hadn't known it. Damn the little bitch, how did she do it?

"Who was her friend, I wonder?" Who could she have found to help her? She wouldn't contact people who had known her before, because she couldn't be certain their first phone call wouldn't be to the police. It had to have been someone she had met afterward.

"Perhaps that is why we couldn't find her," Conrad suggested. "We have been looking for a woman alone, instead of a couple."

The idea infuriated Parrish. He ground his teeth as they walked swiftly to the computer room and he opened the door. Everything looked normal, except for a chair that was out of place.

Conrad pointed at the ceiling. Directly over the chair, a panel was slightly out of place.

"Find her," Parrish said in an almost soundless whisper. She had been there, so close; she had taunted him, coming there with another man. He didn't know yet if she had actually found anything of use in his computer system, but just the fact that she had dared invade it made him shake with rage. "Find both of them. And kill them."

Chapter 16

GRACE'S SECOND SLEEPLESS NIGHT IN A ROW MADE HER EYESIGHT blur, but she couldn't stop reading parts of the Hitler file over and over, couldn't get it out of her mind even when she laid it aside. She kept coming back to it, rereading it to assure herself she hadn't imagined any of it.

The Foundation had been founded in 1802 by a strange assortment of men; Napoleon Bonaparte had been one of the original members, perhaps the most important one and the moving force behind the forming of the organization. Certainly he had been the only one at that time who had ambitions to conquer the world. A grandiose scheme, on the surface of things, but not so unexpected when the entire picture was seen.

The Hitler file gave a different and disturbing look at well-known history. In 1799, Napoleon invaded Turkish Syria, advancing as far as the fortress of Acre. He hadn't managed to take the fortress, which the Templars had built in 1240, but perhaps he had heard something there, or found something. It was after he returned from Acre that his ambition had become full-blown; he had immediately made himself dictator of France, and then Emperor. He conquered Spain, Italy, Switzerland, Holland, Poland, attacked Russia and Austria.

Perhaps a lot of men wanted to rule the world, but few, luckily, really tried to do it or even thought they could. Napoleon had thought it possible; his intention was plainly stated in the Hitler file. He had launched an all-out search for the lost Templar Treasure, certain that when he found it he would be unstoppable, for it was promised in the papers: he who controls the Power controls the world. What was the Power? Not gold, but certainly something tangible, such as the Ark of the Covenant. Whatever it was, the Foundation believed it controlled unimaginable power, and for almost two centuries the Foundation had devoted all its resources to finding the Treasure.

There were three distinct levels within the Foundation. At the lower level were the employees, paper pushers or hired muscle. The center tier was made up of "contributors," people who were members of the Foundation and who contributed large amounts of money to it, whether by choice or coercion. From what she read, coercion was most common. At the top level were relatively few names; she recognized most of them. Napoleon. Stalin. Hitler. Two American presidents. A Middle East dictator. A French general. A British prime minister. A famous labor leader. Tycoons, both male and female. One name particularly surprised her, for he was an extremely wealthy man known for his humanitarian works. And Parrish Sawyer. His name seemed minor compared to the fame of the others, but they hadn't been famous at the beginning of their careers, either. The presence of his name on the list was a testament to his ruthlessness.

The power to rule the world. The concept was far more ridiculous now than it had been no more than fifty years before. How could any one person, or Foundation, rule the entire world? But when she looked at it in terms of national power and influence, something most nations lacked, it was indeed possible to control the world by controlling key nations. A political takeover wouldn't even be necessary, so long as the politicians obeyed the money men. Media, banking, commerce—take control of those three elements, and one did indeed control the world. World rule wasn't measured in terms of military conquest, but in economic ones.

To rule the world was a strange ambition, reasonable only to the megalomaniac personality. What was unusual was that so many of these men had joined the Foundation, for by their very personalities each would have thought himself smarter or greater than all the others. But each one had been drawn in, and in his way served the Foundation while he thought he was serving himself.

The Foundation of Evil.

Hitler and Stalin had been overtly evil, their twisted, conscienceless psyches exposed to world view. Most of the others on the list appeared, or had appeared, normal, but she knew from Parrish's example how misleading appearances could be. All of these people had pursued unlimited power and ambition, their actions guided by the Foundation. Did they use the Foundation, or did the Foundation use them?

What was the nature of evil? What face did it wear? Was the capability to do evil in every person, and like any seed it flourished in some places but not in others? Or did the impetus for evil come from without? Was evil itself a separate entity, or nothing more than a result?

Was the Foundation evil because evil people served it, or was it evil in and of itself? Had the Foundation existed, in some other guise, far longer than a mere two centuries?

When had the Guardian been created? Had the Templars created the post, or served it? Had the Order been destroyed by the servants of the Foundation? Certainly the motives of Philip IV and Clement V were suspect, greed and jealousy and a thirst for power.

Evil.

In the silence of predawn, exhausted beyond sleep, Grace paced and thought, wondering if sleep deprivation was making her crazy or if she was indeed battling nothing less than Satan.

Just when she would decide she was definitely crazy, she would remember the Gaelic papers. "The Evil one shall be called Parrish." And "In the Year of Our Lord 1945, the Guardian slew the German beast." The words had been written more than six hundred years before the event actually happened, and were accompanied by a recipe for time travel. The papers were either masterpieces of prophecy, or the Templars had known the secret of time travel.

Perhaps that was the Power the Foundation sought. Time travel! The possibilities were endless. One could zip around in history and make enormous profits by using prior knowledge. What if someone made a large bet against enormous odds that the *Titanic* would sink, or invested heavily in munitions manufacturing before the onset of World War II? Why, just knowing who would win the World Series would make someone rich beyond belief. The possibilities were endless: take out life insurance policies on someone who would soon die, lotteries, horse races, political elections.

On the other hand, it seemed the Guardian had used time travel to protect the Power, so she was still in the dark.

Finally dawn lightened the sky, and she watched it through her dingy window. A sane person would call in sick and try to get some sleep, but instead she showered and drank a pot of coffee. She felt strangely restless, and it wasn't caffeine jumpiness. Instead there was a growing sense of urgency, as if she should be doing something but she didn't know what.

Perhaps it was time to pack up and move on, find another job, another room. She had been Paulette Bottoms for a couple of months now, as long as she had kept any identity. Her instincts had kept her alive this long, so she saw no reason to ignore them now.

She hadn't made the mistake of accumulating a lot of possessions. A few clothes, the truck, the revolver. The coffeemaker was a two-dollar yard-sale find. It took her exactly ten minutes to have everything she owned packed and loaded in the truck. The room was paid for through Saturday, so she dropped the key in the super's mailbox and walked away.

The day was Friday. She would work, collect her pay that afternoon, and quit; that would be the end of Paulette Bottoms. She would pick another name, find another room, get another job. Perhaps she would even leave Minneapolis. She had come back because it seemed the best hiding place, under Parrish's nose, and with a fierce need for vengeance. She had never managed to come up with a reasonable plan, but neither had she devoted herself to it; instead she had concentrated all her energies on translating the papers. That task was finished. With Kris's help, she now knew more than she'd ever imagined about the Foundation. She didn't know yet what she could do with the information, but she felt she should leave and she could barely control the urge to get in the truck and drive until she couldn't stay awake any longer.

Leave Minneapolis. The realization eased through her, bringing a sense of relief. Yes, that's what she should do. Get away from Parrish, from the memories that always hovered at the edge of her control, threatening to crush her if she ever relaxed her guard. She didn't know yet what she was going to do with the information she had, but she wanted to get away from the snow and cold, from the short winter days. She would drive south, and not stop until she found warmth and sunshine.

All she had to do was this one day of work. Clean a few houses, collect her pay, and then she would get on I-35 and head due south.

Paglione sipped on the last of the coffee in his thermos. Winter stakeouts were the worst. You had to drink coffee to stay warm, and then you had to piss all the time. Took two people to do a decent stakeout, because one of you was always off somewhere taking a leak.

At least staking out a McDonald's wasn't so bad. He could always get something to eat, more coffee, and there was a toilet handy. He had been there three days, though, and he was getting damn tired of Big Macs. Maybe he'd try those chicken things next time—

A car pulled in beside him, interrupting him, and he glanced over. The shape of Conrad's head was instantly recognizable. Despite his years of working amicably with the man, Paglione always felt a little uneasy when he first saw Conrad each time, as if he had somehow forgotten exactly how cold and ruthless he was. Paglione had known stone killers before; he had killed a few people himself. But Conrad was different. Paglione could never guess what went on behind those emotionless eyes. Conrad didn't panic, and he didn't give up. He was like a machine, never tiring, wired to pick up on details everyone else missed. Of all the people

Paglione knew, and that included Mr. Sawyer himself, Conrad was the only one he truly feared.

On a rush of cold air Conrad slid into the passenger seat. He wore an expensive wool overcoat that failed to impart any stylishness to his stocky frame.

"Glad you're here," Paglione said. "I been drinking coffee all day and I gotta piss. You want me to get you something while I'm in there?"

"No. Has anyone used the pay phone?"

"A couple of people. I wrote down their descriptions." Paglione took a small notebook off the dash and laid it beside Conrad, then heaved the door open and hurried across the parking lot to the restaurant.

The car windows were beginning to fog. Without looking away from the pay phone, Conrad leaned over and turned the ignition key to start the engine. He picked up the notebook but didn't begin reading it. That would wait until Paglione returned. Reading was too distracting; before you knew it an entire minute could pass, and a lot can happen in a minute.

He was still annoyed with himself. Grace had probably still been in the computer room when he walked by; he had glanced in and seen nothing out of the ordinary. But when he and Parrish had gone back, Conrad had noticed immediately that a stack of manuals had been moved.

So close. He could have gotten her then, and all this would be over.

She had changed. He discounted what was obviously a wig. He no longer looked for any particular length or color of hair, because that was too easily changed. She had lost a lot of weight; when they watched the film again, trying to get some clues to the identity of her companion, Parrish had remarked disappointedly on how thin she was now.

But the biggest change wasn't even the weight loss; it was how she walked. He had watched a lot of clips on her over the months, and he knew her walk as well as he knew his own. She had strolled instead of strode, and there had been something completely feminine in the subtle sway of her hips. Even he could see the sensuality that had Parrish so obsessed. But she had walked like an innocent, with no street awareness, her balance that of someone completely at ease and off guard.

That innocence was gone. Now she walked purposefully, her slight weight balanced on each foot so she could move immediately in any direction. Her head had been up, her attitude alert. Her shoulders were squared, the muscles prepared to swivel. Sometime during her eight months on the run, Grace St. John had gotten street smart, and learned how to fight.

He regretted her lost innocence. She hadn't been insipidly sweet; she was too witty, too sharp. But she had been radiant; that was the quality that had come through in the videotapes he had watched. Both husband and brother had adored her, and she had passionately loved them in return. Parrish had compulsively watched over and over one tape made at Christmas, when her husband had pulled her down on his lap and thoroughly kissed her, and been thoroughly kissed in return. There had been a lot of laughter and teasing in those tapes. The little family had been happy.

A lot could happen in eight months on the run. She could have been beaten, robbed, raped. He didn't like to think of her being brutalized, but he was realistic. Parrish wanted to use her before he killed her, drag her soul in the dirt, humiliate her, and Conrad strongly disapproved. She deserved more respect than that.

Paglione trudged back to the car, carrying a paper sack. He slid behind the wheel and the greasy aroma of french fries and chicken filled the car. He opened the plastic lid on the coffee cup and set it on the dash, then dug out his fries and little cardboard container of poultry pieces.

Now that Paglione had returned, Conrad opened the notebook. Six people had used the pay phone. A black woman at 7:16. A teenage boy, about fourteen, had used it at 9:24, when he should have been in school. An elderly man had approached, fumbled with some change, then left without making a call. An Asian-American male driving an electric utilities truck had placed a call at 10:47. Two young men had arrived at 12:02 and camped on the phone for almost an hour. Damn! When Grace called before, it had been during the lunch hour, so if she had needed to make another call those two idiots would have forced her to go elsewhere.

"Melker's watching the drive-through," Paglione said.

"Bayne's inside. Melker's been bitching because he don't know what kind of car to look for. Just look for frizzy blond hair, I told him."

Conrad sighed softly. If he had been a step faster, he would have seen more than a split-second flash of taillights, almost more of a reflection than the actual lights. Not that she would necessarily be in the same vehicle; it could belong to her companion. The important thing was that she was no longer dependent on public transportation, making her much harder to track.

But he was patient. She had been here before. She would be here again.

Grace finished her last house early, a little after two. She stopped by the cramped little office of the cleaning service and collected her pay, and told the owner she wouldn't be back. Personnel turned over so regularly that her departure didn't elicit more than a grunt.

She needed to call Kris; he would go crazy with worry if she disappeared without a word. She regretted leaving him behind once again. His company, his friendship, had been like a warm cocoon; actual conversation was rare in her life now, but for a brief time she had been able to talk to Kris, and not feel so isolated.

She pulled into the McDonald's parking lot to use the pay phone, but someone was already using it. She didn't stop, but swung the steering wheel to go around the cars lined up for the drive-through window. One of the cars in line abruptly pulled out in front of her and she slammed on the brakes to keep from rear-ending it. Her computer case was on the seat beside her, and the abrupt stop sent it pitching off the seat. The zippered section was open and several pages of her notes came out, scattering on the floorboard.

"Damn it," she muttered, pulling to the side. Computers weren't delicate, but neither were they meant to be tossed around, either. The case was padded, but still—

She leaned over and picked up the case, but some of the scattered papers had slid under the seat and, with her possessions stacked in the way, she couldn't reach that far. Swearing again, she left the truck running and got out, walking around to the passenger side.

She opened the door and began gathering the papers. She had just reached for one on which she plainly saw the words "Creag Dhu" when a gust of wind swirled into the truck and sent the sheet flying over her head. She whirled to catch it, and saw the man almost on her.

She didn't stop to think. Instantly she dropped to the ground, lashing out with a booted foot and catching him solidly on the kneecap. His leg went out from under him as if he'd been shot, and he fell on his face.

Grace rolled away from him, coming to her feet and swinging herself into the cab of the truck. Another man was suddenly there, a man with a simian head and cold, expressionless eyes. She tried to slam the door and he knocked it open, his heavyset body crowding into the opening. Grace heaved herself back but one meaty hand closed around her ankle, inexorably drawing her forward. She kicked at his face. He jerked his head back, and seized her other ankle.

The knife hissed as she drew it out of the scabbard, the blade glinting as she jackknifed to a sitting position and slashed at his hands. She held the knife the way Mateo had shown her, palm down, blade jutting outward so that the attack came from her midsection and was much harder to block than a wide, sweeping slash. The knife sliced across the back of one hand and he jerked back, releasing one ankle.

The first man was slowly climbing to his feet, groaning and favoring his knee, but within seconds he would be able to help. She could hear someone running, a third attacker hurrying to the truck. She wouldn't be able to fight off three at once, or even two.

Oh, God, the one holding her ankle was as strong as a bull. He pulled her forward, ignoring the pain in his cut hand, blocking her efforts to kick him. The pistol was stuck under her stack of clothing, easily reached if she were in the driver's seat, but now she was lying on top of it.

She threw the knife. He saw the blade coming at his face and no training in the world was strong enough to override the instinct to duck. He threw himself to the side, but even so he retained his grip on her ankle, pulling her partially out of the truck. Desperately she scrabbled under the pile of clothing, her hand striking the pistol and knocking it away. She grabbed again, and this time found it.

She bolted up, both hands folded around the butt, firing as soon as the barrel was clear of her own feet. She heard the shots but they sounded far away, muffled. In slow motion she saw the gorilla-man flinch, then falter. She heard the strange wet thud of a bullet hitting human flesh. She saw the eyes flicker with both surprise and annoyance, as if he shouldn't have let himself underestimate her.

But he didn't let go of her ankle. He set his teeth and pulled.

"I'll kill you," she said, her voice barely audible. She held the barrel centered between his eyes. Her hands were steady. She began taking out the slack in the trigger, and the hammer moved back, poising for the strike.

Their eyes met, and he saw his death in hers. She saw a cold, dark intelligence in his, an awareness that went beyond the moment, as if he knew her down to her soul. There was a flash of acknowledgment, then his hand loosened and he slumped to the ground.

The man she had kicked in the knee began to back away, his hands held up to indicate ʰe was unarmed. She didn't believe that for a minute.

She jerked her head around to locate the third man, and heard the driver's door opening behind her. She threw herself on her back, held the pistol over her head, and shot through the door. Sitting up again, she shot at the first man as he pulled his pistol from under his jacket. She missed, but he dived for cover.

She had two shots left; she couldn't keep shooting back and forth, she had to make them count. She clambered over her jumbled possessions and settled behind the steering wheel, and jerked the transmission into gear as she jammed her foot onto the gas pedal. The old truck shuddered as it leaped forward, tires slipping on the icy patches in the parking lot. The third man's face appeared in the window beside her as he grabbed for the door handle. She shoved the pistol at the window and he ducked, letting go of the door. The truck shook as the first man jumped up on the rear bumper, trying to climb into the bed.

Grace jerked the steering wheel hard to the right, then to the left. It was like playing crack the whip, except the stakes were a lot higher. His feet slipped off the bumper but he managed to hold on. Watching in the rearview mirror, she barreled out through the parking lot entrance into the path of a car turning in. A horn blared, she jerked the wheel again, and the man lost his grip on the tailgate. He went rolling across the parking lot, and fetched up hard against the rear tire of a parked car.

The passenger door still swung open, but she couldn't take the time to stop and close it. Stepping on the gas, she took a hard left at the first corner, then a right at the next one. The door slammed itself.

She tried to think what she should do. They had a description of the truck, and probably the tag number as well. The truck was registered under Louisa Croley's name, the same name that was on her passport and her driver's license. She should ditch the truck, steal a car somewhere, and get as far from Minneapolis as she could. The police would be looking for her within minutes; a shoot-out at a McDonald's was bound to attract attention.

But she didn't ditch the truck. She didn't take the time to drive to a mall and look for a car with the keys left in it, though Harmony had assured her there were at least two fools shopping at any mall at any given time. Instead she hit 36 and drove west until she got to I-35. Then she got on the southbound lane and headed for Iowa.

"A mysterious shoot-out at a McDonald's in Roseville has police puzzled," the talking head earnestly announced. "Witnesses say several shots were fired, and at least six people were involved, with two seriously injured. But by the time police arrived, all those involved had vanished, including the wounded. Witnesses said one person, perhaps a woman, was driving a brown pickup truck. By law, all doctors and hospitals are required to report all gunshot wounds to police, but thus far no one has requested treatment."

Parrish paced back and forth, furious. Conrad sat silently on the sofa, his shoulder bound and his arm supported by a sling. A doctor who belonged to the Foundation had removed the bullet, which luckily had struck his collarbone instead of tearing through the complicated system of cartilage and ligaments in his shoulder. His collarbone was cracked, and the insistent throb seemed to pound through his entire body, but he had refused any pain medication. The cut on his hand, though it had required eight stitches, was minimal.

"Four men couldn't catch one woman," Parrish said, seething. "Bayne didn't even know anything was going on until it was too late for him to help. I'm very disappointed in the quality of your men, Conrad, and in you. She caught you with your pants down, and now she's gone to ground again. With all the people we have in this city, no one has seen her. She's one inexperienced woman; how in hell can she keep getting away from me?" He roared the last sentence, his face flushed dark red, his neck corded with rage.

Conrad sat silently. He didn't make excuses, but as soon as he was able, he would personally take care of Melker. As soon as he spotted her, the fool had run up to the truck without waiting for the others to get in place. If they had all come at her at once, taken her by surprise, she wouldn't have escaped. Instead Melker had tried to take her by himself, and she'd kicked the hell out of him.

Conrad was deeply annoyed at himself, too; he should have expected her to have armed herself by this time, but instead he had allowed himself to be caught off guard, first by the knife, then by that unwavering pistol. She hadn't hesitated, hadn't panicked. She had said, "I'll kill you," and the warning was sincere. She would have done it. In that moment, looking deep into her pure blue eyes, he saw the strength none of them had suspected.

He could have held on. She would have killed him, but the delay, and the hindrance of his body dragging on her, would likely have resulted in her capture. He had chosen to let go and pretend to lose consciousness, to save himself. He didn't want to die, he had too much left undone. He didn't want anyone except himself to capture Grace St. John, and he wanted to be alone when he did it. Parrish would never know what happened to her. To that end, though he had noted her license plate number, Conrad kept it to himself.

Rather than get involved in a tedious police investigation, they had all gotten into their cars and left. Despite his pain and blood loss, Conrad had managed to drive to a secure place and arrange for medical care. Parrish was in a rage, not yet paying attention to the sheet of paper Paglione had picked up in the parking lot, the paper that had blown out of Grace's truck.

The paper lay on the table. Conrad hadn't yet looked at it, but his gaze kept going to it. After all these months, searching for both Grace and the papers, a sheet had virtually fallen into their hands. How important could one sheet be, out of all those papers? But it drew him, and he couldn't stop glancing at it in a mixture of dread and anticipation.

At last Parrish noticed that his temper tantrum was being mostly ignored. He followed Conrad's look and stalked over to snatch up the sheet of paper. "What's this?"

"Paglione picked it up," Conrad said. "It blew out of her truck."

"It's some notes she's made," Parrish said, his tone growing thoughtful. He walked over to the desk and sat down, turning on the lamp. "I don't know this language. *'C-u-n-b-h-a-l-a-c-h'* means 'steady,' *'c-u-n-b-h-a-l-a-c-h-d'* means 'judgment.' I'm so glad to know that. This is gibberish. It must be a code that's in the papers. *'Creag Dhu'*— this doesn't have any interpretation beside it. Then there's 'fear,' and beside it *'gleidhidh.'* This looks like Welch without all the *y*'s and *w*'s."

Conrad didn't comment, but the feeling of dread was growing stronger. He stared at the paper, hearing his heartbeat pounding in his ears, throbbing in his shoulder. Perhaps he had lost more blood than he had thought, and was about to lose consciousness for real.

Parrish lapsed into silence, his head bent over the paper. He was an educated, sophisticated man, well traveled. He had seen this language before.

"It's Gaelic," he said after a moment, his tone soft. "It isn't a code. *Dhu* means 'black,' and I think *creag* means 'rock,' or 'rocky.' Black rock." He stood abruptly, his eyes narrow and intent. "Get some rest, Conrad. I'll have this translated. Grace's little slip may be just the break I've been needing."

Chapter 17

ONE OF HER PAGES OF NOTES HAD BLOWN OUT. GRACE COULDN'T stop thinking about it, her insides clenched tight with dread. She had made a dreadful mistake.

She drove carefully through the snow-dusted Iowa night, well aware she was long past exhaustion and operating on sheer instinct. She needed to sleep, but she couldn't make herself stop. She felt driven, somehow, and so she drove.

She had lost one of the sheets. It was just a sheet of her notes, not one of the document sheets, but still she clearly remembered seeing "Creag Dhu" on it as she reached for it. What were the odds against one of those men picking it up? Not very good. They had to know they weren't just after her, but some papers as well.

She had given Parrish the location of the Treasure; all he had to do was figure out what it was. She had to assume he would. After all, the Foundation's business was archaeology. Parrish had access to any number of old maps, files, cross-references. He would learn Creag Dhu had been a fourteenth-century castle, and with a little effort he would be able to pinpoint its location. He could throw the Foundation's enormous resources into excavating the site—and he would find the Treasure.

Her fault. Her fault. The words drummed ceaselessly through her head. She had failed Ford and Bryant, letting Parrish attain the knowledge for which he had killed them.

She had failed Niall.

She should have done something, should have shot both the other men if necessary, and chased down that errant sheet. But all she had been thinking about had been escape, survival; she hadn't remembered the paper until she was already in Iowa.

She had actually shot a man. All of Matty's advice had worked, and she had functioned well enough to *do* something, instead of simply flailing in terror and hoping for a lucky blow. Eight months ago she wouldn't have had any idea how to use a pistol, and would have been horrified at the thought of doing so; this afternoon she had used both knife and pistol. Thinking of the moment when she had pulled the trigger, Grace wondered numbly if she was still the same person at all.

But what good had all of it done? She was alive, yes, but still she had failed Niall. She had failed to protect the papers. Parrish had won, through her own negligence.

Eaten alive by guilt, sick in the aftermath of battlefield adrenaline, it was almost ten when she thought of Kris. Swearing softly to herself at her lack of consideration, she began looking for an exit occupied by people and equipped with a pay phone. Perhaps she simply hadn't been paying attention, but it seemed as if most of the exits were nothing more than lonely intersections, access to empty roads leading off into empty night.

She must not have been paying attention. There was a brightly lit truck stop at the next exit. She pulled into the crowded parking lot, her truck dwarfed by the huge tractor-trailer rigs that sat idling, their motors rumbling like enormous sleeping beasts. She decided she might as well gas up while she was there, so she pulled up to one of the islands and stood shivering in the icy wind as the tank filled. At least the cold woke her up; she had sunk almost into a stupor, her eyes half closed, hypnotized by the endless zipper of stripes between twin banks of dirty snow, where the snowplows had cleared the highway.

It had started snowing again, she realized, seeing the white flakes blowing through the bright vapor lights of the truck stop. She couldn't go much farther; she was too exhausted to battle snow too. She paid the attendant for the gas, then got in the truck and moved it to the restaurant.

The warmth inside went right through her, making her shudder with relief. Truckers sat at a long counter, or in pairs in the booths that lined the wall. A jukebox played some rollicking honky-tonk song, and a cloud of blue cigarette smoke hovered against the ceiling. There was a tiny hallway to the left, decorated with an arrow and a sign that said "Rest Rooms," and two pay phones were crowded into it. One of the phones was in use by an enormous bearded fellow whose gut strained his thermal-knit shirt. He looked like a cross between Paul Bunyan and a Hell's Angel, but when she neared she heard him say, "I'll call you tomorrow, honey. Love you."

Grace squeezed past him and dug change out of her pocket. A quarter bought her a dial tone. She punched in the numbers, then waited until a recorded voice told her how much more change to feed the beast.

Kris answered immediately, his voice anxious.

She turned her back on the big guy, and lowered her voice. "I'm okay," she said, not giving her name. "But they almost caught me this afternoon, and I had to leave. I just wanted you to know. Is everything okay on your end?"

"Yeah." She could hear him gulp. "Are you hurt, or anything?"

"No, I'm fine."

"That was you, wasn't it?" His voice shook. "That shooting at the McDonald's. They said—on television—a woman in a brown truck. I knew it was you."

"Yes."

"The police don't know what happened. All those men vanished before the cops got there."

Grace blinked. That was surprising news. She had expected the cops to be hot on her trail, too. Evidently Parrish didn't want the cops to catch her, preferring to do so himself. She didn't know why; she had seen about half the city's muckety-mucks on the donor list, so she had no doubt he could pull enough strings to get the papers out of the evidence room, or whatever they called it. He could also have her killed in her cell, and she would be just one more jail violence statistic.

The implication was startling. Parrish wanted her alive, and he wanted her as *his* prisoner. A wave of revulsion swept her at the thought, but she didn't analyze it.

"I have to go now," she told Kris. "I just wanted you to know I'm okay, and tell you how much I appreciate what you did."

"Grace—" His voice cracked on her name. "Take care. Stay alive." He paused, and his next words came out quiet and strained. "I love you."

The simple words almost shattered her. She had been too alone; too many months had passed since she had heard them. She gripped the receiver so tightly her knuckles turned white, and the plastic creaked under the strain.

She couldn't blow off his youthful devotion as an adolescent crush; he deserved more respect than that. "Thank you," she whispered. "I love you, too. You're a wonderful person." Then she gently hung up, and pressed her forehead against the wall.

Beside her, the trucker was saying his own good-byes, more "I love yous" and "I'll be carefuls." He hung up and glanced at her.

A meaty paw patted her shoulder with surprising delicacy. "Don't cry, little bit," he said comfortingly. "You'll get used to it. How long you been on the road?"

He thought she was a truck driver. Amazement chased away all other emotion. Did she *look* like a truck driver? Her, the poster girl for academia?

She looked down. He wore boots; she wore boots. He had on jeans; she had on jeans. Baseball caps topped their heads.

She looked like a truck driver.

She was so tired she was giddy, and nothing seemed quite real. For the first time in eight months, her lips quivered with amusement. She didn't laugh, but she was astonished at the impulse. Quelling it, she cleared her throat and looked up at Paul Bunyan. "Eight months. I've been driving for eight months."

He gave her another pat. "Well, give it a little more time. It's tough, being away from your family so much, but the freight has to move and somebody's gonna get paid for hauling it. Might as well be us, huh?"

"Might as well," she echoed. She nodded to him and escaped out to her truck. She hoped he didn't see her driving off in an ordinary pickup, instead of one of the snoozing behemoths; she didn't want to destroy his illusions about her.

The snow was falling faster, and more trucks were leaving the interstate, rumbling up the exit ramp to take overnight refuge at the truck stop. There was a small, ratty-looking motel next door, and its "Vacancy" sign was lit. Grace decided not to chance driving any farther, and to take a room before the new arrivals got them all.

The room was just as ratty-looking as the exterior. The carpet was worn and stained, the walls were brown, the bedspreads were brown, the lavatory bowl was brown—and it wasn't supposed to be. But the heating unit worked, and so did everything in the bathroom; good enough.

She stuck the pistol in the waistband of her jeans and dragged out the computer case, and a change of clothes for the next day. If the rest of her clothes weren't safe in the truck overnight, well, she hoped the thief was small enough to wear them, because she didn't have the energy to cart everything inside.

She undressed, then reloaded the pistol. Her hands trembled, and she fumbled the bullets. She thrust the gun under her pillow, then climbed into the lumpy bed and was unconscious even before her head hit the pillow.

She dreamed.

"And so came Grace to Creag Dhu."

Niall wrote the words, the pen scratching across the page. He signed it, dated it, then turned to face her. "Aye, lass, that will bring ye to me." His intent black gaze moved over her, starting at her feet and lingering at hips and breasts before reaching her face. She drew a deep breath, knowing what that look meant. He was the most intensely sexual man she had ever met, and the challenge of that burning appetite only fed her own sensuality. She could feel her body readying itself for him, growing warm, softening, her nipples standing upright and her cheeks flushing. Excited desire began coiling deep in her belly.

He knew it, saw it. His hard mouth took on a sensual curve and he dropped the quill onto the table, turning on the high wooden stool to face her. He held out his hand. "Dinna wait near seven hundred bluidy years," he said softly. "I want ye *now.*"

Grace took the five steps that carried her to him, her hands lifting to sift through the thick black silk of his hair. He bent his head, and his mouth covered hers. No one else kissed like Niall, she thought dazedly. His taste was as potent as fiery whisky, his kiss was both dominating and seductive, taking what he wanted but giving pleasure in return.

His big hand covered her breast, his thumb rubbing gently over her extended nipple. Her hands clenched in his hair and she crowded closer to him, shivering.

They had already made love so many times he knew exactly how aroused she was, knew there was no need for love play. With a soothing murmur he pulled up both her skirts and his kilt, and lifted her astride him as he sat propped on the high stool. Their loins came together with ease, and she gave a little whimper of relief as his thick erection slipped up into her. Niall gasped, his teeth set, then he gathered her close and they clung together, their need deeper and sharper than physical desire.

'Twas *her.* Niall awoke, fiercely aroused and aching, but grimly triumphant. This time he had seen her face, this damned wench who tormented his sleep, who watched him from hidden places. He sat up in bed and thrust both hands through his hair, pushing it out of his face as he tried to firm his memories of the dream.

He had been sitting on a stool at a high table, writing something, while she stood off to the side. He couldn't remember what he had said, he just remembered looking at her, and the wench looking back at him, and lust abruptly burning through him. He held out his hand to her and she came to him, into his arms, and he had not even carried her to bed but taken her there, lifting her skirts and hoisting her onto his shaft. She was like liquid fire, flowing over him, lovely blue eyes closed and her face tilted back, exalted, as she pleasured him and he pleasured her.

She felt fragile in his arms, her body tender, her skin silky. She had a great swath of dark hair hanging down her back, thick and sleek, and her eyes were as pure a blue as a Highland lake under a clear summer sky. Her face . . . a chill ran over him. Her face looked like an angel's, solemn and slightly distant, as if she had some greater purpose. Her brow was clear and white, her delicate jawline slightly squared, and her mouth . . . "Ah, weel, perhaps not an angel after all," he said aloud, relieved. That mouth put him in mind of a number of things, all of them very carnal.

Still and all, there was something about her that made him uneasy, and Niall was a man who trusted his instincts. He snorted to himself. Aye, and so he should be uneasy, for she was likely a witch; how else could she watch him without being seen, and slip into his dreams whenever she wished? Witch or no, should she ever appear in the flesh he would be glad to give her the measure of his shaft in truth as well as dream, but he would not trust her.

She had to have some purpose for watching him; perhaps she had somehow learned of the Treasure.

It would be her ill fortune if that was what she sought, for he was sworn to guard the Treasure against all threat, be that threat from male or female. He had yet to kill a woman for it, but her sex would not save her. If she came for the Treasure, though he ached at the necessity, she would have to die.

Grace slept past the eleven o'clock checkout, awakening only when the maid pounded on the door. She stumbled to her feet, told the maid to come back later, and fell back into bed. She woke for good at three, groggy from so much sleep.

She stood in the shower for a long time, alternating hot and cold water in an effort to dispel the mental fog. She felt physically rested but mentally tired, as if her brain hadn't shut down all night. She had dreamed endlessly, it seemed, her mind going over the short, violent scene in the McDonald's parking lot, replaying it like a loop of film. Time after time she saw herself reach for the sheet of paper, saw "Creag Dhu" on it. She would feel the wind coming, know what was going to happen, and over and over she grabbed for the paper but every time it sailed out of her grasp, straight into Parrish's hands. He had looked at it, smiled, and said, "Why, thank you, Grace." Then he pointed a pistol at her and fired, and the dream would start all over again.

She had also dreamed of Niall, of making love with him. His black gaze had pierced straight through her, as if he knew she had failed to protect the precious papers given to her. But he had held out his hand to her, demanding she come to him, and she had gone.

"Come to me," he had said. "Now."

A violent shudder wracked her, starting at her feet and moving upward until her entire body shook. Her knees gave out and she leaned against the shower wall, her mouth open and little whimpers coming from it. She couldn't stop shaking, couldn't control the sensation of flying apart. Some external force pulled at her, tore at her, compelled her. Her eyes dilated and the dingy shower walls suddenly looked very bright, as if they were glowing.

Come to me. Travel the years, six hundred and seventy-five of them. I have given you the knowledge. Come to me.

The voice boomed inside her head, and yet it was from without. It was Niall speaking, but the voice that was low and devastatingly sexual in her dreams now sternly demanded, *Come to me.*

The glow began to fade, and the quaking in her muscles gradually weakened until she was standing upright and steady. Cold water pelted down on her and hastily she shut it off, grabbing a thin towel to wrap around her head. She used another to roughly dry herself. God, she was freezing! How long had she been standing like a dope, hallucinating, under the cold water? She had almost given herself hypothermia.

But she hadn't been hallucinating. She knew it. It had been real. There really was a Power; she had felt it from the first moment she had seen those old documents. That was why she had been driven to keep translating them, lugging both them and the laptop around when doing so had been a lot of trouble. She had protected them when common sense should have led her to abandon both.

Everything that had happened in the past eight months had led her inexorably to this moment, standing naked and cold in a dingy little shower in a truck-stop motel somewhere in Iowa, facing an unbelievable but suddenly crystal-clear conclusion.

If it were possible, she had to travel through time. Parrish had the sheet; perhaps that was preordained, and there was nothing she could have done about it. But now that he knew, she had to prevent him from getting the Treasure, and the only way to do that was to force Niall to hide it somewhere else. Or perhaps—silly thought, because she wasn't made of heroic material, but still—just perhaps, she was meant to find the Treasure, and use the Power to destroy the Foundation.

She had to go to Creag Dhu—six hundred and seventy-five years ago.

Chapter 18

SPRING CAME SOFTLY TO THE HIGHLANDS. IT WAS MAY, AND THE mountains were carpeted with green. The cool, misty days could suddenly give way to bright sunshine and air so clear it hurt her eyes to see it. From somewhere would come a fragment of sound, the faint echo of a bagpipe, and the haunting sound made her soul weep.

It had taken her four months to get here. At first she had simply kept on driving, going south, angling toward the east. The seasons changed as she drove, winter loosening its grip more and more the farther south she went, and it was in Tennessee, in mid-February, that she saw the first flower blooming. It seemed like such a miracle, in the form of a cheerful yellow jonquil, that she stopped driving then, and rested, and planned.

An early spring, the locals said, after a mild winter. The jonquils were blooming a couple of weeks earlier than usual. The winter hadn't been mild in Minnesota, but eight hundred miles farther south put her in a different climate, a different world.

She had quickly realized she couldn't do this alone, and there was only one person she could think of to call.

Harmony had listened silently to Grace's request to travel with her to Scotland for an unspecified length of time.

"Scotland," she finally said. "They don't still paint their faces blue, do they?"

"Only in movies."

"I don't have no passport."

"That's easy to get, if you have your birth certificate."

"You said you need my help doin' something. Reckon you can bring yourself to tell me exactly what it is I'd be doin'?"

"If you go," Grace said.

"I'll think about it. Call me in a couple of days."

Grace gave her three days, then called again. "Okay," Harmony said. "If I go, would I be doin' anything illegal?"

"No. I don't think." Given that she had to expect the unexpected, Grace couldn't swear that she would stay on the side of the law.

"Dangerous?"

"Yes."

Harmony sighed. "Well, hell," she drawled. "You do make it hard to resist, don't you? How long would I be gone? I got my house to look after, you know."

"I don't know. A couple of days, a couple of weeks. I'll pay all your expenses—"

"I'll pay my own way, if I go. That way, if I get pissed, I won't feel beholden to stay." She was silent for a moment, and Grace could hear her tapping her nails on the phone. "I got one more question."

"Okay."

"What's your real name?"

Grace hesitated. It felt strange to say her own name. The only time she had heard it spoken in months was when Kris had said it. She had gone by so many names that sometimes she felt as if she had no identity. "Grace," she said softly. "Grace St. John. But I'll be traveling under the name Louisa Croley; that's the name on my passport and driver's license."

"Grace." Harmony sighed. "Shit. If you'd lied to me, I coulda said no."

* * *

Finding where Creag Dhu had stood took some time. Grace and Harmony had been in Edinburgh more than a week before Grace managed to track down the name, and then it was in such a remote section of the western Highlands that it was almost inaccessible. While Grace researched, Harmony did Edinburgh. She toured the castle, she toured Holyrood House, she took day trips to St. Andrews and Perth. It wasn't until Grace actually found Creag Dhu that she told Harmony what she was going to do. Harmony laughed in her face, but when Grace quietly went about her preparations, Harmony sighed and pitched in. She didn't laugh when she heard about Ford and Bryant.

When she had everything gathered, Grace rented a car and they drove to a small Highland village five miles from where Creag Dhu had supposedly stood. The only accommodation in the village was a small bed-and-breakfast, which they took, but the local tavern was a hotbed of gossip. Harmony could stand elbow-to-elbow with hard-drinking Scotsmen and hold her own with them, whether it was beer or whisky, and as a reward they answered all her questions. Aye, a fancy American had arrived some two months ago, bent on digging up a great pile of rock. A storm had delayed him a bit, turning the ground to mud and making getting to the site a bit difficult, but the weather had since turned fair and word was he was making a great deal of progress.

"It won't take him long to find it," Grace said when Harmony reported back to her. "I can't wait any longer; I have to go."

"You talk like this is a guaranteed trip," Harmony said irritably. "Like as not all you're gonna do is give your ass a major shock."

"Maybe," Grace replied. During her own more reasonable moments, she knew that was exactly what was likely to happen. But then she would think of the documents and the things she had read, and the dreams, the sense of compulsion, and she knew she had to try no matter how crazy it sounded.

She hadn't had any dreams since arriving in Scotland. Everything felt so strange, as if a veil were hanging between her and everyone else. Nothing quite touched her, not fear or anger or even the more mundane things such as hunger. An essential part of her was already gone, turned away from this time. She knew she was going, and she had prepared as thoroughly as she could.

They set out just after lunch the next day, driving as far as possible, then they got out and walked. Storm clouds hovered to the west, out over the ocean, and the mountain shadows were purple under a gaudy blue and golden sky.

Grace had carefully considered the logistics. The documents had given the formula for time, but not for location. She decided that location didn't change; where she was when she went back would be where she arrived. Standing in the middle of Creag Dhu's ruins would have been perfect, but she hadn't dared go close enough even to see it. She had to settle for getting as close as possible, then walking the rest of the way to the castle when she arrived in that time.

The narrow road they had chosen was little more than a path, and it gave out while they were still some three miles from the ruins. Gathering Grace's things, the two women left the car and walked higher into the mountains.

The air was sweet and fresh, a bird's cry high and lonely. Grace could already feel something tugging at her, a quiet anticipation, a need.

"Why don't we just shoot the son of a bitch?" Harmony suggested suddenly, lifting her lemon-white head into the wind. Her nostrils flared, her pale green eyes narrowed. She looked like some exotic goddess of war, ready to slay her enemies. "It's easier, neater, and a hell of a lot more likely to get the job done."

"Because it isn't just Parrish, it's the Foundation. Even if we kill him, another will take his place." She had finally reached that conclusion, and found a measure of peace in it. She would love simply to kill Parrish and be done with it, claim her vengeance, walk away. She couldn't do it. *The Foundation of Evil* . . . she couldn't let the Foundation get control of the Treasure.

She spotted the place where she wanted to be, and pointed it out to Harmony. The nest of rocks was almost at the peak of the mountain. Carefully they climbed up, their feet alternately sinking into damp sod and slipping on loose rock. When they reached their goal, they stood quietly looking at the empty glen below, at the mist blowing in from the ocean. The Creag Dhu site wasn't visible; it lay beyond the next mountain. The local folk said it was a bed of black rock, jutting against the ocean. Grace tried to picture it in her mind, but even though she had seen numerous archaeological sites, the image that formed was of the great castle when it was whole, looming dark against an angry gray sea.

"Are you sure you have everything?" Harmony asked, placing her bundle on the ground and quickly arranging the items.

"I'm sure." She had made a list while still in the States, and had begun making her preparations even then. According to the instructions, she had altered her diet more than a week ago, tailoring it to the specifications. She bent down and attached the electrodes to her ankles, taping them in place.

She sensed that her detachment worried Harmony. "I'm all right," she said in answer to an unvoiced concern. "If this doesn't work—well, it just won't work. I'll get a shock, but it won't be enough to kill me."

"You hope," Harmony snarled, her irritation growing.

"If it *does* work—I don't know if any of this stuff will go with me, or if I'll suddenly appear there stark naked. If it doesn't go, carry it back to the village and do what you want with it."

"Sure. I've always wanted a velvet dress that's three sizes too little and a foot too short."

"I'm leaving the laptop anyway. I've deleted all my notes from the hard disk, but my journal is still on there. I've put everything down. If anything happens to me and I don't make it back . . ." She shrugged. "At least there will be a record of what happened."

"How long am I supposed to wait?" Harmony asked furiously.

"I don't know. I'll leave that up to you."

"Damn it, Grace!" Harmony turned on her, face red with fury, but she bit back her angry words and merely shook her head. "I can't reach you, can I? In your head, you're already there."

"I know you don't understand it. I don't, either." The wind plastered her gown to her form and lifted her hair, streaming it behind her. The glen stretched below her but she didn't see it, her eyes looking beyond. "It's been a year since Ford and Bryant were murdered. I haven't been able to cry for them yet. It's as if I don't deserve to, because I haven't done anything to avenge them."

"You haven't had time to cry." Harmony's voice was rough. "You've been busy just stayin' alive."

"I haven't been to their graves. I was back in Minneapolis for six months, and I didn't look for their graves. I didn't put flowers on them."

"Damn good thing. From what you've told me, this Parrish bastard would have men watching the cemetery. They'da nailed you for sure."

"Maybe. But I couldn't have gone even if I had known it was safe. Not yet. Maybe when I get back."

After that, there didn't seem to be anything left to say. Harmony hugged her, green eyes wet, then walked quickly away.

Grace sat down on the rocks and opened the laptop, turning it on. She logged into her journal and tried to gather her thoughts. It was useless; they darted about like swallows. Finally she stopped trying and simply began typing.

"May 17th—Revenge takes over your life. I never realized this before, but then I've never hated before. One moment my life was ordinary and secure, happy—and the next moment everything was gone. My husband, my brother . . . I lost them both.

"Odd how things change, how in the blink of an eye one's life goes from the ordinary—even mundane—to a nightmare landscape of horror, disbelief, and almost crippling grief. No, I haven't cried. I've held the grief locked inside me, a wound that can't heal, because I don't dare let it out. I have to concentrate on what must be done, rather than allow myself the luxury of mourning those I've lost. If I falter, if I let my guard down even the slightest, then I'll be dead too.

"My life feels as if it belongs to someone else. Something is wrong, discordant, but what: before—or now? It's as if

255

the two halves don't match, that one or the other simply isn't my life. Sometimes I can't feel any connection at all with the woman I was, before that night.

"Before, I was a wife.

"Now, I'm a widow.

"I had a family, small but familiar, and achingly dear. Gone.

"I had a career, one of those obscure, intellectually challenging jobs in which I could, and did, lose myself in dusty old parchment and precious, unknown little books, where I mentally wandered in the past for so long that Ford sometimes teased me about having been born in the wrong century.

"That too is gone.

"Now I have to run, to hide, or I too will be killed. I've spent the months scurrying from hole to hole like a rat, lugging around some stolen manuscripts and ancient translations. I've learned how to change my appearance, how to get a fake ID, how to steal a car if necessary. I eat occasionally, though not well. Ford wouldn't recognize me. My husband wouldn't know me! But I can't let myself think about that.

"How did I come to this?

"A rhetorical question. I know how it happened. I watched it happen. I saw Parrish kill them both.

"There was no transition between before and now, no time to adjust. I went from respectable to fugitive in the space of a few shattering minutes. From wife to widow, from sister to survivor, from normal to . . . this.

"Only hatred keeps me going.

"It's a hate so strong and hot and pure that sometimes I feel incandescent with it. Can hate purify? Can it burn out all the little obstacles that might keep you from acting on it? I think it can. I think mine has. I want Parrish to pay for what he's done to my life, pay for the deaths of those I love. I want him to die. But I don't want Ford and Bryant to have died for nothing, so I have to go after the Foundation too, not just Parrish.

"I don't know how long it will take me to reach my destination. I don't know if I can do it in time (a bad pun) or if I'll die in the effort. All I can do is try, because hate, and revenge, are all I have left.

"I must find Black Niall."

She stopped typing, staring at the words on the screen. When she was in college she had kept a paper journal, with a butter-soft leather cover. Ford had given it to her the first Christmas after they started dating. She had intended it to be a record of her work, her thoughts on it, how the research and translations were going; instead it had become a diary of her private life, and when she switched to a laptop computer the habit had carried over to the electronic page.

In the journal she had recorded her flight from Parrish Sawyer. In it, too, was the only relief she had from the grief she kept bottled inside, for only there had she mourned Ford and Bryant. She had also chronicled her deepening fascination, and her warring senses of disbelief and awe, with what she had discovered in the old manuscripts for which Parrish had killed. She had wanted to dismiss them, but she couldn't; there were too many details that tied together, too many coincidences for them to be mere coincidences after all. Certainly Parrish didn't dismiss the secrets contained in the documents. And in the end, she too had believed.

Carefully she closed the file and turned off the laptop, setting it safely aside. She didn't know if any of the articles she had gathered would make the trip with her, or if she would arrive there—or was it *when*—without anything, even a stitch of clothing. She hadn't been joking about being stark naked.

She didn't know anything for certain, not even if the whole damn procedure would work. If it didn't, at least only Harmony would be a witness to what a colossal fool she made of herself. And if it didn't work, she would find some other way to stop Parrish and the Foundation. But if it did—

She took a deep breath. She had everything ready. She had checked and rechecked her figures, then checked them again. She had found the correct mineral surroundings, the rocks, for better conductivity. She had drunk the correct amount of water, calculated according to her weight and the time she needed to travel, so much that she felt bloated. She had eaten the correct things, subtly altering her body chemistry. She had prepared herself mentally, rehearsing what she would do, the sequence in which she would do it. Even the weather was cooperating, with the offshore storm advancing nearer and nearer, so that the air was crisp and crackling with electricity. The storm wasn't needed, but its presence seemed like a blessing.

It was time.

Grace picked up the big, rough burlap bag she had sewn herself, and hugged it to her chest. She and Harmony had also handmade the heavy, old-fashioned garments she wore, though neither of them was particularly skillful at sewing. At least early-fourteenth-century fashions had been simple. She wore a plain cotton gown, with long sleeves and a scoop neck, not formfitting at all. Over it was another gown, a sleeveless one, of good, soft wool. The undergown was called a kirtle, the overgown a surcoat. In the bag was a heavy velvet surcoat, should she need to convey a bit of status. A length of wool was folded in the bag, to be used as a shawl should she need it.

She had taken the precaution of buying a pair of hand-made moccasins while she was in Tennessee, and the soft leather molded to her feet. She wore long white stockings, secured with old-fashioned ribbon garters which she tied above her knees. She wore no bra or panties, for there hadn't been any such thing as underwear back then. There were no elastic bands or garment tags to make anyone suspicious. Her long hair was secured in a single thick braid, in the style she had worn a long time ago—before. She covered her head with a thick cotton scarf, tying the ends behind her neck.

The only thing she carried in the way of money was a few pieces of jewelry, the earrings and wedding band set she had been wearing when it all happened. There was nothing about her appearance, she hoped, that would be glaringly out of place. What she carried in the burlap bag would be enough to get her burned for witchcraft if she were caught.

The storm was growing closer, thunder echoing like a brass gong. *Now or never,* she thought. She had to hurry so Harmony could collect the laptop; rain wouldn't do it any good.

Carefully she placed her foot on the pressure switch she had rigged, holding her weight just short of tripping it. She could feel the electrodes where she had taped them to her ankles, and wondered how they had managed this in the days before electrodes and batteries existed.

Closing her eyes, she began breathing deeply, slowly, and forced herself to focus on Black Niall. She had done all the right things so she should go back exactly six hundred seventy-five years, but she felt as if she needed a target. He was the only target she had, this man who had lived almost seven hundred years before. There were no portraits of him, not even a crude drawing such as had been common back then, for her to bring to mind. All she could do was concentrate on *him,* the man, the essence of him.

She knew him. Oh, she knew him. He had haunted her for months, owning her waking mind while she struggled to decipher the ancient documents, then invading her dreams with images so vivid that sometimes she woke herself talking to him in her sleep, and always—always—she felt as if he'd just *been* there. He had made love to her in her dreams, tormenting her with her subconscious's sensuality. Black Niall had in some ways been her savior, for he had given her hope. The force of his personality, of the bigger-than-life man he had been, had reached out to her across the span of seven centuries. He drew her, somehow, and kept her from sinking into the tar pit of despair. There were times, during these past months, when he had been more real than the world around her.

His image began to fill her mind, forming against the darkness of her closed eyelids: a man as vivid as the lightning, as forceful as the thunder. Dimly she was aware that it was dangerous to focus on her imaginary picture of him, rather than on facts, but she couldn't change her mind to a blank screen. She could feel him, drawing closer. He was there, he was *there* . . .

Breathe, deep and slow. Draw the air in one nostril, circle it around, expel it out the other nostril. Complete the circle, again and again. Breathe. Breathe . . .

She saw his eyes, black and piercing, burning through the fog of time until it was as if he glared straight into her eyes. She saw the high, thin blade of his nose, the thick mane of his black hair as it swung against his muscled shoulders, the small braids that hung on each side of his face in ancient Gaelic fashion.

She saw his mouth open as he roared a command. She faintly perceived around him the din and horror of battle, but he was the only clear figure. She saw the glint of a weak, watery sun on his sword blade as he swung the massive weapon with one powerful arm. The other arm wielded a fearsome axe, rather than a shield, and both weapons were stained with blood as he hacked and parried, felling one foe after another.

In. Out. The air circled around and around inside her, drawing ever smaller, tighter, her mind fastening ever more firmly on the man who was her target. The spiral began to shrink, hugging around her, creating a sense of suction, and she knew she was almost ready to go.

Niall! Black Niall!

Mentally she called to him, screaming his name, her yearning so fierce and intense that it ached in every cell of her body. There was a sensation of being compressed, condensed, concentrated. In her mind she saw his head jerk around in surprise, as if he heard the distant echo of her cry, and then his image too began condensing, tugging on her, pulling her down into a pit of darkness. She fastened on the pure beacon of his essence, like a pilot surely guiding an airplane down on a beacon of radio waves. With her last remnant of consciousness she let her foot relax on the pressure switch, and the world exploded in a flash of blinding heat and light.

Chapter 19

GRACE LAY ON HER SIDE IN THE COOL GRASS. SHE FELT DAZED, bruised. Around her she heard a confusion of noises but they came from a great distance, and she couldn't quite tell what any of them were. Her mind, lingering between times, struggled to grasp any detail of existence. She felt as if she were waking up from anesthesia, aware first of external details but with no clue of who or where she was. Then details began seeping back; first was a vague "Oh, yeah, I'm Grace" moment of self-recognition. After a moment, or an hour, she wondered drowsily if the procedure had worked or if she had merely succeeded in shocking her ass, as Harmony had phrased it.

She became aware of various aches, as if she had been beaten, or had rolled down a hill.

The noise was steadily growing louder. The din became annoying, and she struggled to open her eyes, to gain control of her body so she could sit up and tell whoever was yelling like that to shut up. Then the smell hit her, and she gagged.

That involuntary reaction seemed to complete the transition from unconsciousness to complete awareness. The noise exploded into a roar, a horrifying din of what seemed like hundreds of men yelling in battle, screaming in pain. The discordant clash of metal against metal hurt her ears. Horses thudded the ground with steel-shod hooves, neighing shrilly. And the smell was an unholy combination of hot, fresh blood, urine, and emptied bowels.

She sat up, then gasped and hurled herself to the side as two dirty, long-haired, plaid-wrapped Scotsmen clashed almost on top of her. A bloodstained blade swiped through the air, barely missing her.

Dear God. She had landed in the middle of a battle.

Her breath caught. She had seen Black Niall in a battle, focused on him, and the procedure carried her directly to the place in her mind.

He was *here*. Somewhere. An almost painful excitement seized her insides.

Clutching her bag, she scrambled farther away from the clash of bodies. She stumbled over something soft and heavy and pitched hard onto her back. Winded, she sat up and saw that her legs were draped over a bloody dead man. A shriek caught in her throat, hung there unvoiced. Instead she hastily jerked herself away and came to her feet, swaying unsteadily as she swiveled her head, trying to orient herself.

They were in the glen, just below the rocks where she had gone through the procedure. The scene was madness, some men on horseback but most afoot, running, attacking, pivoting, slashing. Panic seized her; she couldn't see Black Niall anywhere, couldn't find a big man with a flowing mane of black hair, who effortlessly swung a huge sword with one hand. God, oh God, was he lying somewhere in the middle of this carnage, his own blood adding to the red flow?

Reality asserted itself with a thud. Despite her dreams and imaginings, she had no idea what he really looked like. The Guardian wouldn't glow like an archangel with a fiery sword; he would look just like everyone else. He could have been one of the grimy combatants who had almost stepped on her and she wouldn't have known him.

So how was she to find him? Climb the hill and scream "Black Niall!" at the top of her lungs?

"Niall Dhu! Niall Dhu!"

She heard the screaming, the sudden roar from one end of the battlefield, and all the seething bodies seemed to surge in that direction. Grace backed up, climbing a little way up the hill so she could have a better view.

"Niall Dhu!"

She started, the hoarsely screamed words suddenly making sense. *Dhu* meant "black." They were yelling his name.

Blood drained from her head. Had he fallen under a sword? She stumbled forward, her feet slipping in the red mud created by many feet churning a blood-soaked ground, driven by an insane need to reach his side. He couldn't be dead. No. Not Niall. He was invincible, the most fearsome warrior in Christendom.

The surge abruptly reversed, coming back to her. Grace halted, transfixed by the sight of all those screaming, dirty, long-haired men, bare legs flashing as they ran toward her. Hard reality slapped her. She was in the middle of a fourteenth-century battle, and if any of these men got their hands on her she would likely be raped and killed.

She turned and ran.

It was like waving a cape at a bull. They were already in a blood lust, and a collective roar burst from a hundred throats when they saw her. Grace pulled up her skirts and hurdled bodies, the bag she clutched in one hand banging heavily against her legs. She struggled to draw breath but panic clutched her throat, squeezing, threatening to cut off her breathing altogether.

The ground shook under a horse's thundering impact and a beefy, bloodstained arm swept around her. Grace shrieked as the world abruptly whirled off kilter and she was jerked into the air, flailing, to land heavily across a stinking, wool-covered lap. The man roared with laughter, roughly fondled her rump, then kneed the horse around. He yelled something, his tone obviously gloating, but she couldn't understand anything he said except "Niall Dhu."

Helpless, upside-down over a horse, all she could do was hang on to the bag and hope against hope that the ruffian who had captured her was Niall himself. She had caught a glimpse of a beefy face with a dirty beard, a dreadful disappointment compared to her dreams, but if he were Niall at least that would save her the trouble of hunting him down.

She didn't think she was that lucky.

The bastard was in high spirits, laughing and yelling as he rode. Others on horseback were around them, but most of the men were afoot. There was a great deal of activity in a group just out of her limited view, more yelling and laughter.

The man holding her put his hand between her legs, roughly feeling her through her skirts. Fury swept over Grace in an abrupt, unthinking tide, and swift as a snake she turned her head and sank her teeth into his bare, dirty calf. He roared in surprised pain and jerked on the reins. The horse half reared, neighing, and its hooves hit the ground again with a bone-jarring thud, jerking her teeth out of the man's leg. She gagged at the taste, and nausea overwhelmed her. She began to heave, and vomited over his foot.

Laughter rose around them, men pointing and howling with glee. Her captor seized her and furiously jerked her upright, his fetid breath hitting her full in the face as he roared at her. She couldn't understand a word he said, but his breath made her gag again. Hastily he pushed her off the horse and she sprawled in the dirt, landing with the bag under her stomach and knocking the air out of her.

She was jerked upright, held there while she swayed and gasped for breath, and a rope was tied around her waist. The beefy man tied the other end around his own waist and kicked his heels to the horse's sides, and she had to walk or be dragged. She walked, wheezing, desperately clutching her bag in both hands.

She expected the bag to be taken from her at any moment, but the men evidently didn't see any need to carry anything extra when she could do it. She wasn't going anywhere, and they could relieve her of her possessions whenever they reached their destination.

At least now she could look around. She didn't know if it was morning or afternoon, so she had no way of telling in what direction they were traveling. Not north or south, though, because the sun was behind them. If it was morning, they were traveling west; if afternoon, they were going east.

Behind her, a group of men were carrying a long bundle, completely wrapped and tied in a motley collection of dirty plaids. The bundle heaved occasionally, and was rewarded by a thump from one or more of the men. She looked around and one of the men met her gaze, grinning to display a few remaining teeth, the rest rotted to mere stumps. "Niall Dhu," he said proudly, indicating the bundle.

Aghast, she stopped walking, and was jerked forward when the slack was taken out of the rope. Niall! She looked over her shoulder at the bundle, struggling to make sense of the situation. These couldn't be his men, or they wouldn't be hitting him. Obviously he had been captured, and his own men hadn't been able to pursue for fear he would be killed.

Her mind buzzed with possibilities. He might be ransomed, or his captors might take pleasure in torturing and killing him. If he were held for ransom, he would likely be well taken care of; she thought she remembered reading that medieval Scots had practiced kidnapping as a fairly normal means of income, which of course would work only so long as the captive was returned unharmed. If killing them had been routine, obviously no one would have been willing to pay their hard-earned gold to no avail. The Scots were too practical for that.

But if they intended to kill him . . .

She had to find some way to help him. The problem was that she was a captive herself, and whenever they reached their destination she was likely to find herself in much more dire straits than she was in now. She was a captured woman, vulnerable, nothing more than a piece of meat to these men. Grace knew she was facing rape, probably multiple rapes, unless she could come up with some miraculous plan. Fear chilled her, but she forced it away. She was here. She had actually traveled through time. The circumstances weren't good, but she had found Black Niall almost immediately. Whatever happened later, she had to keep her mind focused on her objective. If necessary, she would endure. She would survive.

She was *here*. The amazement of it suddenly pushed out all other concerns, and her head swiveled from left to right, trying to take everything in. Her heart pounded in her chest. There was nothing really different to see; odd how little the Highlands had changed. Even in the twentieth century they were still mostly deserted, as if time had passed them by. The craggy mountains looked the same, perhaps a bit rougher, with patches of mist clinging to them.

She looked around her at the men, curiously examining their faces. Even under tangled thatches of dirty, uncombed hair, and sometimes an equally dirty, untidy beard, they looked so identifiably Scottish. She saw a long, thin nose here, high slanted cheekbones there, over there a cheerfully round cheek.

The men weren't in a good mood, despite their success in capturing Black Niall. Their losses had been heavy, and none of them had escaped completely unscathed. They laughed whenever one of them punched Niall, but the laughter was mean.

They talked among themselves, but she couldn't understand them. Learning to read Gaelic was a far cry from speaking it, and she doubted any of them could read even if they were inclined to let her write notes to communicate.

The bearded beast who had captured her looked around and scowled at her, and snapped something in Gaelic. Grace started to shrug her shoulders, but a risky plan popped into her head. She didn't give herself time to think about it. She found herself smiling and saying, "I'm sorry, I can't understand you," in the softest, sweetest voice she possessed.

His eyes popped wide open. The men around her gave her startled looks. Until then they had probably thought she was one of Black Niall's crofters, perhaps his woman or belonging to one of his men, but when she spoke in a foreign language they all realized she wasn't what they had assumed.

The beast's small, piggy eyes roamed over her clothes, and for the first time he noticed she wasn't wearing the rough, shapeless clothing of a crofter. He reined his horse to a stop and said something else. Everyone was watching her now. Even the bundle that held Black Niall had stopped wriggling. Grace didn't stop, but walked up beside the horse and gave the beast, the mounted one, another smile. She hadn't smiled in so long that the movement of her face felt strange, but if the beast noticed how false it was his stupefied expression didn't change.

"You stink as if you haven't bathed in your entire life," Grace said pleasantly. "And your breath would knock this horse down if he got a good whiff of it. But you seem to be the leader of this war party, so if being nice to you will protect me from them, I'll take my chances with just one man instead of a crowd any day of the week." She accompanied this with the sweetest smile she could manage, and held her arms up to him.

He was so startled that he automatically leaned down and lifted her onto the horse in front of him. The beast was strong as an ox, she thought, daintily settling herself in a proper position and arranging her skirts. She tried not to breathe through her nose so she wouldn't smell either his body stench or his breath, but she didn't let herself flinch. She acted as if it were her right to ride instead of walk, gave him a regal nod, and said, "Thank you."

They were all gaping at her, and they began gabbling excitedly among themselves, pointing at her clothes. She hadn't realized what good quality her plain cotton and wool garments were, until she compared them to the rough-woven fabric the men wore.

The beast lifted her hand, fingering her rings, and Grace held her breath. She expected him to tear them off her fingers, but instead he grunted and turned her hand over to look at her palm. She looked down, and saw the difference in their hands. His was thick and beefy, callused, the ragged nails black with encrusted dirt. In contrast her hand was soft and pale, the skin smooth, her nails well shaped. Her hands didn't look as if she did any physical labor; in this age, that meant she was at least nobility. She could almost see the ponderous thoughts forming in his brain. She was foreign, and wealthy, and of value to someone somewhere. Perhaps he didn't intend to ransom Black Niall, but here was a little godsend who could add considerable weight to his purse.

He prodded her bag and said something. Guessing he

wanted to know what was in the bag, Grace obligingly
opened it. The men crowded close, craning their necks in
curiosity. She took out one of the books she had brought,
flipping the pages to show him the paper and words, then
shoving it back into the bag. She hoped no one would be
very interested in it, because books didn't exist yet. Priests
and monks did illuminated manuscripts, but the printing
press wouldn't be invented for another hundred years or so.

The beast wasn't interested in the book, waving his beefy
hand in dismissal. She pulled out the velvet surcoat, just
enough to let him see the fabric. He murmured in pleasure,
rubbing his dirty hand over the plush texture, and grinned
in anticipation of riches. Next she showed him a larger
book, hoping he wouldn't want her to flip the pages in it too,
because this book had photographs. He grunted, shaking his
head, and she shoved it back into the bag.

She had brought several books, chosen with care. There
were also several kinds of drugs in the bag, but she didn't
want to display the pills. She had gotten prescriptions for
them and gone through customs without any problem, but
the beast would either eat them or scatter them on the
ground. So she pulled out another book, and he looked
impatient. He probably wanted to see something he recognized as valuable.

Perplexed, she pulled out the length of wool. Again, he
fingered the fine weave, then shoved it aside. She pulled out
another book. He said something rude, causing the men to
laugh. She shrugged, and brought out still another one,
hoping that would allay any suspicions he might have about
the weight of the bag, should he investigate.

Abruptly he decided to do just that, grabbing the bag and
shoving his hand inside. Grace held her breath. The pills
were carefully rolled in a handkerchief, then placed in a
small wooden box to keep them from getting crushed, and
the box secured in a pocket she had sewn into the inside of
the bag.

He didn't notice the pocket or the box. His searching
fingers found the Swiss Army knife, and he pulled it out
with a triumphant expression that swiftly changed to puzzlement as he stared at it. With all the blades and utensils
folded in, it didn't look like much. She didn't want to lose

the knife, but if he figured out the blades she knew she would. She drew a quick breath and reached for the knife.

He drew it back, scowling. Grace made her expression impatient. She untied the scarf from her head and unbound her hair, letting it fall free. He blinked at the long, thick mass. She reached for the knife again and this time he let her have it. She closed her hand around it so the blades didn't show, and turned it so he could see the head of the small tweezers. Delicately she plucked it out, and he blinked in astonishment. She held the tweezers in the palm of her hand, letting him look at it, then she quickly gathered her hair and began rolling it up around the knife, forming an oblong bun. When the roll was tight against her nape, she stuck the tweezers into her hair to secure it, and gave the beast a beatific smile.

He looked at her, then at her hair. He blinked again. Then he evidently decided ladies' hairstyles were beyond him, and turned his attention back to the bag.

Next he found a small penlight, luckily the kind that came on when the top was twisted instead of one with a button. Grace sighed, pulled the tweezers out of her hair, and started to unroll the bun, but he got the idea and dropped the penlight back into the bag without examining it very closely. He missed the book of matches, but it had probably gotten stuck between the pages of one of the books.

Next he found an extra pair of stockings, rolled into a ball. To her relief, she didn't have to put them in her hair. He found her comb, and exclaimed over how well made it was. She had searched for a wooden one that wouldn't cause comment, then carefully scratched off the maker's name. The comb was one thing he really could have used, but he dropped it back into the bag without further interest. A few more halfhearted pawings, and he decided she didn't have any valuables hidden from him. He gathered the horse's reins, and with a click of his tongue and a touch of his heels they rode on, with her held carefully in front of him like a queen—a queen with a Swiss Army knife rolled up in her hair.

Chapter 20

THE GRIMY GROUP OF MEN AND THEIR TWO CAPTIVES REACHED A castle just before nightfall. The setting sun had given Grace their direction of travel, and she had carefully noted what landmarks she could. Luckily, they seemed to be traveling due east, so if—when—she managed to free Niall and they escaped, she knew they should go due west.

The castle was surprisingly small, little more than a keep with a great hall added, and in ill repair at that. Grace was ushered into the dark, smelly interior, but at least she walked on her own. She watched, trying to hide her anxiety, as Niall was carried in. The bundle had stopped squirming a couple of hours before, and she wondered if they had inadvertently smothered him. Evidently the same thought occurred to the beast, because he shouted something and one of the four men carrying Niall cuffed him on the side of the head. A muffled growl reassured them, and Grace.

Securing Niall was much more important than dealing with her, at least for the moment. A smoky torch was fetched, and Niall was carried down a narrow, winding stone staircase, deep into the bowels of the castle. Grace trailed along because she didn't know what else to do, and the dirty, sullen women who had watched her arrival didn't seem welcoming. Besides, she needed to know where Niall would be held.

The dungeon was creepy. It was dank and dark, with moisture oozing from the slimy stone walls. The air was noticeably colder. There were three cells dug into the earth, each of them secured by an enormous wooden door. There weren't any grilles in the door; the prisoners in this dungeon would live in total darkness, cold and damp, and likely die of pneumonia within a week or two.

The beast cut the ropes that bound the plaids about Black Niall; he and his men all stood with weapons ready, should Niall try to escape. Grace stood on tiptoe, her eyes wide as she tried to get a glimpse of the man who had haunted her for so long. Her movement drew the beast's attention and he scowled at her. He barked an order, and one of the men reluctantly took her arm and forced her to the stairs. She tried to resist, slow him down, but he wasn't happy to be missing the fun and he literally hauled her up the stairs, wrenching her arm in the process. Below, yells burst from male throats and she twisted her head, trying to see, but she was already too far up the curving stairs. There was a crash, and curses, and the sounds of a scuffle, feet scraping on stone and the thud of fists into flesh.

She flinched, wondering if they intended to beat him to death. Her guard jerked at her arm, scowling at her. She gave him a frustrated glare. Yelling at him wouldn't do any good, because no one understood her.

They reached the great hall and he shoved her toward another flight of stairs, this one curving upward into the keep. This staircase was just as dark and narrow. Grace glanced down and saw the sullen faces watching her.

The guard paused in front of a crude wooden door, opened it, and shoved her inside. Immediately she whirled but he closed the door in her face, with a snarled order that she took to mean "Stay there!"

There was no keyhole in the door and the bar was positioned on this side of the door, meaning she wasn't locked in, but when she laid her ear against the wood she heard the guard settling himself on the other side.

She turned and looked at her jail. The room was small and dark, lit by a single smoking torch whose light didn't quite reach all the corners of the room despite its lack of size. The only window was a narrow slit, cut so an arrow could be shot from it at any angle. The floor was covered with rushes gone black and smelly with age, and the only furniture was a roughly made bed that was about the size of a modern double, a single chair, and a wobbly table. A small chest sat against the far wall, and a single candle stood on the table. There was a fireplace, but no fire. A leather bottle stood on the table beside the candle, and a single metal cup.

Grace took advantage of her privacy, which she was sure was only temporary. Unless she missed her guess, this was the beast's bedchamber. Hastily she removed the tweezers from her hair, which had held up remarkably well, and unrolled the knife. After replacing the tweezers in their slot, she thrust the knife inside her stocking and retied the garter, determined to keep the combination weapon and tool with her from now on.

Taking the small wooden box from its pocket inside the burlap bag, she opened it and removed the handkerchief, carefully unrolling it so she didn't lose any of the precious pills. She had brought a full course of antibiotics, and prescriptions of painkillers and Seconals, in addition to picking up some over-the-counter stuff in Edinburgh. The Seconals were an impulse, an effort to cover all bases; it was strange that they would be the first drug she would need to use.

The reddish capsules were hundred-milligram doses, enough to put someone to sleep. What she had to figure out was the delivery system, because she couldn't hand one to the beast and say, "Here, take this."

She looked at the leather bottle, thinking. Alcohol intensified the effects of Seconal; what wasn't a lethal dose of the drug could become lethal if the user also drank. She didn't want to kill the beast, just knock him out. Two or three pills were enough to put someone to sleep; the pharmacist had carefully told her that she shouldn't take more than one, because she didn't weigh very much.

The beast was a heavy man, not very tall but she guessed his weight at two hundred pounds. She picked out three capsules, and returned her drug stash to the burlap bag.

She opened the leather bottle and sniffed the contents. Her eyes watered at the smell of raw, strong ale. He wouldn't notice anything wrong with the taste if she dissolved the entire thirty capsules in his cup.

Three should do the trick, however. Carefully she pulled the capsules apart, pouring the powder into the battered metal cup. Then she poured a little ale into the cup and swished the liquid around until the powder dissolved. She peered into the cup. The color of the ale looked a little cloudy, but in this light he wasn't likely to notice.

Then, forcing herself to calm and patience, Grace sat down in the chair with the cup in her hand.

She waited a long time. The noise that drifted up made her think there was a revelry going on downstairs. She was hungry, but she wasn't anxious to join them. If someone thought to send food, fine. If not, she had been hungry before.

She grew drowsy. The flickering torch was as sedative as watching a fire in a fireplace, and gave off enough warmth that she wasn't cold. She thought of Niall, and knew that he was neither warm nor comfortable enough to sleep. He would be hungry, too; if they hadn't fed her, they certainly hadn't fed him. That was assuming he was even still alive, but she didn't think they had killed him yet. If the beast intended to kill him, he would want to gloat a bit first. He struck her as that kind of man.

Finally she heard voices outside the door. She didn't jump up, but continued sitting relaxed in the chair, or at least as relaxed as she could be on something as hard as rock. The door opened and the beast came in, his shaggy head lowered and his small, mean eyes bright with anticipation. He looked at the cup, at the open bottle of ale on the table, and his lips spread in a big grin, displaying terrible teeth and remnants of the dinner he had eaten.

Grace yawned and leisurely came to her feet. She pretended to sip the ale, then looked at him and raised the cup in a silent question, nodding at the bottle. He rumbled what she took to be agreement, and she filled the cup, then passed it to him.

He downed the ale in two gulps, then wiped the back of his hand across his wet mouth. His eyes never left her, and lust burned hotly in them.

She fought the impulse to gag even as relief filled her. Dear Lord, how long would it take the Seconals to work? He had eaten, which would slow the effect, but from the look of him he had also had a good deal to drink. She had to stall for time, anything that would keep him from assaulting her now.

Genius struck, and she made an eating gesture, her brows lifted, and then she rubbed her stomach to indicate hunger. He scowled, but went to the door and bellowed something, she hoped a call for food. Evidently he didn't intend to starve her, but had merely forgotten.

He stomped to the chair and sat down, and poured himself another cup of ale. Grace smiled at him, pointed to herself, and said, "Grace St. John."

"Eh?"

At least she understood that sound, she thought in relief. She said again, "Grace St. John," then she pointed at him and waited.

He caught on now. He thumped his bull-like chest. "Huwe dhe Hay."

"Huwe," she repeated. She tried another smile. "Well, Huwe, I don't wish you any harm, but I hope the Seconal knocks you flat on your butt. I know you have big plans for tonight, but so do I, and you aren't included. As soon as everyone is asleep, I'm going to see what kind of damage you and your goons have done to you-know-who, and then I'm going to get him out of here."

Huwe listened to her speech with growing impatience, and he cut her short with an impatient wave of his hand. Then he spouted something involved at her. She made a helpless gesture, spreading her hands and shaking her head.

A brief thud sounded at the door and it swung open. A plump, slatternly woman with wiry dark hair came in, carrying a small platter on which rested a thick piece of coarse bread and a hunk of cheese. She set the platter down with a thunk, glaring at Grace all the while. Either no one here liked outsiders on principle, or the woman had a thing for Huwe, which gave her a new appreciation of the old saying that power was an aphrodisiac.

The woman left, and Grace pinched off a piece of bread. She sauntered around the room, nibbling daintily at the bread and making an occasional comment to Huwe. His gaze still followed her, but after ten or fifteen minutes she noticed he was blinking owlishly. She continued to pace, her manner completely relaxed, returning to the table to taste a tiny bit of the cheese. It wasn't bad.

Huwe's eyelids were drooping heavily. Grace walked over to the narrow window and stood still, looking out at the night while she pretended still to eat. In the shadows as she was, as drugged as Huwe was, he likely couldn't tell her hand was empty.

The night was bright with starlight, and a soft mist was gathering in the glens. Grace quietly watched, listening for Huwe's snores, but the inaction gnawed at her. She felt—she felt as if her body couldn't contain the force of her blood, pounding through her veins. She felt excited, anxious, burning with energy. The constant wariness with which she had lived the past year, the sense of doom hovering over her, was gone. Parrish couldn't reach her here. There were very real dangers she might face but still she felt oddly light, as if a weight had been lifted from her.

She felt alive.

The realization shocked her. She had become so accustomed to the numb bleakness inside her that she hadn't even noticed its absence. Until today, all she had felt for a year had been fear and rage and hate, punctuated by moments of a pain so sharp the numbness had been welcome. But today she had felt excitement, and interest; she had even smiled like mad at Huwe—*Huwe!* The smiles were totally false, but they were more than she had managed in a year.

She was really here. She ached in every muscle, she felt sore inside, but she was here and Black Niall was just two floors below her. They were both captives, he was likely wounded, by their captors' fists if not their swords and daggers, but she could feel his presence like an energy field, making her fingertips tingle.

A soft rumble reached her ears. She looked over at the table, where Huwe was slumped across the surface, his head pillowed on one outstretched arm.

She tiptoed over to the table and moved the bottle to a safer location. A swipe of his arm would have dislodged it, and perhaps awakened him, though she thought likely not even a cannon would do the job tonight. She wasn't going to take the chance.

She had no idea of the time, so she gingerly sat down on the bed and forced herself to wait. The ale would have flowed freely that evening; the men would be tired and sore from the battle earlier, and the ale would ease their aches. They would sleep early that night, and deeply.

Still she waited, until she was in danger of falling asleep herself. When she jerked herself to attention for the second time, she knew she had to go now.

She picked up her bag and walked silently to the door. She eased the door open, peering through the crack to see if a guard stood outside. Empty darkness greeted her, lightened only by a dim glow from down below.

She slipped out of the chamber and eased down the stairs. Men slept in the great hall, snoring lumps rolled in their plaids. She didn't tiptoe; she walked quietly, as if she had a right to be there. Anyone who woke and saw her in the dim light might think her nothing more than a serving wench, but if she were sneaking about, her furtiveness would rouse suspicions. Harmony had told her that: "Walk as if you have a right to the entire sidewalk, and the bad dudes will leave you alone."

A big iron candlestick was set on a table, the thick candle burned half down. Grace picked it up in case there was no light below; she didn't want to use her penlight and try to explain it to Niall, at least not yet.

The staircase to the dungeon was at the back of the great hall, hidden behind a door so dark she almost didn't see it. She set both candlestick and bag on the floor, and eased the door open by increments, taking care the leather hinges didn't creak. A light came from below; there would be a guard, then, for a prisoner wouldn't need light.

She eased her body into the opening, holding the door while she retrieved both bag and candlestick. She didn't need the candle, but she did need a weapon. She blew out the candle and pinched the wick with spit-dampened fingers, then removed the candle from the spike atop the stick and placed it in the bag. Carefully setting the bag down on the top step, she took a deep breath, then another, and silently prayed.

The stone wall of the dungeon was cold and damp against her back as Grace eased down the narrow, uneven steps. There was no railing, and the flicker of the torch below didn't penetrate up the inky, curving stairs. She had to feel her way down, wishing for the candle after all, but it would have alerted the guard to her presence.

The weight of the heavy iron candlestick pulled at her arm. When she was halfway down the curve of steps she could see the single guard, sitting below on a crude bench with his back resting against the wall, a rough skin of wine at his elbow. Good; if she were lucky, he had drunk himself into a stupor. Even if he had a Scotsman's hard head for spirits, at least the liquor would have slowed his reflexes. She hoped he was asleep because given where he was sitting, she would have to approach him almost head-on. The light was poor and she could hide the candlestick against her leg, but if he stood up it would be much more difficult for her to hit him hard enough to knock him out. She was so sore and battered from the trip through time that she didn't trust her strength; better if she could simply lift the heavy candlestick and swing it downward, letting gravity aid her.

Grace cautiously edged her foot forward, searching for the edge of each step while trying not to scrape her shoe against the stone. The air was cold, and fetid; the smell assaulted her nose, making it wrinkle in disgust. The odor was composed of unmistakable human waste, but beneath that lay the sharper, more unpleasant odors of blood, and fear, and the sour sweat of pain. Men had been tortured, and died, in these foul depths that never saw the sun.

It was up to her to make certain Black Niall didn't join their ranks.

She had a guilty thought: was it her fault he had been captured? Common sense told her that was ridiculous; it was impossible for Niall to have heard her mental call to him. She couldn't have caused a split second of inattention that could have resulted in his capture. She hadn't actually seen what had happened, anyway, so it was silly to feel guilty. But then, her very presence here was evidence that the impossible was possible, so she couldn't say for certain that Niall hadn't heard her call him.

She didn't know how much time she had. Huwe of Hay would sleep until late morning, under the double influence of alcohol and Seconal. Given how much he had drunk, she only hoped she hadn't overdosed him. Crude and disgusting as he was, she didn't want to kill him. But she was heartily grateful she had brought those drugs; without the Seconal, she could never have escaped from Huwe at all, much less avoided being raped.

Her searching foot found no more steps. The floor was nothing more than hard-packed dirt, uneven and treacherous. She stood still for a moment, taking deep, silent breaths as she tried to steady her nerves. The guard still sat slumped on the bench, his head nodded forward onto his chest. Was he truly asleep, or drunk, or merely playing possum? As careful as she had been, had he still heard some betraying rustle, and was now trying to lure her closer?

It didn't matter; she didn't have any choice. Even if his capture wasn't her fault, she couldn't leave Black Niall here for Huwe to kill. Niall was the Guardian, the only person alive who knew both the secrets and the location of the Templars' Treasure. Unless she could find the Treasure herself, she needed his knowledge, his cooperation, to prevent Parrish from getting his hands on the Treasure. She wanted Parrish stopped, and she wanted Parrish dead; for that, she needed Black Niall alive.

She considered the guard. If he were awake and merely being crafty, then she would arouse less suspicion by approaching him directly, as if she had nothing to hide. Harmony's theory, again. Moreover, if he saw her, he wouldn't expect any threat from a woman. Her heart thumped wildly in her chest, and for a moment black spots swam before her eyes. Panic made her stomach lurch, and she thought she might throw up. Desperately she sucked in more air, fighting back both nausea and weakness. She refused to let herself falter now, after all she had already been through.

Cold sweat broke out on her body, trickled down her spine. Grace forced her feet to move, to take easy, measured strides that carried her across the rough floor as if she had nothing at all to hide. The torchlight danced and swayed, as if under the spell of some unheard music, casting huge, wavering shadows on the damp stone walls. The guard didn't move.

Ten feet. Five. Then she stood directly in front of the guard, so close she could smell the stench of his unwashed body, sharp and sour. Grace swallowed, and steeled herself for the blow she had to deliver. She sent up a quick prayer that she wouldn't cause him any lasting damage, and used both aching arms to raise the heavy candlestick high.

Her clothing rustled with her movements. He stirred, opening bleary eyes and peering up at her. His mouth gaped open. Grace swung downward, and the massive iron candlestick crashed against the side of his head with a solid thud that made her cringe. Anything he might have said, any alarm he might have given, dissolved into a grunt as he slid sideways, his eyes closing once more.

Blood trickled down the side of his head, matting in his filthy hair. Looking down at him she saw that he was younger than she had thought, surely not much more than twenty. His grimy cheeks still held a certain childish curve. Tears stung her eyes, but she turned sharply away, need shouldering aside regret.

Of the three cells, only one was barred. "Niall!" she whispered urgently as she grasped the massive bar. How was she best to communicate with him? Today had taught her that Gaelic wasn't a possibility. He was a Templar, though; he would almost certainly speak French. She felt capable in either Old English or Old French, but Latin hadn't changed at all since his time, so that was the language she chose.

"I have come to free you," she said softly as she struggled with the bar. My God, it was heavy! It was like wrestling with a tree trunk, six feet long and a good ten inches wide. Her hands slipped on the wood, and a splinter dug deep into her little finger. Grace bit off an involuntary cry of pain as she jerked her hand back.

"Are you hurt?"

The question was voiced in a deep, calm, softly burred

voice, and came very clear to her ears as if he stood close against the other side of the door. Hearing it, Grace froze, her eyes closing as she struggled once more with tears and an electrifying surge of emotion that threatened to overwhelm her. It was really Black Niall, and oh, *God,* he sounded just as he had in her dreams. That voice was like thunder and velvet, capable of a roar that would freeze his enemies or a warm purr that would melt a woman into his arms.

"Only . . . only a little," she managed to say, her voice shaking. She struggled to remember the correct words. "A splinter . . . the bar is very heavy, and it slipped."

"Are you alone?" Concern was there now. "The bar is too big for a mere woman."

"I can do it!" she said fiercely. Mere? *Mere?* What did he know? She had survived on the run for a year; she had managed to get here, against all odds, and moreover she was the one on the *free* side of the door. Anger mixed with exhilaration, surging through her veins, making her feel as if she would burst through her skin. She wanted to scream, she wanted to hit something, she wanted to dance. Instead she turned her attention back to the bar.

Abandoning any attempt to lift it with her hands, she bent her knees and lodged her shoulder under it, driving upward with all the strength in her back and legs.

The weight of the bar bit into her shoulder, nearly drove her downward again. Gritting her teeth, Grace braced her legs and strained. She could feel blood rush to her face, feel her heart and lungs labor. Her knees wobbled. Damn it, she *wouldn't* let this stupid piece of wood defeat her, not after all she had already gone through!

A growl of refusal burst past her lips and she summoned every ounce of strength in her aching body, gathering it for one final effort. Her thigh muscles screamed in pain, her back burned. Desperately she shoved upward, forcing her legs to straighten, and one end of the bar slowly rose inch by inch. It teetered for a moment and she shoved again, and the bar began sliding down through the other bracket. The rough wood scraped her cheek, snagged her clothes. Using both hands, ignoring the need for quiet, she shoved the bar forward until it was free of the right bracket.

Instead of continuing its slide through the other bracket, the heavy bar slowed, its weight tipping it back toward her. Grace scrambled out of the way as one end hit the dirt floor with a reverberating thud. The bar stood braced there, one end on the floor and the other balanced against the second bracket.

She stood still, breathing hard, trembling in every muscle, but triumph roared through her, fierce and sweet. Heat radiated from her, banishing the cold as if she stood close to a fire, and she couldn't feel any pain in her injured hand. She felt invigorated, invincible, and her breasts rose tight and aroused beneath her clothing.

"Open the door," she invited, the words coming out breathlessly despite her efforts to steady her voice. Then she couldn't resist a taunt: "If you can."

A low laugh came to her ears, and slowly the massive door began to open, pushing the huge bar before it. Grace took a step back, her gaze fastened hungrily on the black space yawning open between the door and the frame, waiting for her first glimpse of Black Niall in the flesh.

He came through the door as casually as if he were on vacation, but there was nothing casual in the black gaze that swept over the unconscious guard and then leaped to her, raking her from head to foot in a single suspicious, encompassing look. His vitality seared her like a blast, an almost palpable force, and she felt the blood drain from her face.

He could have stepped straight from her dreams.

He was there, just as he had been in the images that had plagued her for endless nights, as he had been when his essence had pulled her across nigh seven centuries. Slowly, like a lover's hand drifting over the face of a beloved, barely touching as if too strong a contact would destroy the spell, her gaze traced his features.

Yes, it was he. She knew him well, his face memorized in countless dreams. The broad, clear forehead; the eyes, as black as night, as old as sin. The thin, high-bridged Celtic nose, and chiseled cheekbones; the firm and unsmiling lips, the uncompromising chin and jaw. He was big. Mercy, she hadn't realized how big he was, but he stood more than a foot taller than she, at least six-four. His long black hair swung past his shoulders, shoulders that were at least a two-foot span of solid muscle. The hair at his temples was secured in a thin braid on each side of his face.

His shirt and plaid were dirty, and dark with dried blood. Bruises mottled his face; one eye was swollen almost shut. But for all that, he was strong and vital, impervious to the cold that was making her shiver, or at least she told herself it was the cold. He was wilder than she could have imagined, and yet he was exactly as she had dreamed. The reality of him was like a blow, and she swayed.

He looked around, his face hard and set, every muscle poised for action. "You are alone?" he asked again, evidently doubting that she had managed the bar by herself.

"Yes," she whispered.

No enemies rushed from the inky shadows, no alarm was raised. Slowly he returned his gaze to her, and with the torch behind her outlining her form she knew he could see how violently she was trembling.

"Frail but valiant," he murmured, coming closer. Despite herself, she would have shrunk back, but he moved with the deceptive speed of an attacking tiger. One hard arm passed around her waist, both supporting and capturing her, drawing her against him. "No, don't fear me, sweetings. Who are you? No relation of Huwe's, I'll wager, not with such a pretty face—and a command of Latin."

"N-no," she stammered. The contact with him was going to her head, making her feel giddy. Oh, God. His voice had taken on a deep, unmistakable note. Her stomach clenched in panic. She lifted her right hand to brace against his chest; the touch jammed the splinter deeper into her finger, and she flinched from the sudden pain.

Instantly he caught her hand, hard fingers wrapping gently around it and turning it toward the light. Her stomach clenched again at the contrast of her hand lying in that callused palm. Like Huwe's, his hand was dirty from the battle he'd fought that day, but that was the only resemblance between the two men. Black Niall's big hand was lean and powerful, the long fingers well shaped, the nails tended. For all the obvious strength in that hand, it cradled her much smaller one as delicately as if he held a baby bird.

She glanced at the small, burning wound on her hand. The long, jagged splinter had entered her finger lengthwise, and the end protruded just above the bend of the first knuckle. He made a softly sympathetic sound, almost a croon, and lifted her hand to his mouth. With delicate precision he caught the end of the splinter in his animal-white teeth, and steadily drew it out. Grace flinched again at the pain, sucking in a hissing breath and rising on tiptoe against him, but he held her hand steady in his powerful grip. He spat the splinter out, then sucked hard at the sullenly bleeding wound. She felt his tongue flicking against her skin, laving her hurt, and a moan that had nothing to do with pain slipped from her lips.

That black gaze moved back to her face, so close to his now, and his eyes grew heavy-lidded as he sensed how it was with her. His thin nostrils flared like a stallion's, drawing in her female scent. And then his expression changed, shifting into furious recognition.

"You!" He spat the word as if it were an epithet. His hands bit into her shoulders as he whirled her toward the light. She hadn't put her hair back up after removing the knife, and he sank one hand deep into the heavy mass, lifting it as if to measure its length. His olive-toned face was savage.

"M-me?" she squeaked ungrammatically, in English. She caught herself and returned to Latin. "I?"

"Who are you?" he asked again, and this time the question was hard with barely contained fury. "It was you, screaming my name, who distracted me today and caused me to be captured. You have watched me for months, never showing your face until you invaded my dreams. Are you a spy, a witch?"

Grace went white, staring at him in horrified dismay. He had felt her dreams, shared them with her? *Oh, no.* She felt a fiery blush begin to heat her cheeks. Then she jerked as his last words registered. "No! I'm not a spy, or a witch!"

"Then why have you watched me?" he asked grimly, releasing her to cross swiftly to the unconscious guard. He looked briefly at the young man's bleeding head, then at the iron candlestick lying beside him, before taking both sword and dagger as if he felt the need to be armed in her presence.

The dagger disappeared inside his soft leather boot, and he turned to face her, eyes narrowed and watchful. "How have you come to my bed so often I know the very smell of you? How came you to be with Huwe today? I heard your voice, I know you were there."

"They c-captured me, too." The unsteadiness of her voice annoyed her, and she took a deep, irritated breath. She was mortified that he had shared those erotic dreams with her; she didn't know how it had happened, but everything about this went beyond the normal and there was nothing she could do about it.

"A likely tale. You hardly bear the look of mistreatment."

"Huwe intended to ransom me, I think."

"That would not keep him from rutting on you, sweetings."

She blushed again, unable to control the heat in her cheeks, but it seemed as much in response to the rather biting endearment than to his crude words. "No. *I* kept him from that."

"How did you accomplish that feat? A spell?"

"I am not a witch! I gave him a drink that made him sleep. He was drunk, anyway."

"And all the others?"

"They are all asleep from drink. They think you safely locked away, and that your men will not dare attack while they have you."

"No, but they will be nearby." He didn't seem as angry now, though his gaze was still hard when he looked at her. "You have not yet answered my question. Who are you?"

"Grace St. John." She said it in English, because she didn't know the specific Latin applications.

He repeated her name as she had said it, slowly duplicating the pronunciation, his tongue sure on the syllables with the deftness of someone who spoke several languages. Then he stepped closer to her, the sword still in his hand, so close that his big body blotted out the light of the flickering torch. "And how have you watched me?"

"I haven't." She made a helpless gesture. "I dreamed."

"Ah. More dreams." He was still angry, she could feel it, but his voice had taken on that low, seductive note again, making her shiver as she fought the pull of it. "In your dreams, sweetings, was I inside you?" he whispered, moving even closer, his left arm sliding about her waist and slowly, inexorably, pulling her against him. "Were you beneath me in my bed, did I ride you hard?"

Grace struggled to breathe. Her lungs weren't working properly, only drawing in fast, shallow breaths. She braced her hands against his chest, feeling the incredible heat of his body through his rough linen shirt. She felt hot, too, restless and panicky, her skin almost painfully sensitive.

His gaze was sharp and hot, startlingly aware. His lips parted slightly, his own breathing coming a little too fast as the hard arm around her waist urged her even closer, closer, until her breasts touched him. "I'm a fool," he murmured, this time in Scots, but somehow she understood him. "I've no time for more, but I'll at least have the taste of ye."

He lifted her, turning to pin her against one of the cell doors. His big, iron-muscled body ground against her from shoulder to knee, and her breath snagged at the fullness of his arousal. Instantly he took advantage of her parted lips and set his mouth to hers. His kiss was ravaging, not in force but in effect. Her blood surged wildly in response, and her body instinctively molded to him. His taste was hot, tart and uncivilized, shatteringly familiar. He used his tongue with soul-searing skill, demanding her response, then deepening his advantage when she helplessly gave it. His hands moved over her body, cupping her breasts, her bottom, moving her against him. His long fingers slipped between her legs, feeling her through her gown. Grace had a second of warning, an almost painful inner tightening, and frantically she pushed against him but it was too late. Sensation splintered into a thousand piercing shards, and with a hoarse cry she arched into him.

She felt his surprise as his mouth muffled her cry, then he gathered her tighter while her climax pulsed through her, those devilishly knowledgeable fingers gently rubbing to give her a full measure of satisfaction. The spasms finally slowed, diminishing to tremors, and she sank weakly against him.

She jerked her mouth from his and pressed her head hard against his shoulder, her face hot with mortification. She had never been so embarrassed and humiliated in her life.

Reaching climax in a dream was unsettling enough, but to do it in front of him, with no more stimulation than a kiss and a bold caress—she burned with shame.

"Lass," he said, his voice low and husky, almost a whisper. His lips pressed briefly to the exposed curve of her neck, the touch hot and tender. His breath came in soft, short pants as he let her slide to her feet, all down the length of his body.

She would have kept her head down but he cupped her chin, lifting her face so he could see it. His thumb swept over the soft bloom of her mouth. His own lips were swollen and shiny, his eyes narrow with lust. "A pity I must go," he whispered in Scots. "Ye burn a man to a fair crisp, but I'd turn to ash wi' a smile on my face." He bent and brushed her mouth with his, then patted her bottom and set her away from him.

Shaking, Grace leaned against the door, her mind a blank and her knees like water. He moved so fast that he had already reached the stairs before realization sank into her brain. She struggled upright, her eyes wide. "No, wait!" she cried. "Take me with you!"

He didn't even pause, his powerful legs taking the stairs two at a time. He tossed her a grin. "I give you thanks for my liberty, but gratitude doesn't make me a fool," he said, returning to Latin, and he disappeared upward into the darkness.

Oh, damn! She didn't dare call out again. She launched herself after him but her legs were still shaking, and she barely had the strength to climb the stairs. There was no sign of him when she emerged from the dungeon.

She couldn't sound an alarm, for after all she didn't want him recaptured. Nor did she herself dare to remain. She collected her bag and tiptoed toward the kitchen, thinking that the most likely avenue of his escape. If there were a guard there, Niall would have taken care of him. She had to get out of this grimy hold and find him again. He wasn't a hero, damn him, no knight in shining armor. He was just a man, though bigger than most, more bold and vital. He was arrogant and rude, and he was her only hope.

Chapter 21

GRACE WAS A LITTLE GRATIFIED TO REALIZE SHE HAD GUESSED right. Outside the kitchens she found a guard's body, slumped on the ground in the boneless attitude of death. There was an uproar in the stables, torches being lit, men running and cursing. Niall must have stolen a horse and escaped through the postern gate. There was no chance of her stealing a horse now, and the keep was coming awake behind her. She dodged into a small storeroom, little more than a shed built against the side of the keep. It was evidently the granary, for the dusty smell of oats made her stifle a sneeze.

She heard rustlings in the oats that made her grit her teeth. Where there was grain, there were rats. She was acutely aware of the vulnerability of her legs beneath the long skirts. What she wouldn't give for her jeans and boots!

But she stood grimly still, even when the noisy search discovered the guard's body just outside her hiding place. Even though she couldn't understand the words, she could grasp their anger and agitation. Their chieftain couldn't be roused; the dungeon guard was injured, perhaps dead; both captives were gone, though only one horse was missing. She only hoped they would assume she was with Niall, that somehow they had simply failed to see her, because otherwise they would begin a thorough search of the keep.

Damn Niall, she thought violently. Why couldn't he have taken her with him? Even if he refused to take her to Creag Dhu, he could at least have gotten her away from Huwe. Gratitude didn't make him a fool, indeed!

The uproar eventually died down. They couldn't pursue Niall in the dark, and without Huwe they weren't inclined to take action anyway. She waited, rustling her feet whenever the munching rats seemed to get too close, sending them squealing and scurrying. She would never forgive Niall for this.

At least security would be lax, now that their prisoner was gone. The Hay stronghold wasn't very strong anyway, from what she had seen. There had once been a wall around it, but it hadn't been maintained and the mortar had crumbled, leaving big gaps. Unfortunately, someone would still be watching the horses.

His tough luck, she thought when she finally crept out of her hiding place. She didn't know the time, so she didn't dare wait much longer. Dawn could come at any time, and with it her only opportunity to escape.

A soft mist was falling, not much more than a heavy fog. Her heart sank. That was probably why they hadn't pursued Niall, because they couldn't see in this pea soup. Unfortunately, she didn't have any choice, even though she didn't know where she was. She had carefully noted the direction from which they had come the day before, but the fog greatly increased her chances of getting totally turned around.

She walked quietly into the stable. A guard snoozed against a pile of hay, a small candle with a protective globe over it guttering by his side. What was she supposed to bash *him* with? She looked around and spied a rough pitchfork, its handle made of a sturdy length of wood. She picked it up, gripped it like a bat, and gave it a healthy swing. The wood swatted him in the side of his head and he jerked once, then fell heavily limp.

"I'm going to go to hell," she whispered into the night. That made two innocent men she had knocked in the head tonight, and for all she knew she had killed both of them. Severe head injuries in medieval times likely resulted in death. If Niall had taken her with him, hitting this last guard wouldn't have been necessary.

She bit her lip, looking at the curious equine heads surveying her. She knew how to ride, because it was a convenient skill to have when out on a dig, but she wasn't an expert and in any case hadn't been on a horse in more than two years, except for being held in front of Huwe on his horse yesterday, and that didn't count.

"Pick a horse, any horse," she muttered to herself. Geldings were always less fractious than stallions or even mares, but in the darkness she couldn't tell anything about her available choices except their size. She settled on a brown horse that was neither the largest nor the smallest, hoping that moderation was the key to success.

The horse stood quietly as she saddled it, and followed obediently when she led it to a keg. She stepped up on the keg, then mounted the horse. After tying her bag securely to the saddle, she clicked her tongue to the animal and carefully rode it out of the stable. Behind her, she heard a quiet groan as the guard began reviving. She was glad he wasn't dead, but that meant she had only a minute or so to get away before the alarm was raised.

She rode the horse at a walk to one of the gaps in the wall, and let it pick its own way over the tumbled rock. In the dark and the fog, the run-down keep was soon out of sight.

The safest course would be to find a place to hide, and wait until dawn when both she and the horse would be able to see. But if she remained close by, that increased the chances the Hays would recapture her and she doubted she would escape abuse so easily again.

When she saw Black Niall again, she was going to throttle him, even if she had to climb on a stool to do it.

She clicked to the horse and nudged it with her heels, but she let it pick its way at its own cautious speed. She could barely see past the horse's nose, so it seemed wiser to trust the animal's instincts; it at least had its feet on the ground. Still, she hoped sunrise wasn't several hours away.

To be fair to Niall, she hadn't tried to explain herself or her presence. Part of her reticence was pure caution, because as Guardian his duty was to protect the Treasure from all threats, including herself. If he discovered she knew the procedure for time travel, he might feel it necessary to kill her. If she could get the Treasure herself, without his assistance, she preferred to do so. If she found she needed him, then would be the time to confess.

But all the logical reasons for remaining quiet weren't what had kept her from telling him. She had simply been too shocked, first by the embarrassing discovery that he had shared the dreams with her and then by the way she had humiliated herself in his arms. She had been hard put even to speak, much less launch into a detailed explanation.

Her cheeks burned again as she remembered what had happened, and she lifted her face to the chilly mist.

She had been agitated from the moment she had arrived back in time, nervous, excited. She hadn't thought that agitation could so swiftly convert into sexual response, but it had. It was as if her body had been numb for a year, but something had happened to her during the time transition and now she felt everything too much.

Niall had fascinated her from the moment she had first read his name. She had spent so much time concentrating on him, dreaming about him, it was no wonder all her senses had been so acutely focused on him. All those hours she had been so aware of his actual presence that it had been difficult for her to think of anything else, her skin hypersensitive, prickly. She should have recognized the sexual charge underlying her jitters, but she hadn't. While she had accepted and rationalized the sexual aspect of her dreams, it hadn't occurred to her the physical attraction would be as strong in reality.

It wasn't. It was stronger.

She had been unfaithful to Ford in every way except the actual act, but she couldn't find any solace in that detail. If circumstances had been different, if they had been alone in a safe place, she had no doubt Niall would have had her. But now that she recognized her weakness, she could safeguard against giving in to it. She must never let Niall so much as kiss her again.

But as she rode through the night, she was uncomfortably aware that if Niall wished to kiss her or do anything else to her, her defenses were very weak indeed.

Creag Dhu was a massive stone castle, the rock from which it was built as dark as a stormy sky. Unlike the Hay keep it was in excellent repair, with thick stone walls surrounding four huge towers. The big main entrance was guarded by two sets of gates twenty feet apart, and the men who guarded it looked healthy, well clothed and armed, and well trained. Everyone who entered was stopped and questioned, and no carts or bundles went through those gates without being thoroughly inspected.

Grace knew she should have expected as much, given Niall's military background, but when she looked at Creag Dhu she felt overwhelmed by the task she had set herself. Just getting in looked impossible; how on earth would she manage searching it?

She had to stay hidden, because a stranger would be immediately noticed. The castle was busy, having attracted its own small village as people moved closer to safety, but everyone would know everyone else. She was hungry, and tired from having ridden for two days. She had wandered off course in the fog, and a journey that shouldn't have taken an entire day had instead taken two.

At least the horse was content, because there was plenty of grass and water.

The animal was a gelding, blessed with a calm and forgiving nature. If it hadn't been, Grace was certain she never would have survived. She ached from head to foot, and her bottom was so sore she didn't think she would be able to climb back into the saddle even if Huwe of Hay suddenly appeared in front of her.

She had tethered the horse in a copse of forest, while she assessed the situation, which wasn't promising. Perhaps she should just walk up to the gates and ask to see him. He might not be pleased, but she *had* freed him from the dungeon; if she told him she was hungry, could he turn her away?

Of course he could, she thought. He was the Guardian. He wouldn't let anything as paltry as gratitude stand in the way of his duty.

She had to think of some way to get inside the castle.

She couldn't smuggle herself inside by hiding in any of the carts she saw going in; all the carts were searched, even when the guards obviously knew the owner and they chatted genially together while the goods or produce were inspected. She didn't even speak the language, so when they asked questions she wouldn't be able to answer. She could try speaking Old English, but that wouldn't win her any friends here in Scotland; the two countries had been at war for years. She could understand most of the Scots dialect, but speaking it was useless because the parts of it she understood were English, so she wouldn't gain anything.

Even if she did manage to get into Creag Dhu, what then? The castle inhabitants would certainly know one another far better than they knew the village folk, so there wouldn't be any way she could escape notice by mingling with the crowd. Exploring the castle would take time; she needed to be able to come and go without being questioned. Grimly she arrived back at one inescapable conclusion: even if she got into the castle, she would need Niall's permission to stay.

She decided to face one problem at a time, and found herself back at the beginning: how to get into Creag Dhu?

She began making her way back to the horse, stumbling over rocks and roots, catching her skirts on bushes and twigs and having to jerk them free. She was becoming more and more irritated with the nuisance of a long gown. To tell the truth, she was irritated with everything, but at least her ill humor had distracted her from the humiliation of what had happened with Niall.

By the time she reached the horse, she was sweating from the effort of fighting her way through brambles and bushes. The wool surcoat, which felt good on cold nights, now suffocated her. Irritably she stripped it off and tossed it over the saddle, sighing in relief as air seeped through the lighter cotton kirtle. She loosened the laces that held the neckline and sleeves tight, pulling the neckline completely open and then pushing up the sleeves as far as she could, which was only to the middle of her forearms. Under the scarf, her hair was wet with sweat. Off came the scarf, and she unwound the heavy knot of her hair, running her fingers through it and letting fresh air reach her scalp. She had expected Scotland to be uniformly chilly even in May, but that wasn't the case today.

There was no way she was putting that heavy wool gown back on, and the velvet one would be just as hot. Grace looked down, checking the kirtle for modesty. She was dismayed to find it failed miserably, unless she didn't mind any casual observer being able to see both her nipples and the darkness of her pubic hair. Inspiration struck, and she shook out the big scarf, then tied it around her waist so that it draped strategically over both front and back. Then she bloused the kirtle out from the waist so the fullness gave her a bit of modesty up top, too. Satisfied with her effort, she stuffed the dirty wool surcoat in the bag and remounted the horse. She hadn't solved any of her problems, but at least now she was comfortable.

Five minutes later, as she watched a group of five women trudge along the rutted road, obviously heading to Creag Dhu, inspiration struck again.

The business of the women wasn't in any doubt. Their skirts were hiked up farther than any Grace had seen since arriving, and their bodices were pulled low. They hadn't bothered with long-sleeved, high-necked kirtles; their undergarments were short-sleeved and loose. No kerchiefs covered their heads, and though their hair was for the most part unkempt, as Grace watched they began finger-combing the tangles, pulling strands over their shoulders to curl flirtatiously around their breasts. They pinched their cheeks and bit their lips, and there was a good deal of laughter and obviously naughty observations.

Whores, or at least loose women, on their way to the castle for a night of recreation or commerce, or both. And Grace now looked remarkably like them, with her scanty clothing and loose hair. She kneed the horse into a walk, approaching the group from an angle.

"Good afternoon," she said pleasantly when she neared, trying to alter her accent so the "good" sounded like "guid." No help for it; she would have to speak Old English, which was at least close enough to Scots for her to be largely understood.

The whores watched her suspiciously, no hint of welcome in their faces.

"My man left me," she said baldly. "I've no coins, no food for two days, and I have no place to sleep."

An overblown redhead who had seen better days looked her up and down. "Aye?" she said in a tone that clearly meant, "So what?"

"If you are going to the castle, could I go with you? A night's work would bring me a coin or two, and at least food for my belly."

"Ye have yer beast," the redhead pointed out, nodding at the horse. A horse was a valuable animal, worth more than all their possessions put together. They weren't likely to have any sympathy for her so long as she possessed him.

Grace thought quickly. "You can have him," she promised, "if you will take me with you."

The five women put their heads together, and a swarm of Gaelic buzzed around her ears. Finally the redhead held up her hand and nodded to Grace. "'Tis a bargain." She waited expectantly, and Grace climbed down from the horse, not without a great deal of relief. Her bottom was so sore after two days of riding that she was much happier walking. She untied her bag from the saddle, and presented the reins to the redhead, who looked triumphantly around at her friends.

They resumed their trek up the road. As they trudged around a bend and the castle came into sight, the redhead said, "What's yer name?"

"Grace."

"I am Wynda." She nodded in turn at the four other women. "Nairne, Coira, Sile, and Eilidh." Introductions accomplished, they completed the walk to the castle.

Both guards stepped forward to meet them, stubbled cheeks stretched in huge grins. A great deal of giggling, pinching, and butt patting went on, then both guards looked questioningly at Grace. Evidently the other five were well known by the men-at-arms.

"Grace," Wynda said in reply to their questions. "She's a Sassenach hoor."

The guard took the bag from Grace and opened it, thrusting his big hand within. He pawed through the articles of clothing and pulled out a book, looking at it in puzzlement. Grace was too tired and hungry to do anything but stand there. Wynda repeated Grace's tale of her man leaving her behind. Perhaps it was the explanation, Grace's lack of anxiety, or that the bag obviously held no weapons, but with a shrug the guard handed the bag back to her. He called out to the guards on the other side of the double gate, and the six women walked through.

She was in. Her heart began pounding with excitement, the rush of adrenaline dispelling her fatigue.

Wynda proudly led her horse to the stable, while the others made their way toward the barracks. Grace fell behind them, slowing her steps until they were well ahead of her. They were chatting, laughing, paying her no mind. Calmly she changed direction, looking around with interest.

The inner ward was neat and busy, people going about the daily business involved in running a castle. To the left were the stables and barracks, to the right a training ground where a number of men, stripped to the waist, practiced their swordplay. She could see a well-shaped head with long black hair, towering over all the others, and quickly she looked away as if he might feel her gaze.

Black Niall was there, so she wanted to go in a different direction. Now that she was inside she could see that in addition to the four tall towers which stood at each corner, there were two smaller inner towers, one on each end of the center great hall. The entire thing was huge; she couldn't begin to guess how many rooms the castle contained.

She walked into the great hall, and a wave of dizziness swept over her. The hall was just as she had seen it in her dreams. She knew where Niall sat, and exactly where the kitchens were. The smell of roasting meat filled the air, and she wondered if her dizziness was caused by hunger.

Men and women alike were looking at her strangely, and

she ducked her head, walking quickly toward the kitchens. Perhaps she could beg a piece of bread; if not, perhaps she could steal it. She had already stolen a horse, so why worry about bread? She doubted either was as serious a sin as the rash of head bashing in which she had recently indulged.

Her appearance in the kitchen went unnoticed for a few moments, largely because there were so many people bustling about, chopping and stirring and pounding. A young boy slowly cranked a spit on which turned what looked like an entire pig. Fat dripped sizzling into the fire, sending out a wonderful smell to mingle with the yeasty scent of baking bread.

Finally a buxom woman spotted her, and snapped out a question in Gaelic. "I've come a very long way," Grace said. "I've had no food for over two days—"

"Sassenach!" the cook spat in disgust, and made a shooing motion with the cloth tied around her waist.

Evidently being thought an Englishwoman was more to her discredit than being dressed like a whore. Grace shook her head and said, "French." Then she abruptly turned white as another wave of dizziness hit her, and she swayed, reaching out to the wall to support herself.

The dizziness was all too real. Gasping, Grace bent over from the waist, trying not to faint. The need for food was becoming more pressing by the minute.

Perhaps it was the reassurance that she wasn't English, but supporting arms were suddenly around her, leading her to a bench. The buxom woman pressed a piece of bread into her shaking hand, and poured ale into a shallow bowl for her to drink. Slowly Grace chewed on the bread, which was of much better quality than that she'd had at the Hay keep. She didn't dare take more than a few sips of the ale, not after being so long without food.

The work went on around her, though the buxom woman kept looking in her direction, perhaps assessing the return of color to her face. After a bit, when the bread stayed down, another piece was placed before her, along with some cheese and a few slivers of cold pork. Feeling stronger now, Grace ate as greedily as good manners allowed, and drank more ale.

The cook clucked her tongue approvingly and put even

more meat and bread in front of her. "Ye're scarce as thick as a strae, lass. Ha' a bit more. Ye'll need yer strength tonight."

Grace tried, but she was full. After a few more bites she sighed, replete, and smiled at the woman. "Thank you. I was very hungry."

"Ye're welcome. Go on wi' ye, now." Charity served, the woman made shooing motions with her cloth again, and Grace went.

Her first priority now was to find a secure hiding place, at least until she decided what to do. When everyone's attention seemed to be elsewhere, she dodged into a curtained alcove and gingerly sat down on the floor, prepared to wait.

She leaned her head back against the cold stone wall. What had she gotten herself into? Coming back had seemed reasonable when she was still in her own time, but in the three days since her arrival she had accomplished exactly nothing toward her goal. What had seemed fairly simple— find the Treasure and return to her own time—had taken on gargantuan proportions.

Now that she had seen the size of the castle, she knew it would take days, weeks, to search it thoroughly. She certainly couldn't stay hidden the entire time. Unless she enlisted Niall's help, which didn't seem a viable alternative, she needed an excuse to stay in the castle. To do that, she had to have Niall's permission.

She had to face him again. She didn't look forward to it, but she had done more difficult things than this during the past year. What was humiliation, after all, compared to seeing her husband and brother murdered, to being hunted like an animal?

She was very tired. Now that she had eaten, she was so sleepy she couldn't keep her eyes open. She hauled the heavy burlap bag around behind her back and reclined in a more comfortable position, her head pillowed on books and clothing. She slept within minutes.

After declining enthusiastic offers of company from both Jean and Fenella, a lusty serving wench, Niall climbed the stairs that curved along the outside wall of the tower, leading to his private chamber. He was in a foul mood. He ached for a woman, but not one with Fenella's overripe charms. Not even Jean tempted him, and over the months she had become his favorite, if not only, bedmate.

"Damn the witch!" He swore viciously as he slammed the door to his bedchamber. He strode to the table and lifted the bottle of wine that sat there, then thumped it down unpoured. He didn't want wine; he'd had wine when he supped. What he wanted was what he had left to Huwe's untender mercies.

Witch or spy, still he should have taken her with him. At least then he wouldn't feel this gnawing discontent, this sharp-clawed lust that refused to be slaked on other women's bodies.

The feel of her was still in his arms, along his body. No woman in his life had ever responded as she had, so swiftly and completely, her body pulsing to his touch as if she had been made for him alone. It had been like holding fire, delicate fire, and he wanted it again. He wanted more. He wanted to push deep into her and hold himself there while she spasmed around him, arms and legs clinging, hips pumping.

He groaned aloud. He had done so in his dreams, *their* dreams, but when at last he'd had his hands on her, like a fool he had left her behind. He had been so angry to find her with the Hays that all he could think was that she was somehow in league with them, and had spied on him apurpose. His sense of betrayal had made him furious with her.

Later, when he had found his men and was well away from the Hay keep, logic had returned. She wasn't a Hay; one look at her had told him that. He should have discovered why she was there, who she was, where she was from. She had said her name was Grace St. John, a name he didn't like repeating even in his own mind. It was somehow mocking, a reminder of the faith he had lost. Her clothing had been uncommonly fine, her accent strange. She spoke Latin; that alone was so unusual it raised an internal alarm. Why would a woman speak the language of the Church?

The hour had grown late while he sat downstairs, trying to work up a bit of interest in any of the women available to him, but he wasn't inclined to sleep. He paced around the chamber, thinking of clear blue eyes and a swath of shiny dark hair. She had smelled as sweet as in his dream, and her mouth . . . he closed his eyes, whispering a strained profanity under his breath as he helplessly imagined her mouth sliding down his body, closing over his shaft, and his entire body jerked in reaction.

Furiously he threw off his clothes. He was fully erect, aching. All he had to do was open the door and call for one of the women, or two, and he could ease the ache. He didn't open the door. Instead he paced, and he wondered what had happened to her. She had helped him escape, after all; had anyone seen her? He had initially thought his escape a trap, to what end he couldn't imagine since Huwe could have killed him at any time anyway, but perhaps he had overlooked something. But nothing had happened, and he had soon found his men. What had happened to her? Had she suffered for aiding him? Huwe wasn't gentle with women at the best of times; if he knew the lass had released Niall, he would kill her.

Even if no one had seen her aid him, by now Huwe would have taken her to his filthy bed, used her harshly. Niall ground his teeth. The thought of that delicate, fine-skinned body lying beneath Huwe enraged him. He would take his men and ride on the Hay keep, take her from that pigsty, care for her, gently bring her to trust and respond to him again—

The door began to creak slowly open. Niall whirled, automatically grabbing his sword, the woman forgotten as he balanced his weight on his bare feet and began the lethal swing of the blade.

Pure blue eyes peeked around the door. They flared wide in alarm as she saw the naked warrior and the shining blade whistling toward her, but she didn't scream. Instead she ducked, dropping to the floor, and at the last split second Niall deflected his aim so that the blade bit deep into the edge of the door just above where her head had been.

Cursing viciously in every language he knew, Niall worked the blade free of the wood and leaned down, gripping her arm and dragging her on her bottom into the bedchamber. She gasped, and then somehow she turned in his grasp, her legs whipping out. One dainty foot hooked behind his ankle, the other foot kicked hard at his knee, and he went down on his back. His body reacted even before he landed, flowing into the momentum, tucking, rolling, and with a lithe backward flip he came to his feet in a perfectly balanced crouch, sword in his hand.

She was still sitting on the floor, glaring at him, her skirts above her knees. He glowered down at her in silence for a moment, then with very deliberate movements walked to the table and laid the sword on it. Calmly he wrapped his plaid about his hips and turned back to face her.

She hadn't moved. Her gaze jerked up to his, and with primitive satisfaction he realized where she had been looking.

"If ye wished to see my arse, lass, ye had only to ask," he said rather mildly, considering he was so furious with her for nearly causing him to kill her that his hands ached to give her a good shaking. He approached her, reaching over her head to slam the door and flip the bar into place, then he leaned down and hauled her to her feet, standing her before him. "Now. How in hell did ye get here?"

"I stole a horse and rode," she replied, lifting her chin.

His brows lifted. "So ye speak English as well as Latin. What other accomplishments have ye?"

"French," she said readily enough. "And Greek."

"Then we may converse in any of four languages," he observed in French, as if to test her. "Given that, there should be no misunderstandings between us."

"No, there should not," she said in the same language.

He reverted to English. "Then perhaps you will tell me now how you evaded my guards and come to be in my castle, in my bedchamber."

She squared her shoulders, facing him as steadily as if he weren't more than a foot taller and easily twice her weight. "I freed you from Huwe's dungeon," she stated. "I am alone, and have no home. I came to ask you for shelter."

"Ah." His voice was soft. "You've told me the why, but what I asked was the how."

"I came in with the whores, and hid."

His teeth ground together. "And no one saw you? Asked your cause for being here?"

"I told you, I came with the whores. My cause seemed

obvious enough, given the way I'm dressed." With her hand she indicated the thin cotton garment she wore, laces loosened, the shadow of her small nipples dark against the fabric. Her hair flowed sleekly down her back, hanging below her hips.

For all the provocation of her dress, no one with eyes should have mistaken her for a whore. She had none of the look about her; her skin was too fine, her hands soft and pampered. Nor was there any vulgarity in her speech or her manner. Remembering her searing response to him, he thought she was a woman who had been well loved, not well used. But that night in the dungeon her eyes had been fierce with excitement, her awareness of him plain on her face. Tonight she was guarded, wary, despite the way she had looked at his nakedness.

There were depths and shadows in her eyes that made him wonder what she had left unsaid. A simple request for shelter? No. She had watched him for months, caused his capture, then conveniently rescued him from the dungeon. There must be a deeper purpose behind her actions, and he knew he could not risk trusting her.

His loins throbbed. He wanted to toss her onto the bed and sink himself into her. He wanted it with a ferocity that knotted his gut. He knew what it was like, knew how she felt beneath him, how she moaned with that little catch in her throat as he slowly pushed all his swollen length into her. He knew it with his mind; he wanted to know it with his flesh.

But because he wanted her so violently, he didn't dare relax his own guard.

He unbarred the door and opened it, bellowing Sim's name, then stood watching her while the castle came awake and running feet thundered up the stairs. Sim arrived gasping, clutching his sword, and behind him were ten more men.

"Aye?" Sim fought for breath, relieved at seeing Niall standing there unhurt and apparently unalarmed.

Niall opened the door wider, allowing them to see the woman standing in the middle of his bedchamber. "Put her in a bedchamber and post two guards at the door. If ye canna keep her out, perhaps ye can keep her in."

Sim gawked at her. "Wha—?" Then he recovered and grabbed her arm.

"Mind her feet," Niall advised, stepping aside so Sim could lead her from the chamber. She went easily enough, though she gave him a long, quiet look over her shoulder. The guards thrust her into the small chamber next to his and locked her in, then two of them took up position on each side of the door.

The chamber was dark and chilly. The only light was a thin sliver of starlight coming through the narrow, cross-cut window. Grace fumbled around, searching for a candle and flint, but found nothing. If she had kept her bag with her she could have struck a match and briefly surveyed her surroundings, but she had thought it safer to leave the bag hidden.

The room was unfurnished. There weren't even rushes on the stone floor. Her skin roughened with chill bumps, and she hugged her arms.

Abruptly the door was opened, banging against the wall. One of the guards thrust a burning candle into one hand and a thick plaid into the other. Without a word he closed the door again, and she heard the massive key turning in the lock.

She dropped the plaid onto the floor and carefully shielded the flickering candle with her hand as she set it down. She looked around. The room was small, empty, but she had already discerned that.

At least she had light, and a plaid to keep her warm. She was in Creag Dhu. Sighing, she wrapped herself in the plaid and lay down on the hard floor. Things could have been worse.

Chapter 22

GRACE WOKE THE NEXT MORNING TO THE SOUND OF THE KEY grating in the lock. She sat up in her plaid nest, pushing her hair out of her face. She had merely dozed for most of the night, until fatigue had finally taken its toll and toward dawn she had finally slept. Niall stood in the doorway watching her, his face expressionless, and she rose creaking to her feet. She was stiff and sore in every muscle but her legs in particular didn't want to cooperate.

"Come wi' me," he said, holding out his hand, and she limped to the door. She reflected that if he had only said those same words the night in Huwe's dungeon, she wouldn't now be aching all over.

He led her to his chamber, ushering her inside with a big, warm hand on the small of her back. A fire leaped merrily in the big fireplace, dispelling the early-morning chill. A large round wooden tub had been placed before the fire, and steam rose gently from the water that filled it.

"For you," he said, indicating the tub. "For all ye

knocked my feet from under me last night, I saw ye moved with care. Ye've a sore arse, I suspect."

She took a deep breath, staring at that wonderful hot water. "I do."

"Then get ye in the water, lass, afore it cools."

He reached out and untied the scarf from about her waist. Grace slapped his hand, backing away. "I can undress myself," she said warily. "But I won't do it with you in the room."

Those expressive black brows rose. "Ye saw me naked," he pointed out. "And it isna as if there's no been any intimacy between us."

She flushed. Having a sword swung at her head the night before had distracted her from the embarrassment she expected to feel, but now he'd been kind enough to remind her. "That was a mistake," she said evenly. "It won't happen again."

"I'm no of the same opinion," he said softly, his gaze sliding down her body. Remembering how thin the kirtle was, she turned away from him, her blush growing hotter. He chuckled, and though she didn't hear him approach he was suddenly right behind her, so close she could feel his heat. With one fingertip he lightly stroked the side of her neck, the tender underside of her jaw.

"I'll give ye privacy to bathe," he murmured. "Then Alice will bring your porridge, and we'll talk."

Grace shivered as he left the room. The first two things sounded wonderful; the last terrified her. Talk? Seduction had been in his voice, in the small touches, the way he had stood so close to her. For whatever reason he hadn't tried to take her to bed last night—anger, surprise, suspicion—this morning he had evidently decided that reason no longer held sway.

He wanted her. The thought made her knees watery as she quickly undressed and slid into the hot water, moaning aloud as the heat soaked into her sore muscles. Underlying all his suspicious questions was that sharp animal awareness between them, forged during months of shared dreaming. He had been fully aroused during that devastating kiss. He had the same memories she did, of those dreams. Just as she knew how it was to lie beneath him, he knew how it was to mount her. Yin and yang, she knew the inward thrust that stretched her around his erection, he knew the hot, moist inner slide and clasping. She knew the hardness of his hands; he, the softness of her breasts.

How could she resist that? For Ford's sake, how could she not?

She distracted herself by vigorously washing, first her hair and then the rest of herself. Just as she finished, the door opened and a sturdy gray-haired woman came in, carrying a wooden platter on which rested a covered bowl, a spoon, and a cup.

"Such hair!" she exclaimed, hurrying to the table and setting the platter on it. Lifting a heavy ewer, she came to the side of the tub. "My name is Alice; I manage the household for Lord Niall. Stand up, then, lass, and I'll pour the clean water o'er ye."

Grace felt her face heat again, but she stood up out of the protective water. Alice poured the water over her head, rinsing away the last of the soap. She was given a sheet of linen with which to dry herself, and another, smaller one to wrap about her head.

Alice made a clicking sound with her tongue. "Ye need meat on yer bones, lass. I'll keep ye fed, now ye're here. Sit ye down, now, and eat while the parritch is hot."

Wrapped in the linen cloth, Grace sat down on the bench and dipped the spoon into the porridge. It tasted nothing like the oatmeal she had eaten before, being rich with butter and milk, and having a salty taste. She ate all of it, and drank the water in the cup. "That was wonderful." She sighed. After a year's absence, her appetite seemed to be making a reappearance.

Alice had sat quietly while Grace ate, but now she bustled into action. Soon Grace found herself dressed in a soft linen smock, looser than the cotton kirtle and with short sleeves, and then a plain brown overdress was dropped over her head.

Clean stockings were provided, and ill-fitting leather shoes that had been made to fit either foot. Her hand-sewn moccasins were set aside to be cleaned. Then Alice set to work on Grace's hair, sitting her down on the bench before the fire and slowly drawing a wooden comb through the wet strands. "What's yer name, lass?" she asked comfortably.

"Grace." The motion of the comb in her hair was soothing. Grace's eyelids drooped almost shut.

"Ye've lovely hair, so thick and shiny and smooth. Takes a bit to dry, though, aye?"

"I braid it while it's still wet, sometimes," she said in answer.

The door opened behind her, and she recognized the booted footsteps. "I'll finish, Alice," Niall said, taking the comb from her hand. Alice took the wet linens and the platter with her when she left.

"Turn," Niall said, and Grace swiveled on the bench, turning her other side to the fire. He was as skilled as Alice with the comb, sliding his muscular forearm under her hair and lifting it, letting the heat of the fire dry it more evenly.

Her heartbeat had speeded when he entered. Though she sat quietly while he combed her hair, the sedative effect had vanished. Instead that feeling of being hypersensitive had seized her again, tightening her skin, sending twinges through her nerve endings.

Panic began to tighten her stomach. She had been braced for a full-scale seduction. This subtle gentling was far more dangerous to her resolve.

"Ye asked for food yesterday, in the kitchens," Niall said conversationally. "Ye were weak wi' hunger, having not eaten for two days, ye said. Then ye vanished, and no one saw ye for hours, until ye came into my chamber. Where were ye?"

"I told you last night," she said, her tone as even and without heat as his. "I hid, and I fell asleep."

"Where did ye hide?"

"In an alcove." She turned her head to glance at him over her shoulder. "Or did you think I turned myself into a bat and perched in your belfry?"

"Creag Dhu doesna have a belfry," he said in amusement. "Tell me where ye've been for two days, if ye left Hay Keep hard on my heels. Why did ye come here? Creag Dhu is for broken men and outlaws, not lovely lasses with hands soft as a bairn's."

"I couldn't escape right away," Grace explained. "I had to hide in the granary for several hours, until everyone slept again. I stole a horse, but there was fog . . . I got lost." She turned around again, this time to glare at him. "If you hadn't left me behind, I wouldn't have gotten lost."

"Sit still," he commanded, turning her back. "Ye'll pull your hair." The comb resumed its strokes through her hair. "As for why I didna bring ye with me, the reason is the question I just asked, and ye didna answer. Why did ye come *here?* Last night ye said for food, and shelter, but when ye got here ye didna even try to ask those things of me."

She was silent, searching for a plausible answer. She couldn't say because of the dreams, because for the most part they had been so blatantly sexual in nature, and yet she had rebuffed him not an hour ago.

"Also," he continued softly, "there was other shelter, closer than two days' ride, if that is truly what ye wanted. And once ye were here, all ye had to do was ask for me, instead of tricking your way into the castle. If ye thought I would refuse ye, lass, then your insistence on coming here is no verra logical. I still have the same question. Why Creag Dhu?"

He was relentless, and he hadn't missed any of the holes in her logic. She hadn't come to this time expecting everyone to be ignorant barbarians, easily outwitted, but still she was dismayed by the sophisticated nature of his reasoning. Niall wasn't at the disadvantage here; she was, tripped up by her own actions. He was right; simply approaching the gates and asking for him would have been far less suspicious.

She bowed her head, looking at her hands twisting together in her lap. She fingered her wedding ring, and for once deliberately tried to bring up Ford's image in her mind. She needed him now, sitting here before the fire with Black Niall's hands gentle in her hair. But it was difficult to concentrate, and she couldn't pull the details together.

"I was too embarrassed," she blurted.

The comb paused. "Were ye, now?" The deep voice was little more than a murmur. He slid his hand around her neck, under her hair, and she jumped in surprise. He crooned something soothing in Gaelic, and his thumb began to rub the nape of her neck. "Because I gave ye pleasure, in the dungeon? I'll admit to a bit of surprise, but then I greatly enjoyed it. A man likes for a lass to shiver and moan in his arms."

She shivered now, in response to both the memory and the caress of his thumb on her neck. He moved his hand just a little, so that he rubbed and massaged the cords that joined neck and shoulder, and she bit back a moan. Desire pooled deep in her belly, between her legs, and her breasts tightened. It was a dangerous man who knew the sensitivity of a woman's neck, where a caress was like a bolt of lightning through her body. A touch on her breast was more intimate—but a touch on her neck was more seductive. Niall knew well what he was doing.

She tried to control her breathing, which was coming in short, erratic spurts. "I haven't—I mean, there's been only . . . we had just met!"

He laughed, the soft sound totally male and self-confident. "That isna true. Ye've been in my bed many times."

She gathered herself, tried to inject a note of firmness into her tone. "Those were dreams, not reality."

"Were they not? When I wake wi' my seed spurting from me, it feels verra damn real to me." The words were full of masculine wryness.

Her breath caught on a surge of yearning so abrupt and intense it felt like pain. She wanted to feel him come inside her, wanted to feel that powerful body surge and convulse while she held him close, wanted to watch his face.

"Ye like that thought, do ye? Your wee nipples ha' gone as hard as berries."

She wasn't the only one aroused; she could hear it in the slight thickening of his accent. She closed her eyes and for a moment the only sound was that of their breathing, fast and erratic.

The comb was tossed aside and he stepped over the bench to stand in front of her. His hands slid down her arms, lifting her to her feet. She stared at the pulse throbbing in the base of his strong throat.

"Come lie wi' me on the bed," he murmured, rubbing her

back now, each caress subtly urging her closer and closer to him. Her nipples tingled in anticipation. Closer . . . their bodies touched, and she swallowed a gasp.

"No—I . . ." Her disjointed refusal trailed off, lost as his arms closed around her, lifted her on her toes to bring them together more firmly.

"I willna hurt ye." His breath was hot on her ear as he nibbled the lobe, and licked the small hollow beneath.

She knew he likely would, though not deliberately. She had seen him naked, though she had tried not to dwell on it; she had *felt* him in their dreams. His size wasn't limited to his height. To her dismay, the thought of such intimate discomfort wasn't the deterrent she would have preferred.

Her hands were flattened against his chest, and she had to clench them into fists to keep them from sliding around his neck. Even that small a surrender would be the one step too far, because they were both trembling. Amazed, she felt the quivering of that strong body, the result of fierce need tightly leashed.

"Lass . . ." His mouth slid across the underside of her jaw, planting small kisses as it went. His hands knew no boundaries; they cupped her bottom, lifting her to even closer contact. His erection pushed hard against the juncture of her thighs.

Ford.

In despair Grace wrenched herself away and fled to the other side of the table, a flimsy barrier he could dispose of with one flick of his hand if he chose, but she knew he wouldn't force her. Seduce her, yes, with his devastatingly successful technique of alternating subtlety with boldness. He wasn't a man who found force either desirable or necessary.

He was very still, watching her from beneath heavy lids.

She clenched her hands together, turning her wedding ring around and around, using the small symbol to remind her of both loyalty and betrayal. The ring was so loose now she worried about losing it, and had developed the habit of checking to make certain it was still there.

He was waiting.

"I'm a widow," she said, forcing out the word. Her throat constricted, and she swallowed. "My husband is the only man I've ever—" She stopped, and couldn't say more. She didn't need to.

"Did ye love him, then?"

She swallowed again at his swift understanding. "Yes, I do." The words were almost inaudible.

He walked around the table. She stood her ground, though she wanted to flee. Niall cupped her face, a hint of a smile on his firmly molded lips, understanding in his dark eyes. "'Tis new to ye, wanting another man. Ye think it a betrayal of him that yer body, which has known only him, should quicken against mine."

"It is," she whispered.

"And yet ye came here, knowing how it is between us. Your body is ready. Your mind needs a bit more time." He leaned down and kissed her forehead. "I'll not force ye, lass, but I'll no leave ye for long in an empty bed. Ye'll learn my kisses, and my touch, while your thoughts settle."

She thought he would kiss her then. Her lips parted in anticipation of the pressure, the taste, the wildness. Instead he dropped his hand and strolled to the door, his tall, muscular body as graceful as a dancer's. "I would like to think you came to Creag Dhu because of me, and what we both want." He spoke now in precise English, the easy burr of his Scots accent gone. "But gratitude did not make me a fool, nor does lust. Until I know your true reason for being here, you'll not be allowed freedom within my castle. Someone will be with you at all times during the day, and at night you will be locked in either your chamber—" He paused, black eyes glittering. "Or mine."

Chapter 23

IT WAS IMPOSSIBLE TO DO ANY SEARCHING AT ALL. ALICE WAS with her every moment of the day, except when she used the garderobe. Rather than intensify Niall's suspicions, Grace willingly followed in Alice's busy footsteps, listening to the chatter and increasing her understanding of both the Scots dialect and a little of Gaelic, as her mind began to associate pronunciation of a few words with the spelling she knew.

The advantage of being with Alice was that the woman's duties carried her all over the castle. Without having to sneak about, Grace quickly became familiar with the different rooms. She tried to think where the most secure hiding place for the Treasure would be; Creag Dhu had a dungeon, much larger than the one at Hay Keep, but the dungeon was such an obvious choice she doubted it would be correct. Nevertheless she would have liked to inspect it, but could hardly ask Alice for a tour.

The wine cellar was an interesting possibility, dark and cool, with casks and racks that could conceal a hiding place.

"Are there any hidden tunnels?" she asked Alice. "A way to escape if the castle is under attack?"

"Aye," Alice said readily enough. "There's a passage leads to the sea, should it be needed, but my thinking is that 'tis safer in the castle than without. Lord Niall has built the best defenses in Scotland," she boasted. "We could withstand a siege for a year or more."

As she followed Alice about, Grace was struck by how natural everything seemed. Of course, she had the advantage of her education in medieval languages and culture so that she was at least technically familiar with much about the normal lifestyle, but not even when she first awoke was she disoriented. It was as if her mind had neatly slotted itself into the time. Why, yes, of course meat was salted for preservation, and milk had to be churned, and herbs had to be scattered on the floor rushes to keep them sweet-smelling. Her taste buds had adjusted immediately to the plain fare, accepting that there was little seasoning to be had. When Alice sat her down with a needle and a linen sheet that needed mending, Grace didn't even think of how easy it would be to go to a department store and simply buy new sheets instead of mending the old ones. Instead she took pains to make tiny, even stitches.

She had made a mistake in her clothing, she realized. Cotton wouldn't make an appearance in Europe for quite some time, and velvet was reserved for royalty. No wonder Huwe had been impressed by her velvet gown! He had probably thought her a foreign princess, and anticipated a huge ransom for her return. Luckily her cotton kirtle was unbleached and the finish wasn't shiny, so at least it didn't look rich. Since Grace obviously wasn't a Scot, her strange clothing hadn't elicited any suspicion from Alice, who had taken the garment to be washed, or from the woman who washed it. She would keep the velvet surcoat hidden, though. She wanted to check her hiding place and make certain the bag was still safely tucked away, but she reasoned that if it had been found she would have heard, and it was more likely to remain hidden if she didn't attract attention to the area.

Niall trained with his men all day, or hunted, or patrolled the area around the castle. If he returned for a noon meal, Grace didn't see him. She heard the clash of swords in the courtyard but didn't go to watch. The sight of his muscled body, sweaty and half naked, would not help shore her resolve.

She hadn't known lust could be so powerful, so consuming. Even though Alice kept her busy, her thoughts went time and again to that expert, devilishly knowing touch on her neck, to his kiss, the silky brush of his long hair against her face. He was so wonderfully barbaric and untamed, yet astonishingly well educated and sophisticated. She managed in his time with prior knowledge and training; she suspected he would manage as well in hers without those benefits, by the sheer determination of his character and the force of his intellect.

She tried to think of Ford, but he seemed so far away. A year had passed, a year in which she had had none of his things to touch and hold and weep over. She hadn't dared let herself think of him too much, and now when she needed to she couldn't quite capture his face, or the quality of his voice.

It had been easier before she came back, as if the distance of time was a veil that blurred her other life now, making it seem like a dream. *This* was real, *now* was real. Niall was all too real, too vital and dominating. Everyone in the castle bowed to his wishes, obeyed his slightest command.

The men returned for the evening meal, disturbing the efficient peace of the castle with their boisterous, chaotic masculinity. There were shouts, curses, rumbling voices, the clang of swords and shields, the stomping of feet and excited barking of dogs, the sharp muskiness of male sweat. When Niall appeared all eyes went to him; he looked around and located Grace immediately, nodding his head toward the table where he sat.

She hesitated, and Alice gave her a nudge. "He wants ye to sit wi' him," the older woman said, stating the obvious. "Best do as he says."

Grace hadn't had any thought of disobeying, only a reluctance to be so close to him again. She wanted to, too much, and there was where the danger lay. With slow steps she walked across the great hall to where the head table was set. Niall stood beside his chair, waiting for her.

He had either dunked his head in a barrel of water or taken time to bathe, for his long hair was wet and sleeked back. His simple linen shirt was clean, his plaid belted about his lean waist. A knife was thrust into his belt, and another into his right boot. The huge claymore was slung in a scabbard over his back; he removed that, hanging it on the back of his chair. Even here, in his own hall, he kept his fearsome weapons to hand.

Looking around, Grace saw that all the men did. Niall had called them broken men and outlaws; they were hard men who had lived hard lives, yet they chose to be governed by Niall. They were the castoffs of clans all over Scotland, but here they had formed their own clan, with Niall the unelected but undisputed chieftain, and he had transformed them into a prime fighting unit with pride and discipline. These men would willingly die for him.

A smaller chair had been placed beside Niall's. Those were the only two chairs there; everyone else sat on benches. Grace was burningly aware of all the curious glances coming her way, especially from the men. The women of the household had gotten accustomed to her during the day; some of *their* glances were hostile.

Niall cupped her elbow as he seated her, his hand very warm on her bare arm. "Ye asked Alice about the escape tunnel," he said, his tone mild, his eyes sharp.

Grace blinked in amazement. She had been by Alice's side almost every minute of the day; she was certain Niall had had no opportunity to speak to her since the morning. "Yes, I did," she admitted without pause. "But how did you know?"

"I was displeased that ye managed to enter Creag Dhu on false pretenses, and no one questioned ye or even saw ye for the rest of the day. Nothing ye do now goes unobserved." He leaned back in his chair as the meal was set before him, roasted pork, turnips, fresh bread, cheese, and stewed apples. Taking the knife from his belt, he carved several slices of tender ham from the haunch and placed them on the trencher set on the table between him and Grace.

"Have ye a knife?" he asked Grace.

She thought of the Swiss Army knife in the bag she had hidden, and shook her head. Niall drew the smaller dagger from his boot and surveyed it, then thrust it back into his boot. "I dinna think I trust ye with something so wicked sharp. I'll cut your meat for ye."

"I wouldn't stab you," she said, shocked.

One eyebrow lifted. "No? When first I met ye, ye were with the Hays."

"You know I was captured! You could hear what they were saying."

"It could have been arranged, aye? I was half smothered with plaids, as ye remember; I couldna see anything. Ye might have been captured, or ye might have been with them from the start. Ye released me from the dungeon, then followed me here to Creag Dhu, knowing I wouldna cast ye out. Now ye've asked about the tunnel. Do ye plan to tell the Hays, and let them into my castle to murder us in our beds?"

Furious, Grace turned on him. "Huwe already had you at his mercy. Why would he scheme to help you escape, when he could kill you and be done with it?"

"As to why, if Huwe wanted only to kill me then, aye, he could ha' done it then. But he wants Creag Dhu as well, and he kens well he couldna take it from without. To take the castle, he must find a way inside." Expertly he cut a small piece of meat and offered it to her.

She ignored it. "I only asked about a tunnel because I was curious. I didn't even ask where it is, as you should know since you've obviously had my every word reported to you!"

Niall eyed her flushed face, and saw that her eyes had gone as dark as a stormy sea. "And will continue to do so," he said. He offered the meat again. "Eat, lass. A good wind would blow ye away."

Grace took the meat with her fingers and neatly popped it into her mouth, then deliberately turned her head from him to watch the others. He paid no attention to her ire or her efforts to ignore him. He fed himself and her, alternating between the two of them, and patiently holding each bite until she took it. She could see people watching them, and good manners prompted her not to make a public scene.

His consideration undermined her efforts to remain angry. He didn't try to force her to talk, didn't belabor his point; having made it, he was content. She knew now how closely she was watched, which had been his intention.

His leg pressed against hers. Instantly she moved away, then glanced at him to see if the contact had been deliberate. It was. He was watching her, his gaze steady. He took a drink of spiced wine, then put the cup in her hand so she too could drink. "Do ye remember a time," he said in a low voice, "when I was sitting on a stool, and ye came to me, and I lifted ye astride—"

Her hand shook, and she hastily set the cup down before she spilled the wine. She didn't reply, but the hot color in her cheeks gave him his answer.

"How can it be?" he wondered.

She shook her head, and whispered, "I don't know."

"At times I wasna asleep, and still I could feel ye watching me." He lifted her hand, holding it in his palm and tracing his fingertip over the slender bones that fanned in the back of her hand.

"Sometimes when I was awake, I thought I heard you speaking." She couldn't look at him as she made the confession. The words felt torn out of her, a reluctant acknowledgment of the awareness between them that had tormented her for months, and tempted her now. It would be so easy to turn her hand in his, lace their fingers together. He would know what she wanted. He wouldn't ask any questions, simply lead her up the stairs to his chamber.

She stared at the saltcellar. She had once had this unspoken intimacy with Ford; they had known each other so well that a lot of times words hadn't been needed. When he died, she thought that wonder, that sense of belonging, had died with him and she would never know it again. How could it be duplicated? They had forged that mutual knowledge during years of dating and marriage, of making love, of quiet talks in the darkness as they lay together, of working and laughing and worrying, of *living* together.

She couldn't feel it now, with Niall. Her imagination was working overtime again, making her think the link was there when it couldn't be. From the moment he had walked out of that dungeon cell until now, the total time she had spent with him was less than two hours. He couldn't possibly know what she wanted, nor could she predict what he would do.

"All ye have to do is take my hand," he murmured, watching her, drawing her gaze. "My bed is big, and warm, and ye won't be alone."

A chill ran over her, and her eyes went blank with shock. No. It wasn't possible.

"Such big, sad eyes. What do ye see, lass, when ye look

through me as if I'm not here, when ye go away in your mind? Does Huwe hold someone ye love, a child perhaps? Does he force ye to do his bidding?"

Her throat felt tight. "No," she managed. "I have no one, and I'm not in league with Huwe."

An expression passed over his face, tightening his flesh over the chiseled bone structure, giving him a remote, austere expression as old as the one in his eyes. So must the ancient saints have looked, stripped down to the essentials of character by the burdens they had borne. "Tell me," he said. "And I will aid ye."

How matter-of-fact he was about assuming yet another responsibility! His friends had been tortured and burned to death, he was excommunicated and under a death sentence should he venture outside Scotland; as a young man he had been made Guardian of the Treasure, his entire life dedicated to and dominated by the burden he had accepted. He had created a disciplined fighting force out of loners and misfits and outlaws, then extended his protection to the crofters and villagers living around Creag Dhu. The burdens he had accepted onto those broad shoulders would have crushed most men, but not even knowing how he could help her, he offered to assume responsibility for her, too. Her throat tightened even more, this time with unshed tears. Silently she shook her head.

He sighed as he stood, lifting her to her feet too. "Ye will tell me," he assured her, walking with her to the stairs. At a nod from him, two men rose from their benches and followed. "Ye will tell me, willingly or no. Ye'll come to my bed, too, and lie soft and yielding beneath me. I'm a verra patient man, lass, but never forget I hold all the power here."

Her mouth went dry. Was that a warning that he suspected she knew about the Treasure and wanted to find it? Her heart hammered painfully against her breastbone. She was struggling with him on both a personal and an impersonal plane, and uncannily he sensed it. Viewing him as a man, she desired him with a ferocity that terrified her; seeing him as the Guardian, she feared him. Defeat on either level could destroy her.

He opened the door to the small chamber where she had been locked the night before, and ushered her inside. She paused in surprise. Sometime during the day a small bed, not much more than a cot, had been moved into the chamber. A small fire crackled in the hearth, dispelling the chill, and two thick candles appeared to have been lit only moments before, for the tallow was only now beginning to melt down the columns. To her relief there was also a chamber pot, and a small basin and ewer of water.

"Thank you," she said, turning to him. The small chamber felt almost luxurious to her after some of the places she had slept in this past year.

"I dinna intend to freeze ye to death," he replied, his brows quirking in amusement. He smoothed his hand up her arm. "I like ye warm and tender."

He kissed her, his arms folding around her and molding her to his body. Grace gripped his biceps, concentrating on holding tight to her self-control even though she could feel the foundation of resolve crumbling beneath her. He slanted his firm mouth so that it fit perfectly to the soft contours of her lips, and despite her best intentions her mouth parted under the pressure. His tongue gently penetrated, cajoling rather than demanding.

Desire clawed at her, hot and sharp. She jerked her mouth from his and buried her face against his chest, breathing hard. The question of loyalty to Ford aside, how could she even consider making love with Niall? She intended to be in this time only for as long as it took her to find the Treasure and discover if she could somehow use the mysterious Power herself, to stop Parrish and the Foundation. If she could, she would steal the Treasure and return to her own time, leaving Niall behind.

Success or failure, she would not be staying. Any relationship she had with Niall would only be casual—God, she thought, could making love with Niall ever be considered *casual?*—and even were the circumstances different she wasn't a woman who had casual affairs. Perhaps he would be content with only sex, but she knew she wouldn't be; for her, making love was a commitment, something she couldn't make.

He cradled her so carefully in his arms, rocking slightly back and forth as he stroked her back, that she wanted to weep. She had never met a man like him before, and never would again; he was extraordinary in any century. Just for a moment she gave in to temptation and slid her hands around him, flattening her palms on his back and absorbing the vital heat and power of his body. His muscles subtly flexed with every breath he took, and his heart beat strong and steady under her ear.

"When a woman has been wed," he said low, into her hair, "she becomes accustomed to her man in bed beside her at night, and if aught happens to him, she loses not only her husband but that comfort of no being alone in the dark. I offer ye that, lass. I'll hold ye close against the dark and the chill, give ye the comfort of my body."

She almost groaned aloud against him, aching from temptation. To sleep with his arms around her, to wake and be able to reach out and touch him, stroke his hairy chest, slide her hand down the flatness of his belly, hold his penis while he slept and feel it soft in her hand—how had he known the way she hungered for that, for the intimacy that went beyond sex? He was in her mind again, reading her with uncanny accuracy.

"No," she whispered, and knew that she wanted to say yes.

His lips brushed her forehead. "I wish ye a good night, then. If ye decide ye need comforting in the night, ye've only to knock on the door, and the guards will bring ye to me."

When he was gone, Grace pressed her shaking hands to her lips. She was walking a tightrope between passion and danger, but the knowledge didn't lessen the need. If she gave in to him, would that incline him toward a greater indulgence than he would normally show, if he discovered her true aim?

No, it would not. She knew from the documents that Black Niall was ruthless in his protection of the Treasure. Perhaps he had merely meant he held all the authority here, but he had said "power," and that could be a warning. Being a woman, and moreover a woman he wanted to bed, wouldn't protect her if he should discover she was after the Treasure. He would kill her, and she knew it.

Chapter 24

THE NEXT DAY DAWNED COOL AND RAINY, THE MOUNTAINTOPS
to the east lost in mist. There was no hot bath waiting for
Grace that morning, only a basin of cold water and a hasty
scrubbing in front of the fire. Breakfast was porridge again,
and then Alice swept her up in another whirlwind of
activity. Then men trained in the courtyard despite the
rain—"Lord Niall says trouble doesna wait for a fair day,"
Alice explained—and clotted the rushes with mud when
they all tromped in, soaking wet and grousing.

Alice warmed them up from the inside with *colcannon,* a
cabbage stew, and the men occupied themselves with games
of dice, flirting with the serving women, sharpening their
swords and daggers, and swapping tales that grew both
louder and taller. Not all the men were there; Niall and ten
others patrolled around Creag Dhu.

The rain dripped monotonously, and the dark gray sky
made torches necessary for light. Grace yawned, thinking
that a rainy day was better suited for napping in front of a
fire than anything else. She wasn't the only one yawning; a

few of the men sought the darker corners and nodded off. Others' thoughts turned to bed for a different reason. Grace saw hairy masculine arms wrapping about plump waists here and there, and soon there were noticeably fewer women going about their work.

They were all startled by the shouts from the gate, the sudden alarm. Sim had Alice on his knee, teasingly pinching her bottom and trying to cajole her away from her work; he jumped upright at the shouts, dumping Alice on the floor. His hand closed over his sword and he was running before his plaid had settled around his knees.

Alice scrambled up and ran to the huge ten-foot-high double doors that opened into the great hall. Her heart in her throat, Grace ran too. Niall was outside the safety of the gates; had something happened to him?

The scene was chaotic, confusing. A crowd of people rushed toward the gates, yelling in alarm, their heads covered against the pelting rain. Behind them was the sullen red glow of burning huts. "The Hay!" they howled. "The Hay!" Men surged on horseback, waving axes and swords.

"Open the gates!" Sim yelled.

Men roughly pushed Alice and Grace aside as they rushed to their posts in a well-ordered drill, some going to the top of the walls with their crossbows, some to the stable to get the horses, others falling in behind Sim.

Grace ran into the courtyard, heedless of the rain. The Hays were attacking, and Niall was somewhere outside. Had he and his men been attacked by a much larger force? Her chest clenched, panic welling. No. *No!* She couldn't bear it again, couldn't lose—

Alice grabbed her arm, jerking her around. "Come inside! Arrows—"

The gates were open, the pounding crowd only yards away. Grace gave them an agonized look as Alice dragged her toward the doors, and her gaze fell on the beefy man who ran in front of all the others, his plaid pulled over his head. She saw him grin suddenly, saw his rotted teeth, and she jerked away from Alice, running forward as she screamed, "Close the gates! It's a trick!"

Sim's head jerked around and he gaped at her, then her words sank in and he spun back toward the gates. "Close the gates!" he roared, rushing forward. The guards began pushing the massive doors closed but it was too late. The Hays poured into the narrow gatehouse, shoving the gates open. Swords and axes were pulled from beneath plaids, and the "victims" attacked.

"Run!" Alice screamed, pulling on Grace's arm again and hauling her back inside the great hall. Women were screaming and rushing about, excited dogs barking and leaping about their feet, getting in the way. "The doors!" Alice gasped, and she and Grace turned to throw their weight against them, closing them so the massive bar could be dropped in place. Alice outweighed Grace by fifty pounds or more, and she got the right door closed first, then darted over to aid Grace. They almost made it.

Heavy bodies thudded against the doors, bursting them wide, and the fighting spilled into the hall. The impact knocked Grace to the floor. Alice ducked under a slashing blade and grabbed Grace again, bodily lifting her and shoving her down the hallway toward the kitchens. "Run!" she screamed again, and Grace lifted her skirts and ran.

From in front of them came thundering feet and the rattle of metal. Grace skidded to a halt just outside the larder. "They're in here, too!" she yelled, trying to reverse her direction. Then the door to the larder slammed open and Niall came through it at a dead run, claymore in hand, black hair flying around his head and his eyes like murder. He was followed by the ten men who had been on patrol with him.

Grace flattened herself against the wall to keep from being smashed to the floor. Niall didn't even glance at her as he ran past but he barked to Alice, "Get to safety!" Then with a roar he ran into the hall and threw himself into the battle, pushing Hays back a few steps with the sheer force of his size and the swing of his blade. Screaming, his men followed him.

"Come!" Alice screamed to make herself heard over the din of battle, and she dashed into the kitchen without looking behind her.

Grace started to follow, then looked at the larder. That had to be the secret passageway, for otherwise how could Niall and his men have gotten back into the castle? She hesitated only a second, and plunged into the cool, dark room. There was a small store of candles just inside the door and she grabbed one, her hands shaking as she took up the stone and flint lying beside the candles and struck a spark to light the candle. When the small flame flickered to life, she hastily shut the larder door and looked around.

A whole section of the back wall had been swung open. Blackness yawned beyond the opening.

Her breath came in quick spurts as she approached the open section. This might lead to the Treasure's hiding place; it might not. But this was the first time she had been alone to search, and in the chaos of battle it would be some time before she was missed. She thought of Niall hurling himself into the fight with terrifying abandon and she bit her bottom lip until blood welled. He might be hurt, even killed—

And there was nothing she could do.

Here was her chance, likely her only chance, to accomplish what she had come to Creag Dhu for.

The deafening roar of battle was only slightly muffled in here. Men screamed, in fury and in agony, sword clashed on sword, wood splintered. She had come into this time in the middle of a battle; perhaps she was meant to leave during one, too.

Niall. Her heart whispered the name, and her hands shook, making the candle flame dance. Then she thought of Ford and closed her eyes, trying to see his face. The only image that came to mind was the last one, his eyes blank in death as he toppled over.

A wordless sound of pain vibrated in her throat, and she stepped through the opening.

The air was immediately colder, danker, and had a faint smell of salt water. Steep, narrow stairs plunged straight down into complete darkness. She took them cautiously, guarding her candle so the flame didn't go out.

Everyone knew of the secret passage, she thought. Was it likely Niall would hide the Treasure there?

But where there was one passageway, perhaps there were others.

She reached the bottom of the stairway and found herself in a narrow, rock-lined tunnel. The smell of the sea was stronger there, and she could hear the muted thunder of crashing waves. The passageway was a short one, then, leading straight out to the rocky shoreline.

Her supposition was right. Though she moved slowly, she reached the end of the tunnel within two minutes. A jumble of boulders before her almost completely filled the opening, so that only a sliver of gray, rain-washed light filtered through.

No Treasure there.

She retraced her steps, and began to climb the treacherous stairs. She held the candle in her right hand and put her left against the wall to steady herself. She had never had claustrophobia, but the inky darkness seemed to clutch at her feet, trying to pull her down. She shivered and moved closer to the wall, and her fingers slid over a section of rock that jutted out a quarter inch from the other stones.

She stopped, lifting the candle higher to enlarge the pool of light. She could hear her own breath eerily echo as she examined the section that was out of alignment. Could there be a secret passage within a secret passage?

She pressed around the edges of the rock, feeling foolish but doing it anyway. Nothing happened. She held the candle nearer to see if there was a minute seam in the mortar, or if she was wasting her time.

The mortar was cracked, but when she examined the rock around that particular section she found hairline cracks in that mortar, too. There were no hinges that she could see, no way of opening the door—if it was a door.

Archaeology and translations had taught her to approach the unknown logically. If this were a hidden door, there had to be an easy way to open it, easy because a method that took a lot of time or trouble would increase one's chances of being discovered in the act of opening it. A hidden door would be silent and fast.

The easiest method would be to put an opening mechanism behind one of the other stones, but given the steepness and narrowness of the steps, it stood to reason almost anyone going up or down them would put a balancing hand against the wall, making it too likely a hidden door would be opened by accident.

She climbed a few steps and surveyed the section of rock from above. Yes, a rectangular section definitely jutted out a fraction of an inch. Where could a mechanism be hidden? It had to be someplace accessible, easily reached.

Easily reached. Grace's eyes widened. In this time, she was of average height for a woman, with most of the men she had seen in the range of five-five to five-eight, with very few taller than five-ten. Sim was a large man, perhaps reaching six feet; only Niall was taller. Niall was six-foot-four. He could reach higher than anyone else in the castle.

She looked up. If this was a door, and there was a mechanism to open it hidden behind one of these rocks, logically it would be behind one of the higher rocks, one that only Niall could comfortably reach.

She stretched on tiptoe, pressing every rock she could reach. The rectangular section remained stubbornly stationary and rocklike. There was a flat stone that looked promising, being slightly smoother than those surrounding it, but it was half a foot out of her reach. She climbed another step and leaned to the side, balancing precariously on the edge of the step as she stretched, her fingers scrabbling on the rock, trying to pull herself just a fraction of an inch farther. She almost lost her balance and quickly flattened herself against the wall, gasping in fright. A fall down these steps would break her neck. Cautiously she lifted herself on her toes again, perched on the very edge of the step. Her extended fingers couldn't quite brush the edge of the rock.

Swearing in frustration under her breath, Grace sat down on the step and removed her left shoe. Once more she stood on tiptoe, stretching outward, and she slapped her shoe against the flat rock.

Silently the rectangular section slid inward, leaving a black hole in the wall.

Holding the candle before her, she leaned in, not setting a foot inside that hole until she knew what was in there.

The blackness was Stygian, swallowing the feeble light of her small candle. She could see a solid stone floor, and nothing else, not even walls.

She stepped inside, squeezing past the stone door. She waited, ready to throw herself back through the opening if the door began to close on its own, but it remained reassuringly open. Probably there was another mechanism on this side of the wall that one had to press to close the door, which she had no intention of doing.

Warily she moved forward a few feet, and made out a wall

three or four yards in front of her. She turned to her left, squinting her eyes at a darker patch. She went closer, and saw that it was another door, this one made of a very dark wood, and the bar that lay through the brackets was attached like a lever on one end so it could be lifted up and swung over to unbar the door, but not removed.

A breeze from somewhere made her candle flicker, and she quickly cupped her hand around the flame to steady it. She glanced over her shoulder at the opening in the wall, but the breeze didn't seem to be coming from there. It was coming from the direction of that dark, closed door, which didn't make sense. The air must be coming in through the rock opening and swirling around the antechamber, confusing her.

Grace approached the door and tried to lift the bar, but though it was a small bar compared to the massive ones in other parts of Creag Dhu, it was heavier than it looked and she couldn't manage it with one hand. She set the candle on the floor, and seized the lever with both hands. By bracing her weight below the bar and shoving, she slowly inched it upward. The pivoting connection was smooth, but the action was incredibly difficult for so slender a bar. There was a definite mechanical click when she forced the bar straight up, and it locked in the upright position.

The door itself swung silently inward, and more stairs yawned at her feet, a stone wall on one side and black emptiness on the other. The breeze was more pronounced now, and the candle flickered wildly, almost going out. Grace crouched and cupped her hands around the flame again until it steadied, picked up the candle, and stood with one hand still held in front of it.

How much time had passed? she wondered as she went down the stairs into nothingness. Had the battle ended? Was Niall unhurt? The compulsion to turn around and return to the upper reaches of the castle stopped her with one foot poised to take another step downward. *Niall,* she thought in despair, terrified for him. He was a fearsome warrior; she had seen him fighting in skirmishes and in pitched battles, and understood why his name had struck terror into the hearts of his foes, but still he was human. He bled if cut, he bruised if struck. He could be overwhelmed, as he had been when Huwe's men had captured him.

There was nothing she could do to affect the outcome of the battle overhead. If she found the Treasure, then according to the documents for which Parrish was so willing to kill, she could affect the outcome of events in her own time. Her choice was simple, but more difficult than she had ever imagined. She had been in this time less than a week; how could Niall have so quickly become important to her?

Because she had known him much longer than a week, her inner soul whispered. She had known him for a year, through the documents given into her safekeeping, and she had been fascinated, obsessed, beguiled by him even before her world had been destroyed by two bullets. If she hadn't been so anxious to have her modem repaired so she could access files and learn more about Niall, she would have been at home when Parrish and his men came, and she too would be dead now.

She wanted to go back. Instead she went forward, step by cautious step.

"Ahhhhh!" Mouth open, screaming, Huwe rushed at Niall, claymore held over his head with both hands. For a split-second Niall jerked his attention away from the Hay clansman on the other end of his sword; Huwe was behind him, the other in front, and he had only one more second in which to keep Huwe from splitting him from gullet to arse. He ducked under the swinging sword of the Hay clansman, grabbed him by the arm, and slung him into Huwe's path. Huwe's great sword was already arcing down and it bit deep into his clansman's shoulder and neck. A great spray of blood drenched his clothes, but Huwe kept coming, his small eyes mad with rage.

"Bastard!" he howled. "Bastard!" He lifted the sword again and brought it whistling down, intent on separating Niall's head from his shoulders.

Niall parried the blow with his axe, the force of it numbing his arm. He went in low with his own sword but Huwe was more nimble than he expected, jerking away from the long blade. "Ye kilt my son," he roared. "Ye bastard, I'll have yer head!"

Niall didn't waste his breath on speech; aye, he had killed Morvan, and would again had he the opportunity. He was filled with a cold, merciless rage, that the Hay filth had dared invade Creag Dhu, his home. Not only was the Treasure endangered, but Grace; he remembered the terror plain on her face as he raced by her, and he knew the fate that would befall her, and all the women of Creag Dhu, if he and his men failed to repel the invaders.

He would not allow that to happen.

He seized the offensive, attacking with silent ferocity, the steel of his sword clanging as it met Huwe's. He advanced steadily, axe and sword swinging, driving Huwe before them. A Hay clansman ran screaming at him from the left and he hurled the axe, burying it in the man's chest. The man gave a strange gurgle and dropped like a stone, his heart stilled by the massive blade that had cleaved it in two.

Niall had only the sword now, but he hadn't dared let the man engage him. He gripped the hilt with both hands to better balance himself, holding the weight centered with his body. Huwe rushed forward, heartened by Niall's loss of the axe. Niall parried the downward arc of Huwe's sword, steel sliding along steel with a hissing sound, disengaging, slashing in from his left and burying the blade deep in Huwe's right side, in the kidney. Huwe jerked, his face turning gray. His sword clattered to the floor. He rose on his toes, convulsing as his body reacted to the massiveness of the injury. Niall jerked his blade free and struck again, straight into the heart, a death stroke.

A howl rose above the roar of battle as Huwe's clansmen saw their chieftain slain. Disconcerted for a moment, it was a moment that cost them dearly, for Niall's men took swift advantage, their training bringing the struggle to a swift finish.

Niall leaned on his bloody sword, panting. Slowly he surveyed the ruin of his great hall, noting which of his men lay sprawled in death. There was a moment of eerie silence; then moans began to rise, the sobs and curses of wounded men. Here and there he saw a tangle of longer skirts, gently rounded limbs, and he knew some of the women had not found safety.

What of Grace? She had been with Alice, fleeing to the kitchens.

Sim slowly walked toward him, his face so covered with gore Niall almost didn't recognize him. The big man limped, his entire left hip wet with blood. "What do we do with the Hays who live?" he asked.

Niall's first impulse was to kill them all, but he stilled it. 'Twould cause Robert difficulty if he destroyed the clan. There were Hay women and children, too; they would need what men survived. The clan would not recover for many years from Huwe's stubborn stupidity. "Turn them out," he said.

The women were creeping from their hiding places. There were tears, of both joy and sorrow, as they identified both the survivors and the dead, and then as women do they set about restoring order, tending to the wounded, laying out the dead, bringing drink for those who wanted it, sweeping out the bloodstained rushes. Alice took charge, her manner brisk and capable, though her cheeks were still pale with fright.

Niall's black gaze darted from one woman to another, searching for a dainty form, a long, thick fall of hair. He listened, but could not catch that voice with its strange accent, the emphasis on all the wrong syllables. "Alice!" he called. "Where's the lass?"

Alice had no doubt which lass he meant. She looked around in puzzlement, but reached the same conclusion as had he. Grace was not there.

"She didna follow me," Alice said slowly. "But she was there behind me when ye came from the larder. Perhaps she hid there." She paused. "The lass saved us, gave us warning. She recognized Huwe."

So she had not been in league with Huwe. The thought brought him relief, but another worry sent him striding rapidly from the great hall. Inside the escape passage was yet another passage, one that he had sworn to protect with his life. There was something mysterious about the lass, something she kept hidden. What if she were the most serious threat to the Treasure he had yet encountered? Could he keep his vow, if it meant killing her?

Cold sweat beaded on his brow as he took a candle and

ducked into the escape passage. Halfway down the long, narrow stairs an area of the wall was even darker, as if a hole had been knocked in the stone. Niall felt his heart still, his skin going cold with dread. Then rage came, saving rage.

Silently he took his bloody sword and followed her.

The stairs ended. Grace lifted the candle but couldn't see anything except cold stone walls, made of the same dark rock as the rest of the castle. It was very cold down there, and she began shivering. An odd pulse hummed through the air, not a sound but a sensation, brushing against her skin.

Her skin prickled, but not from the cold.

Slowly she paced around the walls, looking for any indication of a door. Blank stone was all that met her searching fingers.

The subtle pulsing was mildly disorienting. She must be below sea level, and what she felt was the force of waves battering against the rock.

Beneath the stairs was a deeper darkness. Her heart pounding in her throat, Grace stepped forward, and the frail light of her candle illuminated another opening, a black hole leading . . . where?

The pulsing was stronger. She could feel it on her face. It was coming from the dark opening.

She stopped, the small hairs on the back of her neck lifting. Dear God, what was *in* there?

She could do this, she told herself. For Ford, and for Bryant, she could do anything. She had proven that to herself time and again during this past year of hell.

Bone-aching cold seeped from the stone straight through the thin soles of her shoes, crept beneath her skirts to curl its icy fingers around her legs. She had to act quickly, before the dangerous cold began to sap her strength. Her small candle wouldn't last much longer, and she didn't want to be caught down there without light. Calmer now, driven by necessity, she moved toward the black hole in the wall.

It engulfed her as soon as she stepped through, the darkness, the sensation of trembling on the edge of . . . something.

Was that warmth she felt?

She went deeper, her candle fluttering madly. The light

picked out the dim shape of what looked like a large chair ... a throne? ... carved with lions. A tattered banner, the sort carried into battle and woven with fire in the strands, hung over the throne and in it golden lion eyes shimmered in the candle's light. Beside the throne was something else, something she couldn't quite see, and she took another step forward.

"Ah, lass." The deep voice was low, regretful, controlled. It came from no more than a few feet behind her. "I dinna want to kill ye."

The fine hairs on her body lifted in sheer terror, and for a moment Grace felt herself sway as the blood left her head.

Blood. She could smell it now, hot and metallic. The blood of battle was on him, the fierceness of it singing through his veins, intensifying the rage she could feel blasting from him in waves.

He was going to kill her. She could feel his intent, the cold resolve that had guarded the Treasure all these years. Underlying that, however, was his barely restrained rage at ... what? Her trickery? How close she had come to succeeding? It was the rage she felt most, a fire burning beneath ice, and it ignited her own rage.

She couldn't let him kill her. If she died now, then Parrish would win. There would be no vengeance for Ford, for Bryant; their courage in death would have been in vain. She would die knowing she had failed them, and that, more than anything, was unbearable.

Niall's hand closed on her shoulder, turning her, his fingers gripping like iron. Grace dropped the candle and it rolled away, its fragile flame glinting on the sword in his hand, wavering, almost extinguishing before flaring to renewed life. She turned into his grip, stepping closer, whirling. Warrior that he was, he began reacting even before she could complete the move, turning his hip to the side to catch the brunt of her knee. But it wasn't her knee she used, it was her elbow. She jabbed it hard into his midsection, aiming for his solar plexus. The impact with his hard stomach jarred her arm all the way to her shoulder. She missed her target but the force was enough to make him grunt and bend forward a little, his grip on her shoulder loosening for a fraction of a second.

It was enough. She jerked backward, wrenching herself from his grasp. His fingers caught in the cloth of her bodice and a seam gave, the ripping sound almost unbearably loud in this deep, silent sepulcher. The fabric tore loose and she stumbled at the sudden release, going down almost to her knees before literally throwing herself back to her feet, panic lending her strength. She pulled her skirts high and raced into the darkness beyond the candlelight, instinct guiding her to the stairs.

Her chances of outdistancing him were slim, and getting out of the castle even more unlikely. Still, she had to try. The soles of her shoes slipped on the stones and she banged into the wall, hard. The light of the candle behind her was no more than a faint glimmer, of no use in finding her way, but now she had the wall for guidance. She put one hand on it and ran.

She tripped on the bottom stair and fell, hard. Instantly she bounded up, knowing he was right behind her, *feeling* his presence even though she couldn't see him, couldn't hear him over the thunder of her own heartbeat, the harsh gasps of her breathing. He was close, that terrible bloody sword in his powerful hand, his rage pulsing through him.

Grace ran up the stairs, hurling herself upward into the inky darkness. If she missed one step she would plunge off the side, down onto the stone floor, maiming if not killing herself outright. If she faltered, he would be on her. There was certain death behind her, possible death waiting at every step. She could do nothing but throw herself forward, hoping she had that one extra step on him that would allow her to gain the top of the stairs and bar the door before he could reach it.

Just one extra step. She had barely been able to move the bar, but she would manage, somehow. If she could get the bar in place, she would make it. Niall would hack his way through but that would take time, time enough that she could flee the castle. One step.

No. She couldn't flee, not now, not when she was so close. She would have to hide . . . and return.

There were no more stairs. She staggered off balance when her lifted foot came down hard on a level surface. She reached desperately for the door.

And she heard him, heard his breath, felt it hot on her neck.

No time for the door.

Her scrabbling hands had barely closed on the frame when his weight hit her in the back, overwhelming her, driving her forward and down and crushing her beneath him.

Grace put out her hands to break her fall but still landed heavily. Stunned, she lay helplessly beneath him, her cheek ground into the grit covering the cold stone floor. He was so heavy she could barely breathe, and so big that he surrounded her, his heat burning her back, scorching through her clothing. His hot breath stirred her hair. She inhaled his pungent scent, the hot, mingled odors of sweat and blood and man, primitive and dangerous. The smell of him filled her, warming her within as his body warmed her without.

Caught. Captured. This was the end, then. He could snap her neck with one hand, and perhaps he would, for she could feel the great rage seething within him. She was down, and helpless. He would kill her now.

He didn't move, didn't lift his heavy weight from her.

She couldn't see him; the darkness was almost total. Far away there seemed to be some lessening of the darkness, perhaps a torch set in a sconce on the outer stairs, but it was too dim to be of use. He didn't speak. All she could do was feel him, his body stretched on top of hers, his iron-muscled limbs controlling her. She could feel his chest move with his controlled breathing, feel the strong thudding of his heartbeat against her back. He wasn't even winded, damn him. She wanted to scream at him, claw at him in her own frustrated rage, but all she could do was press her face against the icy stone and wait.

The silence grew as they lay there, and then she felt the prod of his stiffened penis against her buttocks, the slow and deliberate movement of his legs, pushing between hers.

Grace's breath stopped.

She had known great emotions; she had thrilled to love, been devastated by grief, ridden the sharp blade of hatred. The riptide of lust that seized her body now went beyond the force of even those things, smashing through her barriers as if they had never existed, sweeping everything away in the sudden, blindingly intense need for him that overtook her. She had known she was weak where he was concerned; the first time he kissed her, her lonely, yearning flesh had exploded into climax at his touch. He aroused her as no other man ever had, ever could, aroused her to a response so overwhelming she couldn't control it.

He wasn't Ford . . . *he wasn't Ford!* How could she want him so much, this big, violent man who held the key to her desperate quest in his powerful hands? He was sworn to protect the Treasure, he had killed in its defense, and he would kill her . . . afterward. For now, lying there on the cold stone floor in the darkness, there was only the sound of his breathing, and hers, coming faster and harsher as his rage transmuted itself into lust.

A low moan slipped past her lips, a husky, helpless sound of want. *Yes. Oh, God, yes.* Even if he killed her afterward, before she died she wanted to feel him within her, absorb his driving force, cool this insane, inexorable fever that burned in her flesh for him.

Her hips lifted the scant inch they could, instinctively pushing upward against him, grinding her buttocks harder against his rigid shaft. Just that, a slight movement at best, but it sent shards of pleasure spearing through her. Her breasts hardened in painful need of his touch, her loins moistened and clenched, aching with desire and frustration and emptiness.

"Damn you," she whispered into the silence, almost weeping. Damn him for being a man like no other, for being hard and ruthless, for being more dominant in the flesh than she could have ever imagined. Other men paled beside him; he was too vital, the force of his personality and the strength of his sword arm smashing any resistance to his will. And damn herself, for how could she resist him, when he had only to touch her and her weak, traitorous body instantly began preparing itself to yield to him?

"Damn me, then, if ye must," he murmured against her hair, accepting her despair. Subtle, instinctive bastard that he was, he knew she was his for the taking now, all resistance gone, and he moved to claim her willing flesh.

He slid her skirts up, bunching the fabric on her back, and the cold air washed over her bare legs and bottom. Her skirts were still caught under the pressure of his knees, anchoring her in place. Grace quivered, fear and desire twisting sharply together until she couldn't separate them. The coarse wool of his kilted plaid scratched the tender backs of her thighs. His hand moved between them, pulling his plaid up and to the side, and his naked flesh was suddenly against her own, thighs to thighs, groin to buttocks. His heat was startling, almost unbearable, as if she touched fire.

He slid his right arm under her, curving around her belly, and lifted her up and back, onto her knees, raising her hips and positioning her for him. Grace squeezed her eyelids tightly shut as she struggled with the abrupt, startling exposure and vulnerability of her sex. His rigid penis stabbed at her soft folds but he wasn't trying to enter her, not yet. Her loins pulsed, throbbing as she waited in paralyzed agony for the thrust that would carry him deep inside her, and at last this terrible need would be eased.

His sustaining arm slipped from around her but she maintained her position, on her knees with her bottom lifted. Her fingers scraped against the icy stone, trying to sink into it. Why was he waiting? Why didn't he just do it, before she went mad?

He touched her then, his warm palm shaping itself over the curves of her buttocks, learning her. His hand slid between her legs and he cupped her sex, his hard fingers opening the closed, secretive folds. He searched out her small, exquisitely firm nub, pushing back the protective hood of flesh and exposing her to the rasp of his callused fingertips. A soft cry exploded from her, and her hips writhed. Oh, God, another touch and she would explode, just as she had before. But he didn't give her that touch. Those damnably knowing fingers withdrew after the brief caress, dragging through her swollen folds to find and stroke the entrance to her body. He circled her soft opening with one finger, spreading her moisture but not probing inside her even though he had to feel the convulsive clench of her loins. He touched between her buttocks, exploring, and murmured a soft reassurance when her entire body jolted in shock.

He bent forward, his entire body covering hers, his weight supported on his left elbow and forearm. "Lay your head on my arm, lass," he whispered, and blindly she did so, pressing her forehead against the hard muscles of his forearm, her right hand entwining and clinging to his while her left hand curled around the iron swell of his biceps, anchoring herself against what she knew was to come. With his free hand he guided his jutting penis to her prepared opening, and slowly pressed within.

Grace couldn't prevent her sudden intake of breath, her involuntary whimper of feminine distress. She had known he was big; she had seen him naked. But until she felt him pushing into her, her body hadn't known the true measure of him. He was thick, and hot, and so hard she felt bruised by the inexorable advance of his shaft into her. He wasn't brutal, just relentless. Her hips undulated, instinctively trying to ease her clasp of him as inch by slow inch he completed his penetration.

Her fingers dug into his biceps, and she pressed her forehead harder against his arm. Surely she couldn't take any more; he was too big, he was hurting her, and helpless little cries broke from her throat. But he continued to push, and her hips rocked back and forth, adjusting, taking. Then he was in her to the hilt, seated hard, his pubic hair coarse against her bottom, his heavy testicles swaying between her spread legs and brushing against the burning nub he had exposed.

He moved carefully within her, just a little, the sensation setting off tiny explosions in her nerve endings. "Here?" he asked softly, his deep voice rustling against her ear. "Or . . . *here?*" He moved again, his swollen shaft nudging a place inside her she hadn't known existed, and her wild, helpless cry gave him his answer.

Slowly he began moving, a subtle flexing of his hips that wasn't a thrust at all, but instead a tenderly ruthless internal stroking of that place deep inside her. Grace cried out again, her entire body clenching under the lash of a pleasure so intense she couldn't bear it. She shuddered convulsively, her loins shivering around the thick intrusion of his penis. Oh, God, she had climaxed before with less arousal than this, but somehow she couldn't quite reach that blessed relief. This was exquisite torment, paralyzing pleasure, and she couldn't fight it. She couldn't pump her hips faster to gain her peak, for his body too completely controlled hers. All she could do was quiver just short of fulfillment, each slow rub of his cock taking her almost there, but not quite. Low, rhythmic cries wrenched from her with each inward movement he made, and her arousal grew even more intense, until she thought she would faint. She heard herself pleading with him, wild, disjointed words of need. "Niall—please! More—*do it!* Please . . . I can't—no!"

"No?" he panted softly in her ear, his voice low and raw. The next incremental movement tore a groan from him. "Ye'll bear it, lass, for I say ye must."

"I can't," she said again, moaning. She tried to move, tried to end this delicious torture, but he locked his right arm around her hips and held her still for yet another deep stroking. She strained against that warm, iron-muscled band, knowing it was useless, that his strength was far greater than her own. In this sensual battle she was helpless to take anything except what he gave her, her body too slight and delicate to resist being overwhelmed by a man who was a foot taller than she, and who had spent his life either in battle or training for battle, so that he was stronger than anyone she had ever known before.

Tiny red sparks exploded behind her closed eyelids. Her heart thundered, reverberating against her rib cage. She couldn't drag in enough air; her lungs strained, her entire body strained, and with a thin cry of despair, of pleasure taken beyond bearing, she turned her face into the crook of his arm and wildly sank her teeth into the bulge of his biceps. She heard his answering growl, and his big body flexed, a guttural sound rattling in his throat as his control shattered.

Like a stallion he set his teeth into the curve of her neck and shoulder, gripping the sensitive cord that ran there, and his hips plunged. She screamed, electrified by the primitive bite, the sudden hard thrust, and everything in her body gathered, concentrating, pushing, clamping down until she broke apart in cataclysmic upheaval. The sensual fury that seized her was so intense she was only dimly aware of the power of his own convulsions as he pumped violently into her, and the contractions went on and on, deep and hard, gripping him, shattering her.

The silence afterward was like death, black and complete.

Perhaps she lost consciousness; she didn't know. Reality returned in bits and pieces, first the awareness of the cold, gritty stone floor beneath her, and the heat of his body above her. His arm was wet, from her bites and her tears. There was the smell of sex, sharp and musky, added to the other scents of man and battle. The cord in her neck throbbed, an echo of pleasure like the lingering pulse in her loins. She felt the wetness of his semen. He was still inside her, not as large or as hard as before, but still firm, still *there*. Her vagina contracted in a sated, gentle caress and he grunted, shifting a bit upon her as he dealt with his own final wave of orgasm.

Perhaps he would kill her now. The thought formed out of the nothingness of exhaustion. So be it. She couldn't fight him, couldn't even move.

Slowly he withdrew from her body, taking away his support, his warmth, leaving her sprawled half naked and exposed on the floor. She could hear the hard rush of his breathing, the scrape of steel as he picked up his sword, and she waited to feel the cold bite of death.

Then he picked her up too, standing her upright for the barest second before he dipped and set his left shoulder to her belly, then stood with her draped like a limp bundle of rags over that broad shelf. At least her skirts had fallen into their proper position, she thought vaguely, so that her bottom wasn't exposed as he carried her to . . . where?

He strode through the darkness, his step sure and strong as he effortlessly carried her on one shoulder and his huge sword in his other hand, climbing steps as easily as if he hadn't just fought a battle and then emptied his body's seed into her in a shatteringly intense coupling.

He was still furious. Not just angry, but raging. She could feel the force of it inside him, controlled but unabated, and she knew their personal battle wasn't over.

Chapter 25

GRACE LET HER EYES CLOSE, UNABLE TO DEAL WITH ANYTHING right then, unable even to worry. She felt disconnected, drifting apart from reality. Her world had just been shattered, again, and she couldn't quite accept what had just happened between them.

She had never before made love *without* love; she had slept only with Ford, known only his touch, and known that when he took her it was with love. With Niall, what was there? Lust, definitely. Lust beyond measure, beyond comprehension. Desperation on her part, rage on his. And yet he had forced from her a response deeper and far more powerful than any of the joyous loving she had felt with Ford. She hated him for that, hated him for taking something that should have been Ford's, but which she hadn't known was within her for the giving.

Lights danced beyond her closed eyelids, and the icy cold of the hidden passageway changed to the greater warmth of the castle.

"Alice!" Niall called, his deep voice like thunder. "Bring hot water."

"Is the lass hurt, then?" asked Alice, her tone startled.

"Nay," he curtly replied, then he was going up more steps. After a moment she heard a door creak on its leather hinges as it was opened, then closed again with a thud. A few more steps and he stopped and dragged her off his shoulder, holding her briefly while she found her balance. Startled, she opened her eyes, swaying a bit as he moved away from her.

They were in his chamber. She looked around as if she had never seen it before, for she couldn't grasp why he had brought her there. She looked at the sturdy table, and the carved, massive chair that sat to one side of the fireplace, in which a fire was springing to life as Niall bent and struck a spark to it. On the other side was a bench, large and heavy. A big wooden trunk occupied the space at the end of the bed . . . the bed. It was at least four feet high, and looked to be seven feet square. A huge bed, more than large enough for the man who slept there. It was piled high with furs and rugs, and looked as if she would sink out of sight in it.

The fire grew, chasing the shadows to the farthest reaches of the chamber, sending its waves of heat out to flow over her chilled body. She looked out the narrow window and saw that night had fallen while she had been below. The castle was quiet, the intruders repelled or killed, repairs and recovery going on in the hush that follows a battle.

Niall unbuckled his sword belt and dropped it across the bench; the sword he kept in his hand, however, as he took a piece of straw and stuck it in the fire, then used the flaming twig to light the tall tallow candles on the table. Grace stood where he had deposited her, afraid to move lest he wield that wicked, bloodstained blade against her.

In the flickering mellow light of fire and candle she could see now the signs of battle on him, see the dark patches of dried blood. His shirt was splattered with it, there were dark splotches on his kilt, and smeared on the leather of his boots. The blood of many others adorned him, this warrior, and she wondered if hers would soon join the stains. His black hair swung about his shoulders, freed from even the small braids that were usually at his temples.

Without glancing at her he sat down on the bench and took an oiled rag to the stained surface of his sword, meticulously cleaning it, inspecting the edges for ragged chips. He would sharpen it himself, as she had seen him do before in her dreams, not trusting the weapon to anyone else's care.

The sword restored to its previous gleam, he laid it on the table. Then he stood and began to strip.

The bloody shirt had been pulled off over his head and dropped on the floor when Alice softly knocked on the door, and at his growled permission she entered with a pitcher of steaming water, and cloths for washing. As she set the water and cloths on the table beside the sword, Alice cast a curious glance at Grace, who stood white-faced and silent.

Alice picked up Niall's bloody shirt. "Will ye be wantin' food, and wine?" she asked.

"Nay," he said, then changed his mind. "Aye, bring bread and cheese, and wine."

Alice left with another furtive glance at Grace. It hadn't happened to Lord Niall before, but mayhap the strange lass was less willing than others, and he thought to soften her resistance with wine. He was angry. Alice knew his mood, knew he was in a rare rage, and it was centered on the young woman whose eyes made one want to weep.

Niall moved to the table and poured some water into the washbowl. Wetting one of the cloths, he scrubbed it over his face and shoulders. By the time his chest and arms were clean, Alice was back with the wine and food, curiosity having given her feet wings. He denied her the opportunity for observation, however, by going to the door and opening it only enough to take the platter, then closing the door and dropping the heavy bar in its brackets.

Now he stripped completely, removing his boots and stockings, dropping his plaid. Splendidly naked, he stood in front of the fire and washed himself clean of the grime and blood and sweat of battle. He gave Grace no more attention than if she were part of the furniture, unconcernedly washing his armpits, his muscled legs, his genitals.

She had been blessedly numb, but this last act brought reality intruding again, making her sharply aware of his body and hers, of the aches from fight and flight, of the throbbing tenderness deep inside and the stickiness between her thighs as his semen dried on her skin.

Firelight played across his powerful muscles. She stared as if mesmerized at the gleam of his shoulders, the flat ridges of his stomach, the round hard buttocks, the long, brawny muscles of thigh and calf. Black hair grew in a thick patch on his chest, around his genitals, and to a much lesser extent decorated his forearms and lower legs. Sheer perfection. She had never before seen a man so acutely male, his body as God had surely meant His creation to be formed. The beauty of bone and muscle and sinew, honed by a lifetime of work and battle, made her weak.

Warmth began to pool deep in her belly as she stared at him, and in despair she recognized the return of sexual desire. This unreasoning need felt like the deepest betrayal of all Ford had meant to her but she couldn't stop it and, it seemed, couldn't sate it. How could she possibly want him again, so soon after that soul-searing upheaval of body and mind? But she did. She wanted to know it again, take him within her, milk him with the internal caress of her body. Even when he came to her covered in the blood of battle, she wanted him. Should he take up that sword now, and take her life from her, she would die with her flesh aching for him.

Her gaze dropped to his groin. His testicles swung heavy against his thighs, evidence of his recent climax, but her heart jolted in her chest when she saw his penis jutting out, thick and erect. She remembered the tales she had read, the whispers she had heard since coming there, of how he could ride a woman all night long when a hungry mood was upon him, of how he sometimes required two women before his appetite was slaked. Suddenly she knew that his moods weren't hungry, they were savage. She could see it in him now, feel it pulsating beneath his skin. He gave no outward sign of it, except for his erection, but she felt the rage that still burned in him and manifested itself in the stiffness of his cock—a rage that somehow didn't feel as if it were directed at her.

He poured the bowl of red-stained water into the chamber pot, then refilled the bowl with fresh water. He looked at her for the first time since carrying her into the chamber, and the expression in his black eyes made her shudder with both dread and anticipation.

"Remove your clothing," he said quietly, but she heard the underlying iron. If she didn't undress voluntarily, he would perform the service for her.

She obeyed in silence, removing shoes and stockings, her bare toes curling with nervousness. Next came the overgown, then the kirtle. As that garment dropped to the floor, she stood in complete nakedness. Twentieth-century clothing revealed more, she thought irrelevantly, but it provided much more protection. A man had to deal with hooks and snaps and zippers, had to peel off layers of formfitting clothing before he could get to a woman's private parts. Medieval clothing, all-covering as it was, offered a woman little protection. All a man had to do was lift a woman's skirts and he could take her. The Scots had simplified matters even further, for a man had only to do the same to his own garments.

He looked at her, leisurely inspecting her breasts, the narrow curve of her waist, the dark curls at her pubis, her trembling legs. Then he held out his hand and said, "Come," and those trembling legs moved, carrying her to him.

He dipped a clean cloth in the warm water and began cleaning her as gently as a mother would a babe. He bathed the grime from her face, the smears of blood from her skinned palms and knees. His callused hands were careful with her, easing over the dark bruises forming under her pale skin. He knelt down and parted her legs, steadying her with a warm palm on her bottom as he gently wiped the cloth between her thighs, washing away his dried semen. Her thighs quivered, and she gasped for breath. The cloth felt raspy on her oversensitive flesh as he moved it along and between her folds. He even covered his fingers with the cloth and washed inside her, gently probing. He was very slow, very thorough with his washing, and the warmth in her belly grew into a fire. Her hips arched, seeking. Without a word he tossed the cloth aside, leaned forward, and set his mouth on her.

He knew exactly how to handle her, how to drive her insane. He sucked at her clitoris, drawing it forth, then licked it until she writhed and could barely stand up. All the while his long fingers probed, sliding into her, withdrawing, circling her tender opening. Then he kissed her, holding her hips with his iron hands and arching her forward while his tongue moved in and out of her, and helplessly she gave in to her exploding senses.

She went boneless, collapsing over him. He lifted her and sat down in the chair, and she lay limply across his lap, unable even to lift her head.

With his free hand he reached to pour the wine, holding the goblet to her lips, and she sipped. He drank after her, the expression in his black eyes shielded by his lashes. Grace relaxed against his chest, feeling warm and hollowed out, and oddly reassured. He might have taken her while still planning to kill her, but she doubted he would have pleasured her the way he just had if he intended to kill her afterward. It wasn't just his manner of pleasing her, but the fact that he'd done it at all; executioners generally weren't concerned with their victims' pleasure.

The heat of the fire licked over her bare body, chasing away the last of the chill. His thighs were hard and warm under her bottom, his shoulder a wonderful resting place for her head. He fed her bits of bread and cheese, feeding himself, too, and held the goblet to her mouth again. Again she drank, more deeply this time. When he raised the goblet to his mouth again he turned it so that he drank from where her lips had been, and the subtly erotic action squeezed at her heart.

"I have to tell you—" She stumbled into speech, not at all certain what she would say, but he pressed the back of his knuckles to her mouth.

"Nay. We'll not speak of it tonight. In the morn will be time enough." His voice was low and quiet, his Scots accent gone. He spoke now in the precise, measured tones of the Guardian. "For now—I like the taste of you, and I mean to have more of it." He leaned over and set the goblet on the floor, and then he kissed her as he had not since the night she had freed him from the Hay's dungeon, as he had not even during those other kisses they had shared. The kiss was wild and deep and she put both hands in his hair and held him, almost moaning with delight and arousal. He could make a fortune with his kisses, she thought dimly. What woman wouldn't give her gold to experience such sweet, wild mastery, such play of lips and tongue, such a blend of teasing and promising and authority? He kissed like an angel, or perhaps it was the devil, for surely an angel wouldn't know such carnal delights.

Swiftly he carried her to the bed and placed her on it, then joined her there, his broad shoulders blotting out the light as he came up over her. Panting, Grace opened her legs and took him between them, gripping his hips with her thighs even as she pushed hard on his shoulders. Willingly he rolled onto his back, and Grace sat astride him, gripping his penis in both hands and lowering herself onto it.

The penetration was just as shocking, just as full. She braced her hands on his belly and pressed her hips down, taking all of him. Her breath shuddered between her lips. God, oh God, she felt frenzied, unable to get enough of him. Her body had been starved for a man's hardness, the hunger shoved into her subconscious where it could surface only in her sleep, and now that hunger was released in an ungovernable flood. She rode him hard, and he squeezed her breasts, and she came again.

And still it wasn't enough.

He hadn't climaxed, he was still iron-hard within her. The hunger built again even before she had the energy to deal with it. Lying on his chest, his hands moving comfortingly over her bottom, stroking her back, she felt her inner muscles tighten around him.

He laughed, the sound rough and male, his white teeth gleaming in the golden firelight. She sat up, the motion pushing him deep inside her once more. She rode him hard again and this time he came before she did, his powerful body arching between her thighs, his hands gripping her hips and grinding her down on him. Wet with his spurting seed, she climaxed again.

They dozed a bit, with her lying on top of him and one of his hands threaded through her hair. Grace woke to find the fire still warmly blazing, so she knew not much time had passed. He slept, his penis soft. She slithered down his body and took him in her mouth, feeling him wake, feeling him grow hard. And then she mounted him again.

The hours blurred together. He gave his body generously, letting her do as she would with him. He gritted his teeth and fought his own climax, not letting himself reach pleasure again so he would remain hard until she was sated. She didn't know if the frenzy would ever stop, if her body, so long denied, would ever tire of her almost intoxicated enjoyment of his body. She stroked every inch of him, her hands shaking with delight at the textures of his skin. She kissed his jaw, his ears, his wonderful mouth. At the last, when finally she was exhausted and emptied out and at peace, she tormented him by taking him deep in her mouth. Knowing how he fought to control himself, she swirled her tongue around his shaft and sucked at the swollen head, and with a strained, hoarse sound he bolted upright, lifting her away from him and tumbling her onto her back.

He mounted her, pushing her thighs wide. "You've put me to hard use tonight," he whispered, sliding into her. "Now 'tis my time."

He should have been beyond control, but she discovered that wasn't so. When he climaxed again, he should have been beyond arousal, but that wasn't true either. His use of her was as devastatingly thorough as hers had been of him, and the sensations blended together. His thrusts hammered deep in her belly, over and over, and she held him when he shuddered and convulsed. The fire burned down, the candle guttered, and in the darkness he did things to her she had never imagined she would let a man do, but instead she reveled in his raw sexuality.

And in the darkness, finally, quiet came.

She lay against him, her head pillowed on his shoulder, her body heavy and limp. His hand covered her breast, his thumb absently stroking her velvety nipple. She inhaled his scent, the musky, unique smell of him, and she realized she could no longer recall how Ford had smelled.

Agony rushed out of the darkness, and she had no defenses left. It boiled out of her, deep and wrenching, sharp claws shredding her insides. A guttural cry ripped out of her throat. Niall's arms closed hard around her, and she came apart.

She didn't know how long she wept. Endlessly, unceasingly. The grief had been kept bottled up too long and now there was no holding it back. She cried in deep, wrenching sobs, her entire body shaking. She cried until her chest hurt and her eyes were swollen almost shut, until her throat was raw and the sounds she made sounded like an animal's.

He held her through it all, not letting her go even when she fought him, kicking and scratching. She raged silently against the two senseless deaths that had devastated her, against the terror and fury of the past year. She pounded Niall's chest with her fists until he caught them and held them, rolling over on top of her and using his weight to control her.

She began gagging, and he swiftly dragged her to the chamber pot and held her while she vomited. Then he gave her more wine and carried her back to bed, and held her until she could cry no more.

Dawn's faint gray light was creeping through the narrow window. "You loved him," Niall said quietly, smoothing her tangled hair away from her hot, grief-ravaged face. "You have not wept for him before, have you?"

"No." Her voice was a croak. The sound shocked her. "I couldn't."

The wine was warm in her belly, and her mind was fuzzy from both alcohol and fatigue. His hands were on her body, her breasts and thighs and loins, ensuring she acknowledged his claim on her even as he comforted her. She was so sore from the night's excesses that she flinched when he entered her again, but she didn't resist. He pressed deep, nudging her womb, and held himself deep and still until all the tension eased from her muscles and she lay limply beneath him, breathing deeply.

He didn't climax, didn't even thrust, just maintained the link. After a time he maneuvered them onto their sides, and put his hand on her bottom to keep her anchored to him.

Grace put her hand on his face, her fingers tracing the slope of his brow, the high curve of his cheekbone. "I know who you are," she said numbly, all emotion exhausted except for the uneroded joy of touching him. "I know what you are, Guardian. I came from the year nineteen ninety-seven to find the Treasure, and use it to destroy the man who killed my husband and my brother."

Chapter 26

NIALL SAT AT THE TABLE, QUIETLY LOOKING AT THE BOOKS
Grace had brought. Thinking to convince him she was
telling the truth, she had told him where her sack was
hidden and he had fetched it, but she realized now he hadn't
required proof. He looked at the books out of curiosity, and
for knowledge, not for confirmation.

He rapidly absorbed the changes in the language, saying
once, "I knew the rhythm of your speech was odd, even
though you spoke English." Another time: "So there are
other lands across the ocean. I have always wondered."

He wasn't shocked, he wasn't disbelieving. He was highly
educated; he spoke seven languages, and he dealt daily with
the fantastic. But he was unnervingly calm, and it was
destroying what little of her nerves were left.

"These papers you translated," he finally said, turning to
face her. "You say I wrote part of them?"

"Yes. You signed your name, and dated them. Thirteen
twenty-two."

"I have not written any papers," he said.

"But I saw them—"

"Perhaps you are the cause of their existence."

She digested that, and bit her lip. "You mean they wouldn't have been written if I hadn't come back? But I came back *because* of what you wrote!"

A bitter smile touched his lips. "I have hated God for what He allowed to happen to my brethren," he said calmly, "but I cannot doubt His existence. How could I, when I guard His power on earth? Who knows what the hand of God does?" He shrugged. "I have ceased trying to understand Him, I only do my duty."

"You hate God?" Stunned, she could only stare at him.

"How could I not? I did not want to be a Knight; I was forced into the Order. I have a talent for killing," he said in unflinching acceptance of his skill. "I became the Knights' best warrior. I learned the secrets we protected—in service of God!—and He allowed his servants to be butchered in defense of those secrets. No Knight betrayed his greater oath, not one talked even with the flames of the stake licking up his legs, devouring his entrails. They suffered and died, and He let it happen. Perhaps He directed it, to destroy those who knew. Only I am left, and fool that I am, I have kept my oath all these years, because my last oath was not to God but to my friends who died for Him."

His tone was unemotional, his eyes remote. Grace wanted to go to him but somehow she couldn't, he was too distant.

"Look at me," he said. "I have thirty-nine years. I should be growing old, but my hair remains black and my teeth stay in my head. I never sicken, and if I am wounded I quickly heal. He has cursed me to guard His damned Treasure even after I should be dead."

"No," she said softly. "You're just a healthy man." She could reassure him on this, for she was all too piercingly aware of his humanity, his mortality. "In my time, people easily live into their seventies and eighties, sometimes even over a hundred. I'm thirty-one."

His brows lifted and he looked a little surprised. He surveyed her, noting her smooth, clear skin and lack of wrinkles, her shiny hair. "You look a mere girl."

She didn't want to think of her looks, with her eyes red and swollen from her emotional storm, her face drawn with fatigue from the long night of nothing less than debauchery. She sat down on the bench, wanting to be close to him even if she didn't dare touch him.

"Tell me of this Foundation," he ordered.

She told him what she knew. She had already choked out the details of what had happened to her, how Ford and Bryant had died, and why. He listened, his long fingers drumming on the table.

"I wonder how they discovered the Treasure's existence," he murmured at one point.

"An archaeological discovery, probably," Grace said. She hesitated. "This Power—what exactly is it?"

"It is God's power," he said. "With it, all things are possible."

"But power isn't something you can leave in a chest and take it out when you need it! God can't store His power in the basement of a Scottish castle and—"

He shook his head. "Nay, 'tis not that. Though He could, if He wished. The Knights understood that, the fact that mortal man cannot understand God, that we must not say a thing is impossible, because all things are possible to Him, and our understanding too paltry. God is not limited by our imagination or our small minds. The Church makes rules and says they come from God, but they come only from man and his attempt to interpret God."

Believing God was so powerful, how indeed could he not hate Him? Grace wondered. Niall had long since reached the conclusion that God had deliberately destroyed the Templars, for had He wished to save them they would still be flourishing.

"But why would He want to destroy the Order?" she whispered, and Niall's black eyes flashed.

"To protect the Church," he said tiredly. "Flawed as it is, still the good outweighs the bad. The Church gives the framework of civilization, lass. Rules. Limits."

"How were the Knights a threat to the Church?"

He stood and walked away from her to the window, where he looked out over the wild and beautiful land he ruled. "We knew."

"Knew what?"

"Everything."

She waited, and the minutes passed. Without looking at her he said, "Did you note I never called you by name? Your name! Grace-Saint-John. I want you until I think I shall burn alive, but your name eats at me. There is no state of grace, there is only one of ignorance."

She hadn't noticed, but now she felt a pang, as if he had rejected her. Perhaps he had; he hadn't touched her since her confession. "What did you know?" she whispered.

"They found it all in the Temple, in Jerusalem. The Lion Throne, that great barbaric throne on which are carved both Yahweh and Ashara, god and goddess, male and female. They were two, and they were one; the ancient Israelites worshipped them both. Then the priests deliberately destroyed all the altars built to Ashara, and tried to erase knowledge of her. Yahweh became Jehovah, the one God."

"Yes, I know," she said. Archaeology had uncovered all that, eliciting a storm of conjecture among the scholars of ancient Jewish history.

"There were other things," he said. "The Cup. 'Tis a plain thing, and despite the quest for the Holy Grail it gives no powers. The Banner. The army it flies over is never defeated, its firebirds rising again and again from the ashes. It plainly depicts the same lions of the Throne, though legend has it that it isn't that old, and that only the Knights had it." He sighed softly. "And there is the Cloth."

Her mouth went dry. "The Shroud?"

He made an impatient gesture. "So it would be called, but that is false."

"Then what is it?"

"The cloth in which Jesus was wrapped when he was taken from the cross," Niall explained.

"Then it is the Shroud. He was entombed in it."

Niall's eyes were blacker than she had ever seen them before, looking through her. His mouth had a bitter line. "No, not a shroud, because he lived. He was God's son in spirit and the cross could not defeat him. The Church built itself around the preposterous tales of the resurrection even though its own writings plainly state he did not die, and afterward the truth could not be told without destroying the Church. So we remained silent to protect the Church, to serve God—and He destroyed us in return.

"His face." The words were pulled out of him, taut with fury. "We had his face from the Cloth. We revered it, because he was proof of God's power. Jesus lived! God reached down and saved him, because his duty was fulfilled, and then he left in an explosion of light and heat. We found the record of it! *We know how!* But when our duty was fulfilled, He broke us, He destroyed us. And still . . . still I serve."

Grace couldn't speak. Her lips tingled, and she realized she had stopped breathing. The explosion of heat and light . . . she had felt something like that, when she had come back—

"We knew the *how* didn't matter. The method He used did not matter; we trusted Him, worshipped Him. Others wouldn't understand, though, with their small minds and rigid superstitions. They try to limit God to their own understanding, their own imaginations. They would have turned from the Church. *We* didn't."

The bitterness spewed out of him, his lips drawn back in a snarl. She swallowed her fear, and crossed to the window to stand beside him. She didn't dare touch him, though, not when his anger was like a force field blasting from him. "But you're doing it, Niall. Trying to fit His reasons and methods into your own understanding." She paused, trying to work through her thoughts. She believed in basic goodness and when it came down to it she believed in God, sensed a higher power, a deeper meaning, but she was no theologian. "I think . . . I don't believe God causes all things to happen. I think He gives us the freedom to be either good or bad, because if there is no choice then our actions have no worth, and no blame. I think when people do bad things it's because they have chosen to do so, and we should blame them, not God."

"Why did He not stop Philip? Why did He not strike Clement dead? He could have, but instead He let them act."

"He let them choose, and they'll be judged by their actions."

"Then I'll meet them in hell."

"Oh, Niall." She did touch him now, leaning her head against his arm. She felt overwhelmed with tenderness for him, and admiration. "You won't go to hell. How could you? Even with all your pain and anger you've kept your oath, and served God. Don't you think your service is more valuable to Him than the service of those who have never suffered, never been tested?"

He turned on her, gripping her arms so tightly he hurt her. "I would have preferred not to have served Him at all!" he ground out.

"But you did anyway."

"Aye, and my entire bedamned life is tied to this castle, to His cursed Treasure I am sworn to protect! Do ye not think I would have preferred to live a normal life, with a wife, and bairns?" His Scots accent was back, and thick with his anger. "I could not! The burden, and the danger, have been too great. And now—"

"Now?" she prompted, when he broke off.

He gave her a bitter smile. "Why, now He's sent Grace to me, but only as a means to lead me to another battle I must fight for Him."

She blinked, startled. "I didn't come back for that. If I could find the Treasure I was going to use it myself; if not, I knew I would have to ask for your help, but I only need your knowledge."

"Ah, no, lass," he said gently. "Ye need *me*. I'm the Guardian, and no other may use the Power."

"How does it work?" Grace asked nervously, clinging to his hand as he led her into the hidden passage. The castle slept around them. They had spent the day arguing, sometimes heatedly, over the course they would take. Huwe was dead and that threat ended, so Niall felt he could relax his defenses somewhat, and now was the perfect time for him to go. Remembering the violence of the procedure, Grace couldn't look forward to going through it again. "How do you get the electricity?"

"Electricity?" He repeated the word slowly, feeling his way along the syllables. "What is that?"

"A form of energy. Power."

"Power." He laughed, the sound humorless. "We use God's Power. The procedure is a means of *returning.*"

He walked with confidence, as if he had no need for the candle he held. Grace was less certain. She felt surrounded by the nothingness of space, of emptiness, as if the reality of Creag Dhu was already dissolving around her. Her heart pounded wildly, the pressure high in her throat. She swallowed to contain the panic, the unreasonable fear. She had been there before, and with less trepidation.

But still, now she knew. She felt the breeze, and the subtle throb of the very air against her skin. Niall led her down, down, to the deeper darkness beneath the stairs. He left the candle outside and walked into the darkness, his arm hard around her now to keep her with him.

It lay in the blacker depths, hidden from view but pulsing with that silent energy. The air should have felt dead, empty. It didn't. Though cold and dark, the chamber felt fresh, vibrant with the secrets it concealed. Treasures. Things. And yet the real treasure lay not in what they were, but what they represented.

"We have drunk the water and eaten the salt," Niall said in a low voice. "Take us."

The flash was blinding, the force like a giant blow that knocked her flat. She lay senseless for a time, deafened and blind, not even thinking. When the fog began to clear, she groaned and tried to roll over.

"Let me help you, my love," a voice crooned, and she was lifted to her feet, held upright by strong arms. Grace's head lolled back on her neck. She fought for control, won it. She opened her eyes, and stared up into Parrish's smiling face.

"Imagine my surprise when the workers found you lying in the rubble," he said conversationally. "I sent them all away, except for a few trusted men. I believe you've met Conrad, and perhaps you remember Paglione, too."

Dazed, Grace found herself staring into the cold, emotionless eyes of the man she had shot in the McDonald's parking lot. He didn't so much as blink. The other man, Paglione, looked familiar, but she couldn't quite place which assailant he had been.

A chilly wind stirred her hair, and she turned her face into it. A sea wind, blowing over where Creag Dhu had once stood. All that remained now were a few ruined stone walls, and the rubble that had been unearthed by the workers. Where was Niall? Had they already found him? Had he survived the journey?

"Looking for the gold yourself, were you?" Parrish asked. He pinched her breast, cruelly twisting the tender flesh. Grace bit off a scream, though tears started to her eyes. She didn't want to give him the satisfaction of making her cry out.

"There isn't any gold," she blurted.

He stiffened, and his eyes narrowed. "What?"

"The Treasure isn't gold. It's artifacts. There isn't any gold!"

"You're lying," he said violently, and slapped her. The force of the blow would have knocked her down if he hadn't been holding her arm. He drew back his arm again, and this time his fist was doubled.

"Aye, there's gold."

The softly burred words made them spin, Parrish dragging Grace about, wrenching her arm. She bit her lip, and tasted blood where Parrish's blow had cut her. Niall stood relaxed, the wind lifting his hair, ruffling the ends of his plaid. A faint smile was on his lips, and he leaned negligently on the claymore which he had driven into the ground. He looked wild and barbaric and wonderful, a splendid savage who possessed a sophistication of manner and experience most modern men would never come close to achieving.

"Who are you?" Parrish asked. "Not that it matters." Conrad and Paglione had already spread out, one going wide on each side of Niall, and both of them had guns in their hands.

"Niall of Scotland. And I fear it does matter, for the gold is mine."

Parrish's eyes narrowed. "You've already found it, haven't you?"

Niall looked amused. "It was never lost." He glanced at Grace, and his glance lingered on her bloody mouth, hardened.

"Well, you are a complication," Parrish admitted. "But I don't think you've spent it all, or you wouldn't be dressed like a bag lady. Maybe you don't have it at all."

"But I do." Niall reached into his shirt, the movement prompting both Conrad and Paglione to lift their weapons. Niall's eyebrows rose, and he smiled as if they were no more than presumptuous children. "Easy, lads." He drew out his hand and slowly opened it, palm upward. A crude golden coin lay there, gleaming bright in the sun.

Parrish smiled, too, his handsome face creasing in a benevolent expression that made Grace want to vomit. "Where is the rest of it?"

"It isna here. I moved it long ago, against such a day as this."

"A pity." Parrish shrugged. "You'll tell me; Conrad will see to that. But you won't like his methods, and unfortunately you look like the stubborn type." He jerked his head at Conrad, and Paglione anticipated the order, moving toward Niall.

Something wild flared in Grace's eyes. She had watched two men she loved die; she couldn't watch another. A low, animal sound tore out of her throat and she jerked to the left so that she half faced Parrish, and drove the palm of her hand hard against his nose. Cartilage crunched, and blood poured out of both his nostrils. He staggered back, his grip on her loosening, and Grace tore free. Paglione whirled on her, the pistol rising in his hand.

Calmly Conrad tightened the slack in the trigger and fired. Grace screamed, surging forward, only to be jerked back as Parrish recovered and grabbed her again.

Paglione hung there in surprise, not even blinking. The small round hole in his forehead was neat, bluish around the edges. He dropped bonelessly to the ground and didn't even twitch.

Parrish gaped in disbelief. "Are you fucking crazy?" he screamed at Conrad, his voice high and cracking.

"No," Conrad said, and turned to face Niall. Slowly his simian head bowed. "I serve you, Guardian," he said.

Niall acknowledged him with a single nod.

Parrish pulled out a pistol and pressed the barrel to Grace's temple. He began backing away, stumbling over the raw dirt and tumbled rocks, dragging her with him. "I'll kill her," he said viciously, the words thickened by the blood streaming from his broken nose. "I'll fucking kill her."

Niall pulled the tip of the claymore out of the ground and rested the blade on his shoulder, his hand draped negligently over the hilt. "No," he said. "You will not." He looked at Grace and smiled, a smile so sweet and strangely radiant that her heart stopped in her chest. "Grace . . . move."

She dropped immediately, lifting her feet and simply falling out of Parrish's grip. He grabbed for her and stumbled off balance, going down on one knee in the dirt. Grace rolled, throwing herself away from him, and he fired the pistol. The bullet burned along the top of her right thigh and she cried out, grabbing her leg.

Parrish scrambled to his feet, aiming the pistol first at Niall, then at Conrad, daring either of them to make a move. Niall lifted the claymore off his shoulder, the smile on his face changing to something deadly. "Are you sorely wounded, love?" he asked in the most gentle voice Grace had ever heard him use.

"No," she said, though her voice wobbled and her thigh burned like hell. Blood seeped through her fingers, and she pressed her hand hard against the wound.

Parrish fired at him, the shot echoing with a flat metallic sound across the sea. Niall began walking toward him. Parrish fired again, and still Niall advanced.

"Ye canna kill me, servant of evil," Niall whispered.

"God damn you, you bastard," Parrish screamed, and fired again. Niall was so close Parrish couldn't have missed, yet his hand must have been shaking, the shots going wide.

Niall's gaze was distant, fixed on something both beyond Parrish and yet inside himself. He turned his head and smiled at Grace, that piercingly sweet smile again. "My own Grace," he said. "I found heaven wi' ye, lass, but that time is gone." Then he lifted the heavy claymore and rested the tip against Parrish's chest. Grace saw Parrish's handsome face go slack with shock, and a bolt of lightning split the cloudless sky. The blinding light enveloped Niall, arcing along the long blade of the claymore, and shot straight through Parrish. He screamed, lifting on his tiptoes as if hauled there by an invisible hand. He trembled and shook, and the lightning arced again. The front of Parrish's trousers went wet and dark, and steam rose from his crotch. His eyes rolled back in his head, until only the whites showed. His lips split, and his hands began to scorch. His blond hair was singed, turned to gray ash. He tried to scream, his mouth open, but no sound emerged over the roar and blast of light. The skin on his face shriveled, pulling away from his bones. Through it all Niall stood motionless, wrapped in brightness. Then with a thunderous boom it was over and Parrish collapsed like a sack of rags, lying motionless on the scorched earth.

"Niall!" Grace struggled to her feet, ignoring the pain in her leg. "Niall!"

He strode rapidly across the ruins to her, catching her as her leg went out from under her and she started to fall. Gently he lowered her to the cool ground, lifting her skirts to bare her thigh and expose the wound.

The man called Conrad went down on one knee beside Parrish's smoking, stinking corpse. What he saw must have satisfied him, for he gave a brief nod of his apelike head, then rose and came to Niall's side.

Deftly Niall tore a strip of fabric off the hem of Grace's undergown and wrapped it around the long gouge on the top of her thigh. He glanced briefly up at Conrad. "You are of the Society?"

"Yes. We have known of the Foundation's existence for many years. Someone from the Society has always belonged to the Foundation, to monitor its activities. Only twice has it come close to finding the Power; in 1945, and today."

"You were going to kill me," Grace said, her teeth chattering with shock. She couldn't quite take in that this man with the cold, dead eyes was somehow on Niall's side, at Niall's service.

"If necessary," Conrad said unemotionally. "My concern was the papers, to retrieve them at all cost and prevent Parrish from acquiring them. Then I began to think that . . . perhaps . . . you were meant to have them. You are one of only a few people in the world who could understand what they were, who would know to go to the Guardian and bring him here."

"Be verra happy ye didna harm her," Niall said softly as he glanced up from tying the cloth around Grace's thigh. His eyes were as cold as Conrad's.

"We do what we must," Conrad replied. "As do you."

Niall's mouth twisted bitterly. "Aye." He looked down at Grace's bare thigh, at his rough hands on the silkiness of her flesh. He smoothed her skirts down, his fingers gentle. "Ye'll be all right, lass. Can ye stand?"

"I think so," she said shakily. Her leg throbbed like blue blazes now, but she had seen for herself that the wound wasn't deep. Niall helped her to her feet, holding her until her balance steadied.

He looked around, lifting his head into the breeze. His gaze lit on the two cars, English rental cars parked near where the stables had once stood. "Automobiles," he said on a note of wonder. "Before, I didna see anything, just that damnable dark little dungeon, and the madman."

"Bunker," Conrad said.

Niall shrugged his indifference at the terminology. "I think there must be many wonders now to see," he said absently. "But many evils, too."

"Yes." Conrad's eyes locked on Niall, and for once they weren't cold. Grace couldn't read his expression, but suddenly she knew that Conrad would give his life unhesitatingly for Niall, and in that moment she forgave him for everything.

Niall tilted his head down, his face calm as he studied Grace. "I must go," he said.

"Go?" She realized even as she said the word how stupid she sounded. Of course he had to go; he was the Guardian.

"I couldna stay here, even if I wished." He cupped her face in his hands, his fingers tenderly tracing her cheekbones, her lips. "My duty is there." He bent and kissed her, his lips soft, barely touching hers. Then he released her and strode away from them, and she heard him repeat the words about water and salt. She took a step forward, trying to scream his name, but panic closed her throat. The flash of light blinded her, and when she could see again, Niall was gone.

"Niall!" Too late, she had voice. She stumbled toward the spot where he had stood, a great fear welling inside her, a fear that had no name.

Conrad caught her arm. "He is gone. He is the Guardian." To him, that explained everything.

"He's a man!" Grace whirled on him, her eyes wild. "He's just like every other man!" She felt hysteria building in her, a sense of loss so sharp it was staggering. "He eats and sleeps and breathes and bleeds, he doesn't have supernatural powers or anything like that—"

"No," Conrad said, turning her away from the ruins. "But God does." He began to lead her toward one of the rental cars. "The Guardian has his work there—and we have ours here."

She stumbled, her leg crumpling under her again, and without a word Conrad lifted her in his powerful arms and carried her to the car. She sat numbly as he drove them away from the scene, but inside she was coming apart, because Niall was gone.

"That man gives me the willies," Harmony muttered, watching Conrad as he sat beside Kris, the two of them patiently pulling up Foundation files and destroying them. It was night, the building deserted except for the four of them. Conrad and Kris could have done the work on their own, but Grace had to be there, her nerves not letting her be anywhere else. Harmony had come along because she was worried about Grace, who looked as if she would shatter at the slightest touch.

"He's strange," Grace conceded. She had spent a little more than a month in Conrad's company, and she still knew little more about him than she had the day Parrish had died. He didn't talk about himself. She knew he was ruthless, that some might call him a stone killer and perhaps be right.

He had been invaluable, making arrangements, contacting Harmony to more thoroughly tend the wound on Grace's leg, doing away with Paglione's body. Parrish's body he left to be found, the victim of a freak lightning strike. Grace had moved like a marionette to his orders, so numb she wondered if she would ever feel alive again. Niall was gone. She woke in the night weeping, reaching out for him. She had spent so little time with him, and yet she felt as if he were imprinted on every cell of her body.

"There!" Kris announced in triumph, his hacker's blood excited by what he had been doing. "We can't kill the Foundation, but it's going to be in the dark for a while. All their records are gone."

Conrad nodded, and for a moment there was a gleam in

his dead eyes. "Good," he said, the word filled with satisfaction.

They hadn't told Kris anything more about the situation, except that Parrish was dead, but what he knew was enough to make him willing to help out. Harmony, who still hadn't recovered from the shock of watching Grace vanish in an explosion of light the month before, was even more protective than normal.

Conrad stood, looking at the blank computer screen. "Are you certain an expert can't retrieve the files from the hard disk?"

"I'm positive. Trust me. The hard disk is wiped clean. If you're sure no floppies exist anywhere, or a hard copy, then there's no way all that information can be compiled again."

Conrad grunted. The possibility of a floppy disk floating around out there worried him. He had personally searched Parrish's house and found nothing, but such a valuable disk, if it existed, would likely be in a bank vault somewhere.

Grace had burned the papers she had worked on for so long, and ached as the flames destroyed her link to Niall. She would never again read about him, marvel at his exploits. The written accounts paled in comparison to the real man, anyway. But she didn't want anyone else to find those papers, and use them to threaten the Treasure Niall had dedicated his life to protecting.

The four of them left together but separated when they reached the street. No one talked much; there wasn't much left to say. Kris departed in his Chevelle. Conrad gave Grace an oddly old-fashioned bow, and walked off down the street. Harmony and Grace slowly walked to Grace's truck.

"What now?" Harmony asked. "No more running, no more bad guys chasing you and trying to kill you. Well, the cops are still after you, but from what I see they can't find their ass with both hands and a flashlight, so I guess you're safe enough. I'd live somewhere else, though. Take up some boring stuff, like skydiving."

Grace managed a ghost of a smile. "I don't have any plans after tomorrow," she said.

"So what's on for tomorrow?"

"I'm going to my husband's grave."

* * *

The June morning was bright and sunny, the flowers in full bloom. Grace carried two bouquets of spring flowers, daisies and lilies and bright yellow primroses making a gay splash of color in her arms. Harmony walked silently beside her through the rows of grave markers.

Grace knew exactly where the graves were. Bryant was buried beside their parents, and Ford in the plot nearby that he and Grace had chosen. The day they had bought the plots she had looked at them and thought how many decades it would be before they were used. She had been wrong.

The two graves had markers on them. The life insurance policies would have paid for the markers, but she wondered who had ordered them. Friends, perhaps, or colleagues. It was possible Parrish had done it; he would have found the idea amusing. She didn't mind. If he had, in this case, the end did justify the means. She was glad they had markers, that these two wonderful, precious men hadn't lain for a year in unmarked graves.

Bryant's marker was simply inscribed. "Bryant Joseph St. John. Born Nov. 11, 1962—Died April 27, 1996." That said so little. He had been thirty-three years old. Never married, but engaged once. Several serious girlfriends. Loved his work, doing crossword puzzles, an ice-cold beer and salty popcorn when he was watching a ball game. His second toes had been longer than his big toes, and he hadn't liked anything starched. She couldn't have asked for a better brother.

She placed one of the bouquets on the grave, and numbly walked on. She stumbled a little, and Harmony placed a strong supporting hand under her arm.

"Are you all right?"

"No, not really," Grace whispered. "But I have to do this."

Bryant's grave had been in partial shade; Ford's was in full sun, and the grass that covered it was thick and lush. "William Ford Wessner," the marker read. "Born Sept. 27, 1961—Died April 27, 1996." One more line had been added: "Married with Love to Grace Elizabeth St. John."

Grace's knees buckled and she sank slowly to the grass, despite Harmony's alarmed efforts to keep her upright. She reached out a trembling hand and traced the engraved letters of his name, trying to reach the essence of the man. She missed him so much, ached to see his crooked smile, or the humor in his twinkling eyes. He had died for her, and done it willingly.

"I'll always love you," she promised him, though she could no longer read his name in the stone; everything was blurred. He was a man worth loving, and that feeling for him would never die out of her heart, any more than her love for her parents had died.

The human heart had the capacity to love many people, and none of those loves diminished it for the others. Niall had been in her heart even before Ford died, a tiny burning kernel of interest and respect. Losing Ford hadn't extinguished that spark. Instead it had grown during the long months when she was alone, giving her the strength to go on. At first she had loved him as a person, and later she had loved him as a man. It had been a banked fire when she had gone back to his time, and when he stirred the coals the fire had blazed into an inferno. How many women were so lucky as to have two such loves? They were nothing alike in personality. Ford had been cheerful, good-natured; she suspected Niall could be the very devil to live with, as accustomed to command as he was. Different times, different men—and they *were* both men, in the best sense of the word.

Harmony knelt down beside her, disregarding the effects of grass on her white pants. "Would he have minded?" she asked softly, nodding at the grave. "Or would he have wanted you to love again?"

"He would want me to love again," Grace replied, brushing her hand lightly over the grass. As she would want the same for him. She couldn't help the small spurt of jealousy she felt, ridiculous under the circumstances, but she would want him to be happy, and he had been more generous and openhearted than she was.

She laid the bouquet on the grave and touched the marker again. Since his death she had been able to see only one image of him, that horrible last one, but the words on the marker summoned another, happier memory, that of their wedding day. She saw him in her mind, nervous and excited, the way he repeatedly swallowed, the way his voice shook when he said his vows. When the ceremony was finished a wide grin broke across his face, and it was that grin she saw, relieved and happy all at once.

Tears dripped down her cheeks, and her mouth trembled. "Oh, Ford," she said, her voice shattered. "I miss you so much, and I love you, but I have to go now."

Harmony helped her to her feet and gently led her away. Grace stumbled; the grass was springy beneath her feet, and wet with early-morning dew. She stopped, tilting her head back. It was a beautiful day. She took a deep breath, inhaling all the fresh scents, and with swimming eyes looked at the wide expanse of blue sky.

"You look like you gonna pass out any minute now," Harmony said sternly. "You eat anything yet?"

"No, not yet." Grace gathered herself and smiled. It was wobbly, but it was a real smile. She ached, but she felt at peace. She hadn't had vengeance, but Ford and Bryant had had justice, and it was enough.

"Did you even try to eat, or did you just start gagging?"

"Gagging." Morning sickness had started three days ago, hitting her early and hard. Harmony had said the worse the morning sickness was, the less likely a woman was to miscarry; if that old wives' tale was true, then Grace figured she could play ice hockey in her ninth month without any harm coming to the baby.

She touched her flat stomach. She was five weeks pregnant; she knew the exact date of conception. She would have the longest pregnancy in history, a baby conceived in 1322 and born in 1998. That was one for the record books.

At first it had seemed so unreal, that one night would result in a pregnancy, but when she remembered the night, she wondered how she couldn't have *expected* to get pregnant.

She thought of what Niall had said, of wanting a normal life, a wife and babies. Perhaps a normal life would never be his, but she carried his child and he didn't even know it. He had isolated himself, allowing himself nothing but the burden of his responsibility. Would he want his child, or would he turn away?

He would want it, she thought. There was a great tenderness in him, and great passion. He had shown both of them to her. A man like that would adore his children. It would be criminal to keep such joy from him.

"Are you going back?" Harmony asked as they drove away from the cemetery.

"I think I have to. It may be a wasted trip, he may send me here again, but if he wants me I'll stay."

"Man," Harmony breathed. "That must be luuuvvv. I mean, a woman givin' up hot water and central heat, *Chicago Hope* and Sean Connery, pizza and enchiladas—a man better have somethin' more to offer than a hot love stick, if you get my drift."

"I get it," Grace said, and found herself laughing. "He has a castle, too."

"Yeah, but it's drafty. Better make that a *big,* hot love stick. I dunno about leaving Sean Connery, but at least you're tradin' him for another Scotsman, and one you can lay hands on at that. Must be something in the water up there, growin' men like that. So, when you gonna do the deed?"

"As soon as I can get back to Scotland, and Creag Dhu."

"Reckon it'll hurt the baby?"

Grace touched her stomach again, something she often did these days. "I've thought about that. I can't think why it would. It's low voltage, and the only effect I noticed was a little muscle soreness."

"Want me to go with you to Scotland?"

"I'd like that. Have you thought about *really* going with me?"

"No way. I'll miss you, Gracie; you lead a damn interestin' life. But no way in hell am I givin' up my modern conveniences for no love stick, I don't care how big it is."

Chapter 27

"HOLY CHRIST!"

Grace heard the yelp, the sound muted, far away. She tried to think, tried to swallow, but not even her throat seemed to work. She drifted away into darkness for an unknown time, then slowly became aware of noise again, of being gently lifted and carried. Her limbs were heavy, useless. Her head lolled like a child's.

She was placed on a bed, and she felt the softness under her. Her fingers moved, rubbing the cool linen beneath her. She managed to open her eyes a little, and a face swam before her, a strong-boned, frowning face with little braids of hair at his temples. A piercing joy spread through her. *Niall.* She didn't know what would happen in the next ten minutes but for right now she could see him, touch him, and she was happy for the first time in—how long? Had she been happy when she was there before? She frowned slightly; this seemed very important. No, she decided, she hadn't been happy the time before. She had felt torn, frantic, captivated, and many other things she couldn't quite name. Now, this moment, she was finally happy again.

"Lass?" He stroked her hair back from her face. "Can ye speak?"

The Scots accent was back, she noticed. That meant he was Niall the Scot now, not Niall the Guardian. Like Harmony, he varied accents with his mood, the effect of having seen too much and knowing too many languages. A small smile quivered on her lips.

"If ye can smile, ye can speak." The words were stern, but she heard a smile under them, and another, more serious note.

"Perhaps," she murmured, not opening her eyes.

He grunted with satisfaction. "Ye sound awake enough."

"Awake enough for what?" But even before the words were completely spoken she felt his hands moving on her, loosening laces, sliding over her legs, and lifting her gown. Her heart gave an enormous leap but she lay still, enjoying his remarkable expertise with women's clothing. In little more than fifteen seconds she was completely naked.

His own clothing took even less time. Trembling in joy and her own abrupt urgency, she opened her legs and he crawled up to settle between them, pausing along the way to distribute kisses on her stomach and gently suck both her nipples. She gasped, her fingers digging into his back, electrified by the increased sensitivity of her breasts.

"I've been more than a month without ye," he muttered, reaching down and guiding himself to her. "I canna be slow, this first time."

"I don't want you to be." She had been more than a month without him, too. She held herself still as the heavy invasion began, startled anew at the initial difficulty that wasn't quite pain, the pressure, the sense of being stretched. She breathed deeply, gripping his shoulders hard until her body adjusted.

He paused, his own breathing as deep as hers. He braced himself above her, his expression drawn, urgent. He pulled back, pushed inside her again, and shuddered as he began to climax. Grace held him, her own urgency not quite at the same peak as his and grateful that, with Niall, the second time wasn't long after the first.

He sank down heavily on her, sweating, his heart pounding against her breast and his breath catching on occasional small groans at the last small twitches of his orgasm. She slid her hands into his hair, sifting the long black strands through her fingers. "Does this mean you haven't had any—ah . . . relief—since you came back from my time?" She braced herself for his answer, trying to control the ferocious jealousy that began to burn inside her. They had parted without promises or even the expectation of being together again so she couldn't expect him to have been faithful, but she thought she might skin him alive anyway.

"If by relief ye mean have I had a woman," he answered irritably, "then nay, I have not." He lifted his head from her shoulder and glared down at her, as if his deprivation were her fault.

"Good," she said, with intense satisfaction.

A reluctant smile eased his frown. "Ye like that, do ye?"

"Very much." She arched beneath him, delighting in the rub of his belly against hers, and the way her movement made him harden slightly inside her. She stroked her hands down his back, feeling the powerful muscles flex. His buttocks were cool to the touch, and she cupped her palms over them.

He slid his arms under her and rolled, reversing their positions. Grace sat up, her face glowing with soft sensuality. How freely he gave his body for her pleasure!

He put his hands over both her breasts, tenderly fondling them, rubbing his thumbs around her nipples and making them harden. "I'm verra glad of it, but why did ye come back?"

"Because of you," she said simply. "Because I love you. If you want me, I want to stay." She took one of his hands and moved it down to her belly, flattening it over her womb. "If you want *us.*" Her voice wobbled then, because there were no promises between them and she had taken such a huge chance in coming back. There hadn't been any talk of love between them, but when she thought of the night they had spent together and his tender care when she had expected much less, she had hope.

He looked at her stomach and his pupils flared wide. His expression went completely blank, as if he had been hit in the head and had no idea what had happened. He tried to speak and nothing emerged. He tried again, his voice so hoarse it was nothing more than a croak. "A bairn?" He shook his head, as if the words made no sense.

"Are you surprised, after that night?" She surprised herself by blushing, hot color rushing to her cheeks as she remembered the raw, frenzied mating.

He began to laugh, gripping her hips to hold her in place. His head arched back and he howled with laughter.

"What's so funny?" Grace demanded, frowning down at him. She was glad she was pregnant, but she didn't think it was *amusing*.

"All these years," he gasped, tears of mirth shining in his eyes. "I've held to my oath, hating the responsibility, holding myself apart from the things another man would expect—and now I've no choice! Thank God!"

The words echoed in the room and he stilled, the laughter gone as if it had never been. "Grace," he whispered.

She touched his face, her fingers tracing the beloved lines. "I don't know," she whispered in reply. "You told me yourself, we can't know." Perhaps she had been sent to him, the pain in both their lives healed by the magic that brought them together, the fever and obsession and devotion neither of them could resist.

He pulled her down, cupping her face in both hands as he kissed her, long and slow and very thoroughly. "I won't question fate," he murmured. "Mayhap I question your sanity, leaving behind the life ye did—I read the books ye left. It is a truly wondrous time."

"So is this time, in a different way. You are here, and that's wondrous enough for me. You're the Guardian; you had to come back, you have to remain. So I came back too. It was an easy decision, once—once I had said good-bye."

"To your husband?" His tone was understanding. Niall knew what it was to lose those he loved.

"To him, and my brother. I've no family left there. But the start of a new family is growing inside me, and I want to be with you . . . if you want me."

"Want ye?" he growled. "Grace—I wanted ye months before ye finally came to me. I burned for ye. How could I defend myself against a lass who wasn't there? If 'tis the words you want, then aye, I love you. Did ye doubt it? After I found ye wi' the Treasure, instead of killing ye as was my duty, I came near to killing myself loving ye! I'm glad ye came to stay, because I willna let ye go again no matter your wishes."

Startled, she realized that Niall's dereliction of duty was indeed unprecedented; why hadn't she realized that at the time? "You loved me then?"

"Of course," he said calmly. "Now, lass, I think ye should have your way wi' me."

Having her way with him took quite a long time. Alice brought food to them that night, grinning at the way Niall sprawled in his big chair, modestly covered by his plaid, but his eyes heavy-lidded and drowsy with an absolute surfeit of physical satisfaction.

Grace lay on his lap, wearing only his shirt. The garment would have reached her knees, if Niall had left it alone, but he seemed to be incapable of doing so. If he wasn't feeding her or holding a cup of wine to her lips, he was stroking her thighs, sometimes reaching a bit higher.

Her stomach was peaceful now, lulled by the plain, unseasoned food. She had had one bout with nausea, right after Niall had dragged her down to the great hall and they had pledged themselves in marriage to each other in front of all the residents of Creag Dhu, and everyone had insisted on toasting them. The second cup of spicy mulled wine had been too much. And after that, of course everyone had to toast the coming bairn.

The wine she drank now was weak and sweet, but added to the events and exertions of the day, she was exhausted and sleepy. She rested her head on his shoulder, her heart peaceful.

When a section of the wall beside the fireplace began moving, Grace merely blinked at it, thinking the wine must be stronger than she had thought. Then a man strode through the opening and stopped still, his pupils flaring. "I sent you a message," he said in French.

"Aye," Niall said drowsily in Scots. "Ye did. Ye waste your time speaking French, for she does too. And Latin.

And Greek. If ye've something private to say, best do so in Gaelic; she can't speak that yet."

"Why is she here?"

"Why, because I married her." Niall smiled at Grace, his thumb tracing her lower lip. "Sweetings, my brother Robert. He's king of Scots. Robert, this is Grace, my wife and the mother of my bairn."

Robert looked startled, Grace even more so. She scrambled off Niall's lap and stood before the king of Scotland wearing nothing more than her husband's shirt, her legs and feet bare, her hair hanging loose past her hips. She blushed.

Robert the Bruce was a big, powerfully built man, though not as tall as Niall. He was ruggedly attractive, probably approaching fifty in age, and wore the look of a warrior. He eyed Grace with some appreciation, his gaze lingering on her legs. Niall scowled and came to his feet, placing himself in front of her.

"Ye've told her everything?" Robert asked disapprovingly.

"Nay, she already knew." Niall reached back and made certain Grace was still modestly tucked behind him. "Would ye like wine?"

Robert began to laugh. "Ye rogue," he said with exasperated fondness. "Ye kill a clan chieftain, decimate the clan, and ask me would I like wine? The nobles are demanding that I raise an army to rid Scotland of the renegades of Creag Dhu."

"Huwe attacked *me*," Niall said, his voice hardening. "And I freed all those Hays who survived the battle."

"Aye, I know. I came only to ask—to beg, and me a king!—that ye try not to shed more blood for a time."

"If 'tis in my power, I'll live a verra peaceful life from this day onward," Niall said. "Will ye wish me happiness?"

"Always." Robert stepped forward and hugged his brother, and the glimpse Grace had of his face made her love him forever, for it was filled with love and an aching relief. He winked at her over Niall's shoulder, and she blushed again.

"Can ye speak, lass?" he asked.

"Yes, of course," she said, pleased that her voice was steady. "I'm pleased to meet you—" She stopped, suddenly unsure of what to call him. Sire? Your Highness? Your Majesty?

"Robert," said the king. "With family, I am Robert." He cocked his head. "Your accent is strange, not English, and not French either. Where are ye from?"

"Creag Dhu," Niall said firmly. "This is her home."

Robert nodded, accepting that here would be yet another mystery about his brother. "When did ye wed?"

"Today."

"Today!" Robert laughed again. "Then there's no wonder ye had the lass half naked on your lap! I'll leave ye to your wedding night, then, and may ye enjoy it well!"

"I will," Niall said firmly. "As soon as ye leave."

Robert was still laughing as he stepped back into the hidden passage, though he tried to muffle the noise. Grace watched as the section closed behind him. "Just how many hidden passageways does Creag Dhu have?"

"It's fair riddled with them," Niall replied, lifting her in his arms and carrying her to the bed. He lay down beside her, cradling her close against his side as if he would never let her go. "Ye feel so perfect," he whispered into her hair. "As if ye are part of me, as if ye could be nowhere else."

"I don't want to be anywhere else."

"Then tomorrow morning, love, I think I should write those papers that brought ye to me. I dinna want to chance anything going wrong." He put his hand on her belly, where his child grew, and held her close as they slept, and dreamed.

Two great books—
one great price!

Each book features two classics
by your favorite authors together
in one collectible volume!

Coast Road • Three Wishes
Barbara Delinsky

The Taming • The Conquest
Jude Deveraux

Twin of Ice • Twin of Fire
Jude Deveraux

Velvet Song • Velvet Angel
Jude Deveraux

Angel Creek • A Lady of the West
Linda Howard

Shades of Twilight • Son of the Morning
Linda Howard

Guardian Angel • The Gift
Julie Garwood

Castles • The Lion's Lady
Julie Garwood

Honey Moon • Hot Shot
Susan Elizabeth Phillips

Scandalous • Irresistible
Karen Robards

Homeplace • Far Harbor
JoAnn Ross

The Callahan Brothers Trilogy
JoAnn Ross

POCKET BOOKS
A Division of Simon & Schuster
A VIACOM COMPANY

Visit **www.simonsays.com**

13361